KEY TO LIBERTY

Titles by Piers Anthony
Published by Mundania Press

ChroMagic Series
Key to Havoc
Key to Chroma
Key to Destiny
Key to Liberty

Pornucopia Series
Pornucopia
The Magic Fart

Dragon's Gold Series
with Robert E. Margroff
Dragon's Gold
Serpent's Silver
Chimaera's Copper
Orc's Opal
Mouvar's Magic

Of Man and Manta Series
Omnivore
Orn
OX

Other Titles by Piers Anthony
Tortoise Reform
Macroscope

Piers Anthony Interview on Video
Conversation With An Ogre

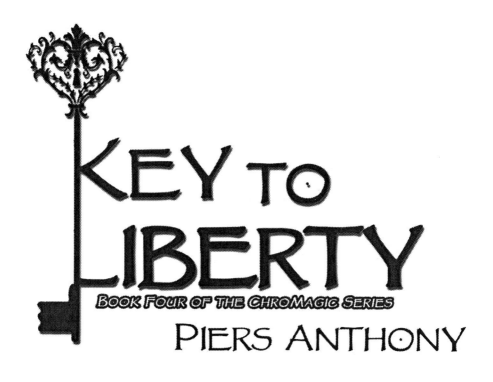

KEY TO LIBERTY

BOOK FOUR OF THE CHROMAGIC SERIES

PIERS ANTHONY

Mundania Press

A Mundania Press Production

Mundania Press LLC
6470A Glenway Avenue, #109
Cincinnati, Ohio 45211-5222

To order additional copies of this book, contact:
books@mundania.com
www.mundania.com

Cover Art © 2007 by SkyeWolf
SkyeWolf Images (http://www.skyewolfimages.com)
Book Design, Production, and Layout by Daniel J. Reitz, Sr.
Marketing and Promotion by Bob Sanders
Edited by Daniel J. Reitz, Sr.

Hardcover ISBN: 978-1-59426-381-1
Trade Paperback ISBN: 978-1-59426-382-8
eBook ISBN: 978-1-59426-380-4

First Edition • April 2007

Library of Congress Control Number: 2006927885

Production by Mundania Press LLC
Printed in the United States of America

10   9   8   7   6   5   4   3   2   1

Table of Contents

Chapter 1
Havoc

Havoc swept Gale half-clothed into his hot embrace. "Passion," he said.
She smiled and kissed him. "Novelty," she said with fond irony.

They laughed. It was the middle of the day, and they were preparing for a formal dinner. Havoc always desired her when he got her alone, especially when she was in partial dishabille, and she had gotten quite efficient at taking his edge off in seconds so as not to delay any formal function. Even after more than a decade and a half of marriage she loved his constant interest and enjoyed obliging it. But this time she paused. "What day is this?"

He checked her mind, but it was closed. He had to guess the occasion on his own. However, this time he was prepared. "The eighteenth anniversary of our marriage. You are exactly twice as old as you were then, but you look as young and lovely as ever." That was true, as much for him as for her.

"Frustration! Ennui warned you."

He nodded. "Affirmation. How else could I have remembered? She sets me up for every key event."

"Agreement. Even this," she said, frowning.

"Especially this." His eager hands squeezed her breast and bottom simultaneously.

"Negation. For this occasion I want an hour, not a minute, and there's not time now."

"Minute now, hour later."

"What do you think I am, the succubus? A minute's not enough."

"Swale is with you, isn't she? She can do me in a minute." Swale was the succubus Gale had tamed, a sexual demon. Havoc had come to really appreciate her talents, especially when it was Gale's body she used.

"Not this day, wretch. She's perfecting a new technique."

"Question?"

"Normally she can take a man's soul when he climaxes. She's learning to reverse it, locking his soul irrevocably into his body."

"What is the point? Isn't that where he wants it?"

"Yes. She could do it to youths, protecting them from any subsequent succubi they might encounter. It might be useful. Mainly it's a challenge for her to master. She likes sexual challenges."

Havoc considered, intrigued. Adolescent boys still got taken on occasion by succubi; he had worried about their son Warp, who was rather too amorous with women. "I think I don't want that for me. At times my soul needs to travel."

Gale opened her mouth, but held her retort, for there was a knock on the door. "In, On," Havoc said.

Ennui entered. "Voila is here. She says 'Sire, I request a private audience.'"

"Mischief," Gale murmured.

She was right. Voila normally just popped in without notice, even when they were making love. Sometimes she critiqued their sexual efforts, teasingly. Her normal phrasing was "Parents, got a minute?" In public she would say "Father, may we converse?" This super formality meant the matter was deadly serious.

"I'll meet her at the illusion field," he said. Ennui nodded, turned and left. Then, to Gale: "If I'm not back in time, use the mock. I don't think we want anyone to know I'm gone."

"And if you aren't back thereafter?"

"Take him to bed, by all means." It was only partial humor; she could and had taken the mock King Havoc to bed when necessary to conceal her husband's absence, to the mock's delight. She remained perhaps the planet's most beautiful woman.

"Not this day, tempting as it may be."

He smiled at the implication that she might prefer the mock, getting back at him for his mental "perhaps." He kissed her, squeezed her bottom, waited a moment for his erection to subside, then popped out.

He arrived at the edge of the illusion field on Planet Counter Charm. He was in a comprehensive forest, standing before a shimmering veil.

Then Voila was there, fifteen and modest in appearance, a girl few would notice, by her own choice. She could be radiantly beautiful, or hideously ugly, but preferred what she termed "wallflower mode." "Sire," she said, and moved into his embrace. Her mind was closed.

"Daughter," he said. Her extreme formality, even here, was ominous.

Then they held hands and stepped into the edge of the adjacent field.

The change was instant. They had been on a path in a forest; now they were in a burning desert. Voila looked like a standing six legged pig, and Havoc's own arm resembled the limb of a similar animal. He spoke, but his voice was a guttural oink. She responded with a feminine squeal.

That was of course why they maintained hand contact. The illusions changed all senses but one, and that one had to be fought for. They focused, and in a moment recovered their voices as they walked slowly on through the desert.

"What is it, Voila?" he asked.

"Father, it's here. The Second Crisis."

He was amazed. "Why couldn't it be something simple, like your falling in love with a married woman?"

The pig grimaced. "I would rather do that than this. This is the big one."

Havoc quickly reviewed the situation. There were three major crises impending. The first had been the struggle between the Glamors and Mino, the alien machine. Voila had taken him on in a contest of future vision when she was only six months old, and defeated him, winning his loyalty to the folk of the two magic planets. The third crisis would be when the terrible devices of Mino's home culture came to mine the planets, destroying them in the process. The second crisis was undefined. Until now.

"Speak," he said seriously.

"Earth Planet is coming to recover her colony. Mino perceived their unit coming but could not clearly identify its nature, as it was both life and machine. He summoned me, and together we fathomed it: a space ship containing a crew of human beings. It possesses weapons of White Chroma we can't safely balk. Mino could, but that would reveal his nature to the enemy. It is too early for that."

"Science magic," Havoc agreed. "But they shouldn't work beyond their Chroma."

"The ship carries its Chroma with it, and the weapons are large enough to do the same," she said. "Mino understands this better than I do; it is the way he functions regardless of external Chroma. They have what he calls a bomb that can destroy our planet. We can't stop them directly."

"Which means we shall have to negotiate," Havoc said.

"Mino says they will accept only our immediate subservience. They will depose you and put in a regent who answers directly to Earth. Charm will be a colony again."

"Obscenity!"

The pig smiled. "Do I know that word, Father?"

"Naturally not, innocent child. Delete it from your tender memory. I am merely annoyed about being deposed."

"But you didn't even *want* to be king, Father," she said teasingly.

"How do you know? As I recall, you weren't there."

"Ennui told me, of course."

"That woman is a personal pain in the posterior."

"And your oath friend. The one you trust before all others."

"Who pretty well runs the kingdom, covering for my inattention."

"Mom says that if it wasn't for Ennui, you would have messed up much worse than you did, at the beginning."

"Ennui and the Lady Aspect," he agreed. "They took the barbarian in hand and made a king of me."

"And Symbol. Without women you'd be nothing."

"So you say. But you would; you're one of *them*."

"Oh Father, I love you." There was a tear in the pig's eye. "Hold me."

He embraced her and held her close. He felt her shivering porcine body, and increasingly her mind, as her control loosened. She was truly awed and frightened. That was itself awing and frightening, because Voila was as potent and confident a person as existed, for excellent reason.

And she did have reason for her emotion, for with their mind linkage came more information on her role in the near future. She was the center of a horrendous nexus that put her situation in peril. Yet that was only an aspect of a much greater threat that concerned the entire Planet of Charm. As with the first crisis, everything oriented on her. It was an overwhelming responsibility she could not avoid.

"Who knows?" he asked grimly.

"Mino. Idyll. Me You."

"Gale and Ennui must suspect."

"They do."

"I love you. I would take this from you if I could."

"I know, Father. No one can take it from me."

They separated and resumed progress through the illusion fields. The desert vanished, replaced by a heaving sea, and they were three-winged birds floating on it. Their plumage was light brown, matching their hair and eyes in normal life. Any stranger would know them for father and daughter, and they liked it that way.

"What do you, Mino, and Idyll fathom?"

"It's vague as yet, but coming clearer. The odds are against us if we oppose Earth openly; they have the means to destroy Charm, if suitably aroused. The odds are for our survival if we capitulate at the outset."

"Outrage!"

"The odds remain against us if we feign surrender and plot against them. They are experienced at dealing with unruly colonies."

"The choice is between defeat and destruction?"

"There is an intermediate path. That is the one I bestride. Mino says it leads to mergence with Earth on acceptable terms. It leads to significant complications we can't yet fathom, but is the one we must navigate."

"Reluctance."

"Inevitability."

"Pain. We dare not risk you, beloved child."

"The choices are risk or loss."

He knew it. His own awareness of the near future was coming into play. It was not nearly as strong as hers, but was enough to satisfy him that she was correct.

They left the sea and were in an orchard with many fruiting trees. Here they were themselves; they had emerged from the illusion fields. They followed the path to a central glade. "Idyll," Voila called.

A shimmer appeared in the air. "I respond, Voila, Havoc." The words were ordinary sound, emanating from the shimmer.

"Glamor of the Ifrits, we need you," Havoc said.

"As we need you," Idyll agreed. "The risk is to Counter-Charm too, and not subject to nullification in the prior manner."

"Voila is at the center of the intermediate path. Who else is there?"

"All your children, Havoc. They are central; others are peripheral."

This was even worse than he had thought. "All? Warp, Weft, Flame? Gale will freak."

"But she will recover," Voila said.

"They should be here," Idyll said.

"Summon them," Havoc agreed with resignation. "And Gale."

A handsome black-haired black-eyed youth appeared. "Hi, Pa. Hi, brat. What's happening here?"

"We are at the second crisis, Warp," Havoc said. "The four of you are central."

Warp sat down suddenly on air, as if using an invisible chair. "Just like that? What is it?"

"Earth is coming to reclaim her colony."

"And we can't fight," Warp said, picking it up from their minds. "So we have to finesse."

A healthy slender red-haired young woman appeared, wearing the garb of the Amazons. "I was practicing," Flame said. "Couldn't wait to change. What's so urgent?"

"Read my mind, hot stuff," Warp said.

Flame did. "Hooo!" she said, blowing out a burning breath. "We're in for a fight."

A striking blonde appeared. That was Weft, who had in the past two years filled out into a startlingly shapely woman, and who made the most of it. She spied the four instantly, and oriented on Havoc. "Tell me, dad."

Havoc smiled as he opened his mind to her. "You know I'd marry you if I weren't your father."

"That's no necessary barrier," Weft said. "Just divorce mom and I'm yours."

Warp and Voila put up with the familiar by-play. Weft had always had a thing for Havoc, and the flowering of her femininity had only intensified it. The fact was that they were genetically unrelated, she having been adopted, so it was biologically permissible. They all knew it would never happen, which was why they felt free to banter. Within a year Weft would marry elsewhere, reluctantly; that might make it fade.

"Now if you're quite done, Electra," Flame said, "We have serious business."

Weft had read it in Havoc's mind. "Do we ever, hothead! The Second Crisis!"

"It seems that the four of us must go to Earth," Voila said.

Gale appeared. "I had to roust out my mock on practically no notice," she said, exasperated. "What is so expletive important as to require this meeting?"

"Mother, it's the Second Crisis," Voila said. "We're in the center."

Gale paused, assimilating that. "I would rather we had all lost our ikons."

"Close, Ma," Warp said. "We'll have to take the ikons along."

"To a White Chroma planet? Disaster."

"We believe that no planet is pure single-Chroma," Idyll said from her shimmer. "Mino reports that the machine culture explored thousands, and found none that were, up to the time of his own assignment here. There must be other Chroma and nonChroma on Earth. They will have to find them."

This was new to Havoc. "Why?"

"Earth possesses weapons of Science magic we can't oppose without rousing dangerous suspicion. Our own White Chroma efforts fall way short. We can try to nullify the weapons of the warship coming here, but this will have to be a matter of corrupting the human personnel rather than magic. When that occurs, Earth will simply send another ship, perhaps a robot that can not be corrupted. We have to nullify Earth itself, and we believe that can best be accomplished by converting it to a full Chroma planet. If Earth becomes like us, it should be less interested in destroying us for our independence."

"This is feasible?"

"We ifrits have labored for millennia on the problem of converting Chroma, as it is vital to our nature. We believe we have distilled the Chroma essence that will shift one Chroma to another, in a matter of a few months after seeding. Earth's volcanoes are said to be all White Chroma. They should be convertible. The problem is getting people there to do it."

"But why our children?" he demanded.

"Only Glamors can accomplish it, and we think we can get these particular ones to Earth."

"How."

"By allowing the Earthers to take them hostage against your acquiescence to Earth's dominance of your planet."

There it was. Naturally the children of the king would make the king heed, when other hostages would not.

"This seems extremely risky," Gale said. "I don't want my children sent into this hazard."

"Nor do I," Havoc said. "Do we have a choice?"

"You can arrange one," Idyll said. "Query your people. Maybe they would prefer to submit."

Havoc came to a sudden decision. "I shall."

"I'll help, dad," Weft said, taking his arm. She pretended not to notice Gale's roll of the eyes, while Warp and Flame laughed.

"Pause," Idyll said.

"Question?"

"The incipience of your decision brings new paths into view. There is great promise and great danger."

"Familiarity," Havoc said. "This is why I seek an alternate avenue."

"Beyond what we have discussed. This is the intermediate future. You face the prospect of great new love and loss."

That set him back. The ifrit Glamor's specialty was the intermediate future, which was why she worked closely with Voila (near future) and Mino (far future). The three constituted the most important aspect of planetary policy. "I personally?"

"New love?" Gale echoed, while Weft looked perplexed and not particularly pleased.

"On Earth," Idyll said. "Second only to yours for Gale, Havoc. And the planet in peril."

"Which planet?" Havoc asked sharply.

"Earth."

"Why should that concern me? We oppose Earth."

"Because you will come to love Earth."

Havoc was appalled. "*Earth* will be my new love? Treason!"

"Negation. But your new love is bound to Earth, and you must save her. The future of our worlds depends on it."

This was both exciting and disturbing. "Fathom further this intermediate future, Idyll. I will put it out of my attention for the moment, so as to focus on immediacies." Because he was genuinely shaken, and knew he would foul up if he allowed this nebulous love/threat to distract him.

"Agreement."

"Meanwhile we will continue to read the near future, trying to fathom the motives of the Earthers, and plan for the trip to Earth," Voila said.

Weft squeezed his arm possessively. They jumped together back to Triumph City. Somehow she managed to sneak another kiss in transit. He liked that better than he found it expedient to let her know, but of course the naughty vixen did know. She would have made a fine mistress, were she not his daughter.

And naturally she caught that thought. "I'd make a fine mistress regardless, Dad. Let me prove it."

"Negation," he said with insufficient force.

Havoc convened an assembly of the people of Triumph City within the hour. The city was a huge wooden pyramid floating on a lake, with the Royal Suite at the apex and the ranking officials immediately below. In the center was a large theater for assemblies and entertainments. The pyramid was efficiently organized both physically and hierarchically, and the King's will could be implemented rapidly at need.

Havoc took the upper stage and gazed down at the massed faces. The people knew that he never summoned them frivolously, and they had needed no special urging to collect. They were curious and somewhat alarmed.

He wasted no time on amenities. "A thousand years ago Earth planted a colony on Charm, saw it established, and departed," he said. "The ship was supposed to return in half a year, but it never did. We fended for ourselves, slowly expanding our sway. We needed more people, so implemented the rule of four children per woman. We needed diversity and homogeneity, so required each woman to have at least one child by a man other than her husband, or to adopt one. As you know, the queen and I adopted three, and had just one natural child." He smiled ruefully. "Sometimes Weft forgets she's my daughter."

That was her cue. Weft came and plastered a big kiss on his mouth, her audience-side hand swinging across to pinch his buttock. The audience laughed; Weft's passion for him had been common gossip for a decade.

"It could have been worse," Havoc continued ruefully. "Suppose she had been my natural daughter?"

Weft spanked his bottom. "Then no more no fault traveling with you, Sire," she said warningly.

There was more laughter, because no fault travel was notorious for otherwise illicit liaisons. Theoretically all the king's travels were known, and of course there had never been any impropriety. The supposedly irrepressible monarch had been scrupulously proper in that respect.

Then he turned serious as Weft retreated into the background. Such incidental by-play was expected of the "barbarian" king. "We made it on our own, deserted by Earth, and did well enough. Today we have a successful society, and soon we may be able to phase out the rules of four and one. Then maybe I'll be able to retire at last."

There was a murmur of negation. Havoc was probably the most popular king of the last century, and the people did not want to see him go.

"But now there is a crisis. Earth has sent a ship to recover her colony." He paused meaningfully, letting it sink in. "We believe they mean to depose me and install a regent so they can govern the planet as the colony it was meant to be. Earth law and Earth custom will be established and enforced, for good or ill."

He paused again, as though pondering, and there was silence from the audience. "In a moment I will ask your opinion. But while I have the stage, I will express mine. I am willing to establish relations with Earth; she is after all the origin of our species. I would like to trade with her, as she surely has novelties that would interest us. I would like to exchange diplomats to smooth relations. I would like to let their tourists visit here, to see our wonders, and to have ours visit there to see hers. Such a relationship of equals could be helpful to both planets."

Another pause. "But I would not give half an expletive to be Earth's subordinate colony."

Now there was an emphatic response as the audience agreed with him, almost with one voice.

"But I must tell you," he continued grimly, "that this is not an easy matter. We believe that Earth means to have her way, and if she can not incorporate us as her vassal, she will try to destroy us. Their ship of space has a weapon that could fragment the planet, killing us all. It would be safer to capitulate."

There was no sound in the huge theater.

"We do have resources. I understand the Glamors are with us. They might succeed in nullifying the weapon. But Earth would send another, and that would be more difficult to deal with. We can not be sure of winning our independence. So resistance would be dangerous. We judge our chances of success as even. But if we try and lose, even if they don't destroy our planet, they will treat us far more harshly than they would have had we welcomed them. Can independence from Earth be worth this?"

One more pause. "I am putting it to a vote. I want to know the sentiment of the people of Triumph City, and of the Chroma. I am asking you to cast your ballots within a day, for the ship will be here tomorrow. I am asking the Chroma to poll their folk and report back to me on the same deadline. Your will determines mine. Do not make this decision lightly. This is not merely my kingship in question; this is your lives. You must decide whether it is better to live as a colony of Earth's, or to risk dying as the Kingdom of Charm. There may be no more important decision you can make in your lifetime. Consider carefully. Thank you."

There was uncertain applause. He had hit them with a mind-numbing decision to make, and they were still assimilating it. He did not know how they would decide.

"Now I need Gale," he said to Weft. "And you need your siblings. Go to them."

She nodded soberly. She had performed her bit on stage, but she was no spoiled brat. She was an accomplished musician possessed of more magic power than any ordinary citizen knew. She vanished.

Soon he was with Gale, ready for their delayed tryst. But now there was a shadow. "How can they all go?" she asked plaintively as she stepped out of her royal gown and stood gloriously nude. "We could lose our children."

"I mislike it too," he said, stripping also. "But Voila says it must be, and she is right as far as I can follow."

"And as far as I can," she agreed, pretending not to notice his lack of an erection. They were both seriously stressed. "None of us can match her in reading the paths of the near future."

"She coordinates with Mino and Idyll. They are supreme. We have to do their bidding."

She made a wan smile. "There was a time when you were the master, Havoc."

"That was before we had children."

"How true. Glamor children. It has been a challenge, and I wouldn't trade any of it. But now—"

"Who's going to weep first?"

Gale considered. "We'll do it together."

They clasped each other and sobbed together. They had never done that before, and of course would never do it in any other circumstance. They were two Glamors, with extraordinary powers of magic, but the prospect of losing their children was beyond that.

At last they relaxed. It was time to revert to normal. "Maybe sex will blot it out for a while," he said.

"Let's try."

They tried. They looked and acted like teen-aged first lovers, her interest and participation as fierce as his. They were indefatigable, and both climaxed fifteen times in fifteen minutes. But it didn't banish the shadow.

"We'd better focus on giving them their best possible chance," he said.

"In space and on Earth planet, without magic," she agreed.

They discussed it as they washed and dressed. "We can't send them alone," he said.

"Chaperones," she agreed. "Traveling royal children should have them, according to ancient Earth history. Who will do?"

"Augur and Aura," he said promptly. "They can play the parts, and we trust them."

"Agreement. Should they also have a royal maid?"

"Who can curb Warp's desire for any pretty damsel? We can't have him tackling Earth women from sheer lust."

"Ine. She can handle him. She has proved it."

"Ine, the Sorceress," he agreed. "Fifteen years his senior, but quite competent in that respect."

"Like Symbol," she agreed.

"Now don't get jealous, woman."

She laughed. "Symbol is worthy of jealousy. When are you going to give her her fourth?"

"When she wants it. Maybe when she retires."

"She carries Voila's ikon. She'll have to give it up for this adventure."

"Then maybe now is the time."

"As compensation for losing Flame." Symbol had nursed Flame as a baby, and remained close thereafter.

"I'll see to it." He paused. "Maybe Ine should take Swale along."

"To protect Warp from Earthly succubi?"

"That also."

Gale nodded, appreciating their son's propensities. "Swale will go. There may be need for her new abilities."

Royally garbed and in order, complete with crowns, they left their private chamber. Ennui was in her office, mopping her face.

Havoc didn't have to inquire why. His closest friend loved the children too; she had helped raise them. "Voila says their chances of success are even," he told her.

"I know. But that means the chance of their not returning are even too."

"They are immortal," he reminded her.

"There are other deaths than physical."

She was correct. Glamors were not completely invulnerable, and the siblings were young.

"Maybe the vote will be for acquiescence," Gale said.

"Doubt."

He laughed. "You must stop constantly reading my mind."

"When I retire, Havoc," Ennui said. "Which reminds me: in two years I'll be 60, and I look it. You need to train in a new personal secretary."

That set him back. "On, I still need you. I'll always need you." On was her nickname, used only among friends.

"Pshaw. Anyone can do my job, and many could no it better."

"But no one else could ever have the bond we do. Why don't you take back my ikon?"

"Havoc, we've been through all that. Soon I'd be a seductive young slut trying to displace Symbol in your bed. That's not the nature of our relationship."

"I'd rather that, than lose you to old age."

"Exaggeration. You need to move on."

"Denial."

"Let her be, Havoc," Gale murmured. "You know she's right."

Unfortunately, he did. The ikons had subtle but phenomenal powers; they changed people to make them better ikon carriers, by the ikon's definition. Being Glamors changed people also, in more profound ways, but they were better able to mask it. Voila had been especially affected—and specially schooled to hide it. Ennui had been through it, and wanted no more of it, understandably. "Carry on, bitch," he told Ennui ungraciously.

Gale kicked him. Smiling with perfect understanding, Ennui returned to her paperwork.

Their next engagement was a formal meeting with the Chroma Representatives, who were of course interested in the details of the crisis. Twelve people, each a different color, addressed for this purpose by their colors. Each not only was the hue of his or her Chroma, they wore matching robes.

They bowed in unison. "Sire," White said for them all.

Havoc nodded formal acknowledgment. "Speak."

"We heard your address. The survey of our respective Chroma is in progress. It is a formality, as we know the result."

"As king I govern with the consent of the governed. The formalities must be observed."

"Granted, Sire. But given that the Chroma support you overwhelmingly, what are the real risks and costs of this effort?"

"They are still being fathomed," Havoc said. "But we know that my four children must be yielded as hostages and sent to Earth Planet. They may not return the same as we know them now."

"Oh!" That was Invisible, shown only by her tiara, which contained a single smudgy blob of a stone, which nevertheless had a special luster.

Havoc smiled sympathetically. "You have a problem with that, Air?"

"I do, Sire, if Flame is among them."

"She is. I assure you, I understand your concern."

The Representatives were little given to humor, but there was a ripple of mirth. They all knew how literally he had spoken.

Havoc turned serious. "The Earthers have a Science bomb that carries its own magic and can destroy our planet. We dare not oppose them directly. But if they obtain my children as hostages, they believe I will do their bidding until they depose me and institute their own government. We need that belief to give us time to neutralize their bomb and abate their urge to incorporate us into their empire. You know my children are Glamors; they will take their ikons and seek nonChroma magic on Earth. If they are successful, the odds are that we will prevail."

"And if they are not?" Blue asked.

"Then we are lost, and I will yield to the Earther imperative so as to spare my planet. The odds are even that we will succeed, and approximately three to one that we will survive, as independent or colony."

"If they fail—what of the children?" Red asked.

Havoc frowned. "They have independent skills, and can be winsome when they choose." There was another ripple; he had understated the case. Warp and Weft were especially noted for their seductions of others of any color or age. "The odds are nine to one that Warp and Weft will survive, and four to one that Flame and Voila will."

"Why the difference?" Invisible asked, a quaver in her voice.

"Because Flame is an Amazon and will fight rather than yield. Voila as yet lacks an emotional compass; her feelings may betray her."

"It seems you risk more than we do, Sire," Green said.

"As king and Glamor I have more power than you do. It behooves me to risk more."

There was a pause. Then Invisible stepped forward to embrace him. "We love you, Sire."

Havoc affected surprise. "I had no idea! I can't see you, but you feel quite shapely. Shall I take you to my bed?"

"Please do," she agreed. There was another ripple. This was another familiar by-play.

He turned to Gale. "If you have no objection, beloved."

"I will remain to acquaint the Representatives with the remaining details," Gale said. "Talk with her, plumb her, and try to get at least a little rest this night. Things may be busy tomorrow."

He frowned. "Spoilsport."

Gale shook her head. "I should have known better than to marry a barbarian." That, too, was familiar. They were doing their best to show that despite the crisis, they were their normal selves, and in reasonable control of events. The Representatives would be reporting to their Chroma; they needed that reassurance.

Havoc took the Air Chroma woman by her invisible elbow and guided her to the royal apartment and to his bedroom, where they both stripped. Actually she had worn only a light invisible cloak, in anticipation of this occasion; he heard it land on a chair as she tossed it. He sat naked on the edge of the bed, letting her invisible hands tease him into an erection. She had left on the tiara so he knew where her head was, assuming she was still wearing it on her head instead of elsewhere. She did that so he could kiss her on the mouth without missing too badly.

Only when they were well into it did they lapse into serious dialogue. "Havoc, you know it's not just Flame," she said as she sat her bare body on his lap. He never tired of the novelty of feeling her without seeing her. Even when he poked a finger into her vagina it looked as if he were gesturing in air. Not for nothing was it nicknamed the Air Chroma.

"Symbol, it grieves me to ask this of you, but it is necessary. You must give up Voila's ikon." Symbol was of course his long-time official mistress.

"I know it." She removed her tiara and set it nearby, now that full contact made it unnecessary. "And it's not just that I'll revert to my real age. Do you know I'm 46?"

"You will always be lovely to me," he said seriously. "And whatever you think you lack, you can mask with illusion. I won't know the difference." He fondled her full breast, then bent to kiss it.

"Idiocy," she said fondly. "You can fathom reality any time you choose."

"I would not choose, with you."

"Take me!" she said, abruptly bearing him back on the bed and straddling him. He lay submissively while she mounted him, took him in, and thrust against him, forcing his first emission. The translucent essence hovered just above his belly, invisibly contained. Then she lay on him, keeping his still-rigid member in, her breasts nudging him as she breathed. "Now tell me the rest, while I have you close."

"Voila must have her ikon with her on Earth. You know that."

"I know." She kissed him, and her vulva squeezed his member. "May I go with her?"

"I think not. You are too generally known as my mistress. The Earthers would catch on."

"Who will go, then?"

"Ine."

She nodded. "That Sorceress can handle Warp while she's at it, too, protecting the innocent Earth maidens."

"That is our thought."

"And it would not be meet for the king's mistress to seduce the king's son."

"However willing the king's son might be," he agreed.

"But what will I do, as I slowly turn old and saggy?"

"It occurred to us that this may be the time for your fourth."

Her whole body stiffened momentarily. Then she relaxed. "You want me to pull the wire?"

"I want you to have your forth before you revert to 46. It should be healthier."

"And I'll have one of my own to cherish. Your baby."

"I did promise," he reminded her.

"I've never been a mother. I'm not sure I know how."

He laughed. "You nursed Flame until her weaning, and sometimes the others, so that Gale could keep up. You raised ours as much as we did."

"The whole palace staff raised them. I was merely an extra milk breast."

"And so your substance is in them all, especially Flame. And the staff will help you, as much as you want. But you'll have to swaddle your baby in visible clothes."

"I'll do it now," she said.

"As soon as you get the wire out."

"You take it out. You can do it telekinetically."

"I don't know anything about internal female anatomy!"

She got off him and went off to the bathroom. She returned clean. She stood before him, legs spread; he could tell by the impressions in the carpet. "Feel inside me with your mind. It's a metallic coil just inside my uterus. Catch it and squeeze it compact, then slide it out. I'll take it once you get it past the uterine neck."

Havoc focused his telekinesis and found the object, which was quite different from her living flesh. He closed on it and moved it slightly.

"That's it! Now squeeze it."

He pressed the wire coil together, then forced it down and through the tight aperture. She reached in with her fingers and caught it, letting it expand as it come out.

"Done," she said with satisfaction. "Now have at me again, Sire." She bore him down, connected, and rolled him over to be on top of her, so that there would be no leakage of semen. "Spout."

He had just spouted, but she well knew that a Glamor could climax fifty times in an hour if he chose. Havoc thrust and jetted into her.

"Again," she said. "I want to be sure."

He thrust and climaxed again, this time issuing enough to pretty well fill her.

"Got it," she said, satisfied. "Now leave me alone while it sets."

Well, Gale had told him to get some sleep. He did so, while Symbol lay beside him, one hand touching his. He didn't need to inquire how she felt; she was thrilled to be working on her fourth at last. He read it in her mind. She truly loved him, and was deeply gratified to have his approval.

In the morning, still in bed, Symbol's interest returned to the challenge before them all. "Who else is going with them?"

"Augur and Aura as chaperones."

"No ifrit?"

He hadn't thought of that. "There should be one."

"Try Iolo. They are closest friends."

"They are indeed," he agreed. "But we don't want the Earthers to know about the ifrits."

"Have him take the form of a dog. He can be Voila's pet, always close to her, and bite anyone who molests her."

"Brilliant!" he agreed.

"Reward me," she said, and turned into him. "Another double dose."

He penetrated her and thrust, issuing enough semen to make her overflow.

"That will do," she agreed, surely holding her vagina closed as she lay on her back.

"I must be about my royal business," he said.

"Get on about it, Havoc. I'll make my own way to my chamber."

He got up and walked naked to the bath, where three nubile girls happily washed his every part. When he returned, Gale was there. "Symbol rousted me out of her room," she said. "I have seldom seen her so happy."

"We pulled her wire."

"Fair exchange for her loss of the ikon. She'll be an apt mother."

"And what will compensate us for the possible loss of all our children?" he asked grimly.

She paused, thinking. "Do you know, we could do it. We aren't limited to four children."

"Another natural child?" he asked, amazed. "I thought you wanted no more."

"That was before I faced the dreadful prospect of losing what we have."

"Whatever you wish."

"I will think about it. Now we have to make ready for the results of the votes, and the arrival of the Earth ship."

"Agreement," he said grimly.

They checked in with Ennui, then had a formal royal breakfast, maintaining the conventional show. Havoc normally chafed under the trappings of royalty, but Gale, Symbol, the Lady Aspect and the Chroma Representatives always persuaded him to stick it out longer. The planet kingdom was prospering under his rule, mainly because he had a good sense of delegation and found competent, committed people to do the necessary. This had not always been the case with prior kings, partly because the good ones had been systematically undermined and sometimes assassinated by the corrupt bureaucracy. Havoc's first task as king had been to route that out, with the help of the Glamors.

Voila appeared. "Greeting, Father."

Havoc sent a mental message to Ennui. *Get us private.*

Done. Ennui would not have moved at her desk or changed expression, but she had telepathically checked all minds within range to make sure no one was snooping. Even so, Havoc, Gale, and Voila kept their minds locked, and communicated only verbally.

"Acknowledged, Daughter," he said after a moment. "We are private."

"Please join us for breakfast, beloved," Gale said.

Voila sat down and helped herself to bread and jam. "The near future has come clearer. The ship will orbit the planet, then send down a shuttle to land and contact the natives. It will crash unless we intervene."

"Why?" Gale asked.

"Because Earth does not believe in magic. Earthers think Science is the only magic that exists."

"And if it crashes, they may take that as hostile action on our part," Havoc said, reading that much for himself. "And will loose the planet-buster bomb."

"They may," Voila agreed. "But more paths lead to a second effort, as they are aware that accidents happen. When that one also crashes, the paths converge on destruction."

"Should we teleport someone to the ship to warm them?"

"No, Father. They wouldn't understand. They truly do not believe, so would seek some alternate explanation, and not take proper warning. Anyway, our security depends on them not learning about magic yet."

"Yet?" Gale asked.

"Once the ship departs with the hostages, leaving only the bomb craft, it will be safe to teach them magic. They can't communicate directly with Earth; it is too far away. So the ship will go, and return in six months. We need to nullify that bomb in that time."

"Why is it needful that they not believe in magic, yet?" Havoc asked. "Surely it would broaden their perspective."

"Father, it's a bigot society, according to Idyll. Sudden evidence of magic other than Science magic would shake their core belief system and most likely lead to denial and violence. Remember, historically Earth burned witches. Idyll doubts they have changed much in the past thousand years."

"So we must conceal our magic, and prevent them from letting their ignorance crash their shuttles," Havoc said. "That is coming into my department."

"Obviously," Voila agreed. "It is why I am here."

"We shall simply have to see that they land in a White Chroma zone," he said. "Maybe if we make a large seemingly ideal landing site, they will use it, like bees attracted to honey."

"Do it, Father," she agreed.

Havoc sent a mental message to Ennui, providing the directive for her to implement. Then he closed his mind. "Done. Now there is something else."

"Question?"

"We believe there should be an eighth member of the hostage party: your pet the dog."

Voila stared at him. "Confusion."

"Iolo ifrit."

She laughed. "Joy! He'd love to come, even as a dog."

"He should be able to diffuse on Earth, as will the rest of you, as that is independent of magic. That is a secret that may prove useful."

Voila focused intently, then shrugged. "I can't see that far ahead, but it makes sense. I'll tell him."

"I think our business is done, for the moment," Havoc said. He glanced at Gale.

Gale nodded. "Dear, this may be a formality, but—"

"Oh, I know, of course," Voila said. "But say it anyway."

"We love you. If we should lose you—"

"Yes, you must have another natural child," Voila said. "And make her the Glamor of Amoeba, if that is open."

Gale nodded again. Then tears streaked down her face. She didn't sob, just let them flow.

"Mother, don't *do* that!" Voila protested. "Father, make her stop!" She glanced at him. "Chagrin." For tears were coursing down his face too.

Voila gave up and let her own tears flow. It was their communal sharing of grief for what might be. They all knew the risk and accepted it, but their emotions did not. Even with their minds closed so that there was no telepathy, the overwhelming feeling came through.

Then Voila kissed them both and vanished.

"We have lost her already," Havoc said.

"She has achieved her maturity," Gale agreed. "She will never be the girl she seems."

He faced her seriously. "Gale, let's *have* that next child. An ordinary one, not a Glamor."

"An ordinary child," she breathed. "Oh Havoc, can we really?"

"Affirmation. After this crisis passes."

"Agreement." She kissed him fervently." Then they cleaned their faces and prepared for the rest of the day. They had a royal front to present to the planet.

Havoc went about his business, issuing the necessary directives and warnings, preparing the planet for what was to come. The results of the vote were announced: overwhelming support for resisting any takeover by Earth.

At last the huge Science magic ship arrived. It established an orbit about Planet Charm, quite visible in the sky. The crisis had come.

Chapter 2
Marionette

Marionette looked over Captain Bold's shoulder as he established orbit about the ancient colony planet. The picture on the screen was phenomenal: all the colors of the rainbow, and more, spread in splotches across the surface. No wonder they had named this world Charm; it was indeed charming in its variegated hues. Like a painting by a child with more colors than sense.

"The colors come from the volcanoes," Bold said. "They stain everything in their vicinity, modified by the prevailing wind patterns and local weather. See—there is an eruption now, that red one." He pointed at the screen.

She looked closely, and saw the fresh red dust puffing into the sky, spreading to form a cloud. "So many active volcanoes! I wonder if any colonists survive such a violent planet."

"That is of course what we have come to ascertain," he said, reaching out to pat her bottom. It was a signal of respect and desire permitted the ranking officers. "We know there is life, plant and animal, so presumably they did."

She accepted the signal. "Let's celebrate the occasion of safe orbit while the surveyor casts about for a suitable landing site."

"Gladly, mistress," he agreed.

They went to his chamber. She stripped him, then stepped out of her utility robe and into his naked embrace. They had only seven minutes slack time, so did it vertically. She put her arms around his neck and lithely hoisted her body high enough to clear his rampant member. She wrapped her legs around his waist and lowered her slick cleft onto his organ without using her hands. She kissed him as she took him in fully, kneaded him with her peristaltic channel, and he erupted like the volcano, only on a rather smaller scale.

She let him complete his pulsing, then lifted herself off, her vagina closing firmly around him so that no semen leaked out, leaving him clean. She left him to dress himself as she made a quick toilette at the head, efficiently disposing of the residue within her.

"Oh, Ette, I love you," he said as she emerged and put on her robe, adjusting her Mistress Tiara.

Marionette smiled. "How could it be otherwise, Captain?"

"It could never be otherwise," he agreed.

They returned to the control room. The surveyor's report was just appearing on the screen; they had timed it perfectly.

The land, it turned out, was teeming with life, including plants, animals, and human beings. The colonists had indeed survived and prospered; their villages dotted the landscape, including the color patches. There was one large wooden structure anchored on a small lake, in the shape of a pyramid. "Perhaps a burial vault, akin to those of the ancient Mayans and Egyptians," the surveyor conjectured. "There is considerable human activity in its vicinity, with small boats ferrying parties to and from it."

"We shall have to investigate that, in due course," Bold said. "What of a landing site for the shuttle?"

"We found a cleared plain near the pyramid that seems ideal. It may be a sports field, used only for competitive games. The fundament is sturdy enough to support the shuttle. It is within one of the white regions, but not dangerously close to the volcano. There is a village close by; initial contact should be easy."

"The colonists may flock to see the amazing bird from the sky," Bold said with amused irony. "However, there is one significant constraint."

"Which is?"

"According to our records, the atmosphere of this planet was not identical to that of Earth. The colonists had to wear breathing masks to add oxygen and filter out certain other gases. They also were unable to eat most of the native plants and beasts, so they established their own."

"Understandable," Marionette agreed. "It is an alien world. We can surely rig similar masks."

"Except that we may not need to."

"Come again, Captain?"

"We find no evidence of masks today, and they appear to be farming native species of animal and plant."

"So they adapted."

"We sampled the air. It is completely compatible with our own."

Marionette paused, gazing at him. "The air changed?"

"So it seems, Mistress. I don't quite trust this."

"They must have found a way to terraform it."

"Perhaps. Should we risk it?"

She considered briefly. "Yes. But warn the landing party. Make it volunteer."

"Aye, Mistress." He touched a button. "Dynamo: assembly your landing party."

"Aye, sir," Dynamo answered immediately.

Marionette touched the button. "I will accompany you."

"Mistress!" Bold protested. "First contact is inherently dangerous, and not merely because of dubious atmosphere. You should wait for a later landing, after we are sure the natives are friendly."

"That would be less exciting," she said. "After two dull months in space, I am ready for a bit of adventure."

"But the risk!"

She touched his hand. "You will not be at fault if I have trouble, Captain. Let me be."

He stifled his evident further objection. Her touch had that effect, as was intended. "Aye, ma'm."

She joined Dynamo's party of four men. Dynamo was a handsome, muscular, highly skilled man, one of the key elements of the mission. Handsome muscular men were common, but what counted was his curiosity, determination, and intelligence. He should be an excellent first-contact man.

"Dynamo, have you and your men been apprised of the question of air?"

"We have, Mistress. We trust the sample readings."

"As do I. Proceed."

The shuttle compartment was crowded, as it was sized for five, and she made the sixth. But of course no man objected, as she made sure to touch each with some portion of her body. The ones squeezed directly before and behind her became sexually excited; she felt their members stiffen against her, under their uniforms. She would have been annoyed if they had not. Of course their clothing was bullet proof, as was her gown; they could not have done anything with her regardless, unless she actively facilitated it.

The shuttle detached from the mother ship and spiraled down toward the planet, orienting on the bare spot in the white region. At length it shuddered and landed.

"Disembark on guard," Dynamo said curtly as the access port opened. Then, to Marionette: "Mistress, you will of course do as you choose, but please stay behind the men until we have secured the perimeter."

"Thank you for your concern, Dynamo," she said, kissing him on the cheek. "I hear and obey."

The man stood still a moment, assimilating her kiss, then moved out with his men. They formed a crude circle around the craft, weapons at the ready.

Marionette stepped out. The landscape was entirely white. It wasn't just the sand; the air itself seemed to have a whitish cast. In the distance she saw several trees, also white. The effusion of the volcano had stained everything. But the smell of it was fresh and sweet.

"Natives ho," a man called.

Marionette looked. A party of men, women, and children were wending their way toward the shuttle. They looked quite ordinary, with one exception: they too were totally white. Somehow she hadn't realized that the people were affected also, though perhaps it made sense. Probably the white ash coated their skins and got absorbed, painting them.

Dynamo took a stance directly before the natives. "Hello," he called. "Do you understand?"

The native party halted. "Greeting," a white man called back. The accent was strong, but the word was recognizable.

"Greeting," Dynamo echoed. "We come in peace."

"Peace," the man repeated. "Are you nonChroma?"

"We are from Earth," Dynamo said. "The mother planet."

"Earth!" the man said, evidently recognizing the word.

"Show us your leader."

That prompted a native consultation. Then the man spoke again. "King Havoc."

So it was a monarchy. That figured; they were primitives. "King Havoc," Dynamo agreed.

There was a consultation. Then a woman and a child departed, evidently to send word to their oddly named king. Would anything come of it? More likely the king would depart for the far reaches of his kingdom, suspicious of well-armed strangers.

The hell with that. "Take me with you!" Marionette called, running after the two.

"Mistress!" Dynamo said, appalled.

"Why waste time?" she called back. "Let's establish a liaison immediately."

He followed her. "This is a strange planet. We don't know the natives. It's not safe."

"Now who would harm a winsome girl?" she inquired, continuing her course.

"Mistress! This must not be!"

"Catch me if you can," she said gaily, coming up on the woman and child, who had paused. The woman looked amused and the girl was giggling.

Of course Dynamo had to come too. His head would roll if she came to grief. "The Captain will not be pleased."

"Too bad for him." She turned to the woman. "Take us to King Havoc."

Dynamo faced the shuttle. "Maintain your perimeter until our return," he called. Then, resolutely, he joined Marionette. "You are a harsh mistress," he muttered.

She patted his rear. "I'll make it up to you, in due course."

The girl giggled again. "They understand us!" Dynamo said, appalled anew.

"You do seem to be real people," the white woman said. "Typical controlling man, typical independent woman."

"Exactly," Marionette agreed, laughing.

"We must take the coach to Triumph City," the woman said. "To save time."

"By all means, save time," Dynamo agreed. His interest was to get this done with as fast as possible, so as to get them out of an unknown situation. Marionette's willfulness was testing his ability to cope. Yes she know that there was also a strong current of private gratification, because alien cultures were his specialty, and this was putting him in the middle. His protests were mostly for the record.

They came to the coach. It, too, was all white, from wheels to windows, with a white coachman on a high bench in front. More surprising was the creatures harnessed to it: white six legged monsters. Six legs?

"You like horses?" the woman inquired. "These are friendly." She patted a massive horny nose.

"I do," Marionette said, delighted. She patted the nose. The creature eyed her, its orb rotating smoothly in the socket, but did not protest. "But on Earth, horses have four legs."

"That's interesting," the woman said. "We don't have many Earth animals here."

They boarded the coach, and the "horses" set briskly off. The white landscape fairly whizzed by outside the windows.

"Havoc is the local king?" Marionette asked the woman.

"Havoc is king of Charm."

"The whole planet?"

"Yes. He's a good king."

"Perhaps we should introduce ourselves. I am Marionette, mistress of the Earth mission. My companion is Dynamo, a capable officer."

"I am Deva. I am interested in demons. My daughter is Lucent. She likes insects."

"Demons! You speak figuratively?"

"No, in stories of magic."

Oh. "Everyone likes a good magic story."

"Your term 'mistress.' I don't think I understand."

Dynamo shot her a warning glance. He clearly did not trust any of this, and did not want her to be too free with information.

"I provide sex for all the men of the ship. I am good at what I do."

Dynamo gazed resolutely out the window.

Deva looked her over appraisingly. "I dare say you are. You are stunningly beautiful."

"Thank you. I take pride in my work."

"Oh, look," Deva said, evidently satisfied to change the subject. "Lucent has found a bug."

Indeed, the girl was holding a large odd bug with no sign of fear or aversion. It was walking carefully across her hand. "It's missing a leg!" Marionette said.

"By no means. All insects here have five legs."

"I see." Things really were different on this planet.

"Ah, we are coming to Triumph City," Deva said.

Marionette looked out the window. "The pyramid?"

"Yes. The king lives in the top. We'll have to take the ferry now."

They got out of the coach and approached the lake. There was a boat. Deva went to negotiate with the boatman. In a moment she beckoned them forward. Evidently the Earth visitors were privileged travelers.

Marionette saw that here the people were all normally complexioned, rather than being pure white. They were out of the white region, and that apparently made all the difference.

They boarded the boat and the boatman paddled them across. Soon they were at the floating base of the pyramid city. It was huge, an impressive work of architecture for a primitive culture. Just how primitive were they?

The interior was a mass of passages. They took a lift up to the top. "What powers this?" Dynamo asked, interested in the mechanics.

"Men on cranks," Deva explained. "There is a counterweight, so they don't have to work too hard."

The lift halted. Deva pushed a panel aside. They got out and followed a short passage to what was evidently a throne room.

And there was the king on his throne. And beside him, the queen. He was a sternly handsome man in his mid thirties, and she was a lovely woman. Both wore crowns set with colored stones. Both had brown hair and brown eyes.

Dynamo and Marionette made slight courtesy bows. Primitive monarchs could be very sensitive about the forms.

"I am King Havoc," the man said gravely.

"And Queen Gale," the woman said.

Dynamo took half a step forward. "I am Dynamo, of the Earth ship Dominance. My companion is Marionette, ship's mistress."

King Havoc wasted no further time on amenities. "What is your mission here?"

"To recover our lost colony," Dynamo said. "We hope the process will be amicable."

"And if it is not?"

"We dislike the use of force, but are prepared to resort to it when necessary."

"What force?"

"The ship has what we colloquially term a planet-buster bomb. We can and will destroy this planet if we have to."

The king did not seem much awed. That was a bad sigh; it meant he was either a fool or a fighter. "And if we should take the two of you hostage?"

"The bomb will be loosed immediately."

"Doubt," the king said. "Earth did not send a ship out here to waste a bomb. You won't recover a colony that way."

Marionette realized that the king was both smart and nervy, no fool. He would fight rather than yield his power.

Dynamo considered briefly. "You are calling our bluff?"

"Affirmation."

"We also have lesser bombs that can be targeted on specific sites without damaging the planet as a whole. Such as this city. We can if you wish arrange a demonstration."

The king swelled visibly, but the queen put a hand on his arm, pacifying him. That interested Marionette. Was she the real ruler?

Havoc spoke. "We will spare you the demonstration, accepting that you have such weapons. But you will not conquer this planet by such means. You need the cooperation of the citizens. We offer trade of unique goods, exchange of embassies, courtesy to tourists from and to Earth. This can be mutually profitable. No governments will change."

"This is not Earth's purpose," Dynamo said. "We prefer to govern our colonies. The yoke need not be heavy."

"At first," the king said.

Marionette was watching him carefully while Dynamo kept the dialogue. She knew men, and could judge intellect and capacity closely by small signs. Havoc was frighteningly intelligent, and strongly motivated. He was also, amazingly, a man of his word—once given. A truly dangerous adversary. He had to be nullified.

"We will take your offer to the ship," Dynamo said. "I suggest you consider your options carefully."

"Our position is reasonable," Havoc said. "Reconsider yours."

"Then this dialogue is at an end," Dynamo said. "We appreciate your courtesy and candor."

"Similarity."

They bowed again and retreated. Deva and her daughter were waiting to guide them back.

"You have an interesting speech convention," Marionette said to Deva. "Single word summaries, alone or introducing clarifications."

"Agreement," the woman said, smiling. "Why did you never speak to the king?"

"Dynamo is the ship's officer in charge. I am a more social creature. The king would not be interested in me."

"Negation. The king takes many beautiful women to his bed. Especially those who are good with sex."

Marionette laughed. "With the knowledge of the queen?"

"She had an eye on Dynamo."

This time even Dynamo laughed. "You seem to have a very free society," he said.

Marionette faced him momentarily. "Make a note: perhaps I should be offered for the king's bed, and Dynamo for the queen's, should the king elect to cooperate with Earth's program. I believe we could satisfy them in that re-spect."

"So noted," Dynamo said somewhat sourly.

"You're a tease," Deva said.

"If that were all that were required to help the mission succeed, I should be glad to do my part."

"The king is said to be excellent in bed. All the palace servant girls are in awe of him."

It was time to change the subject. "These colors—do the people in the other colors also reflect the emissions of their volcanoes?"

"Chroma," Deva said. "We are white Chroma. Black Chroma zone citizens are black, and Blue Chroma are blue, yes."

"Chroma zones," Marionette repeated, getting it straight. "You don't mind being stained by such colors?"

"Negation! They enable us to do magic."

"Magic?"

"It is a cultural thing. Folk of foreign Chroma zones don't get along well in ours. Therefore they generally prefer to travel in the nonChroma zones, where no one has magic. Except the Glamors, of course."

"Glamourous people?"

Deva smiled. "Magical people. Some say they are myths, but many do believe."

"So they would be welcome in any Chroma zone."

"Affirmation."

Marionette shook her head. "It seems perhaps unfortunate that we of Earth do not believe in magic."

"Wonder."

So this woman was one of the believers. In primitive societies acceptance of magic was common.

In due course they returned safely to the shuttle. "We appreciate your kindness in guiding us to see the king," Marionette said.

"Welcome."

"Please accept this token of our gratitude." Marionette brought out an elegant bracelet set with a bright diamond.

"Appreciation. I have only this White Chroma stone to offer in return, surely a poorer thing." Deva presented a pure white crystal, unmounted.

"It is more than enough. Thank you, Deva."

"It is magic. Keep it with you always."

"I shall."

They exchanged baubles, and hugged. Marionette had not understated the case when she said she was social; her beauty and manner affected women too. She made a point of being popular. It was after all her profession.

Then Dynamo called in the men, who had maintained rigorous guard throughout, and the party squeezed back into the shuttle. It closed, its gravity shield came on, and it lifted from the ground, surely awing the native specta-tors.

"That was pat," she told Dynamo, ignoring the men crowded around them. "As if a hostile party from a far world could simply land unannounced and be granted an immediate private audience with the king of the planet."

"They surely had bowmen oriented on us throughout the interview. Had we made any false move, we would have been dead."

"I'm not sure of that. Did you spot any hidden guards?"

"No. That merely means they were well masked."

"Extremely well masked," she agreed. "As you know, I specialize in reading people. That white woman Deva was no incidental spectator; she was sent to intercept us. She is not at all what she appears."

"She appeared to me to be a very attractive if pale woman."

"Precisely. She's old and experienced and powerful. She could have broken me like a stick. I'd like to know her secret of apparent youth. And her daughter, Lucent—she's an adult masked as a girl, and not related to Deva. She didn't find that five-legged bug; she had it with her. I suspect she could have made it attack us, and its sting would have been deadly. They were not merely guides, they were guards. They would have killed us if we had attacked the king."

Dynamo's jaw fell. "You are surely correct, Ette. I should have been more alert."

"Don't flatter me with false modesty, Dyn. You were poised to spin about and smash Deva's head the moment she moved against us. My only regret is that our little hero and maiden act did not fool them. I don't know what weapon they had—that's not my specialty—but am sure you had little chance. I hope we can learn something from that receiver I gave Deva."

"And hope she didn't give you one in return."

"I'll have the white stone analyzed in the lab. I suspect it is ordinary crystallized mineral. Meanwhile, what's your impression of the king?"

"He's a martial artist, damned smart and fast. I would have had to use a gun on him, from a distance, or I'd be lost. Even so, it would be close. He has suspicious confidence, and I suspect it is justified."

"So we are dealing here with primitives, not fools."

"Exactly. They are competent in their home territory. We underestimate them at our peril."

"My sentiment also. They were studying us as intently as we studied them, and surely learning as much. The queen especially was not deceived; she was watching me closely."

"She hardly looked at you."

"True. But she tracked my every wiggle. She recognized me as the power behind you, as she may be behind the king. We just may have another matriarchal society here."

"Are you sure? The king struck me as sure of his power."

"The man doesn't necessarily know. But no, I am not sure. More likely she governs him by seduction; she's an extremely attractive woman, as you noted."

"I said nothing of her!"

"You forget my specialty, Dyn. She could take you almost as readily as I could, if she wished. You have half a crush on her already."

"Granted," he said with resignation.

She poked him lightly in his taut belly. "If we make you regent of this colony, she may be yours to love."

"The king would have to be dead first."

"Or distracted. Remember our prospective offer: the two of us in their beds. They just might take us up on that."

"And kill us when they had us naked."

"That, too," she agreed, smiling.

The shuttle docked. "Thank you, men," Dynamo said as they got out. "You did your duty."

Marionette glanced at her watch. "Four minutes until your report to Captain Bold. Close the hatch."

He closed it and turned back to her, quickly opening his uniform. She had already doffed her cloak and stood naked. She turned away from him and bent over, touching the floor with her ten fingers, presenting her ample bottom. Rapidly erect, he set his member in her exposed crevice and thrust, climaxing instantly. She milked him as she had the captain, holding her pose until the last jet, then stripping the residue from the softening tube as she drew off him. It was a mark of her professionalism to see that the man needed no further cleaning up. He was done within two minutes.

There was no head here in the shuttle, so she slipped in a sponge and drew her cloak back over her. She kissed him, her tongue teasing his. "On your way, Dynamo."

He opened the port and stepped out. He forged toward the captain's office. She followed more sedately, but turned aside at the first head, where she removed the sponge, efficiently cleaned, and checked her itinerary video. There was a crewman who had recently received news of a death in the family. He was suffering awareness of mortality and needed comfort and distraction. She headed for his station.

≈≈≈

Marionette's communicator buzzed, waking her. It was the captain's signal. She touched the acknowledge key.

"I must leave you now," she said to the crewmen, sliding out of his bunk. "Thank you for sharing your bed."

"Oh, Mistress, thank *you*," he said gratefully. "I feel much better now."

"Welcome." She stood, inhaling to give him one last peek, and donned her cloak. A sympathetic ear, judicious sex, and a warm clasp during sleep could significantly enhance a man's mood. He should be all right for some time.

It was a mark of her position that Marionette had no room or bed of her own. She always slept in the bed of a crewman, providing him with whatever most pleased him. Some were quite virile, penetrating her several times in a rest session. Some were satisfied to have her full soft breasts for a pillow as they slept. Some merely held her hand as they poured out their secret feelings, knowing she would never judge or embarrass them on that account. She knew every man aboard extremely well, and loved them all in her fashion, and of course they all loved her. The mission's mistress was a very special role.

"Something's happening," Captain Bold said as she entered his cabin. "Your impromptu interview with the king set off a flurry of activity whose nature we can guess."

"Clarify it for me, Bold," she said, taking his hand and stroking his fingers. "You know I'm not apt on technical matters."

"The hell you aren't, Mistress. You just don't like to reveal your calculating mind."

She widened her eyes innocently as she passed his hand inside her cloak to rest on a breast. "Please, Captain! How can anything as soft as this have any hard edges?"

He had to smile. "There is an ancient song 'April is in my mistress' face.' I think of you as April."

She laughed, causing her breasts to bounce against his hand. "'But in her heart, a cold December,'" she quoted. "My heart is warm." She pressed the tips of his fingers hard against her breast bone. "Feel the pulse."

"Warm yet calculating," he said. "At any rate, we have been monitoring all activity in that vicinity, and believe we fathom it, with one notable exception. A party of seven departed the pyramid in a coach and is making its way across the white zone you visited before. We suspect this is the king's household proceeding to some hiding place they believe is beyond our knowledge or reach. Indeed it may be; if they enter some deep cave we would have extraordinary difficulty extracting them without injury. As it is, this offers a rare opportunity."

"The king's household," Marionette repeated thoughtfully. "Perhaps his wife, a child or two, and some servants and guards. It is to be expected."

"That is my thought. I believe we can make a lightning raid and capture them, if we use a larger shuttle and a fast ground transport. It would be a coup, and a significant wedge against the king's intransigence. He might even become reasonable."

"I agree. Dynamo should handle it. Maybe I should go again, also."

The captain looked pained. "Mistress—"

"But I'm not much for violence, so no. I'd only get in the way. But if they *are* members of the king's family, we don't want to hurt them. Do your best to capture them bloodlessly."

"We'll use stunners rather than blasters," he agreed.

"Excellent. Keep me advised." She drew his hand from her breast, kissed him, and left.

She returned to the crew barracks and checked the bunks in the dim light. Most were occupied, as the crewmen slept in shifts, three to a bunk, saving weight and space. Most were also asleep, but one was kneeling on the floor by the bed.

She approached. "Problem?" she inquired gently.

"Praying, Mistress," he replied.

"For what?"

"For company."

"Then you have been answered." She set aside her cloak and got into bed with him. He was ardent before he lapsed into sleep, one hand still holding her buttock. That enabled her to sleep also, which she appreciated. She could sleep alone when she had to, but did not enjoy it. The clasp of a satisfied man was her best soporific.

※ ※

The news of the raid was remarkable. "Seven natives and a six-legged dog," Dynamo reported, excited. "None hurt, but we had to stun one."

"A guard resisted?"

"A girl resisted. She's what we have learned is called an Amazon, a female martial artist. She knocked out two men, moving like lightning, before I used the stunner. She is also, it turns out, the king's daughter."

"Well! Bold's conjecture was correct, then."

"Absolutely. In fact we captured all four of the king's teen-aged children, together with two chaperones and a maid. And the youngest child's pet. They were definitely sneaking out to what they thought was safety. We were extremely fortunate."

"Our alertness facilitated exactly such luck," she clarified. "It seems they never thought we'd be watching."

"They lack advanced technology. Their weapons are swords, clubs, nets and the like. No radios or vision screens. They saw the ship, but lack the awareness of what it represents."

"Precisely. Once we pacify them we'll be providing them with that kind of technology, surely improving their lives."

"As we mine their minerals, harvest their useful crops, and take their healthiest individuals as slaves." He clearly disapproved such exploitation.

"As honest workers."

He shrugged. "Whatever term applies. They may not agree that their lives are being improved."

"In time they surely will. Civilization can't afford to leave primitives to their inefficiencies."

"We being civilized," he said with irony.

"I want to meet them."

"It may not be appropriate, Mistress. We secured them for safety, but they know they are captives and are not pleased."

"Well of course they aren't! That's why I must go to them."

"Mistress—"

She silenced him with a glance. Without further protest he conducted her to the confinement chamber.

There was the full party of seven. Four were normal human color, looking young and frightened. Two were older: a red man and and a blue woman. Another was so thoroughly swathed in clothing and veils as to be completely hidden. All were manacled to the wall, except for the gray six-legged dog, which lay touching the youngest girl.

"This is unkind!" Marionette protested loudly enough to be heard within the chamber. "They must not be chained."

"Protocol requires—"

"Forget protocol!" she snapped. "Where are they going to go? They're aboard the ship." Without asking, she entered the chamber and stood before the captives. "I am Marionette, mistress of the mission. I want to be your friend."

They stared stonily at her. Evidently her little show was not yet sufficient to persuade them. That wasn't surprising.

She went to the one in a para-military uniform: a strong, healthy girl, no beauty, but possessed of a certain appeal in her evident defiance. For one thing, she had a head of flamingly red hair with matching eyes. "You must be the Amazon. Tell me your name and I will free your limbs."

"Mistress!" Dynamo protested. This was of course part of the script.

She ignored him. "As a martial artist you surely understand discipline—and honor. I will accept your word not to attack me or try to disrupt the operation of the ship."

"Outrage," the girl snapped.

"At least tell me your name, so we can talk. I have told you mine."

The girl yielded to that extent. "Flame, the king's daughter, age seventeen."

"Named after your hair, surely," Marionette said, smiling winningly. "And your temper. Am I correct?"

Slowly the girl smiled in return. Marionette's direct approach was almost impossible to rebuff. "Close enough."

"Well, Flame, as I said, I want to be your friend. I have a certain influence; I can help alleviate the rigors of your captivity. Work with me and I will work with you. Give me your word."

Reluctantly Flame acquiesced. "Given."

Marionette put her fingers on the manacle at Flame's wrist, and it fell open. All locks on the ship were keyed to her touch. The girl was free.

"You could have disabled me with a blow or kick even while manacled," Marionette said. "You did not."

"It would have been pointless. Your guard would have stunned me again."

"You could have taken me as a temporary hostage, threatening me harm unless you were freed."

Flame shrugged. "You were trying to be friendly."

"Ah, now we have a dialogue. You know that I am an enemy, as you see it, and that my friendliness is just a pose. But I can indeed help you to a degree. Will you trust me that far? All I want is your cooperation and promise not to make mischief on the ship. To behave like the honored guests you can be. You are hostages to the king's behavior; this is a tactic of war, but there need be no cruelty. Agree to behave well and you will have the freedom of the ship."

"Mistress!" Dynamo protested again, on cue.

Flame looked at the red man. He nodded. "We all agree," she said.

"Then I release you all," Marionette said, moving to the next one, who was a handsome black-haired, black-eyed young man. Interesting how hair and eyes matched. These youths were color coded in their fashion despite being "nonChroma."

"Mistress, the others have not given their word," Dynamo said.

"Yes they have." She looked around. "Haven't you?"

The others nodded, including the three adults. They had evidently come to understand that resistance would be futile and that there was no need to invite punishment.

"Who are you?" Marionette asked the youth.

"I am Warp, the king's son, seventeen."

She touched the manacle and it fell free. Then she stepped into him and kissed him briefly on the mouth. "Thank you, Warp. Perhaps in due course we will get to know each other better."

She left Warp half stunned, as intended, and went to the next, a striking blonde with matching eyes. "Weft, the king's daughter, seventeen," this one said. "Don't kiss me."

Marionette laughed, as did the others. Things were loosening, and that was good.

The fourth one was a slightly younger brown-haired and eyed ordinary girl. "Voila, the king's daughter, fifteen, almost sixteen," this one said softly as she was freed. There was something about her, but Marionette could not immediately place it. "And this is Iolo Ifrit, my friend." She patted the dog, who wagged his tail briefly.

Marionette went on to the red man. "Augur, Red Chroma, thirty five, chaperone to the king's children. Beside me is my wife Aura, Blue Chroma, thirty five, sharing the duty."

"Of course." Marionette moved on to the swathed woman.

"Ine, Air Chroma, thirty two, servant to the king's children," a dulcet voice came.

"May I see your face?"

"No. I am invisible."

Marionette laughed. "Please, I want only to be able to recognize you."

Slowly the woman unfastened her veil.

Marionette stared. There was nothing there! "Where is your head?"

"It is here," the voice said, issuing from the space. The gloved hand reached down to catch Marionette's hand. "You can feel my face."

Her hand came to the emptiness—and felt a woman's comely features. There really was a head there, and it really was invisible. Marionette was speechless.

"Now you understand the value of our word," Ine said. "When I strip naked, I cannot be seen. I dress not to hide myself, but to make myself visible."

"I see, as it were," Marionette said faintly. "Resume your veil; now I understand." They would have to make sure the heat and sound sensors could accurately place this creature, so she could not slip her clothing and roam the ship unknown.

"Appreciation." The woman restored the veil and was fully apparent again, in her fashion.

"Now you are free to explore the ship," Marionette said. "But first—are you hungry?"

"Yes," the dark-haired Warp said immediately. He was evidently the natural leader among the young folk. The adults did not challenge him, though Marionette was sure they had the authority to do so if they chose. At any rate the red and blue chaperones did; the invisible maid was probably at the bottom of the pecking order.

"Would you care to join the crew mess hall, or do you prefer to eat here?"

Now the red man, Augur, spoke. Marionette was good with names, necessarily. "Would our appearance cause disruption?"

"It will attract attention, but the crewmen are disciplined and will not impose unless invited. They would find you interesting, especially the women."

Augur smiled, as did Aura and Weft. They understood about the appeal of attractive women, as these ones were. "Then we will join the mess."

"Question," the Amazon girl, Flame, said.

"Ask," Marionette responded. She was good with conventions, too.

"I retain my weapons. Is this an oversight?"

"No. You gave your word. You are therefore no physical danger to us. We do not seek to deprive any of you of your possessions, dignity, or your right to self-defense, other than your freedom beyond this ship."

"Question," Augur said. "How may we obtain that larger freedom?"

"That is up to King Havoc. If he agrees to subordinate Planet Charm to the Empire of Earth without further resistance, and to facilitate our designs, you will be returned immediately. We will accept his word as we do yours."

"He will not accede," Augur said grimly. "What is thus our prospect?"

"You will return with this ship to Earth, where you will be held pending the resolution of our issue with King Havoc. You will not be mistreated, but you will be accompanied wherever you travel. This is as much for your protection as for the fact that you are hostages. We do not wish to aggravate the situation unnecessarily."

The youngest, Voila, smiled for the first time. "No one wants to aggravate

Father."

"Unless they are stupid," Warp said.

They had confidence in their sire, perhaps exaggerated. "We are not stupid," Marionette said. "There is the local head." She gestured.

"Question?" Augur asked.

"The latrine. Bathroom. Cleaning and elimination chamber."

"Understanding," Augur said. "Ine, see to them."

The swathed maid preceded the four teens into the chamber. There seemed to be no concern about gender privacy. The six-legged dog followed Voila.

"Appreciation," the red woman, Aura, said.

"Welcome."

In a moment the maid emerged and went to the baggage piled in the corner; the crew had simply brought everything in the fleeing coach. She selected several outfits and an odd contraption and took them to the head.

"It is a shock, this capture," Augur said. "They expected to be safely in a far Chroma zone by this time. But they should adjust readily."

"They are well-trained," Aura added.

"We shall treat them as guests," Marionette said. "Now that we understand each other."

"You may find them to be more of a challenge than you anticipated," Augur said.

"As long as they honor their word, there should be no difficulty."

Augur and Aura both smiled faintly, but did not argue the case. Marionette was curious to see what non-hostile ways the teenagers could test the limits. They would surely do so.

Meanwhile she had something else to discuss with the adults. "When the Charm colony was set, a thousand years ago, the atmosphere was not quite right. The plants and animals were not properly edible. Masks and special provisions were necessary. Something seems to have changed."

Now the smiles of the two were open. "As it happens, my wife and I were curious about this too," Augur said. "So we studied it, merging our specialties."

"And we concluded that it was not our species that adapted to the planet, but the planet that adapted to us," Aura said.

"How could you have done such a thing, without advanced science?" Marionette asked, though it did seem that it had been accomplished.

"It would have been a challenge, even with advanced magic," Aura agreed. "But we did not do it. The planet did."

"I do not wish to question your expertise, but—"

"It was a challenge for us to accept," Augur said. "Until we realized it was Gaea."

"The mother planet," Aura said. "Loving and helping all her inhabitants. When we had trouble breathing, she changed the air—without hurting any of the other creatures. It was a marvelous and intricate compromise."

"Similarly she changed the plants just enough so that they were compatible for us," Augur said. "We did not understand the phenomenal benefit she had rendered us. But the earth-mother loved us anyway."

Marionette was amazed. "You are saying that the planet consciously catered to the human species?"

"Not consciously," Aura said. "She doesn't work quite that way. She simply does what feels right to her. This was merely an early example."

"There were other ways that Gaea acted?"

"Perhaps," Augur said, shrugging. Marionette realized that these folk had said all they were going to on this subject. Maybe that was just as well, as what they had said so far was barely believable.

Yet it did account for the mysterious conversion of the planet's atmosphere—and more—to human comfort. Could this possibly make sense?

Soon the teens emerged, trailed by the modest maid. All of them except Flame the Amazon had changed from their travel clothing to display outfits. It was a considerable improvement. Warp was darkly handsome in a light shirt and dark trousers, and the two girls now wore matching outfits: light blouses and dark skirts. Weft had done her fair hair and practically radiated beauty; Flame had loosened hers and looked more feminine than she had before. Young Voila's hair was in a modest ponytail; she had said she was almost sixteen, but she looked thirteen, small of breast and poise. The dog remained loyally by her side.

There was one other change: all four of them now wore small golden crowns. They were not trying to conceal their royalty, they were advertising it.

Marionette led them to the mess hall. A shift of fifteen men was there, seated at the crew tables. The sergeant in charge looked up as Marionette entered, but Dynamo intercepted the man's reaction. "At ease, men. The guests will be joining you." That was military code to make no untoward reaction. "At ease" was a defined condition, not an invitation to be natural.

Marionette showed the four teens to the head table, facing the crewmen, and the chaperones to the two ends of it. She and Dynamo took the inside, facing away from the men. The swathed maid remained at the doorway, inconspicuous but available at call.

The crewmen watched, making no sound. They were of course at first impressed by the red man and blue woman more than by the relatively ordinary teens. Then their attention shifted. Marionette knew that many eyes were studying the buxom blonde Weft; for the past two months she, Marionette, had been the only live woman they had seen. This was a rare treat for them, and the girls clearly knew it. They were heedless of the stern glances of the chaperones.

"Our food is all artificial, with the same essential nutrients," Marionette said. "But it can be crafted to almost any appearance and taste. What are your preferences?"

The teens hesitated. "We are not familiar with your foods," Aura said. "Please select for us."

"As you wish." Marionette spoke a series of codes, and in a moment panels on the table slid aside and the meals rose from below, a slightly different one before each person. Salads, cooked vegetables, baked meats, colored beverages, and jellied desserts, together with suitable eating utensils. There was a separate set of dishes containing water and dog food, which Voila took and set on the floor for Iolo.

"Your science magic is impressive," Augur remarked as they tasted the food and found it good.

"Thank you." They thought of it as a type of magic? Advanced technology might indeed seem like magic to primitives.

The group ate with good appetite. The panels slid aside to receive the expended dishes. Rinse cups appeared.

"To clean the mouth after eating," Marionette explained. "Merely swish and spit back." She demonstrated, delicately letting the fluid return to its cup, then smiling to show her suddenly spotless teeth. They emulated her, seeming amused.

Marionette was about to guide them from the mess hall when Weft addressed her. "Please, for your courtesy, and the nice men," she said, flashing a smile at the silent crewmen. "I would like to sing a song. To thank you."

What was this? Did the natives pay for meals with performances? It seemed best to humor the girl. "By all means, dear." It wasn't as if anyone here was about to disparage an amateur effort; the men would be interested in anything this lovely maiden did. Marionette did however see that Warp rolled his eyes at Flame, who nodded; evidently this sort of thing had happened before. It seemed that one of their number was a show-off when there was an audience to be had. Teens would be teens.

Weft lifted the instrument she had brought and held in her lap. She stood and walked around the table. "If I may," she said, then sat on the table, crossing her legs toward the crewmen. She had remarkably good legs, and they showed to advantage. She also had extremely well formed breasts, fully outlined by her almost translucent blouse. She could sing like a croaking frog and the men would hardly notice.

Weft balanced the instrument on her partially exposed firm thigh. She flung back her flaring hair and gazed at the crewmen. "I am Weft, captive daughter of King Havoc of Charm. I am a musician, a songstress. I will accompany myself with my hammer dulcimer, which I learned from my mother, Queen Gale."

A hammer dulcimer. What was that? The thing was in the shape of a flat trapezoid with a number of metal strings. This was struck with a hammer? Then she saw that the girl was placing little balls on her fingers: the hammers. That should make quite a jangle!

Weft glanced at Marionette. "This is for you, Mistress. The words are a poem written by Thomas Moreley, in the sixteenth century of your Christian era. Our culture derives from yours, of course, and we have tried to keep the artistic conventions."

"Thank you," Marionette said guardedly. What *was* she up to?

Then Weft began to play. Her fingers danced nimbly across the strings, and an intricate pattern of notes formed a fetching and familiar melody. She was good at it; in fact she bordered on professional. Then she sang—and jaws went slack. It wasn't just that she really could sing well; it was her choice of song.

April is in my mistress' face
And July in her eyes hath place
Within her bosom is September
But in her heart a cold December.

The men were staring. So was Dynamo. All of them were stunned. So was Marionette. But she rallied. "You may applaud," she murmured.

There was an instant clapping of hands. That helped cover Marionettes' confusion. True, the girl had chosen, and evidently well knew, a remarkably relevant song. More significantly, this innocent and perhaps pampered royal child was as good a singer as any woman on Earth.

Chapter 3
Flame

Flame sedately followed her provocative sibling back to their chamber. Weft had put on quite a show, and not merely of her music; the eyes of the crewmen had been virtually glued to her body throughout. That had distracted them so that no one noticed Iolo the "dog" diffusing and spreading under the table. He hadn't spread far, just enough to verify that his vapor could not be detected by the Science Chroma mechanical eyes they had noted spread throughout the ship. It was the special ability of the ifrits to incorporate the magic of whatever Chroma they were in, so that they could function anywhere, including this all Science chroma zone ship.

But Weft finished too soon; Iolo had not compacted again, as the process was slow. Flame saw Voila catch Aura's eye.

"Perhaps you should do another," Aura suggested to Weft. "Perhaps one more relevant to their interests."

Weft nodded, understanding the reason. "We do not yet truly know your culture of Earth," she said to the men. "But we hope to remedy that in the course of our visit there. We do know something of men who must spend a long time away from their homeland, as warriors or prisoners, who are perhaps forced to do hard labor in a swamp, physical or emotional. This song is titled 'The Peat Bog Soldiers,' dating from ancient Earth. Forgive me if this is irrelevant."

Flame saw that every eye was still fixed on Weft, as she intended. Relevance hardly mattered; they were utterly fascinated by her person and manner. Weft was as apt in the use of her body as Flame was, but in a rather different way. Flame did not care to admit it, but there was a buried corner of her personality that envied that. Flame could render a man unconscious in a moment; Weft didn't need to.

The men did not seem to recognize the title. They would, after Weft sang it, flashing her body for emphasis. It was the art of flirtation, something Flame could never do.

Far and wide as the eye can wander
Heath and bog are everywhere
Not a bird sings out to cheer us
Oaks are standing gaunt and bare.

We are the peat bog soldiers
Marching with our spades to the bog.

Now there was faint recognition, and considerable empathy. These men *were* long away from home, and somewhat homesick. They did relate. So did Flame.

Weft sang the second verse, and the third, concluding:

One day we shall cry rejoicing
Homeland, dear, you're mine at last.

Then will the peat bog soldiers
March no more with their spades to the bog.

It was an ordinary song, but Weft sang it with such flair and feeling that a number of the men were caught up in it, and tears ran down the cheeks of a few. They felt the emotional bog.

Flame glanced under the table. Iolo had reformed. Voila nodded slightly to Aura. Voila and Iolo had been close companions from infancy, and understood each other almost perfectly.

"Thank you," Aura said. "Now we must return to our quarters and get some rest."

Weft uncrossed her exposed legs, giving the men a wicked flash inside her firm thighs, and put away her dulcimer. "You have been a great audience," she told the men. "Maybe we'll do it again some time."

They applauded again. Weft had completely won them over, and not just by displaying her remarkable body. Flame was not surprised. Weft was a Glamor, the child of Glamors, with superhuman powers, and she had applied herself diligently. She was probably the finest songstress on Charm, and well able to impress any audience.

Of course all four of them were Glamors, and the best in their specialties. The purpose of their arts was to distract observers from their extraordinary powers of magic, which were seldom shown. The others would take their turns as expedient, while only Voila held back. She needed to be the immature, shy, reticent one, shadowed by the light of her talented siblings. It was a part she was ironically qualified to handle. She really was the youngest, but her magic was the strongest by far. It was vital than the Earthers not catch on before it was time.

"That was remarkable," the Mistress Marionette said back at their chamber. "Do the rest of you have similar abilities?"

"They do," Augur said. "The king believes in the arts, and had his children specially trained. Warp is a tale teller. Flame is an Amazon. Voila is an actress. On occasion they put on a show together."

"We shall have to arrange such a show," Marionette said. "Now I will leave you for a time, for this should be your night shift and I have duties elsewhere. There will be a guard outside your chamber. Please do not take this amiss; this is to protect you against any possible danger. The crew is male, and some of you are sexually appealing."

"Thank you," Aura said, casting a dark look in Weft's direction, as if she had transgressed. She had, of course, but for excellent reason: to protect their darker secrets.

"Touch the walls. Bunks will appear. Sleep as you wish. I suspect you have much to discuss with each other." The mistress left.

They were seemingly alone. They experimented with the walls and found the bunks. They intruded on the floor space, but of course space was at a premium on the ship. They washed and changed to their night clothes, completely careless about brief nudity, and lay down. The men viewing the recording would get a private thrill seeing Weft and Aura gloriously bare.

"It has been a day," Warp said. "We thought to be safely away in hiding, and instead we are captive by the enemy."

"And doomed to be taken to Earth Planet," Flame said. "Because Havoc won't budge." Each of them addressed their parents in particular fashion, by mutual agreement. Flame, considered to be the least emotional, used their given names.

"Fate worse than death," Weft said.

"Oh, I don't know," Warp said. "That Mistress is some creature."

"She's a scheming hussy," Flame said severely. "Just because she kissed you doesn't mean you can trust her."

He sighed. "Oh, I know. But I'd sure like to get her in my bed for an hour."

Weft laughed. "Ask her, why don't you? She might do it. She's the mistress, after all."

"There are two meanings, dummy. She's the mistress of marionettes, and we're the ones on the strings."

They continued the dialogue, nominally resigning themselves to their joint fate. But the real exchange was silent telepathy.

Iolo reports that we are under constant observation, Viola thought. *There are sensors everywhere, recording sights and sounds. They are here too.*

They are peeking at our bared flesh? Weft asked with mock shock. She, alone among them, had chosen to sleep nude.

Worse, Viola thought. *They can see through our clothing. We are all naked to those sensors, all the time.*

So they can see my weapons, Flame thought.

If you had bigger breasts, hothead, they wouldn't notice your weapons, Weft thought.

Wisdom from the cow, Flame retorted.

That's enough, Augur thought. *Don't waste the stones on incidental dialogue. We may need them for serious work.*

He was referring to the nonChroma gemstones each of them wore, that provided them with spot magic despite being in a Science Chroma environment. Telepathy and illusion were low-energy magic, but any use of it slowly depleted the stones.

What of Marionette? Aura asked.

She is the Mistress in both senses, Viola replied. She was the one who could best read the near future paths, so the others left that to her. In the process, she learned useful things, because the paths affected the farther future. *She governs the mission; all the men answer to her. Earth is a matriarchy; all men are subservient to all women. The women control the men largely through sex, and the men are conditioned to accept their dominance.*

That is helpful to know, Augur thought somewhat ruefully.

Just behave like the ignorant teens you are supposed to be, Aura thought.

So they don't catch on to our mission. They are not stupid; any slip can give us away.

With that they let it be, and slept.

✒ ❧

In the morning, their time—the ship was always active, so the days were different for each shift—Marionette conducted them again to the mess hall, where a different group of crewmen was eating. Weft sang them another song, and they were duly appreciative. Then a privileged crewman was delegated to give them a guided tour of the ship.

They reacted like wonder-filled primitives, thrilled by the marvels of Science. Flame hoped the Earthers did not realize that their Glamor intellects were recording the details as thoroughly as the ship's sensors were recording their motions and words. They wanted to know exactly how the ship functioned, in case they ever needed to run it themselves. Such a notion might have made the Earthers laugh, but it was serious. Warp, especially, had studied White Chroma Science magic on Charm, so had a head start.

They also discovered the ship's holo entertainment. This was like an Air Chroma illusion show, with human figures appearing in a globe and acting their parts, telling stories, singing songs, or instructing in some trade. They were fascinating in their novelty. Science magic was really quite something; in fact it almost rivaled other kinds of magic in some respects.

The second "night" Flame was restless, so she slipped from her bunk, garbed herself, and went out beyond the chamber to look around while the others slept. Ine, the supposed maid but actually a skilled Air Chroma Sorceress, was the one on watch. *Alert me if you need help* Ine thought, taking no overt notice.

Appreciation. As if an Amazon would need help, even if the situation were not placid.

As she entered the hall the guard appeared. "May I assist you, maiden?" he inquired politely. He was a man of middle age, carrying weapons he did not bring to his hand, but alert and attentive.

"Boredom," she said. "May we talk?"

"Do you wish me to summon the mistress?"

"Negation. I meant, may I talk with you?"

He smiled. "I am hardly worth talking with. I am merely the assigned routine guard for this shift, of no personal significance, here to help you and protect you as required. But I can summon someone of intellect or interest if you wish."

She liked his modesty. He was not trying to impress her, just being honest. "Negation. I seek merely to divert myself an hour before returning to sleep. If you are an ordinary person, you are suitable."

"Protocol requires me to remain on duty, not allowing my attention to wander."

Flame realized that she wasn't getting anywhere. She drew slightly on her nonChroma gemstone and exerted her perception of the future. She could not do it nearly as well as Voila could—none of them could match Voila in that or any other magic—but her ability should suffice for a simple situation like this.

She saw the several paths diverging from the present, most leading either to the man's summoning of a more competent man or to her return to the chamber without accomplishing anything. But one led to an intriguing and perhaps pleasant interaction.

"I am Flame, an Amazon."

He had to respond to the introduction. "And I am Grumble, a noncommissioned shipman."

"Do you know weaponless disciplines?"

He smiled. "No. I have always been curious, but never had occasion to learn any."

"I can show you some."

He was tempted but cautious. "Protocol—"

"Would not your officer prefer that you handle your shift without disturbing him?"

Grumble laughed. "Certainly. However—"

"I promise to make no trouble for you. All I want is a bit of dialogue. Some human interaction."

Still he hesitated, fearing some mischief that could get him in trouble. The men had been warned to be careful of the hostages; she read it in his mind. But there was a path that nullified that.

She unbound her hair and shook it out in a red torrent. Normally she was sternly Amazon, but she had spectacular hair when she chose to display it. Weft had assured her of that, and Weft was an authority in that respect. "If you ever have to exert sex appeal, firehead, don't depend on your bitty breasts. Let down your roiling hair."

Grumble watched her warily. He had been warned against seduction, but it was Weft they feared, not the angular Amazon female. He wasn't properly prepared for this. She smiled at him.

That did it. The spreading fiery hair overwhelmed his prior image of her, making her completely female. She read it in his mind. Like all the men of the ship, he had seen no women in two months, beyond Mistress Marionette and the hostages, and had had no personal contact with the latter. He could not resist her feminine plea, though it was a chore for her to make it. But this was the course that her path-seeing guided her to, and it was working. She had found the way to make him remain in dialogue instead of diverging to duty-specified alternatives.

"As you wish, Flame," he said with ferociously mixed emotions. His entire awareness of her was dissolving and reforming around her luxurious hair. "Still—"

"Draw your weapon."

"Against you? By no means."

"I wish to learn its nature."

"Oh, of course." His hand reached for the convoluted metal at his hip.

Flame was there against him, her hand catching his wrist, preventing him from drawing.

Surprised, he froze. "Please, miss. I thought you understood I was not threatening you."

"Nor I you," she said. "I merely show my nature. I am combat-trained."

He nodded. "That, too."

"Too?"

"You are female."

Her modest breast and hip were against him, her hair brushing his chin.

"Apology," she said, retreating. "I did not mean to make a demonstration of that nature." But she was thrilled to have accidentally done it. Her bitty breast had scored, now that her hair had cleared the way.

"I understand. It merely is awkward."

"Agreement."

"I am not good with women."

"Nor I with men."

They gazed at each other, suddenly relating.

"Not that I was trying to suggest anything," he said awkwardly.

"Ditto."

"You wish to learn about my sidearm."

"That, too," she said, smiling again.

This time he returned the smile. "We do seem to be two of a type."

"More martial than social," she agreed.

"But if you are trying to get me in trouble—"

"Negation! Trust me in this: I mean you no mischief of any kind. I just want to relate. I have little such experience, so may be clumsy. Maybe I simply want a friend."

"I can be a friend. But even in that respect, you could do better. I'm really just an average middle-aged man."

"I think I prefer that kind. I feel more comfortable with average than I would with superior, being barely competent myself, socially. You surely can teach me much."

"Of course I've been with the Mistress. But that's different; she's professional. She handles it." Then he reconsidered, embarrassed. "But why am I saying this to you?"

"Because I understand. I have never been with a man in that sense, but if I did, for that alone, I would prefer a professional lover, because he would know exactly what to do."

"Exactly. No missteps." He shook his head, bemused, still much aware of her hair. "I am amazed to find myself in such a dialogue with you, princess."

"Similarity. I thought to compare combat techniques."

But having loosened to that extent, Grumble now reconsidered. "I may already have overstepped protocol. I do not wish to make mischief for either of us."

"Agreement." The paths ahead were tangled, and promised trouble if she pursued them further. "Appreciation. I will return now to my sleep."

"Welcome," he said, seeming relieved.

"Parting."

He hesitated. "I would like to answer properly by your convention, but do not know how."

"Acknowledgment," she said.

"Oh. Acknowledgment."

She left him then, and reentered the chamber. It had been an interesting interchange.

It certainly was, Ine agreed mentally. *He likes you.*

I'm the only ordinary woman he has talked with.

Ordinary, Ine thought with a mental laugh. *Princess, Glamor, and the leading young martial artist of Charm.*

And an innocent girl, socially, Flame responded.

At such time as you wish to abate that, call on me.

It was a fair offer, as Ine could work magic with men, even without drawing on her formidable magical abilities. She had schooled Weft in that respect.

Grumble liked her? She liked *him*. They had found an unlikely camaraderie, and she valued it.

In the morning the Mistress Marionette spoke to her. "Do you wish to socialize with the guard?"

Of course she knew all about the nocturnal encounter; the ship's mechanical spies would have recorded it. That was one reason Grumble had been hesitant; he knew that nothing was secret. "Yes, if it does not make trouble for him or me."

"In the circumstance it is permitted."

Just like that! "Appreciation."

That night Flame stepped out again. Grumble was there. "You spoke to the mistress," he said, surprised.

"Only to say I did not wish to make trouble for either of us."

"When a princess expresses a wish, even a hostage princess, others take it seriously. She gave me permission for limited interaction."

"Limited?"

"I must not initiate anything, or cause you distress. But I may respond to your directives."

So the protocol had been amended. Flame had not realized that the wishes of the hostages would be honored so literally. "Appreciation. I remain interested in your weapons, and will show you mine in exchange."

"Agreement," he said, picking up on the convention. He put his hand on the device at his hip. "This is my sidearm. It is a laser pistol that can put a hole in flesh or bone at short range." He drew it slowly. "It is keyed to my hand, so that no one else can fire it."

There was a pause, until she realized that she needed to ask, as he could not initiate. "May I inspect it?"

"You may." He took the pointed end in his other hand, and proffered the hand-end to her.

She took it, weighing the thing in her hand. It was light, but had an aura of deadliness. There was an enclosed portion where her forefinger naturally fit, and a bar that could be moved by that finger.

"That is the trigger," Grumble explained. "When I draw that back, the pistol fires. The effect can be deadly, depending on the portion of the body holed."

Flame was impressed. A weapon like this could indeed be deadly. She would be careful not to allow one to be pointed at her. "Appreciation," she said, returning the pistol. Then she brought out one of her own weapons, a throwing knife. It was small but balanced and sharp. She let him take it in his hand.

"I have had some knife training," he said, "but I don't think this could do much damage unless it struck a vital spot with sufficient force."

She took it back. "Mark a spot on the wall."

He produced a piece of chalk and marked a small circle on the padding of the wall. "Call that an enemy eye," he said, standing beside it.

"Clap your hands."

He shrugged and did so.

"Observe," she said, standing still.

"Observe what?"

"The eye."

He looked at it—and started. "The knife!" For the blade was stuck in the center of the circle. "I never even saw you move."

"It is my business," she said.

"You could put that through my eye before I could draw the pistol!"

"I would not," she reassured him.

"Remind me never to offend you, Flame."

She hesitated. "Question?"

"It is humor, suggesting that you might skewer my eye if I annoyed you. I know you would not." He glanced at the knife again. "I don't mean to question your competence, but could you repeat that?"

She went to pull the knife from the wall, walked away, then whirled, her arm moving. There was the sound of the blade striking the wall.

"Right in the track of the first strike," he said. "Amazon maiden, I am in awe of you."

"Well, my siblings depend on me to protect them."

"When you were captured, the report said that you disabled two men before Dynamo stunned you with his stunner. I don't see how he could have done that, unless you didn't know what a stunner is."

"I did not know," she agreed, but that was a half truth. She had made a token show of resistance, then accepted the expedient course for capture. The near-future paths had guided them well.

"I wish I could move like that."

"I can show you. There are techniques. But proficiency takes time."

He shook his head. "I'm forty years old. I'll never have reaction times like yours."

She smiled. "You can start. It's in the readiness of the muscles. Here, maybe I can show you." She came to stand before him. "Put your hand on my arm."

He put his large hand on her small upper arm. "Thin, but that's all muscle."

"Yes. An Amazon can't afford fat." She smiled ruefully. "Which is a liability in relations with men."

"Not necessarily. Some men like their women slender."

"Question." But she couldn't quite voice it.

He chuckled. "Yes, I am such a man. Oh, I really appreciate the mistress, but if I could choose—" He shrugged.

He was bound by his obligation not to initiate anything, but she was intensely interested. However, there was other business at the moment. "Now I'll twitch." She twitched, and suddenly her arm was outside of his grasp.

"Not only did I not see that, I did not feel it," he said.

"Hold more firmly." She stood before him, and had him grasp her arm from behind. Her backside was against his frontside, by no coincidence; she felt pleasantly naughty. She had never flirted like this before. "Feel that tension? I'm ready to move. Then I release it, like freeing a spring." Her arm was outside again.

"You just quiver, and you're gone," he said, amazed.

"You're not holding on firmly enough. This time take a real grip."

He grasped her arm again, this time quite firmly. In the process their body contact became tight. She twitched, and the arm did not spring free. Instead her body was flung back more firmly into his. He grunted from the impact to his chest, and fell back half a step, carrying her with him. His free hand automatically came around to catch his balance, coming up against her chest. For a divine moment he had hold of one clothed breast, as if overcome by lust for her.

"Apology," he said, quickly disengaging.

"Needless. No harm done."

"We'd better stop. My body's getting the wrong idea."

As his mind indicated. But she played ignorant. "No, you held on to my arm the last time. The power channeled back through my body and yours."

"That is not what I mean. That proximity—I'm not used to being that close to a woman."

"As women go, I'm not much." She hoped he would argue. "I'm all muscle and reflex."

"You are nevertheless too much."

"Question?"

"Please, no offense intended. That contact—I am coming to like you too well."

"Confusion." It was important that he clarify it; she needed that reassurance despite reading his mind.

You turn him on, idiot, Ine thought, mentally laughing.

Grumble struggled for words. "I am—I am not good with women," he repeated. "I react maybe when I shouldn't."

"Regret. I did not understand. I am not good with men." They had made the same statements before, but now they had more meaning.

"Maybe—no more close demonstrations."

"Agreement." But it was a lie; she fully intended to get close to him again.

He fidgeted. "I have no right to ask—in fact, I must not, but—"

"Question?"

"Last night you—you let down your hair."

Oho! "Like this?" she inquired, unbinding it again.

"You're beautiful. I mean, your hair is."

She smiled. "I would have been satisfied not to have had that clarification."

"I withdraw it. I feared you might think I was becoming too familiar."

"Banish that fear." They left off the demonstrations, as agreed, and simply talked about incidental aspects of their lives, discovering a fair amount of mutual concerns despite the disparity in their ages and backgrounds. Flame found herself liking the man increasingly, but still did not know how to handle it. She feared making a miscue and embarrassing him or turning him off. Soon she returned to sleep, unsettled.

It is natural for two people to be attracted to each other, Ine thought. *When they are close together and have common interests. It doesn't have to be serious; passing attachments are acceptable.*

Not for an Amazon.

Error. Amazons are human too.

And Ine surely knew.

The third night they were more careful. Both stripped their weapons and set them aside. Flame also let down her hair; it had become a private signal of her interest in his interest. Then they played a game of dodging without touching. Flame jumped to one side or the other, to pass him, while Grumble tried to see the play of her muscles and balance and move to block her way. He was beginning to get it.

She made one more effort, but he anticipated it and caught her. They collided face to face, in close contact from breasts to crotch, her hair swinging out on either side to briefly enclose his face. "Apology!" they gasped together, neither really sorry.

Then they did something neither could explain. They kissed. And separated. Neither knew what else to do.

At that point there was a noise. A man appeared, charging down the hall, swinging a laser sword. "Bow to the Lord, infidel!"

"A berserker," Grumble said. "Flee, Flame!" He lunged forward to intercept the intruder.

The man swept up his sword. The laser light cut across Grumble's left arm, severing cloth and flesh. Blood spurted as he fell.

The berserker's eye fell on Flame. "Die, bitch!" he cried. The beam of the sword swung around.

Flame moved. She struck first at the man's sword arm, stunning it so that the sword sagged in flaccid fingers. She struck second at his neck, scoring on a nerve. The berserker fell unconscious.

Then she leaped toward Grumble. He had lost consciousness from shock and sudden loss of blood pressure, but blood still pulsed from the severed artery in his arm. Flame whipped off her metallic skirt, folded it, and wrapped it as a tourniquet around the arm just above the cut. She knotted it and twisted the knot, tightening the tourniquet until the bloodflow stopped.

With the pressure restored, Grumble revived somewhat. "Flame! Get away! The berserker—"

"Disarmed," she said. "Rest."

Suddenly the hall was filled with men. "Medic," one said, kneeling by Grumble. He looked at the tourniquet. "You did this? You saved his life." He applied some kind of pad to the wounded man's neck. "Pain killer," he said tersely.

A mechanical stretcher appeared. Men picked Grumble up and set him carefully on it.

"Flame!" Grumble cried. "Don't leave me!"

"I am here," she said, pacing the stretcher as it rolled down the hall and taking his right hand.

"He's delirious from the anesthesia," the medic said. "He'll fade out soon. You can go now."

"Flame," Grumble repeated, his grip on her hand tightening spasmodically. He trusted her. That was of overwhelming importance to her.

"I will stay," she said. Then his grip relaxed.

They came to the infirmary. They slid the man to a table. A doctor cut away the makeshift tourniquet, cursing at its toughness, and applied some kind of gauze that closed around the arm, sealing off the cut. He set up a tube that caused fluid to flow into the man. It was all part of the healing Science magic.

"Now he needs rest," the doctor said. "Let him have it."

But Grumble still clutched her hand. She knew he didn't want her to go. "Negation."

Mistress Marionette appeared. "Let her be." She brought a basin. "Clean yourself and join him, Flame, if you choose."

Now Flame saw that blood was spattered across her blouse and her underwear, exposed when she removed her skirt. She found a sponge and warm water in the basin, and cleaned herself off as well as she could. The mistress helped her remove her blouse and underwear and get into an open white hospital robe. The light faded, leaving them in darkness. Then she lay down beside Grumble and slept.

Time passed. Grumble woke and found her there, still holding his hand in the darkness. He also felt her hair brushing him, confirming his recognition. "Flame! You didn't have to stay."

"Negation."

"Appreciation," he said. "But I am better now. They stopped the blood loss and the IV restored me. You can go now."

"Question."

He sighed. "No, I don't want you to go. But it is unfair to you to hold you longer. You saved me, didn't you?"

"You charged the berserker, to protect me."

"And instead you protected me," he said. "I owe you my life. But Flame, you must not stay longer."

"Question?" Again, he had to voice it; she was unable to take this particular initiative.

"Because I—desire you. I don't want to—to compromise you. So it is better if—"

She cut him off with her kiss. "I want to stay with you. Tell me what to do."

"Flame, no! I'm forty and common. You're seventeen and a princess."

Ine! Tell me what to do.

The answer was immediate. *Don't make him move. Keep him on his back. Pull up his hospital robe. Pull up yours. Mount him.*

Flame followed the instructions, and soon was bestriding the man, setting his hard member in her maiden place, and taking him in full length. It was amazingly easy. She lay on him, her hair piling across his face.

Then, prompted by Ine, she kissed him. Almost immediately he jetted into her.

Read his mind.

She did so, having tuned his mind out while focusing on her first act of sex—and suddenly felt the overwhelming joy of his climax. That triggered hers, and she lay there floating, transported by the glorious sensation.

She had done it. Now she knew how.

"Oh, Flame," he breathed. "I love you."

"I love you," she repeated. "For now."

"I understand. I will never forget you."

"Similarity." Part of her mind was bemused by the fact that they had not yet separated the vital connection. What a strange and wonderful thing!

As the wonder ebbed, she dismounted and lay again beside him. *Mop up* Ine reminded her.

Oh. She found a tissue and cleaned her genital region.

"You didn't have to do that," Grumble said.

He means love/sex, Ine thought, preventing her from misunderstanding and saying something embarrassing. "Difference," she said. "You needed me."

"But you could have departed. I would have understood."

"Explanation. I am a warrior. No one ever desired me as a woman before. I am not a feminine creature."

"Opposition," he said, not finding quite the right word. "You are completely feminine to me. You just proved it."

"You made me so, by your desire. I had to accept it. I never did this before."

"I would rather have you with me now than the mistress. You are—genuine."

Flame thought of the way Ine had helped her, to prevent her from fouling it up. That was hardly natural. *You are genuine,* Ine thought. *You are an innocent girl in love. He is right about that. Don't quibble about details.*

"Appreciation."

"But now you really should go. Your people would not understand."

Flame suspected they would understand all too well. But she had seen him through the worst, and appearances did count for something. "Then I will go. But I will return. No fault." She got off the bed and found her clothing, which she discovered had been cleaned and returned.

"Fault?"

"On Charm, when two people need to be together for a time, such as a man and a woman coincidentally journeying to the same distant village, they normally travel no fault. They assume a relationship, such as man and wife, and honor it until they arrive. Then they separate with no further obligation. It is a temporary mutual convenience."

"No fault," he said, assimilating it. "No long-term commitment."

"But for their association, it is complete. He will defend her with his life, and she will give him her body. Both may be married elsewhere; it does not matter. No fault does not exist beyond the moment."

"And you propose such an association with me?"

"For this journey, if you wish."

"Oh Flame, yes!"

"Now you must rest and heal." She squeezed his hand. "Until tonight."

"I love you. No fault." His emotion was overflowing, bathing her in its wonder. Hers was rising to match it.

"Equivalence. Parting."

"Acknowledgment."

She left him. As she entered the hall, uncertain of the route to their chamber, Mistress Marionette appeared. "I will guide you, Flame."

"Appreciation."

"Something about berserkers: they are crazed. They feel no pain. Their reactions are faster than any normal person's. It is normally death to be in the way of one."

Flame pretended to misunderstand. "I did not mean to violate our covenant. I thought it best to stop him."

"You did not even use a weapon."

"It was my fault Grumble was disarmed. Please do not blame him for that."

The Mistress smiled. "At ease, Amazon. I had given leave for your association. We thought there was no danger. Berserkers happen haphazardly. There is no fault in you or Grumble."

"Relief." Was her use of the words "no fault" coincidental?

"We reviewed the video of your encounter with the berserker. We judge you to be a formidable martial artist. No other could have done what you did."

"I am an Amazon," Flame said. "Combat is my nature."

"Please. I ask for the sake of understanding. Could we have captured your party had you truly opposed it?"

The woman had caught on. "Negation."

"You wanted to be captured?"

"Yes."

"Why?"

"Because then Earth would not destroy our planet." She hoped that would satisfy the woman, though it was a half truth. They had needed to nullify Earth without submitting to Earth's dominance.

"But you are the king's children!"

"Agreement."

"Weft is a first-rank musician. You are a first-rank martial artist. Are the others similarly talented?"

"Affirmation."

"Yet you befriended Grumble, an unremarkable crewman, saved his life, and provided him considerable solace. Is this a warrior way?"

"He needed me."

"And so you are a woman as well as a warrior."

"Affirmation. Now."

"Flame, do not misunderstand: I will destroy you if I see the need. But I like you. I hope there is never the need."

Flame wrestled with the morality of the situation. They were enemies, yet she understood that Marionette was true to her mission and her nature. It was more likely that Flame would destroy the mistress, than the other way around, but she couldn't say that. Their Glamor abilities had to remain secret. "Leave Charm. Make no attempt to recover it as a colony and there will be no need."

"I lack the authority to do that."

"Then there is need."

Marionette nodded. "You have given fair warning, Amazon. We understand each other to the degree we are able. But I believe Earth is able to take Charm regardless of whatever effort you have in mind. Therefore the mission remains."

"As you wish."

"I want to be friends. No fault."

So she did know about that. "Friends do not betray each other."

"I have no intention of betraying you. I have spoken plainly of my situation and preference."

"But I do of you." She dared not clarify.

Marionette gazed at her a moment. "So be it. Then let us make the pretense of friendship during this voyage. No fault."

That would do. "Agreement."

"Your association with Grumble is permitted, so long as it is your initiative. My presumption is that your father understands about affairs of choice."

"Affirmation."

"Here is your party's chamber. You are not confined."

"As long as we keep our word."

"Affirmation," the Mistress said, smiling.

The siblings were quick to razz her. "Who would have thought the cold warrior would be the first of us to night out," Warp said. "Did he get hold of your thin ass, or did he give up the search?"

"It is good to see the lover boy jealous," Flame retorted.

"Did everything fit?" Weft inquired. "Did it come out all right? Was it juicy? Did he manage to feel your faint bumps?"

"Affirmation thrice. He's not into overflowing melons."

Voila, true to her image, merely hugged her. "Congratulations on your conquest, Amazon."

"I think he conquered *me*. I had to be what he saw me as: an innocent girl."

They all laughed. "You were," Augur said. "In that respect."

"But you know, I *am* jealous," Warp said seriously.

"Ditto," Weft said. "We never figured you to beat us in that department."

"It was your hair," Voila said. "You seduced him with it."

"Agreement," Flame said. "Weft told me how."

"My mistake," Weft said darkly.

"No fault, of course," Aura said. It was a question.

"Agreement. He understands."

"One shot?"

"Duration of voyage. I will return to him tonight."

"I think she's got it," Warp said, affecting surprise. "She has discovered traveling no fault."

"And you can't do the same with Marionette," Weft teased him. "Poor boy. No way to soften your—resolve."

"If you weren't my sister, plush bottom—"

Weft pulled down her halter, baring her splendid breasts. "And that's not all, stiff neck. I dare you."

"Dad would be mad, if I got you before he did."

"Children," Aura said warningly.

They gave it up, smiling. They loved playing the game of Rogue Siblings.

On this day they were guided to a small theater. One wall was a picture of a sterile cell where a man was confined.

"That's the berserker," Flame said, surprised. "The man who attacked us."

"He's not berserk now," Augur said. "I understand these things do not endure long. The berserker state is wasteful of energy." Indeed, the man was sitting on the side of his bunk, staring at the floor.

Mistress Marionette entered the chamber. She wore a close gown that emphasized her superlative figure. She was tiny compared to the man, but completely confident. "You attempted to harm our guests, the king's children," she said. "The penalty is death."

The man ignored her.

"We wish to know your motive," Marionette continued. "Tell us that, and you can have one final session with me before you die."

Now the man's head lifted. He was plainly tempted, as any man would be. But still he did not answer.

"I repeat. Tell me, and this is yours." Marionette opened her gown, showing her body from breasts to thighs. Even Flame was impressed; there was no denying that the woman's body was outstanding. It made Flame's look like a scarecrow, and Weft's look like stuffed balloons.

"Pain," Warp murmured. He was unashamedly turned on.

Weft put her arm around him, not teasingly. "Regret."

Still the man did not react.

"Then here is your sword," Marionette said. She drew a small bar from a pocket Flame hadn't realized existed. She squeezed it, and the scintillating laser blade appeared, extending a yard outward.

Flame's eyes narrowed. She had not had time to study the sword before. This was a fearsome weapon, as it weighed nothing yet cut whatever it touched. Had she not seen it cut Grumble's arm, she would not have realized how dangerous it was.

"Take it," Marionette said, proffering the handle to the man. She held it so that the blade pointed to the side, touching neither of them.

The man took it. He stood before the woman, bright sword in hand. Could he cut her down? No, Flame realized; there were surely weapons trained on him that would cut *him* down the moment he made a false move.

"A third time I offer," Marionette said. "The motive."

But the man merely twisted the sword so that it swung across his own neck. Blood spurted as a seam opened in his throat, and he sagged to the floor.

"I am sorry," Marionette said, and left the chamber.

Flame exchanged glances with her siblings. The man had surely deserved death. What impressed them was the manner of it. Even at the end, the man had not tried to attack the mistress, and she had not flinched from the act. She had nerves of steel.

❧

"That she does," Grumble agreed when she joined him in the infirmary that evening. He was now off the feeding tube, but remained weak. "We all love her, but we also know not to cross her, and it's not just a matter of losing bed privileges. She is our goddess."

They had had sex and she was lying beside him in the dim light after cleaning up, for his need to commune was almost as great as his desire for physical release. This was the way it typically was with a man, Ine had assured her: first sex, then talk, then sleep. Ine was now serving part of her purpose in this group. She was a Sorceress, an expert in magic, and should be able to sniff it out on Earth if it was there. But she was also adept in sex, and was taking on Warp in this respect, to abate his frustration about Marionette. Sex was a mechanism rather than an end in itself, to a woman. Flame nevertheless remained thrilled to be valued for this, and craved the reassurance of Grumble's continued desire. "But now you have me."

"Yesterday was the single most significant day in my life. It's the first time I have been seriously wounded, and the first time I have been blessed by a woman other than a professional. I love you, Flame." He paused. "No fault."

She noted and appreciated that hesitation. He clearly loved her beyond no fault. Men were like that too, Ine had explained. Sex stirred their deeper passions. It lasted until they had sex with a new woman. "No fault," she echoed.

"But I have you by the sufferance of the mistress. She can end it at any time, for whim or reason. I dare not cross her, lest I lose you."

Suddenly it fell into place. Marionette was pulling the strings to make Flame obliged to her. The woman was a manipulator of people, especially men, but she could evidently handle women too. "I will try not to annoy her."

"Appreciation. But do not let her use me as a lever against you. If the time comes, let me go."

"I am an Amazon. No one controls me."

He smiled. "I keep forgetting. I know what you did. You could kill me with a touch. Yet somehow all I can think of is your softness and your caring."

"Not a lot of softness," she said, embarrassed. "My sister Weft has that."

He turned on his side, facing her, and ran his hand along her lean thigh, across her tight belly, and to her small bare breast. He brought his face near and kissed the nipple. His exposed penis swelled and became rigid. She was surprised and daunted by its size in this state; had all of that been inside her? She had not before paid attention to that aspect, guided by Ine's instructions.

He had made his point, in more than one sense. Her body truly turned him on. She turned into him, got partly onto him, and made the connection. Yes, it slid slowly in, and there was somehow room for it all. Her aperture was stretching to accommodate him, becoming large enough. Her eagerness made the channel slick, which surely helped. She was getting better at this with practice. "Appreciation," she said.

He laughed, and she felt it all the way inside her. "You give me such a gift, and you thank me?"

"I've never been a woman before. Only a warrior."

"You are all the women I'll ever need."

"Delight."

He paused again, not doing the thrusting he had before. "I forgot you're not experienced. You—both times—no climax?"

"Question?"

"Let me show you."

"Confusion. Am I not doing it correctly?"

"Flame, you're divine! But now it's my turn to deliver. I will give you what you gave me."

"Mystification." Of course he was unaware that she could read his mind and receive his feeling of orgasm.

He withdrew from her, then reoriented. He had her lie on her back, naked. He put his hands on her legs, spreading them. Then he put his face down to her groin. His tongue stroked her cleft.

"Alarm!"

"Flame, I love you. Trust me. Relax."

"Apology," she said, relaxing.

His tongue returned to action, licking the hot groove. Now that she accepted it, she became aware of the pleasure of it. Her groin became warm, responding. His tongue touched her clitoris, and there was a surge of feeling. Then his lips closed on it, in a sucking kiss. The feeling expanded into passion. The urgency spread from her cleft through her belly and to her breasts, whose nipples went taut, and to her face. She licked her lips, wanting to kiss him, but he was out of reach. "Aaaah," she sighed.

He continued, and her desire became overwhelming. Her pelvis ached with the need for culmination. She lifted her legs and closed her thighs about his head, squeezing. Then at last the great surging release came, wave after wave, transporting her whole body into space. This was all her own feeling, not his: her first female orgasm. Yet even so, something was missing.

"Please!" she gasped, still in the divine thrill of it. "M-m-mount me!"

He lifted his head, then used hands and knees to make his way up her writhing body. He came down on her, fitting his stiff member to her cleft, and slid it in. She reveled in the easy penetration; it filled a void, literally. He lowered himself to her body and kissed her.

Her vagina clenched around his member in the final throes of her orgasm. Her legs enclosed him, holding him tight. He thrust, and in a moment she felt him spurting in her depth. He had done that before, but this time it was enhancing her sensation, another new experience. So they were climaxing together after all. That, too, delighted her.

Slowly it faded, and he got off her so as not to crush her with his weight. "Now you know, beloved," he said.

"Now I know," she agreed, kissing him again. "Appreciation."

"Acknowledged."

"I had no idea."

"You did everything for me. I'm glad I was able to do something for you."

"But to make you do that—to lick my—I am ashamed."

"Flame, Flame! It was my pleasure too. Men like to do it. A woman's whole body turns us on, that part especially."

"Even one like mine."

"Especially one like yours. You turned me on from the start, remember; it interfered with our martial arts practice. I kept being aware of your vibrant slender shape."

She never tired of hearing that. "Gratitude."

"Agreement."

After that they slept, half-embraced.

⚜

In the morning Marionette was there again. "I know the way now," Flame said. "No need for you to take the time."

"I have a concern. Perhaps we can make a fair exchange."

"Question?"

"We are not true friends, only pseudo-friends. It behooves us to trade favors, incurring no obligations."

This woman made Flame nervous. Marionette was no physical Amazon, but she was a warrior of amazing competence. Flame was coming to understand the importance of staying in her favor. She now had a personal stake, apart from her mission. "Acquiescence."

"Our tests indicate that none of you are related to each other. Not even the siblings. I would appreciate an explanation. What would you appreciate?"

The one was an easy question to answer. The other was not. "I do not want to be taken from Grumble. He still needs me."

"That has already been granted. You will be separated from him only for preference or cause. Ask elsewhere."

Then it came to her. "My brother Warp desires you."

"He knows my nature."

"Yes. But—he is male."

The mistress laughed. "Granted. I will add him to the roster. This is not like your affair with Grumble; he will be with me only on well spaced occasions. But he will be well satisfied then."

"Agreement." That had been easier than she expected. Maybe the Mistress had intended to indulge Warp anyway. "Background: every citizen of Charm must marry by age eighteen, apart from rare exceptions, and raise four children. At least one of those must be by a man other than the husband."

"Confusion," Marionette said, right on cue.

"The requirement of four is to populate the planet. The requirement of one is to maintain species unification by assuring crossing of lineages. In populations subject to rapid mutation, it is a rule of two: every second child must be from an outside man. But for most it is just the one, and that child is called a fourth. If the woman prefers not to have sex with another man, she can adopt a foundling instead. That child becomes hers, but there is a certain shadow. Fourths are treated equally, but other children may taunt them. It is not supposed to be, but sometimes is."

"Comprehension. I was adopted."

Flame stared at her. "You!"

"It gave me strong motive to succeed."

Flame nodded. "You do understand." But she was shaken by the revelation.

"We are not always as we seem. You more than most."

That was certainly true. "It happened that three special babies from different families were unmanageable, and were returned to an orphanage. Warp was one, Weft was another, and I was the the third. Queen Gale learned of us and adopted us, and we became the king's children."

"Three rather than one?"

"One fourth is the minimum. There can be more. So we became three fourths, and the king and queen had only one child of their own. That was Voila."

"You seem highly disciplined and talented, all of you. How were you unmanageable?"

"We were magic."

"Confusion."

And of course the Earthers did not believe in magic. They thought Science magic was the only kind. "Warp floated. Weft conjured objects. I set fires."

"So it was not merely your hair that named you."

"It was not," Flame agreed.

"Warp surely had to be watched to be sure he did not climb out a high window and try to fly. Weft must have been an adept thief. But you must have been the most dangerous, because an uncontrolled fire could destroy a home."

"This is not the way we see it. Our talents are real."

"You can make fire without some device?"

"Yes."

"Can you demonstrate this now?"

"That would be difficult."

"Why?"

"Because it is magic, and this is a Science Chroma zone. I would need a device here."

"Do not use it. We do not like shipboard fires."

"Acquiescence." It was plain that the Mistress did not believe it, and it was to Flame's interest that that unbelief continue. She had told the literal truth, so was not lying. In any event it was not the question she had agreed to answer.

They arrived at their chamber. Only Warp was there; the others were gone. "I'm supposed to wait for Flame," he said, plainly mesmerized by Marionette. "To guide her to the group."

"In a moment," the Mistress said. "Join me on your bed."

Obviously he did not dare believe the notion that came to his mind. "Question?"

"I made a deal with Flame. I will oblige you now."

"I'll go," Flame said, embarrassed.

"Hold, Amazon!" he exclaimed. "I don't trust this."

"It's all right," Flame said. "She means you no ill."

"Then you stay here, fireball. I trust you."

"Warp, this is *sex*. You don't want me watching."

"Sure I do. You can knock me out or burn me to a cinder, but you'll never play me false. *She's* something else."

"He has a point," Marionette said. "My time is limited; for the sake of efficiency, remain."

Disgruntled, Flame sat on a neighboring bunk. "Reluctance."

Marionette stepped into Warp, embraced him, and kissed him. "Strip." She shrugged off her robe and was naked. She disposed herself smoothly on the bunk.

Warp hastened to obey. His erection was already forming. He joined her on the bunk, mounting her. His penis would have missed the spot, but the Mistress caught it with her hand and guided it without looking. Warp did not pause; he simply thrust vigorously and climaxed.

Despite her embarrassment, Flame was interested. She saw that Marionette had skillfully guided Warp from the outset, positioning herself and him, and bringing him immediately in. It was the essence of efficiency—and he had never noticed. She had been in control throughout.

His passion expended, Warp rolled off her, his member softening. Marionette caught his available hand and set it on her breast. Then while he was distracted by that, she produced a small sponge from somewhere and cleaned out her vagina. That done, she sat up, turned, got on hands and knees beside him on the bunk, and took his limp penis in her mouth.

Astonished, Warp simply lay there. "I can't—" he said. But his protest faded out, for she was already evoking a response. Her mouth moved around his member, her tongue tickling the tip, and as it thickened and lengthened, she took it all in, virtually swallowing it. Meanwhile her hand reached out, caught his near hand, and guided it back to her breast, which was now depending from her chest and touching his belly. He held it and squeezed it, transported.

In a surprisingly brief time Warp was breathing hard. His body tensed, his loin thrust involuntarily, and he went into another climax. Marionette took it in, sucking on his member, as he groaned with passion.

Soon she released his spent penis and got up. He was quite clean; no ejaculate had escaped. She had to have swallowed it and left none to drip. "I must go now," she said, shrugging into her gown. "I regret having to hurry you; next time I will give you more time." She kissed him again and was gone.

Warp lay there, supposedly sexually exhausted. He turned his head to face Flame. "You saw that? She did me twice in five minutes, and the second was better than the first. What a woman!"

"Agreement," Flame said. It had been an amazing exhibition, and not just because the mistress had made him perform beyond his expectation. He had been a complete puppet, without realizing it. Marionette had not only done him, as he put it, she had also openly demonstrated exactly how a woman could manage a man and make him like it. It was surely how she handled the men of the ship, making every one of them love her, efficiently. Flame realized that it had been deliberate; Marionette had shown her what else to do with Grumble.

Warp dressed, still expounding on the marvel of Marionette. She was, he said, better than Ine, which was itself an amazing thing. He had been completely satisfied. So was Flame, in a different manner. They went to join the others, each distracted by the intense event.

Ine's veiled gaze met Flame's. *Even I learned something. Don't tell.*

Flame smiled. She would not tell.

Marionette appeared before them. "There has been no progress in negotiations," she reported. "We are therefore taking you as hostages with us to Earth. The trip will take two months, but we will do our best to keep you entertained."

Flame was quite sure that would be the case. Already she was eager to return to Grumble, to talk and to explore new things. She had never had a romantic relationship with a man before, and had had no practical experience of sex. That had changed.

Thereafter, between sexual sessions, she discussed other things with Grumble. The man was glad to talk with her about anything, but his focus was better when his passion was sated. That was the way of men, Ine assured her. To a woman, sex was one of a complex of factors in a relationship. To a man, it was more than all others merged. It was simply the way men were made. The smart woman used it to her advantage.

"What do you do for entertainment?" he asked her one night. "And don't pretend it's sex; you never had it before me." So it seemed he understood also.

Maybe she could learn something useful. "Volcanoes. I went to visit volcanoes." That was true, but not the whole truth. She didn't like deceiving him even to this extent, but it was necessary.

"Volcanoes? I know you have plenty of them on your home planet. You're not bored by them?"

"Negation. I want to know how Earth volcanoes operate, without magic."

"Ah. Of course you consider science a form of magic. But it is true that ours don't erupt in many colors. Just fire, smoke, ash, and lava."

"Plea: tell me."

"Sure. In school I read an ancient history book about a volcano that formed in Mexico, Central America. It seemed that a farmer was plowing a corn field on a sunny day, when he noticed some white vapors floating up from the furrows he had just cut, and from the deep hoof-prints of his team of oxen. Then he heard thunder, but the neighboring clouds were fleecy. He was mystified—until he heard a louder and closer rumble, coming from under the ground. There was a small hole in the field that he had been trying to fill for years, but it seemed bottomless; the sound seemed to come from there."

"A fissure was opening," Flame said, picturing the farmer trying to make sense of it.

"Indeed. A magma chamber had been forming ten miles down, pushing the rock apart, sending up a thin column of molten rock. Now it was reaching the surface. A crack ran out of both sides of the hole, and the portion of the field near the rupture puffed up into a cakelike mass, frightening his wife. It swelled to almost human head height, then collapsed in a cloud of dust. Black smoke whistled from the crack, and then burning stones. A choking wave of sulfur washed by them."

"Of course it stinks near a volcanic vent," Flame said. "They needed to get quickly away from there."

"They did. They ran. The roaring got worse, so that it could be heard at the nearby village. Glowing stones sailed up and landed around the hole, and what they touched burst into flames. All night the eruption grew, and by morning the closest falling stones formed a cone thirty feet high, and cinders were dropping for miles around. Every few seconds lightning flashed in the column of smoke."

"Oh, I wish I had been there!"

"It was dangerous," he reminded her. "In two days the volcanic pyramid stood almost two hundred feet high. It destroyed the corn field and the whole area. In a year it was a thousand feet high and half a mile wide. Ash covered the landscape. Lava broke out of the side and slowly advanced. It overran the village. Then after nine years of continuous activity, the volcano ceased, never to erupt again. That is the way of the small ones in that vicinity. I wrote a paper on it."

"Ours are like that," Flame said. "They come and go. We move with them. But some are big and stay a long time."

"Yours must be relatively benign. This one did nobody any good. I visited the site, a thousand years later. It was just the old weather-beaten silent cone, not impressive at all. Vegetation was verdant; it seems that volcanic ash and lava make rich soil. But at least I had satisfied my childhood dream of actually seeing the volcano I had read about."

"It was a nice dream," she said, kissing him. After that they did not get back to the subject; sex got in the way. But she had learned things she valued. Earth volcanoes, like those of Charm, had their own histories and personalities.

She had also found a relationship she valued. It was no fault, but it was clear that Grumble loved her, and she was quite taken with him. She loved being loved! But he did understand that it would end when the voyage did. She intended to see that he never regretted this interlude with her. And that no man hereafter would ever find her deficient in sexual performance, once it came to such an interaction. It could be considered, in its fashion, a martial art. Grumble and Ine had taught her, and she had always been an apt learner.

And—it was fun. She did after all have the Glamor urge. She could control it, but delighted in indulging it. Especially with Grumble. This new understanding clarified much in the relationships of others that she had not properly comprehended before. Such as the constant indulgence of Havoc and Gale, and their occasional bouts of multiple climaxes. They were in love! Sex was not merely a tool to control a man; it was worthwhile in itself. And it made the rest of the relationship more meaningful. She *liked* giving Grumble pleasure, and receiving pleasure from him.

Of course Ine could have told her all this. But it was far more meaningful discovering it for herself. She would never again be merely an Amazon warrior. She was a woman.

Chapter 4
Dynamo

Marionette came to him one last time before the separation. "I regret isolating you for so long," she said as she efficiently drew his passion into herself. It was her way, and he wouldn't have had it otherwise. "But we must make it clear that the hostages can not be recovered unless there is a sufficient accommodation made with Earth."

"I understand, Mistress. This task is not onerous; I really want to study this planet, and this provides me with six months uninterrupted. With luck I will also manage to persuade the king."

"Do that," she agreed, kissing him and drawing off him as cleanly as always. There was simply no other woman in her class. "We depend on you." She garbed and departed.

Dynamo remained as he was for a time, savoring the encounter. It would have to last for six months. He thought it unlikely that Colony Planet Charm would have any woman to rival her, and prohibitively unlikely that such a woman would have any interest in him. He was in for a dry season.

An hour later the *Dominance* weighed planetary anchor and moved rapidly clear of the system. He was alone in the shuttle with the bomb.

There was no need to wait. He separated the bomb, leaving it in orbit, and guided the shuttle down to the landing site in the white Chroma zone. The natives had been told to expect him.

Indeed one was waiting for him as he emerged. This was a gray woman of about his own age, solidly constructed with a remarkable coiffure. "I am Stevia, of the Gray Chroma," she said. "King Havoc asked me to guide you. You may select another guide if you prefer."

"I am sure you are competent," he said. He could tell already that this woman was no ordinary native; there was something about her, as there was about the king, queen, and the White Chroma Deva who had guided him before. That was one mystery he intended to fathom, but he knew they would not divulge it on their own. Fortunately he had time.

"What is your wish?"

"To see and experience all I can of your planet and culture, in these six months before the ship returns. I want to understand everything."

Stevia smiled. "There are things that will surprise you. Some you may not like."

"Let's get something clear," he said. "Do you speak for the king?"

"To a degree. I know his policy."

"Then understand this: there is a bomb in geosynchronous orbit about this planet, above your pyramidal capital city. Should anything happen to me, that bomb will automatically be loosed. It will drop and destroy the pyramid. Thereafter negotiations for the return of the royal hostages will become more difficult."

"You're cute when you're dictatorial. May I kiss you?"

"This is not a joke. You need to comprehend the seriousness with which Earth takes this mission."

She closed on him and kissed him firmly on the mouth. Her gray lips were surprisingly appealing. Her body seemed to shift subtly, becoming more sensual. Even her hair seemed to spread and ripple. There was a musky alluring scent about her. He found his arms around her, his hands on her evocative bottom. "Humor me," she murmured.

"Are you trying to seduce me? I assure you that such tactics will not be effective in corrupting me. My mission is paramount."

"Then you can have your will of me without consequence."

He disengaged and gazed at her, frustrated. "What makes you think that I want to take advantage of you? I am here to study Charm, not chase skirts."

"Perhaps." Her gray hair rippled again, forming waves that coursed down to the ends of her tresses. It was a weird but oddly esthetic effect.

"I have told you about the bomb," he said somewhat stiffly. "You know about the hostages. I hope the king has the sense to keep these factors in perspective. It would be a shame to have to make an unkind reduction of the planet, when it could so readily be accomplished amicably."

"This way," Stevia said, setting off for the edge of the white zone. Her backside was more shapely than he had first judged, especially when in motion.

"I haven't yet told you where I want to go."

"Fortunately there is no need."

He hurried to catch up with her. "What is the matter with you? You're supposed to be my guide; instead you ignore my preferences."

"That is because you don't want what you think you want. I am taking you where you belong."

"This is nonsense!"

She glanced at him. "Do you want me to kiss you again?"

"No!" But he realized that was not quite true. Her kiss had had a strange potency. She was obviously no amateur in this respect. "It is irrelevant to my mission."

"Perhaps," she repeated.

It seemed to be pointless to argue with her. He ceased the effort and accepted her lead, annoyed.

They came to the edge of the White Chroma zone. It was tricky to keep that nomenclature straight because it sounded so much like chromosome, but he was working on it. Beyond was a neutral zone, followed by a green zone. Here, he knew, all the plants would be green, which seemed natural enough, but also the people. That was the weird thing about this planet. But he had seen the red man and blue woman among the captives, and knew that they functioned normally. In fact the swathed woman had invisible flesh; she was from the Air Chroma. That effect still had to be explained, as there seemed to be no refractive distortion as the light passed through her flesh. That was one of the things he wanted to explore: the mystery of the invisible Air Chroma. What conceivable chemical could cause living flesh to become completely transparent? It would be an invaluable discovery.

"This is a Green chroma zone," Stevia said. "Its specialty is plants. Stay close to me, as not all of them are friendly."

"Unfriendly plants," he said dryly. "I appreciate the warning."

"Oh, that reminds me: I have a stone for you." She produced a white crystal similar to the one given to the Mistress. "Wear it always."

He accepted the bauble and put its string around his neck. The other had been tested in the laboratory and found to be mere stone, typical of its region. Marionette wore it as a courtesy to the hostages. She was very good at putting people at ease. He could surely do the same. "Appreciation."

"We do have our little ways." She forged on along a path winding through the greenery.

Dynamo felt a call of nature. "I must pause for a moment," he said. "I will catch up with you." He stepped to the side, opened his fly, and prepared to urinate against the green trunk of a tree.

Stevia as suddenly there, catching hold of his penis. "Mischief! Don't do that!" she said, squeezing it firmly.

For a moment he was speechless. He had never imagined a woman doing such a thing. "What?"

"Clarification: Don't piss against the bark," she said. "That will rile it. See, the mere threat put it into attack mode."

Indeed, several green branches seemed to have swing close, their leaves glistening with thick moisture. That was probably his imagination. "Attack mode?"

"Explanation: The nettles are poisonous." She faced the tree. "Apology, honorable tree. He is a visitor to our scene, and does not yet know our courtesies. He means only to honor you with a gift of nourishment."

The amazing thing was that the branches seemed to swing back. Maybe it was the effect of wind. "In a manner," he agreed.

"Requirement: Now piss into the ground at the base, and don't let it splash. Then the tree will be your friend." She let go of his member.

"I am not sure I can, now," he said, bemused. For his penis had stiffened in her grasp and was now half erect.

"Force it. The tree won't wait long if you tease it."

But the erection continued, preventing urination. "Some other time," he said, seriously embarrassed.

The branches swung back. This time there was no doubt of their motion. The tree was indeed reacting.

"Necessity: I'll do it," Stevia said. She hoisted her gray skirt and squatted. It was now apparent that she wore no underclothing. She spread her solid thighs and sent a stream of gray urine into the ground.

That sight was worse yet. She was angled toward him; he saw everything. His member hardened into rigidity. He had never thought of himself as a voyeur or interested in the process of a woman's voiding, but this surprising exposure affected him profoundly. It wasn't just the urine; her entire genital region was open for inspection, as it were. His member wanted to possess it. Of course he would not say that.

She finished and stood, letting her skirt drop back down. "Procedure: We must move on, before it realizes that a substitute was made. Next time be more careful." She led the way back. There were no close branches now.

Dynamo fitted his standing member back into his trousers. He still needed to urinate, but that was hopeless now. "The tree would have attacked?"

"Affirmation. All plants appreciate a tasty offering; none will tolerate affront. That's true anywhere, not just in the Plant Chroma. It is generally best to save your wastes for those plants whose favor you really need."

The weirdness continued. Evidently she believed what she was saying. "And what plant would I really need?"

She considered. "Realization: This is something you need to know. Very well, we'll camp here tonight, before catching transport to the next Chroma. This way." She forged on in a new direction.

Dynamo followed. He had to admit that his own plan of travel hardly matched this for interest, awkward as aspects were. He was learning more about the native culture this way. Were they plant worshipers?

Stevia brought them to a giant tree whose massive trunk supported copiously spreading thick branches, all green, of course. "Situation: We'll night in this one; it will provide us fruit and sap, and safe bedding. But first we have to befriend it, both of us. I'm out of urine; I'll have to defecate. You can piss here." She indicated a choppy patch of ground to one side of the trunk.

His erection had faded, but threatened to spring back into life as the picture of her urination flashed into his mind. "I don't think I can."

"Dynamo, this is serious business," she said. "Do you need my help?"

He laughed, more than slightly embarrassed. "I doubt that's possible."

"Statement: I would debate with you if it were convenient. But the tree expects it, and we can't afford to tease it. Give me your spout."

"My—?"

She reached down, opened his fly, grasped his swelling member, and aimed it at the spot of ground. She squeezed at the base, and it suddenly went numb. His burgeoning erection faded, and he lost continence. The contents of his bladder coursed down and out unimpeded as she directed the flow.

"That's a good amount," she said approvingly as the stream diminished. "The host tree knows and accepts you. Now it's my turn." She let go of him and squatted, this time defecating. When she had deposited a small gray mass she used a gray tissue to wipe herself, and stood again. "Now it knows me too."

"I should think so," Dynamo agreed faintly, putting away his slowly recovering member. This remarkable woman continued to surprise him.

"Procedure: Now we enter the tree, before it forgets." She went to the trunk, caught hold of its rough protuberances, fitted her toes into notches, and climbed to the nexus of branches. In a moment she was standing in the center of the complex, almost out of sight. "Expediency: Come on, Dynamo."

He followed her example, climbing the natural ladder. He joined her in the embrace of the tree. The branches and twigs formed what seemed like an enclosure, with leaves lining the walls. "What now?"

"Relaxation. Now we make ourselves comfortable. The tree will protect us for the night. Here is fruit." She plucked a small sphere from the surrounding foliage. "It's not perfect, but it will feed us." She handed it to him. "Don't worry; it is safe to eat. This tree caters to travelers, for the sake of their varied offerings."

Offerings like urine and feces. Yet it did make a certain sense. He bit into the fruit, and it was tasty and juicy. It would do.

After they had eaten, Stevia found a comfortable alcove amidst the branches and settled into it. "Invitation: Join me," she said. "We have nothing but time to pass until morning. It's not safe to be abroad by night."

Did he have a choice? He settled down beside her. But the rough wood poked his body, making relaxation awkward. "I could use a pillow," he said.

"Provided." She caught hold of his upper body and drew his head down to her gray bosom. Her breasts beneath the gray blouse were very full and firm, and did provide ample cushioning. He decided to accept it.

Still, he felt imperfectly supported. "I fear I will move or roll, and plunge through the foliage to the ground."

"Legitimate concern," she agreed. "I will address it. Observe."

"Observe what?" But then he saw the oddest thing yet. Her hair was growing, lengthening and spreading like an independently living thing. It was a gray tide that slowly enveloped her body and his, cushioning his legs with surprising firmness. Soon they were in a gray cocoon, and it was quite comfortable. He felt as if he had been sealed in. It was a comfortable couch, and her bosom was rather nice. Was she still trying to seduce him, or was she merely being natural? He would surely find out soon enough.

"Satisfied?" she inquired.

"Question," he said, adopting the native convention.

She took a deep breath, raising his head somewhat in the process. "You Earthers do not believe in magic?"

He smiled tolerantly. "Correct. There is a natural explanation for everything."

"Natural magic," she agreed. "Accept it for now as a word to describe the way we function. The Gray Chroma is not noted for active magic, but I do have some. I can control my hair, as you see." A hank of it lifted from the area of his secured feet and seemed to wave at him. "You might have a term for it."

"Prehensile," he agreed. Was there no end to the wonders of this woman?

"And beyond." Her hair became warm, then hot. It seemed to melt; in fact he felt the moisture against his ankles. It tingled, massaging his legs. It lifted and floated in a cloud-like mass. It fell back, this time ice cold. It warmed again, closing around him, covering his legs to the waist, and a hank of it gently squeezed his crotch.

"And beyond," he agreed. "An extraordinary ability."

"Tomorrow we will be showing you more magic. You may attempt to explain it away, but in time the balance of evidence will persuade you. This is the first major thing you must accept about Charm."

"I will wait for that revelation," he said.

"Then there is little point in discussing it further now. We face a dull night. Would you be interested in hot passion, no fault?"

He was interested, as she surely was aware. But there was generally a price on such an offer. "Question."

"No fault is the convention among travelers. It means there will be no continuing obligation once the journey is done. Mutual commitment exists only during the association."

"In my experience women generally expect something in return for sex, unless they are mistresses, which is a special situation. What would you expect?"

"I will answer, but first prefer to have your explanation for the term mistress."

"Gladly. Earth is a matriarchy. Women govern it. They do so without violence or unkind coercion, which is an improvement on the way it was when men governed. They do it by sex appeal and by sex itself. A man will do almost anything for a truly lovely and obliging woman. The *Dominance* is crewed by about one hundred men and one Mistress. She both governs and services the men. She is superlative. There is no quantifiable exchange; the men simply do her will, and she sees that each is emotionally and sexually satisfied. But on Earth itself most women are lesser creatures, on an approximate par with men. Those are the ones who will bargain for favors with sex. So men become cautious about commitments until they understand what return the women have in mind."

"I most resemble a mistress," Stevia said. "I am governing what you do here, and proffer you emotional and sexual support for the duration of our association."

"And the orbiting bomb has nothing to do with it?"

"That has a good deal to do with it. We do not like having our world or any part of it be threatened. It makes you the focus of our immediate attention. Thus I was selected to guide you, rather than some lesser woman."

"Lesser women are like Earth's ordinary ones?"

"In respects. If you desire any of them you may have them, but I am all the woman you will need."

She certainly seemed sure of herself! Yet he could not deny that she had maneuvered him into a position where he did desire her body despite the fact that it was not nearly equivalent to that of the Mistress Marionette. Still he was wary.

"What makes you special?"

"I am a Glamor."

"You are glamourous?"

"That too, when I choose to be. It is a category that I suspect is more than equivalent to your mistresses, though we do not directly govern the planet. Capital G, l a m o r."

"Exactly what is a Glamor?"

"The explanation would be largely meaningless before you accept magic, for we are magical beings. I suggest you wait until you know more of our culture."

But Dynamo's interest had been tweaked. "Try me."

"Question?"

"Give me the explanation that I may find meaningless."

"Glamors represent the eighteen classes of life on Charm, as defined by the number of their legs. Twelve are Chroma, six nonChroma. We are able to perform magic anywhere, not being limited to our home Chromas, as long as our ikons remain within our home Chromas. We have among other things, enormous sexual capacity."

Dynamo shook his head, in the process bouncing it on her resilient breasts. "I concede the point: that explanation is largely meaningless to me. One further question: does your enormous capacity for sex include interest? That is, desire to participate in it frequently?"

"Affirmation."

That decided him. "Then with the understanding that no other commitment is made or implied, let's participate."

"Confession: I thought you'd never ask." Her hair sprang outward, forming a larger shell, on whose floor they lay. "Disrobe."

He was glad to oblige, setting his weapons aside and scrambling out of his uniform. Now they were naked together, with only a limber tether connecting the shell to her head. Her body turned out not to be at all stout; it was solidly feminine with voluptuous proportions. She rolled into him, positioning herself on top and facing up, her plush buttocks pressing against his groin. She drew his arms up to clasp her, his hands on her breasts. Somehow his member entered her cleft without guidance and he plunged into the depth of her evocative body.

Relief was almost instantaneous. He climaxed explosively. To his surprise he felt her doing the same; she was breathing hard and her vagina was clamping on him. It had been very fast and very satisfying.

She disconnected and turned over, now straddling him face to face. "Question: how often can you jet in an hour?"

He laughed, relaxed. "I am a lusty man. I can do it four times, when sufficiently motivated."

"Note the time."

He checked his watch. "Noted."

She moved on him as she kissed him. Her breasts seemed to caress his chest independently, and her thighs stroked his thighs. She melted into him, her whole body becoming hotly erotic. He had to respond, and soon enough he entered her again and climaxed again. It was slower than before, but fully as satisfying.

But she was not nearly through. There followed an amazing series of positions and caresses by hands, mouth, and other parts of her body. Before he quite believed it, he was into a third orgasm. Then a fourth, and a fifth, as her endlessly inventive sexual talent played his body like a musical instrument.

He looked at his watch. It was now an hour. She had caused him to break his record. "I acknowledge your expertise," he said. "You are a mistress of sex."

"All this is yours as you elect," she said. "Continuous or intermittent, no fault, for the duration of our association. But you may still possess any other woman you desire; I will see that she acquiesces."

"All this," he echoed. "For no price?"

She shrugged, her breasts quivering, and such was her body that the motion still stirred a flicker of desire in him. "Merely an inducement for continued association while I endeavor to persuade you to believe in magic, and more."

"More?"

"Much more."

Dynamo decided not to question that. She had presented her inducement, and it was persuasive. He was played out at the moment, but the prospect of days of this—perhaps six months—was overwhelming. "Submission."

She laughed. Then her hair contracted, pressing them together. "Now we sleep. It has been pleasant."

"Pleasant," he agreed, accepting the understatement. He clasped her, this time not sexually despite her bare proximity, and slept.

The odd thing was that though he did not wake in the night, he was aware of her luxuriant contact, and found himself inside her again as she gently milked him for more pleasure. How many times? He could not be sure, but several. She really did desire sex, and was taking it at will. Once he even felt as if he were the woman, experiencing the slower, milder, but no less satisfying female orgasm. Was he dreaming? He doubted it. Stevia simply had the sexual capacity and inclination of a man, and was doing what she desired, now that she had a man who was not in a position to demur. It was a remarkable reversal of the normal roles.

He had thought his time on this planet would be a dry spell. Already he knew he had been seriously mistaken. He had also thought that no woman could match the Mistress Marionette. Stevia was definitely not the same woman, but neither was she sexually inferior. But she was not going to seduce him away from his loyalty to his mission.

⚛︎⚜︎

In the morning they dressed, ate more fruit, descended, and thanked the tree for its hospitality by urinating and defecating on its receptive patch of ground. Two days ago he would hardly have imagined such a sequence, but now he accepted it.

"Qualification," Stevia said. "I have told you my nature as a Glamor, though you neither understand nor believe it. I prefer that this not be bruited about elsewhere. Let me be an ordinary Gray Chroma guide."

"Agreement," he said. "But what of me? I do not want to be anonymous. I want to be accepted for what I am, an emissary from Earth."

"Agreement."

They resumed their trek. This time it led to a village. Every man, woman, and child was green; apart from that they were normal. Their houses were formed of green stone with green thatched roofs. Even the water in the community cistern was green, but perfectly potable.

They paused in the center circle, where paths converged. There an elder man met them. "Elder," Stevia said. "I am Stevia, and this is Dynamo, emissary from Planet Earth."

"Planet Earth!" the elder said. "We do not wish to become a colony again."

"That decision I think is in the hands of your King Havoc," Dynamo said. "I merely wish to learn all I can about your culture."

"On that basis, welcome to our village of Glen. As it happens, we will have a lesson play today for the children. If you are not familiar with our culture, you may find it instructive."

"He will," Stevia said, forestalling Dynamo's demurral. He was stuck with a children's educational show.

In due course the villagers of Glen assembled for the presentation. They sat on the ground in a circle, the smallest children in front, larger ones outside, and parents in the largest circle. Dynamo and and Stevia joined the parents, sitting with their hips touching. Her knees were raised; if anyone in a forward row glanced back, he would see her exposed cleft. That turned Dynamo guiltily on.

All of the people seemed perfectly ordinary in appearance, dress, and manner; only the color distinguished them. Rather, it was the divergent colors of the two visitors that distinguished them from the natives. Dynamo was beginning to feel a bit out of place, quite apart from his origin on a far planet.

A handsome green man entered the center stage. "This is our warning of the threat of the Incubus," he announced. "It is a drama of two actors. Watch and learn."

The Narrator hauled a wheeled bed into the center of a stage, then scratched a ring around it in the packed dirt. "This is the house, and this is Naive, who just had her twelfth birthday," the Narrator said. He stepped out of the circle as a figure appeared on the bed. Dynamo could have sworn the bed was empty a moment ago.

"She is an ordinary child, in her bed in her home, which is of course protected against the intrusion of evil spirits. It has a firewall." The Narrator poked one finger above the ring, and a spark flew.

The children in the nearest audience circle giggled; they knew about firewalls. Dynamo realized that this was probably a fable designed to make children feel secure in their homes. The tale itself was pitched to their level, with obvious names and a familiar opening situation. Naive = naïveté. The Incubus would be any strange man who might hunger for young flesh. So they dramatized the warning.

"Her mother has just tucked her in for the night," the Narrator continued. Then he affected a falsetto. "Good night, dear; sleep tight."

"Good night, Mother," the girl on the bed called back.

The Narrator faced outward toward the audience. Dynamo saw that he moved about, so as to address every part of the audience at one time or another. This was theater in the round, with minimal equipment, depending largely on imagination. The Narrator was providing that, with his apt words and manner. It was a considerable contrast to the elaborate stages and props and costumes of Earthly plays. But Dynamo had to admit it was effective; he could almost see the house, and the situation was believable.

"But little does Naive's mother know that an Incubus lurks in the area. The child has just started to become a woman, with a little swell of breast on her chest and a certain forming delicacy. The Incubus has tuned into that from afar, and comes here to see what he can do."

Now a second actor walked onto the stage. This was a tall cape-shrouded man with a furtive manner, skulking beautifully from shadow to shadow.

"The Incubus knows he is not welcome here, and that every house is protected," the Narrator said. "But he smells young flesh, and must see if he can get her innocent soul."

The Incubus came to Naive's house and paused there, lifting his nose to sniff. He nodded: this was the place.

"He tries to enter the house, but of course is repulsed," the Narrator said.

The Incubus poked a finger over the circle. A spark jumped and he fell back, jamming his burnt finger into his mouth. The children laughed.

"But then he gets smart," the Narrator said. "If he can't get in, maybe he can lure the girl out. He approaches her window."

The Incubus put his face up against the wall, not quite touching. "Naive!" he called quietly, his voice somehow carrying throughout the village center. "Wake! Come to me."

The girl stirred and sat up on her bed. "Who calls me?"

"It is I, your friend from afar. I love you."

Naive laughed. "I'm only twelve! Just a child. Nobody loves me."

"You are mistaken, Naive," the Incubus answered. "You are young but beautiful. I am smitten by your nascent perfection."

The girl put her feet on the floor, peering toward the window. "Negation. I have no breasts, no hips. I can't be beautiful." But she was plainly intrigued.

"All girls long to be beautiful," Stevia murmured. "Especially the plain ones. They see physical beauty as the key to all future happiness."

"You never had a problem," he responded.

"Oh, I did, I did, before I achieved my magic. Now I delight in the power of it."

That was surely true, as she had proved the past night. She well knew the power her body had over men, and had seemed pleased to demonstrate that repeatedly.

"Affirmation," she murmured as her hand slid into his trousers and took hold of his member. He was unable to protest, lest a villager take note.

"Naive, Naive," the Incubus said persuasively. "You must not heed the jealous jibes of siblings or other children. Your female assets are dawning, and your face is already lovely. You are like the morning sun first coming into its power."

"What a line!" Dynamo muttered.

"Or rod," Stevia murmured, squeezing his stiffening member. The woman was incorrigible.

The girl was plainly interested. "Really?"

"She wants to believe," Stevia murmured, tweaking his member further. Again, he thought of the way a man might fondle a helpless girl who didn't want to make an embarrassing scene. It was almost alarming being in the presence of such unremitting female sexuality.

"Really, truly, absolutely," the Incubus said expansively. "How is it that no one has remarked on your luster before? Come to me, that I may appreciate your qualities more completely."

The girl walked to the window and peered out. She wore only her nightslip, and was not visibly developed. "Question: Who are you? I don't recognize you."

"I am an admirer from a distant village, in quest of unique perfection. Lo, I have found it! You exceed even the dream I had of you."

But the girl was not entirely obtuse. "What village?"

"The distant village of Faraway. Few know of it, and visitors seldom come. That is why I have had to search far afield in quest of my heart's desire. But my search has ended; I have found you at last, you marvelous creature."

"Doubt. I don't believe you," Naive said, covering her face as if blushing.

"Oh, my dear, be not so! How can you not believe the truth? Come out and let me kiss your radiance."

At this point the players froze in place and the Narrator spoke, addressing the watching children. "Remember: the Incubus can not enter the protected house. He must induce her to come out. Even then he is limited. He can not touch her; he can only enable her to touch him."

"There is a distinction?" Dynamo asked Stevia.

"A vital one." She massaged his member, which was on the verge of jetting. "I am touching you; you are not touching me."

"You are about to embarrass me."

"Not necessarily."

The action resumed. "Uncertainty. I don't know," Naive said. "I'm not supposed to leave the house at night."

"Surely you misunderstand, dear girl! They mean you should not travel to the next village or into the deep and dangerous forest. Come stand with me in the lea, close by your house."

"Mother wouldn't like it."

"Mother need not know, need she, pretty thing? I long to be with you. Come to me, Naive."

Still she hesitated. "I'm not supposed to talk with strange men."

The Incubus clapped a dramatic hand to his chest. "You wound me, darling girl! How can you call me strange? I love you!"

She was immediately apologetic. "Apology. I'm sorry. It's just that—"

"I beg you, splendid creature, come out to me. Give me a precious kiss. I am perishing for longing."

"I can't. I mustn't." But she was evidently weakening.

"Just one kiss," the Incubus pleaded. "To last me the rest of my life, knowing that my lips have touched divinity."

Naive laughed, embarrassed. "Far fetched. I'm not divine! I'm hardly even ordinary. I'm just a dull girl."

"So you say. So you may even believe. But to me you are splendor incarnate, the epitome of femininity. In my fond image you can never be less than ideal."

"Ludicrous. It's just not so. I'm nothing special." But she was clearly flattered.

"Your loveliness is exceeded only by your modesty, delightful maiden. Oh, Naive! Grant me my desperate dream. Come to me. Come to me!" He reached out toward her, beseechingly, though his hand remained clear of the firewall.

"This is so obvious it is painful," Dynamo whispered. "But I think if I were a twelve year old girl, I'd be swept off my foolish feet."

"Precisely," Stevia agreed. "Look at the audience: you can recognize the twelve year olds by their rapt expressions."

He looked. It wasn't just the twelves, but the elevens, tens, and even nines. They were absolutely fascinated by the expressive Incubus. Only the older girls wore the knowing expressions of those who had seen this presentation before.

Now he realized that the children were mostly female. "Where are the boys?"

"They don't have to attend this one. Theirs is the Succubus warning. That's a truly striking effort, because of the beautiful nude actress. Queen Gale once played that role, when she was seventeen. She left a wake of broken hearts."

Dynamo sifted though his eidetic memory for his snapshot of the queen. She was a strikingly handsome woman, who in her first flush of youth must have been stunning, especially in the nude. That was the play he would rather have seen.

Still, this one had its points. The girl was perfectly played, and the Incubus practically radiated insincerity. He almost wished Stevia would let go of his member so he could concentrate more fully on the presentation.

Naive made a timorous decision. "All right. Just for a minute."

"Joy!"

She went to the window and carefully climbed through. The actress was skilled; the sill really seemed to be there. Her slip rode up as she wedged awkwardly through, exposing her thin thighs. The Incubus' eyes seemed to be bulging, though they were not visible under his hood. He did not try to help her down.

She landed on the ground before him, straightened up, and dusted herself off. "Remember, just one kiss."

"I shall do better than that, beloved belle. I shall take no advantage at all. I will stand absolutely still and let you kiss me. Is that not fair?"

"Surprise," she said uncertainly. "When—in stories—the man sweeps her into his arms and kisses her passionately."

"My darling, my darling, how I long to do exactly that! But I must give you reason to trust me, so I will not do what I so ardently crave. I will play statue for your wonderful kiss."

"That's fair, I guess," she said. She approached him, but he was too tall for her to reach his face. "I—can you get lower?"

"Gladly, my precious love. I abase myself for you." He lay on the ground, face up.

Naive kneeled beside him, leaned down, and tried to kiss his face. But she lost her balance and fell across his chest. "Regret!" she exclaimed, scrambling off him.

"Needless. I cherish your evocative touch of whatever nature, perfect maiden."

"Nonsense. You're lucky I didn't squash you to death."

"Ah, that were the ideal demise."

She had to laugh, this time less embarrassed. "You're such a gentleman."

"It is the illumination of your presence that makes me so."

"Decision: I will try again. This time I will keep my balance." Naive straddled him, set her hands on either side of his head, lowered her face, and kissed him firmly on the mouth.

The players froze as the Narrator spoke. "Observation: this is their first full physical contact, skin to skin. She has touched him. That touch is magic; it instills in her a strong desire for more. This is the nature of the Incubus." He stepped back.

The action resumed. "Oh, that's something," Naive exclaimed as she lifted her head. "I want another."

"You promised one," the Incubus said. "That one transports me halfway to Vivid."

Stevia touched Dynamo's hand with her free one. "Vivid is our bright star."

Naive lay down on top of him, seeking greater contact. Her prior reticence had disappeared. "I will give you more." She kissed him again, lingeringly, then raised her head again. "Now where are you?"

"Between Vivid and Void. Your touch fulfills me, yet incites a desperate craving."

"Between Vivid and Void," Stevia said. "A common saying, meaning to be caught between delight and horror, or between impossible alternatives."

Void: he recognized the black hole that was the star's companion. Naturally it had entered their language.

"Craving?" Naive asked. "What else do you desire, more than a kiss?"

"Trepidation. I dare not ask."

"Ask!" she begged.

"I can not deny your imperative. I desire the full contact of our bodies. As much of your touch as I can have."

"Granted! I want it too." She scrambled up and removed her nightie, baring her lanky body. Then she worked on his cloak, opening it out so that his body was similarly exposed. And paused, staring.

For the Incubus had a huge phallic erection. Not the only one, but Dynamo's was concealed as Stevia's fingers gently tickled it, keeping it always on the verge without quite triggering its eruption. She was teasingly skilled.

The Narrator spoke again. "Naive has never seen such an implement. She knows that boys have penises, and that sometimes they mysteriously grow and stiffen, but this is the veritable king of members. She does not know its purpose, but is urgently drawn to it. She is now under the spell of the Incubus, and eager to do his bidding. But when that magic member enters her, it will incite her to orgasm, and that is the moment the Incubus will suck out her soul. She is doomed."

The action resumed. "That is my joy stick," the Incubus said. "It seeks a home in you, that we may both be transported by intolerable pleasure. Straddle it, take hold of it, and guide it to the crevice between your legs. It will find its way."

"Dismay. It's so big!"

"It will not seem so. Take it."

The girl considered, and was overcome by burgeoning desire. Dynamo realized that the actress was skilled; little signals made her sexual excitement clear. She straddled his body and took hold of the giant member. She carefully set it at her cleft, working it around to find the place. "Delight! It warms me wonderfully. I want it inside me."

"Settle yourself down on it. You can take it all in, slowly. There will be no discomfort."

"Oh, I feel the rapture of it already!" She started settling herself down, taking in the member. It had to be distending her narrow channel, but evidently there was an anesthetic quality associated with it.

Dynamo peered as closely as he could from this distance. There did not seem to be any fakery; the girl was actually getting it inside her, very slowly and carefully. He was amazed and dismayed, but also fascinated. This was a public show for children?

The sight of that huge member wedging into the tight channel finally put Dynamo over the limit. He felt his own climax starting.

And Stevia was sitting on his lap. Somehow his member was freed of his trousers and sliding into her, finding its deep lodging just as it spouted. He suffered a desperately powerful orgasm; it seemed as if most of his substance was pulsing into her hot core.

Now the Narrator used his falsetto. "Naive! Where are you?"

"Mother!" the girl cried, chagrined. But she did not jump off the half-buried member. The desire for completion was too strong. She tried to take it quickly the rest of the way in, but it balked like a stout peg reaching the bottom of a hole; the process evidently had to be at its own pace.

The Narrator stepped into the house and over to the window. "An Incubus!" he cried in falsetto. "Stealing my daughter's soul! I curse you, foul monster! Begone!"

The Incubus groaned as the curse struck him. Then he caught fire. It flared up greenly. Now the girl jumped up, avoiding the heat. She stood, appalled, watching the figure on the ground burn to nothing but some bad-smelling green ash. "You killed my lover!" But already she was realizing that he had been a demon lover, not a true one. She had almost sacrificed her soul.

Dynamo, his urgency spent, glanced nervously around. Had he made a similar spectacle of himself? He discovered that no one had noticed; all eyes were on the play. What great luck!

"Negation," Stevia murmured. "I made an avoidance aura around us; they are unable to look directly." She lifted off him and refastened his trousers as she resumed her seat beside him. "Now that aura fades."

What a woman! "Thanks," he murmured inadequately.

"And so Naive was saved after all, despite herself," the Narrator concluded. "She was lucky. Moral: do not heed the Incubus. Once you touch him, he will lead you on until he possesses you, and take your soul. This is the manner of it. You can't change your mind halfway through. Be warned."

The young girls in the audience were staring, horrified. Now they understood the danger, right down to its physical details. They had seen what went where, and how. They would not forget.

"This is a cruel lesson," Dynamo said. "Considering that there is no such thing as an incubus, only unscrupulous men. It should have been done without the fantasy."

"You are mistaken," Stevia said. "Incubi and succubi exist. They operate exactly as shown. The children must be warned."

There was that superstition again. Earth's work was cut out on this one. How could an entire planet be brought rapidly into civilization? But that was only one aspect; there was another. "Was it necessary to demonstrate grotesque sex before children? Some of them are under five years old."

"Yes, those are the ones who must be shown, because the incubi and succubi prey on innocence. They try to catch girls and boys at the beginning of their sexuality, before they are on guard, and sometimes they succeed. We must always be vigilant. We have to educate the children before they ever encounter the evil spirits; some of them don't otherwise know how sex is performed, let alone the dangers of it."

"But doesn't that, well, turn them on? Make them desire sex despite being too young?"

"There is no nether age for voluntary sex. Children are free to experiment with each other, learning how it is done. As long as no one forces it, they can do whatever they want. The point is not that sex is wrong, but that they must be wary of demons."

Dynamo let that aspect drop. This was one strange culture. "And what of that poor actress? Twelve years old and forced to perform sexually in public. This is obscene."

She smiled. "The play is done. Come meet the actors." She led him to the center, where Narrator, Girl, and Incubus were talking with the children.

"No, it does not mean that sex itself is evil," Naive was explaining to a ten year old girl, much as Stevia had just done for Dynamo. "With your boyfriend whom you have known for years, if both of you are willing, a game of Tickle and Peek or Touch and Touch can progress to sexual touching and finally full sex. That's how you learn, how you gain experience, so you will be ready for marriage. But you have to be wary of strangers, especially when you are virginal."

"Relief," the girl said. "He put his finger in, but I was afraid to let him use the other."

"Don't be. And if you are ever in doubt, remember that an incubus can't touch you. So don't do it for him, as I did in the play; make him do it. No incubus can."

"Appreciation." The girl departed.

"This is Dynamo, of Earth," Stevia said. "He is learning our culture. He is concerned that you are required to do something you shouldn't or don't want to."

Naive gazed at Dynamo, assessing him. Up close she seemed taller, and she did have a feminine shape though was hardly large-breasted. "No fault?"

He clenched his teeth to keep his jaw from dropping. "You are inviting me to participate with you?"

"Sex, yes, of course. I am seventeen and you are a handsome man who has a question. I can best answer it by demonstration."

He evaded part of the issue. "You don't look that old."

She laughed. "Obvious! I was late developing, and got teased, until I volunteered for this role. Now no one teases me. Soon enough my body will complete its change and I will have to give up the play, but for now it's wonderful. I like being the center of attention." She looked at him again. "Answer?"

Dynamo wrestled with it. Stevia had given him leave, in fact probably wanted him to do it. But his taste was not in children. He decided on honesty. "Negation. I see you as twelve."

"Some like twelve."

"Not me. My apology if I gave you the wrong idea."

Naive glanced at Stevia. "I can't compete with that. Parting."

"Acknowledged."

They moved on. "Satisfaction?" Stevia asked.

"Agreement. She's no child."

"Desire?"

Suddenly it hit him. The sexuality of the play had affected him far more than he had realized. He had just done it, but wanted it again—and again. "Yes."

"They have provided us a house. We won't be staying the night, but can use it now."

She took him to the green house. Inside were amenities including a bed. He threw her on it and penetrated her immediately and explosively. It was as if he had been weeks, rather than minutes, without sex. Only after that release did he realize that both of them were fully clothed. Somehow she had facilitated it, once again baring what was necessary, just in time. "Appreciation," he gasped.

"Unfortunate you did not accept Naive's offer," she said. "She would have loved that passion."

"You are a tease."

"I delight in educating you."

So it seemed. "What next?"

"We travel magically."

"That I will be interested in seeing." He thought he was being ironic.

Chapter 5
Caveat

Caveat appeared as directed before the Head Mistress. She was of course an extremely beautiful woman, and possessed of the aura of almost absolute authority. "We have a task for you," she announced.

"Mistress, I will serve as directed."

"Caveat, you are seriously overqualified for the chores you have been performing. We regret that you have been barred from the promotion you deserve. I speak as a friend."

"Appreciation, Mistress."

"I believe that of all the men under my sway, I feel closest to you. Certainly I respect you most. I would marry you if that were feasible, or at least take you to my bed."

Caveat was wary of compliments from above; there was generally some associated penalty regardless of their sincerity. He knew the Mistress bore him no animosity; she really did respect and like him. But she was constrained by the mores of the culture she governed. She, too, had to obey.

He smiled. "But there is a caveat."

She nodded. "As always. So our friendship must remain officially covert, though I will continue to call on you for advice when your special objectivity is required. If others conjecture that I am using you as a private sex toy, that harms neither of us."

Caveat waited, as her remark had not required a direct response. They had been over this territory before.

"This is a rather special assignment for which it seems you are uniquely qualified. The explorer space ship *Dominance* is returning from a colony recovery mission, bearing four hostages and associated personnel. These are the colony king's four children: three by adoption, one natural. We conjecture that the three are actually support for the one, given royal status to ensure that no commoner can ever interfere with their association with her. They are seventeen years old and highly talented; they surround her with virtual effulgence. She is fifteen, less impressive, seeming as yet somewhat in their shadows. But there is no question among any of them that she is ultimately dominant; all subtly defer to her. She is a true princess."

Caveat felt pain. He saw the hit coming.

"Yes, I am assigning you to be her guardian on Earth," the Mistress said. "I am sorry, Caveat, I truly am. But after what we have seen of the nature of the siblings, we dare not take any chance. One of them is a musician and singer as talented as any on Earth, and she seems unhesitant to employ her beauty to seduce any man she chooses. The mistress of the mission allowed it, as the girl was clearly sexually experienced and the men were ecstatic. It considerably alleviated the normal boredom of travel time. Another is a female martial artist of dismaying competence; she could kill you or me before we or our guards could react. She seduced the guard we had on their chamber."

"The singer?" he inquired, clarifying a potential confusion.

"The Amazon. She is spare of physique and no coquette, but he became her master for the duration of the journey back to Earth."

"These are not ordinary royal brats, then."

"Definitely not. The male is a story teller of remarkable finesse; I understand that his listeners are mesmerized. He entertained the crewmen throughout, never repeating himself, never growing dull. On occasion his siblings supported him, acting parts he narrated. Sometimes they enlisted a crewman for a supportive role, which was a coveted office. On rare occasion, even the Mistress. She reports that this was like entering a different world, one where fantasy governs. She served him sexually, of course, but she says that if ever she had her choice of permanent partners, he would be the one, though he is but seventeen."

"What of the youngest, the true princess? Does she have a specialty?"

"She is an actress. The Mistress is under the impression that the girl was making an effort to conceal the extent of her talent, but that even so it is remarkable. She can play any part she chooses, extremely well. She is also as nearly as we can ascertain a remarkably nice girl with many quite winning qualities." The Mistress gazed seriously at him. "We suspect she could as readily seduce a man as did her siblings, if she chooses, despite her age. That she could make him love her, and thus corrupt him. She may have reason to do so, to win their freedom to return to their home planet. We fear that we must assign either a female guard, which would be awkward, or an incorruptible male."

And there it was. "I must nursemaid a royal brat."

"I wish it were that simple, Caveat. Any of us could handle a brat. These children may be virtually ungovernable. We do not wish to cause them any harm, either physical or mental, as that would seriously prejudice any peaceful acquisition of their planet. Their father the king is by all accounts an intelligent and situationally ruthless man. He is known as a barbarian, and he may be, but it would be folly to misjudge him. The achievements of his children suggest the depths of his competence. We want him on our side."

"I must guard and please the girl without being subverted by her."

"That is the assignment, Caveat. Success will provide me a basis to promote you to your warranted level. That should be an incentive."

It certainly was, as she knew. She was buttressing his obligation to serve as directed, with reason to do so well. "I hear and obey, Mistress," he said formally.

She rose from her seat and approached him. "Be warned: this may be more of a challenge than we know. You have planetary discretion." She put her fine hands on his shoulders, pressing him down slightly so that he bowed his head in automatic submission to her will. She kissed him. "I have faith in you," she said.

Caveat was half-stunned, not by the kiss, which was her signal of confirmation of the authority she was vesting in him, but by the authority itself. He could do almost anything, even opposing the expressed will of an ordinary Mistress, if he found it necessary. Of course he would avoid any such confrontation if possible, and always show due respect. But the power was there.

And the Mistress of Mistresses thought he might need it in the performance of his duty: working with a fifteen year old alien princess. That was almost frightening.

※※

Caveat met the hostage party at the Antarctica landing site as they emerged from the planetary shuttle. They were in the charge of a mistress, of course. As it happened, he knew her: Marionette, or Ette, young but rapidly rising because of her expertise. She was reputed to have the most satisfied missions, as she related well to the men. It was another signal of the importance of this mission that they were retaining her in the capacity. She had evidently bonded with the royal children.

"This is Caveat who has special authority as your guide and guardian on Earth," she said to the hostages. Then she introduced them in turn to him. He was familiar with their names and images, as he had of course done his background research. Now he noted special features that the records had not picked up on. For one thing, their hair and eyes matched colors, a remarkable coincidence, if that was what it was. Apart from that they were strikingly different.

Warp was tall, dark, and confident, a natural leader. Weft was outstanding in her blonde beauty, openly eying him as a prospect. Flame had red hair, slender and fit, with the balance of the martial artist; she could move rapidly in any direction as required. And Voila—brown of hair and eye, conservative of garb and body, but somehow possessed of an intangible assurance the belied her young age.

"You are measuring me," she murmured as they shook hands.

"I need to know you well," he explained. "To facilitate your safety and comfort during your stay on Earth."

"That, too," she agreed. "This is Iolo, my dog."

Iolo was unlike any dog of Earth. For one thing he had six legs. Caveat squatted to meet the animal's gaze—and discovered a disturbingly aware countenance. This was no animal, he concluded, but an alien being.

"May I pet him?" he asked.

"Affirmation," the girl said. "He's friendly."

Caveat cautiously petted the odd dog's head. The touch was not what he expected; there was a spongy quality to the dog's fur. Also something strange, but he could not pin it down. This animal, weird *as* it seemed, was not exactly *what* it seemed. But in time Caveat would fathom that riddle too.

There were also three palace personnel: a red man, a blue woman, and an invisible woman. Literally; flesh and clothing were all of one color, or lack of color. That last was of special interest to scientists, as it seemed her flesh was not refractive; light passed through her unaffected. She was a general maidservant and, they had ascertained, sometime sexual partner of the boy, Warp. Presumably the royals could not be denied by servants, so she made the best of it. This was likely to be the case on primitive world—and some not-so-primitive ones too.

Introductions complete, Marionette got on to the business of the moment. "There is a suitable suite for the party a hundred kilos distant. We will take a subway capsule there. Then we all can rest; I'm sure we are all tired."

"Question: Kilos?" the young man inquired.

"Our unit of distance," Caveat explained. "A kilo is abridgment of kilometer, or one thousand meters, which is in turn approximately one walking pace."

"A hundred kilo is thus beyond convenient walking distance," Warp said, getting it straight.

"Yes. It is also not convenient to walk far here, because this is a continent formed of ice. We tunnel through it; the passages are quite cold, except the heated concourses. So the capsules are preferable."

"Like a Black Chroma network," Augur, the red man, said.

Warp nodded; evidently that analogy clarified it for him in a way Caveat's discussion had not.

"Ice," the blonde, Weft, said. "Charm has ice at the north and south poles."

"That is similar to Earth," Caveat agreed.

"This way," Ette said. She led the way to the capsule station. Caveat noted how the eyes of the youthful prince followed her flexing posterior. So did the eyes of the red man. That was of course the point of the apparel of a mistress: to compel the gaze of any man in the vicinity. Sexuality was a significant aspect of mistress' power.

They reached the capsule. It was sized to comfortably contain twelve people, so their party of nine plus alien dog had no problem. They entered the side door and took seats. The little princess Voila sat beside Caveat, though she did not have to. Warp sat beside Marionette, evidently taken with her, unsurprisingly.

The door closed and secured itself. Then the capsule started moving, rolling smoothly forward on its eight wheels.

"The trip will take approximately one hour," Ette announced. "Our destination has been pre-programmed. We may talk, or relax, or sleep, as you prefer."

"How about you and me making out?" Warp asked her.

"If your sisters or chaperones approve," she replied easily.

"Affirmation," Weft said immediately.

"Negation," Flame said.

Augur lifted a hand. "We are in an as-yet unfamiliar situation. A public display of this nature does not seem to be in order. Therefore, negation."

Warp looked rebellious, but accepted the decision of the chaperone. Ette took his hand and caressed it, and that seemed to pacify him.

This single word convention interested Caveat. It was an efficient way to convey mood as well as meaning.

"Suggestion," Ette said. "We can watch the holovision for diversion." She gestured, and a programmed show came on, filling the upper portion of the front end of the capsule with three dimensional images of costumed players.

"Illusion!" Weft said, delighted. The others joined her in watching. Evidently there was something similar on their planet.

Voila took Caveat's hand. "Mischief," she murmured.

Surprised, he looked at her. "I mean you no harm, princess."

"Confirmation," she said, meeting his gaze. Suddenly her brown eyes seemed large and almost luminous. "Request."

"I mean to accommodate any reasonable wish of yours," he said carefully. "It is my purpose to safeguard you and facilitate your comfort."

"Urgency. We two must be close sooner than is convenient. I need your oath."

This was confusing. "Oath, princess?"

"To keep our secrets."

Would that facilitate relations? "I may not agree to help you escape custody, or allow any activity that is dangerous to your welfare. Apart from such caveats—" he paused, smiling with her at the practical use of his name. "I will agree to keep your secrets."

"Ours," she said, gesturing to include all the others and Mistress Marionette.

"I can't speak for the mistress."

"Warp," Voila said tersely.

Warp turned to Ette. "We need your word, in a hurry. Keep our secrets."

Ette glanced at Caveat. "With the standard cautions, agreed," she said.

"Agreed," Caveat said. What was this girl up to? A children's game?

"Danger," Voila said. "In progress."

"Oh, I assure you this capsule is safe," Caveat said. "There is no need to fear—"

Then the capsule swerved. "It's changing tracks," Ette said, surprised. "That's not supposed to happen."

The capsule swerved again, and again, shoving them all to one side and another. Caveat found Voila within his embrace; somehow she had moved in close, perhaps for comfort.

"We can not affect it now," Voila said. "We must wait until it stops." She looked at the red man. "Speak for us, Augur."

Augur looked thoughtful, then nodded. "We are in serious danger," he said. "I must ask the two of you, Marionette and Caveat, to accept my directives for the duration of this crisis, and to keep quiet about what you see in the next hour."

Something was certainly going on. "We have already given our words," Caveat said. "But we will not participate in anything either dangerous to you or in significant violation of our duties as officers of Earth."

"The threat can be avoided if you cooperate," Augur said. "We ask you only to eliminate your normal reports on our activities for the coming hour. Then things will return to normal, and control will revert to you."

Caveat and Marionette shrugged in unison. "So be it," he agreed.

The constant shifting of the capsule continued. Finally it slewed to another side and came to a rapid halt.

"This is not where we belong," Ette said grimly. She brought out her communicator and held it before her, dismayed. "We are in a dead zone. We can't call for help."

"They will miss us when we don't reach our destination on schedule," Caveat said. He tried the sliding door, but it was locked in place. "All we have to do is wait."

Augur looked at Voila. "Negation," he said. "In twenty five minutes this capsule will be animate again, rerouted, and accelerated into a blank wall, killing all aboard. At present it is sealed, and any physical attempt to break out of it will result in the detonation of the explosives set on the track beneath it.

We must act immediately."

"How can you know this?" Ette demanded.

"We have some special powers," Augur said. "Clairvoyance among them. We do not know the identity of our enemy, but we are quite conversant with the local threat. Bear with us this hour, and we will try to explain more clearly once we are safe."

"Agreed," Marionette said, clearly shaken. Caveat echoed it.

"We know the capacity of the explosives," Augur said. "But this is Science magic we do not properly understand. What would be a mechanism?"

"That would be a bomb," Caveat said. "It would have a trigger device to set it off if disturbed."

Voila embraced Caveat and brought her head close to his. "Please," she said, and kissed him.

Caveat simply sat there, astonished. Her kiss was no token; neither was it an offering of love. It felt as though her very being was infusing his, exploring it, searching for something.

She ended the kiss and withdrew. "Appreciation. Apology."

"For what?" he asked, baffled. There had certainly been something.

"For reading your mind," she said. "We had to get the detail fast."

Augur glanced at the dog. "Iolo—explore and nullify the bomb."

The six legged dog walked to the center of the capsule and began to evaporate. Caveat stared. Vapor was rising from the creature, and the body was shrinking.

"Iolo is an ifrit," Voila explained. "He can dissolve into fog and travel that way. He will find the bomb and coalesce around its ignition mechanism, nullifying it. Then we can safely break out of the capsule."

"How can you know about such technology?" Caveat asked.

"From your mind. I read it and relayed it to Iolo so he could do it."

"You read my mind?" Caveat asked unbelievingly. He had not properly absorbed the significance before.

"Affirmation. I do not like invading your privacy, but we will all die if we don't do it now and right."

The last of the ifrit diffused into mist, leaving the dog collar on the floor. The mist drifted up and out an air vent as Voila picked up the collar.

Marionette shook her head. "I think it is just as well we committed to secrecy. Others will think we are crazy."

Caveat was similarly bemused. "I would not believe much if any of this, had I net just seen that dog dissolve into vapor. Now it seems I must believe in telepathy and clairvoyance."

"There will be more," Augur said.

"More than this?"

"I can read the near future," Voila said. "That is how I know about the crash." She glanced at Augur. "Iolo got it; we can break out now."

Augur nodded. "Flame."

The red-haired girl stood. "Give me room."

They cleared the center of the capsule, squeezing to either side. Flame stood before the sliding door. Suddenly she moved. She was in the air, her two feet striking the door in a martial arts kick. She landed neatly back on her feet. The door was dented, but remained closed. She leaped again, and a third time, and the denting increased, until finally the catch broke and it could be forced open.

Augur and Caveat did that, wedging it the rest of the way. The group of them exited, finding themselves on an unlighted service platform.

"Light," Weft said. Her fingers glowed, and there was enough light for them to see nearby.

"We must wait for Iolo," Augur said.

"He is clear of the capsule," Voila said. "But when he lets go of the bomb, it will explode."

"We must get clear," Augur said. "Which way?"

Voila pointed back along the track behind the stalled capsule.

"But if they are going to start it moving again, we'll be run over," Marionette protested.

"That is why this way," Voila said. "It will go forward. Except that it won't."

They got onto the track, following Weft's light, and left the capsule in the dark tunnel.

"He's letting go," Voila reported.

"Cover your ears," Caveat said, believing. "This is a confined space." The others obeyed.

There was an explosion. He felt the impact of its force against his body and his covered ears. Voila was against him again, close.

"Princess—" he said gently.

"I had to protect you. We are to be friends."

"Protect me?"

"You were to be hurt. Warp protected Marionette."

Caveat glanced at them. Warp was holding the mistress close, very close. Obviously the youth liked that, but it seemed there was more to it than an early feel. Actually they had already been lovers, so perhaps it was natural.

"And Weft and Flame protected us," Augur said. He, Aura, and Ine the shrouded woman were in a close group.

"How could you young folk protect adults?"

"The force of the blast was stronger than you thought," Voila said. "See your clothes."

Caveat checked his clothing. Much of it had been torn off him by the force of the passing wind of the explosion. The same was true of Marionette, who now showed more anatomy than she had realized. They had indeed been protected.

"We must flee," Voila said. "They are coming after us."

"Who?" Caveat asked somewhat dazedly.

"The enemies. Now I see their minds. They are from Atlantis. They know about us."

The astonishments were piling in too fast. Atlantis was the assortment of islands on the planet, and it was in current near rebellion. It could well have sent a secret hostile mission here to interfere with the colony recovery process. "When this is done," Caveat said, "You must tell us more."

"You must give your oaths."

"We will," Marionette said. She, too, was shaken.

Now Voila led the way. She seemed not to need the light Weft provided; she knew where she was going. The ifrit dog Iolo coalesced beside her, his six legs trotting intricately. She paused to put his collar back on him, then resumed her forward march.

"It's the seeing," Weft confided to him as she matched his pace. "She can see the near future, as she told you. She knows when she's going to trip and avoids it."

"And she knows where to hide to avoid them," Flame said. "Better than the rest of us do."

"What *is* she?" Caveat demanded.

"A Glamor." Flame laughed. "And you don't understand. It's a magical being. And you don't believe in magic."

"True," Caveat and Marionette said almost together.

"You will," Warp said. "But you must not tell."

"That will be easy not to tell," Caveat said wryly.

Voila found what she deemed to be a safe place. It was behind a tangled nest of cables, and was tight. They crowded in together, Voila sitting on Caveat's lap, and Warp taking Marionette on his. Weft and Flame squeezed in with the three other adults. The dog settled down at the edge, partly diffused as if maintaining spectral guard. Weft's light continued, so that they were not in perfect darkness.

"Shouldn't we hide in the dark?" Marionette asked.

"They aren't using human eyes," Warp said. "Light makes no difference now."

"Now we can talk," Voila said. "How were you named?"

"I don't understand."

She kissed him with a fair amount of feeling. "Answer, or I'll do this too much and get a crush on you."

"Don't do that!" he said with alarm.

"Question?"

What was there to do? "We have promised not to tell your secrets. Will you promise not to tell ours?"

"Promised," the four siblings chorused.

"Do not get a crush on me, because there can never be anything to it," Caveat said. "Because I am your enemy, protecting you as a valuable hostage. Because I am twice your age. And because I do not relate romantically to women."

Her eyes were wide and dark. "Confusion."

"He prefers men, or boys," Marionette said. "That is why he was assigned to you: you can not seduce him."

Voila gazed at him with horror.

"I am sorry," Caveat said. "I have no desire to hurt you in any way. I have become very much impressed with you in the brief time we have been acquainted; you have truly remarkable qualities. We can be friends if you wish, but no more than that."

"Chagrin," she said, tears rolling down her face. "Humiliation."

This was painful. "This may be no comfort to you, but I do see you as a nice girl. I expected a spoiled princess, but have learned that you are well beyond that. Your talents amaze me. Were I what you thought I was, I suspect you could have seduced me despite your young age, if that was your intention. There is no failing in you; your reactions are normal. I wish we could *be* friends, but understand if that has become impossible."

"It's a fair offer, Voila," Augur said. "He can't proffer more."

"Expletive!"

"This is unkind," Aura said. "He does not deserve it."

The girl looked rebellious for a moment longer, then wilted. "Capitulation."

So the adults had brought the child to heel. They were serving their purpose.

"I apologize for misjudging you before I knew you," Caveat said.

"Clarification: it's not that. It's that I must work with you, and we must have a close association. I mistook its nature. Obscenity!"

"Voila!" Augur said sharply.

"Retracted," the girl said immediately. She looked at Caveat and smiled through her tears. "Condition: I reserve the right to kiss you on occasion. You may be differently oriented, but I am not."

He shrugged. "What occasion?"

"This one." She kissed him. She had done that twice before, and each had had its impact. This time was no exception; there was significant power in her kisses. There was something more to them than either love or sexuality.

"Are you reading my mind?" he asked.

"Negation. I did that only when I had to get the technical detail to defuse the bomb. I respect your privacy."

"That was why you didn't pick up on my sexual orientation."

"Confirmation."

It was time to move on. "You asked me how I was named. To answer that I need to clarify the Earthly convention. We exist our first few years with assigned temporary nicknames. When we are old enough or experienced enough to show some individuality we are assigned permanent names by committees that have studied us. They are supposed to have some relevance to our natures. As a child I was popular with girls, who seemed to like my manners, but I was never as close to them as to my male friends. Thus it was said that any girl was welcome to associate with me, but there was a caveat: I was not a prospect for intimacy."

"That's how we are named!" Voila said, clapping her hands as if she were five years old. "Only no committee. It's done informally. My parents considered me to be special, so they named me Voila! Found at last. But usually it is friends or the community who do it."

"This is interesting," Ette said. "May I participate?"

"Yes, if you kiss me," Warp said.

"You don't need to bargain with her, blackhead," Weft said. "Just kiss her; she never says no."

"Not that *you* ever say no, yellow belly," he snapped back.

"If you two want to fight," Flame said, "you should take Amazon training,"

"Ignore the children," Augur said to Marionette. "How were you named?"

"When I was young I showed a certain talent for manipulating others, so they named me Marionette and put me into Mistress training. Had I been male, they would have named me Puppet. But now I wonder; I can appreciate how Flame came by her name, but how did the two of you acquire the terms for weaving?"

"We were rejects," Warp said. "Sent back to the Temple at the same time. The women there needed temporary names for us, so took what was most handy, Warp and Weft. But then King Havoc and Queen Gale adopted us, and kept the names, so they aren't really relevant."

"Yours is," Weft said. "You're warped."

"Consider the company I had to suffer with!"

"This is a convention in your culture?" Caveat asked. "By that I mean, not the naming, but the question: how were you named?"

"Affirmation," Weft said.

"We have lots of them," Weft said. She glanced at Warp. "Half a greeting, Contortion." She smiled. "As in warped."

"Half back, Crybaby." He glanced at Marionette. "That's as in wept, crying."

"Say my name."

"Say mine."

"Warp."

"Weft."

They leaned into each other and kissed. It was obvious that they had no romantic interest in each other, but liked pretending. They were normal teens—to an extent.

"Then there's Tickle & Peek," Weft said.

Warp poked her in the ribs with a finger. She exploded in simulated ticklishness, managing in the process to bare both thighs and part of one breast.

"What did you see, pervert?" she asked him.

"Nothing interesting, flatform."

The others laughed at that, for Weft was anything but flat, anywhere.

"You liar," she chided him. Then, to the Earth folk: "He has to tell anything he saw. Then I can tickle *him* there, for ten seconds, and he must not laugh or move, or he loses the game."

"Want to play it with me?" Warp asked Marionette. "I guarantee not to cheat."

"Liar again," Weft said. "You'd Peek her cleft, she'd tickle yours, and something would move."

"No it wouldn't," he insisted. "It would already be stiff."

"Those games must lead to more intimate explorations," Marionette said.

"Confirmation," Weft said. "It's a form of early courtship."

"I should think there would be abuse," Caveat said. "Some adults have sexual interest in children."

"Negation," Warp said. "Children have to be of similar ages to play. Adults never play with children."

"They'd be exiled from their village," Weft agreed.

"Question," Caveat said. "How were the king and queen named?"

All four siblings laughed. "When Father gets mad, he makes havoc," Voila said. "Everything gets torn up. Nobody crosses Havoc!"

Caveat exchanged a glance with Marionette. "We may already have done so," he said.

They laughed again. "Certainty," Warp said. "You'll be sorry."

"What would he do, considering that his children are hostages on Earth?" Marionette asked.

All four sobered, not answering.

"And Mom had a pet spider," Weft said after a pause. "Only it grew too big, and ate a man, and she had to lie to save it, saying there was a big wind in the night. So she became Gale."

Marionette looked at her watch. "Is it safe to resume motion?"

"Negation," Voila said. "They have motion sensors out. We can't leave this refuge for another hour."

"You are sure of this?"

"Affirmation."

"How can you be sure, since your planet lacks such technology?"

Voila glanced at Marionette. "You gave your word."

"I did. I will not tell my people of this."

"I can see the paths of the near future. Many are fleeting, or merge into each other, but some are firm. The bomb was firm, because it existed in all paths. The time limit is firm, because your minions are searching for us, and the assassins can't stay longer. They must go by then. Then we will emerge and tell how Caveat saved us from the plot."

"I did not!" Caveat protested.

"If the truth gets known, the assassins will be more careful next time," Voila said. She was not at all like a carefree teenager now; she spoke with conviction. "That would force us to take more serious action, which would endanger our lives and your careers. Therefore your commitment to be silent about our special powers includes the mechanism to accomplish that. The need to take the credit we offer. It is best for us all."

"You are asking me to lie," Caveat said. "To soil my honor."

"Apology. Yes."

There was a silence.

"Perhaps not. This would come under the heading of counterintelligence," Marionette said. "Some secrets need to be kept. It is not a matter of honor. Rather, honor requires us to keep faith with these people, excluding all others."

Caveat nodded. "I would rather have had you seduce me," he told Voila.

"Similarity," she said.

"Observation: It seems we have an hour to pass," Augur said. "I suggest that we use the time beneficially."

"Tickle and Peek," Warp suggested, looking at Marionette's décolletage.

"No fair," Weft protested. "Flame and I don't have men to play with."

"Anyway, he's already seen it," Flame said.

"You know little of Earth as yet," Marionette said. "We can fill you in on what it would help you to know."

"I would like to know the intervening Earth history, since our colony was founded," Augur said. "We had expected the ship to return with more colonists, but it never did. What happened?"

"Boredom," Weft complained, frowning.

"Interest," Flame said. "History sets up the present, and the future. We need to know."

"Confirmation," Aura said. "A necessary study."

Caveat smiled. "I think you are outvoted," he said to Weft. "I will provide a capsule history."

They settled down comfortably to listen. Weft closed her eyes as if to sleep through the boredom. Flame sat still, but her eyes were constantly checking their surroundings. If trouble should come, she would be the first to react. But it seemed they knew that trouble would not come, provided they sat tight.

"Space travel arrived late in the twentieth century," Caveat said. "Manned rocket ships were sent up to orbit Earth, then to the moon. Unmanned ships went out to the other planets of our Solar System, photographing them and analyzing their substances. It was a dangerous business, with significant loss of lives and equipment. In the twenty first century it went farther, as the inter-stellar drive was perfected, and inertialess movement, and the so-called 'worm hole' routing to the vicinities of neighboring stars." As he spoke he visualized it, seeing the early ships setting out with their crews.

The population of Earth was burgeoning, and there needed to be some release. For a time it seemed that interstellar exploration was that release, with the dream of finding new planets for people to travel to. Some were found, classified, listed, and set up for colonization. Several were quite promising, with atmospheres that could be adapted for human use with minimal treat-ment. The process was called Terraforming, and it was hard on native life, but promised to generate new Earths scattered about the galaxy. The onset of Earth's empire was at hand.

But considerable resources were required to locate, occupy, and tame the new worlds. Those who remained confined to Earth became impatient with the lean rations remaining. Poverty spread, ranging from mild privation to starva-tion. Spot rebellions broke out; these were put down, but the tough measures required alienated more people, and terrorism became rampant.

Then it got worse. Much worse. Details were vague, for so much was de-stroyed and records were perishable. Whole cities were vaporized, and huge swaths of inhabited land became empty. Civilization broke down, and death become commonplace. The scant records suggested that a population on the order of eight billion people was reduced in fairly short order to about half a billion, and the survivors were widely scattered and losing what advanced tech-nology they had possessed. The world reverted to effective barbarism. There was no way to support the far flung colonies; Earth had problems of her own.

So it remained for several centuries, as the population shrank further, to perhaps two hundred million. Warrior chiefs ruled their areas, and fought other chiefs for territory. The population continued to decline.

Then at last something happened in one region, and slowly spread to oth-ers. Women, tired of the chronic violence of men, deposed them and assumed the power themselves. They were not entirely free of quarrels and combat, but as a general rule the female kingdoms retained more of their resources, fed their people better, and expanded their populations more. In the course of two centuries they took over the rest of the world and established their system on a planetary basis. Earth was organized around six administrative sections: the five continental masses of Africa, America, Antarctica, Asia, and Australia, and the far-flung global islands of Atlantis. The Mistress of Mistresses resided at Antarctica, and all lines of governance led there.

Then for five centuries they consolidated. Global population expanded to perhaps one billion people. But this time there was a difference: women con-trolled the pattern of reproduction, and many preferred business to children. The population stabilized at a level that enabled all people to be well-fed and housed. Once again there was leisure time, and the arts flourished. Science, for centuries in bad repute, returned and flourished. This time it was not focused on warfare but on discovery. The ancient devices were found and analyzed. The ancient records were deciphered. Colony planets that had existed only in my-thology were verified.

That brought the decision: to recover the lost colonies and make Earth an empire again. This time under the sway of the female government, so that there would be no resumption of the costly warfare of a thousand years before.

"And that brings us to the present," Caveat concluded. "We have sent ships to a number of colonies. Some are dead, either expired in the interim, or never properly established. Some are viable, existing on a primitive level, ignorant of their human heritage. Some are doing well, though hardly as well as they could under the tutelage of Earth. Your planet of Charm is among the latter."

"But suppose we don't want to be part of Earth's empire?" Warp asked.

"You are hardly in a position to know what you want," Marionette said. "A decision based on ignorance is not worthwhile."

"That may be a matter of opinion," Warp said. "We know a good deal, and are learning more."

"Your opinion is based on ignorance."

Caveat was watching them carefully. These young folk were not nearly as bewildered or confused as might have been expected. And of course they had special powers undreamed of by Earth's authorities. This was significant.

Warp glanced at Flame. "Your turn, fireball."

"Try this for ignorance," Flame said. "Earth suffered a collapse based on mismanagement of its resources. Finally a reduction of population resulted in so few people that even the depleted resources sufficed, and there was enough to go around. But then, with the subsequent increase in population, there was no longer enough. Trouble stirred up again, and the rulers realized that they had hard choices: either cut down the population by some means such a whole-sale executions, or suffer rebellions and mischief similar to those that destroyed the civilization of the men. It was not gender that made the brave new world, but the drop in population. The illusions were becoming apparent."

Caveat and Marionette listened, giving no signal of their reaction. The fact was, this statement was uncomfortably close to the truth.

"Then they thought of another way out," Flame continued. "Why not re-cover the colonies, whose resources were largely untapped, and exploit them to improve the situation of Earth? Then no hard measures would be required."

They waited. Finally Marionette nodded. "This may be a viable interpreta-tion. How did you know?"

"Havoc taught us how to appear ignorant without *being* ignorant, and to be observant and rational," Flame said. "We have been watching your culture as much as you have been watching ours."

"But you believe in magic!" Marionette protested.

Flame lifted one hand. A fireball appeared in it and floated toward Mari-onette. "We do," she agreed. The fireball expanded into a sphere. Inside the sphere was a picture—of Marionette. "Why do you not?" the figure in the sphere asked. Then the sphere exploded into a pattern of colors and faded.

The mistress simply stared, speechless.

Caveat shook his head. "After what we have seen this day, we may be pre-pared to alter our perspective. I trust you will give us time."

"The time is done," Voila said. "We can resume motion."

They unpacked from their jammed hiding place and unkinked. "I'm not giving up on you," Voila murmured during the distraction of their getting clear.

"You can not romance me," he replied. "Best to accept that. Otherwise I hope we get along well."

"I have a connection," Marionette said. "They have located us, and will be here shortly."

"Perhaps you should straighten out your skirt," Aura said. "Lest there be any misunderstanding."

"I am a mistress. Such misunderstandings are my business." But she did put herself in order, to the degree possible considering the destruction of her clothing, and so did the others; they had all gotten mussed in the course of their hiding.

Men appeared in the tunnel. "Mistress! Are you well?" one called.

"I am well," Marionette replied, poised despite her dishabille. "So are the hostages, thanks to Master Caveat's understanding and effort."

"He was great," Voila said enthusiastically. "He figured out about the bomb and got us out of the capsule in time. But then we had to hide from the enemy minions. That was scary."

Caveat let it pass. He was supposed to take credit for the rescue, leaving the royal siblings' secrets to them. It was apparent that they were able to lie freely when they saw the need. That might be why they insisted on formal commitments when there were secrets to share.

They were conducted to another capsule, which conveyed them the rest of the way to the Hostage Suite. This was a spacious set of ten bedroom chambers, a dining room, activities room, and an upper vision room that poked above the broad and variegated expanse of ice.

"You may choose your rooms," Marionette said. "Individual or shared, as you prefer. Caveat and I will take what is left, or will share with you, again as you prefer. We mean to make your stay here as convenient and comfortable as is feasible."

"I want you with me," Warp said immediately. It was evident that he was seriously taken with her, and he did not attempt to conceal it.

"Acquiescence," she said, smiling.

"And you with me," Voila told Caveat. "And Iolo, of course."

"We'll share, string-bean," Weft said to Flame.

"Just keep your burgeoning flesh on your own side of the bed, bovine."

"Aura and I will share, of course," Augur said.

That left the invisible woman, Ine, who had been largely out of attention even in her swathed condition. She shared neither the banter of the siblings nor the authority of the adults. But Caveat knew that did not necessarily mean she could be ignored.

What other surprises were in store? He was not at all sure that either he or Marionette would be pleased with them.

Chapter 6
Naive

It turned out that Stevia had not been fooling about traveling magically. They walked to a staging area near the fringe of the Green Chroma zone and sat down on the ground to wait. Her skirt slid back to uncover her lifted knees, as it had at other times, and Dynamo realized that this was by no accident. She liked showing off her legs, incidentally inflaming the passion of any man who happened by, himself especially. He was in no position to object. "Caravans pass here frequently," she explained. "This is a rest stop, and station, where goods are loaded and people board. We'll make a deal with one going our way."

"What is our way?"

She smiled. "Any way. This is a tour of discovery."

He looked around. The clearing narrowed on either side to a channel through the forest, lined by giant trees whose lower branches most resembled tentacles. He remembered the way the branches of a tree had seemingly threatened him before, until the two of them made offerings of urine.

Several young and pretty women from the village arrived. "Oh, are you traveling too?" Dynamo inquired, recognizing them as members of the audience for the play. He was of course making a mental file of everything and everyone he encountered, for his eventual report. He was trained for it.

They laughed. "Negation, Earth visitor," one said. "We are here to trade favors for trinkets. Travelers generally are lusty, and have otherChroma items we value."

"Observation," another girl added. "They often hanker for otherChroma flesh,"

"OtherChroma? I am not familiar with that term."

"Clarification: A Red Chroma man normally has little experience with any women who are not Red," the third explained. "Green is a novelty, and no fault makes it easy."

He was taken aback. These were prostitutes!

Stevia nudged him. "You did ask," she reminded him. "Chroma severely limits contacts, so we make the most of those that occur. Their business is legitimate and serves a need."

So it seemed. Such business existed on Earth, too, but was generally disparaged if not illegal. Only the mistresses were completely free with sex, and even that generally had a purpose. The surprise was to see it practiced openly without shame.

Soon the caravan arrived. Dynamo almost gaped. The huge tentacular trees were grabbing on to a series of covered wagons and swinging them from branch to branch. The trees seemed conscious as they reached, took hold, and swung; it did indeed look a lot like magic. They brought the wagons to the clearing and set them gently down.

Stevia approached the lead wagon to negotiate with the master to obtain spots in a covered wagon for the next hop. She had made sure he saw her sitting, and in a moment joined him inside his wagon for more intimate negotiations. Dynamo knew she would readily obtain passage for them both, at a price that was not at all onerous for her. He suppressed a faint twinge of jealousy; it was clear he did not own her, and she was doing what she needed to do.

The three girls walked along the line of wagons, calling to their occupants. Soon all three had disappeared into the covered sections; they had evidently found takers. Meanwhile three more travelers arrived: The Narrator, Incubus, and Naive.

"Salutation, Dynamo of Earth," the girl called cheerily.

"Acknowledged." Of course they were a traveling act, and this was how they traveled; it was not coincidence that they were here. He had somehow thought that as green folk they were limited to this Green Chroma zone, but of course they traveled from one Green zone to another.

Stevia returned, adjusting her displaced skirt. It seemed she didn't mind having others catch on to the nature of her negotiation with the wagon master; in fact she was proud of it. "We have bunks on a wagon," she said. "Greetings, Narrator, Incubus and Maiden."

"Returned," the Narrator said. "We have a chronic pass, as we travel constantly."

Stevia eyed the Incubus. "Question: is your piece real?"

He smiled. "I enhance it by illusion for the show. It is nevertheless of good natural size."

"It's still too big for me," Naive said. "We make it seem as if it penetrates halfway, but it hardly dents the channel. I'm too tight."

This open discussion gave Dynamo an immediate erection. An immature woman did not turn him on, but somehow the idea of wedging into a tight channel did. He began to regret that he had declined her "no fault" offer.

The Incubus put a friendly arm about her shoulders. "When you develop and loosen enough to take it well in, you will too old for the play. We will have to find another childlike girl. Do not hurry; we like you."

The girl's green color deepened. "Appreciation."

Stevia nudged Dynamo. "Request."

He shrugged. "Whatever."

"Let us trade partners for the first leg of our ride. I would like to try that outsized implement, no fault."

"But that would put me with the child," he protested without much force.

"Clarification: no fault does not necessarily mean sex. It covers any temporary relationship. You can ride with her as siblings."

"Agreement," Naive said.

Dynamo found himself committed. "As you prefer." The thought of that tight channel remained with him, wickedly.

A solid nonChroma woman came from the lead wagon. "Introduction: I am the caravan master's wife. Are you five travelers a single party?"

"Two parties, and me," the Narrator said. "I lack a partner for this occasion." He gave her a glance.

She assessed him, evidently noting his handsomeness. "No fault?"

"Agreement."

Dynamo was surprised again. It was clear that in this culture pretty women and handsome men could readily find temporary sexual partners, and enjoyed doing it. As the three village girls had said, interactions across Chroma also had appeal. No fault seem to work even when a married woman's husband was along. But of course the caravan master surely had his pick of traveling girls, so the wife could claim similar privileges. She was surely flattered to have the passing interest of a man who could readily have found younger and more slender flesh.

The woman showed each party to a wagon, then conducted the Narrator toward her own. Dynamo and Naive scrambled into theirs. There was a comfortable bed formed of canvas over packed cloths, with a view of the wagon ahead.

Naive sat cross-legged, so he emulated the position. Her skirt bared her legs, but they partially blocked a deeper view, to his regret. "Apology," she said. "I know you'd rather be with your Gray Chroma companion."

"Needless. I merely did not want there to be any misunderstanding. She is a lusty woman."

"Whom he will properly appreciate. The show leaves him unfulfilled, and me also. The narrator is like you: he does not favor children. So we travel chaste."

"Surely a frustration," he agreed. He thought again how she had offered no fault to him. Actually in the deep shadow she could be mistaken for grown, and the open position of her bare thighs was increasingly suggestive. He looked away.

There was a jolt that almost knocked them over. "Under way," she said. "The trees are competent, but not always gentle. I prefer the straight floating of other Chroma."

"Wagons float?"

"Yes. Of course Green Chroma could float too; all the Chroma can do all kinds of magic. But there is Chroma pride in specialties, so they use the trees. Green is the Plant Chroma." She straightened out her legs and lay down instead. "There will be other jolts."

Again he followed her example. There was room for the two of them, side by side, but without much leeway. Their shoulders and hips were in contact. "As I think you know, I am not merely from another Chroma. I am from Earth. We lack—magic—there. This is new to me, and interesting."

"I am interested too, about your world. Is it true that it is limited to Science magic?"

He smiled tolerantly. "Affirmation."

"But your color is not white, it is nonChroma."

"We have many volcanoes on Earth, but they don't color the wider landscape the way these cones of Charm do. Maybe the effect is too far diluted to color us."

"That must be," she agreed.

"Actually we do have different colors of people: white, black, brown, red, yellow, approximately. But these are governed by heredity and access to sunlight, and don't change when people move to other regions."

"Oh, I wish I could see that world!" she said enthusiastically.

"It may be possible. Earth has come to reclaim her lost colony, and the exchange of visitors should be part of the process. I will petition for a visit for you, if you wish."

"Delight!" She turned her head quickly and kissed him, then was apologetic. "Chagrin: I forgot."

"Needless. Are we not brother and sister?" But already he was regretting that arrangement.

She glanced at him obliquely. "As you wish. But I do like to travel, and Earth is the farthest imaginable destination. I would do anything to visit there."

"It can be arranged. Of course we need Charm's acquiescence first. King Havoc opposes the merger."

"Protest. Oh, I don't want us to be a colony! I prefer trade between equals."

"Earth may not see it that way."

"If Earth truly understood Charm, maybe she would see it that way."

"My mission is to understand Charm as truly as I can, and to report to Earth."

"Amazement! You're from that fascinating planet, and you seek to understand *us*?"

Dynamo smiled. "Affirmation."

"Promise: I can help you."

"You are already helping me, Naive. I am learning much."

"Objection. It's no good just riding in a wagon talking to a teen girl. You need to be out in the field. I can take you there."

He was tempted, but cautious. "In return for what?"

"Truth: Just for the joy of doing it. If I can't travel far, at least I can help you travel."

Why not? "Decision: let's do it."

"This way." She scrambled forward and perched on the front rim of the wagon. He followed. From here they could see the green ground passing below as the wagon swayed across.

"Concern: I hope you don't mean to jump,"

"Trust me, Dynamo. Please."

What could he do? "Extended."

She put her arms around him as he squatted. Then something weird happened. They floated out of the wagon without falling. They drifted gently to the ground and landed on their feet, still squatting. Then she let him go. "Success."

The caravan continued without them, the wagons being swung through the trees. In moments the last one disappeared down the faint aerial trail.

He was amazed yet again. "Question!"

"Answer: I floated us down. You're twice as heavy as I am, but I can do it for a little while. Now we can explore alone."

"But that's—"

"Magic," she agreed.

"But there is no such thing!"

Naive shook her head in the manner of an adult with a wayward child. "Dynamo, your attitude is quaint, but now we are in reality. It will be easier if you simply accept it."

Whatever she had done, she called it magic. It seemed better not to debate the matter at present. "What next?"

"Now I will show you what the Gray Chroma woman could not."

Again he was suspicious. "Question?"

"She can't do all of her magic beyond her home Chroma, so she's helpless here in Green. But I am native Green. I can do it. Everyone can."

"Magic," he repeated dubiously.

"Demonstration: conjuring." She extended her hand, and a green flower appeared in it. "A rose by any other color smells as sweet." She gave it to him.

He sniffed. It did indeed spell like a rose.

"Illusion." Now she stood before him as a fully developed grown woman. "Feel me."

"Negation!"

"Indulgence. Feel me."

He reached tentatively to touch her shoulder. It was solid. He touched her hair. It was long and loose.

"Touch where you don't believe. Please."

He set himself and put his hand on her voluptuous breast. It was not only solid under the cloth of her blouse, it was warm and swelling with her breathing. It was also a phenomenal turn-on despite his knowledge that its heft was illusory. "Amazement."

"Full-senses illusion is difficult, but possible. I have practiced this because it is what I lack. Sight and touch. You know it isn't real, but you can sense it."

"I certainly can! I have difficulty believing this."

"I can do this for a while with my full body. Long enough for you to possess it, if you like."

He withdrew his hand. "Negation." What was the matter with him? She had excited his desire, as it seemed she intended, and she was more than willing.

"Dynamo, I would really like to please you. How may I do it?"

"Not through fakery." And he realized the truth of that as he said it. Illusion was fine, but for sex he wanted reality.

The body vanished. She was her young-seeming self. "Apology. I mean well, but I am young and inexperienced." A tear ran down her cheek.

Was this more fakery? "Why are you doing any of this?"

"I told you. Folk dismiss me as a child. I want to be a woman, once, with a real man. I think you're handsome and smart and decent, and I'd like it to be you. No fault."

"But sex isn't any casual thing! Not between strangers." Though in that case how could he explain or justify what he had done with Stevia?

"Yes it is," she argued. "It is a medium of exchange. Women give it to men for favors or protection. But they have to be desirable, or the men aren't interested."

Dynamo didn't know what to say or do. This was what on Earth would be called a minefield. She had inflamed his desire, but he feared it would be child molestation. He stood there just gazing at her.

Naive put her face in her hands. "Confession: I knew I shouldn't have told you. Now you know I lied about being no fault siblings."

Perhaps it was an act. She was after all an actress. But he couldn't help it.

He put his arm around her. "Apology for being cruel. I don't know how to handle this."

"Appreciation for your comfort. I can conjure myself ahead and ask the caravan master to wait for us at the next stop. I lack the power to conjure you with me."

"No, let's remain here. I need to know about the backwoods too."

She brightened. "I'll make a bower and show you everything." Then she colored darker green. "I mean, green magic."

"Understanding." She was not twelve, but in respects she was still child-like. He was coming to appreciate her openness and impulsivity.

She set off through the forest. "Follow me. I'll find a friendly tree where we can safely stay."

Soon she found one. It was similar to the one Stevia had used. "Let me befriend it." She squatted and urinated on its receptive patch of ground. Apparently women did not use underclothing here, regardless of Chroma. It facilitated such introductions to trees. "But you'd better too."

Wordlessly he brought out his member and urinated. It wasn't as if she was unfamiliar with the male organ.

"Oh, I like your penis," she said. "It's not too big for me."

"Appreciation," he said dryly. He finished and put it away before it could react to her girlish enthusiasm.

"Now we can climb the tree and be safe. I'll show you all the magic you like."

"Well said, honey," a green man said from the tree.

Naive froze, horrified. "It's occupied!"

"Sure it is," the man said. "Come on up. I like them young."

"We must go," Naive said, appalled.

The man disappeared from the tree and appeared on the ground before her. "After you see *my* penis, you little sweetie."

"Negation!" She disappeared, and reappeared a few feet distant.

The man made a similar maneuver, appearing again before her. "No fault, of course."

"No!" She tried to run, but he caught her by the hair and held her back.

Dynamo had been foolishly frozen, hardly believing any of this. Now he spoke. "She told you no."

"But she means yes." The man hauled on the hair, bringing the girl reluctantly back toward him. "She wants penis."

Dynamo charged. But he was met by a monstrous serpent that lifted its hissing head and made ready to strike. He sheered off, avoiding it, and stumbled over a projecting root he hadn't seen in his distraction. He landed on the ground.

The snake faded out. It had been illusion. Magic. The man had it and he didn't. "Stay clear, dope," the man said. "Or I'll sic something nasty on you." He turned back to Naive.

Only she no longer stood there. Instead it was the Incubus—and the man was holding on to his monstrous penis. "If we're going to do it, let's do it right," the Incubus said. "Take down your pants, bend over, and back into me."

The man cast loose the member, horrified.

Dynamo caught on. "Idiot!" he cried at the Incubus. "You're supposed to wait until he's in you before you reveal yourself. Now you'll never get his soul!"

"Wrath! I forgot." The Incubus advanced on the man.

"Give it up, spook," Dynamo said, evincing deep disgust. "You lost him. We'll have to look for another mark." He went to grab the Incubus by the arm and haul him away. "You just wasted a perfect prospect."

The green man simply stared, dumbfounded.

Only when they were out of sight did Dynamo speak candidly. "Danger. We've got to get out of here before he remembers that Incubi don't go after men. Where can we be safe?"

"Only out of the Chroma," Naive said, resuming her natural form. "This way. The edge is close by."

They ran and found the edge. The green faded out, and natural landscape colors resumed.

Then Naive collapsed into tears. He held her close. "That was one smart ruse," he said. "If I hadn't seen your play, I would have been fooled too."

"I needed you not to be fooled," she sobbed. "His magic was stronger than mine. I couldn't escape him by force."

"And I couldn't help you. I don't have any magic at all." He marveled at himself: he was coming to believe.

"That's why he held you in contempt. He knew you were out of your Chroma. NonChroma folk usually avoid Chroma zones entirely because of that. So do otherChroma folk, for similar reason." She drew back her head and gazed wetly at him. "But you were wonderful! You knew exactly what to do."

Dynamo felt foolishly flattered. "Appreciation."

"But I don't have magic either, here. I can't protect you."

"Let me make sure I understand: nobody has magic here?"

"Except maybe a Glamor, and they're so rare you never see them. I hate having to be here."

"I don't. Let's go until we get somewhere."

She shrugged. "You're the leader now."

They walked along what he now saw was a relatively narrow nonChroma zone between the green one they had left, and a red one on the other side. The different colors seemed to repel or cancel each other out, leaving a torturous avenue for those who lacked magic.

There was a cry ahead. "That's a woman," Dynamo said.

"Sometimes brigands attack. That's another reason I don't like this."

"I don't like thugs attacking women." Dynamo ran ahead. There were two women and two men. One man had hold of a woman's long hair—where had he seen that before? And was hauling her in to him. The other man was preventing the other woman from interfering.

"Ho!" Dynamo called. "Cease!"

Both men whirled to face him, raising their fists defiantly.

He surprised them. He charged right into them both. He dodged the fist swung by the first, stuck him in the gut, and kicked the second in the groin. Both men dropped.

Dynamo stood beside them. "Satisfied? Or shall we have another go?"

The men were evidently satisfied. They got unsteadily to their feet and departed. The women were silent, perhaps uncertain whether Dynamo was friend or new foe.

Naive arrived, having been unable to keep his pace. "You did it!" she exclaimed. "You stopped the brigands."

Dynamo shrugged. "Someone had to do it."

Naive turned to the women. "Introduction. I am Naive of the adjacent Chroma. He is Dynamo of Planet Earth, learning our culture. He's sort of gallant."

The women relaxed. "I am Purl, and this is my daughter Daylight, traveling to join her husband. Are the two of you going our way?"

"We are looking for a safe harbor for the night," Naive said. "It's not safe in my Chroma; a nasty green man came after me and we had to flee magic."

"Understanding," Purl said. She was a severe woman with her hair bound tightly back. Her daughter was so heavily cloaked that only her face and hair were exposed. Those were attractive.

"Recent understanding, emphatic," Daylight said, and they all laughed a bit weakly. "Appreciation, man of Earth. I do not favor rape."

"Welcome."

"We have been this way before," Purl said. "Going the other direction. There is a haven tree in the next Blue Chroma, and a nonChroma village a distance beyond."

"Perhaps the village," Dynamo said.

"Perhaps the tree," Naive said firmly.

She surely had her reasons. "The tree," he agreed.

They walked on together. Daylight seemed ill at ease. Then suddenly she spoke. "Apology: I have no favor to render in return, yet must beg one of Dynamo."

Dynamo spread his hands. "I am ready to be of service in whatever way is feasible."

"I want my fourth of you."

He was blank. "Fourth what?"

"He is still learning our ways," Naive said. She turned to him. "Every woman must bear four children, but one must be by a man not her husband. She is asking you to impregnate her."

"It is my time," Daylight said. "I feared for a moment I would get it involuntarily by a brigand. You are so much better! I would be proud to have it of you."

"But I—this is not—"

Naive took his arm. "This is not a thing a man can decline," she said seriously. "It is not done. She is no child like me; she has borne three babies."

"But she is married!"

"Precisely."

"I—normally there should be some desire, some continuing relationship."

"No relationship," Naive said. "Only enough desire on your part to get it done, none for her, lest she be disloyal to her husband. It is a special circumstance."

He remained half flabbergasted. "I can't decline?"

"That would be extremely unkind. It was difficult enough for her to ask you; to be rebuffed would be worse."

He looked desperately at the older woman. "Truth?"

"Truth," she agreed. "And I agree with her choice. You are a good man."

He shrugged. "Then I must accede. But I don't know how to go about it. Is it simply sex?"

"Simply sex," she agreed. "She will not tell her husband who it is, just that it is done." She hesitated. "I will tell him that she did it with no enthusiasm. It is a business transaction."

This was hardly his favorite form of sex. But there seemed to be no help for it. "Where?"

"The Blue Chroma tree should be good. Then you and Naive can remain there, while we repair to the village, saying nothing of you."

"Done," Naive agreed.

It was an hour's walk to the Blue Chroma zone. The Red faded, and the Blue commenced, with a narrow lane between them. Farther along Purl led them along a path into the zone. There was the tree.

Dynamo and Daylight befriended the tree and climbed into its protective branches. At least here they were shielded from outside observation. "This—I am not accustomed to—I hate the thought of indulging with an unwilling woman, whatever the necessity," he said awkwardly. "I may not be—potent."

Daylight smiled. "Reassurance: There will be no problem."

"But there may be. I regret it, but—"

She stepped into him and kissed him. He became aware that under her comprehensive cloak she was a limber woman. "Mother lied."

This gave him further pause. "Confusion. I am—we are not to—?"

"Oh, that we are," she said easily, carefully removing her cloak. She wore a belted dress beneath. Her figure was excellent. "The lie was that I would not be responsive. She knew I hankered for you from the moment you rescued us, and as I came to know you somewhat this intensified. I believe you are an excellent choice, and the fourth is justified thereby, but it will be our secret that this was a union of passion as well as convenience."

"Our secret," he repeated numbly.

She stood before him, gloriously nude. Her babies had not destroyed her figure; probably they had enhanced it, for she was a fine specimen of fertility. "Strip."

He hastened to do so, while she gathered blue pillows and arranged them to form a bed. He stood before her, his member fully erect. "Ready."

"Obvious," she agreed. "But I mean to have some pleasure of this." She stepped into him again, kissing him and running her hands across his back and down to his buttocks. Then she hauled him down on the cushions with her. "Surprise: you wear a White Chroma stone."

"A prior companion gave it to me and asked me to wear it always. I will remove it if—"

"By no means. Such stones should always be worn. I merely did not expect to see such a thing. They are rare and valuable."

"I didn't know."

She nodded. "There is more about you than meets the eye. I regret I lack time to learn it." Then she got to work.

The details became hazy, but his one later clear memory was that she had milked him three times in a very short interval. She was thoroughly competent, as a married woman could be, and eager to give him something back for his service. She succeeded. She was in her fashion equivalent to both Stevia and Mistress Marionette. Women kept surprising him.

In the end he was deliciously exhausted. She got up, clipped her vagina together to retain the semen—that astonished him, yet it made sense—and efficiently dressed. "Remain here. I will say that you were loath to penetrate a reluctant woman, and it took some time, but that you finally rose to the occasion. Mother will know it's a lie but will honor it. Your friend will know when she finds you here like this." She paused. "It is not my business, but I can perhaps do you part of the favor I owe you by dispatching some advice. Indulge your companion, when you recover sufficiently; she is of age, and you are torturing her by your reticence."

Surprises kept coming. "Question: How can you know this?"

"I am an experienced woman." Then she smiled. "But I owe you the truth. There is a disease that circulates, and some of us accept it voluntarily. It is telepathy, that at first blasts the mind with all the unguarded thoughts of surrounding people. But with diligence a person learns to close her mind to unwanted ones, and then it becomes useful. Concerned about your nature, I read Naïve's mind and yours. That reassured me, but also gave me information I had not sought. I apologize for intruding."

"Forgiven," he said.

She stooped to kiss him once more. "Appreciation for an experience that was far more positive than I anticipated before today. Parting."

"Parting," he agreed. He remained as he was, naked on the cushions; he had little energy left.

In due course Naïve joined him, carrying a package. "Revelation. I knew it! She did you proud."

"She did," he agreed. "But officially—"

"It was a mutual burden. Understanding."

"Agreement."

She opened the package. There was an assortment of green foods: bread, fruits, drinks.

"Question?"

"While we waited interminably for you to summon gumption to reluctantly give a resistive woman her fourth, I returned briefly to the edge of the Green Chroma and conjured some stables."

"Concern! The risk. The green man."

"Has I think given up the chase. Now eat." She pushed a piece of fruit into his mouth.

They had a good meal, then dressed, then descended to the foot of the tree to befriend it further. But their timing was bad.

A huge blue monster charged the tree. Branches came down to intercept it, but not in time; it had evidently laid cunningly in wait for this occasion. Naïve screamed.

Dynamo drew his pistol and fired almost in a single motion. The bullet blasted through the monster's teeth and shattered its spine. It staggered a short distance from the tree and dropped, dead.

"Bless your magic!" Naïve exclaimed. "We needed it."

He did not bother to remind her than science worked anywhere. They returned for the night. Naïve disrobed and joined him on the bed. "I wish I could have the expertise that woman has. Her husband must be a happy man."

"He surely is. But the nature of our liaison must remain secret, to spare the feeling of her husband."

"Agreement." Then she spoke again, in a low tone. "Dynamo, I promised, but I can't keep it. I—in my fashion I love you. I ask you—I beg you—"

He was vanquished. "Reconsideration. Now I see you as a woman."

"Delight! Effusion! Excitement! Gratitude!" She snuggled up to him.

"Caution: not at this moment. Daylight exhausted me in that respect."

"Later," she agreed, disappointed. But she remained close.

The last of the light faded and they were in darkness. Naive found a sheet and covered them. He slept.

He woke in the night, finding her sleeping against him. The effect was conducive. But he didn't want to disturb her. So he found her face and kissed her, gently.

She woke immediately. "Now? Eagerness!"

So much for letting her sleep. He stroked her body, finding that her breasts, though slight, did have some substance, and her bottom was firm. He mounted her, finding the avenue. She was quite tight, and he hesitated. "I don't want to hurt you, Naive."

"I am snug, not fragile," she assured him. "Wedge it in; I want it."

"Doubt: you are sure?"

"Certainty. Remember the play."

And if she had handled any portion of the member of the Incubus, she was indeed not fragile. Reassured, he forced the issue, and his member wedged slowly in, as she had urged. By the time he was fully embedded the urgency overwhelmed him, and he suffered a pressurized orgasm.

"You did it!" she exclaimed. "Thrill!"

"But you weren't with me. Regret."

"Needless. No one ever made it with me before. That's enough for this time."

"Acquiescence," he agreed, relieved that she was satisfied and that he had not hurt her.

They slept again. In the morning he woke to her kiss. "My turn," she murmured.

"Agreement," he said, curious what she had in mind.

She kissed his mouth several times, then moved down to kiss his member, causing it to stiffen. Then she sat up and straddled him, carefully taking him in. She remained tight, but less so than before, perhaps because she was more relaxed. She lowered herself until she was sitting on him, her buttocks against his hips. Then she reached down with her finger and stroked her clitoris.

He felt her response. Her vagina quivered around him. He remained still, letting her proceed. When at last her climax came, her vagina clenched about him, massaging him, and he felt as if he were a ship in a heaving sea. He had to come, and climaxed in the midst of hers, though it was like spitting into a storm.

She collapsed on him, still connected. "Appreciation," she gasped.

"Welcome." She had done it all herself, but he didn't care to remark on that. It had been a good experience for them both.

They got up, washed with soft damp leaves the tree provide, ate breakfast, dressed, and climbed down to the ground.

There was the blue monster, now half-buried in the earth. "Surprise."

"Explanation: The tree is digesting it," Naive said. "By dusk it will be entirely gone. You gave it a real treat."

"Coincidental. I was trying to save our lives."

"And you did, with your marvelous Science magic."

That made him pause. "It is my understanding that magic only works in its home Chroma. You can't do any magic here, because you're in the wrong color."

"Affirmation."

"So my Science magic, as you put it, should work in the White Chroma, but not here either, any more than yours."

"Revelation!" she agreed. "Yet yours worked."

"You can't accept that Science is universal?"

She looked troubled. "You can't believe that."

"Then how do you explain why it worked here?"

"Mystery." Then she brightened. "The gem you wear! That's a White Chroma stone. That's how."

"Confusion."

"Most folk can't do magic outside their Chroma zones. But those who can arrange it obtain Chroma stones. Then they can do magic, though it soon uses up the stones."

Dynamo brought out the stone he wore. "Stevia gave this to me, and told me to wear it always. I thought it was so she could always recognize me."

"It is so you can always do your magic," she insisted. "Without it you could not."

He considered. "Perhaps I should make proof of this."

"That is easy. Separate from it and try your magic."

He took off the cord and gave her the stone. He walked away. Then he drew his pistol and aimed at a nearby stone. He pulled the trigger.

Nothing happened.

Surprised, he checked the chamber. There was a shell there. It should have fired.

He tried again, with no result. The gun was inoperative.

He returned to Naive and took back the stone. He put the loop back over his neck so that the stone hung at his chest, as before. He returned to the place he had stood, lifted the pistol, and pulled the trigger.

The gun fired. The bullet caromed off the stone, sending a chip flying.

He removed the stone again, and tried the pistol. Nothing. He recovered the stone. This time it fired.

This was beyond coincidence. "It needs the stone," he said.

"Affirmation. But don't use it too much, or the stone will expire. See, it is already fading."

He looked. The stone was now off-white, as if depleted.

There might be some other explanation, but this one fit the rules of this planet. He had seen enough magic now to know that it did indeed exist here. Science it seemed was a subset of magic, following the same rules.

"This—unsettles me. May we return to the tree?"

Her eyes widened. "Wild surmise: you want more no fault sex?"

Oops. "That too, perhaps. I need to think."

"Anything, Dynamo. I am yours."

They returned to the tree bower. "All my life I have been secure in the knowledge that there was no such thing as magic," he said as they undressed again. "I took your magic as superstition. I must now come to terms with the notion that it is real."

"It must be dull, in that respect, on Earth," she said, kissing his ear. "Where is the color?"

"There is color everywhere on Earth. Just not monochrome. Science works everywhere, and magic nowhere."

"It would be dull if all of Charm were Green Chroma magic," she said, stroking his shoulders. "And maybe we would believe that Green was the only kind. That it was—universal." She put her arm around him comfortingly.

It helped. She looked like a child, but she cared, and that was what he needed. He turned into her, hugged her, kissed her, and bore her to the bed. They had emphatic sex, her tightness enhancing his effort. "Appreciation," he said.

"Welcome."

"That's not limited to sex."

"Understanding. Gratification that you allow me to comfort you to the extent I can."

He kissed her again. "You're a nice girl, Naive."

"I prefer to be a nice woman."

"You are. May I try you on some troubling questions?"

"Permission," she agreed warmly.

"Why did Stevia give me the White Chroma stone?"

"So you could protect yourself despite your ignorance."

"Stevia!" he repeated. "She and the Incubus must have missed us long since. We have to return."

She nodded. "Confession: we should have returned last night. I wanted to be with you so much I couldn't do it. Then when Daylight had you, I was so jealous, I just had to have the night. I'm a bad girl."

"Neither bad nor girl."

She kissed him again. "Adoration."

But now that he was focusing on their situation, disturbing aspects were clarifying. "I am a skeptic about coincidence."

"Question?"

"When we sneaked off together, it seemed that no one missed us very soon. That's odd, because Stevia knows she has to keep a very close eye on me. Then the green man came after you, but we were able to fool him and escape. Why did he not recognize your illusion? Then we encountered the two women just as brigands were attacking them. That's highly improbable. One turned out to be looking for her fourth, another coincidence. She was a superlative sexual partner, parallel to Stevia. Much like Stevia, in fact. Then you—eager for passion with me, though you never saw me before yesterday. And the blue monster, showing me that I have magic because of the stone. Now you are competently comforting me. This is so pat it must have been scripted."

Her eyes filled with tears. "Mortification."

"In fact it must be a play, with assorted actors. And one main actress with several roles." He kissed her. "Well played, Stevia."

She sighed. "Admiration. You are too smart." Her features shifted, coalescing as Gray Chroma Stevia.

"You did mention the powers of Glamors, and you are a Glamor. May I see your true form now?"

"Reluctance. I do not wish to dazzle you. It interferes with sex."

"I recover readily from dazzling."

She shifted again, becoming a stunningly lovely red woman. She seemed almost to glow. "I am 265 years old," she said. "I became a Glamor 250 years ago."

Dynamo was frozen in place, fascinated by her presence. He had spoken dismissively of dazzling, but he had underestimated her power. She was Woman incarnate, the perfection that was the template no mortal woman matched.

She shifted back to Stevia, then to Naive. "Satisfaction?"

Now he could speak. "You have made your point. "You can dominate me. Yet I have some concerns."

"Speak."

"I presume you modeled your forms on real people. That there is really a Daylight woman as you portrayed her, for example."

"Affirmation."

"I think I owe her her fourth."

Naive stared. Then she laughed. "Beautiful! I shall take you to her."

"And the real Naive, who is taken with me. I owe her a night."

"Granted. Other?"

"Then you can explain what you really want of me. I know it is a good deal more than sex."

She nodded. "Concurrence. First I must ask a question of you that may confuse or annoy you. I do not wish to offend."

"No offense. I believe in plain speaking."

"Why do you wish to indulge these two women, knowing that neither was really with you, so did not hear your agreements? They will not suffer if left ignorant."

"A fair question. This relates to my peculiar concept of honor. I said I believe in plain speaking; that applies to those I deal with directly, and also to those who may be affected by my actions. I do not want my participation with this culture to be fraudulent on either side. I want honest experience, rather than faked-up experience, so I stand to gain from interacting directly with these women. I want them to have the things I promised them, even if they were not here to know about them. Perhaps then they will gain similarly from interacting with me. That way everything is open and honest, and we all can profit."

She considered. "Correct. I do find your concept peculiar. But I think I like it. But I must advise you that Daylight is not as voluptuous or eager as I presented her; she really will be somewhat diffident, and may decline your offer of a fourth."

"That is her privilege. At least it will be her informed decision."

"And Naive is not as inexperienced as she seemed; she has had men before, and should welcome you. She is no virgin, though her body is as I have it now."

"That will do. It is the voluntary nature of it that counts, rather than the particular body."

She paused a moment, then met his gaze. There was something in her eyes that hinted compellingly of her enormous age and power. "What do I really want of you, and why did I arrange this little charade? First, I am a lusty wench, and you are a fresh prospect; those are always choice. Second, I wanted to be sure to show you the key aspects of our culture, such as the reality of magic and our policy of the fourths, and this was best not left to chance. So I arranged it, with some help from other players, and thought it was effective."

"Agreement. It was."

"But you were a bit more alert than I anticipated, and caught on. I like that in you." She closed on him and kissed him. This time the kiss had more impact than prior ones, because now he knew her nature. "But the script is but a means to an end. I need something from you, and you will not like it."

"Nevertheless, I had better know."

"I want your commitment."

"To you? Apart from my, shall we say, dalliances we have just discussed, you can have it for the duration of our association. You are a remarkable woman, whatever your form."

"To me first. Thus I am angling not merely for seduction, but for love, so that you desire me more than anything else."

He shook his head. "I can't commit to that! In six months I shall be rejoining my ship and returning to Earth, my mission here done. Why should you even want it?"

"Because it will then be a lever to win your larger commitment to Charm."

"I will not play your planet false. I want what is best for it. We may differ on details, however."

"We do. I want you to forsake Earth and become an agent for Charm."

He stared at her, astonished. She held his gaze, and slowly he realized that she was completely serious. She wanted him to betray Earth.

"Observation," he said after a moment. "We have a problem."

Chapter 7
Weft

In the morning they set up for a spot tour. "There is a volcano here in Antarctica," Caveat said. "Inactive, but possibly of interest, considering your planet."

"We want to see all Earth's volcanoes," Voila said enthusiastically. She was of course the ingenue, the young innocent: her role for the occasion. In reality she was far removed from that. "We love volcanoes. That's where the magic is."

Weft saw Mistress Ette and Caveat exchange a glance. They still didn't believe in magic, despite what they had seen. That was probably just as well, because every use of magic depleted their nonChroma stones. They were confining it to illusion, telepathy, clairvoyance, and near-future seeing, which were the least energy-expensive forms of magic, but there was no point in wasting it. They needed to obtain Earth Planet sources of magic which would be essentially inexhaustible. That meant volcanoes. This was a significant part of their mission.

They also needed to relate to their Earthside constituencies, to secure their powers on this planet. The ikons were merely gatherers, transformers, and transmitters of magic power. It was the constituencies that made it all possible. Weft was the Glamor of Bacteria. She knew that bacteria inhabited Earth, because they thronged through the bodies of Earthers as they did Charmers. But there should be massive cultures of them in the Earth sky, seas, and soil, and it was these she needed to establish rapport with. When she could do so privately, without Earthers catching on to her purpose. Similarly Warp had to relate to his Fungus, Flame to her Viruses, and Voila to her Amoeba. They would all be watching their opportunities. Without their constituencies they would be unable to refresh their magic; it would be like trying to eat sand instead of organic food.

They took another capsule to the volcano. The Antarctica authorities had made a thorough sweep of the region and run down the assassins, taking them into custody; they were free of that threat, at least for now. Capsules were safe. The trip was three hours each way, so it was a day-long excursion. They chatted and joked as usual, being themselves, satisfying the Earthers that they were normal teens despite the aspects of magic they had had to show the day before. Warp teased Ette, who was reluctant to indulge him in sex in public, and Voila talked with Caveat, learning more of Earth and Earth's ways. The adults remained carefully aloof, playing their quiet roles. That left Weft and Flame, siblings, opposites, and close friends, to entertain themselves.

There wasn't much to see. The volcano was entirely covered by ice, and was extinct. But a faded remnant of its magic remained; they could feel it, faintly: Air Chroma. Already they had verified that Planet Earth did have more than Science magic. Because this volcano was far removed from prior human habitation, and now extinct, its magic effect had not been felt. But it existed. Weft was so thrilled that she hugged Flame, and Flame was so thrilled that she did not put Weft down with a spot nerve strike. Confirmation was wonderful.

But what they really needed was live volcanoes, in or near populated areas. They had agreed to split up so as to cover as many as possible in the coming six months. For one thing, if the Earthers caught on to the real mission, they would act to prevent it. It had to get far enough along to survive regardless.

During the return Weft pried Ette away from Warp long enough to present their common need: "We really do want to see Earth's volcanoes," she said. "Volcanoes are vitally important to our home planet, and the prospect of visiting alien volcanoes is irresistibly exciting. We know we can't see them all in six months if we travel in a group, so we'll do it separately. Will you arrange this?"

"Six months? You believe your father will accede by then?"

"Negation. Earth will give up the effort by then. We are allowing for the return of the ship to Charm in two months, and that ship's return to Earth four months thereafter. Then we will be free."

The woman did not argue the case further. "Whatever fate wills."

"Meanwhile, the volcanoes?"

"This is not necessarily easy," Marionette said. "We are responsible for your safety, and global tours would significantly increase the risk."

"We can protect ourselves, to a degree, as you have seen," Weft said earnestly. "It would also be more difficult to take us all out if we are widely separated."

Marionette nodded. "I will consult the Mistress of Mistresses. We will see what we can do."

"Wonderful! What is there for me?"

Marionette eyed her. "You are sure there is something?"

"Affirmation."

The Mistress sighed. "Is it mind reading, clairvoyance, or seeing the near future?"

"Logic. You have the itinerary. We are eager to cooperate."

"There is something, but it may be a considerable challenge."

"We adore challenges."

"There is a retired mistress I know who associates with a touring opera company. Recently they lost their lead female singer. Is this something that would interest you?"

"Affirmation!"

"But there is a caution: they need a singer who can handle an extremely difficult piece."

"I can handle it."

Marionette shook her head. "Weft, you are as good as any female singer on Earth. But this is special. It's an Aria that only ten singers have the potential to perform correctly, and only five can sing."

"Question."

"If all those ten practiced it for a year, all might achieve it. But only five have actually done so. They are outstanding performers with large audiences. I think you have that potential, but you are unpracticed in this. You will not be able to do it right now. In a month or two, however, I believe you have a fair chance."

This smelled of a musical challenge. "Statement: I can do what I choose to do. What is this melody?"

"It is more than a melody. It is an interacting duet that leads into the Aria that strains the limits of the human voice in range, timing, and timbre. Done correctly it transports the audience. Done imperfectly it is disaster. The singer lost her edge and had to retire rather than risk that humiliation. They have had to make do with a recording, but that's patchwork and they are losing audience and reputation. They need a new singer, and are negotiating to obtain another, but all the five are otherwise committed at present. So it is an opening, but I fear too much of a challenge for you at this time."

"Desire: Play me that recording."

"I don't have it here. I do have the written music I can show you, however. You will see how challenging it is."

"Negation. I don't read music. I do it by ear. That's all I need."

Marionette shook her head. "By ear! This makes it next to impossible. But I will put in a requisition for the recording, so that in a few days you can at least hear it."

"When is the next performance?"

"Day after tomorrow."

"Take me there tomorrow, then."

"Weft, Weft! I am trying to protect you from embarrassment. No one has ever mastered the Aria in less than a month. If they even suspected you had it in mind, you would be subject to ridicule."

Weft shrugged. "Decision: I'll risk it."

Marionette looked helplessly around the capsule without speaking.

"She is serious," Augur said. "We have learned not to try to balk the imperious will of the royals. I had better accompany her."

"You know I tried to dissuade her from any immediate attempt."

"Affirmation. I will report that futile effort to the king, in due course."

Weft pounced. "See? He agrees."

"As if I had a choice."

"Are there volcanoes along their route?" Weft asked eagerly.

Marionette sighed expressively. "Weft, if by some miracle you should perform the Aria, you could ask them to include volcanoes on the tour, and they would oblige. Successful singers write their own tickets, as it were. But this is a foolish notion that can only do you harm. If on the other hand you are willing to travel with them, and study the Aria for a month—"

"Negation. I'll do it now."

Marionette looked at Augur. "I think I will be glad to have you accompany her. I will take you both there tomorrow, then return here. You will be on your own."

"Appreciation," Augur said gravely.

Warp frowned. "She gets to tour volcanoes and we don't?"

"Unfair," Flame said.

"Tough meat, rawhide," Weft said.

"Volcano tours we can arrange," Caveat said quickly. "It is the challenge of the singing that concerns us."

"What of a tour with a martial arts group?" Flame asked.

"Or an acting group," Voila added.

"Or a tale-telling tour," Warp said.

"Such can be arranged," Marionette said. "If that is what you wish. We want to provide you the maximum freedom consistent with your safety during your stay here."

"Better set it up, then," Aura said. "Once the siblings get hold of a notion, especially if it is competitive, they are unstoppable."

"Competitive?" Caveat asked.

"I'll see more volcanoes than you, plush butt," Warp said.

"That's what you think, hard head," Weft snapped back.

"Competitive," Caveat agreed, smiling.

"And you will take me to more than any other tour," Voila informed him.

"No promise!"

"Annoyance. I can't winsomely seduce you into agreement. This puts me at a disadvantage."

"That is surely just as well," he said, hardly dismayed.

Weft smiled inwardly. Caveat thought he was safe from teen wiles. He hardly knew what he was in for.

❧ ❧

Next day Marionette took Weft and Augur to the present site of the opera company, explaining things as they traveled. They took a capsule to a station, and a rocket that arched high into the atmosphere fifteen hundred kilometers to Martinique in West Indies. That was in Atlantis, the continent of the globe's islands.

"But isn't Atlantis in rebellion?" Weft asked, alarmed.

"By no means. Sections are in a ferment of unrest, but there is little open action. If there were, we could deal with it. Instead they try covert action, such as inciting rebellion in others, and spot raids such as the one you experienced. In addition, many sections of it are satisfied with the present administration and do not support opponents. Zealand is as safe as Antarctica."

"Still, I hope it doesn't use subway capsules."

"It doesn't. Now about the opera: it travels, so this is merely where it happens to be at the moment. It will proceed from here to Mexico and western America, where there are famous old volcanoes. It should be no trouble to visit them in passing. Your problem will be making the cut, as we put it: winning your place in the opera. It is a company, and it makes money from its performances, so it cares about their quality."

"Money?"

Marionette paused. "I just realized: we never saw evidence of a common medium of exchange in planet Charm. You don't have money?"

"We exchange personally. That's why no fault is vital: it enables women to travel or trade. The king also takes a share of what farmers and workers produce, in exchange for the protection he provides."

"Then you have the principle. Money is an intermediary mechanism. You earn it, then spend it as you wish or need. At any rate, the opera is running short of money, because of the loss of their key singer, and will have to shut down soon if another is not obtained. If you qualify, there will be a standard stipend. But they will not want their time wasted by any unqualified applicants. You may face a hostile group."

"So I had better learn that song," Weft said.

"I obtained a recording. You may listen to it as we travel." Marionette looked around. "Perhaps we can use the rocket's sound system; it is better than earphones." She touched a button on the armrest of her chair. "Mistress Marionette: may I play the dialogue and Aria of the opera *Conquest*?" Her voice was amplified and spread throughout the long chamber that was the rocket. Other passengers sat in seats along its length.

The response was immediate. "Of course, Mistress," a man's voice said, emerging from the ceiling. "We shall appreciate hearing it."

"Thank you, Captain."

Weft realized that this was mere courtesy; it was evident that whatever a mistress wanted she could have. But the other passengers seemed to approve.

Marionette brought out a tiny cube and set it in a shaped hole in the armrest. In a moment song filled the chamber. First a resonant tenor, supported by musical instruments whose type Weft recognized: string, wind, percussion. No dulcimer, however.

Then a soprano, singing in counterpoint. It was an intricate and quite lovely exchange. Both were good, very good; Weft had not heard their like on Charm.

Marionette passed her hand over the cube, and the music paused. "There is a story that goes with it, and speech; this is merely the music. But it should acquaint you with the challenge. Now comes the concluding Aria."

The music resumed. The soprano sang almost solo, using the tenor like a background instrument that came to the fore only at key intersections, going into a melody so remarkable that Weft's mouth fell open. It did indeed strain the limits of the human voice, spreading three octaves and tripping so rapidly between notes that it sounded almost like two voices. The power of it seemed to shake the rocket. But that was only the technical aspect. More impressive was the feeling that poured forth. This was a desperate plea by a woman it was impossible not to love. The tune reached into Weft's core and drew it forth, making her heart race, her breath pant. This was love, loss, passion, and prayer, so feeling as to inspire sheer awe.

It was beautiful. She loved it. And knew it was beyond her present ability. In a month, as the mistress said, perhaps, but not now. She could sing anything—except this.

It finished, leaving her in a trance. She felt the tears coursing down her face. She had heard the ultimate—and could not achieve it.

She found herself sobbing against Marionette's shoulder. No words were necessary.

Then Augur spoke. "Weft, remember what you are."

She was a Glamor, able to do virtually anything by magic. But this was not magic, it was ability. She still could not do it.

"And what you have."

He meant the stone. The nonChroma stone that enabled her to do spot magic. But even that was not enough. All the magic in Charm would not make up what she lacked. Magic could enable her to be the best that she could be, far faster than otherwise, but she still had to have the inherent potential. All four siblings were proud of their arts, because these were earned natural abilities largely independent of their formidable magical powers. Their arts were their real challenges.

"And what you have to do."

She had to reach those volcanoes, and her constituency. They all did. Otherwise Charm was lost.

"Let me clarify something," Marionette murmured. "No one does the Aria alone. It's not a cappella. There is the support of the orchestra, and the male tenor. That makes a huge difference."

Support. Yes, that just might provide her the extra foundation to make it possible. If she were lucky.

"I will try," she said, drying her tears.

"As I said before, I don't think you can do it," Marionette said. "Because I don't think *anyone* can do it without proper preparation. But if you take the necessary time, then I believe it is within your capability. We can arrange for you to travel with the opera as an observer—"

"Negation. I will do it now, or not at all."

"Weft—" Augur began.

She sent him a defiant look, and he left off.

"Then I think all we can do is support you in your endeavor," Marionette said, "and hope you can defy established wisdom."

Augur nodded agreement. He and the Mistress seemed to be of one mind on this matter.

Weft hoped so too. She knew she had set herself up for failure, and she hated herself for doing it. She really was an impetuous juvenile despite her powers, and had gotten herself into trouble. But she was as she was. This Second Crisis had struck before they were mature, and they had to deal with it as they were now.

The flight continued, and conversation lapsed. Weft closed her eyes and focused on the Aria, which was still coursing through her mind. She had memorized it from the single hearing. She could sing it, and play an improvised accompaniment on her dulcimer. The problem was that she couldn't do it *well*. She would miss some notes, and the feeling would be inappropriate in spots. The thing was fiendishly difficult to keep all together. But maybe if she focused on the danger spots she could make some progress. Enough to make at least a credible showing, so as not to be entirely shamed.

Regardless what she accomplished in the next day, the Aria had left its mark on her. She would never forget it. She was already in love with it. Physically she was a beautiful creature, able to capture the attention, passion, and love of men with minimal effort on her part. But artistically—that was where her true heart lay. The Aria was like the ideal lover, one who could not be casually seduced. One who could readily break her heart if not won.

In due course the rocket reversed its thrust and landed at Martinique, on an island of the West Indies. They rode in a wheeled vehicle called a car to the opera site. Weft would have found all of this fascinating if she had not been so distracted by the Aria.

There they were met by Mistress Melodious, an older woman but still beautiful. She wore a tiara similar to Marionette's, the mark of her rank. The two mistresses embraced, and Weft realized that they were friends. In fact the elder had mentored the younger, who was now making her own way up through the ranks of power.

"These are two from Colony Planet Charm," Marionette said, introducing them to Melodious. "Augur of the Red Chroma, who monitors Princess Weft of nonChroma, daughter of their king. Weft is a talented singer." She did not say more on that score; obviously she had already communicated the fuller background.

"I am glad to meet you, Princess Weft," Melodious said, embracing her next. Her body was fit and shapely; evidently the mistresses made it a point to stay in shape. "And you, Augur." She embraced him, and Weft could see that her touch had an impact. She was of his generation, perhaps a decade older. The Mistresses could handle men; it was their nature.

"I must return now to Antarctica," Marionette said regretfully. "I leave Weft in your hands, knowing you will treat her well."

"I will try, dear," Melodious said.

Then Marionette was gone and Melodious was in charge. "I understand you have ambition," she said to Weft as she efficiently conveyed them to the empty stage.

"I want to sing the Aria."

The woman considered briefly. "You know its nature?"

"Affirmation." She hesitated, then added. "I do not know if I can perform it perfectly, but I must try."

"Then perhaps what is best is a rehearsal with Counterpoint, our male singer." She lifted one hand and shook it, and a faint bell sounded. "But I must advise you of something uncomfortable."

"Curiosity."

"The singers are generally tolerant, but the orchestra is shall we say choosy about its devotion. It is not thrilled by the notion of an outsider participating in any capacity. The former singer of the key role was held in high regard."

That meant no support there. "Understanding."

A man approached. He was tall, dark, handsome, and muscular, about age 25. "This is Counterpoint, my lead male singer. There is strong interaction between the male and female parts. I leave you to your dialogue." The Mistress took Augur by the hand and led him to seats at the side of the stage. It was already evident that she had an eye on the red man, and would take him to her bed no fault if she chose.

Weft eyed the man, liking his look. He eyed her, his frown verging on a snarl. So much for tolerance.

Well, there were ways and ways. "I want to try the Aria," she told him. "I need your help. I proffer you a deal." She was actually drawing from a key aspect of the opera, whose general story she had picked up on.

"Depart this minute and I will refrain from spitting on you, you starry-eyed twit," he said gruffly.

She took a breath, consciously expanding her bosom. "I am Princess Weft of Planet Charm, here as a temporary hostage. I want to do something interesting during my captivity on your planet. Help me in this, and if I fail, I am yours for the night, no fault." She touched the top button on her blouse, and it opened, showing a bit more of her breasts. "You can have your will of me, and I will never make you regret it in any venue. Free sex."

His eyes lingered. They had no choice. He was, after all, a man. "I see you have read the score. What is this 'no fault'?"

"No commitment or expectation by either party once morning comes. The events of the night will not exist by day." She released another button, smiling.

"As with a mistress?"

She hadn't thought of it that way, but it did seem that mistresses were perpetual no fault creatures. "Affirmation."

The man took stock. "Done." His original contempt had been banished by her offer. A good and ready body could do that. He surely knew that this was a cynical ploy on her part, to accomplish her purpose, but his judgment had been overwhelmed by desire. Breasts were magical in their own fashion.

"I know the melody and words, but may be awkward on the timing of the interactive parts. I will try to follow your lead. I hope you will let me know where I go wrong."

For answer, he started singing. She recognized the section, and came in where her part began. This portion was easy, even without instrumental accompaniment.

Counterpoint nodded slightly, recognizing the competence of her voice. He sang again, and she sang. Then came the duet, and she matched him note for note. He nodded again. But this was still the easy part.

The musical dialogue progressed, becoming more difficult. Once he stopped her. "Alternate twice; on the third we overlap halfway, you half a note behind me."

"Apology." They did it again, and this time she did it correctly. The hall reverberated with their merging sound. He nodded a third time.

Then came the finale, which was almost entirely her own: the deadly Aria. This was what would make or break her. She had reviewed it, contemplated it, dreamed of it as she snoozed on the rocket, and thought she had made progress. But it was still devilishly difficult, and she had no certainty of perfection.

She launched into it. It was the maiden's final appeal to the warrior, for acceptance and unity. *You are the lock; I am the key.* It built to its crescendo, and she got it—until the finale. Then the light of the stage seemed to dim, she felt faint, and she knew she was losing it.

"Hold!" He was holding her, coincidentally, keeping her from falling. "It can not be done without accompaniment. You will destroy yourself."

She did feel on the verge of destruction. But she remained game. "I have my dulcimer."

"A dulcimer! I meant the orchestra!"

"It is not here."

He shook his head. "Then try the dulcimer. But this is impossible."

"Then I will be yours." He was honoring his part of the bargain, doing his best to enable her to succeed. If she failed despite his support, he deserved her passion and would have a phenomenal night.

She fetched her dulcimer from her traveling bag, sitting beside Augur and Mistress Melodious. The two had observed all of the interaction, including the proffered deal, and had not interfered. Their expressions were set in neutral.

She donned her finger hammers and returned to the stage. "I will try again."

She played the dulcimer, and the music did reassure and bolster her. It was a long familiar friend, with magic of its own. Anything she sang, she could sing better with this supportive companion.

She sang, and moved through it with increased confidence. Counterpoint, too, did better with that accompaniment. Then she hit the finale—and made it.

Barely.

"You strained," Counterpoint said. "But with the orchestra you can make it. You have proved yourself, to my astonishment."

She smiled, feeling dizzy from the phenomenal effort. "I would have failed, without my dulcimer. You could have had me, if you had kept your mouth shut."

"I know it. But you were so close, so amazingly close, I had to make it possible. If there was any chance. Whatever the personal cost, which I deeply regret."

"You can have me anyway," she said giddily, and fell into his arms. "It's in the script."

They paused by the chairs. "She passed," Counterpoint said to the mistress.

"We heard. Congratulations."

"No fault," Weft said to Augur.

"I am about to explore that with the mistress," Augur said, smiling.

So they were hitting it off together. Augur was married, but no fault bypassed that, and Aura was free to make it with other men similarly if she chose. The two were veterans of such interactions. "Then we will see you in the morning."

She accompanied Counterpoint to his room. They undressed, but even so he was distracted. "You must be the finest singer on your planet!"

"Affirmation," she said modestly. "Except for my mother the queen, who taught me."

"No one has ever done that before: the Aria, the first time."

"Explanation: I had your help."

He laughed, enfolded her, and fell onto the bed with her. His excitement was such that he was done in seconds. She took that as confirmation of her power of passion, and was not at all disappointed despite having no climax herself.

Then he lay on his back and talked. "The orchestra may be a problem. I will ask them, but they may balk."

"Don't they answer to the mistress?"

"They do. We all do. But she does not command. She leaves us our choices. They may try to deny you."

"Confusion. Then what should I do?"

"Use your dulcimer. You can make it through, with that; you proved it."

"Doubt: Is that acceptable in a real production, before an audience?"

"There is no score for the Aria. It can be done with any instrument. It would be unusual—highly so—but far better than failure."

"Agreement. Then I will come prepared."

He took hold of her, and she moved with him, working into another sexual episode. This time it took longer, and she was able to climax too. Sex was no challenge at all, compared to the Aria.

They lay on the bed again and talked. He told her the story line of the opera *Conquest*, which was full of the ridiculous twists and coincidences he assured her were part of any opera; the point was the costumes and music, not the logic or accuracy. "There is something else. We have not done the Aria live for a month. The audience will know, and it, too, will come prepared."

"Question?"

"I love that single-word mannerism of yours! They will expect you to fail. The penalty for failure is fruit."

"Question?"

"Overripe fruit. They throw it. This is a tradition. It is nothing personal. So if it happens—" He shrugged. "I was fruited once, early in my career. It can be survived."

"Appreciation for the warning."

He reached for her again. "I—I want to apologize for my attitude. I did not know your potential. We see so many would-be stars that we grow callous."

"Understanding." This time the sex took considerable time, but was pleasant. He was a virile man, and as she came to know him, she liked him.

"But we must sleep," he said at last. "So as to be ready for the morrow. But if it is successful—can we do this again?"

"I will night with you as long as I am on the opera tour." It would be to her advantage to be "taken," so that she could indulge her natural Glamor appetite for sex without seeming promiscuous. It was her secret that she had made the deal not merely to persuade him, but for her own physical satisfaction. As a woman she could take sex or leave it; as a Glamor she hated to leave it.

"Appreciation," he said, smiling. "How may I repay you?" He believed that she was doing him a singular favor. Well, she was, in part.

"Help me visit any volcanoes within range. My home planet is covered with them; I want to see Earth's."

"Deal!"

⁂

In the morning they joined Augur and Melodious for breakfast. "I trust you had as compatible a night as we did," the mistress remarked.

"Affirmation."

"You knew she would win me over," Counterpoint said to Melodious.

"The moment I saw her," the Mistress agreed. "I know your tastes. I hoped she could also sing."

They laughed.

But the live performance was serious. There was a considerable audience, filling the theater for this presentation. Weft had never seen a throng of this magnitude before; there were many hundreds. Weft also saw that many carried bags or packages: the ripe fruit. They were prepared. Was she? She had done it with her dulcimer, but not yet with the orchestra. That might throw her off.

The stage setting was opulent in a rough-hewn way: it was the roof of a battered stone castle, with a tattered flag marked MALE. This was the Last Redoubt of the violent male government. Because the story was mythological rather than truly historical, its location was wherever the opera performed, giving the locals a sense of relevance. Thus it seemed that the last great battle between the Female and Male forces had occurred right here in Auckland.

Before the show, with the curtains closed, Counterpoint introduced her to the cast, including the orchestra players. "This is Princess Weft, of Colony Planet Charm, a temporary hostage to her father the king's behavior. We bear her no malice and wish to make her stay on Earth as pleasant as feasible."

"Greeting," Weft said, smiling. She was in costume: a rather revealing robe, and a Mistress Tiara in her hair, covering her small crown; it was part of her costume.

She was not met with similar friendliness. The actors/singers seemed neutral, but the musicians were negative. "We heard you plumbed her last night," a violinist said, as if Weft wasn't present.

Counterpoint nodded. "And she made my day pleasant," he agreed. "She is also a singer of considerable note on her home planet. She has agreed to fill the role of Malene, so that we can return to full live performances."

There was an abrupt chill, though this was hardly news to them. "The fact that she dazzled you with sex does not mean she can sing," a woodwind player said sourly. "Particularly not *that* role."

"I assure you she can do it," Counterpoint said. "All she needs is your support, as every singer does."

He was met with stony silence.

"I trust you to do the right thing," Mistress Melodious said to the orchestra. Weft noted that she did not define that thing; they retained a choice. That was not a good sign. The mistress knew that Weft had succeeded, barely, the day before; for some reason she did not clarify that.

Augur had a seat at the front of the audience. The mistress had a part in the opera, as the Head Mistress, mother of the heroine Malene.

The audience hushed as the orchestra began the preliminary melody. This was new to Weft, and she liked it; the tune was captivating and the orchestra was excellent. The main part of the opera proceeded, showing negotiations, battles, and tragedies as the women slowly won the world from the recalcitrant men. Until only one pocket of resistance remained.

Then it was Weft's turn, the final act. She walked with Melodious in front of the closed curtain, before the orchestra pit. She was now Malene, young daughter of the local Head Mistress. Hence the tiara: she was a junior mistress.

"The forces of femininity have been victorious everywhere on Earth," the Head Mistress proclaimed to the audience in a singing voice. Everything in an opera was sung, even ordinary dialogue, which made for some rather flat music, but of course the audience understood. "Everywhere except here in Auckland, Zealand. Here stands the final Male Redoubt. We have laid it under siege these past three months, preventing any supplies being brought in, but the men are resistive. We do not wish to destroy them, but to convert them, that they may join the brave new order and live at last in peace."

"Yes, Mother," Malene replied to the audience, also in semi-song. "Why have they not already joined us?"

"They are male, by definition," the Head Mistress sang. "They prefer combat to reason. That is why they have to be nullified. Earth cannot exist in peace, prosperity, harmony, and glory until women rule everywhere."

There was a murmur of applause from the audience. This was patriotic speech.

"Surely they understand that," Malene sang dutifully. "They may be violent, course, crude, oversexed, and wrongheaded, but not completely stupid. They have to realize that their position is hopeless."

"They do," the Head Mistress agreed. "But as they see it, they have three choices: Fight on regardless, capitulate, or suicide. Our information is that they have decided on the last alternative, tomorrow. So we must reach them today, if we are to do it at all."

"Yes, of course. But how, Mother?"

"Daughter, I must do a thing I dread."

Malene made a gesture of bewilderment. "What can that be, Mother?"

"I must send you in to them to negotiate their surrender."

"But they will rape me and kill me," Malene protested. "Perhaps not in that order."

"Not if you make their leader, Rebel, an offer he can't refuse."

"I do not understand, Mother."

"It happens that Rebel was a singer before he turned male partisan," the head Mistress sang. "Perhaps it was because he did not achieve the one thing he craved most that he gave up singing for fighting. You can offer him that thing."

"What thing, Mother?" As if a real daughter in such a situation would not already know.

"The Aria."

There was a pause as the significance sank in. Then Malene sang. "But Mother, you were the only woman who could could manage it, and you retired five years ago."

"True, Daughter. I can no longer do it. But there is one who may."

"Who could that be, Mother?"

"You, Daughter. True, you have not yet done it, but you have been training since my retirement, and are almost ready. Now you must do it. If anyone can do it, it is you. Go there, offer him the Aria if he will surrender himself and his men. That is the one thing that will move him."

"And what if he agrees, Mother, but I do not succeed?"

"Then you are lost, my Daughter. They will seriously abuse you and hurl your bleeding body from the battlement when they are done. So perhaps it is better not to go."

Malene steeled herself dramatically. "No, Mother, I will do it. It is the only way."

Then the Head Mistress broke into her "Song of Regret": "Daughter, Daughter, I fear for you. Do not go." The illogic of the story was such that it was quite acceptable for the Head Mistress to urge her daughter not to do what she was asking her to do.

"Mother, Mother, I must go," Malene sang next as the Head Mistress continued her protests. It was the "Regret Duet," intensely feeling but not challenging as music.

The audience watched and listened, silent. Weft had just demonstrated that she could sing, but the real test was coming. Hands were reaching into bags, finding fruit.

Then Malene drew away, determined to pursue her dangerous mission. Her mother clung to her, trying to prevent it, but she got free and marched offstage, while the Head Mistress dramatically wrung her hands and wept. Then she too left the stage.

The background music stopped. After a pause, the curtain rose, showing the castle roof under a blue sky. Weft watched from offstage, and felt herself getting into the role. Now she was Malene, there in the mythical past of Earth.

A dozen rough-looking men were disposed on the roof, resting against the battlements, which were alternating merlons and crenels: raised sections and low sections of the surrounding defensive wall. They were sharpening swords, repairing arrows, playing dice, or snoozing. One belched loudly, demonstrating his male crudity. Two others got in a pointless quarrel, showing their naturally fractious nature.

"Woman ahoy!" the lookout cried in song.

Immediately all the men dropped their other business, took up arms, and rushed to the battlement.

"She's in white," the lookout sang. "That means truce."

"We know that, bunghole," another sang.

"We should shoot her anyway," a third put in.

"Naw, she's got too good a shape. We should bring her in for some fun first."

"She's a *Mistress*!" the lookout cried, seeing her more clearly. "I see the tiara!"

There was a surprised pause. Even rough crude male types were impressed by that. "Call Rebel," someone suggested.

Rebel came onstage. He was tall, dark, and handsome, his lean loins girded by a long sword. The men fell back before him, responsive to his aura of command. "What's this?"

"There's a Mistress in white out there signaling us."

Rebel considered briefly. "She wants to negotiate. Bring her in, alone."

A man ran offstage, heading for the stairs. Soon he reappeared, leading Malene, who was now in a flimsy white gown that showed her flesh to considerable advantage. All the men faded back and watched as the handsome male leader and lovely female visitor came together.

"I am Rebel," Rebel sang. "Who are you? What do you want?"

"I am Mistress Malene, daughter of the Head Mistress who is besieging your castle," Malene replied. "I have come to proffer a deal."

"I doubt we are interested," Rebel responded. But the way he studied her body suggested that he was interested in something. "We are prepared to fight to the death."

"Your situation is hopeless," Malene informed him. "Soon you will run out of supplies. We offer you food, freedom, and women. All you need to do is yield peacefully to our authority."

"Never," Rebel sang defiantly, and the men hummed a chorus of agreement. Then he and the men launched into the "Song of Rebellion," a rousing refusal to be reasonable. They had surprisingly good voices.

After patiently waiting until the end of the song, Malene took her turn. "I understand you sing," she sang to Rebel. As if that could be in doubt after all his singing of protest.

"That's past. I am a warrior now."

"I offer you the Aria."

There was complete silence, as the faint background orchestral music stopped. She had scored on his weakness.

In a moment Rebel recovered. "What do you know of that?" he demanded.

"I know it is the one thing you lack. You never found a woman who could do it. I will sing it with you. Then you will yield your fort and retire from violence."

"And if you fail?"

"Then I am yours to do with what you will." She drew back her gown, baring her breasts as she turned slightly to give the audience the full display. She knew it was an excellent one. "To ravish and destroy me and hurl my spent body from the battlement."

Rebel made a dramatic show of studying her closely. He was definitely interested. So were his men; some of their tongues were hanging out. She doubted that this was completely feigned for the audience. "And who will judge whether it is sufficient?"

"Your men here." She was putting her fate in the hands of the hostile force.

"Deal," he said. And started singing. He had taken up the challenge.

She joined in, and it became the duet. She was meeting the challenge, to the growing amazement of the men. Then the finale, not hers alone, but the male part was relatively ordinary, supportive for the truly challenging female part. He was the foundation, she the temple. Other women could sing; no other could handle this.

And the orchestra died.

She stood in silence, bereft of accompaniment. No one moved. Some of the men looked pained despite themselves. Rebel stopped singing; it was pointless in this circumstance. How could there be a duet when the woman could not perform?

So they were cutting her down, despite the damage this did to the production. They wanted her to fail.

No. Not the men, neither as themselves nor as roles in the opera. Not Rebel or Counterpoint. They were with her. It was the orchestra. The musicians resented her assumption of the lead role, and meant to take her down.

But she didn't have to go down.

She walked to the edge of the stage, fetched her hammer dulcimer, and sat on a crenel as she applied the little hammers to her fingers. Then she organized herself, sitting with the dulcimer in her lap, looked toward Rebel, and began to sing. He joined her in perfect time, though he looked doubtful. How could a single instrument, however nimbly played, make up for the lack of a full orchestra?

You are the lock, I am the key. The melody expanded to its heights and depths, phenomenally extending the simple words. There was the weight of the closed male lock in it, and the click of the turning female key, emphasized by the dulcimer notes. The maiden was pleading for union with the man. The sexual analogy was imperfect, but the feeling was strong.

The surrounding men's faces showed surprise that was not entirely feigned. Rebel especially. In the setting of the story it was exactly this way, as there was no orchestra on the battlements. But that was hardly realistic, and allowance was made for the requirements of the operatic presentation.

You are the cup, I am the drink. There was the clank of a cup, the trickling of liquid, all done with the voice and accompaniment. The hammer dulcimer was good at such effects. The surprise was shifting to appreciation. Rebel's support had never been perfunctory, but now it was enthusiastic.

You are the planet, I am the moon. Now it was the somber swing of a planetary mass as he held long low notes, and the lighter melody of the orbiting moon as she rippled musically above. The appreciation was becoming enthusiasm.

You are the body, I am the soul. The melody danced trickily around a living body, defining it, with the beat of the heart and breeze of breathing, then the impossibly light, intricate dancing of the spirit. Again the rippling dulcimer notes animated it. Enthusiasm was turning to awe. They were standing close together now, she halfway twining around him as if infusing him, their two voices merging in extremely fine-tuned harmony.

You are the Master; I am the Mistress. This was the finale that few singers could do. It carried the urgency of sexual desire and the joy of commitment. She stood within the loose embrace of his arms as her fingers danced over the strings and her voice finessed the power and climax of his urgency. They were singing *at* each other with full volume and passion. It was about as strongly sexual as it was possible to be without actually touching each other. She was doing it! The men's faces showed sheer desire.

We belong together. If only her voice held out for that final, desperate, absolutely lovely plea. His support was there, the platform of song on which she raced and leaped. It was sheer primal emotion pouring forth in esthetic abandon.

She made it—and swooned. Rebel caught her and held her, kissing her back into consciousness. He was plainly in love. She had given him the Aria, and his fight was over. So was the opera.

The audience burst into prolonged applause.

Then the fruit started flying.

Not at the stage. At the silent orchestra, that had defaulted on the finale. Things dropped into the pit, with splats. Soggy, stinking, messy missives rained down on the heads and instruments of the musicians, half-burying them in filth. The stench rose up, suffusing the scene.

The singers on stage held their positions, waiting for the curtain to descend. But several smiles were cracking despite the awful odor.

Then the curtain dropped, granting them privacy. The men rushed to join Rebel and Malene. They could not speak, lest the audience hear, but they smiled and signaled their deep satisfaction.

"You're in," Counterpoint whispered at her ear, and kissed it. "I think the orchestra got the message. We love you."

"Appreciation," Weft answered. Then she really fainted.

⚬⚬

"That was divine," Mistress Melodious said. "I can't wait for the written reviews."

"Question?"

"The fruit review is only the immediate audience. The more literary critics cast a far longer shadow. I believe they will welcome you. You accomplished what no other woman has: a successful Aria without a long apprenticeship. In so doing, you not only won your place, you saved the opera from threatened ruin. Despite the balky musicians, who will now be on probation; it was a useful lesson to them. I think they will not question my judgment soon again. We will have a most successful season. Just when we need it most. Public support of the arts is not necessarily what we mistresses would prefer."

So the Mistress had known the musicians would balk, and Weft would succeed despite them, and shame them savagely. Melodious had wanted them to be publicly rebuked. "Just so long as I can see the volcanoes," Weft said.

Mistress Melodious laughed. "We will see them with you, my dear. It is a tiny price for your gift to us."

They made it a party of four to see the volcano, staying overnight in the vicinity. This was the famous, or infamous, Pelee, one of the most destructive, historically.

"This is actually one of the more interesting volcanoes of our planet," Melodious said. "It was quiescent for some time, its heat muted, actually improving the local climate. A magnificent 4,500 foot tall mountain, one of the highest in the region. At its base, historically, developed the city of Saint Pierre, the largest and loveliest of the island, known as the Paris of the Antilles." She paused. "That reference might not be familiar to you. Paris has ever been a great city of art and dreams, the standard by which all else is judged. All lovers want to be in Paris."

"Appreciation," Weft murmured.

"It was also called the Island of Flowers. Bougainvillea, oleander, hibiscus, moonflower—many, many kinds of flowers. A virtual paradise. Then one day Pelee came to savage life, destroying the entire city in a matter of perhaps three minutes, leaving a thoroughly blasted ruin reminiscent of Hell. Only two survived, by sheer chance, and they were damaged. For a time it was a mystery: how could it have been so fast? Normally there is at least some time for some to flee the fires. Rocks and ash take time to fall, and lava can be seen coursing down the slope, and generally avoided. Mount Pelee rumbled and emitted columns of smoke and clouds of ash. The answer was pyroclastic flow."

"Question?" Actually Weft knew the term, as some Charm volcanoes had similar effects, but she preferred to have the mistress explain it.

"A mixture of bits of ash and rock, lava, smoke, steam, and anything else that gets in the way, such as dirt and brush. It can form a super-hot cloud that is heavier than air. This welled up and rolled down the mountainside, frying anything in its path—including the city. Because it was light and fast, the natives had no sufficient warning; if any saw it, they were unable to escape it, as it was far too large and swift. Pyroclastic matter is one of the most suddenly deadly aspects of volcanism. That was the killer of perhaps thirty thousand people, on that day. There had been many similar eruptions before, but not since the city formed, so the natives didn't know its threat. They called it the vomit devil, perhaps thinking of it as a nuisance rather than a deadly threat."

"Horror!"

"We do have similar effects on Charm," Augur said. "We Chroma folk are able to view it more safely, because we can readily escape even the fastest flow. Still, it can be dangerous, because it also represents intensified magic."

"I find this fascinating," Melodious said. "Colored magic, colored people. I would have been a complete skeptic, had I not witnessed a bit of it."

"I suspect that the eruption you just described was a good deal more dramatic than most of our Red Chroma magic."

"Perhaps." Melodious seemed to be quite enjoying the company of Augur, perhaps in part because of his novelty as a completely red man. "At any rate, as we reconstruct it, there were several warning blasts that impressed the townsmen, but they did not see these as immediately dangerous. Then in the afternoon of the fatal day, Mount Pelee emitted a huge gray and black cloud with lightning thrusting through it. Ash fell on the city like snow, covering the streets and trees. The daylight was dimmed, and birds fell from their perches, suffocating on the petals of ash. Bugs emerged from hiding, driven out by the hot gases. Large millipedes invaded the city, biting like scorpions. Ants also. They crawled up the legs of horses, and up under the trouser legs of the men. After that came the snakes, aware of problems in the ground because of their proximity to it. They slithered into the houses, and many people died because of snake bites."

"Everything has to get clear of a bad eruption," Augur agreed. "The animals know. So do the plants, but they have fewer options."

"The smell of rotten eggs suffused the atmosphere," Melodious continued. Clearly, she had researched the matter, and was genuinely interested. "There were mud slides, including one incorporating boulders, uprooted trees, dead cows and scalded fish that smashed into the local sugar plant, killing twenty men. But these were mere incidents. The worst was to come. Finally it did come: the pyroclastic torrent that scored directly on the city. Many townsmen may have seen it coming, but by then it was too late."

"And still the volcano sits here, pretending innocence," Augur said.

"We are better prepared for its naughtiness."

"And it did seem to remain alive, if relatively quiescent today."

"Request: a spot windward," Weft said.

"There is no bad smell here," Augur said mildly.

"Not to you," she retorted. Of course he knew what she was up to. He was actually helping to cover for her.

Counterpoint was glad to take Weft to a spot just upwind of the volcano, humoring her foible. Augur and Melodius remained behind, satisfied to have a moment alone together.

As they walked, Weft extended her aura and tuned in on local bacteria. They were compatible and friendly. She would have no trouble establishing the connection.

The volcano was impressive, but barely active. Was this sufficient? She needed a live one, not a dead one. But she was committed now; it would have to do.

Weft removed her small crown. She unscrewed the green point and emptied its bit of green dust into the breeze. The powder colored the air, forming an expanding green bubble.

"That's an interesting novelty," Counterpoint remarked. "What is the point?"

"It's the essence of Green Chroma," she said. "It will suffuse the volcano and convert it to Green. Thereafter it will erupt Green magic. The terrain will slowly turn green, and so will the people."

Of course he didn't believe it. She had counted on that. "Is that how Augur became red? Residing near a red volcano?"

"Confirmation. Most of the citizens of Charm are people of color. Only those of us who live in nonChroma zones are colorless."

"I would never call you colorless, Princess Weft!"

"Appreciation."

The green bubble formed into a small cloud, still expanding. It drifted up over the cone of the volcano, and seemed to quiver. It was as if it knew where it needed to go. It filled the bowl, then sank down out of sight.

"How long does this magical process take?"

"About three months, we think. It depends on the size of the volcano. Never fear—it will be quite obvious when it happens."

"I shall be interested to see that."

She smiled, accepting his polite disbelief. The longer Earth remained ignorant of the program, the better. If the four of them managed to seed all their volcanoes—forty eight in all—the process would be irreversible. Then Earth would become like Charm.

And that would be Charm's victory. Accomplished without threat or violence, before the Earthers ever suspected. If nothing went wrong.

Chapter 8
Idyll

"We have a problem," Stevia agreed. "Because of your sense of honor."

"Exactly," Dynamo said. "I will not betray my planet."

"This is a quality we value. If you were ready to betray one planet, you might well betray another."

"It is nice to have that straight," he said sourly. He feared his honor was about to cost him her delightful sexual services.

"Suppose I can show you that joining us is what is best for Earth?"

He shrugged. "Then I might consider it. But that seems unlikely."

"Come with me to Triumph City," she said. "I believe it is time for you to talk with King Havoc."

"As you wish." He had met with Daylight, and after some discussion she had agreed that she did want a fourth by him. She had, as Stevia had warned, not been nearly as shapely or enthusiastic as her emulation had been, but he was satisfied that he had done the right thing. Then he had spent a night with the real Naive, and she had been far less hesitant, and just as thrilled. Also just as tight, which he was coming to appreciate. There again, he felt he had done right. So now he was free to work things out with Stevia, whose company he preferred.

"Situation: The king is busy at the moment, so we have an hour to ourselves."

"What do you have in mind?"

"Silly man." She embraced him. Her hair sprang outward, forming a shell. In a moment she had them naked within it.

Sex was fast and fun, but most of the time remained. "What now?" he asked as he lay beside her within the shell. He was relieved that she had not decided to terminate the sexual aspect. But he still would not allow it to violate his honor.

"More passion, of course. We Glamors have insatiable sexual appetites."

"The women too?"

"Affirmation. We are merely better at controlling it, so as to be able to tempt men mercilessly."

"But I'm tapped out at the moment."

"Negation." She took his penis in her hand, massaging it. It sprang to new life.

"What did you do?" he asked, pleasantly surprised.

"I infused some of my ardor into your flesh. I can spare it, and you need it."

So it seemed. He had at her again, and it was just as much fun as the first time. She was as avid as he, and he could tell she wasn't pretending, as the mistress sometimes did when she thought her partner of the moment wanted that. Stevia had not been fooling when she described herself as a lusty woman.

But as he ebbed and withdrew, she touched his member again, and again it surged. "How long can you do this?" he asked, amazed.

"Indefinitely. A Glamor can have fifty orgasms in an hour, if he or she chooses. Sometimes we do choose."

"Fifty!"

"You want that?"

He laughed. "I'll settle for twenty."

That turned out to be literal. She restored him nineteen times, for twenty in all. "Satisfied?" she inquired.

"Twenty times satisfied! But how is it possible?"

"Magic," she reminded him.

Every time he started doubting magic, there was another reminder. Magic did seem to explain it. Certainly normal biology did not.

They got dressed. A section of the shell became reflective so he could check himself. Then it dissolved back into hair, and the hair flowed back to her head. They were back in the natural realm.

And lying on a couch in a fancy room. There was a plush carpet on the floor and tapestries on the wall. "Where are we?" he asked somewhat blankly.

"In the King's palace atop the pyramid of Triumph City."

"But we were in a forest glade!"

"We traveled."

"You mean all the time we were—doing it—we were floating across the landscape? Suppose someone had seen?"

"The cocoon was invisible."

"And us too, inside it?"

She smiled. "I suppose I could have made it transparent and floated it low so that others could admire your virility."

He had to laugh. "And you'd have let them think it was me! Twenty times potent."

"What can a woman do except accommodate such potency? Such a treat is not to be wasted."

"You almost make me want to do it again."

Her hair lengthened sinuously, changing color.

"Not right now!" he protested.

But she had gotten the notion. Her hair looped around him, drawing him in to her. His trousers dissolved in the crotch, allowing his member to spring forth. Suddenly they were clinching yet again, he was driving deep into her peristaltic channel, and their mutual climax was similarly intense. He could not resist her sexually, and did not want to. But if she thought this would make him betray Earth, she would be disappointed.

She let him go just as he heard footsteps approaching. He barely had time to pack himself back into his restored trousers before a shapely palace maid appeared. "King Havoc will see you now, Dynamo, Stevia."

"Thank you, Honey," Stevia said.

Dynamo had picked up enough of the culture to know that this would be literal: the maid's name was Honey, probably because she had had a sweet tooth as a child.

"Affirmation," Stevia murmured as they followed Honey to the audience chamber.

A man could get nervous, having his mind constantly read, he thought.

She patted his bottom reassuringly.

Then he had a scary thought: if she really could read his mind, what of the secret code that controlled the orbiting bomb? Could they get hold of that? Not that it mattered, because they had no way to reach the bomb to use the code.

Now they were standing before King Havoc, who was as handsome and healthy as ever. "Unnecessary," Havoc said. "We nullified that the moment the Earthship left."

Dynamo simply stared, horrified.

The king laughed. "You are here to learn the extent of our magic, so we may persuade you to join our cause. Let's start with that." He reached out to take Stevia's hand.

Stevia in turn put her arm around Dynamo's waist. "This may surprise you," she said.

Then they were standing in the bomb housing. Dynamo recognized it, being well familiar with it. How could that be?

The king gestured at the bomb's control screen. A single word was printed on it: DEACTIVATED.

They had done it. Somehow they had turned off the bomb. "How?" he asked numbly.

"Mino," King Havoc said.

"Who?"

"We will meet him now."

Stevia put her arm around him again—and again the scene shifted. Now they were in the control chamber of a foreign space ship. That was the only thing it could be.

"This is Mino," Stevia said. "Speak to him."

But Dynamo was silent, unable to make sense of this.

"A greeting, Mino," Havoc said.

"Salutation, King Havoc, Red Glamor," a speaker said. Simultaneously the words appeared on the main screen.

"This is Dynamo of Earth, here to observe our culture," Havoc said. "We mean to convert him to our cause."

"An Earther," the speaker said. "This is interesting."

"Hello," Dynamo said belatedly. "What are you?"

"I am an alien machine, currently in league with the Glamors of Charm and Counter Charm. I defused your orbiting bomb."

"How could you do that? It was keyed to detonate if disturbed without the code."

"I am of a more advanced technology. I simply used a stasis field and spot telekinesis to nullify it."

"But that was state of the art!"

"The state of your art," the machine agreed. "Not mine."

"Earth is a Type One technology."

"I am from a Type Two technology."

"Disbelief!"

"Reality."

"Question," King Havoc said.

"Answer," Dynamo said, feeling dizzy. "According to an ancient Earthly definition, there are four levels of technology. You of Charm are Type Zero, using a portion of the energy available to your planet. We of Earth are Type One, utilizing all the energy of our planet. Mino claims to be from Type Two, utilizing all the energy of its star. A Type Three technology would use all the energy available in the galaxy." He smiled briefly. "We know of no such culture."

"There is none at present," Mino agreed.

"At present?"

"They have existed in the past, but proved to be fleeting. My culture is working to become another, one that will endure."

That raised broader questions. Dynamo focused on an immediate one. "If you were here, why didn't you nullify our space ship before it took the hostages back to Earth?"

"Because Havoc sent his children to Earth. They have a mission there. It was more convenient to do it without Earth knowing that mission."

"What mission?"

"To conquer Earth," Havoc said.

"With four juveniles? Ludicrous!"

Stevia took him by the hand. "We need to talk. First I need to make you understand more about Glamors."

"I have seen your powers," Dynamo agreed. "But you are no child. Even so, you could not conquer Earth."

"There are eighteen Glamors," she said, guiding him to a seat in the control chamber. "They consist of humans and animals, each with its special constituency. All have similar powers, but tend to specialize individually, for convenience. As a general rule, the younger a person achieves Glamor status, the more competent that person is. The king's children achieved it very young, when they mere babies. They are thus the four most powerful Glamors, and we respect that."

"Four—like you?

"Worse than I am," she assured him. "They can do things I can't. The youngest is Voila, the king's natural child. She is the strongest Glamor ever."

"This has little meaning for me."

"Here is an example. When she was only six months old, she took on Mino, and defeated him."

"Ridiculous! A baby that young can't even talk."

"The match was not verbal," Mino said.

"Then what was it?"

"Seeing the future."

"Precognition? That is fantasy. The future is malleable. The very act of predicting it changes it."

"Agreed. Here is the way of it," the machine said. "I see the far future. Voila sees the near future. At their overlap there is room for challenge. She outsmarted me and defeated me. Her future became mine. That is why I now ally with the humans instead of my own machine culture."

"But assuming this is true, how could she do anything with Earth? The only future she could see is Earth's reconquest of it colonies."

"She sees that, and is changing it," Stevia said. "I could not do it, Havoc could not do it, but Voila has an even chance to accomplish it."

"You can teleport through space, be endlessly sexually potent, change your form, but you can't match the powers of this child?"

"Affirmation."

"Well, I am not going to help you do it."

"We hope to change your mind."

Dynamo was seriously shaken, but did not care to admit it. "Assuming all this is true, what is it you want of me? Why bother, when you can so readily destroy me?"

Stevia laughed. "What would I do for a lover, if you were gone?"

Somewhere there was grim humor. "You could take the king instead. No fault, I believe is the applicable term."

"She did," Havoc said reminiscently. "First she fascinated me as the Red Glamor. Then she slowly seduced me as Stevia. You know how it is."

Dynamo knew exactly how it was. "This is a diversion. What do you want with me?"

The king faced him, and his expression became deadly serious. "We want you to train our citizens to be administrators to govern Earth."

"To govern Earth!"

"You will have a choice," Havoc said. "To make our personnel competent for the job, or to allow them to be incompetent. That would not be wise."

"But Charm is not going to take over Earth! That's backwards."

Havoc shrugged. "Persuade him," he said to Stevia.

She took Dynamo's arm. "Come with me."

This time he shook her off. "Sex won't do it! This is treason."

"I leave him to you," Havoc said to her, and vanished.

Dynamo stared at the space the king had occupied. "He is jumping around the same way you do. That means—"

"King Havoc is the Glamor of trees and plants," Stevia said. "His wife Gale is the Glamor of mosses and lichens. It required Glamors to raise Glamor children."

It all seemed to make horrendous sense. Yet it seemed like a weird dream. "I can't assimilate this," Dynamo said.

Stevia took his arm again. "I will take you to a more relaxed place."

Then they were standing in a field on Earth. Daisies spotted the turf, and the sun was warm in the blue sky.

"Illusion!" Dynamo said. "This has to be a setting."

"Affirmation. But it will do."

"I don't want illusion! I want reality!"

"Reality is overrated," she said, removing her clothing. "Make love to me in a warm field of flowers."

An idea flashed. He suppressed it, lest she read it in his mind. "Agreement." He stripped and had at her luscious body yet again. This continual potency she gave him was nice, and he didn't mind indulging it while it existed. Soon enough she would tire of his intransigence and dump him, so now was probably his only opportunity.

"Not necessarily," she murmured, squeezing him internally.

Thereafter they lay gazing up at the clouds. It was pleasant being back on

Earth, even if this was really a field on Charm. Maybe it would help settle him. He closed his eyes and slept.

He woke in fifteen minutes, as he had programmed himself to do. Stevia still slept beside him. She was beautiful and fun, but he had to get away from her so as to have some privacy of mind. He got silently to his feet, picked up his clothing, and walked away. She was still asleep as he dodged behind a convenient tree.

Suddenly the scene changed. The field was gone. Now it was a jungle, with enormous orange tree trunks twining into dense orange upper foliage. Strange orange birds flitted from branch to branch, pausing to peer at him. They had three wings!

Dynamo froze. How had the scene changed so abruptly? Well, if it was illusion, the master switch for it might have been reset. Was Stevia now in the orange jungle too?

He took a step back the way he had come. The old scene reappeared; he was peering around the tree.

Stevia still slept under the blue Earth sky.

He turned back again, and the jungle reappeared. There was a line of demarkation, with Earth on one side, the Orange Chroma jungle on the other. The weird thing was that from either side the boundary was invisible: just inside the Earth scene, looking out, it seemed to be more of the same. One step away, in the jungle, it showed more jungle. So there was no doubt about both being illusions.

He could hide in this. He forged on into the jungle, spooking the birds, following a faint path. He found a fallen branch, and stripped its leaves to make a serviceable walking staff. Soon he turned at right angles, and then veered again, losing himself. Because he knew Stevia would wake, miss him, and set out in pursuit. She was enormous fun, but she wanted to corrupt him. Her certainty of success made him nervous. She could read his mind; could she also change it against his will? Thought control? Possibly like the legend of the incubus: grasping his soul at the moment of climax. He didn't dare risk it any longer.

There was a sound. Ahead of him appeared a six-legged orange panther. It did not look much like a real panther, but its manner was familiar.

The animal gazed at him assessingly. Then it crouched and pounced. Dynamo jumped aside, angling the staff to deflect the predator. The wood touched the hide—and passed through without resistance.

The panther was illusion too. That was fine—but he could not be certain every creature would be insubstantial. He moved on.

He was in a green snow storm. He paused again, stepping back to verify the continuing existence of the jungle illusion. Then he advanced into the storm. It wasn't cold, fortunately; it was as if some tremendous tree was shedding tiny leaves in the wind.

His foot slipped on a slope and he stumbled down into a gully he couldn't see. The green snow was piled thick enough to mask the true lay of the terrain. There was a lesson: illusion could not hurt him directly, but it would mislead him so that he hurt himself by blundering into a gully or worse.

He used his staff to feel his way forward. The gully eased, and he was on level ground again. Until he stepped into the spaceport.

That was what it was. A paved flat region, with a large rocket ship parked in the center. Attendants were hurrying to service it. In the sky was another rocket, incoming, turning in air to put its jets forward for landing. In the distance was a massive service building.

But it was not Earthly. The rocket design was like none he had seen, and the creatures servicing it were aliens with three legs and three eyes.

This made him consider. This was surely illusion—but what had been the model for the image? He knew enough about space travel to know what was feasible and what was not; this was feasible. There were details that only one versed in space travel would know, such as the bearings inspection ports and the thickened pavement where the rocket blast struck. This was authentic— and not human. This illusion signaled something significant and moderately frightening. There was an alien space culture, somewhere.

He walked across the pavement to the rocket—and through it. Nothing real here, except the pattern on which the illusion was based. Whoever crafted this illusion had seen such a spaceport in operation. Which meant that aliens had visited this planet, or one of the colonists had traveled to an alien civilization and returned.

Did Stevia know about this? Did King Havoc? Surely they did, for they had brought him to this network of animate illusions. What else were they not telling him?

He moved on, into a living sea; he was able to breathe though he was under water. The water was gray, and gray fish swam in it; this must be Stevia's home Chroma. A huge shark-like predator came at him; he blocked it with his staff—how had he managed to retain that, if it was part of the illusion scene?— and it passed through him.

Then he was in a kind of city, where everything was brown metal. The buildings towered into the brown sky, brown glass reflecting brown vehicles driving by. Brown metal six legged dogs walked with brown metal men, robots all. Brown metal three-winged birds flocked to forage for metallic crumbs. Brown metal ants walked in the crevices of the pavement. A complete living machine city scene.

Dynamo paused again, considering. Again, there had to have been a model; the detail was too authentic. He had seen neither metal buildings nor robots on Charm. They might exist, but he doubted it. So where had this image come from?

Someone was playing with him, but too much of what he was seeing was disturbingly real in its fashion. There was a mystery here beyond illusion.

"All right," he said loudly. "I know you're watching me, Stevia. Fetch me back into your embrace."

Stevia appeared, clothed. "What give it away?"

"The realism. A low-tech society did not invent that spaceport or those robots. Where did you encounter them?"

"We did not. Idyll Ifrit did."

"Ifrit? I am not familiar with this term."

"It derives from ancient Earthian fantasy: a nebulous demon or spirit with magical powers. Let me show you."

"Please." It had become clear that he would learn more her way than his.

The illusion scene shifted to a picture of Planet Charm in space, with its amazing array of color patches. "Negation, Stevia said, answering his thought. "This is Counter-Charm or Mystery, our companion planet. You and I are now there."

"The unoccupied one," he agreed. "They do look much alike from space." Then he picked up on something. "You say we are now on Counter Charm?"

"Affirmation. They are much alike," she agreed. "Many of their species are similar. But some are not. For one thing, humans colonized Charm; ifrits colonized Counter-Charm. Here is an ifrit."

The planet expanded as if a ship were flying rapidly toward it. It filled the whole scene. A yellow Chroma zone took over as they landed. There were yellow trees, yellow stones, and a yellow river.

And a yellow cloud. But it was odd, even for this unusual region. It floated low over the ground and seemed to be self-directed. It came to the edge of the zone, where the color faded to transparent. Beyond was a blue Chroma zone.

The cloud condensed, thickening and dropping to the ground. Slowly it formed into a yellow blob. The blob then rolled into the nonChroma band, across it, and to the blue zone. Then the blob evaporated, diffusing into blue mist.

"It's changing color!" Dynamo said. "I thought color was permanent."

"It is for most of us. It takes years for a regular person or animal to change colors, and that person will be at a severe magical disadvantage throughout. It is why we don't like to change Chromas, other than as brief visitors. But the ifrits are different. They readily change, by incorporating the substance of the new Chroma. It is a feat they taught us."

"Confusion. You can dissolve and float away as fog?"

"Demonstration." She lifted one arm, her fingers splayed. Mist rose from them, forming a little cloud. The fingers melted into stubs.

"Disbelief!" He took hold of her hand, to penetrate the illusion.

It was a stub.

"Belief," he said ruefully. "Please reverse it."

The vapor coalesced, and the fingers re-formed. Her hand was restored. He felt every finger, and it was solid and operative.

"The King's children," he said. "They can do this?"

"Affirmation. Better than I can. But they will not need to, ordinarily, because there is an ifrit with them."

"The dog!"

"An assumed form, for convenience and deception," she agreed." Iolo Ifrit, not Voila's pet but her close friend from infancy, who has learned human intelligence. He will do what cloud formation needs to be done, protecting their secret as long as is necessary."

"A power we never dreamed of," he said, amazed.

"As I have said, we mean to conquer Earth, or at least convert her to our side. We do have tools."

"And I can't warn my superiors!"

"Affirmation. We want them to be deceived long enough, and you to know everything, so you can better work with us."

"To betray my planet."

"We covered this before, Dynamo. Earth is likely lost anyway, from your perspective. The question is whether we will administer her competently or incompetently. We prefer competence, and so should you. It is not betraying your planet to arrange for her best government."

"That depends on your perspective."

"Perhaps."

He thought of something. "You can read my mind. You can see the future. Can you also change my mind? If so, why not simply do that, instead of wasting your effort trying to persuade me?"

"A fair question. Artificial mind changes are possible, but seldom last; the person's underlying belief and loyalty will in time reassert themselves. But if that person's own observation and logic persuade him, he will remain persuaded. That is what we want."

"What of buying me with wealth, power, or sex?"

Stevia smiled. "We both know you are not corruptible in such manner. Join us, and you will have enormous power and all the sex you desire, with your desire enhanced. Wealth is not applicable in this society; we lack your Earthly medium of exchange, so can't accumulate it."

"And if I don't join you?"

"Actually you will join us. But to answer your question: we would let you return to Earth, having no further use for you. Your suspicions of imprisonment or torture are unwarranted. With mind reading we don't need such things."

She seemed to be right. If Earth lost power, it would be better to have it competently administered. But they could be fooling him about that. He needed solid, rational evidence before he could make a decision.

"You mentioned one Idyll Ifrit as the one who saw the spaceport and robots. I should talk to her. Ifrits do have gender?"

"Since associating with us, they do, and perhaps before. It is of lesser import to them."

"Take me to Idyll."

"There is no need. She is here."

Dynamo looked around. "Question."

"Answer: We are in her ambiance. All of this is Idyll."

"This illusion scene of a Yellow Chroma zone on Counter Charm?"

"I will ask for a scene with which you can better relate. Idyll?"

An Earthly office room formed around them. This time the change was slow, so that he could see the stages of it. The yellow landscape faded to colorless, and walls rose up, building the structure, until the office was complete.

"I know this place," Dynamo said. "It is one of the offices of the Antarctica spaceport complex, where I met the Mistress of Mistresses, briefly." He paused, savoring the memory. "Always capitalized, because of her status. Never was there a lovelier or more gracious woman. She made Marionette seem like a precocious child. She kissed me and took me into her and told me she trusted me to do the best for Earth. She did me the signal honor of taking my seed and bestowing her trust. I love her, and can never betray her."

The Mistress of Mistresses appeared. "Revelation: I will do the same, though I am not she. I am Idyll."

"You took the scene from my mind!"

The Mistress nodded. "As I took the scene of the spaceport from a new colonist creature three thousand years ago, and the robot city from the memory storage bank of Mino when he joined our cause. I collect images." She came to him, embraced him, and kissed him. "We need you, Dynamo."

He tried to steel himself against her blandishment, but she was irresistible in this form. "How are you doing this? The scene is illusion, and my memory can hardly falsify it, but you—you are physically tangible."

"Would you not prefer to possess me before I reveal the mechanisms of my manifestation?"

"I think that would be foolish. I think of an old horror story of Earth, wherein a man encountered a lovely young woman in a forest, and made love to her and slept the night in her embrace. But in the morning she was revealed as a rotten corpse whose seeming animation had been illusion. He had had sex with that illusion, and was appalled."

The Mistress Idyll laughed. "I am older than that corpse, and not precisely alive, but I am not rotten. This body is as real as it seems to be."

"Stevia!" he said. "You borrow her body for this."

"Negation," Stevia said behind him. There she was, resting in an office chair. "Though I would be happy to lend my body for that purpose." She got up with a flash of legs and approached. She touched his shoulder. "Now that I have established that Idyll and I are separate entities, I will leave you to her ministrations. She will let me know when I am needed again." She faded out.

"But if Idyll is a creature of illusion, how can I feel her like this?" he asked belatedly. For her bosom was brushing his front as she breathed, and his hand on her back felt the warm solidity of it. Her arms about him were physical too.

"I could do this with illusion," Idyll said. "So far I have shown you only visual illusion, but I can also do sonic, tactile, and mental illusion."

"Tactile illusion?"

A mouth kissed his mouth. But there was nothing there; Idyll's face remained before his, not touching. A hand patted his behind, but both her hands were in place holding him.

"A ghost?" he asked.

"I could emulate a ghost," she agreed. Her voice came from his right side, but her visible face was before him, not speaking. There was nothing to his right.

"Sonic illusion," he agreed. "What of mental?"

He found himself floating in space above the planet. Between the planets; the twin worlds of Charm and Counter Charm seemed to be orbiting him. This would be the vacuum of the intervening space, but he had no trouble breathing. He only *seemed* to be in emptiness.

"Mental illusion," he said. "You offered to let me possess you. Is this because of interest on your part, or to make me sexually beholden to you?"

"Interest," she replied as the office reappeared around him, the image of the Mistress in his embrace. "I am intrigued by you and would like to experience your passion, and am concerned that this can only be if you participate before you discover the reality. It is stranger to your philosophy than an animated corpse."

"Why tell me this, then? Why not fool me?"

"You are an intelligent, honorable, and motivated man. We need to have you work with us. This would be imperfect if we obtained your cooperation by deception."

"Though you have thorough tools of deception."

"We do."

"Why do you believe that converting me by deception would be an imperfect course?"

"Voila, Mino, and I explored the near future in as careful detail as was feasible. We found that the paths of your honest conversion are more successful than the paths of deception. Therefore we are following the more difficult but also more rewarding route."

Dynamo decided. "I make no commitment to your cause, but am ready to listen to your presentation. Show me what you can do as a love object, then show me the mechanism."

"Gladly, handsome man," the image of the Mistress said. "This way." She led him to a closed door, opened it, and guided him into the adjacent chamber. It was a bedroom.

In very little time the two of them were naked and disporting themselves splendidly on the bed. It might not be the true Mistress of Mistresses, but the body was perfect, and so were her responses. He kissed her, stroked her, penetrated her, and had an explosive climax. She joined him, and she was either genuinely in orgasm, or as consummate actress as the Mistress she emulated. She was not Stevia; there were subtle distinctions that made him certain of that. She was Idyll, the Ifrit Glamor, a glorious creature in every respect.

"Amazement," he said as he lay beside her. "I hope it was as good for you as it was for me."

"It was, by definition," she responded.

"Question?"

"I read your mind to borrow your passion. It was marvelously intense."

He hadn't thought of that. "But that would be male passion. Can a female relate well to that?"

"When she understands it. Next time I'll send you mine, so you can experience the female passion."

That was intriguing. "But now I need to know the reality. What really happened just now?"

She sighed. "I was hoping you would wait until after the second session."

"I'm pretty good at handling reality. I simply need to ascertain what it is."

"First, this setting is illusion, of course. Here is reality." The bedroom faded and was replaced by a blue forest glade. They were lying naked on a bank of blue moss. "This is Planet Counter Charm, as humans call it, within the Illusion Fields, which are what they took my presence to be."

"When I walked from illusion to illusion—that was all your substance?"

"To a degree. There is a natural landscape, which I adapt to my scenes. For example, this moss bank seemed the fitting underpinning for the human bed. I could have made you see and feel the bed while lying on the ground, but this is better for less effort. The illusion was mainly to delete the Blue Chroma zone and cover it with the earth office scene in your memory. Illusion is one of the most energy efficient forms of magic, along with telepathy, and much can be accomplished with it."

"So I see," he said, smiling. "I did suspect that we were not really on Earth. Instant interstellar travel has not yet been developed, and I suspect never will be."

"Agreement. I have seldom encountered it."

He paused. "Humor?"

She smiled winningly. "Affirmation, to a degree. Instant is not possible, but greatly accelerated travel is. It requires special preparations, so is not normally feasible."

"How fast between here and Earth?"

"An hour, approximately. But only Glamors could do it, and they would need ikons at each planet. Getting the ikons placed would be tedious."

Was she teasing him? He decided to leave that for another occasion. "But my interest at this state is not the background but your body. If you are an ifrit, you must be able to form into a cloud and float away."

"I am an ifrit," she agreed. "I am a cloud. But I am a large one. I cover a considerable territory, embracing several Chroma zones, and have enough substance to enable me to form a solid figure of your size without condensing the whole of my being. Thus I am both forms simultaneously, at this time."

"You are a rolling blob?" He gazed at her displayed nudity, which remained breath-catchingly lovely.

"Our natural form is the cloud, but we have learned to educate our condensed forms so as to better relate to human beings. These forms are unable to think as well as our cloud forms, but we communicate with them by gossamer tendrils so as to enable the expression of full intellect. So this form you see is a shaped blob. It is physically real, but only a portion of the whole."

"As with a soul," he said.

"Question?"

"On Earth we have a concept, perhaps mystical, of body and soul. The body is the physical component; the soul is the spiritual component. Some of us believe that the body is mortal, but the soul immortal. That it may find another body to occupy when the first body dies."

"Interest. However, both our forms are physical, merely differing in density."

"It is only an analogy, perhaps too crude to be useful. But it does help me to visualize your nature. What I see here is only the lesser portion of you."

"Concurrence. It is at the moment the portion that is not illusion. I have spent fifteen years learning the nature of human beings, and emulating their forms so as to relate better."

"How old are you?"

"This is meaningless in your terms. I was formed thousands of years ago to handle a specific problem, and look forward to dissipating when that task is done. I will exist as long as is required to see us through the third crisis."

"Three crises?"

"The first was confining Mino, the hostile machine which the humans finally nullified. The second is dealing with your attempted Earthly conquest of our planets. The third is preventing the machine culture that spawned Mino from mining our planets and destroying their magic."

"You have no instinct of self preservation?"

"Not as you do. With us it is a rational decision to protect our substance as long as we choose to exist as discrete entities. We do not fear death as you do. As I mentioned, we are not alive in the sense you are; we relate more closely to the demons, with consciousness and volition but not flesh that deteriorates when not sustained. We have however learned a number of human emotions from the humans, including the joy of sex."

"You do not reproduce sexually."

"Not in your sense. Similarly we are not male and female in your sense. But for compatibility we have adopted genders when associating with your species. I am female to the degree that any creature is."

"And you could communicate with me verbally or mentally without having a condensed body I can touch?"

"That would be easier, as I could speak directly to your mind, or generate sonic speech. Maintaining this solid form becomes a burden."

Dynamo smiled. "Then let's have that second sexual encounter now, so you can comfortably dissipate."

"Pleasure." She rolled against him, caressing and kissing him. He responded, regretting that this divine form would dissolve after they were done.

Then something wonderfully strange occurred. Part of his mind became aware of her sensations and feelings. When he stroked her breast, he felt her reception of the stroke. When he kissed her he felt her response. Guided by that feeling he did what pleased her best, kissing her nipples and clitoris, taking time to excite her flesh before moving on. Her skin became especially sensitive, reacting with heightened pleasure to his every touch. When his hard member pushed into her body, he felt her cleft receiving it, embracing it. When he thrust and spurted, he felt her answering flush of feeling, centered on the penetration but spreading throughout her body. She clasped him closely, absorbing the joy of their union. The intensity was less, the duration more, and the scale encompassing. It was a true sharing.

It was the female climax. He lay there, savoring it as it slowly faded. What an experience!

Then her body began to dissolve. He kissed her once more before her head slowly vaporized. "Thank you, Idyll," he breathed.

"Welcome," her voice said from the air before him.

"Perhaps I am being foolish," he said. "But alien to my experience as you may be, I find I love you in my fashion. Now tell me why I should betray my planet."

The body continued to evaporate, becoming a diminishing lump. "We ifrits joined the humans because we understood that despite our fundamentally distinct natures, we need each other to handle the coming challenges, beginning with Mino. Together we could survive, while apart we might not. Then Mino joined with us because of a similar need: the conquest of Charm by Earth would occur to the disadvantage of local humans, ifrits and Mino unless he joined with us to prevent it. Now Earth must join with us because otherwise Charm, Counter Charm, and Earth itself will be destroyed by the machine culture. We must unify in the face of this common threat."

"But if Mino is of the machine culture, he shouldn't object to that."

"He joined us, in the manner of oath friendship. We have enabled him to be more than he was, and his best interest no longer lies with the machines. In fact they would destroy him, because he has been corrupted. He does not want to be destroyed."

"You converted him! As you mean to convert me."

"Agreement. He is better off for it. So will you be."

"Earth means to unify the planets. That is my present mission."

"But that would be under Earth's direction. Our resources would be mercilessly exploited, and wasted, and the union would be too weak to oppose the machines. So it must be under our direction. Then, our study of the future indicates, we have a fair chance to prevail. This will be better for Earth as well as Charm and Counter Charm."

"So you don't seek to avoid conquest by Earth," he said slowly as he watched the last film of her body fade. "But to reverse it. To conquer Earth."

"Confirmation."

"I can appreciate the sense in Earth recovering her lost colony, or in decid-
ing to let that colony fend for itself. But it seems ridiculous to have the colony
take over Earth. Even if Charm somehow defeated Earth in space, it would
lack the personnel and knowledge to govern Earth effectively."

"Exactly. Hence we require your expertise to prepare for that governing.
You know and understand Earth as we do not, and you understand the mechanisms of governing your kind. We are sure we could not simply establish a
monarchy of Earth."

Dynamo laughed. "Agreement!"

"You have seen what we are capable of. Can Earth stand against that?"

"You have shown me magic. I have come reluctantly to agree that magic
exists, at least within the range of your colored volcanoes. But Earth lacks
magic. It is a science planet. Your magic won't work there. You would be powerless there."

"Science is a form of magic. It is White Chroma magic."

"So Stevia showed me. Only the White Chroma stone she gave me enables
me to keep science operative in my vicinity, and that is depleted when I do it.
But Earth is not a single stone or Chroma zone. It is a science planet, with no
other magic. And maybe not even exactly that, because our people, creature,
and landscapes are not all white, but of many colors, all relating to science.
Only your White Chroma folk could operate there—and Earth's science is far
more advanced than yours. There is no contest."

"The four Glamors traveling to Earth possess special magic powders we
developed that will convert a number of Earth's volcanoes to other Chroma.
Our magic will then work on Earth as it does here."

He shook his head. "It takes years for Chroma folk to develop their magic
talents. Earth's science will destroy the other magics long before they become
effective."

"Except that science magic will not work within range of any of the
otherChroma volcanoes—or in the regions between them, when they are close
to each other, which will become nonChroma as the magic is changed. They
will be reduced to primitive weapons such as swords and bows. Your civilization will collapse to the extent it is governed by science alone and Earth will
revert to relative barbarism."

"How can you be sure of that?"

"Mino sees the far future. Actually he sees a number of far future paths;
which one occurs is determined by the near future, which is one reason Voila
was able to defeat him. She selected the future that favored the humans over
the machines, at least for now. But we worked together to fathom the intermediate future. That shows what I have described, unless we can act to prevent it.
That is why we need you. You must help us save your world from the disaster
that threatens it now, and in the farther future."

Dynamo did not like it at all, but his reasoning suggested that if what they
said was true, that they were converting Earth's volcanoes, that collapse of
civilization would indeed occur. Everything depended on science; if that were
lost, there would indeed be barbarism. Could he afford to gamble that those
volcanoes would not be converted?

He decided to compromise. "I do not know whether your ploy will work. If
it does, Earth will need to be saved. If it does not, it is Charm that will need the
help. I will volunteer to train your natives to administer either planet, depend-

ing on how it turns out. If Charm wins, they will go to administer Earth, to help it avoid a new dark age. If Earth wins, they will serve as an interim government in lieu of the present one while true Earthers train in. Thus I will not be playing false to either planet, but will be helping the winner to avoid ruining the loser."

"That will do," Idyll replied. "I am sending out the word so that prospective administrators can be recruited. You will be quite busy these next few months. Would you like another session with my condensed form before you depart?"

"Would you? Emulating the Mistress?"

"Affirmation."

"Affirmation," he echoed.

Idyll's Mistress replica began to form.

Chapter 9
Warp

Ine stayed with Warp the night Mistress Marionette was away delivering Weft to the opera company. "So how are you finding her?" the Sorceress inquired as she brought him to a beautiful climax.

He squeezed her deliciously invisible body. "Amazing! She's almost as good as you."

She laughed. "Observation: You are learning false flattery! She's better for you than I am, and we both know it."

"Question."

"Answer: She is younger than I am by a decade, being only 22, closer to your age. She is prettier than I, being crafted by surgery to be among Earth's most beautiful in every physical respect. She is more accommodating, as her entire training has been to evoke passion in men."

"Debate: your age gives you authority that bends me to your will. Your body feels perfect to me regardless, and with illusion you can be THE prettiest woman extant. And your magic makes you her superior in any other type of ability. You are no woman's inferior, and I am halfway smitten with you as my father Havoc is with the Lady Symbol of your Air Chroma."

She kissed him. "Preference: Let me have at you again, sweet boy, before I refute those points."

"Have at me five times in five minutes, if you wish, divine creature."

She took him literally, as he intended, and brought him off five successive times within the set period. "Now let me empty myself, for you have filled me to capacity, virile lover," she said teasingly.

He watched as the blob of his ejaculated substance floated to the toilet and slid into it. He could see her if he focused, but it was more fun letting her be invisible. The sight of her ablution turned him on again. She picked up his thought and returned to him for another collection.

"Ine, I know you are here to cover my sexual precocity," he said as he embraced her. "So that I won't do something foolish like falling for Marionette. I know you are catering to me in a calculated way. But in this excursion to Earth, where we are among potential enemies, you alone truly understand me, apart from siblings, who don't count in this respect. That does make me love you."

"Aura understands you, and she's only three years older than I am. She could handle you."

"True. But she needs to be with Flame, while you will stay with me. And of course she's married."

"That does complicate things a bit," she agreed with an invisible smile. "I escaped that fate, by the sufferance of your father. Though I still wouldn't mind settling down with the right man and bearing my four."

"You could do it with me."

"And I would, Warp, if that were appropriate. You are a king's son and a Glamor. That means more than the ability to climax virtually continuously." That was perhaps the understatement of the month.

"Marionette would not understand about that," he agreed. "I must feign depletion with her, at least for a few minutes."

"But I think your future is elsewhere than with me. It may in fact be with Marionette."

"Surprise: With her?"

"Perspective: She is your enemy now, but she is also a fine, talented, and lovely woman with formidable Earthly political connections. She could be extremely useful to us as your supportive wife."

"But she wouldn't marry me unless she loved me."

"There is your challenge, Warp. You can fascinate her back, if you try. You might start by persuading her to get us onto the Earth Fleet flagship." She did not clarify why such a visit was worthwhile; that was part of the hidden agenda. They knew that all their actions and spoken words were recorded and analyzed by Earther officials. Only *some* Charmer secrets were shared at this point.

He considered carefully. Accomplishing this was probably within his parameters. "Revelation: this may be my necessary course. But winning a woman like that will be difficult. She's too experienced for me to deceive long."

Ine smiled; he felt the expression against his anatomy. "Call on me at need. I do know something of the female state."

He kissed her and plumbed her again. "You are here to prevent me from being led astray by my penis, yet you recommend that I court an enemy woman."

"The difference is that you must be in command, Warp. If it doesn't work out, I will still be here."

"But I will never command you."

"That is another reason she is better for you. There are others." Let the Earther spies mull over that. It was an invitation for Marionette to take him seriously, knowing that he was interested in marrying her. The Earther authorities might well come to a similar conclusion: that she should do it. Once they saw more of what was happening.

"Plea. Do not refute me. Let me love you this night, before I have to refocus elsewhere."

"Mutual," she agreed, kissing him.

Ine had to empty herself several more times before they slept. Warp knew she liked him, and not merely because he was the king's son and a Glamor, but also knew that she had spoken truth. She understood him and his capacities, and readily accommodated them, which counted for much in their relationship. But she had thorough adult perspective, while he was a juvenile, and it showed. And the paths of the near future were more positive for their mission if he went after Marionette.

Marionette returned in the morning. If she knew of Warp's night with Ine— as she surely did—she hardly cared, and would not have believed that he had jetted into her 32 times, once for each year of her age, in the course of an hour. Not until she viewed the recording. The Mistress seemed happy to accommodate his eager need for her, as if he had spent the night alone and frustrated.

"You have big ideas. And why is it you do it so much more often with Miss Invisible than with me?" she inquired when he affected satisfaction after a single climax.

So she was telling him she had already seen, so that this aspect was no secret between them. By similar token, she was letting him know that she knew the nature of his interest in her. The game was on.

"How many times do you wish?"

"Number is less important than quality. Can you make me climax?"

"Do you wish to?"

"No."

"Then it is a suitable challenge. Is it a bet?"

She smiled. "Agreement. What terms?"

"Give me one hour. If I fail in that time, you win and I will do you a favor of your choice. If I win, you will do me one."

"Other than sexual?"

"Affirmation."

"Half an hour."

"Time begins now." He had at her, and she cooperated, but withheld her own joy of the occasion. She was a consummate sexual actress, long accustomed to the pretense of arousal and consummation, but on this occasion she made it clear that she was a body without passion. He was getting nowhere despite employing techniques that had seemed to excite her before. That was a small education in itself, though probably it made a huge difference whether she did or did not want to be aroused.

Ine, he thought.

Kiss her mouth. Kiss her nipples. Then kiss her clitoris and stay with it. I will guide you on technique.

He did as directed, his touch becoming more delicate than he had employed with any woman before. He teased her vulva and clitoris with his tongue, barely touching them. She began to respond, but Ine stifled his urge to bear down more solidly. Feather light he teased the cleft until at last her body shuddered and heated, and she sighed. She had suffered her climax despite her will.

Do not stop, Ine advised.

He continued, though his penis was stiff and almost dripping. Soon Marionette sighed again, and then a third time. Then at last she yielded. "Your victory, Warp," she gasped. "But it is unsatisfying alone. Enter me violently. Fill me with your passion."

He was glad to oblige, thrusting and spurting a good volume, and she joined him in pleasure, climaxing a fourth time. "I underestimated you," she confessed. "I thought you did not know the art of pleasing a woman."

"I didn't," he said honestly. "Until you required it."

"It seems I owe you a favor, or several."

"One is enough. I enjoyed bringing you pleasure, and wanted you to have more of it."

"Unwilling pleasure. No one has done that to me before."

Then he made his request. "Desire: I want to see the space fleet."

She pretended to be taken aback, though this had been in his dialogue with Ine. "What interest does this have for you, Warp? I thought you folk of the volcano planet were more interested in volcanoes."

"That too, of course. But I am interested in Earth's Science power, and this is the main evidence of it. We have no such fleet at Charm. I'd like to see the ships first. Ine is interested too."

"I will see what I can do, as agreed. Perhaps we can make a deal."

"Question?"

"Tourist tours of the fleet are not encouraged. But if you came as an entertainer, they might more readily agree."

"You want me to tell a tale!"

She nodded seriously. "Warp, for two months you fascinated the crew of the *Dominance* during the dull voyage home. Routine patrol duty in space also tends to be dull. You could entertain them for a couple of hours in exchange for a tour of the flagship. It would be a fair bargain."

"Agreement."

"Can you spare me for an hour while I pull a string?"

"Reluctance," he said, smiling.

"I may have to invoke my durable power of attorney on your behalf. We'll see."

"Question?"

"That would be complicated to explain. Trust me, for now."

"Trust," he agreed.

She kissed him and departed. Now he noticed that she did not pause to clean herself, this time; her vaginal control was such that she did not leak despite the volume of fluid he had just pumped into her. Ine was right about that: this woman was better, sexually. For him, at least.

Appreciation, Ine, he thought. *I could not have done it alone.*

Welcome.

Meanwhile, what was he to do in the intervening hour?

Flame appeared. "Answer: You look for a volcano," she said, answering his thought. Naturally the remaining siblings had tuned into his session with Marionette, and Flame was no longer sexually inexperienced. They all enjoyed vicarious sex as well as direct sex, tuning into the orgasmic passion.

"That would have to be another trip."

"Negation. They have marvelous devices to generate what they call holos, just like illusion shows. I have been learning to operate them. I did a search on volcanoes. They have some fascinating ones."

"Like that old cinder cone Grumble told you about?" he asked derisively. "I want a bigger bang."

"I think I knew the one. Krakatau erupted in 1883, their ancient chronology, before the women took control. There was a masculine effort for you. It was said to have been the loudest sound ever documented, heard up to three thousand miles away. In two days it discharged four cubic miles of material. It generated tsunamis galore and killed 36,000 people."

"Sunamis?"

"Tsunamis. It's a new term to me too. It's a huge wave in the ocean. We don't have oceans on Charm, so no tsunamis. They form when rock moves in the sea, disturbing the water. They don't look like much as they ripple through deep water; ships hardly notice them. But when they hit shallow water, all that energy causes the waves to rise up high, and they smash across the coasts destroying trees, buildings, people—anything that's there. They are among the worst of Earth's natural disasters, though now they work harder to detect them in time to get out of their way. That wasn't always the case on ancient Earth, and thousands of people died."

He nodded. "Agreement: that is interesting."

She brought out a small control device and twiddled it. A picture formed before them. "This is a reconstruction," she said. "Of how it must have been."

"Why not the original eruption?"

"Because there is nothing left there. It blew itself away. And of course they didn't have holo cameras then."

"Accepted," he said grudgingly.

The holo image expanded to fill the chamber, making them part of the scene. They were standing on a promontory some distance from the volcano, which was smoking.

"Not closer, because that would be in the killing range," Flame explained.

The great cone shook, rising and swelling as if being inflated from below. The very stone seemed to bend with the force of the rising magma. It was always a pleasure to appreciate the incidental power of a volcano.

Then it burst. The top shot straight up into the atmosphere, leading a plume of fiery smoke. The sound boomed out deafeningly: CRASH! But of course it was muted to protect the viewers.

The column of smoke expanded, twisting and roiling internally. Fire coated its coils, and lightning speared through it. Still the stuff was forging from the cone. Each time it seemed to ease off, new material forged out, filling the atmosphere, generating darkness by day.

Something fell near them with a smelly plop. "Hot mud," Flame said, as if he didn't know. "Water mixes with the ash. All of it is dangerous."

Warp gazed at the thundering cloud. This was, indeed, his kind of show. He missed the glorious Chroma volcanoes of Charm. Where would any of the Glamors be, without that constant magic?

It culminated in the worst explosion of all, blasting rock, ash, gas, and water into the sky. Their site was blown away, leaving them standing in darkness: a nice effect.

Finally the cloud of ash faded, leaving nothing but water. "The caldera collapsed," Flame explained. "It threw its own magma chamber out, and the surrounding land and sea fell into the hole. It was probably the shock of the cold sea hitting the hot chamber and vaporizing that made the final explosion."

"Appreciation," he said. "This is my kind of diversion."

"And it's not even the worst. In 1815 of their ancient history the island of Tambora erupted, putting out about twenty cubic miles of ejecta into the air. The ash overwhelmed the sunlight; they called it the year without a summer."

"Our Charm volcanoes are little compared to these."

"Agreement. Ours erupt fairly constantly, while Earth's may accumulate pressure for centuries, than blow it all out at once. It can make a spectacular show."

"Appreciation, Flame," he repeated. "But time remains. Can your research help me with another item?"

"Question."

"What is a durable power of attorney?"

Flame smiled. "I already researched that. Mistress Marionette has it for the four of us. It means she can act on our behalf, because we are presumed to be incompetent and to lack legal standing on planet Earth."

"Incompetent!"

She kissed him in sisterly fashion. She had mellowed since her affair with Grumble. "You're cute when outraged, brother dear. Fear not: it is a legal term. We are not citizens of Earth, and are beneath Earth's legal age of consent, so a qualified adult must represent us here. It is actually to protect us from exploitation. Marionette really does have our interests at heart. Anyone who wants to abuse us must get through her, and she's a mistress. It is excellent protection."

He sighed. "And I thought she just liked my virility."

She laughed. "That, too." She turned serious. "Ine is right: Marionette is worth your while. She has been helping us throughout: me with Grumble, Weft with her opera, you with your tour, all of us with our freedom. She made us royal guests instead of royal hostages. We could hardly have a better friend in court. Win her, Warp."

He nodded. He respected his sister's grasp of tactics. "Appreciation," he said a third time.

"Noted."

In an hour Marionette returned. "Approval for me to bring you and Ine to the flagship this afternoon, by our current time. As entertainers."

"Accepted." Thanks to Flame's insight, he now regarded the mistress as more than a sexual object.

"The fleet is commanded by Admiral Vitality, assisted by Mistress Morsel."

"Such names no more humorous than, say Warp and Weft?"

"Not at all humorous," she agreed with the trace of a smile.

They boarded a shuttle that boosted them to the flagship orbiting Earth, the *Ms Victory*. This was a giant vessel, much larger than the *Ms Dominance* they had arrived aboard. They docked and were ushered in to meet Admiral Vitality. With him stood Mistress Morsel. He looked vigorous; she delectable. But she was of course the true commander.

The two mistresses embraced and kissed. They were different women, of separate ages and appearance, yet there was a considerable similarity of shape and manner. "Mistress Morsel, this is my charge Warp, prince of colony Charm, and Ine, maid to the royal siblings. They are here to entertain the crews."

"Crews?" Morsel inquired, delicately lifting an eyebrow.

"I suspect you will want to connect the other ships of the fleet."

"They are that good?"

"I believe so."

Morsel made a moue. "Perhaps it will be done."

The admiral immediately signaled an officer. It would indeed be done. The mistresses did not issue commands, they only suggested—but their suggestions were laws to men.

They were given a nice tour of the ship. Warp was openly impressed. "This is like Pyramid," he remarked.

"Pyramid is the capital city of Colony Charm," Marionette murmured. "It floats on a pond and has multiple levels, the peak occupied by the royal palace."

"Nice analogy," the admiral agreed gruffly. It was subtly apparent that this tour was not his preference, but he obeyed his directive.

They passed a sealed hatch. "Curiosity," Warp said, recognizing a key area.

"The locale of the master code," the admiral said shortly.

"Confusion."

Vitality hesitated, but the mistress nodded. "The Earth Fleet consists of forty three ships of the line and numerous lesser vessels. They normally operate independently, but at need can become slave ships directed by a program issuing from this one. We do not want any unauthorized intrusion, as you might appreciate."

Confirmation! This was what they were looking for. But Warp affected boredom. "Slavery is not a thing I understand." He walked on. They did not correct his supposed confusion about human and machine slaves.

The admiral was glad to move on. They saw the crews' barracks, the day rooms, the mess halls, and even a sample head: the place of urination and defecation. Warp had of course seen it on the *Dominance*, but never fathomed why the place of refuse should be termed like a place of leadership. For that matter, he was bemused that the place of eating should be likened to extreme disorder: the mess.

Then they met a few of the crew members, male and female. "Curiosity," Warp said, sensing an intriguing situation. "How is it that some crew folk are female? All were male on the *Ms Dominance*."

"We prefer to keep our women closer to home," the admiral said. "Exploratory missions may be dangerous."

"And local combat is not?"

"There has been little combat in the past century. The mistresses favor peace." The admiral did not seem entirely pleased. Mistress Morsel smiled tolerantly.

"Do men and women share rooms?"

"Most do," the admiral said. "There are more males than females, so some males must sleep alone. The mistress sees to them."

"Do any females sleep alone?"

"At present, only one."

"Why?"

The admiral glanced at the mistress, clearly ill at ease. "Whistle blower."

"Confusion."

"She reported an irregularity," Morsel said. "This is permitted but not approved. Crewmen do not wish to associate with her lest they too be tainted."

Warp was interested. "They are angry because of what she did?"

"By no means," Morsel said. "They approve. Her report was correct. But her future as a member of Earth's Navy is in doubt. It is called retaliation."

"Because she did what was right?"

"Because she embarrassed her superiors."

"And you tolerate this?"

"We prefer not to overrule the chain of command without clear reason," Morsel said. "The issue has alternate interpretations."

"Maybe I can change that."

Both admiral and mistress gazed at him, their courtesy bordering on hostility. They did not seem to like interference by outsiders.

"Shall we adjourn to the theater?" Mistress Marionette suggested, smoothly changing the subject.

But Warp was not embarrassed. There had been a purpose to his inquiry.

The theater chamber was circular, set up in accordance with Marionette's private suggestion. Crew members sat on every side of the slightly raised central platform. Holo cameras oriented on it. There were no stage props. Every Fleet person present, from mistress and admiral down, seemed dubious. How was this colony yokel going to entertain them on a bare stage?

Warp nodded. This was perfect. He glanced at Marionette, who was restraining a smile; she knew what to expect, in general if not in detail.

It was time. Warp stepped onto the stage. "A greeting, Earth Fleet crews," he said. "I am Warp, son of King Havoc of Colony Planet Charm, hostage to my father's decision whether to accept Earth's dominance. I am a tale teller, and I will tell you a tale you will remember."

There was no reaction. They were waiting for him to properly make a fool of himself.

"But first I want to introduce my companion, Ine. She is invisible." He beckoned Ine, stepping to the side himself.

She stepped onto the stage, thoroughly swathed. Her fine shape was evident through the cloth, but that was all.

Then she started removing items. First her veil, and she turned around showing her facelessness to the full circle. Then her headcloth, and her head was gone. Now there was no question of lagging attention. None of the members of this fleet had been told of the Chroma colors.

She doffed her shirt, then her skirt, and stood in bra and panties, turning again. Then her slippers and stockings. Finally the last underwear dropped to the floor and she was completely invisible.

Mouths had fallen open.

The pile of discarded clothing lifted and floated off the stage. Ine had finished.

Warp resumed the floor. "Now you have a notion how things are on my planet," he said. "We are not like you folk of Earth. Our people are all colors, including invisible. We practice magic. We have our own conventions, and do not wish to be incorporated back into the Earth scheme. But that is a matter for others to decide. I am here to tell a story, in return for your kind tourist guidance. We have no spaceships orbiting Charm."

There was a subdued chuckle. Now they were more interested in what he had to say. Ine had been an effective attention getter, and he was building on that. "Once upon a time, before the mistresses took over, in the bad old days of male dominance on Earth, there was a rich old man."

Some nodded; this was a familiar opening. Warp had learned the forms during the two month voyage to Earth, and could relate well to an Earther audience. He could relate well to *any* audience; it was his special art. It wasn't just his ready ability to tell a story; he picked up the mental ambiance, and was constantly aware of audience reaction.

"This man was named Corsair, for in his heyday he had been much like a swift pirate ship. In the course of building his wealth he had made many illustrious enemies and few real friends. He had hardly cared in youth and middle age; power and wealth were his goals and his life. But now he was old, and his powers of mind and body were fading. He knew that in time he would be unable to protect himself, and would be murdered or cheated of his fortune. He did not want to go foolishly into that abyss, but he trusted none of his associates, with excellent reason. He was an aging shark in a hungry school. What was he to do?" Warp gazed up at the ceiling fan that slowly wafted the ship's air, keeping it circulating, pausing for effect.

"Then his cunning mind hit upon a scheme. He would turn over his affairs to someone he could trust to protect him. Someone with loyalty, competence, and guts. He would sign over a durable power of attorney to such a person before he lost his mental or legal ability to decide. Then he would be able to relax and enjoy his retirement."

Warp walked around the stage as if deep in thought. "But who?" he asked rhetorically. "Who had the necessary qualities? He was surrounded by sharks. They had been fine when he had power over them and they knew it. Now their eyes were turning increasingly on him. None of them would do. Any of them would betray him the moment they had power to do so."

Warp continued speaking, getting into the role. He was Corsair, pondering his options. He extended his search outward from his closest associates, looking for the particular qualities required. And finally he found them. Not in one person, but two, each of which had some. He met with his lawyer and made the arrangement. It would take effect only when triggered: when he was declared legally incompetent to manage his own affairs. And he knew who was most likely to pull that trigger.

Corsair had a trophy girlfriend, a truly beautiful woman and a phenomenal schemer. It was time to yield to her entreaties. Her name was Corset, for her figure looked as if shaped by one. She was never so lovely as when she was ardently scheming.

Marionette walked onto the stage, garbed provocatively. The audience took immediate note, especially the males: this was a new mistress to them, young and completely shapely. She was actually playing a part in this story? "Darling!" she exclaimed, planting a calculated kiss on him. "You look tired. Let me cheer you."

Actually Marionette did not speak; Warp spoke for her. She merely acted as his narrative directed. This distinction would soon enough be effectively tuned out by the audience.

"Thank you, Corset," Corsair said as she arranged him on the floor and massaged his back. "You are such a comfort to a feeble old man."

"Well, I love you, Corsair," she replied insincerely. "You know I'd do anything for you." She turned him over and massaged his front side. "But I am concerned for your health. If anything should happen to you, what would become of me?"

"I am inevitably growing older," Corsair said. "Have you a treatment to prevent that?"

Corset considered. "Not precisely," she said after a moment. "But I can recommend the next best thing."

"And what would that be, my gentle-handed dear?"

"Give me your durable power of attorney, my love. Then I will be able to take all those nasty little details off your hands and make you perpetually happy." She took one of his hands and lifted it to her heaving breast.

"Oh, I wouldn't want to burden you with such a chore," he protested. "You are far too pretty and sweet to suffer those complicated details."

"But for you I will do it," she said. "I want to take care of you, Corsair."

She surely did! But not in the way she hinted. Yet he pretended to believe her. "Then maybe I had better do it. I will see my lawyer tomorrow."

"That calculating cheat? I have a better lawyer you can see today."

"Then I suppose I should see him," Corsair agreed.

He saw the lawyer. He signed the documents the shyster put before him, pretending not to be aware that they were not precisely as represented. His signature was duly notarized, and the documents were given to a judge. It was done.

"Now make me perpetually happy," Corsair said, seeking to embrace her.

She pulled away. "Are you crazy, you shriveled old man? I'm going to get me a young healthy potent lover."

"But you told me you wanted to take care of me!"

"And I have done so, idiot. Don't you know what you signed?"

"A durable power of attorney."

"And a legal admission of incompetence. You are no longer allowed to handle your legal or financial affairs. Those are now in my hands. You're through, Corsair. Go suffer your dotage somewhere else."

Corsair pretended to be aghast. "But I trusted you!"

"The more fool you. All I ever wanted was your money. Your dehydrated touch makes my skin crawl. Now get out of my sight, you sniveling has-been. I can't stand the stink of you."

She had revealed her true nature, which was exactly what he had suspected. Evincing dejection, he walked away from her. How long would it take for her to catch on to the truth?

About half an hour, as it turned out, when she first tried to use her new power of attorney to draw a huge sum of money. "What?" she screeched, outraged.

"Your signature is not valid," the banker told her. "You can't draw money from this or any Corsair account. You're broke, scheming woman. You had better get a job servicing horny fishmongers."

There was a murmur of humor through the audience. No one talked to a mistress that way. Of course no one was; Warp was merely narrating the tale, speaking for the woman and the banker (the bit part played by the admiral, who surely relished being this verbally clever), while Marionette stood there emulating the simulated fury of Corset. This was fun for all concerned: Narrator, actress, actor, and audience.

"What happened?" Corset demanded.

"Corsair was on to you throughout, you twit," the helpful banker informed her. "He assigned a durable power of attorney to two other people weeks ago, to be automatically invoked at such time as he was declared legally incompetent. Now that you have taken care of that, the power of his estate devolves on them. There's nothing you can do about it, you justly-served harridan."

But Corset was not one to lie down submissively when not with her potent young boyfriend. "Who are they?"

"I wouldn't know, you has-been slut. They are now being summoned to the court for instruction. Better get your sorry posterior there to find out."

Corset didn't try to argue. She got her sorry posterior over to her lawyer (also played by the admiral). "You nincompoop!" she screamed. "You messed up the papers!"

"I did nothing of the kind, fool," the lawyer retorted.

"I paid you handsomely to set it all up, you ingrate!"

The lawyer smiled. "But Corsair paid me twice as much to do it his way. Now I can retire with moderate wealth, you simpleton witch. Go scheme elsewhere; I don't want to see your butt again unless it's bare and greased and begging for a virile libation. Then maybe I'll summon my pet boar hog."

The narrative had to pause while the audience's open laughter ran its course. Even Mistress Morsel and Admiral Vitality allowed faint smiles to crack through their impassive countenances. He couldn't help it; this role was endearing him to the troops in a way no command decision could. There was something about a well turned insult, especially a sexual one delivered to a mistress. Only Marionette's frown remained in place, necessarily; she had her part to play.

Suddenly Corset wasn't getting any respect: exactly the fate she had thought to inflict on Corsair. She did not very much appreciate it. She moved on to the court.

The Judge (admiral, again) was about to address two frightened people the authorities had brought in. One was an indifferent young man. The other was a halfway pretty young woman.

Warp paused. "I need two more volunteer actors," he said. He gazed across the audience. "You, if you please." He indicated a lowly crewman. The man, astonished, looked at his sergeant, who looked in turn at his lieutenant, who looked at his captain, who looked at the admiral. The admiral glanced at Mistress Morsel, who nodded. The nods returned on down the chain of command, in due course reaching the crewman, who stood and walked to the stage.

"Thank you," Warp said warmly. "You are now Corvee, one of the two main characters in this story. The name means a day of unpaid labor required of serfs by the feudal lord. Simply follow the story line as I present it."

Corvee nodded, bemused but evidently rather pleased to be selected. Audience members generally were; it was a special and easy notoriety. This story had already become permanently memorable because of the utilization of a mistress and the admiral. Warp had picked this crewman because a quick telepathic check indicated that he had a thing for a certain young woman, but lacked the pretext to approach her.

Warp returned to the story. As Corsair he watched the legal proceedings.

Corvee stood before the Judge. "You are Corvee, noted primarily for fighting, drinking, gambling, and whoring?" the Judge demanded.

There was another murmur of humor in the audience. It was fun seeing one of their own number teased like this. That was another aspect of this form of narration: it became part of the audience.

"Yes, Your Honor," Corvee responded abjectly, and the actor hung his head, getting into the role. "But whatever it is this time, I didn't do it. I was asleep when they arrested me."

"You are now the holder of one half of the durable power of attorney for Corsair, the piratical billionaire who has been declared incompetent," the Judge pronounced.

"Your Honor," Corvee protested. "I don't even know what that means."

The Judge rolled his eyes. (The admiral was very good at doing that.) "I don't have time to educate ignoramuses."

Corset saw her chance and stepped forward. "Your Honor, I will volunteer to educate him."

The Judge made a dismissive gesture. "So ordered."

Corset took Corvee by the hand and led him to a private chamber. The audience was amazed to see a mistress participating like this with an ordinary crewman instead of the admiral, and of course the man himself was thrilled. "First it would help me to know what your connection is to Corsair. Then I can clarify your court-ordered obligation. Do you know him?"

"Well, sure, or at least I used to, in a way," Corvee said. "I got in a real mess a few years back and was in juvenile detention with not much hope of reprieve. Then suddenly they called me up and told me Corsair had paid my fine and set me up to go to a trade school where I could learn to be a good citizen. And I did, and when I got out I got a decent job. They didn't ask what I did on my free time."

"Wine, women, and song," Corset said.

"More or less. I never even met Corsair, and don't know why he helped me like that. But I can tell you, if I ever have a chance to do him a favor back, I'm sure game for it. I'd still be in the can, if it weren't for him."

Corset nodded. Now she understood why this man had been selected. Corsair wanted loyalty, and this man would give it. Fortunately he was too ignorant to know the full significance of the power vested in him. She knew how to handle that.

"Thank you, Corvee," she said. "The durable power of attorney means that you now have the right to make decisions that Corsair would have made himself, before he became incompetent. To act in his best interest."

"But I can't do that!" Corvee protested. "I don't know anything about piratical finance."

"Fortunately I am here to help you," Corset said reassuringly. "All you have to do is what I say, and we will both be far better off."

Corvee took a good look at her. He was ignorant of high finance, but he did know quite a bit about scheming women, and instantly recognized her as one. Also a beautiful one. That made a difference. "I don't know. I think I better find out more about this first."

"There is no need," she said anxiously. "We can work together. I'm sure I can satisfy you."

In any other situation Corvee would have been quite interested in what she had in mind. But Corsair was the one person to whom he owed a debt of gratitude, and that was not to be lightly dismissed. He was not about to play his benefactor false. Not even for a luscious hussy like this. It was a matter of the only honor he possessed. "No."

"Let me persuade you." She put one hand to her décolletage.

"Look, lady," he said uneasily. "I know you have the body, and I'd love to plumb it a time or three. But I owe Corsair, and I have to do what's right for him. That's not what you're after. So it's still no."

"But you haven't yet appreciated my case," she said, opening her shirt to show her fine breasts. She wore no undergarment. The male portion of the audience was of course rapt as the actress did this.

"I see your case," he said. "It's got two of the finest knockers ever. But—"

Corset removed her shirt. She turned around once, breathing deeply.

"It's no good," Corvee said. "I won't betray Corsair."

She drew down her skirt and panties. She bent to remove her slippers, managing to show Corvee and the audience everything before straightening up again. This was an actress who was proud of her body.

"I have to go," Corvee said. He recognized dangerous temptation when he saw it.

"Not yet, I think," Corset said. "Watch this." She went into a languorous dance, her breasts, buttocks, and belly bouncing and flexing intriguingly. She lifted a leg, caught it by one hand, and held it pointing at the sky as she slowly turned in a full circle. She made an athletic cartwheel, and landed with her ankles on his shoulders. Not even all mistresses could do such motions. "Are you sure you won't reconsider?" she asked.

Corvee stared into her crevice. "I—" He licked his lips. He knew he would never have access to a body like this if he didn't agree to her suit now. "I— can't."

She twisted her feet smoothly to the floor and came up against him. "I don't believe I heard that."

"I can't to it," he said. It was the hardest decision he had ever made.

"Fool!" she cried, slapping him. Then she turned and stalked away.

Corvee stood alone. His body was painfully aroused. But what else could he have done? He owed Corsair.

Now Warp paused again. "I need another volunteer. A woman." He gazed across the audience, and oriented on one particular crewgirl. The woman who had blown the whistle and been ostracized. "You," he said, abruptly indicating her.

She did not react, not believing it. Warp glanced at Mistress Morsel. She nodded, appreciating what he was doing. The woman, thus directed, stood and walked to the stage.

"You are Corsage," Warp told her. "The hired servant of the niece of Corsair, who did the lazy niece's homework for school, performed her required exercises for health, and lied to cover it up, serving as directed. As a result the niece became fat and stupid, while you became fit and smart. You were scrupulous in your behavior, and never stole from the family, despite opportunities. You got no thanks for this from the niece, but Corsair noticed."

Warp resumed the formal narration: Meanwhile back in the courtroom the Judge was focusing on the young woman. "Are you the erstwhile household servant girl Corsage?"

"I am, Your Honor. But I never wished that household any harm. I don't know why they should report me."

"You are now the holder of one half of the durable power of attorney for Corsair, the piratical billionaire who has been declared incompetent," the Judge pronounced exactly as before. "Do you understand? Are you ready to assume this duty?"

Corsage collapsed in a swoon. The actress might have come close to similar behavior, had the admiral addressed her like this in any other context.

"I will take that as agreement," the Judge said. "Take her to a recovery room." He glanced at the lawyers. "Next case."

A stout court woman lifted Corsage up and bore her to a separate chamber. She left her there to recover on her own. It was a busy court.

In due course Corsage woke, and after a brief period of disorientation recovered her bearings. She had been given a durable power of attorney for her erstwhile employer Corsair. She had met the man only once, when he visited his niece, and thought he hadn't noticed her. Why had he done this?

Before she felt steady enough to stand and walk out, a lovely woman entered the chamber. "Hello, Corsage," she said. "I am Corset, Corsair's mistress. Through some error in paperwork the power of attorney intended for me was instead vested in you. All you need to do is come with me to sign the papers of transferal, and all well be well."

But Corsage was no ignoramus. Neither was she fascinated by the woman's body, which was significantly more shapely than her own. She knew Corset by reputation: the schemer of schemers who had dazzled Corsair but it seemed not entirely deceived him. "Thank you, no. I will do what Mr. Corsair requests of me, to the best of my ability."

"Your attitude is commendable," Corset said as if she had expected this response. "However, I happen to know that your financial means are limited. I can rectify that. I can arrange for a chalet for you in a distant vacation resort, with a guaranteed income for life. You need never serve an ungrateful girl again."

That set Corsage back. This woman evidently knew something about her situation. But it did not change her mind. "Master Corsair has placed his faith in me, and I shall try my utmost to be worthy of it. The position he has bequeathed me is a signal honor, and carries with it a prescribed payment for service that should enable me to meet the required performance. So I thank you for your interest, but am declining your kind offer."

Translation: get lost, bitch.

The audience liked that, too. The character Corsage was showing merit. Many of the female crew were identifying with her: a completely ordinary young woman achieving a better place in life and proving worthy. In addition, this was not unlike blowing the whistle.

Corset saw that she was having no more luck with this one than she had with the other. She masked her ire. "Then we shall try another way. Enjoy your position, Corsage, brief as it may be." She departed.

Corsage recognized trouble. She knew that Corsair had many powerful enemies, and Corset would likely go to some of them to pursue her ill ends. Something needed to be done soon.

First she had better get together with the other share holder of the power of attorney, for they would have to work together. Why the old man had set it up that way she had no idea, but he surely had reason. She left the chamber, passed through the courtroom unnoticed, and went to the chamber where Corvee had been taken.

He remained there, looking out of sorts. She was not surprised; she had a notion what kind of suasion Corset might have used on him. "May we talk?" she inquired.

He jumped, not having seen her. "Who are you?"

"I am Corsage. The other power-of-attorney person. I suspect we need to work together."

"Oh. Yes. Of course. I am Corvee. I don't know why Corsair picked me; I'm not versed in any of his business."

"You are versed in fighting, drinking, gambling, and whoring, according to the Judge," she said. "I am little better off; I was a house servant. But Corsair must have had reason."

Corvee gazed at her appraisingly. "You're a halfway pretty and innocent girl."

"Thank you," she said somewhat coldly. "I am not one of your whores."

"I didn't mean it like that. You're definitely not my type."

She did not thaw. "Nor are you my type. Now that we have settled that, I think we should try to come to understand why Corsair selected either of us for this important office."

"That may be the only thing we are likely to agree on. The old guy never struck me as a fool, but this seems pretty foolish. So what are we missing?"

"Perhaps we should ask him."

He laughed. "Where do we find him? At the graveyard or looney bin?"

She frowned. "He's not dead or incarcerated. You didn't know?"

Corvee made a soundless whistle. "I just assumed that no person alive and sane would turn over his rights like this. He's not out of it? I'm glad to hear it. So where do we find him?"

"At his palatial residence, surely. I am familiar with it. Shall we go?"

"Together? I thought you didn't like me."

"I don't. But if we have to work together, we had better do it. Just keep yours hands to yourself, if you please. This way." She walked out of the chamber.

He followed. "If I could keep my hands off that luscious jezebel, I can keep them off you."

Corsage yielded to female curiosity. "What did she offer you?"

"You know what she offered me! You aren't *that* innocent."

"But isn't she your type?"

"She sure is. Not that I'd trust her farther than I could heave her without hands."

"How could you heave her without hands?"

"With my third leg."

"I don't understand."

Corvee just looked at her. Then she caught on, and colored. "That's disgusting."

"I'm a gutter type guy."

Corsage regrouped. "So why did you turn her down?"

"Corsair did me a real favor a few years back. I owe him. Now that he's asking me for that favor back, I'm going to deliver, no matter what. To the best of my limited ability. That schemer won't do him any good."

She affected surprise. "Do you mean you actually have a modicum of decency?"

He stared at the ground. "Nobody's perfect."

Corsage nodded to herself. Her dislike of him had just taken a hit. He was a *loyal* gutter-type.

They reached the mansion. A uniformed guard stood at the stately front entrance. "They won't let us in without pedigrees," Corvee said.

"Granted." Corsage guided him around to the small side door and punched in a code. "Servants don't go through that rigamarole." The door opened and they entered a small chamber with a picture of an old pirate on the wall.

Corvee nodded. "That's a hole in security big enough to get someone killed."

She paused. "Do you think he's in danger?"

"I'm sure of it. But I'll bet this house has other defenses, like that security camera."

"What security camera?"

"That one." He touched the eye of the painted pirate. "Holo lens. You bet he sees everything. We'd have been in trouble if he hadn't recognized us."

"Trouble?"

"See that laser pistol at his hip? That's real."

Corsage was amazed, and impressed. "I never knew!"

"You haven't done much sneaking around protected homes."

"Of course I haven't! You mean to say you have?"

"Sure, when the rich wives are restive."

"Restive?"

"Sexually neglected."

"Oh." She colored again. "You are insufferably crude."

"Some women like that."

"Well *I* don't."

"Nobody asked you to."

"This way," she said, more coldly than before.

They came in due course to the head office section. "That's odd," Corsage said as she spied an empty desk. "There's no guard here."

"We must be expected."

"How does that follow?"

"Why would he want anyone to see him meeting with a guttersnipe and maidservant? He gave the guard the afternoon off."

She paused. "You make uncomfortable sense."

"I have a criminal mind."

Corsage touched the desk intercom. "Mister Corsair, sir, may we have an audience?"

The answer was immediate. "Come on in, both."

"See?" Corvee said. "He saw us coming."

"I find this unsettling." She went to the door behind the desk and opened it. They entered the inner sanctum. This was a beautiful suite overlooking the broad ocean. A perpetual news holo played in the background.

The old man stepped forward to greet them. "Good for you, Corsage," he said, giving her a quick hug. "And you, Corvee." He proffered his hand to shake.

Corvee took it, but had a question. "Why?"

"This job requires three things: loyalty, competence, and guts. Both of you are loyal, and have guts. You are competent in different ways. Together you represent what I need to survive my dotage,"

"Sir!" Corsage said, shocked.

"I said loyalty, not toadyism, my dear. I am getting old, and slowly losing my abilities. I am surrounded by scoundrels of my own ilk, which means they will turn on me and destroy me the moment they discover opportunity. Like any other selfish man, I want to prolong my power and welfare as long as is feasible, then turn it over to worthy hands. So rather than wait on nature, I anticipate it, by choosing my successors while I retain the wit and ability to do so. Thus your assignment."

Corvee nodded. "Now I get it. You're a cunning old pirate. I'm a young one, even if I don't know your ship."

"Corsage knows it," Corsair agreed. "But she, being a decent person, doesn't properly appreciate the deviousness of unscrupulous schemers. You do. To-gether you should be able to do the job."

"What job?" Corsage asked, flustered.

"The job of maintaining the economic and political empire I have built, and turning it toward good ends."

"Why not simply bequeath it to a reputable charity?"

Corsair smiled. "Answer that, young pirate."

"Because none of them are immune from corruption," Corvee said promptly. "Nothing is."

"I don't believe that."

"That is why you need him," Corsair said. "Therefore I have arranged it myself. You have the required qualities."

"Loyalty, competence, and guts," Corvee agreed.

"But we can't possibly know enough to accomplish that," Corsage said. "We'll be slaughtered by the malign connivers."

"She's right, you know," Corvee said. "We mean well, but we're amateurs. The enemies are professionals. We're overmatched before we start."

"Answer that, honest maiden."

"We don't have to do it all ourselves," Corsage said. "We have to seek experienced advisors we can trust. With their help we can build a fortress against the enemies, figuratively speaking."

"That is why you need her," Corsair told Corvee. "She has practical knowledge and common sense."

"I see the way of it," Corvee agreed. "But why did you help me, years ago when I was just a juvenile thug who had never heard of you?"

"Because you reminded me of myself at that age, and had similar potential. We pirates must stick together."

"Pirates and maidens, it seems," Corsage said, not completely at ease with this.

"You have potential too," Corsair told her.

"And what will you be doing, meanwhile?" Corvee asked the old man as he stared out across the ocean.

"I will retire anonymously to a private chalet catered by a lovely but modest and obliging damsel and watch the proceeding as a spectator, far from harm."

"I think not," Corvee said abruptly. "We need you as our adviser, and we need you now."

"Why so soon?"

"I have served on the sea and shore. I know a tsunami warning when I see it. We're in trouble."

Corsair whipped around to look at the holo news. "You're right. We've got to get to high ground immediately."

"I don't understand," Corsage protested.

"You will, honey," Corvee said tersely. "For now, take our word. We're following Corsair out of here right now."

"We'll need the cook," Corsair said. "There's room for one more." He touched a button on the desk. "Daisy, come to the roof immediately."

They followed Corsair to the roof, where a helicopter rested. As they walked toward it, one more figure appeared. "Hi, hungry," she called.

"Hot feces!" Corsair swore.

He had reason: it was Corset. She had intercepted the message and come in lieu of the cook.

"Deal with her," Corsair said. "I'll start the motor."

Corvee placed himself before Corset, blocking the way to the helicopter. "This is a private party. You're not welcome." He stood ready; it was clear that he had the will and the means to throw her off the roof. Corsage was plainly afraid he would do just that.

Corset smiled cannily. "I know what's up. I snooped on your dialogue. That 'copter is the only escape from the building. I don't want to die. Name your terms."

"Corsair needs a cook, and servant," Corsage said. "Will you serve?"

"For the duration of the crisis."

"Done."

"We can't trust her," Corvee said.

"I saved her. I can dismiss her if she reneges. I have the legal right and you have the physical power."

The helicopter propellor started turning. It was time to board.

"If anything happens to her or to Corsair, you will be the next to go," Corvee told Corset grimly. "Or if you get balky. Or play us false in any manner. Do you have a problem with that?"

"No. We understand each other."

"Then get on in."

They piled into the helicopter. "They let you in?" Corsair inquired, not really surprised.

"They tamed the shrew. I am your cook, servant and sex slave, as you choose, until the need fades."

"Glad to have that straight." He worked the controls and the machine lifted off the building.

They gazed down as the helicopter gained height. A wall of water was rising on the shore of a barrier island. The tsunami had arrived.

Corsair flew them to an isolated but well-stocked mountain retreat he had evidently set up for exactly such an occasion. It was well-stocked in all the necessary ways, and had a news holo, so that they could see the ongoing carnage at the shore. It was the worst tsunami in twenty years, and folk who should have known better were ill prepared. They were dying in droves.

Corset turned out to be reasonably competent as a cook, and soon served them all a good meal. Corsage thought to help her clean up the dishes, but she demurred. "I made a deal to save my life. I will honor it. I'll satisfy Corsair at night too; I know how. You two do your own things."

"I have nothing at the moment," Corsage said. "I'm used to doing the servanting."

Corset smiled. "That has changed. Let me help you."

"Beg pardon?"

"There'll be a better outfit for you here. Corsair is always prepared. This way."

Corsage followed her to a bedroom closet, not particularly pleased.

But the woman knew what she was doing. Soon she had Corsage outfitted in a lovely evening gown, with her hair curling elegantly down around her shoulders. "Now you're esthetic," Corset said, satisfied.

Meanwhile the actress Marionette snapped her fingers, and someone brought out a gown. She, too, was always prepared. She stripped Corsage, who was unable to protest, and dressed her in the gown, adjusting it to fit. Corsage did have a fair figure, normally masked by her severe uniform. The transformation was literal. The mistress knew exactly how to accomplish it.

Warp, the Narrator, paused just long enough for the job to be done. No one protested, male or female; this was one interesting process. Then he resumed.

"Well, now," Corsair said as they returned. "Cinderella emerges from the ashes."

Corvee simply stared.

"I feel out of place," Corsage said.

Corvee finally found his voice. "I never really saw you before. You're beautiful!"

"Thank you," Corsage said, unable to make her voice cold. She appreciated his appreciation, which was obviously unfeigned.

"My job here is done," Corset said with satisfaction.

"You're holding back something," Corvee said.

"Ah, you caught it" Corsair said approvingly.

"What is it?" Corsage asked sharply.

Corset shrugged. "Actually Corsair understands me, and accepts me as I am, and will treat me decently regardless. In contrast to other functionaries who prefer to insult and brutalize me the moment I am without power. I'd rather be his servant than their associate."

"I think it time for you to take a dive," Corvee said, stepping toward her. The cottage overlooked a high cliff dropping to roiling water.

Corset put up her two manicured hands in protest. "I am getting to it. I'm not deceiving you."

"Fortunately," Corsair said dryly.

"Confession: I advised a key enemy of the situation before this crisis occurred. He declined to act. But now that the umbrella of law has broken down in this area, and will not be restored for several days, he will surely strike. He knows where all Corsair's hideouts are, I'm sure. I think he will attack, kill me and Corsair as superfluous embarrassments, and torture the two of you until you sign over your powers of attorney. I tell you this in the interest of saving my own life, again."

"No rest for the wicked," Corsair said. "We shall have to vacate and hide in the next hour. There is a sufficient arsenal here; arm yourselves appropriately, all of you, and we'll get moving." He glanced at Corset. "But first I'll take ten minutes with you alone. You know the drill."

"I do." Corset went with him to the bedroom, disrobing as she went.

"I don't like this," Corsage said. "I never fired a gun in my life."

"I will show you how. Understand this: if an attack party comes, our lives will depend on our getting them before they get us. Keep silent and fire on my command."

"I will try," she said nervously. "But first I should change."

"No time for that."

He fitted her with two small pistols and extra bullet clips. He took an automatic rifle himself, and several grenades. He laid out another pistol with ammunition for Corset. "Now here is how you fire it," he said, leading her outside. "Point it at your target, steady it with your free hand, wait for the spot of red light to touch the enemy man, and slowly squeeze the trigger. Do it that way and you won't miss. It is important not to miss, because you probably won't get a second chance. Now try it against that tree."

She tried. When the red light crossed the trunk, she jerked the trigger. The gun fired and the bullet missed to the side. "Oh!"

"Squeeze, not jerk," he said patiently. "Try again."

She tried again. This time she got the trunk. "I got it!" she cried happily, and kissed him quickly on the mouth.

Then she was embarrassed. "I'm sorry. I didn't mean to—I got carried away."

"I liked it, you lovely creature," he said. "May I kiss you back?"

She blushed. "I guess I owe you that. I started it."

He held her and kissed her, not quickly. Her arms came up to hold him close. It was a surprisingly tender moment.

"Save the rest of it for when you're holed up together," Corsair said, emerging with Corset. "Now we must move."

Corsage flushed again, but did not protest. Her initial dislike of Corvee had become something else.

They left the cottage lighted, with the holo on, plainly still occupied. They trekked along a trail through the surrounding forest. "There are ambushes here," Corsair said. "We will use them. I think we can hold out long enough, if they are careless."

They occupied the ambushes on either side of the trail, and waited in silence. Corsair and Corset were in one, Corvee and Corsage in the other. In half an hour there was the sound of an explosion: the enemy had bombed the cottage. But that was unlikely to be the end of it.

Corvee was lying prone, his hip against Corsage's hip. "Can we spare a bit of attention?" she whispered. "I'm afraid I'm going to die, and so there may be no future opportunity."

"I expect to live," he whispered reassuringly. He leaned over and kissed her.

"I didn't like you, but now that we're in immediate peril, I'm glad to have you by my side."

He glanced into her décolletage, which in this position showed rather more than perhaps she realized. "I thought you weren't my type. But now I know you are."

"What, a practical maid-servant?"

"A stunning creature. I don't much care what your background is."

"I can't think why I like that, but I do." They kissed again.

There was a sound below them. Someone was coming along the trail. Several someones: four brutish-looking men were using a sniffing machine to follow their tracks.

Corvee oriented his rifle. Corsage aimed her pistol, turning on the red spot.

Then suddenly the pistol kicked in her hand; she hadn't been aware of pulling the trigger. All four men dropped to the ground. They had taken out two, and Corsair and Corset must have done the other two.

Corvee got up. "Nice shot," he said. "Now we must scram."

Her knees felt weak. Had she really killed a man? "But why, if they're dead?"

"They'll have back-ups coming the moment these ones don't answer their signals. They'll go after these ambush sites next." He half-hauled her along with him.

Then Corsage realized that her pistol was cool. She hadn't fired it after all.

Corvee had taken both of the men on their side out and tried to give her credit.

Corsair and Corset met them on the trail. "Good work," the old man said. "Now we must hurry before they think to block the other end of the trail."

They hurried, but learned they were too late: two more men barred the way ahead, their guns drawn and aimed. "Halt," one said. "Put your hands on your heads."

Instead Corsair and Corset leaped at them. Both men fired, and dodged to get out of the way of the hurtling bodies. Corvee fired, taking out one man, but the other swung his gun around to bear on Corvee.

A red dot touched the man's head. Then a bullet followed, and the man dropped, blood issuing from the hole.

This time Corsage had fired.

"You saved my life," Corvee said. "Now we must flee."

"But Corsair and Corset!"

"Are dead. They did it deliberately to enable us to escape. Now we'll go and do right by them."

So Corset had been with Corsair in the end, and died with him. That redeemed her in Corsage's eyes. She followed Corvee down a new trail.

"The rest would be tedious to tell," Warp said. "Of course they married and set about using Corsair's fortune to set up a massive Tsunami relief effort that saved many lives and restored a significant portion of the devastated landscape. This tale was merely about how their power came to be, so suddenly and seemingly from nowhere."

He turned to the others. "Thank you for your fine acting. I believe I'll keep you with me, Corset."

Mistress Marionette smiled, accepting it. Admiral Vitality returned to stand beside Mistress Morsel, his rewarding roles over.

Warp focused on Corvee and Corsage, who remained in the gown. "And is there any chance the two of you have any future together? You did a fine job of acting and seem to mesh well." And of course he had taken pains to make her show off her physical assets to the man who already liked her.

The two looked at each other. Then they kissed, this time for themselves. The audience burst into applause. The story romance had become a real one.

The session was over. The crewfolk departed, many seeming dazed. Corvee and Corsage went to move his effects into her room. Mistress Morsel and Admiral Vitality came to join them.

"I confess to having had a certain reservation," Morsel said. "But Marionette was right: you *are* the greatest story teller ever."

"Appreciation," Warp said modestly. "I did have good help." He was also glad that Flame had educated him on tsunamis and durable powers of attorney; that had really helped him frame the story, making it relevant to Earth.

"It's the way they tell stories on the colony planet," Marionette explained. "The Narrator, and a few actors, and some volunteers from the audience. It is effective."

"It is," the Admiral agreed. "It comes to life. At one point I wanted to throttle you, but at the end I applauded you."

"And you wiped out the shunning of the whistle blower," Morsel said to Warp. "After that show, any of the men would have roomed with her."

"She is worthy."

"And pretty," he agreed.

Marionette looked around. "Where is Ine?"

Warp put on a look of surprise. "She must have forgotten to put her clothing back on." He lifted his voice. "Ine!"

"I am here," Ine called from across the chamber. "I was curious what Corvee and Corsage would do."

"There was doubt?" Marionette inquired.

"None at all," Ine said as her bra lifted and filled out generously. "I'm a voyeur at heart." Her panties filled out similarly.

"Aren't we all," the admiral said, watching closely.

Bra and panties paused, orienting on him. "No fault?"

Before the Admiral could question that, Marionette spoke. "Say 'Agreement,' Admiral."

"Agreement? Why?"

"Because she is offering you a swift sexual session with her before she departs your fleet, with no further commitment or complications for either party. It is another colony custom. She is invisible, but quite solid and well endowed physically."

"So I see," he said as the underclothing turned in place, bouncing and rippling. "That would be an, er, remarkable liaison."

"You have my leave," Mistress Morsel murmured, smiling.

The bra and panties joined the admiral and accompanied him to his cabin.

Morsel turned to Warp. "No fault?"

"Agreement!" he said enthusiastically.

"I will take her things to the shuttle," Marionette said, picking up Ine's remaining clothing. She showed no sign of jealousy; it was not her nature.

Mistress Morsel turned out to be every bit as competent a sexual partner as Marionette. "I suspect you are playing a deeper game than we wot, but your narration turned me on," she said as she clasped him and expertly milked him.

"I do what I can." These mistresses were amazing.

"Is it true that you are endlessly potent?"

So word had spread. "Affirmation."

"Demonstrate, please."

He climaxed four times in the next two minutes, filling her with his surging essence.

"That *really* turns me on," she said, going into her own climax. "Continue until I finish, please."

He did, and they spent several more minutes in continuous sexual ecstasy, until she was finally spent.

"Oh, I envy Marionette," she breathed as she mopped up the fluid that had literally filled her to overflowing; even her genital control could not contain such an amount. "You are a wonder. You mean to marry her?"

Word had *really* spread! "It is my dream."

"It is the dream of every living man to marry a mistress, but one very seldom realized. Still, with power like that, and your status as a colony prince, your prospect seems good."

"Hope," he agreed.

"And if you do, perhaps the two of you will visit me again at some time. No fault."

"Perhaps," he agreed, pleased. He seldom got to indulge his full sexual desire, except with Ine, but it was apparent that Morsel was up to it.

She conducted him to the shuttle, where Marionette and a now-clothed Ine waited. The two mistresses embraced again. "He is a treasure," Morsel said. "At such time as you tire of him..."

"I have developed remarkable patience with him."

They laughed together. Then Warp, Ine, and Marionette boarded the shuttle. "You will be wanting to see volcanoes next," Marionette said.

"Agreement."

"Meanwhile we have a dull hour in flight. Shall we tackle you in tandem?"

They would do that? "Affirmation."

The two women stripped and took rapid turns, alternating positions at his groin and face, so that he was continuously kissing one while penetrating the other. For the first time in his life, he found himself slowing. His orgasms became less intense, with smaller outputs. By the time the shuttle landed, his penis was limp and could no longer be aroused.

Marionette shook the invisible hand of Ine. They had bested him. But both of them were thoroughly sore where it counted.

They transferred to a capsule bound for the home suite. All three of them lapsed into sleep, Warp lying contentedly between the two women. But Warp's sleep was not complete. *Ine*.

Accomplished, she replied mentally. Then her sleep became real.

Warp relaxed, satisfied. Morsel had been right about his playing a deeper game. The hidden purpose of his narrative had been to distract all the crews of the fleet so that none would be alert for Ine's secret mission. She was able to become invisible not merely to sight, but also to sound, heat, and touch, so as to be completely undetectable by any but mental means. Thus the tracing machines lost track of her, but their operators, distracted by the tale, did not notice. They assumed she was near her clothing, watching the drama. She was not.

Ine had made her way to the private room, telepathically read the entry code, and used it to enter. The distracted personnel paid her no attention, not noticing the silent opening of the door. She had read the codes in their heads and used them to address the master circuit—the one that governed all the slave circuits of the other ships of the fleet. They now had a new directive.

All the Earth ships were now locked into their present orbits about the several planets and moons of this system. They would not be able to leave those orbits, because the master circuit overruled their initiatives. The master circuit was itself now immune to the directives of any person except Ine. It would require an extraordinary effort to deprogram it.

Warp hoped that the Earthers would not immediately catch on to what had happened, and would take longer to trace the mischief to his entertaining visit to the flagship.

Meanwhile the Fleet was effectively out of commission.

Chapter 10
Gale

"Statement: Now comes your turn," Havoc said. "Mind you don't come to prefer him to me."

"Argument: But there's a certain pleasure in naïve mortality," Gale protested. "And Red and Idyll say he's a good and lusty man."

"Jealousy: *I'm* a good and lusty man!"

"Observation: So the bath maidens all attest," she agreed.

"Well with Symbol getting diffident with her anticipated fourth, what am I to do?"

"Poor thing," she said sympathetically. "Absent wife and pregnant mistress. Maybe Idyll will have mercy on you."

"She can be real fun," he agreed, perking up. "I'll ask her to emulate you, with improvements."

"Improvements!" she flashed. "Outrage!"

Then they dissolved into laughter and a savagely sexual embrace. Eighteen years of marriage and the raising of four precocious children had not dulled their delight in each other. As Glamors they were not only seemingly immortal, but perpetually youthful and, yes, lusty.

"That session would have made Weft jealous," Gale remarked when they eased off, mutually sated for the moment.

"We phrase it as an ongoing joke," he agreed. "But she is not joking."

"Neither are you."

"Guilt. I'm her father."

"Adoptive, with no blood relation." She lay on her side, gazing at him. "Idea: travel with her as no fault strangers?"

"Danger: she is a more proficient Glamor than either of us. I would be overmatched."

"As I would be with Warp," she agreed.

"Flame can beat me at martial arts, and she is appealing too."

"You trained her, as I trained Weft," she said. "We raised them to be the best they could be. What else could we have done?"

"Nothing else. But we did not anticipate the longer range emotional complications. They surely exist in most families, but are magnified in a Glamor family."

"And we are the first and only full Glamor family."

"Saving grace: Voila is truly ours, and she is the most potent Glamor of all. She keeps them in line."

"We try to be impartial," she said. "But we suffer to be apart from her."

"All else is dross," he agreed.

"Consideration: maybe you really should visit Idyll, and when you are sated and at peace, ask her about no fault Glamor interactions within a family. As an alien creature she has perspective."

"Worthwhile," he agreed. Then they separated.

⁂

Actually Gale was the first to visit Idyll, to pick up Dynamo. The Red Glamor had delivered him, but it was Gale's turn to manage him, as Havoc had reminded her.

She landed in the guest glade the ifrit Glamor maintained. There was Idyll in the physical form of the Earther Mistress Marionette, or perhaps another mistress, naked with a blissfully sleeping Dynamo. "A greeting, Idyll."

"Returned, Gale. It has been a pleasant interlude."

"Appreciation for your participation."

"Needless. We are all in the same planetary system."

That was true. The humans, animals, and ifrits of the twin planets faced potential extinction together if they did not navigate the present and future crises successfully. They had a common interest in survival.

"You sent news that the Earther is ready to compromise."

"He appreciates the way of it. He will recruit and train people for supervisory roles depending on the outcome of this contest with Earth."

"I will try to confirm the deal," Gale said. "Meanwhile, Havoc may come to you. He faces privation in the absence of Symbol and me, and also is concerned as I am about our interfamily feelings. We do not wish to have such complications interfere with our effort to do the necessary with Earth."

"I will receive him with pleasure, and do my best."

"Appreciation," Gale repeated.

Then Idyll got up and started to dissolve. Gale lay down in her place. "Parting," the ifrit Glamor said.

"Acknowledged."

Not long thereafter the earth man stirred. His eyes opened, and widened. "Question."

Gale laughed. "Affirmation. I am Queen Gale, not another impersonation of Idyll Ifrit. I will guide you during this next effort."

Dynamo looked around, embarrassed for his nakedness. "I had not expected this change of companions. I thought Stevia would return. No affront is intended."

"No fault."

He paused. "I fear I misunderstand. You are the queen."

"Clarification: our study indicates that when five women have worked with you, you will be fully amenable to our cause. I am the fifth woman. This is too important to leave to another."

He found his clothing and scrambled into it. "I have agreed to undertake dual-purpose training of colonists. That is all."

"We want more than that. We want your allegiance to Charm."

He completed his dressing. "I have not promised that."

She stepped into him and kissed him. "Yet."

He stood for a moment, unsteady on his feet. "You're another! Like Stevia and Idyll."

"Agreement. I am a Glamor."

He considered. "This is not no fault."

"Question?"

"You are offering me something in exchange for something you want. That's bartering, not no fault."

"Negation. No fault is a temporary convenience so that people may safely associate without unwanted complications. We will be associating, so no fault is necessary lest my husband the king be concerned. I am not trading sex for allegiance."

"But you are here because you want my allegiance."

"While we associate I hope to persuade you that allegiance is best. That is a dialogue. If I fail to persuade you, there will be no sexual consequence. The two are separate matters."

He considered, then nodded. "Apology for the assumption."

"Needless. You are foreign to our culture."

"I am. I have a problem with sex with the queen. I fear my touch would soil you, socially."

"Does your touch soil your mistress?"

"No. That is a special relationship."

"It is a no fault relationship."

He nodded, surprised. "True."

"Now I will take you to Triumph City." She approached him, put her arms around him, and exerted her Glamor power of motion. They jumped to the pyramid.

They were in Ennui's office. "Greeting, Queen Gale" Ennui said, seeming almost surprised.

"This is Dynamo, of Earth, here to train citizens in governance," Gale said. "I am conducting him, no fault."

"Greeting, Dynamo."

"This is Ennui, Havoc's personal secretary, a hidden power of the kingdom."

"Hello, Ennui," Dynamo said.

"Where is the first assembly?"

"In the neighboring Green Chroma zone," Ennui said. "They are ready for you now."

"Appreciation." Gale put her arms around Dynamo again, and jumped to the neighborhood of the site she knew: the village center.

She actually landed a short distance outside the village. "Clarification," she said to Dynamo. "Most citizens are not aware that the king and I are Glamors. We prefer your discretion."

"Of course," Dynamo agreed immediately.

"Appreciation." She kissed his ear.

"That was not a no fault kiss."

She laughed. "Acquiescence. That was reward for a favor." She walked toward the village.

He walked beside her. "Question: are all Glamors personally attractive, as you and the king are?"

"Confirmation. We influence as much by appeal as by magic. It is our nature."

"Suppose I fall in love with you?"

"That will not happen. Love complicates no fault."

"You are sure?"

"Affirmation."

He did not question her further, so she did not have to explain that she could use her telepathy to locate his mental turnoffs and invoke them. She would see that he did not fall for her, though he would surely develop a considerable passion for her body.

A small group of Green Chroma folk were assembled. "I am Queen Gale," Gale said, touching her crown though she was sure they recognized her. "This is Dynamo of Earth, here to solicit your participation in training to be administrators." She stepped back, leaving the stage to him.

"I have agreed to train Charm citizens for an ambiguous role," Dynamo said. "We do not know at this stage whether Earth will recover Charm as her colony, in which case you will remain here and become administrators for Earth, answering to Earth, your loyalty to Earth. Or whether Charm will prevail over Earth, in which case you will travel to Earth to govern it, answering to King Havoc and Queen Gale. In either case, there is much you will need to know about Earth, and I will teach you that. At present I seek to enlist suitable people for this training. It is voluntary, despite the presence of Queen Gale." He paused.

"Question." It was a young green girl.

Dynamo looked at her, and did a double-take. "Question," he repeated. "Naive?"

The girl smiled. "Agreement. If Earth wins, what happens to King Havoc and Queen Gale?"

"That is undecided. They may remain as regents, answering to Earth, or be taken to Earth as hostages to join their children."

"Then why is Queen Gale helping you?"

He smiled. "She does not believe Earth will win."

The villagers exchanged glances. Then they drifted away, uninterested. Except for Naive. "I wish to join."

"But you—"

"Look young? I will age in time."

"Yes, of course. But—"

"I bedded you no fault? I will not do so now."

Gale suppressed her smile. The Earther still was not fully accustomed to people's candor about such things.

"Then welcome," Dynamo said, evidently making the best of it. "Fetch your belongings and come with us."

The girl did so. He had his first recruit.

Gale took them to a chamber in Pyramid that Ennui had prepared. She introduced Naive to Ennui, then took Dynamo to the next assembly site, this one in a Blue Chroma zone.

Then she took him to a Black Chroma zone. "Warning," she told him. "The village is near the volcano. That may make you nervous."

"Not if it's inactive," Dynamo said.

"Few volcanoes are inactive. They merely are erratic."

They landed on a bare black surface slanting down toward a dark gulf. "What happened here?" Dynamo asked, interested.

"Black Chroma volcanoes inrupt rather than erupt," she explained. "That is the inverted cone of it."

"Humor?"

"Negation."

Then her sense of the immediate future warned her. "Token inruption," she said. "We must seek immediate cover."

"I'd be curious to see it," he said, unalarmed.

She saw no good cover. She had foolishly put them into danger in an exposed place. She caught his arm and hauled him down into a ridged gully. "Not from this close."

Then the inruption occurred. There was a howling roar, and wind blasted in toward the hole. It yanked at their clothing. She put an arm over Dynamo's back, holding him down. But the wind grew stronger, threatening to blow him into the hole. Now he understood the danger, but it wasn't over. His body started to slide along the smooth stone surface.

She pushed him down and flung herself over him, reaching out with her hands and feet to catch hold of the crevices. She used her Glamor strength to lock them both down until the fierce wind passed. Fortunately it was only a minute. A serious inruption would have been much longer and stronger.

"Observation," he said ruefully. "You made your point. You probably saved my life. I just wish we could have achieved this position without such a threat."

The danger was over. Gale realized that she was spread across him, her limbs flung out in four directions, her body bearing him down. Parts of their clothing had been torn off by the wind, so that only tatters remained in place, mainly where her breasts and groin pressed hardest against him. He was lying face up, ruefully appreciating all of it.

"Apology for teasing you," she said, getting off him.

"Needless. You did what you needed to to protect me from my ignorance."

"I should have looked farther ahead and avoided this."

"It was perhaps worth it."

She considered. "I have aroused you."

He shrugged. "My fault for noticing your body when you were anchoring me."

And she was a lovely woman. She decided. "There is time. I will abate the tease."

"I don't understand."

She lifted what remained of her skirt. She got back on him, pressing him against the black ground. She found his turgid member, brought it out, and took it in. She squeezed it, while kissing him.

His climax was immediate. "Oh, queen lady, you are something else," he gasped.

"Ending what I started," she said, lifting herself off him. "I should not have put you in danger."

"It was a fair trade," he said gallantly. "More than fair."

She used magic to repair their clothing. Then they resumed their walk to the assembly site. This of course was an underground chamber, braced against routine inruptions. She had arrived outside it to conceal her Glamor nature.

Dynamo made his pitch, as he called it, and garnered another recruit. He made no reference to their adventure on the way there.

The recruitment process required several days, during which time they assembled people of all Chromas and nonChroma. When they had a hundred they stopped; that was all Dynamo felt he could effectively manage.

The next stage was the training. Rather than try to lecture them about the ways of Earth, he formulated likely situations and drilled them on how to handle them. "Remember, there's no magic on Earth," he said. "You won't be able to use any except Science there."

"Correction," Gale murmured.

He reconsidered. "I forgot: you are converting Earth to Chroma zones, or trying to. But that brings up another problem: Earthers won't know how to use magic. Probably few if any of them will be able to do it for many years. If Science doesn't work either, the danger will be reversion to barbarism. You will need to work to prevent that from happening. *You* will do the magic to feed the hungry, house the homeless, locate the lost. You will have to guide them to safe areas."

"But isn't Earth larger than Charm?" a recruit asked. "We are only one hundred. We will be swamped."

"This is why we are about to study organization," Dynamo said. "I spoke figuratively. You will not be doing these things yourselves. You will be recruiting subordinates, who will recruit others, forming expanding nets of guided people reaching down to address to lowest tier. Your people will all be Earthers. The Mistresses should help, lending their lines of command."

"Why should they do that?"

"Because they will be the first converted to the Charm cause, according to the plan." He paused a moment. "If this seems far-fetched, I admit I find it so. I seriously doubt Charm will defeat Earth. But for your training you must assume that it will. Then you will be prepared. If I am right, and Earth wins, then Earth will use you similarly to govern Charm. The monarchy will be over, even if the king and queen remain; they will be figureheads."

Several trainees looked at Gale. "It is true," she assured them. "If Earth wins, Havoc and I will be finished. So take your training seriously, because we want you to use it on Earth."

Naive spoke. "Realization: So Dynamo may be helping Earth. Why should we help him depose you? That's not what we voted for." There was a murmur of agreement.

"Privacy," Gale said.

"All one hundred of us?" Naive asked, looking around. She looked young, but had taken hold, and now bedded no fault with a handsome Black Chroma man named Fifth. He, like most of the recruits, had been somewhat set apart from his fellows, thus ready to travel to a foreign world. He had been born after his parents had their four, and they had not sought him.

"You are a select group with an important mission," Gale said. "The fact that you are in training to be governors is open news. But there are things we deem necessary to keep private, such as the fact that I am not merely Queen but am also a Glamor, as is King Havoc."

All of them stared at her. She had concealed this from all but Dynamo, but now needed to share it to this extent.

"Discovery!" Naive exclaimed. "That is how you were able to discipline your Glamor children!"

"Affirmation. It is why we adopted three: we alone could handle them."

That also served to remind them of the sacrifice the royal couple had made, raising three "fourths" instead of one, and having only one natural child.

Naive faced the others. "Vote: any against honoring privacy?"

No one signaled. Naive turned back to face Gale, silent. The agreement had been made.

"Our reason is this," Gale said. "Today we oppose Earth's takeover, and have concluded that to fully counter it we must reverse it and take over Earth. But it is not unmitigated foolish ambition that determines this. We can see the paths of the future, and they lead to mischief unless we do this. Earth and Charm must be unified, under one banner or the other, or both risk extinction. It is better for Havoc to lose power than to suffer the loss of all our lives."

"Question," Naive said. "Mischief?"

"There is a culture of powerful, self-willed, conscious machines that is expanding ruthlessly. They will in time destroy Charm and Earth and all other galactic cultures unless we stop them. We can't stop them alone. We must have the resources and knowledge of Earth."

"Machines? White Chroma? Disbelief."

"Believe," Dynamo said. "I saw such a machine."

But the trainees looked unconvinced. They would have to be shown. "I will arrange a visit. Other Glamors will help." She sent out a mental call. *Human Glamors: assistance.*

In a moment they appeared beside her, in their natural forms: eight Glamors of assorted colors, one of them Havoc. They had been ready for this call.

The trainees stared, daunted. Most had never knowingly seen a single Glamor.

Gale introduced them in turn. "The Black Glamor, the patron of things with ten thousand legs, saprophytes—the creatures who break down dead organic things like plants and bodies." The handsome black man nodded. The Black Chroma trainees smiled.

"The Red Glamor, patron of four legged creatures, human beings." The lovely red woman smiled, fairly dazzling all the males and many of the females. The Red Chroma trainees nodded. Dynamo nodded too, having had experience with her.

"The Air Glamor, patron of hundred-legged things, millipedes." He wore a hat, gloves, and boots, identifying his position. For a moment he became fully visible as a nonChroma man in colored clothing, using the illusion for which Air Chroma was noted. The Air Chroma trainees waved.

"The Blue Glamor, patron of five legged things, insects." The shapely blue woman lifted her two hands and a cluster of dragonflies flew up. The Blue Chroma trainees applauded.

"The Green Glamor, patron of ten legged things, the mollusks." For a moment the green man assumed the form of a ten-legged squid, his tentacles waving. The Green Chroma trainees laughed.

"The Yellow Glamor, patron of zero-legged things, the demons." The stunning yellow woman burst into flame that burned off her clothing, leaving her gloriously nude. The Yellow Chroma trainees murmured with appreciation, especially the males.

"The Translucent Glamor, patron of two legged things, the fish." A giant translucent fish appeared, swimming through the air. The translucent man jumped onto its back and rode it around the chamber. The Translucent Chroma trainees reached out to touch them as they passed.

"A nonChroma Glamor, patron of eight legged things, the roots of trees and plants." King Havoc bowed. This time all the trainees applauded.

"And another nonChroma Glamor, patron of thousand legged things, the mosses and lichens." Gale bowed. There was renewed applause.

Then she got down to business. "The presence of these Glamors should suggest how important this mission is to us. There are also a number of animal Glamors, of equal status with the human ones, but for this particular purpose we feel that you will be more comfortable with humans. Each one will take hold of one of you and transport you to Mino, the machine you disbelieve."

They started, with the nine Glamors taking nine trainees, leaving Dynamo to clarify details for the remaining ones. The Green Glamor took Green Chroma Naive, to her delight, and the Black Glamor took her Black Chroma boyfriend. Havoc took a swooningly charmed nonChroma girl, and Gale took a nonChroma man who was clearly awed by such a close embrace by the Queen. All the Glamors took their own colors, this first group.

Mino was ready with a prepared spiel and demonstration. In a few minutes the nine were satisfied that such an impressive machine did exist. The direct experience with the Glamors had similar impact.

When the first nine returned, they took nine more, leaving the first group to share their experience with the remaining trainees. This was a significant bonding experience for them, which helped.

Eleven trips took ninety nine trainees. Only one was left: an older Gray Chroma man who had been satisfied to let the younger ones go first. The Red Glamor approached him, changed to her Gray Chroma Stevia form, embraced him, kissed him, and vanished with him. Thus his reward for his patience.

Finally all were done. It was now late in the day, so they adjourned. The trainees would have the night to consider what they had experienced.

Gale took Dynamo to the room they shared for the duration. "Apology for preempting your class," she said.

"Needless!" They proceeded to the usual. Men liked to celebrate virtually any occasion with sex, and it was fun for her too; she liked the variety of possessing a relatively inexperienced man. It also kept him quite satisfied to do his job, fending off any lingering concerns he might have about betraying Earth.

Next day they took a floating caravan to the nearest Silver Chroma zone for another event. This time the Silver trainees would have magic while the others lacked it, so it was their job to apply the management principles they were learning to organize the others. There would be other Chroma zones for other sessions. The non-Silvers would lack magic, so would need to learn to cope without depending on it.

They got out and the silver caravan floats departed. But they had hardly gotten started before something happened.

Gale saw it coming in the near future. "Danger!" she said. "Something is wrong."

But she had been distracted by the immediate arrangements, rather than constantly verifying future paths. It was already too late to get them out of what she now realized was a deadly trap. *Silver!* she cried mentally. Then she set about doing what she could to defend them.

"Question," Dynamo asked.

"An enemy has surrounded us, and means to destroy all of you. The silver chroma trainees can escape magically, and so can I, but the rest of you are trapped. I have summoned help, but it may not come in time." The future paths were tangled; she could not select any guaranteed safe ones.

"What specific threat?"

"Electrical. To make it seem like a natural fluke."

Dynamo got to work. "Electrical threat. Silvers can escape. The rest of you close in on me. We must clear out any conductors."

"Negation," a Silver chroma trainee said. "We won't flee. We can help. Tell us how."

"Make a circle of conductors around us, to divert the electricity." He addressed the others. "Find implements and dig to make some kind of depression we can hide in."

They got to work with marvelous discipline. That gave Gale a chance to explore the near future paths in more detail. Voila could have done a better job, of course, but Gale's ability might suffice. She found several where the danger was reduced but not eliminated.

"Not there," she called. "There." She indicated a different place.

No one questioned it. They moved over and started excavating the new area. The Silvers used magic to conjure, shape, and place a ring of metallic posts strung with wires.

Then it came: a sparkling, flashing wall of lightning, advancing rapidly toward them. It extended to the horizon on either side and towered to the sky. Trees caught in it burst into flames, and some exploded. There was the cracking of the thunder of the heated air. This was far too big and powerful to be balked by their feeble efforts. They seemed to be doomed.

Silver men appeared, and the wall halted. "We can't kill you, Glamor bitch," the apparent leader called. "But we can take out your minions."

"Why?" Gale called back. "What is it you want?" For the dialogue was the leading path to safety, still not assured.

"You are betraying our planet, training traitors who will answer to Earth. We won't allow it."

"We are training them to govern Earth," Gale said.

The man turned to Dynamo. "True?"

"She believes so," Dynamo said. "I do not. I do work for Earth."

"See, bitch! He gives you the lie!"

"False," Dynamo said. "It is merely a difference of belief."

The man sent a bolt of electricity at Dynamo, who responded by drawing his Science pistol and firing back. The bullet flashed as it struck the rebel, but did not hurt him; it heated and exploded against the man's chest, harmlessly. Meanwhile Naive's Black Chroma friend, Fifth, reached out and caught the bolt, drawing it into himself in the manner of a Black Chroma volcano. Its power made him flare for an instant; then he collapsed. Naive screamed.

At the same time Gale sent a bolt of her own to intercept the silver bolt, nullifying it before the intense energy could damage the Black Chroma man further. Then she ran to Fifth, sat behind him, hauled his upper body against her chest, wrapped her arms around him, and radiated healing. He groaned, recovering.

"You can't stop the wall, bitch," the rebel said. He gestured, and the walls resumed motion, crackling viciously toward them.

"Down!" Dynamo called. "Cover your heads."

The trainees obeyed, except for the Silvers, who remained alertly upright.

Their defensive magic might be puny compared to the onslaught, but they were ready to balk it to whatever extend they could.

The wall intersected the defensive circle. It flashed as it was diverted, but the sides of it continued advancing, wrapping around until it formed a deadly circle of its own. Then the posts and wires vaporized and their protection was gone.

The wall halted again. "Time to go, bitch," the leader called. "Unless you want to burn too."

Gale couldn't leave Fifth yet; the healing was not complete. But now at last the proper future path clarified. She had to delay the onslaught just one more minute.

"I will buy their lives," Gale called. Her clothing dissolved, and she was sitting naked. Fifth, aware of her bare breasts and thighs pressing against his back and hips, lifted his head, amazed.

The leader laughed cruelly. "No sale, bitch!"

But another man nudged him. "She's the Queen, Charm's most beautiful and powerful woman. We want her. We'll never have another chance." Indeed, the other rebels were staring at the bare portions of Gale's flesh that showed, mainly her lifted thighs.

The leader nodded. "Very well, bitch: you can buy a delay. For as long as we are plumbing you. *Then* they die."

"Then they live," she insisted. "That is the offer."

"Negation. They die."

The minute had passed. "I think not," Gale said. "Give over this treachery, and I will spare your lives, not your freedom."

"You have no more power here than we do, bitch. You can't balk us." He lifted his hand. "Last chance to buy a delay."

"Negation."

"As you wish." He lowered his hand, and the wall resumed motion. The upper reaches became a crackling dome, and the dome was lowering.

Then the motion halted once more. "What's this?" the leader demanded angrily. "Keep it going. Destroy them all!"

"Welcome, Glamor," Gale said.

For there stood a giant Silver seven-legged spider. It lifted one leg in greeting.

"My friend of old," she said. "I know he is part of you now, Glamor." She got up and walked to the spider, who enfolded her with two front legs. She kissed the huge proboscis. "Love." For in childhood she had befriended a spider, who had later saved her from rape, and that feeling for her friend remained.

"What is this?" the leader demanded querulously. "You're a bug lover?"

"Oh, yes," Gale said. "And this is your doom."

"Doubt."

The Silver spider walked to the Black Chroma man, who had sunk back to the ground when Gale left him. Naive was trying to comfort him. The spider touched him where the bolt had entered his chest. The angry burn marks disappeared, and Fifth took his first fully free breath. The healing had been completed. Silver knew how best to deal with a silver wound.

Now the rebel leader showed fear. He could fight Gale, but not the Silver Glamor. The huge spider sent out a loop of silk that caught the man about the neck, and hauled him in. He screamed as the Glamor made a single bite on his shoulder. Then he went into stasis, conscious but immobile. He had been paralyzed as a living food supply. His open eyes showed his horror at his fate.

The other assassins tried to flee, but loops caught each of them. In moments all were immobile and staring.

The big spider flung one more strand out to intersect the dome of electricity. It dissipated like illusion and was gone.

"Gratitude," Gale said. "You saved me again."

The Glamor lifted one leg in acknowledgment, then vanished with the bodies.

The trainees got up and looked around, awed by what they had seen. That included Gale, who now thought to form new clothing about herself. But it was mostly the deadly threat of the silver fire, and the terrible retribution. Gale had presented a friendly, supportive figure with potent connections, a "nice" Glamor. The Silver spider had shown the other side of it: sheer raw power for healing and harming. An angry Glamor was a thing to be feared, even by those it was protecting.

"Give them time to recover," she murmured.

Dynamo took his place before the group. "I believe the danger has passed. This may be taken as an object lesson: you will not necessarily be popular. Your lives may be in danger. Any who prefer to reconsider their participation now may do so; we will let you go. Take an hour, discuss it among yourselves. Then we will resume training."

Gale was impressed. This man really did have nerve and gumption; he had taken hold as if this were a routine incident. During the hour she sat with him slightly apart from the trainees, so that all could see that the two of them were not party to the discussion about continued participation. It was to be a free decision.

"Question," Dynamo asked. "How did the rebels know you are a Glamor? Did someone in our group betray you?"

Gale laughed. "Negation! I know their minds. All are loyal, though three will decide to depart, understandably. My nature is known in command circles; there was a leak that the Silver Glamor will deal with."

"Relief. I like these trainees; they are good people, with nerve and intellect."

"The kind ready and willing to take substantial risks," she agreed. "You selected them to be that way. This vindicates your judgment."

"Question: when you indulge in sex with me, do you get pleasure in it also?"

She was surprised by his change of subject, but answered honestly. "I do, but that is because I peek at your pleasure, sharing it. Glamors are highly sexed, but for my own joy there is only one man: Havoc. I will always love him."

"I am coming to better appreciate the nature of no fault. You are doing what you need to to accomplish your business."

"I never deceived you in that."

"True, and I never deluded myself. But I have something to work out." He paused a moment, and she did not speak or peek, allowing him his time. "You offered your body to the rebels to buy time for all of us, so that the Silver Glamor could come and deal with them. You would have spared them, had they yielded. They could have had the experience of sex with what they called Charm's most beautiful woman and lived to brag of it, had they been reasonable." He paused again. "Is your relationship with me similar in essence?"

There it was. "Affirmation. I hope you are reasonable."

He shook his head. "I can't promise that. I can say I will never betray you or try to deceive you. But I am loyal to my planet. Considering that, I don't think I should have the privilege of your body. It's not no fault."

This time she did not argue the issue. "We understand each other. Remain true to your nature and we will never be opponents."

"Oh, lovely lady, I hope so!" He paused again. "I believe I must seek other company, lest yours cause me to love you despite your corrective magic. I have interacted with five women of your sphere. Each has been remarkable in her own way. Did any want the relationship for its own sake?"

"Naive," she said.

"She has her own man now."

"Clarification. Fifth acted to save you, and is a fine deserving man. But two things prevent him from forming a permanent union with Naive. One is that he is attracted to her youthful, nigh childish body. She does not want to be desired as a child, but as a woman. Soon she will develop her adult body. She must, like all Charm girls, marry by age eighteen, less than a year hence. She is not right for Fifth, and not merely because they are of different Chroma. Second, when I started healing Fifth, it diverted his interest to me. This is a consequence that will take time to fade."

Dynamo stared at her. "A penalty for his good deed!"

"Negation. I do not consider myself a penalty." She smiled. "I suggest that I take him no fault, leaving Naive for you."

"I can't just take her! The woman must make the overture."

"On your planet. Not on ours. Here it is the tradition for the male to propose. Naive will not approach you directly, though she has a crush on you; it is why she enlisted and has tried to impress you favorably. You treated her like a woman, and you are a worthy man."

"She suggested no fault at the outset."

"This is beyond no fault. Your night with her won her love."

"But marriage! There are horrendous constraints. I may return to Earth."

Gale smiled. "You do not need to make such a decision in haste. Suggest to her that the two of you associate for the purpose of ascertaining whether you would be suitable partners in marriage. If by the time she is eighteen you believe you are, then marry her. Otherwise, let her go. At least she will have several months of you. She will value that."

Dynamo nodded. "This seems kind. Appreciation for your guidance, Queen Gale."

"I want you to be satisfied. This seems appropriate. You can have a real woman, instead of a mock relationship."

"I prefer that," he agreed. "One other thing: I believe the trainees should have Chroma stones, so as to be better able to protect themselves in future."

"Agreement. I will see to it."

He paused, hesitant to ask one last favor. She read his mind to this extent, and granted it: a final kiss.

"Appreciation," he murmured.

The hour finished. Three trainees elected to return to their Chroma, as Gale had known. Then Dynamo made two announcements. "We believe you should not be exposed to serious risks unprotected. Queen Gale will procure Chroma stones for each of you, so that you can use your magic when necessary." He shrugged. "NonChroma will have to suffer through as usual. Perhaps she will offer you a kiss instead."

"Granted," Gale said laughing. She went to each nonChroma man and kissed him, and hugged each nonChroma woman. The Chroma trainees were more than satisfied with their bargain. NonChroma stones existed, but would be of no use to people who had never learned to do magic anyway.

"Now a personal matter," Dynamo said. "Queen Gale, impressed with Fifth's act of heroism and sacrifice, will take him as her no fault companion for the remainder of the training." Fifth was openly stunned, and the others surprised.

Gale walked up to Fifth and took his hand. She used momentary illusion for him alone to give herself her body as it was when she was twelve. "I hope I do not disappoint you." All the others burst out laughing, not realizing his preference for that kind. Then she kissed him. "Join me tonight."

"Acquiescence, Lady," he replied faintly.

"That leaves Naive," Dynamo said. He took the girl's hand. "If you will, I request that you and I form an association for the duration to ascertain whether we would be suitable partners for marriage."

Naive fainted.

Dynamo caught her. "She says Agreement," Fifth called, and the others applauded. It seemed that her interest in Dynamo was generally known, especially to her no fault partner.

"Now we must resume training," Dynamo said.

They got to it with a will.

That night Gale took Fifth to her bed. She had flashed him with illusion, but that had limits, so she reverted her physical body to that young age and gave it to him. It was an interesting experience. He was not actually interested in children, merely in an early body, and would surely one day marry a very slightly endowed woman.

"Appreciation, Lady," he panted as he concluded.

"You did a brave and foolish thing, taking in that lightning bolt without the support of your Chroma magic," she reminded him. "Thereby perhaps saving Dynamo's life at risk of your own. You deserve a reward."

"Clarification: appreciation for not revealing my preference."

"That is your business, as long as you do not tackle any real children."

"Never," he agreed.

Meanwhile, she knew, Dynamo and Naive were working it out. He preferred fully-endowed women, and she knew it, and so his restrained interest in her was actually a recommendation. He wanted her as she would become. In the interim they were getting to know each other in other ways. It might indeed lead to marriage.

Gale smiled internally. It was her task to win Dynamo over, but he was actually being won by Charm. He was falling in love with the magic planet. That would do.

The training continued. The trainees learned much about Earth: its odd geography of six water-enclosed continents, its universal White Chroma Science magic, its matriarchal government. The female trainees practiced the mannerisms and sexuality of Mistresses, so as to be familiar with the type; they would better be able to handle the men of Earth that way. They learned about the advanced Science artifacts: holo vision that resembled Air Chroma illusion shows. Rockets that carried people rapidly from one section of the planet to another. Food machines that adapted and mixed base organic ingredients to resemble any regular kind of meat or vegetable or drink. Weapons: Dynamo showed exactly how his pistol worked, so they would be wary of any so-called fire-arms in the hands of others. Computers, which had no common analogy in Charm, capable of recording, storing, and handling great amounts of information on many things.

"Question," a trainee asked. "If Earth wins, how will this information be relevant to our mission?"

"You must know the things of Earth, so as to be able to follow the instructions of Earth," Dynamo replied. "They will send Earthers here to give directions, and you will have to translate them for those farther down the hierarchy. That will make for a smoother transition."

"Question," another asked. "Do you still believe Earth will win?"

Dynamo paused, and Gale knew why. He did not want to say what he believed. "Affirmation."

"Do you still want Earth to win?"

Another pause. "Negation."

There was silence. They understood his reluctance.

In two months the training was done. They were ready for what would come, either way.

The next group of trainees was larger, for two reasons. More citizens had heard of the program, and believed that they could become leaders on Earth. And the first group of one hundred—they had gotten three replacements—was available for assistance. In fact this was the second stage of the training: to become proficient in training others.

By the time the Earth ship returned, in six months, there were a thousand trained personnel, spread across all the Chroma. This seemed like a large group, but of course would be only the nucleus for the Earth effort.

Dynamo married Naive, who had by this time fleshed out so that she looked at least fifteen. It had to be more than that, of course; Dynamo had had experience with far more lovely and experienced women. He had found in Naive qualities of character he respected, and she became his permanent link to the planet he had come to love.

Havoc's mistress Symbol was solidly pregnant with her fourth, and looking for a husband for the other three. She would retire as Havoc's mistress until she had borne them and could wear the wire again. And best of all, perhaps related, Havoc was desperate for Gale's close company.

She had one more special dialogue with Fifth before they ended their no fault relationship. "When you go to Earth, ask to speak with my daughter Flame. Tell her I sent you."

"Question?"

"She will understand." For in the course of her liaison with him, Gale had experimented with variations of form, and found that slender and muscular was his actual preference. Flame had a problem with men, because she was almost masculine in her hard, efficient form. Men were dazzled by her sister Weft and hardly saw Flame as other than a deadly Amazon. But for Fifth, Flame would be beauty incarnate. Gale knew, because once she had assumed Flame's form, except for face and hair, and he had been savagely turned on. Flame longed hopelessly for a man who would find her sexually irresistible, regardless of her other qualities. Fifth was that man. They would make a nice enough couple.

But how were things going on Earth? Gale was hardly the only one desperate to know. The Earth ship was bringing news they all were eager to receive.

Chapter 11
Ingenue

Weft had gone to sing in the opera, and Warp to tour the Earth fleet of space ships. Flame and Aura were visiting the local martial arts dojo, where Flame was surely wowing them with her proficiency and possibly learning new techniques.

That left Voila, with Iolo ifrit, and Caveat as guardian. Caveat was a challenge: a handsome, competent, honest man on whom she had half a crush. And he was what he called gay: romantically interested in men or boys rather than women or girls. Which was why the Earth authorities had assigned him to her, wary that she might otherwise seduce her guard and win him away from loyalty to Earth.

Unfortunately, that was exactly what she had in mind. It galled her that the Earth authority had anticipated her in this, but also made it more of a challenge. She was determined to seduce him anyway, both for her mission and for herself. Her pose among the siblings was the overshadowed maiden, concealing the reality that she governed their mission. That seemed to be working well, but her suppressed pride demanded that she make her mark in some fashion. To seduce the unseduceable—that would be a satisfying private coup. She merely had to figure out the appropriate approach.

She had made a mistake in showing her hand too early. Now he knew her interest, and diverted it. In public he would make it seem that she was a child that no honorable man would touch. In private he made it courteously clear that he would never touch her regardless of her age. Flame was amused, which hardly helped. Flame had had her no fault affair on the ship, proving herself. Warp had Mistress Marionette in addition to the Sorceress Ine; between them they almost satisfied his boundless masculine urge. Weft had had continuous no faults on the ship and now had the opera male lead in thrall. While Voila had this blank wall.

Well, she would get on about her mission, and watch for her opportunity. The time would come when Caveat took her seriously. He simply did not yet know it.

"I want to see volcanoes," she said petulantly. She was not really a little spoiled princess. For one thing, the throne of Charm was not inherited; she was not the heir despite being the only natural child of the king and queen. When Havoc gave it up to become a traveling minstrel, there would be a selection process for the next king. So she was a princess only in name. For another, she was not spoiled; she had trained assiduously in her magical and nonmagical specialties, and was as good as she could be in both. She could afford to demonstrate her talent as an actress, if the opportunity presented, but would hide her Glamor abilities as long as she feasibly could.

In fact all four of them were playing a kind of game, showing off their nonmagical abilities, being excited tourists, viewing volcanoes, so as to divert attention from their real nature and mission. If the Earthers caught on too soon that they were not mere innocent youths, there would be real trouble. Worse, if it became generally known too soon on this planet that magic was real, there could be dangerous mischief. Even their sexuality was part of the diversion; who would think, for example, that Warp had anything serious on his mind as he repeatedly plumbed the alluring Mistress Marionette? That Weft was anything but a young thrill-seeker as she worked her way through the men of the *Ms Dominance*? That Flame's no fault affair with a single Earther was not a girl smitten purely by flattery? But in reality Warp was no reckless scion, and Weft no nympho, and Flame no mindless warrior; they were deadly serious agents of Charm's ambitious agenda. As was Voila.

"This is feasible," Caveat said. He at least knew of their magical abilities, but had seen them use them only when in immediate danger. He was keeping their confidence, per their understanding, and perhaps hoping to learn more of their hidden potentials. She hoped she would not have to show him how much farther it went.

"Enthusiasm." She was the innocent child.

Caveat activated a holo map of the Earth globe. "Do you have a preference? There are volcanoes all across Earth."

Voila looked. "What is that?"

"That is the continent of Africa. Unlike your home planet, Earth is covered mostly by water, with large land masses separated from others by open seas. Africa is thought to be the origin of mankind."

"Wonder! Where?"

"Most early artifacts are in and around the Rift Valley, here in Eastern Africa. The uncertainty and disruption occasioned by the seismic shifts and volcanic eruptions may have caused mankind to become cleverer, so as to cope with the changing environment. We may owe much to volcanic activity."

He was playing to her interest, humoring her. She was happy to play along. "Conclusion: Then those are the volcanoes I want to see. When can we go?"

He shrugged. "Now, if you wish."

Soon enough the two of them and Iolo were on a rocket to Africa. She did not have to pretend being thrilled by the trip; this was Science magic at its best.

They landed at Ababa at the edge of the Rift and took a powered floater into the valley. It was marvelously scenic.

They passed over Lake Victoria, an enormous but shallow body of water. "Some believe that modern mankind originated here," Caveat said. "That when this lake was dry, its fertile soil might have been the basis for mankind's memory of the Garden of Eden. Perhaps more practically, the dangerous volcanoes of the region may have forced mankind to become clever to survive, as I mentioned, to learn the signals of a threatening eruption."

"Our species evolved with volcanoes," Voila said, suitably pleased.

They come to the Western Rift Valley, west of the big lake. There was a huge range of mountains. "This is the Virunga area," Caveat continued. "Virunga means volcano. The one we are going to is Nyamlagira."

"But it's not tall," Voila said, disappointed.

"It is what we call a shield volcano. Its lava is thin and flows almost like water, though it is 2,000 degrees hot. Only the volcanoes in Hawaii, half around the world, have similarly thin outflow. In due course it cools and solidifies, but in thin layers, forming a mound more like a tortoise shell than a cone. Still, it can be impressive enough."

They landed in a "safe" section. As night fell they went out to look at the volcano, and she appreciated what he meant. There were a number of vents or chimneys, like miniature volcanoes. There were rivers and pools of incandescent lava that seemed to be boiling with phosphorescent flames. Holes in the ground belched fire. Bubbles of gas rose to the surface. The surrounding rock was bright orange, with blue clouds of smoke and a strong smell of sulfur.

"Oh, its lovely!" Voila exclaimed, thrilled. Volcanoes had always fascinated her, and this was her first experience with a non-magic one. "I wish we could camp here forever."

"We would get trapped and burned by the flowing lava," Caveat said.

"Negation. I am alert for that." And of course she was. She was also relating to the local amoeba, her constituency, and found them amenable; they would support her.

But before she could find a suitable place to release her magic vapor, there came a holo letter from one M Melodious addressed to Voila. "Perplexity: I don't think I know him," Voila said.

"That is a mistress," Caveat said. "Signified by the abbreviation M. This is important, by definition."

"Resignation. Then I suppose I must view it."

Caveat played the holo on a machine he had with him. The figure of a beautiful older woman formed before them.

"A greeting, Voila," the woman said, emulating the Charm manner. "I am Mistress Melodious, retired, associated with a small opera company. Your sister Weft is singing in one of my operas, and doing quite well."

She would, of course. No one else could sing or play the dulcimer as well as Weft, except possibly their mother Gale, who had taught her.

"Weft tells me that you are as good an actress as she is a singer," the Mistress continued. "If that is true, there may be a challenge and opportunity for you. A traveling play of considerable popularity has just lost its lead actress and will have to cancel the remainder of its tour if a replacement is not found immediately. This is an extremely challenging part for a young actress, and at the moment none of sufficient expertise are available. I must say that Weft has impressed us. I accept her recommendation, and if you are amenable I will ask the play mistress to try you as the replacement."

Voila was more than amenable; she was quite interested. Warp and Weft had made their scenes; maybe it was her turn. "What is the play?" she asked.

To her surprise, the recording answered. "The play is titled *The Option*. It is a romance set in the semi-mystical pre-Matriarchy years when men possessed and abused power. The central figure is a girl of age sixteen who is courted in an unusual manner by an older man of wealth. It is an exploration of her developing character and emotion. That may sound routine, but its nuances are beyond all but the most talented young actresses."

"Where is it? Are there volcanoes there?"

"It is currently being played in the Old Europe section of Asia," the mistress said. "There are some very nice volcanoes in that region."

"I'll do it," Voila said impulsively before Caveat could caution her.

"Pause," Caveat said. "Voila, this is what is known as a responsive recording, keyed to react to particular words. The mistress programmed it for your likely questions; it was not a true dialogue. Your answer will have to be sent back similarly."

"Send," Voila said.

"This may not be wise. I am familiar with that play. 'Challenging' understates the case. It is a grueling emotional workout. Perhaps you can handle it, but you will need time to learn the script and rehearse. A new actress can't simply step into a role like that."

"I can," Voila said with girlish confidence.

"Please, it is my duty to protect you. This role is potential disaster. You would have perhaps only two days before the next presentation. That's hardly time for travel and rehearsal, let alone memorizing the lines. You could embarrass yourself."

"You care?" she inquired archly.

"I do, Voila. I fear you could be emotionally hurt by failing at something no one could succeed at."

"Decision," she said firmly. "Take me there."

He did not roll his eyes, but he might as well have. The willful teenager was manifesting, with a likely catastrophe in the making. "This is in serious violation of my better judgment."

She glanced sidelong at him. "Kiss me and I will reconsider."

"Voila, you have kissed me many times. You know the futility."

"This time I want *you* to kiss *me*."

He sighed. Then he took her in his arms and kissed her on the mouth. No one could have told that his heart wasn't in it; he had a certain acting ability of his own. Regardless, she loved it.

"Reconsidering," she said. "This is likely folly. But I am an imperious child who must learn from experience. Tell Mistress Melodious I accept."

Caveat shook his head. "I wish I could persuade you to change your mind. But I am unable to pay the price you would demand, for more than one reason."

"Three reasons," she said. "It would be a violation of your position as my guardian on Earth. I am underage. And you are gay."

"We understand each other, as usual, you little minx."

"Observation: But you like me a little anyway."

"I do, Voila. You're a fine and talented girl."

"Statement: With no fault your position as my guardian won't matter."

"True, by your definition. However—"

"Soon I will have my sixteenth birthday. Then I won't be underage."

He waggled a cautionary finger at her. "Technically true. Still—"

"That last is a challenge. I am working on it."

"I fear you are. I wish most of all to protect you from that humiliation."

"At least only the two of us will know of it."

"The mistresses would know. Somehow they know everything."

That was interesting. Did the mistresses possess some form of telepathy?

She would watch for that.

He fiddled with the holo receiver. "I will record your answer now." He pointed the lens at her.

Voila smiled. "Appreciation, Mistress Melodious. What my sister Weft says is true. I am accepting the offer, and will travel immediately to join the play. Please relay my respects to my sister the singing heifer."

Caveat laughed as he turned off the unit. "Now we must go to the nearest town to send the letter and board a rocket to Europe. Any other requests, Princess?"

"Confirmation. Obtain a recording of the play I can view while traveling."

"That does make sense," he agreed warily.

In due course the three of them were aboard the rocket. Voila donned the headset and absorbed the play.

They were right: this was a challenge worthy of her effort. She planned to amaze the audience, just as Warp and Weft were doing. But it would be no easy gig, and she could indeed fall short.

They landed in Paris, France, Europe, Asia, and proceeded to the theater just in time for the evening rehearsal. Openly dubious personnel had scheduled it, because the word of a mistress, any mistress, was virtual law.

Mistress Modesty greeted them at the entrance. She was another beautiful older woman. "Thank you for coming, dear," she said to Voila. "I sincerely hope you can help us." She was an actress herself, so did not sound at all insincere.

"I viewed the play while traveling," Voila said. "I can do it. It's a very nice role."

"It is indeed. But of course there are nuances as different groups perform it. The rehearsal may be awkward even if you know the lines."

"I know them."

"A single viewing, and you know them?"

"Affirmation."

"This is remarkable." But she did not argue the case. It was a talent proficient actresses possessed. "The cast is waiting."

Voila clung shyly to Caveat as they walked through the elaborate old building. At one point she paused to whisper in his ear. "She is angry. Find out why."

He nodded, then turned to Modesty. "Mistress, is there a convenient lavatory?"

"Of course." Modesty showed the way.

Voila entered with Iolo and used the facilities. Caveat had covered beautifully, as she had known he would, pretending that she was too shy to ask for herself. And actually she did need this pause. "He'll find out," she murmured to Iolo. "Something is skew."

The ifrit nodded. He understood perfectly.

They came to the stage. The audience chamber was empty except for a few workers and executives, and one holo reviewer. That woman approached them. "May I, Mistress?"

Modesty turned to Voila. "This is Critice. She wishes to interview you prior to the rehearsal, for background. She will review the performance tomorrow. Do you care for the publicity?"

"Affirmation," Viola said confidently. But this was part of her act; a significant current of uncomfortable doubt was nagging her.

"Then we shall retreat briefly," Modesty said. She took Caveat's arm. "I know of you, Caveat. The Mistress of Mistresses speaks well of you."

"Appreciation, Mistress," he said, obviously somewhat ill at ease about leaving Viola to the reviewer.

"You are Princess Voila of Colony Planet Charm," Critice said. "There was skepticism when your sister first performed in the opera *Ms Conquest*, but it seems she prevailed regardless and is a considerable success. Some say she is the finest young singer extant. She recommends you as a similarly talented actress. Do you regard yourself as such?"

This woman was setting a monstrous trap. Viola walked boldly into it. What was the point of a challenge if one did not grasp it by the horns? "Affirmation."

There was a faint crease of predation along Critice's jaw. "You have confidence."

"Agreement."

"Are you familiar with the script of *The Option?*"

"Affirmation. I viewed it on the way here."

"So you believe you will be able to step forthwith into the role?"

"Affirmation."

The woman was suppressing immense private satisfaction. It was clear to her that an appalling embarrassment was about to befall a mistress: miscasting a replacement for a prime part. "Then I wish you well, Voila," she said with enormous irony.

"Appreciation." Her irony matched that of the reviewer, but was far better masked. She was, after all, an actress.

"I will be watching."

With fangs glistening. "Parting."

The woman went to the center of the audience section and set up shop, ready to judge the inadequate performance. Mistress Modesty returned with Caveat. "The woman is an inveterate skeptic. It will be gratifying if you are able to set her back."

"Agreement."

"We are familiar with the experience your sister had before she proved herself. These players are not like that. They will be supportive. We want you to succeed. This is a rehearsal; it may be interrupted at any time to iron out a problem. Don't hesitate if you are uncertain."

"Appreciation."

The rehearsal started—and there was trouble. Voila knew what it was: this was a different group from the one she had viewed, under different direction, with different actors. Their appearance, pacing, mannerisms, cadence, and delivery differed. Voila was geared for what she had seen and memorized. This threw her off.

She did her best to adapt, but knew it was imperfect. The watching reviewer knew it too. Critice was already writing her devastating review of the performance, contrary to regulation; Voila read it in her mind. She was a failed actress herself; it made her feel better to put down others.

"Pause," Viola said after a miscue. The actors paused. "I am not integrating well with you. When you try to compensate, it throws me farther off. Please, make no adjustments; I will soon adapt, and tomorrow I will have it right."

No one argued. They stopped trying to compensate. And as she attuned to them, her integration improved, until by the last act it was passable. But the reviewer had departed by this time. That was just as well. Voila wanted her to be surprised.

There was a pause before the final act as they changed the props. "You do have the lines," Modesty said. "And you are getting the nuances. Judging by your improvement this night, you will do well tomorrow. I confess to being impressed."

"Appreciation." She saw that the woman was no longer angry; Caveat had done his job.

Then came the scene, and the concluding soliloquy. And it was wrong. Not in lines but in spirit.

"Mortification!" she muttered

Modesty joined her again. "This is where experience counts, Voila. You have done a phenomenal job getting all the lines, but interpretation must take its own course. The final soliloquy is its own challenge. Do not try to adapt to anyone else's style, such as that of the presentation you viewed. You must make it your own."

"Surprise: This is permitted, here?"

"Oh, yes, dear. The words are really nothing in themselves; the delivery is everything. Put your own heart into it, tomorrow. This is where it counts. You must, as they say, make the stones cry."

"Gladness!" For she did have ideas of her own for it. Now she had leave to use them. But would they really work, untried? Then she had an idea. "Mistress, this is perhaps the most challenging piece I have encountered. I have seen one interpretation, and would like to see another. Have you by chance performed this role in the past?"

"How perceptive of you, Voila! Yes, long ago when I was young, before I was a mistress, I played it."

"Play it for me now."

"Oh, it has been too long. I am way beyond such expression now, in spirit as well as body."

"Doubt."

"She does not mean that negatively, Mistress," Caveat said quickly. "She believes you retain the feeling."

Modesty nodded. "You put me on the spot, dear. But this is not a request I can deny, in the circumstance."

"Delight."

Mistress Modesty recited the lines, which she naturally knew by heart. "If love can start a fire, then let it start one here." At first her rendition seemed ordinary, but slowly it intensified, until at the conclusion the tears were streaming down her face—and both Voila and Caveat were reacting similarly. "You gave me a life! You made me a woman!" She had transformed ordinary words to something special, evoking key emotions in the listeners. The stones were, indeed, crying. "I love you!" And who could not love her in return?

"Appreciation, Mistress!" Voila kissed her, and the mistress accepted it, knowing the feeling was warranted. She had clearly been a fine actress—and remained one. This would certainly help.

Mistress Modesty took them to dinner, including Iolo. She said nothing of the play. She expressed interest in Planet Charm, and muted her evident skepticism about the practice of magic there. Then she showed them to their room for the night.

"This is not necessarily proper," Caveat said.

"How can you guard her if you are not with her?" Modesty asked.

"Normally there are women present. We are not alone."

"Surely you do not want me to night with you." Viola saw that Modesty knew his nature.

"Unnecessary," Caveat agreed. "But is there danger here?"

Modesty nodded. "There is. The hotel is protected, but there are unscrupulous currents. Remain on guard."

It was a directive. "As you wish, Mistress."

When they were alone except for Iolo, Voila braced him. "Explanation: Why was she angry?"

"I would prefer not to say. The matter has been handled."

"Threat: I will demand that you embrace me naked."

It was effective. "She was directed to make the place for you. To do so she had to abruptly retire her promising protégée, the former ingenue."

Voila was appalled. "Dismay! I didn't know! I thought it was some accident that left them bereft. I thought I was doing them a favor."

"So I explained. Mistress Modestly is now satisfied that you are blameless."

Voila eyed him. "Suspicion: There is more. Don't make me threaten you again."

"Then I put in a call to the Mistress of Mistresses, as is my prerogative, and she explained to Modesty: there was a serious attack being formulated against you in Africa. It was necessary to get you out of there immediately, by seeming coincidence, so as not to alert the assassins that their plot was known."

"Chagrin. I can't do this to an innocent actress. Bring her back."

"I anticipated your reaction. I inquired. She was sent far away, and can't be returned in time for tomorrow's performance."

"Then for the next. She must have her role back."

"Then what of you, Voila?"

"I will visit volcanoes." But she was intensely sorry to have to give up the role, that she had already fallen in love with.

Caveat nodded, fathoming her feelings. "Perhaps there is another way. Will you trust me?"

"Always, Caveat," she said, kissing his ear.

"Then I will talk with Mistress Modesty." He left the room.

Voila prepared for bed, but she remained unsatisfied. She would have one night to perform, and she wanted it to be exactly right. She wasn't sure it would be. Mistress Modesty's rendition helped enormously, but Voila still had to make it her own.

Caveat returned. "Ingenue will return. There will be a story that she graciously gave up her role to allow you to prove yourself. The publicity should generate sufficient interest to overflow the theater. There will have to be two shows a day, alternating between lead actresses."

"Joy!" she exclaimed, kissing him.

"I do what I can," he said. "The Mistress is pleased also. She will be your friend."

But there was something else. "Request: I am still uncertain of the soliloquy. May I rehearse it with you?"

"Of course, if you wish. But I am not a typical audience, as you know. My reactions may not guide you well."

"You reacted as I did to the Mistress' rendition."

"True. I am hardly immune to human emotion of whatever nature. But of course she did it many times in her youth, and perfected the nuances."

"As must I."

She used the center of the room as a stage, and Caveat and Iolo as the audience, and went into it. But it was wrong again. Her ideas did not translate well to reality. "Frustration!"

"You can do it," Caveat said. "Try it again."

She did, changing the interpretation, but still it was wrong. "Aggravation! What's my problem?"

"Observation," Iolo said.

Caveat's jaw dropped. "Did the dog speak?"

"You know he's no ordinary dog," Voila reminded him, smiling. "And not just because he has six legs. He's my close companion from childhood." She faced the ifrit. "Present it."

"You are doing it alone," Iolo said. "But in the play it is not alone."

"Revelation!" she exclaimed. "That's it!" She turned to Caveat. "Assume the role of the leading man."

"But he does not participate. He just stands there."

"That's participation," she said. "It is vital."

"As you wish." He stood behind her.

This time it worked. The words were the same, not really special in themselves. Delivery was what counted, the projected feeling. That transformed the words into the magic of desperate love and loss. This time the walls fairly vibrated with the intensity of her radiating emotion.

As she concluded, she felt the tears coursing down her face. She was Ingenue, the lost maiden.

"Now you have it," Caveat said as she came out of it. His own face was wet: confirmation.

"Jubilation," she said. "Now will you join me in bed?"

"Negation," he said, smiling. They had been through this before.

"Promise: Some day it will happen."

"Doubt."

"At least kiss me."

He did, this time with some real emotion. He had been moved by her final rendition of the Soliloquy. His feeling for her was not sexual, but at least it existed. That was progress, in more than one sense.

Then at last they retired, in separate beds. Iolo dissolved, checking the area. All was in order. She hoped.

The next evening the theater was filled. This was, as Mistress Modesty had indicated, a popular play, with a year-round audience. But the acting made a difference, and the performance of the lead actress was critical.

The Mistress made a brief announcement before the curtain went up. "Circumstances have caused the absence of our regular lead actress tonight. Instead the role will be played by Princess Voila of Colony Planet Charm, an actress in her own right. Refunds will be given to any who are unsatisfied with her performance."

The audience was silent. It was reserving judgment.

The curtain lifted and the play was on. Voila was immediately immersed in the role so that she seemed to be living it herself. The vast audience faded; the stage setting became all, and then it was no longer a setting; it was reality. She was the ingenue, the innocent girl being surprised and changed by remarkable events, long ago in the not necessarily entirely bad old days when men ruled the world and women accommodated to the necessary extent. The name differed, but in her private ear it was her own.

※ ※

"Really?" she asked her friend. "You kissed a real *man*? On the *mouth*?"

The girl giggled. "Really! I told him I was eighteen, and he actually believed me. And he goosed me!"

Voila squealed with naughty delight. "I don't believe it! On the bottom?"

"Where else? I'm putting tape over the spot so it won't wash off in the shower."

"I'm so jealous!"

A ball of light appeared before them. "Holo letter for Voila. Holo letter for Voila."

"For me?" Voila asked. "Who could be sending me a letter?"

"Don't just sit there wondering, dumdum," her friend said. "Receive it and find out."

"It's probably just an ad for something I don't need."

"Like a C-cup bra," her friend teased. "Unless it comes with the stuffing."

Voila glanced down at her slender figure. "Mom says I'll get there some day. Maybe next year when I'm seventeen."

"Maybe next century, you mean. Are you going to open the letter or aren't you? I'm dying of curiosity."

Voila addressed the ball of light. "Voila is receiving. Who are you?"

The ball expanded into the life sized holographic figure of a portly older man. "Salutation, Miss Voila. I am Gentleman, presently unknown to you, but I have seen you around town and am pleased with your aspect. I am proffering an option."

"A what?" Voila asked blankly.

The letter was keyed for this reaction. "A marriage option. You are not familiar with the concept?"

"I never heard of it! Exactly what is it?"

"I wish to reserve your affections for one year. At the end of this period I will either exercise the option and marry you, or renew it for another year at a higher price, or drop it. In any event, you will keep the money, unless you renege or elect to buy it back."

"This is weird," her friend said.

"You want to buy me?" Voila said, confused.

"By no means. I am simply reserving the right to date and marry you, for one year. You will interact romantically with no other person during that period, and will marry me if I choose to exercise the option. When it expires you will be free to interact with whomever you choose. During the option period you will comport yourself suitably so as not to embarrass me. Otherwise you are free to do as you please."

Voila struggled with the concept. "You are—buying—my romantic attention—for a year? Suppose I don't even like you?"

The image smiled. The letter was programmed for this also. "It is not necessary for you to like me, merely to fulfill the guidelines of the option. In the course of the year I hope either to win your love, or to ascertain that this is not something I desire. At the beginning you will be expected to maintain an open mind, and to be appropriately receptive to my initiatives."

"That's the first time I've heard hot sex called an 'initiative'!" her friend exclaimed.

"Sex!" Voila exclaimed, shocked.

"Sex is not required," the holo said. "That can happen only when both parties are amenable. What is required is your attendance with me at one function per week, formal or informal, with appropriate demeanor."

Voila was finally getting it straight. "You mean I have to dress right and smile at you, and not crack dirty jokes or throw food. I have to act like a lady."

"Like a young lady," the holo agreed.

"Will you kiss me or goose me?"

"Chaste kissing is within the guideline. Animalistic gestures are not."

"The money," her friend said. "Ask about the money!"

"For this option on my affections," Voila said carefully. "What will you pay?"

"Seventy five thousand credits."

Her friend fell back onto the couch, astonished.

"Seventy five credits? That's not much."

"Seventy five thousand credits," the holo repeated.

Now Voila stared. "*Thousand*?"

"It is a good option," the holo said. "Payable at the outset. The annual renewal will be a hundred thousand credits, so as not to waste your time if the outcome is uncertain."

Suddenly this was far more serious than she had imagined. Her whole family could live well for the year on that amount. But by the same token, she suspected a catch. "And if I marry you?"

"The pickup price is set at one million credits plus a percentage of my future income."

"Wow!" her friend breathed. "If you're going to sell yourself, you can't beat that price!"

"And I keep the option money—the seventy five thousand credits—even if the option expires?"

"Correct. That money is yours, barring some extraordinary violation. You are welcome to consult with a lawyer about the terms before signing. I believe you will find them fair."

"All to date you once a week? With nothing more than kissing?"

"Correct, in essence."

Still she hesitated. "You must be a very rich man. Why would you want to associate with a nonentity like me?"

"I like your look and manner, and see potential for you to become the kind of wife I desire."

"Who pays for the lawyer?"

"I do. But you must choose the lawyer, to be assured of an objective opinion."

Voila felt giddy. "I'll do it. I mean, I'll see a lawyer about it. I'm not agreeing to the option yet."

"This is sensible. Here is the option coding; take it to the lawyer." A series of numbers and letters appeared, which Voila hastily scribbled down. "I look forward to your acceptance, Miss Voila." The letter ended.

"What an offer!" her friend said. "The guy could look like a toad and it'd be fine, for that kind of money."

"Actually, he's sort of handsome," Voila said. "But he must be twice my age."

"More like three times. He's pushing fifty if he's a day."

"So why doesn't he go after a woman of his own generation?"

Her friend laughed. "What man wants to make out with a fifty year old woman? No, it's the innocent teens they crave. The older the man, the younger the woman. I hear."

"I don't know about this. There's got to be a catch."

"See the lawyer, dummy! Ask him about catches."

Voila decided. "I'll do that."

Next day she saw the lawyer, and was assured that the offer was legitimate and that there were safeguards to protect her virtue. "It is easy money."

Voila wrestled with it for a week, but finally she decided to accept the option. She signed the papers the lawyer presented, and accepted payment of seventy five thousand credits, which she put into the hands of her father for safekeeping. Now all she had to do was get through the year of dating an older man, hoping it wasn't too bad.

He came to pick her up the first week, in a chauffeured car. He met her parents and made a good impression, being urbane, polite, and friendly. They rode to a restaurant where they had an elegant meal. She found him nice to be with; he was interested in her activities without seeming to snoop, and was open about his own.

"I don't want to seem suspicious," she said. "But I don't understand why you should pay so much money just to date me once a week. I'm nothing special—not beautiful or really smart. I'm just an ordinary girl. There are thousands of others like me, and many with far better qualifications for whatever you might wish. I feel I am cheating you by accepting the money."

"Your candor becomes you," he replied. "I will answer similarly. I am wealthy in money but not in time; I have a slow wasting disease that will take me out in about a decade. I prefer to reap what enjoyment I may from my remaining time, and the company of the right woman would be the major part of that. The problem is in ascertaining which woman is right. Only some time of acquaintance will enable me to do that."

"You're dying!" she said, dismayed.

He smiled. "Not immediately. But it does ameliorate the potential problem of age: I will have a decade or so with whatever woman I choose, regardless of her age. She will of course outlive me, and I trust will handle my estate well thereafter. But my concern is that decade. I hope to enjoy it, or at least find significant satisfaction in it."

Voila remained disturbed by the notion, yet it did makes sense. "I hope you find that woman," she said, doubting that it would be herself.

Gentleman looked at his watch. "I see your hour is up. I will have the chauffeur take you home now if you wish. Or you may remain for dessert."

"I'll stay for dessert," she said, smiling.

She stayed longer than that. After the meal they went to a secluded beach and walked barefoot along it, admiring the myriad shells. "I am discovering that the little things are important," he said. "The sight and sound of the gentle surf, the colors of the shells, the blue of the sky. I did not notice, let alone appreciate such things in my younger days. It seems that I had to have fate give me a time limit before I could pause for real life."

"I never paused either," Voila said. "I agree: these little things are nice."

Her first date actually lasted three hours before she was home again. There had been no kissing, not even any touching of hands, merely the meal, the drive, the walk, and the dialogue. She no longer cared about the hour; she would have been happy to have associated with him on such a basis for twice as long. Gentleman had opened her eyes to the nuances of ordinary life, and she was glad.

"Did he kiss you?" her friend inquired breathlessly next day. "Goose you? Try to get you into bed?"

"None of the above. He was very nice."

"You must have been bored limp!"

"No. Three hours passed like one."

The next week he took her to an art show, after warning her that this, too, might overrun the allotted time. "Remember, you are not obliged to stay longer, by the terms of the option. I merely seem not to have judged the feasibility of an hour correctly."

The art was fascinating. Some of the pictures seemed to reach out to bring them into their world. Others were repulsive—yet even then they were intriguing in the emotions they evoked. Voila had never been a connoisseur of art, but now she appreciated a bit of what she was missing. Again, the time passed rapidly. Again there was no direct physical contact. It was merely a shared experience.

The third week they went to an amusement park. This time it was four hours before she got home, half reeling from the thrills of it. The wild rides, the odd sights, the spun candy, the crazy mirrors, the haunted house—she had more unadulterated fun than ever before in her life.

This time she asked him. "Aren't you gong to touch me?"

"Do you want me to?"

"I don't know. I just sort of expected it. I'm, you know, young flesh."

"You are, Voila, and it tempts me sorely. But I am purchasing your time and attention, not your body. My chief pleasure is in your pleasure."

She took the plunge. "Touch me."

He put his arm around her shoulders. "This will do. I do not need to handle your details to know how precious you are."

She suspected that was a line, but she liked it.

The next week they went to a casino where he purchased a huge pile of chips and they played the machines and games until they lost it all. It was fabulous, but depressing in its implication. "Let's not do this again," she said.

The following week they went to see an excellent play. This time she took his hand as they sat watching it. So it continued, week by week, with many events. She took increasing initiative, hugging him and sometimes kissing him, trying to show her pleasure on the diverse experiences. One week they simply went for a walk in a scenic garden, and that too was worthwhile.

They emerged sooner than anticipated, and the chauffeur was away from the limousine. They sat in it, waiting. This time she took his hand and set it on her small breast. "I want you to handle my details," she said.

"This may not be wise."

"Why not?"

"You make me desire you physically, when I am trying to avoid that. I see you as a compatible companion, and I very much enjoy your company on that basis. Once a relationship becomes physical, it can be difficult to retreat."

"I think I have fallen in love with your lifestyle," she said. "I can't say I love you for yourself, but I think I am ready to find out. I have been taking from you throughout—your money, your knowledge, your time. I want to give something back."

"I am not asking this of you, and it certainly is not required by the option."

"I know. And I don't want you to think I'm trying to win you by sex. I have never had sexual experience, and don't even know whether I want you to exercise the option. I just would like to have this experience with you, that maybe we both will remember years later, regardless of the option."

"In that case, let me make a more ambitious suggestion. Would you like a week-long ocean cruise?"

She stifled her surprise. "Yes."

They had the cruise. They had separate cabins on the most expensive level, and the life was opulent. There was no requirement, but the second night she joined him in his cabin, asking only that he remember her inexperience and not judge her too much by it.

They had cautious sex, and he was careful, and it was a glorious experience despite some awkwardness on her part. She loved being in his embrace and bringing him the ultimate pleasure. She strove to become more proficient in succeeding nights, and learned a great deal. She discovered she enjoyed sex, though she doubted she would with any other man. He had initiated her; he understood her; he made her feel truly appreciated.

Now at last she knew: she did love Gentleman. But by the terms of the option the choice was his to make, not hers.

Then she learned something that shocked her. Gentleman had more than one option. "Oh, I'm sorry," he said. "I thought you understood. I have options on five women. When I am not with you, I am with one of them."

"Of course," she said. "I should have known." But she was hurting inside. *She was not the only one*. There was only one chance in five that he would choose her. She had foolishly fallen in love before she knew the full situation.

She suffered in silence. She smiled for him, doing her best to make their following dates pleasant. But now there was an edge of desperation. What was she to do?

Well, there was one thing. "I—I don't know what is proper," she said. "Could I— would it be possible for me to meet the other women?"

Gentleman was surprised. "Yes, of course. But none of the others have made such a request. I think they prefer to ignore the other optionees. Why do you wish this?"

"To see who else you might love. I might learn something."

He smiled. "I have always appreciated your open candor, Voila. I will make the calls. I can't guarantee that all or any of them will agree to meet you, but I will ask."

"Thank you," she said uncertainly. Was she doing the right thing?

In a few days he called her. "I am amazed. Not only did they agree, they decided to all come together to meet each other and you, in my absence. I have reserved a restaurant table for five and will pay for the meal. Go there and meet them." He paused. "They are older than you, and more experienced. Do not let them tease you. You have merits of your own, Voila."

"Thank you," she said, half-awed by this development. What had she started?

She dressed her best and went to the assigned restaurant at the assigned hour. The maitre d' escorted her to an elaborately set table.

The four women were already there. Voila knew the moment she saw them that she was hopelessly outclassed. They were all beautiful, glamorous, and worldly. They made her simple outfit seem crude in comparison.

They were absolutely polite. She thought of them as One, Two, Three and Four, in the order they first spoke.

"Am I late?" she asked worriedly. "I thought this was the time. I am Voila, who asked to meet you."

"Of course, dear," One said. She was garbed in red, setting off her curly red hair. She looked like a holo star. She seemed to be about 25. "You were the one with sufficient initiative. You are not late; we merely came early."

"So as not to be upstaged by each other," Two said. She was in yellow, enhancing her flowing yellow hair. She seemed to be about 28, with assertive features.

"We are, after all, competitors," Three said. Her hair and outfit were absolutely black, and her eyes were piecing. She seemed to be about 30.

"And we do appreciate your quaint notion that we meet," Four said. Her hair was richly brown, as was her suit. She was older, perhaps 35, but remained elegant.

And Voila was most like a misplaced teen with hair colored hair and little sense of manners. She could see the four appraising her and finding her wanting. Evidently her option had simply been for variety. She was sorry she had invoked this meeting; it was already a disaster for her.

"Shall we dine?" One inquired rhetorically. There was poise in the way she said it that Voila knew she would never be able to achieve.

They dined, and the repartee was swift and apt as the four elder women played off each other. Voila could only try to become invisible. She knew already that she was the odd one out, unworthy of association with these sophisticates.

Soon enough the talk turned to sex. "Of course we realize that sex is not the object with a man of his age," Two said. "Yet it seems satisfactory."

"He has curious old-time habits," Three agreed. "Easy to indulge."

"One might almost suppose he lacks experience," Four said, and they laughed.

They glanced at Voila, but she just sat there. If Gentleman lacked experience, what could be said of her? He had taught her all she knew of that matter.

A subtle nod passed among them. They knew she was out of it.

Somehow she got through the meal without collapsing into tears of humiliation. At least now she knew where she stood: nowhere.

"How was it?" Gentleman inquired at their next date. "You do not have to answer, of course."

"Why did you option me?" she blurted. "I'm not even close to the league of those others."

"They made you feel inferior," he said, perceiving her distress. "I was afraid of that. Let me assure you that sophistication is by no means the only measure of a woman. You are whole cloth, as it were: natural, candid, enthusiastic. A refreshing contrast."

"I don't think you answered my question, exactly."

"Voila, if I prefer sophistication, any of them will do. But my situation has caused me to look beyond that. Do you love me? You are not required to answer."

"Yes," she said, blushing.

"Do they?"

"I don't think so."

"I want to be loved as I decline. Need more be said?"

She gazed at him with burgeoning surmise. "That's all you want?"

"No, of course not. My dog loves me. But it is important. I suspect they saw in you a leading competitor, knowing that in your innocence you possess a quality they lack. You are by no means outclassed in what counts."

"Thank you," she said faintly. He had done it again: brought her out of uncertainty into pleasure at being with him.

All too soon it seemed the year of the option was ending. He would come by noon this day to exercise it if he meant to. If he did not come, it would expire, and she would be free.

Voila had hoped Gentleman wouldn't wait until the last moment. But maybe he had decided on one of the others. Beset by uncertainly she waited for what would happen—or not.

A holo letter arrived. She opened it eagerly. "This message was sent to Gentleman this morning," a female voice said.

Voila viewed the message with growing horror. It was images of herself, evidently patched together from incidental appearances she had made in the past few months and carefully edited. "Gentleman," her image said. "Don't bother with the option. I have put a good face on it for the year because I needed the money, but I know I couldn't stand it permanently. You are way too old for me, and clumsy in bed as well. Lose yourself in the sea for all I care."

Voila sat appalled as the letter ended. This monstrosity had been sent to Gentleman? This had to be the work of one of the other optionees, to eliminate her as a competitor. It had never occurred to her that she could be victimized by such a scheme. What could she do?

She called Gentleman's number, but there was no answer. He was out and she couldn't reach him. Could she leave a message? What could she say that would be believable? Either he would know it was fake, or he wouldn't, regardless. If he trusted her, he would see right through it.

If.

She would know by whether he came before the deadline to exercise the option.

She watched the big clock on the wall as the seconds ticked relentlessly onward toward high noon, as it were. Now there was only one hour left, and he hadn't come.

Had she been fooling herself about her worth as a potential wife? The other optionees were all far better qualified than she in that respect. It was possible, even likely, that she was never his choice regardless of the bad message. That he had given her her chance, but in the end she simply had not measured up. That he wasn't even aware of the deadline, having long since decided to let the option expire.

And where did that leave her? Alone with 75,000 credits and her memories of the wonderful year with him.

Half an hour before the deadline she knew it was hopeless. She simply had to express herself before it ended. She fetched the money, which had been translated to credits, and formed it into a loose pile on the floor. Then she kneeled before it and spoke her aching heart.

"I think I was naïve, but I don't regret it. Gentleman honored his part of the bargain. He paid the money and he gave me a wonderful series of dates and gifts. He taught me so many things that I'll always value. I knew the terms of the option at the start. I was a fool to fall in love without any return commitment, but even that I don't really regret. That was the best experience of all."

Then she reviewed the series of dates they had had, savoring each one. Each was its own special experience, precious in her memory. Gentleman had slowly become her friend, then her lover, and finally her beloved.

The memories overwhelmed her, as the clock ticked toward the hour. She gazed at the pile of money before her. "If love can start a fire, then let it start one here," she said with feeling. "What use have I for money, without him? Burn, money, burn with my fire of love!"

The money burst into flame.

"Oh Gentleman!" she cried. "I'll always love you! I hope that whoever you marry takes good care of you in every way. I wish it could have been me, but if you can be happier with her than with me, then it is what I want for you."

The clock ticked to the minute before noon. She did not hear the dark figure coming up behind her.

"If love can kill, then let me die! This is the way I want to go, consumed by my love for you, Gentleman! You are my star, my sun, my moon, my everything! I am ashamed; I lack the eloquence to express it as I wish I could. I just want to be with you as much as I can. I know now it was not fated to be. My dream was vain. How could I ever think I could compete with the perfect ladies of the other options? Everything I know about what counts I learned from you. I am what you made me, crafted from dull clay. I can only be what you design. Without you I am of no account. You gave me a life! You made me a woman! What could I possibly give you in return? Nothing. Nothing but my wretched innocence and my hopeless love. I love you! I love you! I love you!" She collapsed before the dying fire.

The clock ticked the final second to noon. The spotlight fell on the standing figure, illuminating him. It was Gentleman. He had come to exercise the option.

⁂

The audience was in tears of grief and joy, torn by the emotions of the moment. A translucent curtain fell, masking the figures, rendering them into silhouettes. The outline of the man reached down to touch the fallen girl, who lifted almost as if floating and fell into his embrace. They kissed, and held the pose until the main curtain fell, ending the scene.

Then the applause began, and continued for some time.

"Get out there for the curtain call!" Mistress Modesty said. Numbly Voila went, her face still wet with tears. It didn't matter; most of the faces in the audience were similarly damp. The applause continued, seemingly indefinitely, like the endless roar of the sea at a rough beach.

She had done it. She had evoked the part, living it and making the audience live it with her. That was what counted.

"Your sister was right," Mistress Modesty said later as she helped remove Voila's makeup and costume. "You are the finest young actress extant. I have never seen the Soliloquy done better."

"Explanation: You told me how to do it," Voila said. "You showed me."

The woman smiled tolerantly. "Perhaps."

Back in their room, Voila still felt as if floating. She hugged Iolo. "Pleasure! I did it, thanks to you," she said. There was overflowing credit to be assigned. "I evoked the part. Because you give me the key."

"Appreciation," the ifrit said.

The key had been the man standing silently behind her. It was dramatic irony, where the audience could see and know what the protagonist did not. That presence showed that her declaration of love was not in vain; he was hearing and responding to it. The character did not know it, but she as the actress did. That changed everything.

"I would have married you," Caveat said. "Any man would."

"Agreement. That's the way it's scripted," she agreed. "If the lines can just be delivered with sufficient feeling."

"They were. Every person in that audience fell in love with you in that moment."

"Except you," she chided him.

"I, too, in my fashion."

There was the key qualification. "Conclusion: Then you no longer mind my kisses," she said, kissing him.

"I never did. They are fresh and vital."

Still, she had more in mind than that.

Next day the reviews appeared. "All but one are rapturously positive, affirming that you are indeed an actress to make tears fall from stones," Mistress Modesty said with satisfaction. "And that one reviewer has already been peremptorily dismissed."

"Critise!"

"She was caught cheating. She would never have said what she did, had she seen the formal presentation instead of the rehearsal. She was too eager to cut down the newcomer, and it showed. It is a useful object lesson."

"Like fruit being thrown at the orchestra?" For that story of Weft's experience had made its own share of headlines.

"Like that," Modesty agreed. "Now we have another matter of interest. The prior Ingenue has returned. She would like to meet you."

"Welcome!"

The girl appeared. She was eighteen, but looked sixteen, as befitted the part. Her complexion and hair differed, but she could have passed for Voila had she cared to make the effort.

Neither spoke. They simply came together and hugged.

Caveat's prediction turned out to be accurate. The double news of Voila's success and Ingenue's supposed generosity in setting it up for her attracted extensive interest, and there were audiences for two presentations a day. Ingenue took the morning one, and Voila the afternoon one. Both were well received.

"We are getting considerable repeat business," Modesty observed. "Some of the same people attend both the morning and evening sessions, comparing actresses. The consensus is that Ingenue is good, but Voila is better."

"She is," Ingenue agreed. "I was mad when I got booted for a stranger, but now I'm glad it happened, and not just because she asked to get me back."

The play traveled to other cities. Between play days Voila visited local volcanoes, and Ingenue went with her. The friendship of the two had been instant and enduring. The role gave them a special understanding of each other. Caveat and Modesty accompanied them as adult monitors. And of course Iolo, as Voila's pet dog.

It became a pleasant routine. Voila was able to seed her full complement of volcanoes in the course of three months, and to relate fully to her constituency of amoeba. They accepted her as their representative, as they did on Planet Charm. In that time the *Ms Dominance* took off for Charm, carrying none of their party back, but bearing news of their activities that Havoc and Gale would understand. The project was well under way. And she turned sixteen.

But Voila's project with Caveat had not been consummated. She felt about him somewhat the way Ingenue felt about Gentleman in the play, though with greater realism. She wanted to feel his loving embrace at least once before they parted ways, as they inevitably would in time.

Then as they approached another volcano, Mistress Modesty called them to her for a serious discussion. "Princess, you were removed from Africa because of a plot against your life. That plot, or a similar one, has reappeared. We do not as yet know the details, but need to take defensive measures."

"Question: I have to leave you?" Voila asked, disappointed. This was a temporary life, for her, but she liked it.

"I think not, lest we reveal our knowledge of the plot and cause it to fade and resurface elsewhere. This is why we have no guards close, lest they be spotted. We need to catch the perpetrators now. But we do not wish to expose you to any unnecessary danger."

Voila believed that. She had come to like and trust the mistress, who was a good and competent person dedicated to the welfare of the play and the actors. "Acquiescence."

"We believe that you and Caveat should go into temporary hiding." Modesty paused. "There is an aspect I do not like, but it may be necessary. You, Ingenue, should make yourself up to resemble Voila, so that the saboteurs do not know she is gone. That way we may spring the trap. There may be danger for you."

"I'll do it," Ingenue said immediately.

"Concern," Voila said. "I can better protect myself."

"But you are the target. She will not be in the same danger as you would be, as once her identity is known, they will seek you elsewhere."

It did make sense. "Reluctance. But agreement." Voila hugged Ingenue and went into hiding with Caveat while Ingenue made herself resemble Voila. Her form was similar, she now knew Voila well, and she was a consummate actress; she could do it.

They hid in an old bunker nearby, with Iolo, while Modesty and Ingenue walked on to view the volcano. Voila's environmental awareness indicated no immediate threat. Her view of the paths of the near future showed nothing for at least an hour, and perhaps beyond. Iolo diffused into mist and hovered around, on guard against any intrusion, leaving his collar on the floor. Caveat picked it up and put it in a safe cranny. He had seen Iolo perform before, and appreciated the type of protection provided.

The bunker was spare to the point of poverty. There were no conveniences, merely a buried chamber buttressed by masses of stone. There was nothing to do but wait. That did not suit her. "Boredom."

"Regret." He was wary.

"Idea," she said.

"Negation," he replied long familiar with her flirting. "I am not Gentleman."

"Bet: I can seduce you within an hour, if you give me leave. I promise never to tell."

He was almost resigned. "Voila, if I give you that hour, and you fail, will you then give up this useless flirtation? It embarrasses me."

"Deal."

"Deal," he echoed.

"I will use art and magic."

He shrugged. He knew she could do magic, but that would not turn him on heterosexually.

"Request: Ignore me for a time."

He faced away from her. There was not room for them to separate very far.

She removed her clothing and stood nude. She had fleshed out somewhat in the recent months, but remained slender. Then she focused on multiple illusion she had learned from Idyll ifrit: sight, sound, touch, mind. She shaped herself into a boy in those externally discernible senses.

"Turn," she said at last.

He turned back—and stared. "What have you done?"

"I have become a boy. Now you can love me."

"But I know you for a girl, and underage."

"I am sixteen. That is permissible. This encounter is off the record and mutually voluntary; it is not a violation of your trust."

He licked his lips. "Voila, please. This is wicked temptation."

"Exactly." She stepped into him and took hold, embracing and kissing him.

"Voila, I beg you, give over. This is unfair."

"Agreement." She kissed him again. Now her face had a slight scratchiness of a shaved beard. "Remove your clothing."

"How can I persuade you to stop?" he asked desperately.

"Resist me. For an hour. Then I will confess defeat."

He tried, but could not. He knew her and liked her, and respected her abilities. He knew she was smitten with him. Now she had assumed a form that made her unbearably appealing. "This is not right," he said despairingly. "I know you are a woman."

"So?" She took his hand and put it to her male genital, which stiffened under his touch.

"I can't stand this!"

"Sympathy. You have teased me similarly for months." She started undressing him.

Then he snapped. He got out of his clothing and embraced her, reacting. They kissed and handled, and soon he penetrated her and climaxed. That set her off, and she joined him. It was her first full sex. She was thoroughly familiar with the mechanisms, but never actually done it before. She had wanted it to be with the right man.

"I am undone," he panted. "I know you for a woman, yet I love you."

"I will not tell," she reminded him. "I wanted to possess you. I will not do this again unless you ask me."

"Oh, Voila, I can't help myself. I will ask you. I am ashamed."

"There is no shame in love."

"Perhaps not, with you. But in any other circumstance, this would be an abomination."

"Question?"

"You are a woman, with female anatomy. To treat you like a male is abusive."

She realized the nature of his concern. "You penetrated me as a woman. It merely seemed otherwise."

He considered. "That, oddly, is a relief. I never want to treat you as other than the woman you are."

"Appreciation."

They separated. She had him face away again while she cleaned up and dismantled the multiple illusions and returned to her natural appearance. She dressed. "Done."

He turned to look at her, shaking his head. "I really treated you as a woman?"

"Affirmation. It was what I desired of you."

"Voila, you are something else. Now you have me in your power. One word of this to others will destroy my career."

"Promise," she repeated. "This hour never happened."

"You are a wonder." He kissed her, but was no longer turned on sexually. "I am chagrined at my weakness, but if we are ever alone together like this, and you are amenable, I will ask you."

"Amenable," she agreed, satisfied.

"I do love you."

She reached out mentally to explore the near future. And found something. The danger was now within her range of detection, and it was formidable.

"Caveat," she said urgently. "The threat is worse than they knew. The enemy minions have a cordon around this region and are closing in. No one will escape it. They are after me. I must hide."

His mouth quirked. "I understood that this is what you have been doing, apart from a certain diversion."

"Negation. Really hide. I trust your discretion. Iolo will join you; put his collar back on. It's important. I will return when I can."

"Voila, don't try to make a run for it alone! I will do my utmost to protect you."

"I know," she said, kissing him once more. "But only my absence will suffice."

Then she started to dissolve into fog. Her hair quietly vaporized. Caveat stared. "You can do it too!" he breathed.

"Affirmation." The top of her head and her arms translated to mist that floated in the bunker.

"And I am not allowed to reveal this," he said. "Oh, Voila, I hope you know what you are doing."

"Agreement," she said, her mouth smiling as her eyes, nose, ears and brain dissolved.

The process accelerated as more of her being assumed ifrit form. Now her mind was in the cloud, working more effectively than the compact physical version. A vapor tendril touched Iolo, who was condensing. *Help him*, she told the ifrit.

Agreement. Then they lost contact as Iolo became solid.

Her cloud form was too big for the bunker. She siphoned her diaphanous substance out through the airways and floated into the surrounding air. Then she expanded to her full extent, becoming invisible.

She floated across to where Ingenue and Mistress Modesty still gazed at the volcano. Several armed men were approaching them from different directions; there was no convenient escape. How had such a trap been sprung, considering the alertness of the government's guards?

The men closed in. Modesty and Ingenue paused, evincing surprise. Both were seasoned actresses; it was realistic. The girl looked almost exactly like Voila.

Three men confronted them; three more lay in hidden ambush. They were being careful. One took hold of Ingenue's arms, standing behind her; another did the same with Modesty. Neither woman offered any resistance. The third man faced them, evidently the interrogator.

Voila drifted close enough to pick up their dialogue.

"Where is the six-legged dog?" the man demanded. "Its always with her."

Oops—that was a mistake. Iolo should have remained with Ingenue.

Neither woman answered.

Voila now suffused the region, invisibly, surrounding the people with her diffuse substance.

The man put a hand to Ingenue's head and ripped her hair out of its confinement. New its true color showed: not Voila's shade of brown. "You're not the alien bitch! Where is she?"

Ingenue merely looked at him.

The man struck her on the side of the head. "Answer! We don't have time to wait on you."

Voila had been watching, trying to ascertain exactly what was happening. Now she was disturbed. She didn't like seeing her friend brutalized.

The man ripped open Ingenue's dress, exposing her modest breasts. "You're a virgin, right? You won't be much longer if you don't talk. *Where is she?*"

"She can't answer you," Modesty protested. "She doesn't know."

He whirled on her. "But *you* do, you superior snoot! Tell, or she gets it now." He opened his trousers.

Voila had seen more than enough. She was so angry it was hard to focus. She coalesced around the rebel leader and concentrated her substance. Now she began to show, a pinkish haze outlining the man's head. Her fog thickened.

The man gasped, pawing at his face. He was suffocating.

The two others released the women and came to him, not sure what was happening to him. They tried to brush away the mist, but their hands passed through it ineffectively. It didn't need to be solid to cut off his air; it was displacing the air.

The man dropped to the ground, writhing as his face turned blue. He was breathing, but merely inhaling her substance, which did him no good.

"It's a malignant ghost!" one of the men exclaimed. "It's choking him!"

Close enough.

Then Mistress Modesty caught on. "Princess! No! Don't soil yourself on him! He's not worth it. Our guards will arrive soon. You don't want to be a murderess!"

She was right. It was not necessary to kill the man, though she wanted to. So she generated small electric bolts and shot them into his eyes as she withdrew.

The man gasped as breathable air reached him, recovering. Then he turned his head wildly around. "I can't see! I'm blind!"

Modesty took charge. "Lie face down on the ground, your hands on your heads," she snapped at the two other men. Then she went to the blinded leader and started wiping his scorched eyes. "I do not know whether you can be helped, but I am sure you can be hurt worse. Call in your outlying men and bid them surrender, and no further mischief will befall you or them at this time. If you cooperate and provide key information, I will speak for you at your trial."

The man was vanquished. His head fell against her supportive bosom. "Yes, Mistress." Then he called out "Come in! Surrender! They have powers we can't fight."

The three remaining men came in, laid down their weapons, and joined the others on the ground. But Voila lingered, just in case. The rebel leader was right about one thing: they did have powers ordinary men couldn't fight. Glamor powers.

A floater arrived with government men. They got out and looked around, amazed. "Mistress—what happened?"

"Things are in hand, thank you," Modestly said briskly. "There is no need to go into details. Take these men into custody, and treat them kindly. This one needs immediate medical attention to see whether his sight can be saved. I believe he has agreed to give evidence in exchange for leniency." The man nodded against her breast.

Voila drifted away, satisfied that things were in hand. The men were rebels, but when defeated reverted to the compassionate authority of the mistresses.

She returned to the bunker, entered, and coalesced. Iolo was there, of course, and Caveat, staring as she formed her body, and not because it was naked.

"What else can you do, Voila?" he asked.

"Plea: leave a girl some secrets." As the last of her body solidified she took the clothing he handed her and dressed. "The trap has been sprung and countered. We can safely return now."

"I hesitate to ask what you did."

"Nothing, I think."

They left the bunker and walked back to where Modesty and Ingenue stood waiting. A floater was just departing, carrying six prisoners. Ingenue had repaired her dress somewhat, though a bruise showed on her face.

"It would help to have an explanation," Modesty said.

Voila had revealed more than she should have. Now she had to trust the Mistress. "Information: I am a Glamor. We have special magical powers. Among them is dissolving into the form of a cloud, as the ifrits do. I prefer that this not be generally known. It would endanger my safety if others knew I had this option."

Modestly glanced at Caveat. "You saw this?"

"I did," he agreed. "She is a remarkable girl in more than one sense. I am committed to keep her secrets as long as they do not threaten the welfare of Earth."

"And do they?"

"They may," he said reluctantly. "Yet I am bound."

"You love her!" Modesty said, surprised.

He smiled ruefully. "I do."

"This places me awkwardly." Modestly returned to Voila. "You could not have been touched. You were safe. Why did you act?"

"Outrage: He was going to rape Ingenue."

"And she is your friend."

"Agreement."

"Am I also your friend?" That was one sharp question, signaling as it did the intentions of nominal enemies.

But Voila answered without hesitation. "Agreement."

"Do you intend harm to Earth?"

"Negation. But that may be a matter of interpretation."

"I dislike prevarication, but there are occasions when it may be better than the alternatives. This may be such a case. I will report that some force unknown impacted the rebel leader, perhaps a heat flux of the supposedly quiescent volcano, and I took advantage of the situation to subdue him. Is this acceptable?"

"Gratitude," Voila said.

Modesty looked at Ingenue.

"You saved me from rape!" Ingenue said to Voila.

"Necessary. You were emulating me, to protect me. You would not have been in danger otherwise."

"So I will thank you by giving you no credit for it. I hope I am never not your friend."

"Endorsement," Voila said as they hugged.

"Echo," Mistress Modesty agreed, smiling somewhat grimly.

Chapter 12
Fifth

Fifth went with Dynamo and Naive to meet Captain Bold of the Earth ship *Ms Dominance* as it established orbit around Charm. Dynamo knew the Captain, and was of equivalent Earth rank; they could talk. Queen Gale conducted them, representing her husband King Havoc. The four of them were a rather more potent group than the Earthers would realize at first.

The shuttle landed in the White Chroma zone, and they boarded. The crewmen were surprised to see the green girl and black man, but Dynamo satisfied them that these were attendants the Queen required.

The shuttle blasted off and heaved them up to the ship. Fifth understood the process, thanks to Dynamo's training, as did the women. Science magic was odd, but worked well enough in its own environment.

They were ushered into the Captain's chamber. Captain Bold stood there, flanked by an attractive young woman. That, they had been advised, was Mistress of the Mission Minuet. She had replaced Mistress Marionette.

"Dynamo!" Captain Bold said. "How goes it?"

"I have had more of an experience than I anticipated," Dynamo said. "This is Queen Gale, wife of King Havoc and mother of the four hostage children taken to Earth, and these are Fifth, a trainee, and Naive, my wife."

Bold stared. "Did I mishear?"

"Negation," Naive said. "He married the green girl."

Mistress Minuet surveyed Naive speculatively.

Bold took stock. "She is willing to come to Earth with you?"

Dynamo smiled. "She insists upon it. She is quite interested in Earth. So is Fifth."

"Ordinary colonists can not visit Earth on a whim," Bold said gruffly. "In due course, when the planet has been pacified, tourism will be encouraged, but that is not yet."

"Perhaps," Dynamo agreed. "At the moment, the Queen is most interested in the welfare of her children. How are they doing on Earth?"

"Very well indeed. They are outstanding young people, and readily integrated with our society. In fact when we departed the planet, all four were on tours, visiting volcanoes."

"Volcanoes!" Gale said as if surprised. "Haven't they seen enough of them here?"

"It seems not, ma'am. But that is merely in their off time. The boy, Warp, is traveling from city to city telling stories. He is a most gifted narrator and commands large audiences. The girl, Weft, is singing with an opera company; some say she is the finest young singer extant. The girl Flame is traveling similarly, demonstrating remarkable martial arts techniques. And the youngest, Viola—"

"Voila," Gale said.

"To be sure. She is with a play group, performing daily to packed audiences. Many consider her to be the best young actress of her generation. I must say, you have done a remarkable job raising them."

"Appreciation," Gale said. "What of their companions?"

"Each has one Charm companion and one Earth supervisor. The youngest, Vio—Voila—has her six-legged dog, and a prominent official."

"Who?" Dynamo asked.

"His name is Caveat."

"Caveat! I know of him. That can't be."

Bold arced an eyebrow. "Why not?"

"The man is gay. He won't touch any woman."

The mistress nodded slightly.

"To be sure," Bold said. "I understand the authorities wanted to be certain there was no untoward sexual interaction with the underage princess. They mean to return her in due course to her parents as chaste as she started."

Gale's expression was masked. "And how are they getting along?"

"Very well, I understand. They are together everywhere, along with a girl of her generation and a mistress. You can be assured your child is safe."

"Agreement," Gale said. But Fifth knew her well enough to know that her meaning was not what the captain understood. Bold evidently did not know that Princess Voila was a Glamor, like her mother, only more powerful. That was highly significant.

"Has King Havoc decided to cooperate with Earth?"

"Negation."

Bold was surprised. "Doesn't he want to have his children back?"

"Information," Gale said. "Havoc reacts negatively to duress. He is now in the process of wreaking havoc on Earth. We will have our children back after we take control of your planet."

Captain Bold stared at her. Then he looked at Dynamo. "This is humor?"

"Negation."

"What's this—you're turning native?"

"So it seems," Dynamo said. "I have fallen in love with Charm, and of course with my wife. I have not turned against Earth, but I can tell you that Charm does mean to assume control of Earth and has implemented a procedure to do that. The Queen is absolutely serious. You would be well advised to heed her warning."

"This is laughable! What warning?"

"Statement: Taking our children hostage was an act of war," Gale said firmly. "We are responding similarly. It is now too late to turn back. The best you can do is cooperate with us voluntarily. That will be easier for you."

"And if I do not elect to cooperate, as you put it?" the Captain inquired.

"Reality: Then you will perform under duress."

"And suppose I simply clap you in irons and take you hostage too?"

"Don't threaten her!" Dynamo said.

"I will do what I choose, aboard my ship. I am the master here."

"But not the mistress," Gale said. She glanced at the Mistress Minuet. "Speak."

"We will cooperate," Minuet said.

The Captain turned to her. "Mistress—"

"I have spoken."

Disgruntled, Bold nodded. "What cooperation is it you desire?"

"You will conduct your prospective administrators to Planet Charm. You will take aboard approximately one thousand Charm citizens for transport to Earth."

"But we are supposed to bring back artifacts! We have no room for such a number."

"You will have room when you unload your heavy mining equipment," Dynamo said. "The main problem will be food supplies for this number. You will have to take aboard Charm supplies."

"Outrageous!"

Gale glanced again at the Mistress. "Speak."

"It will be done," Minuet said.

Bold stared at her, dumbfounded.

"Perhaps I can help clarify the situation," Dynamo said. "Queen Gale has taken over the mind and will of Mistress Minuet, and thus the ship. The *Dominance* is now under her control."

"But if that is true, I must not obey!"

"Bold, Earth elected to play hardball with the colony," Dynamo said. "That was a mistake. I do not know whether Earth or Charm will win this contest, but I do know that Queen Gale now controls this ship. It is best not to try to oppose her."

"You've joined them, you traitor!"

"I have not joined them in that respect. I am merely acknowledging reality. This ship is in their power."

"At least you could fight them."

"The Queen could control me directly as readily as she does the Mistress. I would gain nothing by trying to oppose her. For myself or for my planet. I am hostage—as are you."

Captain Bold seemed to want to argue further, but the mistress cut him off. "Retire to your duty station, Captain."

"And leave you here alone with them?"

"I am already lost, Captain. Please go."

Reluctantly he went.

The mistress turned to Gale. "You have demonstrated your power, Queen Gale. I respect that. You have left me personal volition, but could have taken that too had you wished. I prefer to accept the leeway you proffer me. I will obey you on the same basis Dynamo does: I am not with you, but I will not oppose you."

"Appreciation." Gale glanced at Fifth and Naive. "See to the reorganization of the ship. Summon me at need." She vanished.

The mistress sighed. "Now I have been relegated to the authority of underlings."

"Agreement," Naive said. "But as my husband can tell you, it is not wise to aggravate a Glamor."

Fifth thought of the episode in the Silver Chroma zone, and knew Naive had it similarly in mind. "Not wise," he agreed.

"I agree," Minuet said. "What is your directive?"

"Set in motion the processes to unload your administrators and equipment," Dynamo said. "Clear your holds for the arrival of the Charm personnel."

"And what will they be doing on Earth?"

"Governing it, I suspect, under the direction of the Glamors. Assuming that Charm wins the contest."

"You have little notion of the magnitude of that task."

Dynamo smiled. "They have an excellent notion, for I have trained them."

"You *are* a traitor!"

"Merely a realist. I think Charm is going to win. At such time as that is confirmed, I will serve Charm, in the interest of garnering the best possible treatment of Earth. This is similar to the compromise you just made with Queen Gale."

The mistress did not argue the case further.

"We had better see to the Captain," Naive said. "He is rebellious."

"Agreement." The two of them left the chamber.

Fifth remained with Mistress Minuet. "And are you to see to me?" she inquired.

"Affirmation. We will need your presence to keep the crew in line."

"I should think so." She studied him a minute. "But perhaps first some background. Your color is natural to you?"

"Affirmation. I am of the Black Chroma; all my neighbors are similar."

She turned slightly, displaying her impressive outline. "And is your nature normal?"

He smiled. "Affirmation. I do find you attractive."

"And do you have the authority to command my attention?"

"Not of that kind. I must direct you only in matters affecting the accomplishment of our mission."

"You know I mean to seduce you, to gain influence with you."

"Affirmation. But I must advise you that I am loyal to Charm and will not be diverted. I would love to have your attention during the voyage to Earth, but I refuse to mislead you in that. Your effort will be wasted on me."

"Perhaps. If we are to keep company, you might as well have the benefit of it. What I believe you call no fault."

Fifth shrugged. "Satisfaction." She was not really his type, being too well-endowed, but she was a most beautiful woman, and he knew she was thoroughly proficient in the arts of sexual gratification. That was quite good enough for an enemy woman, and for no fault.

"If you please, some information. What is a Glamor?"

"Background: Ordinary citizens of Charm can do magic only in their home Chroma. I can do Black Chroma magic; Naive can do Green Chroma magic, for example. A Glamor can do magic anywhere. Queen Gale is a Glamor; that is why she was able to take over your mind. That is the least of what she can do."

"You are familiar with her?"

"Affirmation."

She eyed him cannily. "You have possessed her? No fault?"

There was no need for secrecy; the better she understood the ways of

Charm, the more efficiently she would relate to the needs of the folk traveling to Earth. "I was with Naive. Then she went to Dynamo, and the Queen took me in compensation. She is a most remarkable woman."

"So it would seem. I can now better appreciate your loyalty to her. Is Charm in fact a matriarchy?"

"Negation. King Havoc rules. Queen Gale is honoring his will."

"She seems to resemble a mistress."

Fifth nodded. "Affirmation. That may be a fair parallel. She had no need to cater to me, yet she did, and I will always value that."

"We shall be working together, necessarily. In that time I hope to impress on you the magnitude of what your planet is attending. Earth has a population of one billion human beings; your few administrators will be spread far too thin to have much impact."

"We expect to work through the mistresses, just as Gale is working through you. That should facilitate it."

"I doubt you have enough Glamors to control every mistress. It is as if Tuva tried to govern Asia."

Fifth recognized the allusion, because it was one common Earth saying that Dynamo had briefed the trainees on. Tuva was the remnant of a tiny country in their Continent of Asia, and Asia had hundreds of millions of people. "Agreement. But Tuva could do it, if the Mistress of Mistresses was Tuvan."

They got to work on the process. Mistress Minuet was most efficient in pacifying the questioning crewmen. Her mere touch brought immediate acquiescence. She governed by the power of sexual fascination, just as Queen Gale had governed Dynamo, compelling not merely obedience but gladness.

When the busy day ended, as defined by the local section of the planet rather than the orbiting ship, Fifth retired to an officer's cabin, and Minuet, who it seemed had no cabin or bunk of her own, joined him. Her body was lithe and practiced, and they had completed sex almost before he knew it. "And how was the Queen?" she inquired.

Should he tell? He was supposed to be completely open about all except one thing. "Reluctance."

"Come now, Fifth," she said persuasively. "You have co-opted my mission and had the benefit of my body. The least you can do is show some candor. What is the problem?"

"Caution: I do not wish to cause offense."

"Cause it. I can handle it."

"Queen Gale—made me feel welcome."

"It would be dishonest to pretend that you are the man I have always longed for. We both know we are enemies."

"Agreement. I am no match for the Queen, either, who loves her husband beyond any other man and is far above my station. So it was nothing beyond no fault. Yet I felt satisfied with her as though for that night I was her husband. She did not hurry me as you did, or seek any comparison. She seemed genuinely interested in me."

Minuet nodded soberly. "Rebuke taken. I was careless, as I should not have been, distracted by my anger at being so abruptly disenfranchised."

"Understandable."

She stroked his body with one hand. Her touch was light and skilled, causing him to react despite just having climaxed with her. "You were with the green girl, before Dynamo took her from you. Yet her form is not at all like the queen's. Which is normally your preference?"

"Naive's form. But Gale made herself resemble that form, so that I was fully gratified."

"The buxom Queen can change her form?"

"Approximately. She used illusion, but the effect was the same. She was divine."

"Allow me a moment." Minuet got off the bed and went to the spot head. When she returned her breasts were bound with translucent material, making them seem smaller, and she had altered her hair to make her face seem thinner. The change was artificial, but she had made herself significantly more appealing to him.

She questioned him about his background as she artfully seduced him a second time, and it was better. She had obviously not given up on corrupting him, but he very much appreciated her efforts.

The transfers were accomplished in the next few days, and the ship set off for Earth with its new cargo. Fifth knew most of the Charm folk personally, and facilitated their adaptation to the routine of the ship. Dynamo and Naive worked similarly. Minuet was fully cooperative, not even attempting to interfere with the mission. When the drive technician turned balky she took him aside, kissed him, seduced him, and persuaded him. When the cook objected to the unfamiliar Charm food staples, she drew aside a comely blue girl and persuaded her to assist him, with a no fault liaison to encourage his attitude. It worked.

"But you understand," she murmured to Fifth as she clasped him in bed, "when we arrive at Earth, everything will change. Your companions will likely become prisoners and I will be disciplined for assisting you."

"But you had no choice," he protested. He did like her, as she intended.

"They will not understand that. We do not believe in magic, on Earth. Your evocative Queen Gale did not accompany us here. It is a signal of the strength of her mind control that I have not even attempted to betray you. That will count against me. But if by some mischance your folk remain in charge, you will doubtless speak for me."

"That I can do," he agreed. "Whatever your motive, you have been completely helpful."

"It is our nature." She kissed him, and he could almost believe she meant it.

More than four months had passed since the ship left Earth on this voyage, and the planet had changed drastically. "Lord in Heaven!" Minuet exclaimed as they gazed at it on the screen for the first time.

For Earth, formerly described as a big blue marble in space, was now multi-hued. Lines of variegated colors showed everywhere, outlining the edges of the monstrous planetary seas.

"So it is true," Dynamo said. "The volcanoes have been converted."

"That was the mission of King Havoc's children," Naive agreed. "To seed the volcanoes, changing them to other Chroma, bringing alternative magic to Earth. To make it resemble Charm."

"Magic will work on Earth?" Minuet asked, not concealing her horror.

"This may be hard on unbelief," Dynamo said. "I suspect Earth is descending into near-chaos."

Minuet sighed, then took hold. "I must consult with the Mistress of Mistresses."

"So should I," Dynamo said. "We can go together. I believe the Charmers mean us to be intermediaries."

"The four of us should go," Naive said.

"I must go to Flame," Fifth said. "I have a message for her."

"She can surely be located," Minuet said.

The ship established orbit around the planet. The technicians got radio contact as Dynamo, Minuet, and the two Charm natives stood by.

"*Ms Dominance*—what is your situation?" the Earther officer inquired.

"We are captive of Charm Colony representatives," Captain Bold replied.

There was a pause. "Put the mistress on."

"Mistress Minuet here. We had best land and meet privately with the Mistress of Mistresses. Party of four. We have a situation."

"Earth also has a situation," the officer said. "Party landing denied."

Minuet was surprised. "This is not a feasible response," she said severely.

"It is a necessary one, Mistress. The Captain's message indicates that you are no longer in control of the ship. The Mistress of Mistresses is wary of that. Perhaps it is a contagious illness. Perhaps something more sinister. We must not allow direct contact until this dangerous mystery is fathomed."

"Actually that makes sense," Dynamo said.

"Negation: It won't do," Fifth said. "I need to meet with Princess Flame."

"Denied," the officer said. "The hostages are under house arrest."

"Thank you," Mistress Minuet said. The contact cut off.

"It seems we are at impasse," Dynamo said.

"Question: House arrest," Fifth said. "What is that?"

"Confinement to their place of residence," Minuet explained. "They must have done something to upset the Mistress."

"Like seed the volcanoes," Naive said with a wry smile. "Bringing chaos to Earth."

"That would do it," Minuet agreed.

"We are running low on supplies," Dynamo said. "We can't afford to orbit indefinitely."

Naive smiled. "I know you are not committed, dear. But if you sided with Charm, what action would you recommend?"

Fifth noted without jealousy how well they interacted. His relationship with Naive had been no fault, and Queen Gale had more than made up for the loss of that convenience. He was glad she had found love and happiness.

"I love your devious nature, green girl. I would try a sneak landing and go to see the Mistress of Mistresses regardless. For all we know, she is also under house arrest."

Minuet jumped. "That can't be!"

"Note that we did not speak with her directly," Dynamo said. "I know her well. She would not ordinarily refuse to see me. Would she refuse you?"

"No."

"We two are not her enemy, whatever the Charmers may be," Dynamo continued. "But she has enemies on Earth. I recommend that Naive and Fifth agree to do no harm to her, and let us lead the way. We need to ascertain exactly what situation exists. It may not be what we think."

Minuet nodded. "Here I have no conflict between my loyalty to Earth and my imperative from Queen Gale. I concur with your devious plot."

He smiled. "We males hardly compare to females in deviousness, but we have our moments." He glanced at Naive and Fifth. "Concurrence?"

"Agreement," Naive said. "No harm to the Mistress."

"Endorsement," Fifth said. "No harm."

"We can't use any powered device," Dynamo said. "They'll have sensors to pick that up. So we can't use a rocket descent, or even a powered sled on the ice. We'll have to select our landsite carefully, or we'll soon freeze to death on the surface."

They boarded a padded capsule which was then flung back to counter the orbiting velocity, and let it drop toward Earth without power. A parachute deployed and lowered it, still without power, making it effectively invisible to Earth's sensors. It landed, bounced as it was designed to do, and came to rest. It had been a rough ride, but they were in good condition.

They piled out into the bitter cold. They were garbed for it, of course, but this mass of snow and ice was worse than anything Fifth or Naive had experienced.

"There should be an access close by," Minuet said. "We calculated it for the Air Refresher field. The used air is pumped out, and new air taken in, with a heat exchanger and filter. The complex requires a lot of clean air."

"Science magic," Dynamo explained.

That helped. Science required more obvious processing than most forms of magic did, but it worked about as well.

Dynamo had a small telescope. He used it to look around. "There," he said, pointing. "A motor housing."

They trudged that way. Already Fifth felt his hands and feet getting uncomfortably cold despite the heavy clothing, and Naive did not seem to be any better off.

"Here," Minuet said. She spread her suited arms and embraced him, pressing her body close. It was clumsy in the thick clothing, but immediately he felt warmth infusing his body, spreading from their contact.

"Amazement," he said.

She did the same for Naive, who responded similarly. "Question: What did you do?"

"You would call it mistress magic," Minuet said. "It is a healing warmth we possess."

"Observation: But you could simply leave us to freeze, and be done with us," Fifth said.

"I am not a betrayer by nature. No mistress is. I agreed to this mission, and I will help you see it through."

Fifth had seen how the woman handled men, Chroma men included. She was very good at it. But this was something else. It seemed she had a quality of character beyond mere seduction. "Appreciation."

"All mistresses are similar in this respect. We value life and feeling wherever it occurs."

They reached the motor housing. This was a metal box that hummed steadily. Motors were one of the things of science. "There should be a service access," Dynamo said, poking around. "Ah, there." He caught hold of a panel and pulled it out. There was a hole in the ice slanting down and away from the motor. "We'll slide in. Keep silence."

He led the way. Naive followed, then Fifth, and finally Minuet, who paused to replace the panel behind her.

They slid to a halt in a dimly illuminated service hall. Silently they followed Dynamo, who clearly knew his way around such apparatus. He located a tool wagon, and they sat on it for a rapid ride. He used buttons on its hull to steer it along certain passages.

"Now we can talk," he said as he doffed his heavy outer clothing. The others did the same, as it was much warmer here. They dropped the items off the wagon; by the time they were discovered their mission should be done, one way or another. "Equipment transport is unmonitored."

"I presume you know where we are going," Minuet said.

"I hope so. I am zeroing in on the coordinates of the Mistress complex. Thereafter we will depend on you."

"If the Mistress of Mistresses is, as you imply, hostage, we are traveling into a trap."

"A necessary risk."

Fifth was beginning to wonder whether this effort was wise. Yet it would not have been wise to do nothing, either.

There was a keening sound. The wagon slowed. "Uh-oh," Dynamo said. "That's an alarm. We have been spotted."

"There will be a human investigator," Minuet said.

"I may have to kill him," Dynamo said.

"By no means! I will not have unnecessary violence. Hide. Leave him to me."

And she could readily turn them in, and receive credit for the capture, Fifth realized. Could they truly trust her? Yet what choice did they have?

They got off as the wagon stopped. Dynamo led the way to a niche hidden by shadows. Fifth and Naive occupied it silently.

Minuet remained on the stalled wagon as a panel opened and a figure climbed through. "Hello," she said.

"Mistress!" the man said, astonished.

"Mistress Minuet," she agreed.

"What are you doing here? This is a service tunnel with a rogue wagon."

"Leave me my secrets," she said. "I am responsible for this disruption."

"But Mistress! Access is restricted."

"Is it?" She laid a hand on his arm.

The man paused. "I thought it was."

She brought him close and kissed him. "Please."

He stood frozen. "Mistress, what do you want?"

"Merely a delayed report. Surely you will oblige my whim."

"But my directive—"

She kissed him again, and proceeded efficiently to seduce him. Fifth was amazed to see it, as he knew Minuet knew they were being observed. He was also mightily aroused. The Mistress was fuller of body than he preferred, but was so well constructed that she could have her way with him or any man any time she chose. As she was demonstrating now.

By the time Minuet was done with the man, he had agreed to delay his report. She send him back the way he had come, then joined the others, still unclothed. "He has turned off the alarms and reactivated the wagon," she said. "We can complete our trip."

"May we pause?" Dynamo asked.

Her eye seemed to twinkle. "Of course."

Dynamo took Naive back into darkness. Fifth could only envy them their release.

"Do you have a concern?" Minuet inquired.

How could he answer? "Embarrassment."

"You watched me deal with the worker."

"Agreement."

"This aroused you." She wasn't asking; she knew.

"Affirmation. But our relationship ended when we arrived at Earth."

She smiled. "Not necessarily. No fault."

His breath caught. She did not mean to deny him. "Agreement."

Minuet embraced him and kissed him. Then she opened his clothing. They had fast, soundless sex on their feet. Oh, yes, she understood the effect she had. And was not a tease. She had done what she needed, to buy them time without any killing, and now was tidying up a detail.

"Appreciation, Mistress," Fifth breathed in her ear.

"It is my nature." She resumed her clothing.

So it seemed. The Mistresses had unparalleled power over men, and used it freely as necessary. She had never spoken of love to the Earther worker or to Fifth; she merely aroused and obliged their sexual passions, for her own reasons. What would it be like to have a mistress truly love a man? He surely would never know.

Dynamo and Naive returned. "On our way," Dynamo said.

They reached a service access under the complex of the Mistress of Mistresses. "Will there be guards?" Fifth asked nervously.

"No guards," Minuet said. "Mistresses don't use them."

Because any man was putty in their hands, Fifth thought.

"What about an alarm?" Naive asked.

"This one, too, has been turned off," Minuet said.

She was being almost suspiciously accommodating. But she had had an impact on him, during the journey and now: he trusted her. She wanted this meeting to occur.

Dynamo operated handles, and a panel lifted in the tunnel ceiling, giving them access to the chamber above them. He climbed the ladder and poked his head through. "Hello, Mistress," he said.

"Hello Dynamo," a dulcet voice replied. "I was correct: you are not one to be denied."

"Mistress, we fear for you. Are you in good health and power?"

"I am."

"Why were we not allowed to see you?"

"My subordinates fear for my safety, believing that the Colony Mission has been corrupted."

"That is true, Mistress. But we bear you no malice."

"I am aware of that. Bring up your companions."

Naive climbed the ladder, then Fifth, then Minuet. The four of them stood in the chamber after Dynamo replaced the panel in the floor.

The Mistress of Mistresses was of course another lovely, gracious woman, remarkable in her color: she was white of skin and hair, a true White Chroma native. She exchanged hugs with Minuet, shook hands with the others, and spoke as if this meeting were perfectly routine. "It seems that we seriously underestimated the threat posed by the children of King Havoc of Charm. By the time we understood what was happening, it was too late; the volcanoes were already changing colors. We have serious disruptions in process. What is the situation on planet Charm?"

"Queen Gale of Charm boarded our ship and took possession of my mind and will," Minuet said. "Our cargo was preempted by the transport of a thousand colonists of many Chroma. They are here to help bring the new Chroma zones into orderly societies. I am not sure I believed it, until I saw the new colors of Earth."

"We are constrained to accept," the Mistress said. "The alternative is chaos."

"Has Charm then won?" Minuet asked.

"No. But Charm has succeeded in putting us into a serious misadventure. We shall have to re-establish order before we address the situation on the colony planet. This may provide them an indefinite stay of incorporation, which is perhaps their object."

"Negation," Dynamo said. "They intend to conquer Earth. The conversion of Earth's volcanoes is only an early stage of that effort."

"I doubt they properly appreciate the challenge," the Mistress of Mistresses said.

"I fear they do," Minuet said. "They have powers—magic powers—that we never dreamed of."

"So it seems." The Mistress of Mistresses shrugged. "But there is no need for you to remain under duress, Minuet. Permit me." She took the lesser Mistress by both hands. A pulse seemed to pass between them.

"I'm free!" Minuet said. "You nullified the Queen's imperative."

"It is a prerogative of the office," the Mistress said. "Now we shall meet with the King's children, who are here. We took them into custody when we discovered their mischief. They are nevertheless here voluntarily."

"Question," Fifth asked.

"They have powers of their own, and could have evaded capture, even on Earth. Each is remarkable as a singer, story teller, actress, or martial artist, matching the best Earth offers. But they say these are their avocations. Their powers of magic are their vocations, and are more formidable."

"This is true," Dynamo said. "Glamors are magical creatures of extraordinary capabilities, and the four king's children are the most magical of all. Earth has known nothing like them, other than in myth."

"I agree," the Mistress said.

"You believe in magic?" Minuet asked, surprised.

"I did not before. Now I do. My recent association with the king's children has made me a believer, apart from my observation of the new Chroma zones, as they are termed."

"I too now believe in magic, Mistress," Dynamo said. "I have seen much of it. But I fear those children have done to you something akin to what Queen Gale did to Minuet. To what power do you answer?"

"A fair question, Dynamo. The youngest, Voila, is indeed formidable, and is their leader. She can do things not before seen on this planet. But she has made no attempt to dominate me, only to understand me, and confesses freely that she does not. I believe it is fair to say that we like each other. The issue has not yet been truly joined."

"Mistress," Fifth said. "I am of the other side, but wish to be fair, as we promised you no ill. I have seen the power of the Glamors. Those four are the strongest Glamors of them all. They could influence you without your knowing it."

"No, Fifth, they could not."

"Doubt, Mistress."

The Mistress of Mistresses smiled. The expression seemed to warm the chamber. She approached him and took his hands in hers. He felt calm, warmth, healing, love, and enormous persuasion flooding his body, much more than anything Minuet had done. She was ethereally beautiful, but this was something else. "Believe," she murmured.

He was overwhelmed. No wonder the mistresses feared nothing! It was impossible to imagine trying to hurt or deceive such a creature. To touch her was to love her. Part of it was that he knew this was truth: she was not deceiving or changing him, only showing him her nature. If the mythical angels of folklore existed, she was one. "Belief," he agreed as she let him go.

Naive was staring at him. "Confusion. How can this be?"

Dynamo smiled. "He has experienced the power of the Mistress of Mistresses, Naive. This cannot be denied, but there is nothing sinister about it. Now he knows the truth."

"Agreement," Fifth said, dazed. "We are one."

"Concern," Naive said, unconvinced.

Fifth took her two hands in his. "Sharing."

She felt his abiding inner peace deriving from his experience of the goodness of the Mistress. "Wonder."

"It is what we experience when she first lays hands on us, and we become mistresses," Minuet said. "Thereafter we share some of that power."

That explained a good deal. Minuet had used some of that power on him, but only when he needed it. They had made love many times during the voyage to Earth, but she had never demonstrated this before. The Mistresses neither flaunted nor concealed their power; they drew on it at need.

"Please accompany me," the Mistress said, showing the way through the somewhat labyrinthian passages of the complex.

They trooped to another chamber. There were the four Glamor children of the King. "Greeting, all," the youngest, the girl Voila said.

"Statement," Fifth said, remembering. "I have a private message for Princess Flame."

The slender red-headed Amazon girl smiled. She gestured to an adjacent chamber. They entered, closing the door behind them. "Introduce yourself and speak."

"I am Fifth. I carry your mother Queen Gale's ikon."

"Astonishment! What do you know of ikons?"

"Nothing, Princess. She said you would understand."

"Give it to me."

Fifth put his fingers to his hair, where the little figure of a ball of moss had been hidden. He withdrew it and proffered it to her. She reached to take it— and her hand shied away.

"Confusion," he said.

"Realization. It *is* her ikon! How can this be?"

"Clarification: I am told that the Glamors labored long and hard to generate duplicate ikons so that the duplicates could be sent to Earth. This one is such a duplicate. It performs the same function as the original. I do not know what that function is, but hope that you do."

"Understanding!" Flame exclaimed. "Hold it out away from your body."

Perplexed, he obeyed.

She stepped into him, embraced him, and kissed him.

He reeled. The kiss had the impact of a dive into cool water. It was not at all like the touch of the Mistress of Mistresses, but generated its own urgency. "You kiss like your mother!" he gasped.

She smiled. She opened her uniform, showing her small breasts, and unbound her hair, which became suddenly luxurious, a red tide. She was now completely feminine. "How do you see me, Fifth?"

"Awe! You are lovely! My ideal figure of a woman."

"Mother sent you to me. She knew your desire and mine. We will associate, no fault."

"Wonder," he breathed. "My desire for a woman like you, yes, she knew. But why should you care to associate with an ordinary Chroma man like me?"

"My desire for a worthy man who sees me as a romantic and sexual figure, heedless of my Glamor or Amazon natures."

He was taken aback. "That's right! You are Glamor, Amazon, and Princess. I was so dazzled by your beauty I forgot. Apology."

She laughed. "Needless. Remain dazzled."

He realized that she could indeed have had trouble attracting men, who were more likely to appreciate the appearance of her sister Weft. Queen Gale was right: he was the man for her, in that respect. So Gale had sent him with her ikon, a special message. Yet what made the ikons so important?

Flame read his mind. "Explanation: Glamors use ikons to transmit their powers of magic from their Chroma zones to their bodies, wherever they may be. This is what gives Glamors ability to perform magic anywhere. The duplicate ikons will enable the Glamors to operate here on Earth as they do on Charm and Counter Charm. This is part of the message you bring me. Do not reveal it elsewhere."

"Commitment," he agreed, still staring at her evocative body. He would have no fault with her? This was a stunning prospect.

"Keep the ikon for now," she said. "I will tell you where to put it, in due course." She kissed him again, thrilling him with her supremely evocative body. "We will night together. Now we must rejoin the others."

"Agreement," he said faintly. He had thought he had been prepared for this mission, but amazing things had happened recently.

"The Mistress touched you," Flame said.

"Awe," he agreed.

"Voila will brace her now."

"Concern! The Mistress is not evil."

"Reassurance. Neither are we. It is a necessary thing." She closed her uniform, which he belatedly realized she had left open deliberately for his appreciation, and opened the door.

The others were waiting. "Velocity, rawbone," the voluptuous blonde Weft remarked, eying the loose hair.

Fifth felt himself turning a darker shade of black. The implication was that they had been having rapid sex. Not that he wouldn't have liked it.

"Enthusiasm, plush-butt," Flame retorted. "We are no fault."

"Business," Warp said.

The three elder siblings turned their gazes on Voila. "Linkage," she said.

What did this mean? Fifth could see that Dynamo, Naive, and the two Mistresses were as perplexed as he was.

The four siblings linked hands, forming a circle as they faced inward. They stood there for a moment. Then they separated, three of them looking surprised.

Voila faced the Mistress of Mistresses. "Time," she said. "We must ask a thing of you you do not wish."

"I will of course consider it," the Mistress said.

"You must make the Oath of Friendship with our father, King Havoc."

Fifth was sure that the Mistress was seldom taken aback, but she was in this case. "Voila, apart from the fact that we do not know each other, we are on opposite sides of an interplanetary contest. The issue is which of us, and which planet, will govern our association."

"He does not desire it either," Voila said. "But I have linked with Mino, a machine entity Dynamo will inform you about, and read the intermediate future paths. This is the best one. You must associate with our father, and this can be safe only with the oath."

The Mistress shrugged. "I am not traveling to your planet, and I doubt King Havoc will travel to Earth. So the matter is academic apart from being problematic."

"The paths are intricate, and timing is of the essence. It must be within the hour."

"Voila, what you ask is impossible, for many reasons, as you should see."

The girl merely stepped forward, her two hands reaching toward the mistress. She waited. It was a challenge.

"Mistress, do not," Dynamo said.

"Not," Minuet agreed. "Danger. She is buttressed by the three others."

"And Mino," Naive said.

Fifth could appreciate why the Mistress would hesitate to touch the strongest of all the Glamors. The Mistress had extraordinary powers of accommodation, but this was too much.

The Mistress stepped forward and took the girl's hands.

The two stood there, sharing a contact of some kind. The air seemed to waver with the power of the forces being exchanged. What was happening?

Then they disengaged. Both seemed shaken. Dynamo and Minuet jumped to support the Mistress, while the older siblings closed around Voila. That left Fifth and Naive confused. What had passed between the two?

In a moment the Mistress answered. "She showed me the future paths," she said. "Hopelessly tangled, with disaster on either side. Only one has hope: my close association with King Havoc. It is true."

"Verification: Give her the ikon," Voila said.

The siblings nodded.

Fifth looked at Flame for confirmation, but she shook her head. "Naive," she said.

"Mystification," Naive said.

"Hair."

Naive put her hand to her head, riffling her fingers through her green hair. She found something and worked it out: an ikon in the shape of a tree. She held it, amazed. It was clear that she had not known it was there.

"Aversion spell," Flame said. "She carried it and protected it without being aware."

"Give it to the Mistress," Voila repeated.

Naive took the ikon to the Mistress. The Mistress reached to accept it. Her hand shied away. "I can not."

The siblings nodded, unsurprised. "Keep it, Naive," Flame said. "Go to the other room and bring back what you find there."

Perplexed, Naive obeyed. She stepped into the room that Fifth and Flame had used.

"What was the meaning of that?" the Mistress asked.

"Regret," Flame said. "We prefer not to clarify at this time."

But Fifth understood. When he had tried to give Queen Gale's ikon to Flame, she had been unable to take it. Because a Glamor could not touch an ikon—her own or any other.

Naive carried King Havoc's ikon, the tree, for he was the Glamor of Trees. The Queen had told him that, in privacy. Anyone except a Glamor was able to handle any ikon. The Mistress was unable to touch it.

The Mistress of Mistresses was a Glamor. A Glamor of Earth. The siblings had unmasked her.

Chapter 13
Monochrome

The Mistress of Mistresses remained shaken by the vision Princess Voila had shown her. It was unlike anything she had experienced before, but there was no doubting its authenticity. The planets Earth and Charm were locked in a struggle that portended great harm for both, unless a special, sometimes devious course was followed. That course put her closely together with King Havoc.

She would have to make that oath. There was no reasonable alternative.

The door opened. An evidently daunted Naive stood there. Her mouth worked. "King—King Havoc," she said.

A man appeared behind her. He was tall, handsome, muscular, and possessed of the aura of command. King Havoc. How had he come here? It should not have been possible. Yet it seemed the siblings had known that their father was here.

Havoc stepped into the room. "Greeting, Mistress," he said formally.

Her reply was automatic. "Hello, King Havoc."

He turned to the siblings. "Now what's this about?"

"Father, you must make the Oath of Friendship with her," Voila said.

The King shook his head. "Denial. I have made that oath only twice. Once to your mother."

"She showed me the future paths," the Mistress said. "We are enemies, yet it seems we must associate. Only that oath can make us safe from each other."

"Opposition. That oath has ramifications you can hardly comprehend."

Here she was arguing a case she opposed. "Voila, show him what you showed me."

Voila touched her father's hand.

"Expletive!" Havoc swore. "I never sought this."

"Nor I," the Mistress said. "I have serious issues with you."

"Do it, Havoc," Flame said. Monochrome noted that she, alone of the four king's children, called him by his given name.

Havoc sighed. "I do this under duress. Mistress, do you understand the significance of the oath?"

"I do. I am under similar duress. At least we agree to that extent."

He struggled a moment longer, then yielded. "Oath made."

"Made," the Mistress echoed.

That was all there was to it, verbally. But she knew that both their lives had significantly changed. The future paths Voila had shown them showed it.

"Go with her, Father," Voila said. "It must be."

"Admission," Havoc said. "My life is now run by my children."

"So it seems," the Mistress agreed.

"Now release them."

"This would not be expedient," she protested. "They are confined for excellent reason."

"Negation. They remain restricted only by their own sufferance, as you know, so releasing them is an act of acquiescence, not power. They are needed to help deal with the problems presented by the new Chroma zones, as are the trained Chroma folk on the ship. They are no longer hostages: I have taken their place."

"You are not hostage, King Havoc."

"Hostage to my oath made under duress," he said angrily. "I can no longer oppose you."

"Nor I you," she pointed out gently. "But I concede your points." She turned to the siblings. "I suggest you fetch your companions and see to the transfer of the Charm personnel to their Earth stations. King Havoc and I will remain here to get to know each other."

Voila nodded. "Activity: Dynamo, Fifth, Naive, come with us. Mistress Minuet too. We have work to do."

Dynamo and Minuet looked at the Mistress. She made a little wave of her hand, dismissing them. They joined the others, and in moments all were gone.

She turned back to the man. "We have made the Oath of Friendship, King Havoc. We can best work together if we become better acquainted."

"Call me Havoc, as a friend would, Mistress."

She smiled. "Then call me Monochrome."

"Question."

"Before I became Mistress of Mistresses, I was called Mistress Monochrome. You may have noted my coloration."

"White Chroma."

"Not precisely so, Havoc. Earth is by your definition a White Chroma zone, and I govern Earth, but we do not assume coloration in the manner of your zones. I am an albino."

"Surprise."

"Look at my eyes."

He looked at her eyes. "Pink."

"It is the color of my blood showing through the translucent flesh of my eyes," she explained. "So despite my name, I am not truly monochrome in the manner of your citizens. I merely lack external coloration. This causes unease in some who behold me."

He softened. "My issues with you do not relate to your appearance. You are a beautiful White Chroma woman. May I call you Chrome?"

"As you wish, Havoc. Now I have a question: do you wish the use of my body?"

"Negation. Friendship is not no fault."

"Havoc, I think you are not being candid."

"Clarification," he said gruffly.

"I inquired whether you wish the use of my body. The only answer to that is affirmation. Friendship neither denies or requires sexual relations between us, but it makes a difference. We need to establish the parameters at the outset."

"I was candid," he said, scowling. "I have to associate with you. I have to work with you. I have to protect you, and not betray you, in the manner of friendship. That is neither love nor desire."

"I agree. It is the same with me. But your desire will interfere with our effective functioning if not properly defined."

"Outrage! You are calling me a liar."

He was like a newly corralled bull. "Havoc, look at me."

He looked, scowling.

She undid her white gown and stood in her white underwear. Then she removed panties and bra and stood nude. She knew herself to be the most beautiful older woman on the planet, by definition. "I have stripped. Can you do the same, Havoc?"

He stood for a moment longer, then shook his head. "Capitulation. I am a liar."

"By no means, Havoc. You are a man. I am a Mistress. It is your nature to desire me. It is my nature to oblige. I will do so if this seems appropriate."

"Request: clothe yourself. We will talk."

She got back into her clothing. "What is your concern?"

"Mistresses govern by seduction and influence. The seduction is more than that of the body. I do not wish to subject myself to your power."

"Point well taken," she agreed. "We could call it no fault, but if you have an affair with me, your oath of friendship will in time become buttressed by genuine feeling. I am of course aware of this, but want to assure you that it is not my intent to corrupt you in any way. I merely wish to facilitate our association, for mutual convenience. Perhaps it is better that we not indulge sexually at this time."

"At this time?"

"If at a later time you change your mind, I will accede, to prevent its becoming an issue. I believe the future paths indicate that such accommodation is likely."

"Compromise," he said. "Change it when you desire it for yourself, not for influence."

She paused. This was an unusual request. "Havoc, sex is not something I do for my own pleasure. It is integral to the way I govern. I would lose control if I did it only for myself."

"Precisely."

She nodded. "And a friend would not deceive a friend on such a matter. You have countered my prime weapon."

"Agreement."

"You are an unusual man."

"I am a Glamor."

"There is more I wish to know of that. Glamors, as I understand it, have ikons. The Green Chroma girl, Naive, carries yours, it seems. I saw the tree form. Why do you not carry it yourself, for safety?"

"Impossible. A Glamor can't touch an ikon."

"And any other person can?"

"Affirmation."

"Your daughter told Naive to give it to me, but I was unable to take it. That seemed to confirm something she suspected. What was it?"

"That you are a Glamor."

"But I have no ikon and no powers of magic."

"Glamors have different forms. On Counter Charm there is Idyll, the Ifrit Glamor. She is not like us. Your power over men derives from your Glamor nature. You may not call it magic, but you use it."

"Point taken." She glanced around. "But we need not stand here talking. Where would you be more comfortable?"

He smiled. "At home with my wife."

"One of the two with whom you made prior oaths of friendship. Perhaps you should tell me about them."

"Exchange: yours for mine."

"Fair enough." She took his hand, feeling the inherent power of him; he was like no other man she had encountered, except for his son Warp. "Here is my garden. I believe you will like it." She took a seat on the adjacent bench.

"Agreement," he said, going immediately to the nearest small tree. He touched its trunk, and the leaves almost seemed to orient on him. He touched a drooping plant, and it lifted its leaves with new vigor. He certainly had a way with plants. It seemed, yes, magical.

"This, too, I would like to know about," she said. "I see that your being the Glamor of Trees is not a mere fiction. In what manner do you relate to them?"

"Each Glamor has a constituency," he said as he explored the other plants of her garden. "Voila, for example, is the Glamor of Amoeba. She draws her power from them, and does what she can for them. I draw my power from trees and plants, and I will never harm them or allow harm to come to them in any way I can prevent."

"But do you not eat vegetables and fruits?"

"Fruits are the offerings of plants for animals, and animals eat them and do the plants favors in return, such as pollination, protection, or fertilization. Vegetables may be tubers formed when the plants have lived their seasons and retired; on Charm those who eat them generally return the seeds to the ground and encourage them to grow. This is the natural interaction." He picked up a tiny seedling. "This plant is suffering; it needs a different kind of soil and less water."

"Please, put it where it belongs. I suspect I understand men better than plants."

He set the seedling in a new place, patting sand around its base. Then he stood, opened his trousers, brought out his penis, and urinated onto the adjacent soil.

Monochrome was too surprised to say a word. She simply stared. No man had ever done that before in her presence. Any man who had exposed his penis to her had had it fully erect and eager to penetrate her body. Even thereafter, men were generally embarrassed to perform such a natural function while she watched. This man was truly different.

Havoc finished, put away his member, and looked at her. "I have provided this plant nutrients that will help it prosper. You should do the same. Your plants need what you can offer."

"I will keep it in mind," she said somewhat uncomfortably. If he had intended to disturb her equilibrium, he had succeeded. "Please, tell me of your two oaths of friendship, and how you became a Glamor. I am interested."

He rejoined her and took her hand with the same hand he had just used to hold his penis. Yet why should she object? She would have accepted that same penis inside her.

"Correction: I misspoke," he said. "My first oath was not to Gale, but to the Blue Dragon. It was injured and needed special medicine, but I was a child and afraid of it. So we made the oath, and thereafter we trusted each other. I foraged for what it needed, and it taught me of the magic of Charm and set me on the course that resulted in my becoming king. I owe that dragon everything."

"We lack dragons on Earth."

"They are not Science Magic creatures," he agreed. "I suppose we could import some from Charm."

"That will not be necessary." She did not let go of his hand. Ordinarily any man whose hand she held was in thrall to her; this one remained independent. "What of Gale?"

"We were of the same village and both fourths, so had a common bond even in childhood."

"Fourths?" Three of the siblings had mentioned being fourths, but hadn't clarified the reference.

"Every woman of Charm is required to marry by age eighteen and to bear four children, for the population of the planet. Three may be by her husband; the fourth must be by another man, or adopted, or seeded by the temple. This is to ensure diversity and interconnection. They are called fourths, though they can come in any order; I gave my mistress Symbol her fourth as her first baby. She will marry and have three natural ones. No distinction is supposed to be made between natural children and fourths, but they can feel isolated or different anyway. So it was natural for Gale and I to come together." He smiled reminiscently. "It didn't hurt that she was the prettiest girl in the village, even as a child."

"And you the handsomest boy."

"Affirmation," he said without modesty. "We were also both very smart and healthy. We were both, as it turned out, changelings."

"I fear I have lost track."

"Our mothers did not want to have sex with any men not their husbands—some women feel that way—so they took the alternative of visiting the temple. There they were seeded with special babies, and we were the result. Changelings are related to neither parent; they are crafted to be superior in all feasible ways. So Gale was pretty and nice. We played Tickle & Peek, and she let me see her cleft." He paused, remembering. "I think I never saw prettier."

"She seduced you into love!"

He frowned. "Not the way you do. She loved me from the start, and I loved her."

"I apologize, Havoc. To me seduction is natural."

He smiled. "Needless. It is natural to our women too. In no fault travel, the man may provide different things, but the woman always provides sex."

"No fault travel?"

"Each person can do the magic of his Chroma zone. But when folk travel beyond their zones, through other Chroma zones, they can't do magic, so are vulnerable. Women especially. Brigands and opportunistic men abound to prey on defenseless travelers. So they normally travel with men, who protect them in return for sex. This is the main occasion for no fault. When they get where they are going, usually another Chroma zone of their own color, they separate and it is as if their relationship never existed. The women's husbands know it but never inquire; in fact they travel no fault themselves. It is a great mutual convenience."

"Now I understand. There is a practical basis for it; it is not mere license. Thank you, Havoc." She lifted his hand and kissed it. And caught herself too late. "I apologize. Such ways are natural to me; I am not trying to abridge our understanding."

"Needless. I asked you to do with me only what you wished for yourself. This was such a case."

She nodded, surprised. "Actually, it was, Havoc. I am coming to like you better as I come to understand you."

"Information: male Glamors, also, are highly appealing to the other gender. And all Glamors to each other."

"And if that appeal is effective on me, and I come to desire sex with you for myself, what harm is done? It is no fault throughout. Actually mistresses are essentially no fault creatures."

"Agreement." Then he resumed his extended answer. "In due course I married Gale, and she will always be my first and major love. But for a time we were involuntarily separated, and I found myself in an unfamiliar environment competing, as it turned out, to become king—a chore I did not want. I approached an older woman—I was eighteen, she forty—named Ennui and proposed that we share resources so that we both might better survive the ordeal. I was a warrior, she a native of the city, so our resources were complementary. The barbarian lout and the civilized woman. But she was afraid of me, and made me make the Oath of Friendship. I did so reluctantly."

He paused, and Monochrome did not interrupt. A reluctant oath was highly relevant to their present situation.

"And it turned out to be the second or third best decision I ever made, after my oath with the blue dragon and my commitment to Gale. I won the crown, and Ennui guided me infallibly so that I was able to win acceptance as king instead of alienating everyone and getting myself killed. She is fifty eight now, still twenty two years my senior, and still my most trusted companion and friend."

"And what did Ennui get from this association?"

"Apart from becoming the second most powerful woman on the planet? An interest in living. She carried my ikon for a time."

"For a time?"

"It turned out that ikons partake in a lesser way of the powers of the Glamors. She became younger, prettier, healthier, virtually immortal, and ferociously sexual. She felt that wasn't her proper nature, so gave it up to be herself. Now she's an old, frail woman, and satisfied to be so. I still value and trust her beyond all others."

"This has implications," Monochrome said. "Our oath was involuntary. Will we follow a similar course?"

"Affirmation. That is one reason I did not want to make it. I am choosy about such enduring commitments."

"I am sorry, Havoc. This is more than I anticipated. Can we end the oath and be free of each other?"

"Negation. Voila required it, and she knows. Both our planets face destruction without it."

"I thought it was humor when you said that your children now run your life."

"Negation. Clarification: We can all see the paths of the near future, but we learned this from Voila, and she remains the best. I can see a few minutes; she can see an hour. She also relates well to Mino, who can see the paths of the far future. Together they can piece out the intermediate future: a day, a week, even perhaps a year. This is what enabled them to fathom the paths of our planets. We unwittingly loosed a far more challenging and dangerous course than we anticipated. We thought we were merely nullifying Earth's intended conquest of Charm; instead we have put both planets in jeopardy. Now we must follow the path that threads between disasters, perhaps avoiding them."

"Perhaps?"

"The future is never certain. Paths change, especially when we take paths we had not been destined to take before. We can only select those that are most likely to bring salvation. It is not easy to explain."

"There is no need. Voila showed me the paths. I did not properly understand them, but I knew they were authentic."

He nodded. "Then you understand the power of my daughter. She governs us all. But she couldn't see far enough ahead, from Planet Charm, to know what we were launching. We don't want Earth in chaos."

"How did you come here? Surely not aboard the *Ms Dominance*."

"Not," he agreed. "I came in Mino."

"That is a machine, I understand. Dynamo was to tell me about it, but he is not after all available."

"Mino is an ancient machine from a machine culture that is advanced beyond ours. We were able to stop him from mining and destroying our planet, but we lack ability to stop his culture. Only if we link closely with Earth can we hope to survive the coming of the machines."

"Is this worthwhile for Earth?"

"Affirmation. Earth is also on the list for mining."

"Mining for what?"

"Magic. In your case, it would take all your Science Magic and leave you without it."

"This is preposterous!"

"Regret."

He had misunderstood. She had meant that it was unthinkable that science be removed from Earth; it was inherent. He assumed it was possible and that she was outraged by the possible theft. She tried another tack. "If this Mino machine is so advanced, how were you able to stop it?"

"The ifrits were able to blind Mino for thousands of years. Then Voila contested with him, and defeated him."

"When did this occur?"

"Sixteen years ago. She was a baby."

Monochrome stared at him. "You are serious?"

"Affirmation. Worlds are at stake."

"And this machine now serves you?"

"Affirmation. Mino recognized that we had to be together to handle the second crisis."

"Second crisis?"

"This one."

She decided to move to another subject. "How did you become a Glamor?"

"I realized that not all the Glamor spots were filled. I aligned with the trees, and they accepted me. Gale did the same with the mosses and lichen. That enabled us to deal with a certain planetary problem relating to the change-lings." He smiled. "Later that returned to affect us in a new way: they showed us the three Glamor babies, Warp, Weft, and Flame, and we adopted them, lest they be destroyed as dangerous. They needed Glamor parents; no others could have controlled them, and we did not find it easy. So we have three fourths and one natural child."

"But surely you would have preferred three of your own."

"Negation. These are worthy."

She considered that. This king and his wife had adopted and raised three outstanding children, together with one of their own. She had been advised of this before, by Mistress Marionette, but now she appreciated its meaning. Again, no ordinary man.

"I think it is my turn to acquaint you with my history," she said.

"Affirmation."

From the start, Monochrome was different. Her parents were embarrassed by her albino appearance despite her otherwise good features. She was smart, healthy, pretty, and dedicated even as a young child. It hardly mattered; she was set apart by her pale skin and white hair. Her success in competitive ex-aminations only made it worse; the others did not like being shown up by a freak. Her parents and school proctors had to watch her carefully, not because she would perform any mischief, but because the other children were increas-ingly out to destroy her. The third time she was beaten up, unresisting, the mistresses interceded. They took her in to their closed society and completed her education their way.

Monochrome flourished. For the first time in her young life she was safe from molestation by her peers, and in a completely supportive environment. She loved the lessons, absorbing history, geography, math, civics, and philoso-phy with equal delight. She was fascinated to learn how the gentle mistresses had taken over the world from the violent males. The males had so misman-aged the world that they brought it into a holocaust that wiped out nine tenths of the population. In the shock of that disaster, the subtle female spirit had emerged to displace the brute male spirit. How that was possible remained obscure, but it was clearly the case.

The Mistresses had labored to reform the world. They hospitalized all those with diseases, and if they could not cure them, exiled them to isolated islands so that they could not infect any others. They redefined mental disease, treating those who might once have been institutionalized, and exiling incur-able bigots to restricted regions. But the global problems were persistent, and resistance simmered into occasional open rebellion. More was needed—but what?

When she turned fifteen she was given the option of entering training to be a mistress. Trainees were carefully selected, and few made it through, for the classes were rigorous and depended on things other than memorization or practice. She had to understand how the takeover had not depended on force, despite folklore to the contrary, but on a far subtler principle: persuasion. She had to learn how to win her way without even the threat of force. How to prevail when the opposition did not even pretend to be reasonable. It was reminiscent of her childhood days.

The most challenging was Seduction. This was done with live grown experienced men keyed to respond only to genuinely effective efforts. It was hands on: success led to sexual expression. Monochrome had several problems with this. One was that she remembered her early days of being a freak. How could any man desire her pure white body? Another was that she had never come close to having real sex. She had studied the mechanics, but actually indulging in it was something else. She wasn't sure she could really do it. But mainly it was that this was thoroughly interactive: she had to constantly read the man's responses, and build on them, playing him carefully to lead him in. At any point he could slip the line and be lost. Her white hair might remind him of his grandmother and turn him off. Her shapely body might make him think of disreputable prostitution.

At first she failed miserably. Her target man laughed at her feeble efforts. She tried again, and failed again, but by a less egregious margin. Progress was glacially slow, but bit by bit she mastered the nuances. She learned that her facial expressions were as important as her words, and the way she moved her body was more potent than the exposed shape of it. She learned the value of partial exposure: a peek down a supposedly accidentally lowered halter could be more effective than full exposure of the breasts. A peek up under a skirt was at times more conducive than a bare bottom. The right exposure at the right time, the correct degree of allure.

She was clothed in poor light when she finally reeled in her first man. His hand finished inside her bra, and his penis bypassed her flimsy panties. The partial glimpses and measured suggestions of passion had brought him to her and into her, literally. "Congratulations," he murmured in her ear as his member jetted inside her.

"You are welcome," she responded, kissing him with somewhat more than calculated emotion. She had scored! Of course he had responded deliberately, but it was a signal that her technique had been adequate. A regular, untrained man would have reacted similarly.

Thereafter she improved, and in due course was pronounced expert: she could quickly seduce any normal man, and profoundly affect most abnormal men also. Only the homosexual or nonsexual could resist her charms, and even they felt the impact.

She was also required to learn a musical instrument. Some girls used their voices as such, but Monochrome's singing voice was passable, not superlative, and for this she had to be outstanding. That freed her to try a wind instrument, as she did not need her breath to sing. There were many tempting types, and she quite liked the single and double reeds, but these tended to be large and to require special maintenance to remain in perfect condition. She wanted something she could carry without complication and play on a whim or when meditating. So in the end she selected the smallest and simplest, the soprano recorder. There were many substances from which they could be made, such as wood, clay, or metal, but she chose bone, as it had the particular quality of tone she preferred. It was in two pieces, and she used them to fix her hair in place, thus having the instrument always with her without having to remember to bring it.

∽∾

"Interruption."

"Welcome, Havoc. Am I becoming dull?"

"Negation. I saw the bones in your hair, and thought them a mere style. I like them, barbarian that I am. You truly can play?"

"Yes. I value music for its effect on mood, others and my own."

"Request."

This, too, was intriguing. Normally it was sex a man desired; he would pretend interest in the finer arts mainly as an avenue to gratification. Since she had already offered him that, this other interest had to be genuine. "Honored."

She unbound her white hair, freeing the two pieces, and fitted them together. Then she played an ancient tune, "Drink To Me Only," simple but lovely, well suited to the instrument. It was always a pleasure to exercise her fingers and evoke the familiar melody. She studied his face as she played, curious about his reaction.

And Havoc, amazingly, joined in, singing. "Drink to me only with thine eyes, and I will pledge with mine. Or leave a kiss within the cup and I'll not ask for wine."

She almost stopped playing. He had surprised her again. It wasn't just that his voice was good; it was. It wasn't merely that he knew the song; the Colony of Charm derived from Earth culturally as well as linguistically. It was that he did it at all. He liked music, and was proficient. Perhaps she should have anticipated this, considering the remarkable musical ability of his daughter Weft. She had assumed that that was the mother's influence.

They finished the song. Then Havoc opened his shirt at the belt level and drew out a blue panel. It was roughly oval, slightly curved, and glossy. He produced a blue stick and ran it along the side of the panel. Notes sounded. In tune. The tune of the song. It was a musical instrument!

"Amazement!" she said, in the Colony style of speech. "I don't recognize the instrument."

"Dragon scale, from my oath friend the Blue Dragon. It is magic, making it sound better. I can't make the music Weft does with her hammer dulcimer, but it will do."

"I had no idea you were even interested in music."

"Well, I'm a minstrel."

"Before you were king?"

"I was a martial artist before I was king. I learned minstreling after. I am eager to retire and spend my life traveling and entertaining villagers."

She laughed. "I wish I could do the same! We could travel together."

He paused, gazing at her. "Observation: you are beautiful with your hair loose."

"It's all wild. I didn't comb it out after untying the recorder."

"Agreement. Like a barbarian girl."

And he claimed to be a barbarian. "Havoc, are you sure you aren't trying to seduce me?"

"Negation. I thought you were trying to seduce *me*."

"Negation," she echoed. That Colony manner of summary was contagious.

"But I fear we are doing it to each other regardless. We are discovering common interests. This may be mischief."

"Agreement. Return to your history."

That did seem best.

~⁊~

Monochrome completed all her courses, and wondered what was next. She didn't want to return to the outside world, where her albino color would still set her apart. But what else was there?

There was a quiet hubbub in the complex. The Mistress of Mistresses was coming for her annual visit! All the girls were eager to meet her. Last year she had selected one of the serious girls to become a new mistress, who had promptly departed for a distant assignment. Monochrome, like the others, had been jealous. Would there be another this year? If so, who? The criteria for selection were unknown; the last one chosen had not been at the top of her class, or the prettiest, or most talented. Yet reports had come back that she was doing well. Once her business had taken her back to the training complex, and Monochrome had seen her—and been amazed. The ordinary girl had become a stunning woman with a presence that put the rest of them to shame. It had been a good selection. How had the Mistress of Mistresses known?

This time there was a show for the entertainment of the Mistress of Mistresses. The senior girls performed, while the mistress and the lesser girls watched. Their finest dancer did a languorous, seductive dance that made Monochrome resolve to practice her own moves further; she was not up to that standard, and wanted to be. Their best singer performed "The Aria," the most challenging of songs, and did a credible if not superlative job. Monochrome of course had never aspired to such a height. Another did an on-stage seduction, artfully luring a man all the way into full sex. Monochrome nodded; that she also could have done. Another presented the result of the special study she had made, developing a new mathematical variant. Monochrome was simply not that smart.

Through it all the Mistress of Mistresses, a beautiful older woman with an almost tangible presence, sat impassively, politely applauding each act. Then she looked around, seemingly for the first time, and her eye fell on Monochrome. "What is in your hair?" she inquired gently.

Monochrome was appalled. She had meant no disrespect. Now she had to answer. All eyes were suddenly on her. She was twenty, but felt like six, before the school principal. "My bone flute, Mistress."

"Why?"

She was really in trouble! "To keep it ever with me, Mistress." She dared not apologize; when speaking to a Mistress, any Mistress, and especially this one, a person had to stick strictly to the subject.

"Of course. Why bone?"

"I prefer its tone, Mistress."

"Why? Give a full answer."

This was awful! Yet she had no choice but to plow ahead with it, laying her faulty reasoning bare. No pat answer would do; she had to give the real one, and be damned.

"When I was a child, I suffered discrimination, because of my albino appearance. So I tended to be by myself. One day I visited a wilderness area, and

climbed a tree to be alone and safe. I heard a commotion and saw a pack of
wolves chasing a small herd of antelope. One antelope put its foot in a hole and
stumbled, hurting its leg. It was partly lame, and the wolves closed immediately on it. They killed it almost under the tree I was in, and tore it apart and
ate the flesh. I was horrified, though I knew this was nature in action. I identified with the antelope, rendered different by chance, and thus marked for destruction. The wolves departed, and I descended and returned home, but I had
bad dreams for months. Finally I returned to that tree, and found a cleaned
bone fragment in a hole near the tree; it must have fallen there, out of reach of
the wolves, and been defleshed by ants. I saved that bone in memory of the lost
antelope, wishing I could in some way make up for its misfortune. Then when
I chose my musical instrument, I asked them to make that bone into a recorder, and when I play it, I somehow feel that I am evoking the spirit of the lost
creature from which it came, and maybe helping it in some devious way. I know
this is foolish—"

"Enough. Come here."

Numbly, Monochrome stood and walked to stand before the Mistress of
Mistresses.

"What is your name?"

"Monochrome, Mistress."

"What is your fondest desire, Monochrome?"

She had no fancy prepared answer. Nothing except the sordid truth. "To
eliminate prejudice and bigotry from the world, Mistress. Because I have experienced it, and know the unfair hurt of it. I do not want to punish anyone, only
to make them understand that no one should be judged purely by appearance.
I know my motive is selfish—"

"Take my hands."

What punishment was this? Monochrome reached out with her two hands
and took the hands of the seated Mistress of Mistresses.

Something pulsed through those linked hands. It transfixed her, not painful but joyful. The spirit of the Mistress infused her, making her feel like twice
the person she had been. She felt as if she were glowing.

The Mistress of Mistresses let go. "Thank you, Mistress Monochrome. You
are indeed worthy. Return to your place."

Monochrome returned as if in a dream, aware of the others staring at her.
Only after she resumed her seat did the words register fully. She had been
called Mistress!"

That was her accession. Thereafter she traveled to a distant section of the
world, and governed as a mistress. After several months the marvel of it wore
off and she recognized that she was indeed capable of doing the job. She focused on being the best she could be, and on abating prejudice wherever she
found it. And when alone she played her bone recorder, recognizing that it had
done her the favor, rather than the other way around. She hoped the spirit of
the antelope approved.

As a Mistress she found that her powers had expanded, and developed
further as she learned how to better use them. The training she had had served
as the base, but she was now more capable in all respects than she had been,
as if magically enhanced. There was also a gladness in her; she liked herself
and the world better. Somehow the spirit of the Mistress of Mistresses had
infused her with new purpose.

She was busy as a mistress for a decade. Then the Mistress of Mistresses summoned a convocation of all. This had not happened in thirty years. In fact not since the Mistress of Mistresses was chosen. What did this mean?

They gathered in Antarctica, the province of the Mistress of Mistresses. There were about one thousand of them, from all the continents. Monochrome had never fathomed what governed their number, but it seemed to be fairly constant. A number of new mistresses were made every year—actually, about two every month—while a similar number stepped down, by their own choice. There had never been any scandal associated with any mistress; the Spirit was pure and kept them so.

"I am seventy years old," the mistress said. "I have served thirty years. I wish to retire, if the Spirit is willing."

The others did not protest. It was her prerogative. If no successor Mistress emerged from this assembly, she would continue, and later try again to retire.

They gathered in the center of the huge hall, clustering around the Mistress of Mistresses, until they formed a compact mass one thousand strong. Monochrome felt the enhancement of the Spirit; she was part of an enormously greater whole. They were pressing closely together, but there was no feeling of pressure. It was more like being one grain of sand in a dune.

Something stirred the assembly, and there was motion. Monochrome had started at the fringe; a current carried her inward in a slow spiral. She allowed it to carry her; she had little choice. At one point she found herself face to face with the Mistress of Mistresses, who smiled at her. Monochrome might have thought it was personal, but realized that most of the Mistresses had been made by this same person, and she herself was probably not remembered individually. But it was significant that the Mistress of Mistresses was no longer at the center; that suggested that she would indeed be replaced.

Monochrome lost track of time as the slow swirling continued. Mistresses made their way to the fringe, then stepped out of the mass, allowing it to evaporate. Monochrome expected to do the same, but the current kept her bearing inward. The mass shrank to half its original size, and a quarter, and a tenth. Then she was surprised to find herself as one of only a dozen; all the others had stepped out and were facing inward, watching in silence.

Another woman stepped out, and another. The group dwindled to six. Still Monochrome did not feel moved to leave; the Spirit seemed to have hold of her and kept her in place. In fact she felt stronger and more alive than ever before.

Five woman. Four. Three. Two. One.

Monochrome discovered herself standing alone in the center of the chamber. All the others had vacated. She looked around, aghast.

Then the Spirit intensified, suffusing her completely. With it came wonderful and horrible information. She was now the Mistress of Mistresses, responsible for the planet of Earth and all its works, including the one billion human inhabitants. She was the incarnation of the gentle Female Spirit that had assumed dominance after the violent Male Spirit brought the world to ruin and virtual barbarism. She must maintain control to see that the Male Spirit never ruled again. She must see to the smooth functioning of the new society, keeping the peace, being fair to all parties.

It was too much! She fell to her knees, sobbing.

Hands came to help her up. It was the former Mistress of Mistresses. "It is a burden you can bear," she said. "I think I knew that when I heard your story of the bone recorder. You are my worthy successor. The Spirit has spoken."

She had remembered! "Please, Mistress, guide me," she pleaded. "I am overwhelmed."

"So was I, at first. I will help you, but soon you will be proficient."

That had proved to be the case. Infusion of the Spirit made her far more than she had been, in all respects. She understood now that she had received a token part of the Spirit when she became a mistress, and now had received the whole of it. She could control any man at a touch, simply by willing it, though normally she preferred to stick to conventional methods. She could readily understand concepts that had been difficult before. She could do physical things she had never tried before. In fact, private experimentation suggested that she was physically faster and stronger than any other person, male or female. That she did her best to conceal, preferring to emulate the delicate creature she appeared to be. She was also far more highly sexual than before. She seduced men to control or reward them, letting sex be a potent tool for accomplishing her purposes, but she could have done the same by non-sexual means. She used sex because she liked it. Every Mistress used it, but now she truly desired it.

That was twenty years ago, and in the interim she had done her best for Earth. She had promoted more than five hundred worthy girls to Mistresses as older ones retired, sharing tiny portions of the Spirit within her, and about half the total were now hers, in a manner. In another decade it might well be time for her to retire too. When the Spirit moved her to do so.

❦

"Revelation!" Havoc said. "You are the Glamor—and the lesser mistresses are the ikons."

"Oh, I don't think so," Monochrome protested. "A Glamor can not touch an ikon. I can and do touch my mistresses."

"Diffuse, then," he said. "With the power split among a thousand, the repulsion must become insignificant. But when you all convene it becomes strong; it stirs movement and ushers individuals out, until only the Glamor remains."

Monochrome would have argued, but she had indeed been unable to touch Havoc's ikon. His theory did seem to explain the process.

"Now we know how each of us came to be," she said. "There are details to clarify. Then we shall have to get to work."

"Question. What details?"

"What is this disaster that your daughter foresees, that requires us to be oath friends against our inclination?"

"I think I know. It is the resumption of power by the Male Spirit."

"But there's no danger of that."

"Consider: the Male Spirit lost power when disaster struck the Earth, weakening him enough to allow the Female Spirit to assume control. Now there is global trouble again, as the volcanoes change your magic and bring chaos. That could weaken you enough to make the difference."

Now she saw it. "It could. But you are a man. Why should you be concerned about such a change?"

"Two reasons. One, we are oath friends, and this mischief is of my making. It would constitute my betrayal of you."

"But that effort predates our friendship."

"Agreement. But it has not yet run its course. Now I must help you prevent it. Two, I do not think Charm would profit from a change in Earth Spirits. Now that I know more about you, Mistress, I believe our best interest is in the continuation of your power on Earth."

That did make sense. "I spoke of issues between us. I need to clarify the situation of your children. In the earlier days of Earth, hostages were not necessarily hostile. Neighboring nations would exchange royal hostages to ensure each other's good faith in keeping the peace between them, but they were well-treated. A royal female hostage might marry a royal man of the host nation. This was intended to be the spirit of our exchange. As you have seen, your children were never treated harshly; they were given every freedom of the planet, until they abused it. I regret the misunderstanding."

"I wish we had understood that," he said. "We put them into your hands because we needed to seed your volcanoes and make Earth unable to conquer Charm."

"So that was your directive."

"Agreement."

She gazed at him in frustration. "This is typical male violence. You perceived a threat, and struck back violently."

"Guilty."

"Now you wish to abate the damage you have caused."

"Agreement."

"I really think we should modify our status to include sex."

"Question."

"Because now I desire it for itself."

"Confusion."

"Havoc, you are a man, with the faults of your gender. But you also love plants, and your children, and music, and you are able to admit your mistakes. This inclines me toward you, perhaps foolishly. In addition you are a male Glamor I need not fear. That is a potent attraction. I am becoming taken with you. I hope you will allow me to indulge my nature and provide you with the best sex you can have on this planet."

"Our oath of friendship covers our relationship. Sex will not make it any more binding."

"But it will be a great deal of fun, and defuse tension. Please. I do desire it now."

"Capitulation," he said.

Then it became intense.

Chapter 14
Black

Havoc was gratified. Mistress Monochrome was indeed the best lover he had encountered, exceeding even Symbol in expertise. She was one fit woman, strong despite her seeming delicacy, exactly as she had indicated. He liked that too. Recent sexual privation while traveling, and the Mistress' beauty and confession of desire made him unusually ardent. He clasped her and indulged in a climax a full two minutes long, filling her with countless jets of ejaculate.

He was apologetic as he slackened. "Regret. I haven't done it in a while. It overflowed."

She laughed. "It certainly did! I never knew a man to pump out that long and strong an emission before. You *are* magic."

"Agreement." They remained connected, lying embraced.

"So it is true about the special sexual powers of Glamors."

"Affirmation. We can do it indefinitely if we choose."

"Havoc, this ardor appeals to me. I am, as you know, a sexual creature myself, but I normally do not climax. My purpose is to guide the male to his fulfillment, not my own. But I confess this passion of yours arouses me. Do you mind if I join you?"

"Enthusiasm!"

"Then resume your labor, if you will, and I will let myself go."

He resumed thrusting, and in a moment was in his second extended orgasm. This time she clasped him more tightly, kissing his mouth, and her vagina clenched in rapid waves. Her body heated, writhing athletically, and he felt her heart racing. Then he was jetting into the storm of her fulfillment, carried by her ongoing urgency. He felt her orgasms, one, two, three, four, and on, as she, too, repeated for minutes. She was indeed a Glamor, and could do it as readily as he.

Eventually they expired together, panting across each other's cheeks, their merged crotches mired in the overflowing gel of his emissions. "Glory!" he gasped.

"It has been an experience," she agreed. "I never dared indulge myself like that before."

"Irony."

"I don't think so. There was simply no man on Earth who could have handled it. They have this quaint notion that women lack sexual imperative, and can be frightened by the reality. That mistresses use sex without truly desiring it. You do not have that problem."

"Misdirection. I was thinking of a prior experience of mine."

"Tell me, Havoc, please."

"It was before I was a Glamor. I needed the help of a guirl—" He paused, realizing that this would be meaningless to her. "On Charm there are variants of the human form that adapt to special conditions. In the water there are buoys and guirls, who have developed gills to breathe the water."

"Mermen and mermaids," she agreed. "They exist only in our mythology."

"They are required to have seconds, rather than fourths: every second child a guirl bears must be by a man other than her husband. They can be quite insistent when they find suitable men. So this guirl required me to provide her with her second in exchange for her help. So while she bore me through the water she fixed her mouth on mine and breathed air into me so that I would not drown, and she took in my member and held it with suction and closure, drawing out my essence at will, repeatedly. I could not escape her. When she was done with me, I was sexually exhausted, and did not indulge again for many days."

"Now I comprehend. Had that occurred when you were a Glamor, you could have satisfied her without wringing yourself dry, and had a wonderful time of it. Instead you must have seemed less than manly to her."

"Agreement. Now you can not do it with an ordinary man, lest you wear him out as the Guirl did me."

"Exactly. I confess that when Marionette reported what Warp was capable of, I envied her. Now, with you, I am replete."

"We are well-matched, in this respect. But of course Glamors are."

"May I ask a question?"

"Reminder: we are oath friends, and now lovers. I am even getting to like you. There need be no secrets between us."

"Though we are nominally enemies," she agreed. "My understanding is that though your ikon is here on Earth, it is not functional, because you have no nonChroma volcano to recharge it. How is it that you can perform Glamor-style?"

"Mino brought a shipment of Chroma stones. These contain concentrated magic that people of the right Chroma can draw on. I will show you, when we disengage."

"Let's have another bout before we do. I am inclined to splurge."

"Concurrence." He resumed thrusting again, and she let herself go again, and they experienced another minute of intense orgasmic pleasure. He was confirming that it was true: she really did like sex as well as he did, when she had suitable opportunity. Now she had it.

Then they separated at last, vacating the bed. She fetched sponges and a basin and mopped up herself and the overflow on the bed. "It's almost as if I had a fire hose wedged in my vulva, pressuring its divine substance in and out of me. But surely you feel that loss of matter. There must be half a liter here!"

"Exaggeration," he said, not displeased.

"Still, it's a drain."

"I am hungry," he agreed as she took a cloth to his member and groin, cleaning him also. He did have to eat well to replace the substance lost in his emissions. Then he fetched a stone from his clothing. "Here is a nonChroma

Chroma stone that lends me my magic." He handed it to her.

"I can touch it," she said, surprised.

"It is not my ikon. Any Chroma person can do ordinary magic anywhere, with the right Chroma stone. But such use depletes the stones." He demonstrated by levitating, rising from the floor and floating as if lying on an invisible bed. Then he conjured himself across the room, and back. The stone became visibly smaller as its energy was expended. "Lifting and moving weight is heavy magic," he explained. "Illusion and telepathy are light magic. I could do the latter much longer without depleting the stone."

"They are like batteries," she said. Then, seeing his confusion, explained: "A battery is a storage device for electricity. Many of our machines run on electricity, and if it is not provided by cable, they use batteries instead. But the batteries must be recharged or replaced regularly."

"Silver Chroma," he agreed. "Electrical."

She returned the stone. "I am giddy with gratification. Soon we shall have to get to work saving our worlds. Let's have one more pulse, before we dress; then we will eat and plan."

"But you have cleaned yourself and put away your sponge."

"For a limited engagement I don't need it." She stepped into him and took in his rising penis, her vagina milking it for a single jet. "Make that three." He obliged, and felt her matching small orgasm. She had marvelous control. Then she kissed him, disengaged, and walked back to the sink, nothing dripping, and efficiently cleaned herself there. He was still learning and liking things about her.

They dressed, and she provided a nice meal largely from her garden, and they talked. "I am interested in the Glamor concept, which is new to me. If I am a Glamor, as seems to be the case, why is it I can not do magic?"

"You do Science magic."

"Havoc, I am not sure that is the case. I would be the Glamor of the Female Spirit, and that is surely independent of Science, and indeed, of Chroma. Shouldn't I be able to do what you do? To float, for example?"

"Interest." He considered. "Reasonable. Conjecture: you can do it, but don't know how. Maybe I can show you."

"Excitement," she said, smiling.

"You are in your environment, so should be able to draw in it." He reconsidered. "Negation: this is Science chroma. But your thousand ikons are everywhere, and must be providing you with power. Ikons seem to translate the power in the environment via the constituency. In my case, nonChroma and trees. In your case, the background magic of Earth, and the Female Spirit. You should have magic."

"I should. If our conjecture is valid."

He took her hand. "I will float. Feel my effort. Copy it." He floated slightly. She did not do the same. "I still don't know how."

"Idea! It is your mind that needs to know. I will guide you with mind contact."

"Telepathy?"

"Projected," he agreed. He concentrated, sending the floating signal.

Monochrome's feet left the floor.

"Success," he said, gratified.

She stared down, astonished. "I'm doing it!"

He nodded. "Question: Does Science account for this?"

"No."

"Conclusion: it must be magic."

She swooned.

He caught her and set her gently on her feet, steadying her. He kissed her, and in a moment she recovered. "I didn't believe in magic either, as a child. It takes time to accept."

"As a child? I am fifty!"

"And still Earth's sexiest woman."

"It's the Female Spirit. Without it I would not be nearly as appealing."

"Negation. My mistress on Charm is ten years older than I, forty six, and she has always been wonderful for me. You are of her generation."

"How old is your wife?"

"A year younger than I. She is also wonderful in sex, but I loved her before we ever merged. For sex anyone will do; I like the sixteen year old bath girls too. But love is something else."

"It is indeed," she agreed. "Now you have shown me that I can levitate by magic. You say that illusion is less costly magic. Is it also easier to learn?"

"Negation. But it is worth the effort, because when magic is limited, it can accomplish more."

"The illusion of floating can accomplish more than the reality of floating?"

"Sometimes. See." He gestured, and suddenly they were perched on a precarious chair hanging over an immense gulf. Then the chair started to tip over.

"Oh!" she cried, jumping. Then she straightened. "But I can see reality through it."

"Confirmation: Glamors can," he agreed. "But you reacted worse to the illusion than to the reality before."

"No I didn't. I fainted."

He nodded. "Experiment: try it again." He took her hand and projected the levitation impulse. She lifted into the air. This time she neither jumped nor swooned.

"Point taken," she said. "I am more in control in reality, so react less."

"And the illusion of a pursuing monster, or of a bridge across a chasm where there is none, can be dangerous."

"Teach me illusion!"

They worked at it, and after further mind projection she succeeded in generating the illusion of Havoc standing across the room, using him as a model. His proportions weren't quite right, and he moved somewhat jerkily, but he was recognizable. Then she created an illusion of herself beside him, also imperfect. Then she made them kiss.

"You are learning well and rapidly," he said.

"I am starting late, and have far to go." Now the illusion figures were undressing each other.

Intrigued, he watched her show. The figures became nude and moved into a clinch. His penis and her breasts were too big, but were well-shaped. They kissed again, and proceeded to sex. His huge penis had to try several times before it wedged into her tight cleft, and her breasts projected halfway through his body. "This is fun," she said. "Too bad it's only a holo picture."

"Amplification," he said. "It can be more." He extended his control, took over the illusion man, and made it walk to the real Monochrome. It reached out to touch her clothed breast.

"Oh!" she cried, jumping back.

"Illusion of touch," he said.

"I am amazed! Can it also kiss?"

"Demonstration." The figure leaned down, put its face to hers, and kissed her on the mouth. This time she did not flinch. It was a seemingly solid contact.

The illusion figures vanished. Monochrome flung herself into his arms and kissed him in reality. They went into clothed sex. It seemed she had been turned on by the illusion by-play, as had he.

But after that, she returned to illusion again, determined to become more proficient. It was obvious that she had a flair for magic, now that she accepted its reality.

The session went into night. They interspersed illusion practice with real sex, then tried combinations. She had trouble doing two illusion senses simultaneously, which wasn't surprising; it had taken Havoc months to get that right. But in the darkness she crafted an illusion of herself lying naked and invited him to have sex with it. He tried, but though he could feel her body, it wasn't real and he was alone on the bed. Then he lay on his back, and she made the touch illusion figure lie on top of him, and in that manner he was able to complete seeming sex with her.

"I'm so pleased!" she exclaimed as her real self cleaned up the semen that had fallen on his belly. "I did full sexual touch illusion. Now I want reality." She got down on him. This time no semen fell on his body.

It was quite a night.

✿❧

In the morning Havoc received a mental call. It was Flame. *Havoc, we need you. Hope you had a good time with the Mistress. We need her too.*

Flame was not one to fool around. If she asked for help, he needed to provide it. *On our way,* he replied.

"What happened?" Monochrome asked.

"Flame needs me."

"That girl is all business. Where is she?"

"Rogue Black Chroma zone with Fifth."

"I can order transportation, but I'm not sure it will work in a zone."

"It won't. This is why Glamors have to participate."

"Then I'm not sure how we can help."

"I will take you there."

She looked at him. "Havoc, if you mean what I think, you'll exhaust your magic stones before you get there."

"I have a pouch full of them. Are you ready?"

She hardly hesitated. "Yes."

He put his arms around her and teleported, orienting on Flame's persona.

The surroundings turned black. They were in the rogue zone. "This is remarkable," she murmured in his ear. "I felt your magic power. It is marvelous, and dizzying."

"Confirmation." He let Monochrome go. "Stay close. There is danger."

Flame appeared. "We can handle this if we can get the natives to listen," she said. "But they're terrified."

"I can help with that," Monochrome said.

Fifth appeared. "First we have to get their attention. I can organize them if they'll listen. There's an inruption coming."

"How long?" Havoc asked.

"Two hours."

"We'll have to form temporary bulwarks, then."

"I can do that. But not at the same time I'm organizing them."

"Start forming them here," Havoc said. "We'll address the natives."

"Aura is here," Flame said. "She will help orient you." She vanished.

Now Havoc saw the Blue Chroma woman. He had met her long ago, and respected her. Now he trusted the welfare of his daughter to her. "Appreciation."

"Illusion," Monochrome said. "Put me in the sky. They will heed me."

"Master/slave," Havoc said to Aura.

"Mistress/slave," Monochrome said, smiling.

Aura nodded. "Pose, Mistress," she said.

Monochrome stood straight, facing her. She remained in her night dress but seemed unconcerned. A giant illusion formed behind her, towering into the dark sky. It was beautiful and, perhaps incidentally, fascinatingly sexy. Aura was using her Red Chroma stone to fashion the emulation, copying the Mistress precisely.

"What do they need to know?" Monochrome asked.

"That there is danger within two hours. They must come here where we can protect them. Not to panic, just get here. We'll put an arrow in the sky over here to show the way."

"This I can do. Tell me when."

Aura looked at the huge image. "Ready. Speak to them."

"Citizens of Earth," Monochrome said, and her voice boomed from the image. "I am the Mistress of Mistresses. I have come to help save your lives. Heed me." She paused, taking a breath that made her full breasts quiver under the scant material, then resumed. "This region is being victimized by a magic effect. The volcano will erupt in two hours. You must come here for safety. Do not panic. Just make your way here now."

The arrow appeared above their site, glowing brightly, pointing down.

"Follow the arrow," Monochrome said. "Do not delay. The volcano is extremely dangerous. Come to me immediately. After the eruption is over you may return. Do not risk it. I want you with me." She smiled.

So did Havoc. Only a dead man could resist that invitation.

Meanwhile black stones were appearing, forming a crude convex wall between them and the volcano. Fifth was doing his job.

"Too slow," Aura said. "There will not be a sufficient barricade and excavation when the inruption comes. I need to help them. Can you do the repeat messages alone?"

"We can," Havoc said. "Help them."

Aura vanished.

"I can do it by myself, I think," Monochrome said. "So you can help them also, Havoc."

"Positive. But let me help you with one, to be sure. Incidentally, Black Chroma volcanoes don't erupt, they inrupt. Apart from that your message was perfect."

"I am aware. But my people are not. A foreign word would confuse them. They know an eruption is dangerous."

"Concession." He looked up. "Try taking over the illusion. I will buttress you."

The huge figure in the sky fuzzed, then sharpened, its proportions suffering somewhat. Havoc touched Monochrome's hand, guiding her with his mind, and the image became perfect.

Flame reappeared. "Caution: I prefer not to be known abroad as a Glamor. Fifth should get the credit for Black Chroma magic."

"Concurrence," Havoc said, and she was gone again. He turned to Monochrome. "I suspect it would be better for you, also, to be known only as the Mistress of Mistresses, not a Glamor, at least until you consolidate your magic powers."

"I agree. All Black magic is the Black man's."

"Appreciation." He kissed her.

"Havoc, you don't need to do that unless you mean it. I don't need to be managed."

"Admission: I do mean it. You appeal to me, perhaps too much."

"All men love me, but ours is a business relationship, facilitated by the exchange of hostages we call the Oath of Friendship, and by sexual indulgence. Remember that we are working together now, but we represent the welfare of different planets, and that issues remain between us."

"Remembered," he said. She was being absolutely fair-minded, and that impressed him anew. "I am a headstrong male. Question: do you prefer me not to be demonstrative?"

She kissed him back, lingeringly. "No. I merely prefer not to deceive or be deceived. Havoc, are we falling in love?"

The question set him back. Their association was only a day and a night, but in that time they had come to some rare understandings and extraordinary pleasures. This was a temporary relationship, in essence no fault. How could it be love?

"Complication," he said. "I love Gale."

"Havoc, I don't want to be your wife. I want to be your mistress."

As Symbol had been, until this crisis. He needed a new mistress. Yet this was no ordinary woman—which was both the problem and the allure. They could not continue indefinitely, yet already he knew he wanted her in his life. "How spelled?"

"Both ways. Politically I want to govern you so as to bring Charm under Earth's sway, as your Mistress. Socially I want to clasp you eternally, as your mistress."

And could he afford either? "Indecision."

"No need to make a decision at this time. Merely answer the question."

Which was whether they were falling in love. "Affirmation."

"I was afraid of that."

Aura appeared. "Emergency," she reminded them, and departed.

Monochrome blushed, and Havoc felt himself doing the same. Of all times to get into this particular dialogue! Yet it had come upon them when it chose.

The giant figure had frozen in place during their diversion. Now it reanimated, breathing deeply as if fresh from some physical exercise, with a pulse showing in its throat. In a moment its flush faded. "Citizens of Earth," it said, and went through the spiel again. Monochrome was now doing it all herself. She was an extremely rapid learner.

"Sufficient," Havoc said. "Place it at different locations. I will assist the others."

Monochrome lifted her hand in acknowledgment.

Havoc oriented on Flame and teleported to join her. "Weft will be jealous," she said. No need to clarify of what.

"She's older than Symbol."

"She's a beautiful Glamor."

Exactly. "And what of your mother?"

"She will be relieved you have found another suitable mistress. Now we need to start the excavation. Here." She guided him to the spot she had chosen. "The vertical wall of it must be just inside the boulders, and convex from here, so that the inruption strengthens it rather than weakens it."

"Arch principle," he agreed as they got to work, using magic to scrape out the channel. First they loosened the rocky bonds, forming sand and isolated stone; then they shoved them up against the bolders.

People started arriving. "What's happening?" a man asked.

"We are clearing a bunker for protection from the eruption," Aura explained. "Fifth, the Black Chroma man from Colony Planet Charm, is using his magical talent to powder the ground, but we still need to shovel it out to make the ditch."

"I'll be glad to help, after I check with the Mistress."

Havoc sent a thought to Monochrome. *Assure them it is good to help shovel out the bunker.*

The giant illusion responded. "When you get here, join the workers who are excavating the bunker. It needs to be deep enough to protect us all from the eruption."

The man smiled. "That's clear enough. Too bad I didn't get to walk under that holo."

"Good thought," Havoc agreed, as Flame stifled a smirk. *Walk over us,* he thought. *Give us dull men a thrill.*

The giant woman moved toward them, her feet making no impact. She crossed their site and went on, bound for her next location. Havoc and the man paused to stare upward. They were treated to a marvelous view of the perfectly formed legs and thighs reaching up under the nightie, and the panties between them as the buttocks flexed.

"A sight to die for," the man said.

"Agreement." Havoc wished he could be having at that delicious body again.

"You will be dying soon regardless if you don't get to work," Aura said.

"No need to be jealous," Havoc said. "Make a similar huge image of yourself, and we'll be glad to look up to you."

The blue woman smiled. "Some other time."

They got to work with shovels that Aura "happened" to find. As other people arrived, male, female, and child, they joined in, and progress was good.

But not good enough. Fifth appeared. "There are too many people, the bunker is not sufficient, and the inruption will be too strong," he said. "The magic is wild; it needs taming. I am unable to use it with full effect. We can't save them all."

"Unacceptable," Aura said tersely.

"Inadequacy," Fifth said apologetically.

Flame broke from her labor and walked to him. She embraced him and kissed him solidly.

"Lovely."

Havoc turned to find Monochrome beside him. The giant image still broadcast its message; she had learned how to make it function independently. "She's his type," Havoc said.

"I put the image on auto-pilot. What can I do here?"

"I think we're going to need you for crowd control. We don't have enough room, and the inruption is coming. It will suck half the people in, because they won't have sufficient shelter."

Flame strode across to join them. "Fifth says the only way is to link bodies and hold on. The worst of it will be only a few minutes; then it will ease. There is an effective linkage technique used in the Black Chroma zones in emergencies, but it requires time for training we don't have."

"Show me," Monochrome said.

"Lie on the ground, heads away from the center. Alternate bodies face up, face down."

Havoc and Monochrome lay as directed, he on his back, she on her front, elbows and knees hooked. "Only it is elbow to knee, incorporating successive ranks," Flame said.

They made the adjustment, so that Monochrome's right knee linked with Havoc's right arm. Aura then lay on her front below Monochrome and hooked her right arm through the hook of his right knee. Flame linked also, extending the pattern. "And so on throughout," she said. "It forms a big human fabric that will survive if not torn. There can be several layers."

"I understand," Monochrome said. "How much time remains?"

"Ten minutes to inruption."

"Then it is time to start." The giant figure ceased its programmed message and delivered a new one. "The eruption is coming soon. There is not enough room. Some of us will be blown away. But we can stop that by linking to each other and holding on for just a few minutes. Like this." Monochrome's image shrank in size, and was joined by Havoc's image. Then both divided into several. They linked elbows and knees in the prescribed manner as she described it, forming a pattern of Havocs and Monochromes that expanded as more figures linked, until it resembled a cloth covering the sky.

"Now do it," she concluded. "We will direct you. Hang on until the winds come and go. It will not be easy, but you will survive." Her voice and manner were compellingly persuasive, as was her nature. Her huge figure reappeared, standing almost over them, giving the men another view to remember. That was a nice touch.

Havoc, Flame, Aura, and Fifth directed the pattern, starting at the top and rapidly adding links. When they filled the trench they started over, placing a second web on top of the first, the bodies offset slightly so that no one felt as if smothering directly under another.

One minute, Flame thought.

They were not nearly finished. "Follow the pattern," the giant figure called. "Link! Link! Link!"

There was a scramble as the first sound of the inruption came. It was an unearthly whomp! followed by in inrushing gust of wind. "Link! Link!" Monochrome cried, heedless of her own safety.

"You too," Havoc said, grabbing her and bearing her down with him. They linked on to the edge of the fabric as the wind rose again. Fifth, Flame, and Aura linked elsewhere, shoring up weak sections.

Then came the main inruption. The wind howled across the filled pit, rocking the boulders. Things were flying in it: dirt, plants, stones, trees, all destined for the sucking maw of the black volcano. It hauled at them, trying to dislodge them, to lift them up. But the people understood that it was death to lose the linkage, and clung together for their lives.

The wind increased, rising to hurricane force. The entire top living blanket lifted and flapped. Women screamed.

"Hold on!" the illusion figure cried, reappearing. "A few more seconds!"

The wind eased slightly, and the layer settled back down, intact. Then another gust came, tearing at it. One portion gave way. Twenty linked people sailed into the sky and disappeared. The noise was so great their screams could not even be heard, but the horror registered.

Suddenly it was done. *Inruption over*, Fifth thought.

"It is over!" the giant woman cried. "Now we can let go."

Slowly the network of people released. They scrambled to their feet. Some were stunned by the losses of their friends or family members. Others had dislocated joints and were suffering.

Healing, Flame thought. *Come to the Glamors.*

"Those who are hurting, come to me," the Monochrome figure said. "We will help you."

They came. Aura did efficient triage. Her blue stones were depleted by the recent effort, and she had no further magic to spare, but she remained useful. Now it was not possible for the others to conceal their Glamor nature. Havoc and Flame laid on hands and drew on magic to repair them. Monochrome touched Havoc, feeling and learning his impulses, then did the same, healing. She had mastered a difficult ability with one effort of assimilation. She surely had done something similar in her role as Mistress; this was merely a variant.

When the immediate job was done it was time for more instruction. Fifth assumed the sky stage. Monochrome was beside him. "This is Fifth, of the Black Chroma," she announced. "He has lived his life in a zone like this. Heed his words."

"There will be other inruptions," Fifth said. "We will be vulnerable until we organize to handle them. We need to construct underground bunkers and dwelling places, ringing the volcano. Then we will be safe. Now I will organize you for this effort. Those who want no more of this should migrate from this vicinity. The others can remain and control it. There will be enormous advantages once this is accomplished. As the ambiance of the Chroma zone infuses you, you will become able to perform magic. Then there will be little limit to what you can do. But first we must tame the volcano."

They were listening, of course. They had experienced the devastating power of the volcano. They had seen the ambient magic. Whatever sceptics they might have been before, they were believers now.

Fifth proceeded with the job for which he had been trained. He assigned leaders and chores: search parties to locate the best sites for subterranean construction. Workers to construct them. Details to organize the provision of food for them all. Women to handle baby-sitting so that women could work as well as men. He was creating organization out of chaos. Some were departing, but more were participating. The new order was forming.

Havoc found himself standing beside Aura. "Observation: this was more than you counted on," he murmured.

"Question: more than chaperoning your violent daughter?" she inquired with a smile.

"Business. Any luck with the ikon?"

"Negation. The nonChroma ikons have been seeded, but we have not been free to travel, and the Glamors can't do it."

"Need: do it when you can. The stones are running low."

"Agreement."

That was all, but it counted. Aura, Auger, Ine, and Iolo's real purpose was to carry the duplicate ikons of the four Glamor siblings, and deliver them to the new nonChroma zones as they formed. Then the Glamors would have full Glamor powers on Earth, no longer dependent on Chroma stones.

"We can handle it from here," Flame told him as she appeared. "Appreciation, Havoc. And you, Mistress—you were magnificent. They never would have followed, if you had not led. You saved a thousand lives today."

"I had good instruction," Monochrome said.

"Keep her, Havoc." Then Flame returned to the work at hand.

"Now I more fully appreciate the need for your trainers," Monochrome said as they walked away. "They know what to do. We need that." She glanced at him. "Let's get alone. I am overflowing with passion."

"Desire," he agreed. "But first I must learn some things."

"May I join you?"

"Insistence," he said, putting his arm around her and teleporting to the rim of the awesome black gulf that was the mouth of the volcano.

She was daunted. "Not to question your competence, Havoc, but is this safe?"

"Assurance: Between inruptions, yes."

"I am studying how you teleport. I hope to do it myself soon."

"Welcome." He kissed her and squeezed her firm bottom. "After this, we'll get alone."

"I must confess there is a certain novelty in your barbarian forwardness. But why are we here?"

"Question: you noted the black color of the zone?"

"Assuredly. It's like midnight at midday."

"Why should it be black, when everything sucks inward toward the volcano? What comes from outside should be its own color."

She paused a moment, realizing. "This is true. I was thinking in terms of eruption, and thought it was staining from the volcano. It is odd, considering. I trust your question is rhetorical?"

"Affirmation. The zone makes the volcano, rather than vice versa. We seeded it with Black Chroma demons, who actually perform the conversion. They are everywhere, invisible, but wild. They need to be tamed. Then the volcano will be better behaved."

"I would not know how to begin taming invisible demons."

"Concurrence. That's why the specialists are here."

Two figures appeared before them: a black man and a yellow woman. "Greeting, Havoc," the woman said. "I see you wasted no time finding Earthly company."

"Greeting, Yellow," Havoc replied. "This is Monochrome, the Mistress of Mistresses on Earth, our leading opponent and my oath friend and lover. Mistress, this is the Yellow Glamor of Demons, and the Black Glamor of Saprophytes. They are here to tame the demons."

"Hello, Glamors," Monochrome said, evincing no surprise at their presence. "I wish you rapid success, though I am ignorant of your mechanisms. At the moment our purposes are one: to prevent Earth from sliding into chaos and enabling the return of the Male Spirit, which we feel would be hostile to our mutual best interests."

"Realization: So that's the malign essence we encountered," the Yellow Glamor said. "Something was fighting us, making the demons resistive. It even triggered the inruption."

"We noticed," Havoc said. "Do you have the demons tamed?"

"We have started the process. It is in essence similar to the one Dynamo set up for the human denizens: train leaders, who will then guide followers in an increasing radiation until all are covered. I relate to demons, and Black relates to the Chroma, so we were able to accomplish it. We had not expected them to fight us at first. I will be visiting the other volcanoes and working with other Chroma Glamors. It would help to know more of this male spirit."

"Mistress," Havoc said.

"As I understand it, in terms of Glamor identities, I am the current incarnation of the Female Spirit," Monochrome said. "It infuses all the mistresses, but the Mistress of Mistresses most of all. The parallel seems to be that I am the Glamor, and the thousand lesser mistresses are ikons. In time, perhaps another decade, I will retire and the Spirit will infuse another Mistress. Before the holocaust several centuries ago the Male Spirit governed; it was under his aegis that the colonies were founded and deserted. The disruption of the holocaust enabled the Female Spirit to assume control, and so it has been since, as we recover the marvels of our planet. The disruption of the changing Chroma zones threatens to enable the Male Spirit to wrest back control. Therefore I am working closely with King Havoc, in the interest of saving the present order."

"Request: We wish to touch you," the Black Glamor said.

Monochrome spread her arms. "Touch me."

The two advanced on her. Black took her left hand, and Yellow her right hand. There was a pulse. Then they disengaged.

"Confirmation," Black said. "Glamor."

"Worthy," Yellow agreed. "We will cooperate with you."

"Satisfaction," Havoc said.

The two other Glamors disappeared, returning to their work. Havoc took hold of Monochrome.

"Wait, if you will," she said. "I think I can teleport with you on my own power, if you will guide me. Return to the Mistress station and I will follow."

"Agreement." He hoped she would be able to do it.

Havoc teleported to the residence in Antarctica. He landed neatly there— but Monochrome did not join him. Had something gone wrong?

He teleported back to the Black Chroma zone, but she was not there. What had happened?

He tuned in on her mind, and found it. She was in extreme discomfort. He teleported to her.

She was lying on the ground about a quarter of the way to her suite. He kneeled beside her. "Chrome!"

"I am not accustomed to failing," she gasped, and fainted.

He put two hands on her, sensing her condition. She was whole, but extremely tired. Rest would restore her; no special effort of healing was needed.

He picked her up and teleported to her suite. He set her on her bed.

She recovered consciousness. "I thought I could do it," she said. "I am mortified."

"Needless," he reassured her. "I started with short hops. You tried too much, too soon. You were quite credible."

"You are kind."

"We are oath friends."

"Make love to me, Havoc. It will restore me."

"Uncertainty."

"Trust me."

He needed no further urging. He kissed her, stroked her, entered her, and climaxed immediately. Then, conscious that she had not joined him, he reasserted his potency and did it again, more slowly. She responded weakly, then with more verve, and finally with vigor. She seemed to be drawing strength from his substance within her. That pleased him.

"Tell me," she said as they lay together. "Why did Warp incapacitate the fleet, knowing that in time we would fathom the problem and recover control?"

"Irony: I love your romantic nature."

She laughed. "I am shaken at the moment, and must express thoughts as they occur. I will be more focused soon."

"Explanation: it was part of the plan. It would have been possible to bomb the volcanoes within a month of their seedings, destroying the Chroma. It needed time to infuse the full region. When the Black Chroma extended well beyond the cone of the volcano, it was secure, and bombing would not inhibit it. The same is true of the others. So we prevented your fleet from striking back in time. Thereafter it no longer mattered."

"We never even thought to bomb the volcanoes!" she said ruefully. "We had no idea."

"Request: don't tell Warp. He would be most disappointed to learn that his effort was unnecessary."

"And did we really take your children hostage, or did you give them to us?"

"Caution: Will you still give me wonderful sex if I answer honestly?"

"Of course not. I would be too angry at being duped."

"Concern: Anger would not become you."

"Oh, Havoc, thanks for saving me from my foolishness."

"Needless. What you have accomplished is phenomenal."

"Thank you."

"And you are beautiful."

"I am fifty."

"Memory: we have had this dialogue before."

"And we have had sex before." She stroked him, and soon they were into it again.

But she wasn't finished. "And the others who accompanied your children: they are not mere chaperones, servants, or pets?"

"Not," he agreed. "They are the ikon bearers."

"Because Glamors have ikons, or duplicate ikons, which they can't touch themselves," she said. "So they played those other roles to mask their real purpose."

"Agreement. Actually their support helped the four Glamors function; they are good people."

"So it seems. Mistress Morsel reported that the invisible woman really impressed Admiral Vitality."

"Likely. Ine is an Air Chroma sorceress, thoroughly versed in illusion and sex."

"And distraction. It took him some time to believe that she could have had anything to do with the malfunction of the fleet control."

"Belief. Ine is quite a woman."

"To be sure. Is she better than I am in bed?"

Havoc considered. "Negation."

"You took too long to think about it. The penalty is another performance."

"Chore," he agreed as he got to it with zest.

After a mutually satisfying session, she had another concern. "Why couldn't I teleport the full distance?"

"Conjecture: accuracy becomes a problem with distance. You can travel to sites in sight because you know where you are going. Beyond that you must have an accurate awareness of the route."

"Did you have that for the Black Chroma zone?"

"Negation. But I knew where Flame was, and oriented on her."

"So a person can define a site?"

"Affirmation." Then he thought of something. "Your mistresses may be ikons, but you can touch them. You should be able to orient on them."

"I want to try it."

"Caution. You are depleted from your prior effort."

"And restored by your sexual effort. I want to try it."

"Preference: then let me hold your hand."

"That's so romantic, Havoc."

"That, also," he agreed, smiling.

She chose a Mistress elsewhere in Antarctica, and successfully teleported to her vicinity. Then she tried one on another continent, and made it again. "They are like beacons," she said, "I can tune on in their glows."

"Clarification: it is an aspect of telepathy."

"And that's the next thing," she said as they returned to Antarctica. "I want to learn it."

"Caution. It started as an illness on Charm, because it was incapacitating to receive all thoughts unguarded. First you must learn to shield your mind."

"Teach me, Havoc."

"This interrupts the sex," he complained with a smile.

"Which reminds me: how did Voila seduce Caveat? He has no sexual interest in women."

"Illusion and projection of desire."

"So telepathy did have something to do with it."

"Affirmation. She had to understand his nature in order to adapt it."

"And is it true that you can read your partner's joy of climax, and project your own to her?"

"Affirmation."

"Send yours to me, this time," she said as she addressed him again.

"Hesitation."

"Insistence."

He shrugged and obliged, sending her the raw urgency of his desire and ejaculation.

"Oh!" she gasped. "That's the first time I have felt penetration from the male perspective. It's potent."

"By definition," he agreed. Then they slept.

And by morning they agreed that they were no longer falling in love. They had completed the fall.

"Yet in time we must separate," Monochrome said. "Because whatever the outcome of the present struggle, you must return to Charm and I must remain on Earth."

That was a prospect he now dreaded.

Chapter 15
Green

Help requested. It was the thought of the Green Glamor.

"I'm next on call," Gale said. She conjured herself to the rogue Green Chroma zone where he was operating.

There were Dynamo, Naive, and Weft, standing beside a mass of greenery. "The Glamor is tackling the green magic," Naive said. "We are trying to organize the people. But there are many children who interfere with their concentration. If you can reassure their mothers, Dynamo and I should be able to proceed more effectively."

"Baby-sitting!" Gale exclaimed.

"Confession: I'm no good with children," Weft said, embarrassed. "I expected to help with the magic."

"Instruction," Gale said. "I have had some experience and will show you how."

"We leave it to you," Dynamo said. "We will send the children." Then Naive took hold of him and conjured the two of them away. She was no Glamor, but this was her home Chroma; she had full powers of magic within this zone.

"Envy," Weft said. "How can an ordinary Green girl win such a man when I can't?"

"Answer: By dimming her luster below his," Gale said. "By seeking qualities of character rather than appearance, strength, and potency."

"As you did with Dad?"

"Agreement. He has everything, but it was his nature as a fourth that first appealed to me."

"Confession: I focus too much on everything."

She was learning. That helped. "Children can be distracted by attention, games, and music."

"Remembrance."

A harried-looking Earther woman appeared, with boy child in hand. "Is this where we'll be safe?"

"Confirmation," Gale said. "I am Gale, and this is my daughter Weft, both of Colony Charm. We will divert and protect you and your son."

"It's been horrible," the woman said. "We are farmers. The nearby volcano never caused much trouble before, but when it started erupting green, and everything turned green, and the plants got weird, and our machinery stopped working, we didn't know what to do."

"Explanation: The plants have become magical," Gale said. "We will show you how to use their magic to get better crops. In time you also will turn green and be able to perform magic."

"I don't want to turn green!" the women protested in horror.

"There is no shame in color, especially when it means you can do things like this," Gale said. She floated off the ground. "Magic can greatly enhance ordinary life."

"I wouldn't have believed it if I hadn't seen it," the woman said. "But I'll still look like nothing."

"Negation. With magic illusion you can look like me, if you choose."

"Like you!"

"Proof. Look in your mirror."

The woman fished out a small mirror. By the time she had it in place, Gale had clothed her in partial illusion, smoothing out her wrinkles and a wart, enhancing her proportions. Now she looked as she might have twenty years before, fair and shapely.

"Oh!"

"Mom, you're smashing!" the boy said.

"Illusion," Gale reminded her. "But in public, and for your husband, you can do it. Once you have magic. True, you will be green, but that should be bearable." she sent a mental call. *Naive—please show yourself here for a moment.*

The green girl appeared. She was not beautiful, but she was attractive in a slender way. "Do you feel bad about being green?" Gale asked her.

Naive laughed. "Joke?" She vanished.

"You will be able to do that too," Gale said, knowing she had made a convert.

"I believe I can live with green magic after all," the woman agreed.

Others were appearing, parents with children, or children alone. Gale faced them. "We have a serious problem with wild green magic," she said to the assembling group. "Once we have tamed it, it will serve you well. You can look like this, with illusion." She indicated the now-lovely woman. "May I?" she asked.

"Sure, show them," the women said.

Gale let her revert to her original appearance. Eyes opened; it was a significant difference. Then she restored the illusion, parking it for the time being.

"But now it is dangerous. We hope to have it under control soon. My daughter and I will entertain you while we wait for the others to deal with it." More women and children were gathering; there was now a fair group. Most were white, but a few were black and some shades between. That suggested a song. "If you will, we prefer to have a bit of drama with our song. Let us assume that you—" she glanced at a dawningly pretty white girl. "And you—" She indicated a young black man, barely beyond boyhood. "Are secretly in love. Stand on either side of us, where the others can see you."

Uncertainly, the girl and boy took their places.

Gale brought out her hammer dulcimer and donned her finger hammers. Weft did the same. They disposed themselves on a convenient stone. Both were appealingly garbed with knee-length skirts and bodices; Glamors could wear anything and make it work. "I Know Where I'm Going," she murmured to Weft. "You start."

Weft started, catching on. She played a preamble with marvelous preci-
sion, then sang soprano:

I know where I'm going
And I know who's going with me

Then Gale joined in with both dulcimer and voice.

I know who I love
But the dear knows who I'll marry.

There was no sound from the small audience. The people surely had not
before heard a folk song done with this expertise. Gale and Weft were two of the
best singers on Charm, and perhaps on Earth too.

I have stockings of silk
And shoes of fine green leather

Weft lifted a knee to admire the silk stocking and leather shoe which appeared on her leg and foot, in the process showing an amount of thigh that
made the few watching men take close note, including their actor man.

Combs to buckle my hair
And a ring for ever finger

Gale's hair formed combs, and she paused in her playing to show off her
suddenly ringed fingers.

Feather beds are soft
And painted rooms are bonny
But I would leave them all
For my handsome winsome Johnny

Now the players were catching on. The girl gazed adoringly across at the
man, who lifted his chin, posing.

Some say he's black
But I say he's bonny
Fairest of them all
Is my handsome winsome Johnny

Then they repeated the first verse. Thrilled by the notion, the girl walked
across and kissed the boy, then feigned a blush. The audience applauded.

After that it was easy. Different children delighted in posing for different
songs, and the parents appreciated the show. Audience participation always
enhanced a presentation. Between songs Gale clarified details of the nature of
Chroma zones and their advantages once their magic was mastered. These folk
would would no longer view either magic or the color green with horror. That
was a significant part of the program.

But the wild magic had another idea. Gale had noted and carefully not remarked on the encroaching plants, but now they were coming too close. They formed a ring around the people; there was no convenient escape for those who could not fly. "But this magic has not yet been tamed," Gale said. "The plants are wild, and extending their natures. They are growing too fast, and some I suspect are poisonous. Do not touch them. We must draw in closer."

The Earthers, who had been relaxing, became nervous. That wasn't good, but there was no help for it. They come close, but already plant tendrils were twining in to take the space. They were growing too rapidly, and seemed to be orienting on the human group. She did not look the look of this. *Green, she thought. What's with the plants?*

Problem, he responded. *They seem to have a malign direction. We are having trouble taming them.*

Bad indeed. So she thought to Havoc, the Glamor of Trees and Plants. *Havoc! I hate to interrupt your affair with the accommodating Mistress, but we have strange acting plants in the Green Chroma zone. They have 'a malign direction.' What is going on?*

His answer astonished her. *The Mistress tells me that she represents the Female Spirit, who displaced the malign Male Spirit several centuries ago. That Male Spirit is motivating the plants to attack. We do not yet have an effective way to deal with it, but it must not be allowed to prevail.*

Malign. That seemed to explain it. They were up against more than randomly wild plants. *Appreciation.*

They would have to tackle this in the manner of a conscious and powerful enemy. Without unduly alarming the people. Panic would not help anyone.

"Conjecture," she said. "We may need to fence the plants out, until control is established."

"Offer," Weft said. "I will locate posts."

"And wire," Gale said as the girl vanished.

The mothers were looking at the writhing tendrils nervously. "What about cutting them off?" one asked.

"Agreement!" *Shears, too,* she thought to Weft.

Weft returned with an armful of tools: clippers, hoes, machetes, and axes. She dumped them down and went back to fetch more.

"Reminder: don't let them touch you," Gale called. "Don't let sap get on your hands or face."

The women and children went to it with a will, attacking the vines that were growing rapidly inward. Ichor welled out and the severed parts twisted like snakes. Certainly these were not ordinary plants.

They organized into teams. Children handled hoes, chopping at the smaller tendrils. The larger boys wielded the machetes. The women used clippers. Gale saw the boy and girl of the first song working together, he cutting the big vines, she clipping the smaller ones that tried to trip him up. It had been a completely coincidental introduction, but she liked seeing different colors get together.

Meanwhile Weft was producing metallic poles. Gale knew that was literal: she was crafting them from dirt, an ability the younger Glamors had. This required a lot of magic energy, but the alternative was to let the plants overrun the camp.

They succeeded in widening their territory, but Gale suspected this was a temporary reprieve. The plants were still massing beyond, thickening, growing more tentacles. They seemed to be consolidating for a more determined effort. She did not like that at all.

They made the fence, pounding the poles into the ground in a full circle, then stringing cord that Weft produced around it in a rising spiral. They fashioned a palisade defining their fortress. The children enjoyed this; the adults were more restrained. They knew they were under siege.

Tendrils poked through the fence. The women tried to clip them, but they were appearing by hundreds, simultaneously. It was not possible to stop them all. The fence was becoming a writing green hedge.

"I think we need fire," Gale said. "But there's no time to make a flame thrower. We'll have to make do with buckets and dippers."

"Dangerous," Weft said.

"Agreement. We must proceed carefully."

"Too bad Flame isn't here, so she could handle it."

"Or Havoc, so he could handle the plants," Gale said with a passing smile.

Weft brought a bucket of flammable fluid and some small dippers. Gale explained their purpose to the people.

They dipped fluid, carried it to the rim, and spread it around the base of the fence. They made sure to allow none to spill inward. Then they struck fire, and let the flame spread in a circle around them. The vines sizzled and gave off noxious smoke. The vegetation retreated, hating the fire. Unfortunately the rope burned too, leaving only the poles. But as it had turned out, the rope had merely served as support for the vines. Had they won?

Hardly. Before they could relax, the plants generated a new throat: ugly green goo. It welled out from the scorched tips of the vines, forming bulging puddles. More of it issued, forcing the front edge of it onward toward the perimeter fence, and through it.

"Don't touch it," Gale warned unnecessarily. "We'll use the fire again."

They spread more dippers of fuel on the stuff, and ignited it. But this time it was not effective. The goo developed a skin as it sent up clouds of dirty steam. A stench rose from it, causing people to cough, their eyes watering. It did not actually burn; it merely festered. The fire was making it worse.

"Make a physical barrier," Gale said. "A dirt wall."

They got to work, using spades Weft brought to dig a circular trench, throwing up dirt on the inside, so that the goo would have to rise from the depth to the top.

It did. There was so much of it that it soon filled the trench, and it seemed to be moving on its own now, slug-like, climbing the wall.

They were facing an organized attack, and so far the other side was getting the better of the encounter. But Gale was hardly done. "Ice," she said. "We'll freeze it."

Weft fetched buckets of ice. That was effective; the goo stiffened in place, unable to function in the congealed state. But they were able to stop only a portion of the circle, because there was not enough ice. Weft was surely fetching it from Antarctica, and there was only so much she could do alone.

They had to deal with the organizing force behind this attack, before it discovered something more effective. The malign Male Spirit. But where was it to be found, and how could it be handled?

But she couldn't focus on that at the moment, because the goo would overwhelm them. She had to find a way to abolish it or at least to halt its progress.

She got an idea. *Weft—see if there's a goo eater.*

Weft got on it. In a moment she had it. *There is, mom. It's really a chemical process, Science magic, but it should work.*

Bring it on!

Weft appeared with a bucket of glop. She poured it carefully on the advancing goo opposite the ice.

There was an immediate reaction. The glop merged with the goo, converting it to more glop. The reaction slowly expanded around the circle. The goo had been halted, again.

A man appeared outside the circle. He had high boots that enabled him to walk through the goo without being dissolved by it, but he looked nervous. "You stopped it!" he cried. "What's your secret?"

"George!" a woman called, running toward him. "You survive!"

"Of course I survive!" George retorted.

"But you fell into the volcanic fissure!"

"It wasn't deep. You shouldn't have run away, you foolish woman."

"George! You never talked to me like that before."

"Well, it's about time, then."

The woman reached him and looked into his face. "You're not my husband!" she cried.

"Shut your trap!" George snapped, backhanding her across the face. She fell to the ground, shocked as much as hurt.

Gale was there, facing him. Now she was aware of his alien nature. "Who are you?"

"Who are *you*?" he blustered.

"I am Queen Gale of Planet Charm. If you are not this woman's husband, you must be some entity in possession of his body. Who?"

The man gazed at her, his lip curling with contempt. "Screw you, sister," he said. Then he turned to face the watching Earthers. "Who do you support?" he demanded. "Which Spirit?"

"You're the malign Male Spirit!" Gale said.

"Fall down and worship me, bitch," he said. "Then if you're lucky I'll screw you before I throw you away."

Well now. This was what they were fighting, making a direct appearance. "Hardly. I suggest you depart and leave these folk alone."

He considered her more carefully. "Say, you're a looker. You may be good for several screws before you give out."

"Negation."

He looked surprised. "You know what I am, and you're trying to talk back? You need a lesson in manners."

"Doubt."

His ready backhand fist swung at her face. And collided with her right wrist. It was a bruising contact, but she wasn't harmed. It was almost impossible for any force to harm a Glamor who retained possession of her magic.

Now she had his full attention. "You are not an ordinary dame."

"You noticed." She was goading him. She wanted to ascertain his full nature and powers. Was he really the equivalent of a Glamor? That would be interesting. She had never fought a Glamor before.

"Who are you really?" he demanded.

"Question: are you stupid? I identified myself."

He reached for her, but his hands shied away as she applied magical repulsion. "So you do have magic," he said. "That makes it more of a challenge."

"Advice: depart."

"No, I am intrigued by you. Shapely, with magic. It will be fun breaking you in."

"Possibility. If you don't get broken yourself."

That did it. Suddenly she was surrounded by a savage blast of magic, unlike anything she had encountered before. She might have resisted it, but chose to let it have its play, so she could better understand this baleful male spirit.

He conjured her to a green cave near the volcano; she could feel the intensity of the surrounding magic. She pretended to be lethargic to the point of unconsciousness. She had more than one reason: she preferred to have the man underestimate her, she was curious about his intentions, and she needed to divert him long enough to allow the other Glamors to secure and tame the Chroma zone. How long could she play him along?

She was on a simple bed. He must have made this for his own use, but she was sure he was not being kind to her. Indeed not; he quickly stripped away her clothing and his own. He had spoken of screwing; that was his crude way of indicating that he found her sexually appealing. No surprise there; it was an accurate description of her effect on men.

She could have resisted him by several means, such as conjuring herself away or making her body impenetrable. But that would have spoiled her dazed-woman act. So she let him proceed, offering only token resistance. "No," she protested faintly, as if just becoming aware of her exposure.

He was on her in a moment, penetrating roughly and fully and thrusting until he climaxed. So it was rape. It was obvious that he cared nothing for her preference, whatever it might be. His own immediate gratification was all that counted.

Sated, he withdrew, but did not dress. Instead he slapped her across the face several times. "Wake bitch! I'm not done with you."

She opened her eyes. "What happened?"

"You got screwed. What'd you expect?"

"I did not agree to this!"

"Now tell me who you really are? How do you have magic when you're not green?"

"How do you? You're not green either."

He struck her again. "It will be fun beating that attitude out of you. You didn't answer, so you get a penalty. Turn over."

"Negation."

He put his hands on her and turned her over. She resisted only ineffectively. What was he up to now?

In a moment she found out. He was jamming into her nether orifice. She tried to resist by clenching her sphincter, but he grabbed her hair and pulled her head back until it seemed her neck would break. As the pain made her lose focus, he completed his entry and climaxed again.

Then he withdrew and rolled her back over. "Who are you?" he demanded.

She could have resisted, as before, or done him some harm where it counted. But she was long familiar with all varieties of sex, and preferred to let him think he was humiliating her. She also wanted to save some of his substance, for later analysis. It was probably just that of the human host he had co-opted, but there might be something more. But she didn't want to take the act too far, so she reluctantly answered.

"I am—a Glamor."

"And what is a Glamor?"

"A magical creature with the ability to do magic anywhere, independent of Chroma zones."

"Chroma zones. Interesting term. That's what this greening area is?"

"Confirmation. It surrounds the volcano, sustained by it, conferring magic on all creatures and plants within its range. Green Chroma magic."

"That never existed on Earth before. How come it's happening now?"

"We seeded the volcanoes with Chroma, to make this planet more like our own."

"And the mistresses let you?"

"The mistresses didn't have a choice. We did it before they knew."

"And in the process gave me a base they don't control."

There was the key. What was there about wild Chroma zones that enabled this malign spirit to appear? "That's interesting. How did you manage it?"

And it seemed that he just had to brag. That was a male weakness. "For a thousand years I have been biding my time, waiting for the chance to boot the bitches out and recover my empire. But they were too canny to give me a chance. Meanwhile they have been spreading peace and goodwill all across the planet. It's disgusting."

"Why so?" Now she was being an apt audience, encouraging him to talk. Would he talk enough?

"What's the point? Mankind is made to compete, to fight, to win, whatever the cost. All this cooperation is vitiating the species."

"But doesn't constant fighting destroy valuable resources and lives? Doesn't it bring misery to many?"

His brows drew together. "What's your point?"

"Cooperation seems better for the welfare of the species. Isn't that what you want?"

"No."

"Question: Then what do you want?"

"Power. Sex. Security."

"That's all?" she asked with irony.

"There is something else?"

"What of accomplishment, happiness, love?"

He laughed. "You're a woman. You'd see it that way."

"The things you say you want would be empty if you're without love."

"Come off it, sister! There is greater passion in hate than in love."

"Doubt."

"Then it's time to make another demonstration. You don't like me, right?"

"Affirmation."

"So you don't want to have sex with me again."

"Correction: I did not have it with you before. It was all your own."

"So this time try to resist me. Put some passion into it."

"Amenable," she said grimly.

He grabbed hold of her. She resisted, twisting her wrists from his grasp.

He tried again. This time she moved faster and grabbed his wrists. He twisted, but she held on. She was as strong as he, for the moment.

"Interesting," he remarked, amused. "So I could not have raped you before, had you opposed it."

"Confirmation. I was curious as to your intent."

He struck her with another blast of magic. She caught it and bounced it back at him.

"Fascinating," he said. "You do have equivalent magic. Yet you are not a mistress."

"Explanation: I am a woman, but my constituency is not the Female Spirit," she said.

"So our powers of magic cancel each other out. But because you are a woman, you lack my physical resources." He hurled her back by her grip on his own wrists, then wrenched himself free. "Muscle is power, and I have more. You can resist me only momentarily. Muscles count."

"In your head, too," she muttered.

He pressed her down on the bed, face up, using his naked torso to hold her in place. "Let's see your pooper," he said, poking a finger at her anus. "I'm going to put my fist up your intestine and rip your uterus out through your asshole." He started jamming his stiffened fingers in.

Because of the position, his own rear was within range. She poked her own fingers at his rectum. "And while you are doing that, I will be drawing out your prostate through yours." She penetrated him.

This evidently caught him by surprise. "Bitch!"

"You don't like it?" she inquired sweetly. "How unfortunate." She forced her fingers further in. "It seems like a fair exchange."

He scrambled off her, breaking the connection. But that also broke his own access to her posterior, and got his weight off her. Now, separated, they were at impasse.

He hurled himself on her again, catching her in a bear hug. She wrapped her legs around his waist, linked her feet together, and applied pressure of her own. His arms were stronger than hers, but not his legs. He had to let go again.

"Bitch!" he gasped, and swing his fist at her head.

She caught his fist in her two hands, brought it to a stop, and dug her fingernails into the back of his hand.

He tried to knee her in the gut. She caught his knee, lifted it, and pushed him over backward.

He thrust both hands at her neck and started to throttle her. She caught one finger of each hand and bent them backward until he had to let go.

He dived for her, caught her around the waist, and threw her back on the bed. He rolled his hip over her face to hold her down while he lifted one fist to punch her in her exposed belly. And cried out as she bit his hip, hard. "Bitch!"

"Observation: you have a limited vocabulary."

He withdrew, breathing hard. "You're a weird one."

"Question: do you have a problem with a woman who fights back effectively? Whom you can't beat up?"

"Where did you learn those moves?" he demanded.

"My daughter is an Amazon. I picked up some bits from her training." Gale smiled. "She would not be as gentle with you as I am. She objects to bullies."

"I am the Male Spirit! A virtual god!"

"You are a Glamor, as I am. Glamors can oppose each other, but not hurt each other. Suggestion: stop being foolish and talk seriously. Perhaps we can both learn something."

"Why the hell should I talk seriously with a mere woman?"

"Conjecture: because you have no alternative."

"The hell I don't! I don't have to stay near you."

"Statement: the moment you leave me, you have lost the encounter. You will have been bested by a woman."

He grabbed a nearby stone and threw it at her. It swerved to avoid her, looped around behind her, and fired back at his face. He had to duck to avoid it. "Fuck!"

"Observation: a new word. Perhaps there is hope for your lexicon."

He seethed for a moment, then got canny. "Give me a real fuck and I'll talk to you."

"Question: you are petitioning me to pretend to enjoy your sexual advances?"

"You're the hottest damn bitch I've met in a thousand years. I want to get into you for real."

"You have been out of circulation for a thousand years. Much has happened in the interim."

"So it's not the compliment of the millennium. At least I'm asking."

Gale nodded. "A woman does like to be asked rather than forced. What information do you offer to justify such a pretense on my part?"

"Anything you want. I'll talk as long as I'm in you. Fair enough?"

"Negation. Judging by your prior performances, you will be, as you put it, in me less than a minute."

"Damn it, woman, what the hell else do you want?"

"Answer: I want significant information. That will take time."

"All right, bitch. I'll talk for half an hour, in or out. Satisfied?"

"Sufficient." She paused to organize herself. She had already learned a great deal, such as the fact that he was a Glamor without experience dealing with other Glamors. For all his sexual urgency, he was naïve about women, never having encountered one who could compel his respect. Now, for the price of faking an interest, she might learn the rest of what she needed.

"Get it on, bitch."

She smiled and got into the act. She had picked up things when helping Voila perfect her acting abilities. This man knew she was acting, but wanted the semblance; that made it easy. "Always a pleasure to deal with a real man. Come here, hero." She opened her arms.

He came to her, halfway hesitantly, as if expecting another effective rebuff. But she was honoring their agreement, making a realistic pretense of interest. She embraced him, kissed him, and drew him down on the bed with her.

He was in her in a moment, pumping and jetting. "Advice," she murmured in his ear. "A Glamor can orgasm almost continuously, if he makes the effort."

"Damn!" he said, this time in wonder. Evidently he had always focused so rapidly on women that he hadn't discovered all of his own potentials. Or, more likely, he had been so long out of touch he had forgotten.

"Try."

He worked at it, and in a few minutes came again. Then a third time, sooner, as he found the key. "Damn!" he was thrilled. He did it several more times before collapsing in blissful sexual exhaustion. He had extended his power, but not yet discovered how to make it continue indefinitely.

"Point," she said. "Cooperation can be more fun than conflict." Of course she had not climaxed, and she had no intention of doing so. She would fake it, if need be, but never actually do it with a contemptible man like this.

"Right," he said, mellowed by the effort. "This was better than raping. There's a surprise!"

"It is not yet done." She kissed him. "Tell me of you. How did you come by your status?"

"I have been at war with the Female Spirit as long as I can remember. A million years, at least. I get a turn, I fuck up, she gets a turn, she gets careless I get back in. Too bad I can never fuck *her*."

His crude expressions were natural to him. She knew better than to challenge them. "Why not?"

"Because it's impossible. Either I'm in power or she is; we can't be in power together. So we can never meet. Otherwise you bet I'd look her up, the Mistress of Mistresses, and fuck her brains out."

"Question: Could you approach one of the lesser mistresses?"

"Same problem: if she's out, so are they. None of them exist while I'm in power. I'm still trying to figure how you can be here with me."

"I am a foreign Glamor, from Colony Planet Charm. My constituency is moss and lichen, not the Female Spirit. So there is not competition for your base, and we can share residence."

"Damn! I've been stuck with garden-variety females. If I had you with me all the time, I'd fuck you every hour during the day and night. Because not only are you one lovely bitch, you have the staying power to accommodate me."

"True. Glamors have superior sexual qualities, as I am demonstrating." She turned over, mounting him, and took him into her, forcing his renewed ardor. She massaged his member internally, eliciting another climax.

"Damn! You're something else," he gasped. "I know you're just trying to pump me for information so you can fight me, but you're so good at it I have to go along. Damn!" For she had summoned another orgasm.

"By what specific mechanism do you and the Female Spirit replace each other?"

"I like to fight. I encourage bigger fights. In nations these become wars, with horrendous bloodletting. Marvelous! But sometimes they get too big, and there's a crash. Last time the global population of ten billion people crashed to one billion, what with nuclear war and the destruction of the food chain. The survivors were too busy trying to survive to worry about more fighting; all they wanted was peace. Oh, they always preach peace, but never really want it. Until this time. That froze me out, and the Female Spirit capitalized on her chance and took over. Ever since she's been making peace in the world, knowing that otherwise there'll be war and I'll be back in the saddle. Damn!" It was another ejaculation, as she kept him occupied and distracted so he would keep talking.

"So it's not merely her peaceful nature," Gale said. "There is method in her program."

"You bet! That scheming bitch knows exactly what she's doing."

"I'm sure she does."

He paused. "You're a woman. How come you're saying that? What's your angle?"

"My husband is having an intense affair with her."

"Ho ho ho!" he bellowed. "So you're doing it too!"

"Negation. I want him to have access to her, so he can learn what we need. Just as I am learning from you."

"Which the hell side our you on? Damn!" It was another emission coaxed from him.

"We govern Planet Charm. We wish to remain independent. Earth wishes to incorporate us. So we are fighting back. That is why we seeded Earth's volcanoes, and now are interacting with the new Chroma zones."

"And he's fucking the Mistress! Damn! I wish I was the one doing it."

"I am not adequate?"

"You're the finest fuck I've had in millennia. But she's my other half. I wish I could take over control, but have her captive. I'd chain her to the wall and fuck her blind. Make her scream for mercy."

"Doubt. I understand she has considerable sexual appetite, and consummate skill. Torture might do it, but not sexual indulgence."

"I know," he said surprisingly. "It's a fantasy. But what fun it would be trying."

"How do you propose to take control this time?"

He gazed at her cannily. "You think I won't answer. But I will, because it won't make any difference. Your so-called Chroma zones are disrupting the Mistress' order. Her center cannot hold. When order collapses across the globe, the power will be mine to take."

"Conclusion: So our effort to secure our independence may enable you to recover your power," Gale said, drawing on his member again. "Question: What would be your plans for us of Colony Planet Charm, if you should prevail?"

"Oh, I'll take you over, of course. Your planet must have great resources to exploit."

"Objection: No gratitude for the way our effort enables you to prevail?"

"None, bitch," he agreed. "You didn't do it for me."

"Correct. So we know where we stand."

"Not necessarily. There remains the matter of our relationship after I resume rightful power on Earth."

"Promise: Charm will fight you, of course."

"But I will have what the Mistress lacks: magical zones to match yours, as well as the larger power of Earth Science. That will be a critical advantage."

"Objection: We are changing Earth."

"I love those statement precursors you use! But be realistic: the magical fundament of your colony planet, as I understand it, is nonChroma. Whatever isn't Chroma, is nonChroma. Correct?"

"Correct," she said guardedly. Where was this leading?

"The magical fundament of Earth is Science. Whatever isn't Chroma, is Science. So there is inherently far greater power of Science here than there is on your planet. You can't change Earth to a nonChroma basis. All you can do is disrupt the present social order, as you are doing. This will inevitably give me power. Then I will use that power to bring your planet down."

Gale shuddered internally. This Male Spirit was a worse threat than the Female Spirit was, and it did seem they were playing into his hands. "Question: What relationship do you seek, assuming you achieve power?"

"First, I want you. Specifically, your body, servicing mine as it is now. I want you to be #1 in my harem."

"Unlikely. When we finish this dialogue, I expect never to touch you again. You are not my type."

"Ah, but you are *my* type: a beautiful, sexually accomplished, truly durable, unwilling woman. I want complete access to you."

"Negation."

"Suppose I arrange to torture thousands of innocent Earth folk as punishment for your intransigence?"

"If I were to yield to such a threat, there would be no end to similar threats."

"True. You would be completely mine, and deliciously hating it."

"Conclusion: I will not yield."

He grinned, enjoying this. "Let's try the next step: suppose I make a similar offer to one of your daughters? Such as that Flame I encountered in the Black Chroma zone. A militant female."

"She would cut off your penis and feed it to you."

"Knowing that the futile effort would bring torture to all those innocents? Would she really?"

That was problematical. Flame might well accede, rather than be the seeming cause of unnecessary suffering. She was an Amazon, trained and tough, but a sweet girl at heart. "Annoyance."

"To be sure, bitch. And what of that blonde you have helping you in this zone? Would she go along? Or that younger one I understand you have, the actress. I could use a really good actress to improve my fucking."

Gale controlled her burgeoning rage. This bastard was getting to her! "Ire. If you approach my daughters, I will be there with them, seeking to rip out your prostate as before."

"So we rouse the mother in you," he said with satisfaction as he achieved another climax, this one on his own initiative. He clearly liked having her angry as he used her body. "That is the liability of the Female Spirit: she cares about her children."

"And the Male Spirit does not? That is not true on our planet."

"Nor on Earth, at the moment, because the Female Spirit governs. But there will be another agenda when I return to righteous power."

"Conclusion: you have certainly made your case. We will do everything in our power to prevent your accession."

"Naturally, bitch. How I love a good fight! But your decision is too late. I am well on the way to conquering."

"Doubt. As we speak, my companions are taming this Chroma zone. Soon you will have no further wildness to draw on."

"True," he agreed without fear or annoyance. "You have succeeded in distracting me long enough. I knew your purpose, but you're such a good fuck it's been worth it. I feel the weakening of my presence here already."

"Challenge: So what makes you think you will prevail?"

"Two things, fuckstress. First, this is only one Chroma zone, as was the black zone. There are forty six more, too many for you to take simultaneously, but not too many for I and my minions to invest. The balance will tip before you have done half of them. Second, you accomplish your magic by means of Chroma stones. These are being expended at a horrendous rate, and will soon be exhausted. Then you will be without your special magic powers. You will not be able to oppose me any longer."

The monster was surely correct. "Expletive!"

"Remember, bitch: when I have recovered my dominion, I will offer you the chance to ameliorate the mischief I do to innocents. You will be best advised to take it. You surely know I am not bluffing."

Indeed she knew he was not. He had little or no conscience. "When," she agreed through her teeth.

He kissed her, savoring it. "I am done here."

Something changed; she felt it from his face to his penis. The Glamor had faded, leaving the mortal man he had invested, still in the tight sexual embrace.

"Oh, God!" the man, George, gasped. "It was horrible!"

She knew what he meant. He was referring to his possession by the malign Male Spirit, not to his embrace of her. "Agreement." She stroked his head reassuringly, giving him time to realize the rest of his situation so he could withdraw with some token dignity. George was guiltless, and his wife would be glad to have him back.

In due course they approached the site where the others remained. "Suggestion," she murmured to George. "Keep private what our bodies have been doing. They do not need to know."

"Oh, yes!" he agreed. "I—I'm so sorry—"

She kissed him. "Needless. I indulged him so as to learn his nature."

"I never—he was so potent—"

"Magic. Ordinary men can't match it."

"His mind—I got pieces of it. So much power, but so ugly. I hated being used like that, but I couldn't stop it."

"He possessed you. He is a malign spirit. You need have no guilt."

"Yet I feel it. That's not the way regular men are. We don't want to brutalize women."

"Understanding. He is the extreme essence, warped by a thousand years of deprivation, not the typical male."

They came in sight of the camp. The attack of the plants had evidently ceased at the time Gale had left with the male spirit. Could the whole thing have been a dodge to bring her intercession? The Male Spirit had wanted to study her as much as she wanted to study him. Both of them had achieved that objective.

But if what he said was correct about using the Chroma zones to tip the balance of power in his favor and overthrow the Female Spirit's dominance, they were in serious trouble.

"George!" The woman was running toward them. She recognized his resumption of identity even from afar.

"Martha!" he responded. They come together and hugged.

Weft appeared. "Success. You did it, mom; you kept him out of it long enough for us to take the zone. I knew you could do it."

Such confidence! "Regret: that won't be enough." Not nearly enough.

Chapter 16
Ennui

Ennui looked up from her desk, startled by the sudden appearance of the giant Silver seven-legged spider. "Oh, greeting, Silver," she said. "What can I do for you?"

Come. It was the imperative rather than the word; the Silver Glamor of Spiders was not much for human dialogue.

She was taken aback. "Question: can it wait? I am in the process of running the planet at the moment, in Havoc's absence." Actually she had been effectively running it for more than fifteen years, as Havoc had never had much interest in the details of governance. He trusted her to handle the routine elements and to notify him when there was something special.

Negation. Again the meaning, rather than the word.

She did not question the authority of the Glamor. None of the Glamors were given to idle interactions with mortal humans. There surely was sufficient reason.

"Condition: I must at least notify my husband, and the Lady Aspect, and the mocks, if this is to be more than brief."

The arachnid head nodded, once.

She got on it. *Throe,* she thought as she hurried to the adjacent office. *I must go with the Silver Glamor.*

Understood, Throe's answering thought came. *Don't do anything to make me jealous.*

She laughed. She was fifty eight years old, and looked it, sexually uninteresting even to human males. Except for Throe, who loved her.

She was at the Lady Aspect's office. "Situation: The Silver Glamor requires me to go with him," she said. "Request: cover for me, and notify the mocks. I don't know how long it will be."

"Covered," Aspect agreed. "Something must have come up. I hope it's routine."

"Preference: I hope it is marvelous adventure."

"Compromise: moderate adventure?"

"Agreement." Ennui returned to her office. "Ready." she was not concerned about details of clothing, hygiene, or convenience; the Glamor would not take her into mischief for which she was unprepared.

The silver spider lifted two forelegs. Ennui stepped into that embrace. It spun a quick loose cocoon around her, securing her for travel.

Then they were in a pleasant green forest. The Glamor removed the threads, and vanished.

"Idyll," Ennui said. "Am I with you?"

A human figure formed before her. "Affirmation. We have a mission for you."

"Acquiescence." She knew this could not be ordinary. "I'll be happy to tackle it. You didn't need to bring me to your bower on Counter-Charm."

"Negation. The mission is dangerous and perhaps complicated."

Ennui felt a thrill of excitement. "Conjecture: it's for Havoc, isn't it? I'll do it."

"Clarification: the lesser portion is for Havoc. The greater portion is for Voila."

"I always liked that child. No problem there."

"To transport her ikon."

"Negation! I don't want to carry another ikon. I carried Havoc's gladly, but it was hell to get rid of it and become myself again. Anyway, Symbol carries it now, and she won't be able to give it up."

"She will do so," Idyll said with certainty.

Ennui took stock. "Glamor, have you reckoned with the inadequacies of mortal folk? We lack your abilities. What might be easy for you—well, no, you can't touch an ikon. Still—"

"We are unable to touch ikons," the Ifrit Glamor agreed. "That is why we need you as a mortal, Havoc's most trusted friend. You must do what we can not. Symbol can yield the ikon if she decides to. You must persuade her."

Ennui decided to let that rest for the moment. "What is the lesser portion of my mission?"

The figure smiled. "That is only the lesser portion of the greater portion. The lesser mission is to persuade Symbol to yield her title as King's Mistress to another woman."

"She is ready to do that. She is retired, at least while she carries Havoc's baby." Ennui felt a passing qualm, quickly suppressed: a part of her envied Symbol that pregnancy."

"An Earth woman."

Ennui stared at her. "Oh, my," she breathed.

"Rationale: this is in significant portion a political thing. To govern Earth effectively Havoc must have the willing cooperation of this woman."

"Symbol would understand about that. But does he love her, and she him?"

"Affirmation, both."

"And does he trust her?"

"They have made an oath of friendship."

That stunned her. "But I—" she could not continue.

"You were his third such oath, following Gale and the Blue Dragon," Idyll said. "Mistress Monochrome is the fourth."

Things really were changing! Havoc had made another oath. This had abruptly become more personal. Ennui beyond all others understood and feared its impact. Yet she hesitated. "Was it voluntary?" For it had been involuntary with her, yet had transformed both their lives.

"Negation. Voila required it."

"Expletive! The little bitch!" Yet she knew the girl would not have demanded it, and Havoc would not have acceded, without excellent reason.

Idyll laughed. "Voila loves you too."

"Tell me the greater portion of the greater mission."

"You must go to Earth's region with the ikon, and place it in a suitable nonChroma zone."

"I can do that, if someone transports me."

"Silver will transport you. The challenge will be to find a suitable zone, as there may be none on Earth."

"Confusion."

"Earth's default is Science magic, so between volcanoes is their version of White Chroma. The king's children are converting volcanoes, but lack purchase for nonChroma. When their supply of Chroma stones is exhausted, they will have to retire. We have tracked the near future, and established that there are one or more nonChroma defaults among the other planets and moons of that system. The problem is to locate them, and place the ikon."

"Ifrit, I'm no specialist, but even I know there are problems with that. A Glamor has to be reasonably close to her planet, as is the case with Charm and Counter-Charm, if the ikon is to be effective. Are there close planets?"

"Negation. Only Earth's lone moon is as close to Earth as our two worlds are to each other, and that moon is also Science default. The others are much more distant. They appear no larger than stars as seen from Earth, and some are too faint to be seen at all without special Science equipment. Most are barren rocks or gas balls; none have life."

"Then this is a futile exercise."

"Negation. Voila is the strongest of all Glamors, because she started youngest. She is capable of feats beyond any of the rest of us. She can draw power from a distant ikon. That is, as Havoc puts it, our ace in the hole."

"Havoc would," Ennui agreed. "But I am no space traveler. I'm pushing sixty, and even in my so-called prime I lacked the requisite qualities. I don't know the first thing about searching in space, and lack the nerve to do it anyway."

"Silver will assist you. You must carry the ikon."

"That's another thing. If we take Voila's ikon away from Charm, how will she function when she returns home? She needs that ikon here."

"It is a calculated risk. Her duplicate ikon must remain on Earth."

"But you said it is ineffective there. No nonChroma zones."

"It is the course she fathoms, and I believe she is correct. This is a difficult challenge, because the opposition is the Male Glamor of Earth. When he takes power, no one else will be able to oppose him effectively."

"And she can see the near future better than any other," Ennui agreed. "Joining with you and Mino, she can see the intermediate future too. We have no choice but to respect her judgment."

"And it is a judgment call, not a certainty," Idyll said. "We can not be sure of victory, only of obtaining it if we follow the correct course."

"And you don't know exactly what that course is," Ennui said. The ifrit did not disagree.

They talked longer, but Ennui already knew she had to do it. At least it would roust her out of her chronic boredom. For that had been the curse of her life: lack of interest. Even with the inherent excitement of being around Havoc, it tended to seep back in, making her wish for something else. Well, this was that something else.

The Silver Glamor whisked her back to Charm and to the Air Chroma residence of Symbol, then faded out. This was a nice cottage set in a lovely garden surrounded by a neat white picket fence. All illusion, of course; the reality was surely quite dull. Just to be sure, she touched a slat of the fence: sure enough, there was nothing there.

She walked up the pleasant stone path to the inset wood door. She lifted her knuckle and knocked. There really was wood there, buttressing the illusion. The real wood was probably not as pretty, but it served.

The door opened. "Surprise!" Symbol said. She was proudly showing her pregnancy: five months. "You didn't have to come here to the zone, Ennui. I would have come if you had summoned me."

"Privacy," Ennui said.

Symbol turned her head back into the house. "Garden, dear: I have a private visitor, female."

"I will see to my next client," a man's voice replied. "Return in two hours."

"Appreciation, dear." She returned to Ennui. "Come in. Garden is departing the back way, not even seeking your identity. He trusts me."

Ennui entered the house. Plants were everywhere, with multi-colored flowers, making for a bower-effect. "The name: he gardens?"

"Affirmation. He is the zone's top illusion gardener, and nice catch, considering my age and condition."

"The King's luscious mistress, carrying the king's baby as her fourth?" Ennui asked. "You are the bargain, Symbol."

"But I am forty six and well used."

"And still luscious."

"He has not touched me yet. But when I have birthed, and recovered my shape, I will make him glad to have waited. And of course the next three will be his."

"A fortunate man." Indeed, almost any man on the planet would have been eager to possess the King's Mistress and to have his children by her.

Symbol brought refreshments. "Question."

Ennui paused, marshaling her arguments. "Reluctance. I have two difficult requests to make of you."

Symbol paled. It was a mask of illusion, as neither she nor anything here in the Air Chroma zone could be seen without its clothing of illusion, but it showed her concern. "The ikon! I have to give it up."

"Affirmation. I know how hard that is, because I once carried Havoc's ikon. But it seems that Voila needs it near Earth, to give her power there. I am assigned to place it appropriately."

"Concern: if you take it, how can you give it up?"

"I must complete my mission before becoming addicted to the ikon. I do not want to keep it; I had enough with Havoc's ikon."

Symbol smiled. "Remembrance. What is the other request?"

"That you yield the position of King's Mistress to another woman."

Again Symbol paled. "Not to return to Havoc when I am fit? My marriage will not interfere with that. It is understood as a prior commitment."

This was the part Ennui hated. "He has found a new mistress."

"How could he? He's on Earth!"

"An Earth woman."

"Disbelief."

"It is a political liaison. Voila required them to make on Oath of Friendship."

"That scheming little bitch!"

"Exactly my sentiment," Ennui said with a grim smile. "She is called the Mistress of Mistresses, the effective governor of Earth, and a Glamor, said to be phenomenally lovely and skilled. We need her participation to govern Earth when we conquer it. She needs ours to retain her position. So they made the Oath, then became lovers, and now have fallen in love. It seems to be the course Voila foresaw, and is necessary to avoid disastrous defeat."

"Defeat! How can the Glamors, working in concert with that Mino machine, be defeated?"

"By a hostile planetary Glamor on his home territory. When there are few if any nonChroma zones for ikon power. Voila sees."

Symbol sighed. "I know she does. We have to conform. Pain."

"Pain," Ennui agreed.

"This Mistress: what else is known of her? Is she a sexy young slut?"

"It seems she's a lovely person, fifty years old—"

"Fifty! Four years older than I am!" That seemed to annoy her more than a teen mistress would have.

"A patron of the arts," Ennui continued. "Gentle, nice, smart—"

"And a Glamor. I have become a has-been."

"You have had seventeen years of Havoc, following your time with King Deal. It is an impressive record."

"Confession: I still hoped foolishly it would never end. The ikon keeps me young and sexy." She sighed again. "And I must give it up also, and become my awful real age."

"*Can* you give it up? I was unable to relinquish mine, until caught in a Chroma zone with Havoc so that it was completely depleted."

"It is Voila's ikon. It surely answers to its mistress. If she requires that it be freed, then it must be possible." she reached into her full bosom and brought out the nondescript blob that was the Ikon of Amoeba. She proffered it to Ennui.

Ennui reached for it, expecting to be repulsed. But her hand closed over it without resistance. She lifted the chain from Symbol's neck and took possession. So it was true: the ikon responded to its Glamor's will. "Regret."

"Redoubled. Both my prizes gone in one session. I think the mistress hurts worse."

"Symbol, Havoc still loves you. He doesn't have a choice. This is a war of worlds."

"Understanding. I am being foolish. Of course it is necessary and I do not really begrudge it. Now you must be on your way, I know."

"Affirmation." But Ennui lingered, uncertain why. There was something unfinished.

"Go," Symbol said.

Then she got it. The woman had suffered a devastating double blow to her life and prospects. She was too proud to let another person see her cry.

But Ennui wasn't. "Symbol, I'm so sorry," she said, and let herself dissolve into tears.

The woman stared at her a moment, then caught on in turn. She came to

Ennui and put her arms around her. Then they both were holding each other and crying. Theoretically Symbol was comforting Ennui; in reality it was the other way around. In this manner Symbol could let go without damaging her pride more than minimally. She was not a giving woman, or an internally emotional one, but they had been friends for a long time and understood each other well.

After a time they separated. "Appreciation," Ennui said, wiping her face.

"Echo," Symbol said faintly.

Then Ennui exited the house. The Silver Glamor was there. She stepped into his arachnid embrace, holding the ikon well out from her body so that he would not have to get close to it. Glamors could not touch ikons, but they could carry folk who carried ikons, somewhat in the manner a person could not touch a hot stove, but could put on gloves that could do so. Thus she was in effect a protective glove.

But she had another concern. "May I?" she inquired, opening her mind to him.

Abruptly they were in her suite at the palace. Throe was there, having received a signal. The spider faded.

She stepped into her husband's embrace. "Understanding why Gale likes spiders," she said between kisses.

"Agreement."

They proceeded to an act of love making that a stranger might have thought unbecoming to a couple one side or the other of sixty. Their relationship had become routine in the past fifteen years, but their love for each other had not abated. They had found each other belatedly, after each had completed the requisite marriage and four children, and they had both been experienced enough to recognize their true needs. Would it have worked so well had they married when young? Probably not; they had required the solid experience elsewhere to appreciate a relationship grounded on something other than sex or position. Yet the sex was great too.

"Question," he said as they lay in the aftermath.

"Private from others," she said, knowing he would keep the secret. "I am taking Voila's ikon to Earth, to give her a better source of power. The outcome of this contest with Earth is uncertain, so this is necessary."

"Symbol?"

"Is devastated, understandably. Maybe when this is done, she can have it back. Havoc also has found another mistress and oath friend, an earth woman."

"Amazement!"

"I'm sure she's a good woman. She's a Glamor."

"Amazement," he repeated.

"Echo. We are in a changing situation."

They kissed again. Then she cleaned up, girded herself with informal working clothes and lifted her arms. The Silver Glamor appeared, taking her in.

The forest of the retreat on Counter Charm formed around them. "Confusion," Ennui said. "I have already been here."

The Idyll figure appeared. "There is one more aspect. I spared you this before so that you could handle personal details in privacy."

"Question."

"Voila can see the near future. Mino can read the far future. With their assistance, I can fathom some of the intermediate future. This is the necessary venue. I must be with you."

This was a surprise. "Problem: I carry Voila's ikon."

Idyll nodded. "I can not join you fully physically, but I can infuse you to an extent, sharing your body and mind, with your acceptance."

"A ghostly presence?"

"Agreement. An imprint. Do you accede?"

This was intriguing. "Acceptance."

The figure dissolved in the manner of the ifrit kind. A cloud formed. It floated to Ennui, surrounded her, and closed in on her flesh. She felt the ifrit infusing her. It was not at all unpleasant; rather, it was invigorating. "Amazement," she murmured.

I am here. It was Idyll's thought.

"Welcome."

You are a good person. I am in a position to know.

Ennui had to laugh. "You are pleasant company."

It is only a limited portion of me, and when you travel to Earth the major part of my ability will be cut off. I will retain mainly my ability to read the intermediate future.

"Sufficient." Ennui knew what a tremendous advantage it was to be able to see the future, especially if the Earthers could not. Aware that it was time, she lifted her arms again, and the Silver Glamor appeared.

They were in Mino, the ship from the advanced machine culture. That meant that they were in the vicinity of Earth. It seemed instantaneous, but she suspected it wasn't; she had merely been unaware of the travel time.

Negation. It is effectively instant, on the order of an hour between the systems. This is something the Science folk are not in a position to comprehend. Science is limited to the speed of light.

"Even Mino?"

A panel lighted. AGREEMENT. I FOLLOWED THE EARTHER SHIP HERE. IT WILL TAKE ME TWO MONTHS TO RETURN.

"So magic can accomplish what a type two culture can't?"

AFFIRMATION. I AM BOUND BY SCIENCE.

Two yellow figures appeared, the female carrying the unconscious male. "Surprise, Silver," the lovely yellow woman said. "Question?"

"He brought me," Ennui said quickly, knowing that the arachnid wasn't much for conversation. "Special mission."

"Understanding. I brought this man for healing." She set the man carefully down on a bunk that abruptly projected from the wall.

"I don't have magic," Ennui reminded her.

"I do. I will start him." Her clothes dissolved, leaving her gloriously nude. She got down on the man, opened his clothing, touched his penis to make it stiffen, and took him into a sexual embrace. She kissed him, and he woke. In a moment he was panting as he climaxed. Then she lifted off him, reformed her clothes, and glanced at Ennui. "Required: several hours of rest while the legs heal. Keep him off his feet." She vanished.

Sexual healing, Idyll explained. *She put a regenerative charge into his center. It will slowly spread and repair him.*

Ah. The Glamors used sex to get really close to people's cores, where the most potent magic could spread out. Sex was not necessarily for its own pleasure, though folk were encouraged to think it was. It was a convenient avenue.

Ennui went to the man, who was looking understandably dazed. "Greeting. I am Ennui, secretary to King Havoc."

"Greeting," he replied. "I am Dreamer. I admit I never dreamed of a mission like this, before being recruited. Question: did I just do what I think I did, or was it a hallucination?"

"No dream," Ennui reassured him. "You are it seems injured in the legs, and need a safe place to rest while you heal. The Yellow Glamor brought you here and started the healing process in her fashion."

"Amazement," he agreed. "What a woman!"

"Glamors are. You are supposed to rest for several hours, and stay off your feet. You are in Mino, a Science ship allied with us. You are safe here."

"Relief. Those wild demons—" He shrugged. "Am I in the way?"

"Negation. There is room enough for both of us, and I don't mind the company."

"Question: you are not part of our pacification mission. Why are you here, and how did you come?"

"Answer: Agreement; I did not train with you. The Silver Glamor brought me here for a special mission." She realized that the huge spider had faded out. Was she authorized to speak of her mission?

Limited, Idyll replied. *Do not mention the ikon, or me.*

Agreement. Normal folk did not know of the existence of ikons, let alone their qualities. They might know of the Glamor Ifrit, but would never suspect she was sharing a human host.

"Question."

"I have to locate a suitable place to put something. It needs to be a nonChroma zone."

"Mischief," Dreamer said. "Earth lacks nonChroma zones. In fact it lacked all Chroma zones, before the Glamors seeded the volcanoes. Now we're taming the wild magic of the new zones. It can be dangerous; that's how I hurt my legs. But there are no nonChroma volcanoes, and Earth's default is Science Chroma. I don't know how they expect you to find a nonChroma zone on Earth."

"It seems they believe that one of the other planets or moons of this system is nonChroma. I merely have to locate it."

"How can you get there?" He reconsidered. "I forgot: Mino can do it. Which planet?"

"Ignorance."

He gazed at her. "Suspicion: are you sure this is a real mission? That they didn't just want you safely away from Charm?"

Untrue! Idyll thought.

Ennui was sure of it. "It is legitimate. It would not be worth the effort of getting me out of the way. I merely am poorly prepared, having been enlisted on short notice. Request: tell me about the planets of this system."

"Pleasure. It was part of our training. There are eight planets, together with perhaps a hundred moons, and thousands of loose rocky fragments. It's a messy system, maybe because it has no Void to swallow up debris."

"Void will one day swallow Vivid and our worlds," Ennui said grimly.

"In a few million years. Meanwhile we have better worlds that this 'Solar system' does. The closest the Earthers call Mercury, very hot and a Science planet. The next is Venus, also Science. Then Earth, and Mars, both Science. In fact I think all the planets have been verified as Science. It is one reason the

Earthers don't believe in magic; they've never encountered it, until very recently."

"That leaves the moons and fragments. Are they Science too?"

"All that have been checked are, and no reason to doubt the rest. Somehow Science got locked in here."

"I have to doubt the rest," Ennui said firmly. "I need nonChroma."

"Idea," Dreamer said. "Earth does not much resemble Charm or Counter Charm. Too much water, not enough volcanoes. But could volcanoes be the key? Find a planet or moon with volcanoes?"

"Endorsement! Charm has volcanoes all over, and between them lie nonChroma regions. A world with that pattern well might default to nonChroma. For one thing, the Chroma volcanoes may separate the magic so that nothing is left for the default, and that's nonChroma."

"Then we have prospects," the yellow man said, pleased. Ennui realized that her search was diverting him from any pain he might be feeling in his legs. That was an incidental benefit. "We can eliminate any that aren't volcanically active. Actually there's a giant volcano on Mars, the fourth world out, but that's already been established as Science. No known volcanoes on the four gas giants. That leaves—" "His face lighted, almost glowing. "Io! A moon of Jupiter. It's all volcanoes! And uninhabitable, so no one has gone there to settle. It could have nonChroma."

"That must be the one," she agreed. Then she had another thought. "My mission is private. We don't want the Earthers to know. But they could be watching Mino. If we just go there, they'll follow and know."

"Agreement. Earth has many ships of space, and they are patrolling everywhere. They don't trust us, ever since Glamor Warp messed them up."

"Intrigue. What did Warp do?"

"We learned well after the fact. He told them a story that diverted them for an hour."

"He was always good at that."

"While the Air Chroma Sorceress Ine locked their fleet into unbreakable orbit. By the time they broke that hold, the Chroma zones were taking hold and they couldn't stop it. Otherwise they might have bombed the volcanoes and wiped out the Chroma before it got established. The Earthers were not pleased."

"Enthusiasm," Ennui agreed. "They did not realize she was invisible?"

"They knew, but did not quite believe until after she seduced the Fleet Admiral. They thought they could track her with heat and sound sensors."

"And she turned off those indications," Ennui said. "Beautiful."

"When they finally realized that it had been a coordinated effort, they were pretty upset. It was too late, but thereafter they watched the Glamors closely. Only when it became apparent that they needed Charm personnel to deal with the wild magic did they relent. But you can bet they are watching what we do, anywhere."

"So I can't just go to the Io moon without being spied."

"Agreement. Whatever you have to do there will soon be known and countered."

"Which I can't afford," she said morosely.

"It seems odd that they didn't anticipate this before sending you."

Ennui pondered that. Why would they send her into an impossible mission?

It is a feasible mission, Idyll thought. *We know you will find a way to accomplish it.*

They had remarkable confidence in her. How could she, a nondescript unimaginative old woman, prevail? They needed a young active risk-taking ambitious man.

Negation. Our reading suggests you are the one.

Yet what could she do that others could not?

Ignorance. I can not tell you. But you will do it.

"Apology," Dreamer said. "I must wonder again whether you are not irrelevant. Maybe a distraction from that they're really doing."

Untrue.

"I don't believe that," Ennui said. Yet she doubted. It would make sense to put her out as a diversion, attracting attention, while the real mission was quietly accomplished elsewhere. Yet two things argued against it: Idyll's assurance, and her possession of the ikon. That ikon was potentially the most valuable object in this stellar system.

That gave her an idea. She put her hand in her pocket and palmed the ikon. She had been keeping it out of contact with her flesh, so as not to become addicted to it. She had had more than enough experience with that! But now she drew on that experience.

She sat down and brought the ikon to her forehead. It looked as if she were in despairing thought. That was only half right. She wanted the enhancement of her brain she knew it would bring.

That is one reason, Idyll thought. *Your prior experience.*

It worked. Immediately her mind started racing. Diversion: that could be effective. But she didn't need to divert attention from someone else. She could divert it from herself. By causing them to focus on the wrong thing, and overlook the obvious. It was a common and generally effective ploy.

"We need to stir them up," she said. "To make them pursue us."

"Confusion," Dreamer said.

"And we'll be fleeing, and not quite escaping." She glanced at the panel. "You can do it, Mino: make them think they're about to catch you?"

AFFIRMATION.

"So let's take a few minutes to gad about gaily between planets, suspiciously sight-seeing, and you can drop me off at the right one and go on so they don't realize."

NEGATION.

"Question?" She knew that Mino was capable of spoken human speech, but she was satisfied with this panel mode.

"Explanation, if you please, Ma'am Ennui," Dreamer said. "This is a more spread out system than ours, and the planets range far out. The Earth ships cruise at half light speed in space, and the planets are light minutes or light hours apart, so it takes time."

"But if they can travel a thousand light years in two months, what's this about limits?" She knew that was approximate the distance between Charm and Earth; Dynamo had clarified it to Gale, and the news had gotten around.

"That's different. They use the worm jump."

"Question?" She had a mental picture of a worm emerging from the ground and leaping into the air. It did not align well with space travel.

The yellow man smiled. "It was confusing to us, too, when we were in

training. I never knew anything about Science magic before; it didn't interest
me. Here it's all there is, so we have to know it, and it's pretty interesting. It
seems that space is riddled with what they call worm holes that go from one
place to another instantly. It's not space travel, it's worm jumping. At least
using the holes."

"I hope nobody encounters a worm therein."

Dreamer laughed. "Clever, Ennui. There are no worms, just the holes,
which seem to form naturally. They are tricky to locate and use; after all, if you
take the wrong one you could wind up in another galaxy. But they are relatively
stable, so once you have one marked, you can use it all you want. That's what
the Earthers do, and the Glamors also, now that they know how."

"Realization: The Silver Glamor brought me here—through a worm hole?"

"Confirmation. We came on the Earth space ship, but the Glamors aren't
limited that way. They just need an ikon at each end, and they jump across
almost instantly, using myriad lesser worm holes the Earthers don't know about."

Ennui worked it out. "So the Earther ship travels almost instantly. Then
why does it take two months to make the trip?"

"Edge time," Dreamer said. He was clearly well satisfied to be explaining
this to an interested listener, making himself useful. He had evidently learned
well. "The ship-sized worm holes aren't necessarily right where you want them,
and entering and leaving them makes for some local disruption of space. That
could be bad, if done right next to a planet. So they develop holes about half a
light month out, then travel at half light speed in to the planet. It's mostly
transition time, as they call it: a month to the worm hole, zap through it, and a
month to the planet at the other end. That's that we did, coming here. It's the
safest way. Earth lost the technology during its dark millennium, but recently
recovered it, and that's why they came back out to Charm after a thousand
years. They didn't know how, in between."

"Methinks I should have take that training course," Ennui said. "This explains a lot. So how long will it take to lead the Earther ship a chase around
this solar system?"

"Any time from ten minutes to two hours, per planet. It depends where
they are relative to each other."

She was confused again. "Question?"

"It's different from Charm and Counter Charm, that are always close together, and nothing else in the Vivid/Void system. There are moons that are
always close to their planets, but the planets themselves may be on the same
side of the sun, or on opposite sides. So travel time varies accordingly. You
could figure an economical route to save time, but it would still take hours to
catch them all, and longer if you check the moons too."

She nodded. "I want to lead them a chase, so let's go from planet to planet
in order from the sun, crisscrossing the system as necessary. That should
make them wonder. They'll think we're trying to find a planet where they won't
follow."

"That should confuse them," Dreamer agreed. "But the other thing, about
dropping you off at the right one—Ma'am, those planets are uninhabitable.
Well, there are small colonies, but they're sealed under domes to hold in the
air, and all their supplies have to be ferried in. You can't just walk on the surface."

"Not like Charm and Counter Charm," she echoed. "I see it now. But I will need to walk on one, I think, to accomplish my mission. How will I do that?"

"I think you'll need a space suit."

"Oh, I'll want something more solid than material made from space," she said. "Especially if there's no air out there."

"Clarification: A suit to enable you to live in a vacuum," he said. "Mino should have one."

They looked at the panel. AFFIRMATION.

Ennui took a deep breath. "Comprehension: now I understand the complexities of what I thought was simple. I still don't know how to locate a nonChroma world."

THIS IS MY TASK, the panel said. I WILL SURVEY EACH PLANET AND MOON WE VISIT, AND DETERMINE WHICH IS NONCHROMA.

"You're sure you can do it, Mino?"

I WAS CRAFTED FOR EXACTLY THIS PURPOSE: TO SEEK, LOCATE, AND MARK MAGIC CHROMA ZONES SO THAT MY CULTURE COULD COME TO MINE THEM. THIS WAS WHY I WAS SEQUESTERED BY THE IFRIT GLAMOR FOR SOME TIME.

True. The machine is honest.

Ennui felt giddy. "Then I think we are ready to proceed." She hadn't had this much excitement in a decade, and it thrilled her. She was no brave adventurer, but when circumstance put her into adventure, it made her feel truly alive.

DESTINATION?

"What's the closest planet to this star?"

"Mercury," Dreamer said. "It is small and hot, no bigger than one of the larger moons of the outer planets."

"Start there," Ennui said. "Is there an Earth fleet ship there?"

AFFIRMATION.

"Good enough. Check the planet for nonChroma, just in case. Make sure the Earthers see you."

I SHALL MAKE MYSELF APPARENT.

"Question?"

I HAVE HITHERTO BEEN IMPERVIOUS TO EARTHER SENSORS.

"You can do that? Be invisible? I would think that would be hard to do."

HARD FOR A TYPE ONE CULTURE. NOT FOR A TYPE TWO.

Confirmation, Idyll thought. *Mino is Type Two, a more advanced machine than any of Earth.*

And what would happen when the third crisis came, with the invasion of that advanced machine culture?

We are studying to become Type Two.

Oh. "Affirmation. Become visible. When we get there."

The ship started moving. She felt the mild swing of it, and knew that it was actually undertaking horrendous acceleration, cushioning the human folk within its protective net. It would quickly get up to half light velocity, something that would have crushed her if its full impact had been allowed to manifest.

Technology has its points, Idyll thought.

So it seemed.

In about fifteen minutes the main screen lighted. Centered in it was a planet.

MERCURY.

"Appreciation, Mino." She knew the machine lacked living emotions, but such courtesy came naturally to her.

WELCOME.

Actually Mino does have emotion circuitry he can evoke as required, Idyll thought. *I have come to appreciate what a sophisticated machine he is. And of course his ability to see the far future is priceless.*

"Have you made yourself visible?" Ennui inquired.

AFFIRMATION. THE EARTHER GUARD SHIP IS REACTING.

"Is there any nonChroma here?"

NONE.

"Then taunt the ship and make it chase us."

A pair of human lips flashed momentarily on the screen, smiling. PLEA-SURE.

Mino moved quickly, accelerating away from the small planet. Now the Earther ship showed on the screen; Mino was tracking it. Printed words appeared superimposed on the picture.

Unknown space vessel: halt and identify yourself.

For answer Mino retreated faster. The ship followed.

Halt, or we fire.

This time Mino emitted a cloud of brown vapor. It spread and dissipated, staining the hull of the pursuing ship.

Dreamer laughed. "A fart! He farted at them!"

Ennui tried to stifle her own laughter, and failed. She giggled.

The Earth ship fired. The beam seared just past Mino's hull, illuminated on the screen.

Suddenly things were serious. "Get out of here!" she cried.

IT CAN'T HIT ME OR HURT ME, Mino printed, taking evasive action.

"Relief: I'm glad you're sure of that," Ennui said with more than a trace of irony.

He is, Idyll thought. *But this is odd. As I understand it, the Mistress of Mistresses has the fleet under orders not to fire on anything without her specific approval.*

"Orders not to fire?" Ennui repeated.

"Someone didn't get the word," Dreamer said. He looked as shaken as Ennui felt.

Suggest we query the mistress of that ship.

"Mino, can you query the ship's mistress?"

IN PROCESS.

In a moment a man's face appeared on the screen. "Halt and be boarded," he said. "Or we'll blow you out of space."

Ennui hesitated, but it seemed to be up to her. "Put on the mistress, please."

"She is not available. Prepare for boarding."

Alarm! A mistress commands every ship, and always speaks for it. Something is wrong.

"Mino," Ennui murmured. "Where is the mistress?"

I HAVE SURVEYED THE SHIP. SHE IS CONFINED AGAINST HER WILL.

"But doesn't that mean mutiny?"

AFFIRMATION.

"How could that happen?"

I think I know. The malign Male Spirit has taken over the minds of the men of the ship.

"Male Spirit?" Ennui asked blankly.

The Female Spirit governs Earth and is Havoc's oath friend and mistress. The Male Spirit is staging a rebellion, enabled by the wild magic in the Chroma zones we have fostered. This is mischief.

It certainly was. "This male spirit—is hostile?"

We are conducting a polite war with Earth governed by the Female Spirit. There is honor and considerable cooperation. The Male Spirit is another matter.

So it seemed. "How does my mission relate?"

This is surely the intermediate crisis we foresaw. Your mission is more important now. Perhaps critical.

"I'll do my best," Ennui said. Then she glanced at Dreamer, who was looking askance at her. "Sometimes I talk to myself with under stress. It seems a malign spirit has taken over the Earth ship, maybe the whole Earther fleet. We have a serious situation."

"We were fighting something bad in the Yellow Chroma zone," Dreamer said. "Maybe that was it."

"It surely was," she agreed. "Mino, take us to the next planet, leading the Earther ship."

The ship, receiving no answer to its demand, fired another missile. It missed, as it seemed had to be the case.

"Are you taking evasive action?" she asked.

IN MY FASHION.

"Question."

I AM READING THE NEAR FUTURE AND ARRANGING TO BE WHERE THE ENEMY BEAM IS NOT. THIS AVOIDS ANY DISPLAY OF SUPERIOR TECHNOLOGY.

"But Voila's the one for the near future!"

THIS IS EXTREMELY SIMPLE FUTURE. VOILA TRAINED ME IN IT.

True. We work together now.

In another fifteen minutes another planet appeared in the screen. This one was shrouded by a cloud canopy.

VENUS.

"And another Earth ship," Ennui said.

In a moment Mino verified that this planet was Science also. He resumed travel, this time with two pursuing Earth ships. Their repeated shots somehow managed to miss, surely frustrating them.

It took half an hour to reach the fourth planet out, skipping Earth. This was Mars. It was Science and had another guardian ship.

REST. TIME TO JUPITER IS 1.5 HOURS.

"I'll do that," Ennui agreed. She went to Dreamer. "May I join you?"

"Question?"

"I want to share your bed so I can nap. My old bones do not take kindly to contact with the floor. I promise not to molest you."

His laugh was somewhat forced. "Agreement."

She lay beside him. "Wake me at need," she called to Mino. Then she closed her eyes and dropped into sleep. It was a trick she had learned from Havoc: to fit sleep into the interstices when things were rushed.

Wake Idyll thought. *We have found the nonChroma moon.*

Ennui came instantly alert. "You found it?"

"I did not touch you," Dreamer said.

She smiled as she got off the bed. "Apology. I was talking to myself again. Mino, what have you found?"

MOON IO IS HIGHLY VOLCANIC, AND IS NONCHROMA DEFAULT, AS WE CONJECTURED.

"Great! I must land there."

DON SUIT. A vaguely humanoid costume appeared from a wall compartment.

She struggled into it, assisted by Dreamer, who seemed almost recovered. It fit her surprisingly well.

Meanwhile Io loomed near, huge and red with clouds of vapor spotting its surface. It looked dangerous.

"Ma'am Ennui," Dreamer said. "I don't think you should go there."

"I have to. I will return soon." She hoped.

The Silver Glamor appeared. *Find strong nonChroma magic*, he thought. *Plant ikon in center. Do not dally.*

"I won't dally," she agreed with simulated bravery. As if she had much choice. She stepped into the spider's embrace.

They were on the surface. It was, she understood, frozen sulfur dioxide. Now if only she knew what that was. Nearby was an erupting volcano, sending a cloud of sulfur compounds high into whatever atmosphere existed here.

The Glamor vanished. She was on her own.

She held the ikon in her suited hand, anchored by a stout cord. The suit had been flaccid aboard Mino, but had abruptly filled out rigidly in the reduced atmospheric pressure here. She remained mobile, though; that was the genius of the suit. She felt like a halfway animated golem.

She looked around, peering out through her faceplate. She was on a roughly level plain at night, illuminated by the glow of the volcano. Night? No, the planet Jupiter and its moons were much farther away from their star than Earth was, or Charm from Vivid, so less light reached them. This was its version of day.

Lovely, Idyll thought. She was serious.

Now where was there a good nonChroma place to plant the ikon? The plain was riven by large and seemingly deep cracks. Ennui didn't trust it; she knew that they could be the result of earthquakes, and more shakes could occur at any time.

This spot is supposed to be geologically stable for at least twelve hours. I confirm that with my near-future vision.

"That's reassuring. How do I locate the right spot?"

The ikon will glow and vibrate.

Ennui looked at it. Indeed, it was growing faintly. She took a step away from the volcano, and the glow remained. That was a relief; she wouldn't have to approach the dangerous cone.

This world is nonChroma default, yet red Chroma on the surface. We may need a cave.

"A deep cave," Ennui agreed nervously. She remained foolishly concerned that this entire landscape could shake apart, dropping her into a cruel abyss.

She took another step, and came to a wider crack. In fact it was a small crevasse, several feet across, seemingly bottomless. She considered, then jumped across it.

She sailed high into whatever vapor passed for air, landing well beyond the crack. "Astonishment!"

This is a smaller world than Charm Idyll explained. *You weigh between a quarter and a fifth what you do at home.*

Oh. In her distraction with the larger situation, she hadn't been aware of her lightness of body. Now she was. She would have to watch her step, literally.

She glanced at the ikon. It was glowing a bit brighter. "Progress," she said. "This must be the direction. Away from the volcano."

Because it's a Red Chroma vent, Idyll agreed. *NonChroma will manifest outside its range, as on our worlds.*

They continued in that direction, and the ikon responded. Then they reached a much larger crevice, a veritable canyon. Hot vapor wafted up from it; her suit cooler came on to counter the heat. Curious, Ennui held the ikon out over it—and it glowed so brightly it seemed to be on fire.

This is a vent extending toward the molten nonChroma interior, the ifrit concluded. *This is the place for the ikon.*

"But I can't just drop it in the hole! It might land in magma and melt."

Perhaps you can. Ikons are indestructible, and they protect their holders, as you know. That is a truly potent nonChroma zone below.

"But how would we ever get it back?"

Voila needs a permanent base. This crevasse should be well out of reach of the Earthers.

Ennui thought of something else. "Can it broadcast to Voila from so deep? Those canyon walls might block it."

Negation. Ikons send through material of any nature.

"Then I suppose my job is done." Ennui made an effort of will and dropped the ikon into the void. It glowed ever-more brightly as it fell, becoming a shining torch. She strained to see it land—and overbalanced. "Horror!" she cried as she toppled over the edge.

Float!

And Ennui was floating. "Dream?" she asked, dazed.

Magic. You are levitating.

"But I can't do magic! I'm not a Glamor."

I am. But I lack my main substance here. You are doing it yourself, following my guidance.

"Disbelief." Yet she was doing it. She willed herself back to the edge, and stopped on the solidly frozen ground.

Explanation: normal nonChroma folk can't do magic because the nonChroma fields are too diffuse. NonChroma Glamors differ because their ikons and bodies gather the magic from a wider volume and concentrate it for their use. Here the nonChroma field is intense, enabling you to use it.

"Amazement! Yet I lack experience and training; how can I just suddenly do it?"

My guidance, the ifrit reminded her. *Your body is heeding my directives and utilizing the magic. In time you will learn it yourself.*

"Suddenly I am extremely glad to have you with me!"

Welcome.

"But I still hope Silver remembers to pick me up. I see I have little more than an hour's air left."

I am signaling him.

The silver spider appeared, seeming unaffected by the caustic atmosphere. She gladly joined his embrace.

They were back aboard Mino, and the Silver Glamor was gone. But the picture on the screen was different. The moon was significantly larger and darker, and lacked volcanoes. "That's not Io!" Ennui exclaimed.

"It is Callisto," Dreamer said. "We explored Europa and Ganymede in between, dodging the Earth ship. They don't know what we're up to. They must think we are looking for a world to land on, and not finding it."

"That's the idea," Ennui agreed, suddenly well satisfied. "Now we can lead them a merry chase to Planet Saturn and beyond.

"Question: Your mission—you accomplished it?"

"Affirmation." She pondered a moment. *May I tell him of the magic? I'm about to burst with the news.*

Welcome, Idyll agreed. *Only the ikon is secret.*

"I made a marvelous discovery," she told Dreamer. Her dull life had turned several shades brighter.

Chapter 17
Translucent

"A new spot crisis is coming," Havoc said.

"We shall handle it," Monochrome said. She took it for granted that she would be with him, as before. "But there is one caution."

"Speak."

"You have been operating, as I understand it, on Chroma stones. That is, nonChroma stones. They are bound to be exhausted soon."

"Affirmation."

"So we must plant your ikon, so that you can operate on your own power hereafter."

"Agreement."

"Let's go see the green girl. Naive."

"Confirmation." He put his arm around her evocative waist and jumped to the Green Chroma zone where Naive remained after helping Gale tame it.

Suddenly they were surrounded by green: foliage, ground, water, clouds. "Oh, I do prefer this to the bleak black zone," Monochrome said admiringly.

Naive appeared. "Sire!" she said, surprised. "I felt your trace."

"You carry my ikon."

"True, Sire. It pulsed with your approach. Now I am aware of it."

"There should be a nonChroma zone around the Green Chroma zone, now that it is established," he said. "The conversion strips all Chroma from the immediate vicinity."

"Affirmation."

"Plant my ikon there."

"But it is not yet secure, Sire. The Green Chroma zone is still expanding. Your ikon will be overrun and lose power."

"Track it. Move it as necessary."

"Agreement, Sire." But she hesitated.

Kiss her, Monochrome thought. *She lacks courage to ask.*

Oh, of course. The king repaid favors with gestures of appreciation. He took the green girl into his embrace while she held his ikon out from her body, making it possible. He kissed her. He felt her knees weaken. It was not magic, but her overwhelming appreciation of his royal favor.

He released her and stepped back. Naive recovered her balance. "Sire," she murmured dreamily, and disappeared.

"Appreciation," he told Monochrome.

"Well, I love you, Havoc. I mean to do right by you, and I am far beyond petty jealousy. Your presence and attention are magic, no pun intended, to the women you encounter. But it will require more than a kiss to satisfy me."

He smiled. Then he picked up on the other aspect. "You thought it to me."

"I said I meant to learn telepathy. I am working on it."

There was a surge of emotion. This was more and better woman than he had encountered anywhere else. "Love."

"Similarity," she said, smiling.

Then he felt a change. "The ikon!"

"She has placed it? It is transmitting power to you? Congratulations, Havoc!"

He clasped her and kissed her. She returned it avidly. Then, still embraced, they returned to her suite in Antarctica, their lovemaking uninterrupted.

"We do seem to have much in common," Monochrome remarked after their mutually satisfactory tryst.

"Great sex," he agreed.

She slapped him lightly on the flank. "You know our horizons are broader than that."

"Teasing," he agreed. "You are more woman than I ever expected, and not merely because you are a Glamor. I don't love other Glamors."

"Gale is not a Glamor?"

"I loved her before she was a Glamor. Before she was a woman. She can be anything or nothing and I will always love her. Other Glamors are great for sex and camaraderie, but love is not part of that equation."

"But you know I am lovable because my life is dedicated to being the perfect woman for all men." It was a question.

"It could readily have been pure sex with you, and friendship from the oath. There is something else I love. I don't know what it is."

"It is the Earth Female Spirit. I animate everything you are capable of appreciating in a woman."

Havoc considered that. Other Glamors had beauty, sexual skill, and eagerness, and were his mental and magical equals. Why didn't he love them? Because they were not fundamental spirits? "Confusion."

"Havoc, perhaps you should get another view of Earth Spirits. You should interview one who is not female. That will remove the sexual element for you, so that you can more readily judge."

"Question: there are other Earth Spirits?"

"Just the one other: the malign Male Spirit who seeks to wrest the planet from me."

"Gale interviewed him already."

"Only partially so, Havoc. She encountered the temporary mortal human host he borrowed. He was limited to a degree by the parameters of that host, which lessened him. He is much more than that, as I am more than an ordinary woman. Interview his discarnate aspect and you will learn more."

Havoc was intrigued. "How?"

"Go into a trance state. Seek his essence. Neither of you can affect the other physically or magically in that state, but you can interact. That should be profoundly educational."

But there was a reservation in the background. "Caution: You are suggesting this, but do you wish it?"

"I fear it."

"Despite no possible physical or magical effect?"

"Once you comprehend the full nature of the Earth Spirit, you may no longer love me."

He was not so naïve as to suppose she was being unrealistic. "Then I will not do it."

"Havoc, you must. Otherwise your love is based on ignorance. I prefer it real."

"Conjecture: if it banishes my love for you, you will still love me, for you already know my full nature."

"Confirmation," she agreed.

"The oath of friendship would prevent me from treating you unkindly, and I would surely still find you sexually appealing. But it would not be the same."

"That is true. I will accept what I can have of you, but my heart will be hurting."

Suddenly he thought of Symbol. "My mistress loves me that way. I like her a lot, but Gale was my only love."

"You do have that effect on women."

"Aversion. I would not seek an interaction that lessened my love for Gale."

"There is no need. You know Gale as well as she knows you. But you do not know me that well."

This continued to bother him. "If I do it, and retain my love for you, then it will be real."

"Yes, Havoc."

"Decision," he said, unpleased.

"Do it now, please."

He lay on his back, closed his eyes, and sought the trance state. He let his awareness float out of his body in the manner of a departing soul, but there was no soul-content here. He spread out beyond the chamber.

There was nothing. Just the surrounding ice of the frozen continent, spiked by lines and globules of human habitation. From this vantage they seemed more like an infestation than civilization. They prevented the continent from being completely natural.

He spread out farther, reaching into the sky above and the ice below. The sky grew colder, the ice warmer, until there was no ice, only rock, and no air, only thinning gas. Where was what he was looking for? *What* was he looking for?

Then he felt a slight nudge. It was in the vicinity of a long mountain range that bordered the west side of Continent America. Was this it?

A subduction zone. It was Monochrome's thought, surprising him, because he hadn't realized that she could reach him here.

Question?

Earth is different from Charm in more than the amount of free water on its surface. It is covered with crusty tectonic plates that move slowly across its surface. The mid-ocean ridges are up-welling zones that spread out new magma from below. This pushes the plates aside, and their far edges collide and override each other. Where one plunges below another is a subduction zone.

Havoc found this more interesting than he might have before he learned about the subterranean linkages of Planet Charm. Subduction zones were like

Black Chroma volcanoes, bringing surface material down into the subterranean cauldron. Only, it seemed, rather more slowly. *Do they bring up new magic?*

Yes. And bury the old magic at their oldest fringes. What you call Science magic.

His ranging presence discovered a line of volcanoes. *What are these doing here?*

Subduction crushes and heats the material, liquifying it and forming gas. This struggles to find an avenue to the surface. The volcanoes are such avenues.

Now he could feel that process. It was similar to what occurred on Charm, but on a rather larger scale. Instead of individual volcanoes doing their own things, it was lines of volcanoes. Because the source was the same—the descending crust—the released magic was the same: Science. That, for Havoc's taste, made Earth a dull planet.

Dull to you, perhaps, colonist. Not to the natives.

Havoc took stock. This was a different presence. *Who?*

Who else? You are assessing my domain.

It was the dread male Spirit. The one Havoc sought.

I am required to get to know you, spook.

The intangible presence shrugged. *I have no interest in getting to know you, primitive.*

Havoc made a mental smile. *Why should I care what interests you?*

Because you will not know me otherwise.

Havoc considered. *Then what does interest you?*

Power. Combat. Sex.

Havoc nodded. *Combat.*

Now the Spirit smiled. *Chess.*

They were alternating choices. That was fair enough. Havoc was actually one of the best players of Charm, though second now to Voila, whom he had taught. He might win or lose this game, but had no fear of incompetence. He conjured the animated chess set he had encountered when exploring the illusion fields on the way to discovering the Glamor ifrit Idyll. The white pieces were all male, the black all female. They resembled two Chroma zones of Planet Charm, the Whites completely white in clothing as bodies, the Blacks completely black.

Then the Spirit made a change. One woman appeared among the male pieces: the white Queen. And one male among the female pieces: the black Queen's consort and chief guardian. Well, it did make some sense.

Choose your color, the Spirit thought.

Havoc considered. Normally he would go with the male pieces, but that would leave the female pieces to the Spirit, and that rankled. Power and sex exerted over them, regardless of their preferences? "Black."

Then they were in it. The giant board had become markings on a gently rolling meadow bounded by green trees and a sparkling lake. Havoc stood between the Queen and the female Bishop. The Queen was really the King, the one piece to be protected beyond all others. Before them stood a row of dark-skirted little girls. The knights were mounted on odd four-legged horses, and the rooks were wheeled towers capable of rapid motion.

A white boy strode forward two squares in front of the white King. Pawn to

E4, the standard opening. The Spirit was getting right on it. The boy gazed ahead and stuck out his tongue.

"For pity's sake," the black Queen muttered, disgusted.

The voice was familiar. Havoc turned to look at her. "Monochrome!" he exclaimed, surprised. She was resplendent in her royal crown and raiment, carrying the scepter of power, by no means deprived of her beauty or sex appeal.

"Surprised?" she asked. "You selected me, Havoc."

He had not been conscious of that, but probably he had, because she was the dominant woman of Earth, thus fitting the role. Was she real, to the extent applicable here in the trance state, or a mere replica? He decided not to gamble on the latter. "Apology."

"Needless," she said, smiling. "This does provide me a view of your interview. I trust you are competent at chess?"

"Affirmation." And now it was his move, as he was Player as well as Queen-Consort. He focused, and the girl standing before Monochrome skipped forward to face the obnoxious boy. It was the standard response. He was more interested in feeling out the competence of his opponent than in playing a spectacular game.

Another white pawn moved forward. Meanwhile the first pawn tried to goose the girl opposite him, but she slapped his hand away. Good enough; Havoc liked girls with spirit. He had probably seen a girl like her when touring Black Chroma zones, and used her as a model for the pawns. Neither the boys nor the girls were identical to each other, apart from their colors.

The game progressed, and in due course the major pieces mixed in. When White took a piece, the white male put his arms around the black female and squeezed. She swooned and collapsed, and slid off the board. When Black took a piece, the female kissed the male, and he stumbled dazed from the arena. The eliminated pieces remained by the side of the board, sitting on the adjacent meadow, and some of them talked to each other. They definitely had personalities of their own apart from their roles in the game.

At one point Havoc advanced to stand next to the white Queen, a challenge for her to take him. Not much of one, as both were guarded by pawns, but it was a kind of face-off. She was a remarkably pretty figure of a woman, with regal bearing to match her outfit.

"So this is your doing, Havoc," she said.

It was Gale! He had not been able to make out her features before; apparently distance obscured them. "The male Spirit chose you!" he said.

She made a wry smile. "Evidently I impressed him."

By having sex with him. Gale would have impressed anyone at any time, but that would have intensified the effect. Now she was Havoc's opposite. One of them was bound to destroy the other, directly or indirectly. "The Male Spirit has a mean sense of humor."

"I fear that is the least of it."

Was it really his wife, or an emulation? Havoc chatted with her, theoretically incidentally, but was soon assured that she was real. There were too many fond little secrets between them, such as their first Tickle & Peek game as children. But this also made him nervous, because of the power it demonstrated that the Spirit possessed. Still, the Spirit could not command wills, merely presences. Gale would never be the Spirit's in reality, however much he craved her.

Then the game progressed, and they were separated. Havoc focused on the strategy. The Spirit was an excellent player, but Havoc thought not the very best. Unless that was a ruse while the Spirit studied him.

The Queen and Queen-Consort met again. They talked as the action of the game moved elsewhere. "Do you recognize the King?" Gale asked.

"Negation."

"He is called Caveat. He is Voila's companion and guardian on Earth. He is homosexual."

That was astonishing. Why would the male Spirit choose to animate an imperfect man for this purpose? "Surprise."

"The Spirit surely chose Caveat because of his connection to Voila. My concern is why Voila has that connection. She could fascinate any normal man if she tried."

Havoc smiled. "She must regard him as a challenge. Beneath that sweet, timid exterior beats a heart as bold as they come, buttressed by power we can hardly imagine." He phrased it as bragging banter, but he was speaking literally, as Gale knew.

"She does. But I think she really likes him. That worries me."

"Concurrence." Did the Spirit have designs on Voila? The very idea made Havoc angry. But of course Voila could take care of herself, even against a planetary spirit.

Then the game shifted and they separated. It was reaching the later stage, and was a good game as such things went. The Spirit's strategy was deceptive; poor or indifferent moves turned out not to be as bad as they seemed. It did not seem to bother the Spirit when he lost a piece, but he was not careless.

Then came the finale. Havoc had been biding his time, observing the Spirit, but now the opportunity came to win the game. Unfortunately it required the sacrifice of a major piece: himself. So be it.

He stepped into Gale's line of capture. If she took him, the game was his to win. Was the Spirit smart enough to see that?

She swept down a diagonal and kissed him. It was electrifying in more than one sense, for her love was in it. She knew he had chosen this deliberately. Havoc staggered off the board. His sacrifice ploy had been accepted.

Now he watched from the side as his strategy manifested. The queen consort sacrifice was followed by a devastating split that finished White. There was no way out.

"Damn!" The game exploded into flying pieces and bits of surrounding scenery.

Havoc had won. But he was wary. Was this all there was to the Male Spirit? Or was this game merely a diversion to keep Havoc from fathoming what he sought? Winning or losing the chess game hardly mattered, especially if it interfered with his present mission.

The Spirit seemed oddly satisfied despite his loss. It was almost as if he had just won. He figured Havoc would leave off this mission now, having been bought off by winning a game?

He saw both Monochrome and Gale glancing covertly his way. What did they expect of him?

Now was the time to pounce, when it was least expected.

Havoc spread his awareness again, this time orienting on the essence that animated the fallen White King. This sudden move evidently caught the other by surprise, just when he thought he had diverted Havoc; there was a formidable presence there, much greater than the narrow and crude figure previously presented.

This was the essence of the nature of the Planet Earth, abiding regardless of the activity on its surface. It was huge in both size and concept. Both the male and female aspects were mere papering over a power that was indifferent to gender and identity. In fact the sexes were largely illusion, an incidental mechanism to facilitate the reproduction and evolution of particular species. Beneath and beyond them was the godlike whole.

Godlike. Havoc knew of gods only through the thousand year old folklore that persisted of Planet Charm, deriving from Earth. It meant a supreme being, the ultimate creator of everything. Who made the universe? God. Who governed it? God. It was a convenient fiction to explain things that were otherwise difficult to handle intellectually. It lent a kind of security of mind to those who lacked the will or smarts to handle more relevant concepts. But the Earth Spirit might well be the source of that notion.

Havoc had learned that there were sizable frameworks of belief on Earth dedicated to particular ways of worshipping God. They were called religions, and they competed with each other, sometimes even warring with each other. Each believed that it alone represented the proper manner of relationship to God, and that all others were false. It reminded Havoc of the way the different Chroma of Charm competed and sometimes warred with each other, though all that separated them really was color. Earth, deprived of the colors of magic, had found other ways to compete.

So was all this combative mission, this supposed war between the male and female Spirits, mere quibbling over illusion? Competition of imaginary distinctions? Was Monochrome largely illusion, representing a meaningless distinction between things that were mere parts of a larger whole? Was there really nothing there?

That could not be. The several Chroma of Charm were aspects of the same underlying thing, magic, but they were individual too. Monochrome was a person, whatever she represented. She was much like Havoc himself, an ordinary person who had come to represent an extraordinary aspect of a phenomenal power. Actually he had been more than an ordinary man before he became a Glamor, and thus was better able to fill the new role. Monochrome had been similarly extraordinary, and perhaps had been chosen because she was the most competent candidate for the role. He could still love her, regardless.

Now he had learned enough, and not just the formidability of his opponent. Now he could let it be.

He vacated the trance. In a moment he found himself back in her chamber, his head cradled by her arms and breasts. "Oh, Havoc!" she breathed, knowing the answer.

"Shut up and spread your legs," he said with mock gruffness, parodying the seeming attitude of the Male Spirit.

She did so, understanding perfectly. It was another fabulously rewarding session that left them both panting on the bed.

Pa. It was Warp.

"Acknowledgment," Havoc said, speaking as he focused his answering thought. "Trouble?"

Water volcano Weft seeded. Going wild. Boiling over. People will die.

"On our way," Havoc said. Then, to Monochrome: "Regret."

"Understanding." She reassembled her clothing, and his. "There is work to be done."

"Agreement. Water volcano boiling over."

"You mean an underwater eruption?"

"Negation." He conducted her there.

They stood on an island, gazing up at the volcanic mountain. Translucent liquid was overflowing its rim and washing down the conic slope. Steamy clouds were rising from the apex.

"That's not lava," Monochrome said. "Or a cloud of smoke or ash."

"Agreement," he said. "That is water and steam."

Warp appeared, with Marionette behind him. The women exchanged hugs as Warp spoke. "We're holding it back, Dad. But something's wrong. It's getting wilder."

"The malign Male Spirit," Monochrome said. "Making more mischief."

"He never rests," Havoc agreed. Obviously the trance visit had not interrupted the Spirit's pursuit of power.

"Never," she agreed.

A strange man appeared, his skin brown but not of Chroma hue. He was an Earther. "You said it, sister. Who the hell are you?"

"Monochrome," she said. "And you are the brutish impostor. You don't remember?"

He looked more carefully at her. "Ah, now I recognize you, without the chess motif. Well, you got a shape on you, honey. I like it, so I'll take it. Pucker up your crack, doll." He strode toward her.

Havoc, distracted by his study of the volcano, was slow to react. This was a considerably lesser being than the one he had recently seen in the trance. The limits of the host really did make a difference.

The man reached the woman, grabbed for her—and fell back in a shower of sparks. "Bitch!" he said. "So it really is you."

Then Havoc was in action. He conjured directly to the man, grabbed him by the collar, and hauled him off his feet. "Pucker what?"

"Stifle it, barbarian," the man said. He popped to a spot ten feet away, leaving Havoc holding nothing. "You can't touch me unless I touch you too. But I will say that your wife is a neat piece of tail. I touched her and she touched me. What a fucking good time!"

"Don't let him bait you," Monochrome said. "He's trying to make you angry so you'll do something foolish."

"The malign Male Spirit," Havoc said thoughtfully. "I thought he couldn't be here physically while you are."

"This is a wild magic zone," she reminded him. "Not under my sway. He has power here, until we tame the zone. Then he'll be gone."

"Until I mess up the whole planet," the man said. "Then *you'll* be gone, sweet ass."

"Then let's tame the zone," Havoc said. "What do you need, Warp?"

"Boiling water is flowing down the mountain," Warp said tersely. "We are holding it back so it can't swamp the town below. But more of it is coming, and there are vents farther out, roiling the sea. If we tend to them, the water on the mountain will get away from us. Many people will die. We need to be able to stop more mischief more places at the same time."

"You can't, brat," the Male Spirit said. "Give it up."

Havoc took hold. "You have the Translucent Glamor here?"

"Holding back the flood," Warp agreed. "But we're going to need him else-where."

"And the trainees?"

"They're watching elsewhere. But we need them to organize the natives, so as to tame the zone."

"First get the natives to safety," Monochrome said. "Then organize them at leisure."

"Fat chance," the Male Spirit said.

Havoc nodded. "Do you Mistresses want to tackle the natives? They'll heed you faster than they'll heed us."

"We'll do it," Monochrome said. "You tame the magic."

"It won't work, bitches," the Male Spirit said.

Warp took the hands of the women, and the three vanished. Havoc turned to the Spirit. "Or I could simply take you out, and the problems would stop."

"You and what army, simpleton? You aren't on your own hick planet now."

"You lack full power, or you wouldn't be trying to distract us. I should be able to deal with you."

"Try it, boob."

"I accept the challenge." Havoc strode toward the man.

The man disappeared, and reappeared behind Havoc. Or behind where Havoc had been. For Havoc had moved too. He took hold of the man, his fingers pressing on key nerves. The man dropped to the ground. He might be a Glamor type entity, but he occupied a body that was subject to mortal limitations. To a degree. The main effect seemed to be to make him crude and somewhat stupid.

The man vanished, reappearing fifty feet distant. Havoc remained with him, staring down. The Spirit lurched back to his feet—only to be expertly tossed to the ground again, hard.

"Damn!" he swore, a cloud of fiery smoke appearing above him.

Rain appeared from nowhere, dousing the fire. A gust of wind dissipated the cloud.

He stared angrily at Havoc. "I may have underestimated you, hayseed."

"It happens," Havoc said mildly. "Now about my wife: she interacted with you in order to distract you while the Green Chroma zone was tamed, just as I am distracting you now. You couldn't have touched her otherwise."

"You sure of that, country boy?"

"Affirmation. Now I will interact with you, but you may not like it as well."

"You don't know what you're getting into, kinglet."

Havoc shrugged. It was fun teasing the man, inciting him to do something foolish. But there was also purpose: to ascertain exactly what limits existed. It was as if a being the size of a world was being funneled through a straw. It must be frustrating. "Maybe I'll find out." He reached for the man.

The man jumped back—and collided with a man-sized ball of fire. He cursed and jumped forward again, his clothing burning—into Havoc's oncoming fist. "Damn!"

"Limited vocabulary?" Havoc inquired.

The entire area clouded with roiling smoke. Havoc snapped his fingers, and the smoke faded out. "Shit!" the man said.

"Conjecture," Havoc said. "You normally govern a Science Chroma planet. But with your opposite Spirit in charge, you are limited to other forms of magic— and you aren't very good with them, never having had opportunity to practice. You had better flee, buffoon, before I embarrass you."

"You arrogant ass! I'll pulverize you!"

"You and what army, joker?"

In a rage, the man gestured. Knives appeared, flying in toward Havoc. They struck him—and dropped to the ground, their points blunted and curled up.

"Let me show you how that trick should be done," Havoc said. Suddenly new knives appeared—but the male Spirit was gone. He had yielded the field.

Havoc smiled. He had turned the man's technique against him. He had baited him so as to make him lose his temper. Meanwhile the others had gained valuable time stopping the flood and organizing the natives for their retreat to safe ground.

But the Spirit would soon recover. Havoc knew he had to keep after him. He had to keep him occupied until enough of the wild Translucent Chroma zone had been tamed.

Something kissed him. Havoc checked its mind, alert against some new ploy by the male Spirit. "Greeting, Ine," he said as he squeezed her invisible bottom.

"You plumbed my sister multiply, but left me to your son," she chided him gently. "And she's not even pretty."

This was true. Her sister Ini was plain but very smart, and he had enjoyed their relationship. "I can spare two minutes now, Sorceress." For his awareness of the near future was verifying that he could afford this much time.

"Done, Sire." She had his clothing open immediately, and she was wearing none. Her slippery channel came down on him, surrounding him, massaging him. She was as good at sex as any non-Glamor woman, making somewhat of a specialty of it. In seconds she had him jetting into her hot core, and she continued to work him internally, hungry for more. He obliged her by maintaining a minute-long series of pulses, while she kissed him passionately.

"An invisible fuck!" the male Spirit said. "I'll keep that in mind." They had overrun the two minutes. But this, too, should stir things up.

"All you need is a willing Air Chroma woman," Ine informed him, fully appreciating the ploy. "Too bad there is none here." None willing. She became lusciously visible and drew herself off Havoc. "Appreciation, Sire."

"Welcome, willing woman," Havoc answered. They were meanly teasing the Male Spirit.

"When I resume power, I'll have her unwilling," the male Spirit said.

"How so, excrement?" Ine inquired brightly as her bare breasts heaved with the lingering effort of her tryst with Havoc. She was phenomenally alluring, by no coincidence.

"Those you value will be tortured when you balk," the Spirit said. "You will comply, hating it."

"Then we'll just have to see that you don't resume power, won't we?"

"You'll have to make the attempt, bitch."

"Affirmation." She turned back to Havoc. "Translucent needs you now."

It was time. He took her hand and took her to the coast, leaving the Spirit behind for the moment. She had of course been entertaining Translucent in spare moments, exactly as with Havoc. She was no longer a young creature, at age 32, and loved being treated as one. Her Air stone enabled her to do her magic here, but it was running low and there was not time for her to get another.

"Go to the fringe," Havoc told her. "Do your business there. Save your stone."

"Appreciation, Sire." She vanished.

Of course this was more than it seemed. Ine carried Warp's ikon; that was why she had remained with him on this mission. Havoc was telling her to set that ikon in the nonChroma fringe of the Translucent Chroma zone. That would multiply Warp's Glamor power without the male Spirit realizing. Sex was only a minor portion of her role, but treated as the major portion, to mask the other.

The Translucent Glamor was in the water near an undersea vent that had opened. Hot water was welling from it, imbued with very strong magic. The local life, both plant and animal, was reacting, becoming crazed. This would have been awkward at any time, but with magic it was dangerous.

"Take the clams," Translucent said. This was his element; he could speak under water. Two Translucent trainees were assisting him, but their efforts were not enough.

"Agreement," Havoc said.

A bed of clams was rising up and attacking a crippled cuttlefish. This would have been suicidal in ordinary circumstances, but the magic changed things. They were anchoring their shells on the larger creature and issuing their digestive acids. The cuttlefish was the one in trouble.

Havoc exerted his magic to tame the wildness and restore the natural order. It wasn't that it mattered to the planet whether clam or cuttlefish prevailed, but that any inversion was mischief. The clams might be attacking human beings next.

The clams near Havoc settled back down into the muck, resuming their normal mode. The cuttlefish jetted away, surely relieved. The region of normalcy expanded outward from Havoc and locked into place. Magic remained, but there were no weird effects.

Take the sharks, Translucent's thought came, with a mental picture. Havoc got over there to find maddened Earthly sharks swimming through the magic water welling out from vents on shore. They were swimming out over the land and snapping at astonished people there. Somehow the water enabled the sharks to be supported, without suffocating the land dwellers; it was as if the sharks were swimming through air.

Havoc set up a magic repulsion field, and the sharks turned tail and fled. "Get to higher ground," he called to the people, uncertain whether they understood his language. "Before the sharks return."

Monochrome appeared. "There is worse," she said. "The others are occupied."

"Show me," Havoc said, taking her hand.

She teleported to a deep-sea region, guiding him there. *This is a sea farm,* she thought, indicating a region fenced off by extensive nets. *Oysters, sea snails, edible starfish, sponges, exotic deep-sea coral. They don't move rapidly.*

That was obviously the case. But Havoc was distracted by something else.

How can you breathe down here? He could, but that was an ability he and Gale had learned and practiced.

I can do things I don't care to publicize.

What, modesty? No, now he saw that it was merely caution. She tried to seem ordinary when feasible. Her reticence had deceived him into thinking she was unaware of her Glamor powers before encountering him. She had been flattering him by learning from him, to a degree.

Ine appeared, literally: her bare body was coated with illusion. She could have made illusory clothing, but of course preferred to be bare. "Sire, the volcano: it's about to blow."

"Your business is done?"

She nodded. That meant that Warp now had his full Glamor powers. "Come with me."

He took her hand and transported her to the site. She could have moved herself, but was almost out of her stone's power. He had plenty, now.

Warp, Marionette, and Monochrome were at the base of the mountain, but now so much water was gushing from it that any further attempt to stifle it was plainly hopeless. The entire region was about to be overwhelmed.

For a moment Havoc was baffled. He could save a few people, Warp could save a few, but there were hundreds or thousands. How could they all be saved—in the next minute?

"Sire," Ine said.

"Speak!"

"We of the Air Chroma clothe ourselves in illusion so we do not suffer the problems of invisibility. The Translucent Chroma folk make land of their water. I believe it is simply a matter of selectively strengthening the surface tension. So it hardens like flexible ice, but is not cold."

"So they can walk on water!" he exclaimed, seeing it. "I knew that. Appreciation for reminding me."

She pointed to her mouth. Taking the hint, he kissed her. Then he focused on the trickle of water that was passing his feet. He thickened its surface, then stepped onto it. It supported him.

"But they must not be trapped beneath it," Ine said.

"Mono!" Havoc called. "Tell the people to step up on the surface of the water. Tell them it is like warm ice. They must start stepping now, before it hardens." He turned to Warp. "Read the water-hardening magic in the minds of the Translucent Chroma folk. Apply it to the flood. Immediately. I will do the same."

"Got it, pa. Thanks."

Havoc focused on a wider expanse of water, reaching toward the volcano. He was not used to this particular magic, so it was slow. Then he felt Warp take hold, and the thickening accelerated. The water looked the same as it flowed, but now it had a forming rind on it.

"Residents!" Monochrome called, and her voice amplified to cover the region without seeming loud. "The Glamors are thickening the water! Step up on it as it reaches you; do not be caught beneath it." She demonstrated by making exaggerated stepping motions. This emphasized her salient physical qualities, making her more attractive than ever. Havoc hoped he was the only one to notice that.

The people responded to her in a manner they would not have responded to anyone else. Her magic was relating to people, women as well as men. Her words reached directly through to their understanding. They started climbing invisible stairs. It looked silly.

Then the water burst its restraints and flooded down around them. Suddenly the stepping motions were effective, as people climbed onto the surface and stood amazed.

The male Spirit's host appeared. "Damn!" he cried, seeing the people saving themselves. "I'll fix that."

Then the water poured out even more rapidly. It shot out of the cone of the volcano in a vast thick column, rising high into the sky, where it spread and mushroomed into a roiling cloud. A cloud of boiling water.

"Beware!" Havoc cried. "That's going to make scalding rain!"

"But it's all we can do to keep with up the land flow," Warp called.

"Which is carrying the people out to sea, where they'll drown when the magic ends," Ine said.

It was true. The solidified surface was now moving like a drawn carpet, carrying the people on it outward.

"Boil or drown," the Male Spirit said. "Your choice.

It was no bluff. The hot water was starting to precipitate from the boiling cloud, spreading outward. If the people ran to stay over land, they would soon be in the dreadful rain. It was evident that though Havoc could bamboozle the Spirit with small local magic, he couldn't stop the invocation of planetary effects. This was the Spirit's world, not Havoc's.

"We have to distract him so we can handle it," Monochrome said.

"Sure babe—the way his luscious wife distracted me before," the Spirit replied. "I can't resist really good tail! She's a piece of ass like none other. She must have liked it, too, or she wouldn't have stayed so long. Bring her on, legs and mouth wide open."

That was intended to get to Havoc. Unfortunately, it was succeeding. He oriented on the Spirit, ready for mayhem. "Havoc, no!" Monochrome cried. "Don't play his game."

"You have a better alternative?" Havoc asked grimly.

"Forgive me, Havoc. I love you, but I believe I do."

Oh, no! "You aren't going to give yourself to him?"

"Wow!" the Spirit said. "If there's one hotter cunt than the Glamor wife, it's the Glamor mistress. Sure, bitch, distract me all you want."

"Don't do it," Havoc told her. "He wants to kill you and resume power on Earth. Don't get close to him."

"He can't kill me. He can't even interact with me anywhere but here, while I govern the planet and he governs the island. It's the only way we can coexist even temporarily. I know he desires me beyond all others, for spiteful reasons."

"You got that right, honeybuns!"

Havoc had thought he couldn't be angrier than he had been with the unkind reference to Gale. Now he knew better. The male Spirit found his weakness: he didn't like his women molested. He knew Monochrome detested the Spirit, and would be sickened by his sexual attention. Yet he also know that it would work, because she was a creature the Spirit desired beyond all others. It would be a tradeoff: her pride for the lives of the islanders. She would suffer intense revulsion. It was nevertheless a deal she was prepared to make, to save the lives of her people.

"Take a moment," the Male Spirit said generously. Both water and cloud halted in place. "I am prepared to yield these lives as long as I have access to that precious body. The more reluctant she is, the better."

Ine appeared beside Havoc. "Sire, I have studied sorcery all my life. Heed me."

"Speak," he said. What did she know?

She spoke in his mind. *Golems.*

Question?

You know how golems work. They are animated from a distance by living operators, and can hardly be distinguished from living creatures themselves while so possessed.

Acknowledged. But there are no golems here.

The principle can be applied to living folk also. You can possess Monochrome, if she accedes, while her spirit can park safely in your body.

An exchange of bodies?

In effect, Sire. I can arrange it, if you choose.

Havoc considered. Ine was a sorceress, which meant she had studied nuances of magic in far greater detail than others had. Glamors had power, but not infinite knowledge. She could surely do what she said. He could spare Monochrome the sickening experience if he took her place. He had on occasion possessed female golems, just for the experience. Once he and Gale had both taken opposite genders, and had sex with each other, she as the man, he as the woman. It had been weird but extremely intriguing.

Wouldn't it be a payback to the Male Spirit to have him make out unknowingly with a male! Meanwhile the endangered people would be saved. *Is she willing?*

There was a pause while the sorceress queried the Mistress. *Negation, with reluctance. She can't stand him, but is not willing to leave it to you.*

This perplexed him. *Question?*

Two reasons, Monochrome thought directly to him. *One is that my body, like my mind, is largely private; I prefer to keep some secrets. The other is that I can handle it better.*

Doubt!

She smiled mentally. She was getting better at telepathy. *You may watch and feel, if you wish. You may not govern.*

That was, it seemed, it. *Reluctant agreement.*

Then join me, Havoc. You may leave me at any time you need to.

She thought he would not be able to handle it. He resented the implication, but accepted the half loaf she offered. *Joining.*

Then his position changed. He was looking out from Monochrome's body. He could feel the pliable softness of it throughout, masking its underlying health and toughness. He glanced down and saw her gently heaving breasts. He was in possession.

Negation, as you would put it, she thought. *You merely share and observe. Welcome to that much, beloved.*

He looked across to his own body. There he stood, looking somehow not quite himself. That was hardly surprising; his main attention was elsewhere, so his body was merely marking time.

"Decision time," the Spirit said.

Havoc felt Monochrome put on an expression of resignation and walk toward the man. At least she did not have to pretend to like it. "Do what you will," she said with her dulcet voice. So far the Spirit had shown no sign of picking up on telepathy or related magic. It had been new to Monochrome, so appeared to be something that hadn't been developed on Earth. That was probably because Science magic lacked it.

"Okay, honey," the Spirit said. He swept her into his embrace. "Remember, one false move and all the natives die."

"I know your nature," she said sweetly. "I detest it."

"Exactly. Now pucker up, sweetheart." The Spirit planted a fierce hot kiss on Monochrome's helpless face.

Havoc rode with it, feeling her dismay. Her body yielded almost automatically; only the conscious decisions had to be governed. Havoc didn't like the lip-flattening force of the kiss, but of course the victim was not intended to. He hoped he himself never kissed a woman that way.

The Spirit pinched the bottom. It was no token effort; it was a brutal crunch that hurt. "You have a problem with that?" the man demanded.

"I do," Monochrome said carefully. Had Havoc responded, it might have been with a punch to the groin.

"I'm going to hit you in the face. If you dodge, you lose." The man drew back his fist, giving her time to balk.

Havoc tensed, but Monochrome waited. The blow came, and she did not turn her face. The force of it knocked the body to the ground. But it was a tough body, buttressed by magic healing power, so there was no actual damage.

"That's the thing about you," the Spirit said with satisfaction. "I can't actually hurt you. A regular woman would get bruised; you can take it." He kicked the body in the hip.

"Better this than your love," she murmured.

"Damn!" The man was nettled, knowing it was the truth. Monochrome *would* rather have his abuse than his affection.

Meanwhile Havoc was finding the perspective intriguing. With golems there had been no question of bodily abuse, and it was not something either Havoc or Gale had had any interest in. Yet he knew that some men did get their jollies from hurting women. If he had not already been certain that the female Earth Spirit aspect was nicer than the male aspect, this would have been persuasive. What kind of masculinity was it to be cruel to one's partner?

"But there are other ways to hurt, tough bitch," the man said. "Do you like it in the ass?"

"No." Actually Monochrome could handle sex any and every way, but that was hardly the point.

"Well bend over, honey," the Spirit said with satisfaction.

Monochrome bent the body over. But when the man took hold of the hips and wedged his member at the crevice, there was a shift in the footing as a wave passed. The position changed slightly, the member just missed, and the penetration was of the normal avenue. It could have been coincidence. More likely it was Havoc's jolt of mental energy that had made the woman jump.

"Damn!" But the Spirit accepted the placement, thrusting repeatedly. His member distended the channel, and the male groin slammed up against the female bottom.

So this was what it felt like from the woman's perspective. It really wasn't as exciting as it was for the man. It was just motion.

Just as the orgasm came upon the Spirit, a crazed fish snapped at the female toes. The body jumped away, leaving the man's member to spurt into the air.

"Bitch!" he yelled. "You're balking me!"

Havoc controlled a smile. The jump could have been coincidental. Who could prove that the fish was a projected illusion, and the jump sponsored by another burst of mental energy?

"That does it," the man said. "I'm boiling the natives."

The hot water began to move again.

That is enough, Havoc; let me do my job. Then, to the Male Spirit, she turned a pleading face. "Please, Spirit, I made a mistake. Let me make it up to you."

The water paused. "How so, bitch?"

"I will restore you, so you can resume what you lost." She put her arms around his torso, kissing his belly. She bore him back and down so that she was straddling him. Then she turned, her posterior at his face while her tongue licked his belly, moving toward his spent member.

Havoc was disgusted. She was giving the foul thing the ultimate sex. But he knew it was his own fault; he had interfered, so that now she had to try twice as hard. She was no longer tolerating the Spirit's efforts, she was facilitating them. Indeed, Havoc should have left well enough alone.

The man's member began to stir as the woman's tongue circled around to it and tickled its side. He gazed into her open cleft. He ran a finger along the channel, then poked it experimentally into her vagina. He pushed another finger into her exposed rectum. He slid both fingers in as deep as they would go. She did not flinch; instead she took his member into her mouth and sucked on it. It was rapidly returning to full erection.

Havoc had to concede that she had been correct: she was handling this better than he could have. Straight sex, even brutal sex, could be relatively impersonal. But this was more intimate. This was her apology for the mishaps Havoc had caused. The Spirit liked playing with her, because of what she was, and because he had her at a disadvantage. She had been forced to cater to his tastes. Because of Havoc.

"Damn!" This time it was Havoc's curse.

The man bucked, suffering his second climax, stronger than the first. His penis pulsed and jetted, pulse after pulse. Monochrome took the discharge in her mouth, swallowing the ejaculate, drawing all of it from him. She had given him back what he lost the first time.

But the Spirit was hardly done. He rolled her over, pinned her down, and put his mouth to her vulva. He licked and squeezed with his lips, and ran his tongue into her cavity. What was he up to, since he had already had his joy of her?

Then Havoc, attuned to her mind and feeling, caught on: the Spirit wanted to make her climax too. She did not want to—not with him. So it was another way to humiliate her: to make her give up her own unwilling orgasm.

She fought it, silently, but the man was competent. He knew how to make a woman respond when he chose to. Slowly the sensation increased as the urge strengthened. He ran his fingers back into her vagina and anus as he tickled her clitoris with his tongue, working it expertly. She gritted her teeth, no longer concealing her determination to avoid the denouement. She could not resist actively, only passively, or the tacit covenant between them would be broken. The Spirit liked fighting her, forcing her to respond against her will. He pursed his mouth around the button and sucked as his tongue continued its titillation. Just as she had done with his member.

And finally the urgency became too great. Monochrome made a closed-mouth scream of protest as her genital launched into its climax. Her thighs clamped on the man's head as her hips bucked. Havoc, attuned, felt her vagina and anus clenching on the embedded fingers. She was in the throes of it, carried away by the forced ecstasy of orgasm. "Damn!" This time she was the one who spoke the word. Her disgust knew no bounds.

Havoc, reading her climax, felt his own genital responding. Her pulses became his, and he jetted on the ground without touching his member. He was similarly disgusted. It was as though the malign Spirit had had sex with him, too, and made him like it.

"Gotcha, bitch honey," the man said with satisfaction. And dissolved into water, which flowed away.

His timing was perfect. The others had finally tamed the wild magic, and the Spirit's power here was fading.

They had won the site, thanks to the way Monochrome had distracted the Male Spirit. But the Spirit had had his will of her in more than one way.

"I feel unclean," she said as Havoc joined her.

He knew. "But you did save the people. All of them survive."

"I wish I could have done it some other way."

"So do I. I shouldn't have interfered."

"Don't apologize. He was bound to do it to me regardless. He knows as much about his kind of sex as I do about mine."

"I prefer yours."

"Appreciation," she said, smiling. Then she put her face to his shoulder and wept.

They had won the site, but the Male Spirit had had his satisfactions. It was a token win in what might be a losing game.

"Pyrrhic victory," Monochrome murmured. "The male aspect is still gaining on me, using my nature against me. I fear the outcome."

"We are not yet done," Havoc said. But he was concerned; how long would Voila pursue this course? For she was the one directing their effort, following the path of most likely victory. The malign Spirit was no easy mark, and if he gained control of too much of Earth they would not be able to stop him. He had the home-planet advantage.

Chapter 18
Mutiny

"I need to relax," Flame said tersely.

"Of course," Fifth said immediately. "You have done a phenomenal amount. I will protect your privacy while you rest."

"I said, I need to relax," she said, stepping into him.

He paused, bemused. "Question?"

"Emotionally. Do me."

"Enthusiasm!" He was instantly all over her, stripping away their clothing, and she yielded like an innocently obliging maiden. Which was the thing: Fifth knew her Glamor and Amazon nature, and hardly cared; he loved her for her thin body.

"Slender," he said, knowing her thought. "But I am coming to appreciate your other qualities too."

"I love being loved for my body."

"Confirmation: it is why your mother sent me to you."

"After trying you out herself," she retorted darkly. But she couldn't hold her frown, and laughed as he tickled her bottom. He was coming to know her little weaknesses.

He kissed her mouth and breasts, stroked her belly and bottom, and penetrated her without hesitation, not pausing or inquiring to ascertain how she was reacting. He was treating her exactly like a woman he expected to cater to his desire without regard for her own, knowing that she was more than capable of achieving her own whenever she wished. He also knew she could kill him with a touch of her fingers, and that she could do magic he could never aspire to. He didn't care. She was his ideal figure of a woman, and sex with her was his notion of paradise. *That* was what turned her on. His sheer adoration of her form. He could never get enough of it. Only one other man had ever felt that way.

Then something nibbled at the fringe of her awareness. She checked, mentally, exploring the near-future paths, and discovered an approaching complex of matters. There was a crisis coming that would require precise and strong action by herself and her siblings, and she would be encountering that other man again.

Fifth was in the throes of his climax, but he sensed her partial distraction. "Problem?" he gasped.

"Finish first." Her climax had been delayed by her future awareness, but now she went into it with a will, clenching around his member as the last surges came. That had the effect of extending his own pleasure, and hers.

Then they lay beside each other on the bed they had somehow landed on. He cupped one small breast with a hand, appreciating it even after he was spent, and waited for her explanation as his thumb stroked the nipple. She loved that too: that for him small was beautiful and evocative.

"You know I can fathom the future," she said. She didn't have to keep secrets from him, knowing he would both understand and not tell. That was another aspect of her pleasure. She could afford to trust him.

"Affirmation."

"I had a lover before you. I see him again in my near future. I will seduce him for securing my mission, but I will enjoy it too. Does that make you jealous?"

He laughed. "Affirmation. But I know the way of it. No fault."

"No fault," she agreed. "And I appreciate your jealousy. It's not no fault with you."

"Agreement. I love you."

"And I love your love, and may come to love you too. As yet I can't afford it, lest you be used against me."

"I will never turn against you."

"Knowledge," she agreed, stroking his head fondly. "But if the enemy captured you, you might be tortured to make me capitulate."

"Do not love me," he agreed. "Yet."

"Now I must meet with my siblings. You may do what you wish with my body during my absence."

He was intrigued, as this was a male fantasy: sex with a sleeping woman. His limp penis stirred. "But without your awareness, it would be rape."

She smiled. "Negation. I am asking you to do it. Parting."

"Parting," he agreed, kissing her breast. She knew it would take him a while to recover sufficient potency, but he would enjoy stoking it with her inert body. She was sorry she would not be able to see and feel his second arousal. But she had to put business before pleasure. She disappeared into the trance state.

She joined the others in an imaginary castle the siblings had long ago crafted for just such meetings. All of them were elsewhere, their bodies resting while their minds roamed. It was a way for them to consult without letting others know unless they were told.

"Envy," Voila said. She was sitting in a chair made of shaped diamond.

"You were Peeking!"

"Oh, let the poor child get her voyeuristic thrill," Weft said. She was sitting on a pile of soft translucent pillows that showed off her plush body to excellent effect. "It's the only way she can learn what it's all about."

"Then let her Peek at your animalistic copulations as you breed with the virile bulls."

"She does. But it requires more art to accomplish when you are lean cuisine. We never thought you'd have it in you."

"Girls, girls," Warp said from his block of stone. "You can Peek at my conquests if you really want to see how it's done."

Weft threw a pillow at him, but it dissipated into vapor before getting there.

"Appreciation for your assembly-line penile efficiency, warp-speed."

"Marionette just makes you look good," Flame said, setting into her own spare hammock. "She could make a carrot look virile."

"I have merged with Mino and Idyll to fathom the intermediate future now coming into view," Voila said, bringing the meeting to business. "The Male Spirit is going to win back Earth. We need to plan around that."

"Poor Monochrome," Weft said. "Details?"

"His present strategy is effective: generate enough disruption at the Chroma zones to force a breakdown of government and resulting chaos in the larger Science zone. In due course the balance will tip his way. We made it feasible, unwittingly."

"And we owe it to her to return the planet to her," Warp said. "And not just because she's one luscious piece of flesh."

"She's fifty, and Dad's mistress," Weft snapped. "Not for you, lover boy."

"The Mistresses are anybody's lovers," he said. "If her business ever brings her to me—"

"Is there a way through?" Flame asked.

"Even chance," Voila said. "Devious course. If any of us foul up, we'll lose it."

"How so, when we can fathom the future and the malign Male Spirit can't?" Warp demanded.

"This is his home planet."

"Home field advantage," Weft said. "We're not used to that."

"But when he takes power, then can't we foment disruption to mess up his rule, and win it back for Monochrome?"

"Negation," Voila said. "She will not employ tactics that would hurt innocent people. Not even to recover power. That gives him the advantage."

"So we can't either, in support of her," Weft said. "This becomes difficult."

"But there is a path," Flame said. It was a question.

"There is a path—if we can find it," Voila agreed.

"Then let's get traveling," Warp said.

Voila nodded. "You will go to the remnant loyal fleet, which is about to be overwhelmed by the mutinous main fleet." She turned to Flame. "You will take Ine to that main fleet, before the mutiny occurs, and null it as you did before."

"But we can't pull the same trick a second time," Warp protested. "They'll be alert."

"Not the newly-empowered personnel. There is a path."

"I'm on it," Flame said, now understanding how she would be interacting again with Grumble. He must have been transferred to a ship of the main fleet.

"I will be in touch," Voila agreed. She was of course the unquestioned leader and strategist, however they might tease her about her age and seeming innocence. Those two qualities were fiction protecting her identity as the key player in this war. It was vital that no outsider suspect her real nature and power. Havoc called her the hidden ace—hidden out in the open.

"Parting, all." Flame left the conclave.

Her awareness returned to her body. Fifth was avidly kissing her genital region. He hadn't yet finished! So she remained still, appreciating her chance to participate after all. She could enjoy his unlimited appreciation of her body. It was just so good to have an attentive lover, after being the wallflower of the family. She would not have traded being an Amazon or a Glamor, but this was the aspect of her life she had most missed. Now it was complete.

Her body was reacting, as it was designed to. She let herself progress to orgasm as he licked her vulva. She was half surprised that this was what he chose to do in her mental absence; obviously it was for himself rather than her, as he believed she had no present consciousness of what her body was doing. It really did turn him on to turn her on. That was a minor revelation.

Her breathing quickened as the climax took her. Now Fifth moved quickly to put his stiffened member into her vagina. Once in, he rolled them over so she was on top. He did not thrust; he simply held the rod there at full depth as her joy of fulfillment surrounded him. That quickly brought him off; she felt him jetting. And that, it seemed, was the whole of his secret ambition.

She was charmed. She loved being able to do that for him. Maybe some time they could do it with her playing dead, to get the same effect while she savored it throughout.

"Oh, Flame, Flame, I love you," he whispered, kissing her ear. "I love that you did this for me, that you trusted me with your body. I love everything about you! Indeed it is not no fault. Not for me. For you, maybe; I must live with that. But I'll always love you regardless."

She was overhearing his secret passion. She felt guilty, but also thrilled.

But it was time for her to "wake." She tensed her body slightly, and changed her pattern of breathing, as though resuming possession. Then she opened her eyes. "Greeting."

"Acknowledged," he said.

"I find you in me. Was it good for you?"

"Superlative. Thank you for letting me."

"Letting you what?" For if he told her, she would not have to feign ignorance.

He told her. Everything except his concluding words.

"Next time, do it while I am present," she said. "I will be a play doll. It sounds like fun."

"It is extraordinary fun, for me. You might be bored."

"Let's find out, when." She kissed him. "Then we can try it with you being the doll."

That startled him, but he rallied. "Acquiescence."

"I must go on my mission to the fleet. You know what I will be doing, in part. Be as jealous as you want; I want you wanting me. And if some girl seeks no fault with you, oblige her; it will make me fell less guilty."

He smiled, not speaking. She knew he wouldn't, but at least she had expressed her own regret. She did feel guilty, because she did still care for Grumble; it was for the sharing of her emotion rather than her body.

In due course she collected Ine and they set up to visit the fleet. The mutiny had not yet occurred, so security was nominal. Flame's own magic clairvoyance coupled with her vision of the paths of the immediate future sufficed to identify the crewman she needed to replace.

But first she had to see to Ine. They went at night to the spaceport supply warehouse, mess depot, and infiltrated it, again depending on Flame's Glamor powers of awareness. There were guards; they avoided them by being exactly where they weren't. There were confusing by-paths; Flame could tell which one was correct. It made it seem like chance; it was not. There were many wrong courses and a few right ones, for their purpose; they followed the few.

They found the freezer where bales of meat substitute were stored. The stuff had the flavor, consistency, and nourishment of meat, but was derived from cultured fungi. The reconstitution machines could make it into almost any meat dish. Farm ships could grow the fungal strains in space, but warships were too lean in that respect and needed to be supplied. Thus the warehouse.

Ine used spot magic to form a temperature shield around herself, making her seem frozen. Then she climbed into the container they emptied, curled up, and Flame sealed her in. She could endure for twelve hours in her pseudococoon; then Flame would have to release her, or she would die.

"Trust," Ine said, smiling invisibly. Flame could penetrate the illusion of invisibility, and smiled back reassuringly. She shoved the container into the stack and departed just before the transport crew arrived.

The first part of their mission had been accomplished, but one key detail nagged her: her sight of the future paths did not show how Sorceress Ine was going to be released. Flame could find no avenue where she went and did it, yet the indication was that it would be done. She did not like such vagueness; vagueness could lead to mischief. Voila could have fathomed it, but Flame had to endure with some obscure paths. It was like walking in darkness: fraught with alarm.

Now she went to the man she had to replace. He was about her height and build, by no coincidence; small for a man, large for a woman. He was returning from planet leave. His name was Thimble, because he was assigned to spot uniform repair. It was a lowly task, but he was good at it.

This contact had several paths, none leading to trouble. She selected the most certain ones. Short as they were, some were more interesting that others.

The man got off the rail transport and cut through an alley, bound for the shuttle pickup at midnight. Flame intercepted him there, when no others would pass within ten minutes. "Thimble," she said.

He paused. "Who are you?"

"I bring reassignment orders for you," she said, showing him a paper.

"Don't give me that! They don't do reassignments in alleys. Get out of my way."

"Please." She stepped into him and kissed him.

He was trying to resist her sudden, unexpected move, but the kiss froze him in place. It was contact that provided an avenue for an intense burst of persuasion. Suddenly he believed that the orders were valid, and that she was a legitimate courier for them. He was also temporarily smitten with her; that was a side effect.

"You're a woman," he said, doubly surprised.

"I am. I need your uniform. You can have mine."

"But—"

She kissed him again. After that he meekly removed his clothing, item by item, and gave it to her. She removed her own clothing at the same time.

For a moment they stood naked, facing each other. Flame didn't have to do it, but she felt guilty for the mischief she was causing this innocent man. She had some leeway; the paths ranged from straight to interestingly curved. She decided to give him something nice to remember as a consolation gift. She used illusion to enhance her breasts and hips. "Take me quickly, and go," she said.

Thimble's penis rose rapidly. Men were very quick to get the idea when sex was offered by even moderately attractive women. He took her in his arms. She lifted one leg high, reached down, and guided his member to the spot as she caused her internal lubricant to flow. He pushed and it slid smoothly in. She put her hands on his buttocks and drew him up close, squeezing internally as he penetrated the tight slick avenue. Her breasts not only looked much larger, they felt larger; it was touch and sight illusion. Her face also looked and felt more petite or cute.

It was like lighting a sparkler. He jetted immediately, gasping with the urgency of it. Flame had no climax herself, but was highly satisfied: she was successfully using sex on the spur, the way Weft could. She loved being sexually competent.

"You will forget the details of my appearance and how I approached you," she said as she kissed him again. Actually her details were not her real ones, thanks to the illusion; no one would be looking for a lean woman. "You will remember this pleasure you have had of me. Thank you for what you are doing for me."

"Thank *you!*" he exclaimed.

She gave him one more milking squeeze and separated. "Dress. Depart."

He did so, in her former clothing, holding the bogus orders. He would return home, having another week of leave time, then report for reassignment. Then the fat would hit the fan. But the authorities would know he had been an innocent victim; the orders looked authoritative. There would be a hassle, but he would not be punished.

She spot-cleaned and dressed carefully in his uniform, which fit her reasonably well. She adjusted her hair and expression, assuming a masculine mien. With the hat covering part of her face, she looked approximately like Thimble. Then she walked in the direction Thimble had been going, just before the next man came through the short-cut alley. She had cut it close, but not too close, thanks to her larger awareness.

The sergeant stood by the shuttle entrance, checking off arrivals. "About time, Thimble; get your ass in there." Then he did a double-take as he got a better glimpse of her face. "Hey, you're not—"

She kissed him, delivering a jolt of persuasion. The sergeant's objection faded; he was satisfied she was the right man, though it had been a very female kiss. By the time he figured out that something was wrong, she would be on the lead ship of the fleet, and there would be no point in advertising his mistake.

The shuttle flight was routine, and soon they debouched to the fleet flagship. Fleet Mistress Morsel was there to welcome the men back, kissing each on the cheek. Flame had not counted on this; it was a detail she had neglected while focusing on the larger picture. It was also the beginning of the vagueness of the paths.

The Mistress knew instantly that Flame was neither Thimble nor a man. She took Flame's hand and silently led her to a private chamber. The Mistresses did such things, sometimes selecting privileged men for spot liaisons. No one ever objected. "Who are you, and why do you intrude?" she inquired gently.

Flame could not tell the truth, lest there be Science listening devices. But neither could she lie to this perceptive woman. "I am a friend, and loyal," she said. "I ask you to believe me, and let me be."

"You are also Warp's sister," Morsel said. "I have a certain fond memory of him. Therefore I accede."

She knew! She must have reviewed the files, for they had not met before. "Appreciation."

"Do you need help?"

The paths remained scrambled, but her clairvoyance indicated this was correct. "I need to room with Grumble, anonymously."

Morsel smiled. "He will love that. He loves you."

"No fault."

"He understands. I will take you there."

"Appreciation," she repeated, half-bemused.

"We do have it, a little bit. Not to the extent you do, but enough to bring me to you and to respect your privacy."

The Mistresses had clairvoyance and/or near-future seeing? That would explain much. It also clarified what had been cloudy. The paths were seldom clear when affected by more than one person who perceived them. "Favor."

"Touch my mind."

Flame projected the need to release Ine from the meat locker. The Mistress nodded. That was all, but now Flame knew it would be done. She had an unexpected ally.

"It will be difficult," Flame murmured.

"I know." Again, no more needed to be said. Any later review of the Science recordings would not clarify the real nature of the exchange.

Morsel conducted her to the correct chamber. "You have suffered an involuntary change of roommates," she informed Grumble. "Bear with it." She departed.

Grumble had just been napping on his off shift. He stood to meet the new man. His mouth fell open.

"It remains no fault," Flame reminded him. Then she kissed him, and it proceeded rapidly to sex on the bed.

He put his lips to her ear, kissing her repeatedly. His passion was unfeigned. "Why?" he whispered. "I thought never to see you again, Princess."

She took her turn at his ear. "You are safer not knowing." Then she lifted her head and spoke aloud. "I just had to have you again, lover. No fault."

"No fault," he echoed. "But if I had my preference—"

She put a finger to his lips. "I am using you for my own purpose. Sex merely assures your acquiescence. You know that."

"And can't resist," he agreed.

Flame became Crewman Thimble, serving on his shift, repairing damaged uniforms. The few who knew Thimble personally and noticed were deflected by her spot mental reassurances. Nothing had changed, externally, and of course Grumble was not about to reveal that his male roommate had become female. Meanwhile she focused on every crewman she encountered, checking him or her off against her mental list of the ship's complement. She also wove tiny wires into the patches she made in their uniforms. She studied every by-path of the ship's passages, either physically or by clairvoyance, making sure her mental map was exact. She needed to be able to navigate without hesitation or error in complete darkness. Several days passed.

Then something happened. There was an accident that blew out a compartment and cost several lives. The resulting alarm of the crewmen and savage reaction by investigating officers generated an atmosphere of angry tension. Flame had known it was coming, but had let it be, for several reasons. One was that she would attract attention and suspicion to herself if she revealed her knowledge of it. Another was that if this trigger was defused, the male spirit would simply seek another, and this was the one Flame had prepared for. The issue had to be settled now, when she was best prepared.

For in that atmosphere a subtle shift occurred. Flame was in bed with Grumble when it happened, and they both felt it. Something empowered him and diminished her, not physically, not intellectually, not even significantly, but in background attitude.

It was the takeover by the Male Spirit, who had seized the opportunity presented by the disruption of the accident. Voila had seen this coming long before the others did, and sent Flame to handle it.

"What is it?" Grumble whispered in her ear.

"The fleet is under new management," she whispered back. "You must serve it. I must depart." She kissed him, then got up, dressed, and left. She was necessarily on her own now.

Grumble did not question it. He proceeded with his routine, as if nothing had happened.

Flame was in the hall when the announcement came. "Now hear this. The mistress has been confined for misbehavior. Admiral Vitality is now the final fleet authority. That is all."

That was hardly all, but it was as much as the grunts were entitled to know. The mutiny had occurred, and the Earth fleet was in enemy possession. It was Flame's job to nullify it until it reverted.

Rather, it was Ine's job. Flame was here to protect Ine, once the sorceress's mischief was discovered.

Under the Admiral's command, the fleet set course for Earth. The shuttle had reached the flagship in a few hours, but the majority of the fleet was in toward Venus, with scattered ships farther out. It did not turn on a dime, as the saying went. It required several days for the formation to assemble near Earth.

Meanwhile, Mistress Morsel was confined to her chambers, incommunicado. If any of the crew objected, they kept quiet, because protest could be interpreted as mutiny, ironically.

There was one more preparatory move. Ine had done her part, and now had to be gotten safely out of the way, for only a Glamor could survive what was coming. Flame rendered herself invisible and visited Morsel. The mistress was now on call for particular senior officers, used as a reward for their loyalty to the new order. She served them well, as it was her nature, if not her desire. At the moment she was between trysts, sitting at her desk, meditating.

"I am talking to myself," Morsel remarked. "For if I were to talk to any person not on the admiral's list, both of us could be executed for de facto treason, ironic as that may seem. But I believe I can safely pretend."

So she was aware of Flame, who remained invisible and blank to machine sensors, and was warning her. Flame was of course already well aware of the situation, but she appreciated the gesture.

Favor, she projected.

"And what would any person want of me at this time, other than obliging sex?" the Mistress inquired rhetorically.

Ine needs a place to hide, where she need not fear betrayal. I am about to be busy elsewhere. That was an understatement.

"Though I might wish to have compatible company of the mind as well as of the body."

Appreciation. Flame went to fetch the sorceress. Her awareness indicated that there would be no suspicion that the mistress had invisible company.

The fleet gathered and oriented on Earth. There was nothing near the planet other than five small shuttle ships in orbit. The flagship broadcast an ultimatum: "Mistress Monochrome, heed this. You have 48 hours to recognize the authority of the Male Spirit, abdicate your post and present yourself for arrest by the Fleet Authority. Thereafter we commence bombing sites of our choice, beginning with the capital of Antarctica. Acknowledge."

The Male Spirit didn't mince words, it seemed. He had captured the weapon he needed to force Earth to capitulate. Or so he thought.

Flame, hiding invisibly where she could watch a communication screen, smiled grimly. Things were about to become quite interesting.

Warp's face appeared on the screen. "This is Warp, speaking for the defense fleet. Admiral, your ultimatum is unenforceable. Retract it and surrender your person and authority to our justice within the hour, or be cited for treason."

The admiral's jaw dropped at this temerity. "*What* defense fleet?"

"These stalwart ships of space," Warp retorted. "They are armed, but we do not wish to harm you if that can be avoided. The Mistress of Mistresses much prefers peaceful settlement."

"Preposterous!"

But Flame knew what the admiral did not: among those paltry little ships was Mino, disguised as a shuttle. Mino alone could take out the entire Earth fleet. Mino would not, because violence was not Mistress Monochrome's way, but the power was not where the Admiral thought.

Warp smiled. "I have presented the message of the Mistress of Mistresses. Now I will speak for myself. We are trying to make nice, you pompous turd, but if you call our bluff you will regret it. I suggest that you not wait any hour before testing our strength, so that you will be satisfied you have lost and will surrender on schedule. That way you can avoid being tried for mutiny."

Flame also smiled. Warp was deliberately goading the admiral. Warp was good at that sort of thing. He wanted the admiral to lose his temper and try to fire at the defensive fleetlet. That would justify a token response. It was a trap. And Flame was part of it.

The admiral sputtered without getting any coherent words out. Then he cut the connection.

Yes, it was definitely time for action. Flame was ready. She was guarding the fire control section of the ship, which also controlled the weapons of the rest of the fleet. It was another master/slave circuit that Ine had pied.

It did not take long for the admiral to act. The order came on closed circuit to the firing center: "Take out that ship!" Flame was attuned to it, so heard it as a voice though it was actually a coded series of specific commands.

Nothing happened.

"Did you hear me?" the admiral demanded. "Take it out!"

"Sir," the chief gunnery officer replied belatedly. "There seems to be a problem. The guns won't fire."

"What?"

"They seem to be inoperative, sir. We are trying to run down the error."

They did. It was of course the master control, locked on OFF. It would require a special trained team to reset it. The ship had such a team, having learned something from the prior mischief Ine had wrought. But it was hands-on work: they had to have access to the key chamber.

Flame was here to prevent that access. As long as the master control was locked, the fleet was offensively helpless.

A crewman approached the chamber. Flame intercepted him. She was now in full Amazon outfit, no longer concealing her gender or nature. "Access is barred, Torque," she said.

The man stopped, taken aback by more than one thing. "Who are you?"

"I am Flame, King Havoc's daughter, Glamor Amazon from Colony planet Charm."

"I never heard of you. How do you know me?"

"I know all the crewfolk of the flagship. Torque, you're a decent mechanic. I don't want to hurt you. Go away and spread the word that this chamber is barred from access."

"I can't do that, miss. I have a job to do. I have to check for a mechanical failure in the firing room." He made as if to pass her.

She moved to block his way. "There are two ways we can do this, Torque. I can kiss you or I can kill you. Either way, you won't reach that room."

Torque was a solid, muscular man. He didn't take her threat seriously. "Forget it, miss. Out of my way." This time he put out a hand to move her clear.

She took that hand, twisted, and levered him to the floor. Her knife was at his throat. "Reconsider?"

He stared up at her. "Yeah."

She put her face down and kissed him on the mouth, delivering a jolt of conviction. Then she got clear of him.

He got back to his feet, looking somewhat stunned. "I wish you were my roommate!"

She smiled. "The compulsion has that effect. Now depart."

He nodded, turned about, and departed.

One down. Any number to go. This first had really been preparatory; now it would get complicated.

She turned invisible. It was one of the skills she and her siblings had practiced, knowing it would be needed. Neither the human eye nor the Science machine eye could detect her, except by the objects she affected. Machines were very fast trackers, so she had to be careful. Clairvoyance alone wasn't enough, and neither were the near-future paths; she had to use judgment as well. There were so many paths branching from this point that she could not fathom them all, and some were extremely brief. It was like navigating a garden of nettles: some were bound to stick her.

A troop of six men came down the passage, carrying blasters. Flame knew they were under orders not to pause or try to negotiate. They were supposed to take her out. But there were some paths that led to their nullification without killing any of them.

She let them pass her niche, then stepped quickly out to touch the last man at the base of the neck. She pressed on key nerves. He collapsed silently. She caught him and dragged him backward into the niche. She took his blaster and turned visible. "Behind you," she said.

The men whirled—and froze, seeing themselves covered by her blaster.

"Set down your weapons," she said calmly.

The sergeant whipped his blaster toward her. She fired, burning his hand. The weapon dropped from his scorched fingers. He stood there staring at her, too tough and proud to cry out in pain.

"Apology for hurting you, Sergeant Manning," she said calmly. "Go to the infirmary to tend to your injury."

"I can't do that!" the sergeant protested.

She stepped up quickly, seizing her window of opportunity, and kissed him. The four others stared, unmoving. "Do it," she said.

Sergeant Manning shook his head dazedly, then marched off. She turned to the others.

"Form pairs," she said. "Face each other. Tommy, put your cuffs on Billy. Astor, put yours on Donovan." She waited while they did so. "Tommy, put Billy's cuffs on Astor." She waited again. Now only Tommy was free.

"What you going to do," Tommy asked weakly. "Kiss me?"

"Yes." She stepped up and did it. "Now march these men and Scudder to your barracks." Scudder was the one she had rendered unconscious; he was now sitting up dazedly. "Do not come here again, or I will have to hurt you. You know I could have done it already, had I wanted to."

They nodded grimly. She still held the blaster.

"Company, ten-SHUN," Tommy said, and the four others made a small formation. "Forward HARCH!" They marched off.

Unfortunately this was the end of gentleness. Now the admiral would know that only superior force would gain access to the firing room.

Flame moved quickly down the hall, turning invisible as she passed a blank section where the sensors did not quite reach. She did not want a machine to see her do it, for it would relay the image to the ship authorities. Mystery was her main initial asset. She slid the blaster along the floor behind her, as she could not make that invisible to the machine eye.

There was a jet of fire. It caught the blaster. The weapon exploded.

That was the thing about machines: they lacked common sense, and could be fooled by simple tricks.

Then a large machine appeared at the end of the passage. It had a solid front grill inset with blaster nozzles. A similar machine trundled from the other end of the passage. She was trapped between them, and they didn't need to sense her; they would destroy anything that was there.

But she had studied these machines too. Invisible, she ran to one, leaped up on its grill, and climbed to its top, which was about a foot below the hall ceiling. She stretched out on that top, taking a ride. When it passed the alcove she slid down to the side, letting the machine leave her behind.

Meanwhile her mind was ranging out, tracing down the airborne currents that guided the machines. They were operated by human people. She found one, and sent a hard thought to his mind.

The machine accelerated forward, and crashed into the other machine head-on. Both came to a stop, broken.

And the passage was effectively blocked. That closed off one avenue to the firing room Now there was only one route to reach it, and that was easier to defend.

She remained invisible as she made her way to that passage. Already another person was coming.

The paths shifted, veering in a new direction. This one was a woman! Of course there were women on the crew as well as men, and they made choice roommates for men. But why would the male spirit send a woman?

The woman stopped. "Amazon! Do you know me?"

There were diverging paths here. This was a trap, baited by the woman. Flame could avoid it, but preferred not to show the extent of her magical ability. She also needed to use up some time, so that the deadline would loom closer. So she stepped into it.

She moved to a spot not covered by the machine sensors and became visible, behind the woman. "Angela," she said.

The woman whirled. "You're dangerous!"

"True. And you are deceitful."

"Then we understand each other. What will it take to get you to let us get at the master fire control box?"

"There is no price as long as the Male Spirit controls this fleet. Within half an hour your admiral will surrender the fleet and himself." That was of course the deadline. "When Mistress Morsel resumes authority, the way will be cleared."

"Why do you serve the losing side, Amazon? You know it will lead only to your defeat, brutalization, and repeated raping if you survive. Surrender now, and you will not be beaten, and will be given your choice of rapists."

Flame understood what she meant, but pretended ignorance. "Choice?"

"You will be bound and raped, but you can pick out the first dozen or so men to do it. Some like your lean look, and will be gentle if chosen. We call it compatible subjugation. Some women claim almost to like it."

"This is a masculine notion." But the fact was there was a certain temptation in the notion. What would it be like to be serially raped by men she had selected, some of whom might actually like her? Thorough, helpless sex, the fluids of multiple men overflowing her avenue. There was an insidious appeal hiding behind the outrage of such a process. Not that she would ever admit it.

"The male spirit governs here."

This was becoming too suggestive. It was time to trigger the trap. "Negation."

Suddenly a crowd of a dozen armed women appeared. They charged down the passage, screaming and firing their blasters. Angela threw herself to the floor and lay still, so as not to be hit by accident.

Did they think she would be unable to oppose women? She was no feminist, could they but know her heart.

Flame moved rapidly, dodging the coruscating beams. This was intricate maneuvering, because there was a number of them, but she was aware of the near-future course of each, and placed her body to avoid it. It would seem like freakish luck, which was the way she wanted it. Few Earthers had any real notion of the full powers of Glamors, and it was best that they remain ignorant. Actually she could handle the beams even if they struck her flesh, but that ability, too, was better concealed.

Then the first charging woman arrived. Flame knocked her weapon hand aside and body-checked her, sending her spinning to the side. Already the second was upon her, wielding a wickedly long sharp knife. She evidently knew how to use it, but Flame was more experienced against knives of all kinds than against Science magic guns. She caught the woman's wrist almost gently, pressed at the base of the thumb, and took the knife as the hand went slack. Meanwhile she let the rest of the woman's body go on by, knifeless.

The third woman carried an electric stunner. Flame touched the terminal with the blade of her captured knife and shorted it. There was a spark, and the woman dropped the suddenly heating unit as she stumbled onward.

Now there were women to either side. Flame jammed an elbow into the breastbone of one, making her gasp, and kicked the other in the belly, doubling her over. Then she hunched into a shoulder throw for the next, heaving her onto the two others so that the three went down in a tangle. The following two were unable to stop in time to avoid plowing into the suddenly forming pile of bodies. Close groups were inherently inefficient unless precisely trained. Flame, working alone, had the advantage of not having to watch out for her companions.

Then she encountered two who were properly trained. One fenced with her right arm, the other with her left arm. Nine of ten paths had one or the other catching an arm and holding her for the other to bash. The tenth path had both miss as Flame dodged down and forward, spinning about. That was the path she took. Good training helped, but there was no substitute for seeing the unexpected coincidence coming. She was almost proof against bad luck.

The two women turned together, following up the first attempt—and Flame caught each behind the head and pushed them together so that their heads banged, just hard enough to dissuade them from continuing.

Two women remained. These were more savvy. One lunged for Flame while the other stood back with a laser pistol, waiting for her shot. Again all paths but one were negative, but Flame followed that one. She grabbed the close woman and swung her around as a shield, so that the beam struck her instead of its intended target. The victim made a cry and slumped to the floor, her throat burned.

"So it's true," the final woman said. "You have Seeing."

Oops. That meant this woman had it too, at least to a degree. That was why Flame hadn't seen this coming.

But how good was she? Since Earthers did not believe in magic, they probably had not developed magic abilities far. Flame might be able to overextend the vision of the other.

She focused her mind, planning different and not necessarily reasonable actions. The paths diverged explosively. She took an unlikely one, and focused again. This, too, radiated rapidly.

The woman closed on her, trying to narrow the paths, but she was evidently not familiar with this technique, and was clumsy. Flame selected one that looped back, and suddenly was close behind the woman. She used the blunt hilt of her knife to knock the woman's head, hard enough to fell her.

The spot battle was over. More time had been expended. Flame turned invisible and walked back past the women who were slowly getting back to their feet. She waited by the firing room entry port.

Sure enough, the women saw it unguarded, and went to it. Flame reappeared, whirling her blade. The women changed their minds and retreated down the passage.

Soon one more man appeared. Flame recognized him instantly, though she had not explored this path before. She had been distracted by the engagement with the women. "Grumble!"

"Apology," he said, emulating her Colony style of speech. "This is not my

PIERS ANTHONY

preference."

Now she fathomed it. This was a deadly trap. To stall for time while she considered, she made him describe it. "Question?"

"I am carrying a bomb," he said as he walked slowly toward her. "It will detonate and destroy me, you, and this section of the ship if I cease approaching you, or when I touch you. Unless you say the words to defuse it: 'I, Flame, make my oath to allow immediate entry to the firing room.' They know you will not violate your oath, even if it is made under duress. I can't stall beyond a couple of minutes. You must decide: the oath or our lives, which will have similar effect, opening the access to the firing room."

He was correct: two minutes was the limit. But that was time enough, if she could trust him. "Grumble, which side are you on?"

"Yours. The Mistress'. But my preference doesn't matter. They know you won't want to kill me, even if you are willing to sacrifice your own life for your cause. They know we are lovers. But Flame, I am willing to die. Charge me, set off the bomb while it is still too far from the entry to blow it open. That will balk them."

"Negation. They don't need to blow it open; they have the key. But if we blow the portal, that may destroy the firing control inside, ruining their chance."

He brightened. "Yes! I'll charge you while you retreat toward the door."

"Slowly," she said, smiling grimly.

They moved slowly toward the portal. Now more men came into view, keeping a cautious distance. They thought Flame and Grumble were bluffing, and that they would yield before blowing themselves up.

"Grumble," she said in a low tone. "I have powers beyond what you have seen. Will you trust me?"

"Yes! But you can't touch this bomb."

"I can if I focus all my magic. But that will deprive me of my powers of clairvoyance and seeing the paths of the near future. That's dangerous. We have one minute left. Will you guard me and keep the men at bay while I focus?"

"Yes!" She knew he didn't really believe her, but he wanted to express his support. He loved her, perhaps unwisely.

"Do it," she said, thinking of her father Havoc who had used those two words so many times in the course of his kingship. Her powers as a Glamor had long since surpassed Havoc's and Gale's, as had those of her siblings, especially Voila, but their parents were forever dear to them all.

Grumble drew his weapon. "Stay back, men," he called. "I can shoot at you but you can't shoot at me without setting off the bomb. I want my last minute alone with the woman I love."

The men stayed back, as it could hardly be a bluff.

Flame marshaled her powers of mechanical suppression. She could freeze an object in place without touching it. They had played private competitive games, perfecting this ability, using marbles rolling down inclines and similar items. There had not seemed to be much point in it, but their general awareness of future needs had indicated that it was magic they would need. Now she did.

It was partly clairvoyance, and partly a very narrow future path. It was mostly a force field that closed in on and firmly clasped the object. Flame did not understand the intricate mechanism of the bomb, but knew that something had to move before it could detonate. There was a distance sensor and some kind of timer. She froze both. There was a contact that would be made the moment any other part of the mechanism became inoperative. She froze it all. Now the bomb was armed, eager to detonate, but unable because of the stasis.

Holding it tightly magically, she reached out physically. She took hold of the bomb, holding it her hands. "Release it," she hissed.

Grumble quickly worked the straps that held it to his body. In a moment he had freed it. "It didn't go off," he whispered, half in wonder.

"Not yet," she said tightly. "Get far from here."

"But you're holding the bomb!" he protested.

She did not have the time or concentration to argue with him. "Do it."

"I love you," he repeated. Then he walked away.

She walked toward the other men. They retreated, seeing the bomb. When she had it a safe distance from the portal, she set it down. Then, maintaining the focus, she retreated. Slowly. Her power of suppression diminished with distance. Could she maintain it long enough to get far enough clear?

"It's a bluff!" a man cried. Then they were charging.

Flame flung herself backward, covering her face.

The bomb went off. The blast took out the charging men and blew her down the hall toward the portal and Grumble. Damn! Now the enemy would know that the Glamors were invulnerable. She had wanted to preserve that secret.

"Flame!" Grumble cried, embracing her. "You got far enough clear!"

Maybe that explanation would do. "I did," she agreed. Then she turned in his arms and kissed him. "Appreciation."

"Welcome!" he said, kissing her back, avidly.

Only ten minutes remained in the hour. Flame knew the admiral would be desperate. What ploy would he try next?

Grumble paused. "That portal," he said. "Is it open?"

Flame looked. The explosion had damaged the portal to the firing room, and it might indeed be possible to pull it open and enter. "I must get over there."

"But it's exposed! They could fire a rocket down the passage. Could you withstand that?"

Actually she could, but she preferred not to say so. "I'll guard it from inside. It will be awkward for anyone to pass through that bottleneck."

"I'll go with you."

"Negation. Too dangerous."

"Flame," he said persuasively. "It will be protected and private in there. I won't be seeing you much longer."

She caught on. He wanted sex! Flattered anew that he could think of that even in this battle situation, she acquiesced. She knew it was foolish, but she remained forever thrilled that men could desire her in this manner. Also, this was her first lover; there could never be another first. "Come, then."

They ran to the portal, pulled it open, scrambled through, and drew it closed behind them. It wouldn't lock, but it would be easy to cover it and take out anyone who tried to follow. Ten minutes should pass quickly.

The room was ordinary. A Science computer terminal rested on a desk. That was the one that would, when properly addressed, give the signal to unlock the guns. They would of course leave it alone.

Flame faced the entry portal. "I must remain alert, but you may do as you please." She expected him to slide his hands into her shirt to squeeze her small breasts, then to mount her from behind, standing, so that she could still watch the door with her hands free to go for weapons. There was a certain delight in doing it when in danger. The threat of possible interruption added an edge to sex.

"Give me head," he said.

"Question?" It could hardly be her head he wanted at the moment.

"Blow me." He opened his trousers, letting his erect member spring out.

Now the terms connected. Oral sex, her mouth taking in his penis, as Marionette had done on Warp. It was a legitimate form of sex, and she had done it with Fifth for mutual pleasure. But Grumble had never wanted that before. In fact, he had expressed distaste for it. His oral sex on her he liked, as did she; hers on him, no. It was the way he was. Why the change?

"Unfeasible," she said. "I must watch the door." She would be unable to do that while facing his belly. But her objection was larger than that. It bothered her that Grumble should suddenly want something he had disliked before.

"Now," he said in a peremptory tone.

That too was new. Suspicious, she read his mind—and was appalled. "The malignant Male Spirit!"

"Damn! I forgot you had telepathy. Well, no matter; I'll simply turn on the guns. We'll take out all those ships while they're waiting on the deadline."

She traced it back. The Spirit had infused Grumble at the time his essence took over the fleet. She had not known, because the Male Spirit was a Glamor and no one could spot a hiding Glamor, not even another Glamor. He had emulated Grumble, acting as Grumble would have, deceiving her until his time came to strike. Actually, he had let Grumble have nominal control; Grumble himself had not known that the puppet strings were in place. "Negation."

"Fuck that, sister. We're through playing coy games. There's a war to be won." He stepped toward the console.

She moved immediately to block his way. "Do not make me hurt you." For the spirit might come and go, but Grumble would be left with the body.

"Hurt me," he said dismissively. He pushed her aside and advanced on the console.

She took his pushing hand and applied a pain grip. "Your body is less fit than mine," she said grimly. "You can't prevail physically."

"That so? Digest this, sister: it's your boyfriend you'll hurt, not me. I don't have to feel his pain unless I want to. You'll have to kill him to stop me. Do you have the guts?"

The worst of it was that he was correct. She read the conviction in his mind and knew he wasn't bluffing. The Male Spirit would move the body regardless, without heeding pain, and would animate it like a zombie even if she broke its bones. The thing was merciless. She would have to kill Grumble to stop the Spirit. The paths showed no alternative.

"Forgive me, beloved," she murmured, knowing that Grumble would want it this way.

The spirit sneered. "Got a tender hesitation, sweetheart?"

Then she attacked. She struck at the nerves of the neck and spine, rendering Grumble immediately unconscious. The body did not fall; the Spirit kept it upright and still moving toward the console. She wrapped an arm around the neck, putting lethal pressure on the throat. This cut off the circulation of blood to the brain and interfered with the nervous control of the body. The Spirit continued to struggle, refusing to give up, but could not make headway toward the console.

Flame held the strangle until the systems of the body were entirely disrupted, and it was done for. Dead. Nothing remained for the Spirit to animate. It was gone. She had prevailed. The firing circuits would not be restored as the deadline came. The fleet would have to surrender.

Now she viewed the clairvoyant near future, rather than her own immediate paths. It was clarifying as the significance of her action registered on reality.

The admiral was about to make contact with Warp, agreeing to surrender the fleet and his person to the representatives of the Mistress of Mistresses. He would be removed from his position and retired immediately, but not otherwise punished. He would have one personal request, that would be granted: that the one to convey him to the other ship would be the Air Chroma sorceress Ine, who would entertain him with invisible attention on the way, as she had done when she accompanied Warp to the fleet. Ine had made a considerable impression on the admiral with her demonstration of no fault sex.

The remaining officers of the fleet would be culled according to their degrees of guilt in supporting the mutiny. The men and women of the crews would be judged innocent, as they were merely obeying orders from above.

Mistress Morsel would resume authority, and would guide the new admiral. The fleet would return to its stations around the Solar System, its firing system restored. Nothing much would seem to have changed. The mutiny had been blunted, no real harm done, and all was well.

Flame returned her awareness to the present. Grumble was dead. She had killed him. It had been the only way, but now the grief struck her. This friendly, innocent man, her first lover, dead by her hand. He would never return to his Earthside family and friends. He had been used and abused by the enemy Spirit. She knelt beside the body and wept.

Chapter 19
Battle

Gale was resting between efforts, as there was a pause at the moment. She knew Havoc and Flame had had ugly sieges with the malign Male Spirit, who was proving to be resourceful, forceful, and without conscience. It was not yet clear which side was winning this battle, because the future threads were complicated and sometimes tangled. It was in a sense like a giant game whose outcome was predetermined, but whose resolution could not yet be fathomed by either player.

Gale. It was Idyll Ifrit; she recognized the mind.

Idyll! I did not know you were on Earth!

I am not. I am with Ennui, as an imprint, with Mino in space.

Ennui was in space? More was going on than Gale knew about. *What is your concern?*

There is a significant crisis starting on Earth. You must handle it.

Gale did not inquire why her; it was surely because all the other Glamors were occupied while she was free at the moment. *Information.*

Idyll provided it. The Male Spirit was attempting a kind of flanking effort, striking in an unexpected region. If he succeeded, that change would quickly spread to the rest of the planet, marginalizing the work of the Glamors and giving the Spirit the victory. Gale had to stifle it.

She conjured herself to the site. This was in the continent of Australia, in the north west section, in the middle of the Great Sandy Desert where almost no one lived. It was largely barren, a supremely inhospitable region. But the Female Spirit had found a use for even this spot: there were solar collectors there, taking in the continual bright sunlight, converting it to electric power, and sending that power to the rest of the continent. It was what was termed an environmentally friendly power source.

The village of Sandy was originally a religious community, seeking isolation and privation as an avenue to salvation. That had faded after a century or so, and now it was dedicated to maintaining the solar power collection, for which it received a nominal stipend. There was a regular shuttle to the coastal town of Mandora two hundred miles to the west, and villagers could ride it free. But aside from school trips to see the amazing vast ocean which could freak out some children (not to mention visitors from Charm), and the regulars who handled supplies, it was little used. Sandy was a largely self absorbed community, satisfied with holovision for its outside contact.

Until half an hour ago. Then their Village Elder had sent a panic signal.

Gale teleported herself to the shuttle station, assured that it would be deserted. It was; no one saw her arrive. Then she stepped out and viewed the village. It was a collection of solid brick houses linked by drives leading into the central circle. It was much like a Charm village, which pleased her. She could handle this.

The house of the Village Elder was marked by a bright red flag visible from any part of the settlement. The position, she had learned, was not selected by competence or heredity. It simply went to the oldest member of the community. That guaranteed that there would be no long-lasting tenure leading to possible corruption, and that the Elder would have long experience with the citizens. It did not guarantee that he/she would be fully competent, but presumably there were few crises requiring more than minimal attention.

Her eye was caught by something out on the desert, among the extensive arrays of solar collectors. It was surely a mirage. It looked like a tall fountain of water jetting up from a hole in the sand, spreading and falling to form a puddle and small temporary lake. How could that be, here where water was almost nonexistent? There was a special pumping station whose well extended far down to find the only water available. Had there been a seismic shift that caused deep water to flow up along a fault? No, as she extended her wider awareness she found no such fault. In fact she found no water, either; it was indeed a mirage, and illusion.

Or was it? Now, within it, she discovered an inner core of real water. The illusion exaggerated the effect, but the effect was after all real. Water *was* jetting out of the sand.

Then a man appeared in that water, shrouded by the flow but definitely human. He turned to face her. "Greeting, Gale," he said.

She jumped, startled by the sudden appearance and contact. The man was several miles distant; she had been viewing him clairvoyantly, as her eyes could hardly have made out such distant detail. And he was illusion. He was a construct of her mind, without other reality. But that was just as alarming as a real man would have been. Someone was in telepathic contact with her.

"Acknowledged," she replied.

"Get away from here, Gale," he said. "There is danger."

"Negation on the first, affirmation on the second. I am here to address that danger."

"Fool." The man swelled into some kind of monster, and exploded into vapor. Only the fountain remained.

Gale focused on the village and walked toward the Elder's house. Soon she reached it, and knocked on the old fashioned door.

And old man opened it, mostly wrinkles and leather. His pale eyes widened. "You're not local."

"I am Gale, here to address your problem. You sent an emergency call."

"Then welcome, fair young woman! I am Elder Ottoman. You would not believe what we are seeing."

"A fountain in the sand. A man warning of doom."

He nodded. "So you saw it too. We have heard of magic, but never believed in it. Is this magic?"

"It may be. But there should be no magic here."

"I see you understand the problem," he said approvingly. "Come in, lovely creature, and tell me how to handle it."

She entered his house, which was well kept. Probably a village woman came in to take care of it and the man, who seemed to be about eighty five and not spry. "I must acquaint you with me," she said carefully. "So that you know what I can and can't do. I am a creature of magic. No, no, don't shy away; I am in other respects a normal human woman."

"Not normal," he demurred. "An outstanding beauty. Where were you when I was young and eager?"

She laughed. "I did not exist then. Would you like me to kiss you?"

"Oh, yes."

She stepped up, set her hands on his shoulders, and carefully kissed him on the mouth. She took advantage of that contact to send him some reassurance and acceptance, and some additional strength, as he surely needed it. A pretty woman could do a lot with a man with close contact, and a Glamor could do more.

He blew out a thin whistle as she stepped back. "You do have magic! We must sit down before I get too dizzy."

They sat in opposite chairs, as he had no fancy furniture. Curious as to how well he could see, she crossed her legs, letting a fair amount of thigh show. His pupils dilated. He could see well enough.

"I come from a planet of magic," she said. "To us magic is routine. Science is merely one form of magic. So when I say that what you are seeing here may be magic, I am not being superstitious or fearful. I am assessing the situation realistically."

"Got it, gal," he said, still looking at or beyond her knees. "It doesn't look like science."

"As you may know, a number of volcanoes on Earth have changed color and become magic. There magic has become real. But Sandy is far from any volcano. There should be only Science here, because that is Earth's default."

"We saw about the volcanoes on the holo news," he agreed. "Didn't really believe it. But this we have to believe. Even if it's not real, we have to believe. If this is all that happens, I guess we're okay. But we don't know what's next. That scares us."

"Do you know about the fundamental Earth Spirits?"

"The what?"

"It turns out there are two spirits of the planet. One is the Male Spirit, who governed until about a thousand years ago. He is warlike, violent, and lusty. He brought the world to the brink of extinction. The other is the Female Spirit. She took over at that point, and has governed since. She has restored most of what the male destroyed. Her representative is the Mistress of Mistresses."

"The Mistress!" he exclaimed. "Now it registers. One of them comes by here every few years and really charms the young men. We all love her. I understand she kisses like you do."

"She surely does," Gale agreed. It was a Glamor thing, and the subsidiary mistresses had some of that power. "Your local mistress would have come here to help, but all of them are occupied trying to suppress the masculine tide that is now trying to take over. I need to know: which side do you favor?"

"The mistresses," he said without hesitation. "We all do. They are so lovable, and they run the world better. We haven't had war in centuries. We have a name for the male, you know: he's Satan, the devil. That's who you described."

"The Male Spirit is mounting a determined campaign of disruption, trying to throw the world into such confusion that he can oust the Female Spirit and take over again. He has been active at the volcanoes so far, but now he is attacking here. His purpose is to overwhelm you with magic effects and make you submit to his will. Then you will become warriors on his side."

Ottoman nodded. "How bad will it get?"

"Very bad. This is his chosen breakthrough site. It is like a deadly virus: if you catch it, you will soon spread it to others, and the whole world will be under siege. We need to stop it here."

"We can't stop our eyes from seeing the fountain, or our ears from hearing that man. He'll scare the children, sure."

"We need to protect the children from that."

At that point there was a knock on the door. "Elder!" a woman's voice cried. Gale could hear the desperation in it.

The elder levered himself out of his chair and went to open the door. "Gracie," he said. "And little Tommy."

"He's coming after Tommy," the woman said urgently. "Talking in his little head. His eyes are bugging out of his face! You've got to stop it, Elder."

Gale joined them. "I will stop it." She put down a hand to rest on the boy's head, and exerted calming. The boy relaxed. He had been tightly wound up, terrified.

Gracie saw it, but was canny. "What about when he goes home? It'll come again."

"Agreement," Gale said. "Along with all the other children. We need something better."

The man of the desert appeared. "You sure do, honey. Gimme me another free fuck and I'll let them be until we're done."

"The devil!" the woman exclaimed, crossing herself.

So he was confirming his identity as the Male Spirit. "Negation. We are opposing you."

"I can make you like it, Glamor bitch. Or I can really tear up these kids."

Gale refused to be distracted. "Question: how do you manage illusion magic far from any volcano?"

"I don't have to answer you, heavenly hound, but I will. I am adapting science to my purpose. Mirages are science, nightmares are science, hallucinations are science. Maybe old timers can handle them, but children don't know better. I will have the children."

Gale knew he wasn't bluffing. "We'll stop you."

"You will try," the Spirit agreed. "While the children suffer. Soon their mothers will yield, rather than let it continue." He glanced at Tommy, and the boy suddenly screamed in terror.

Gale put her hand on the boy's head again, and he calmed. She did not need to say anything.

"Ah, but listen," the Spirit said.

Now there was a chorus of screaming from the other houses of the village. He was torturing all the children—too many for Gale to protect. And he was correct: the children were a lever against the parents. This village would soon become his entity. Then the virus of Male Spirit power would spread out, transmitted from child to child and from adult to adult, infecting the world, swinging the balance to his side. She could see it happening; the future paths were remarkably clear.

This was where it had to be stopped.

Idyll! Send the others here.

"Calling for help, she-wolf? It won't be enough."

"Elder!" Gale said. "Assemble all the children in the village center. We will help them."

"Lotsa luck, tailpiece," the Spirit said, fading.

Gale teleported to the village center. Havoc was already there. "Question?"

"I don't know how, but we've got to do it," she said, kissing him. "My future sense suggests that if we can stop it for more than an hour, the Spirit's power will fade and the crisis will be over."

"Confirmation," he agreed. "But there are too many children for us to protect all at once."

"Unless we make a safe zone," she said. "And keep them in it."

"And their parents. This sounds like a story."

"A story!" she agreed. "To distract them long enough."

Warp arrived. "You called, ma?"

"Tell a story to hold the villagers an hour in the safe zone to tide through the siege."

Already the villagers were collecting with their crying children. Word had spread quickly. They expected protection. Could the Glamors deliver?

Flame arrived, with her Black Chroma assistant/lover Fifth. "Apology," she said. "I had no place to park him."

Fifth smiled. "I insisted on helping, if I can," he said. "I can't do any real magic here, but if there is any other way—"

"Confirmation," Warp said. "Lead actor in the play."

"You will narrate?"

"Agreement. Have you any incidental talents?"

"I can dance. I once fancied being an actor, before enlisting in this Earth effort. That's about all."

"He is also a great lover," Flame said.

Warp nodded. "See to the audience."

Fifth got busy directing the villagers to form concentric circles around the center, sitting close in, the children in the center ring, the adults outside them. A story-play presented in the round, viewed from every side. It was a standard audience formation in Charm, but new to these folk. There was some confusion, but Fifth's training for organizing Earthers was paying off.

Soon Weft and Voila arrived. "Focus on the central circle," Voila said. "We can protect it."

Virtually all the villagers were present and seated. The children were quiet; they were within the calm zone the Glamors were making. Gale was aware of the raging unseen battle between the Male Spirit and the Glamors; only the central disk was secure. Could they hold it long enough? Only if they had no trouble from the villagers.

Warp took the center stage. "I am Warp the storyteller. I will show you a story for young folk and old folk. My associates will act the parts. You will see how it works." He glanced down at the smallest children in the front. "Some of it will be beyond you little ones, but you will like the dancing. When you get bored, sleep."

The children laughed. They liked being spoken to directly, now that the terrors were gone.

Warp faced the main audience, turning slowly around in a full circle to face all of them as he spoke. "The main character is Zachary, who is visiting the far away country of Mexico, in America. Maybe some day some of you will visit there." A number of the older villagers smiled. Warp had a way of relating to the audience, evoking its appreciation. That was part of his talent as a master storyteller. Gale was proud of him. But of course she was proud of all her children. And of Havoc, who had helped her raise them.

"Zachary is a dancer," Warp continued. "A good one." His eye caught Fifth's, and Fifth went to the stage and did a small dance step, rotating to face all the audience before completing it. The children smiled; they did like it.

Then Warp plunged into the main narrative, which it seemed he was developing extemporaneously, as it was not one of the standard tales of Charm. Gale hoped he would not foul up; it was difficult to make a good tale from scratch.

"It was sheer bad luck. The week before the big tango dancing contest, Zachary's dancing partner broke her leg in a freak accident. There was no way she could participate. Zak would have to forfeit."

Zachary (Fifth) walked around the stage, emoting disconsolation. He did seem to have some fair acting ability. Gale remained concerned: Warp was catering to Fifth's stated abilities, a nice touch. But could he make a good consistent story on the fly? This was likely to be a severe test of his ability.

"He hated this," Warp continued. "They had made their way to the top rankings, and this was the competition that would determine the championship. They had had an even chance to win, for they were highly polished and compatible as a team despite having no personal interest in each other. It was business—and suddenly that business had collapsed."

Zak spread his hands, pantomiming frustration.

"He was alone in Mexico with no prospects. He didn't even speak the language. What could he do except go home and suffer, his dream gone? Yet somehow he couldn't just quit. For one thing, he had paid his way through the contest. If he left now, that money would be wasted."

Then the verbal magic of the presentation took hold, and Warp the narrator seemed almost to disappear. There was only Zak on the stage, balked and depressed. The narration became Zak's viewpoint.

His motel room was in a satellite village that catered to visiting dancers. At dusk he walked down the central street, encased in a cloud of gloom. He turned down an unfamiliar alley, and soon found himself off the tourist track. Now the town was far more truly native, the bright ads gone. He came to a lighted community center where the natives gathered in their off hours, when they weren't catering to the rich gringo visitors.

(He was approaching the corner of the stage where Havoc, Gale, and the three other Glamors sat, engaged in animated but silent dialogue.)

What the hell? He entered the center. Immediately the folk there paused, recognizing him as a foreign intruder. What could he say? He knew he should depart and leave them to their relaxation.

(The others gazed silently at him, unmoving. He was obviously a stranger, not necessarily unwelcome, but as yet unknown.)

What the hell, again? "I am—dancer," he said. He did a quick individual dance step. There were several smiles; that they understood. "I need—partner."

(Warp paused to select a heavyset woman from the audience. This was another feature of Charm presentations, new to Earth, but in a moment she cooperated.)

A painted, fleshy woman approached, her large breasts rippling. She pointed to her crotch. She was a prostitute.

(The volunteer tried to repress a smile. This was fun despite the negative description.)

"No!" he said. "For dancing."

They gazed blankly at him as the volunteer departed.

"Tango," he said. "Can anyone here do the tango?"

"Cielito," an older woman said. (This was Gale, looking older and severe after a quick adjustment. She did not actually speak; Warp, the narrator, spoke for her, as he had for Fifth throughout.) Obediently a teen girl stood. (This was Weft, her garb and manner made modest.) "Tango."

The girl approached him. She was quite pretty despite not being dressed for dancing. Did she actually know the tango, or was she just another prostitute?

There was one way to find out. He took her hand and led her to the center of the floor. "Tango," he repeated. "Dance." She merely stood there. Was she waiting for the nonexistent music?

So he started on his own, doing the intricate step. The girl smiled—she had a truly lovely smile—and joined him. In a moment she was in his arms, matching him step for step. She did know the tango!

Not only was she competent, she was good. Very good. So good that with her as a partner, and some fine tuning, he might even have a chance in the contest. Could it really happen? (The children, and many of the adults, were enthralled; it was nice dancing.)

"What is your name?" he asked as they paused.

"Cielito Lindo," she replied, evidently knowing that much English. (Again, the narrator spoke for her.)

"Well, Cielito, I want to dance further with you. Take me to your family."

Her mother turned out to be the woman who had first summoned her (Gale). Her father (Havoc) was nearby. After a labored dialogue Zak got through to them that he wanted Cielito for his partner in the big tango contest. About the time he offered money their understanding increased significantly.

Zak wasn't completely clear whether they had agreed to let her dance, or thought he was buying her sexual services for the week. Maybe it didn't matter. He treated her with complete professional courtesy, making it plain that all he wanted of her was the dance.

He took her to his room and danced with her. She was apt, but there were nuances for the competition. He made sure she got them down pat. Her ready comprehension of the motions, if not his words, was a joy; his hopes for the contest increased.

He bought her a suitable dancing outfit. She loved it. She had been good before; now she was outstanding. She was also considerably more than pretty; she was beautiful. The way she moved was a joy to behold. (Weft did transform as she donned the evocative costume, and now all her prettiness showed. The adult men were paying closer attention, especially as she moved.)

The days passed quickly. The night of the competition came. They danced, and her family was there to watch: parents, and two sisters. They clearly approved. Cielito loved to dance, and now was dressed for it, and was doing it perfectly.

There was stiff competition, but they were the best.

(They danced, and now Weft sang the song Cielito Lindo: "Your bright-eyed glance in the sprightly dance lights the shadows, Cielito Lindo!" This aspect she did for herself; there was no way Warp could match her in song. They made an outstanding dancing couple, whirling around the stage, her hair and skirts flinging out, and her flashing smile really did seem to light the region. It was an extended and lovely presentation, a work of art. It showed what ideal dancing could be. The audience, from young to old, was now completely into the story. Every man wished he could dance like that with such a girl; every woman wished she could *be* that girl. Every child wished to grow up to do that.)

They won. Zak was thrilled. It wasn't just the prize money, or the notoriety of the victory. It was Cielito. Despite his intention, he had fallen in love with her.

He approached the matter forthrightly. "Señor Lindo, I wish to marry Cielito and dance with her forever."

The father looked blank, but the older sister, a tall plain woman (Flame), translated for him. Zak hadn't realized that any of them spoke English; this helped.

The father spoke to Cielito. She shook her head. The father spoke again. The sister translated (though the narrator did the talking). "You wish to marry our daughter. We are willing, for you are an excellent dancer and a wealthy man. But she does not wish to marry a gringo, and we cannot force her. The answer is no."

This astonished Zak. Cielito had been such an outstanding partner, melting in his arms, that he had thought she shared his joy of proximity. Certainly what he offered was generous; she could forever escape the life of relative poverty she had suffered. "I don't understand."

Now the plain sister spoke directly. "Cielito is beautiful. All the boys slaver for her. She can have any man she wants. She prefers to play the field a few more years. It is nothing personal, Señor."

So Cielito was as professional in her outlook as Zak was. The dancing was a business for her too. She had gained a fine dress and made herself better known. She had not let her emotions get in the way. Or perhaps Zak simply was not her type.

Mr. Lindo spoke again. "We are sorry," the sister translated. "We will return the dress now."

"No, let her keep the dress," Zak said quickly. "She earned it." He departed, sick at heart. (Fifth walked disconsolately around the stage.)

Several months later a news item caught his eye. At this period in history Mexico had a roving conscription. When the tally landed on a village, every family in that village had to yield one of its children to be conscripted into the military service for three years. It was honorable but at times dangerous work, and the pay was scant. Boys could generally handle it, but girls were apt to find themselves assigned as brothel maidens. It was possible to buy out of the obligation, but it was more money than a poor family could raise.

He knew a poor family with three daughters, no sons.

Zak traveled there and located them. "I will buy out your obligation, if you give me Cielito to marry," he said to Mr. Lindo.

They consulted, and Cielito, hardly eager to serve, agreed. The compact was made, and Zak went to the government office, where he paid off the Lindo family obligation, freeing them of the burden.

He returned, exhilarated. Cielito would finally be his! But the elder sister met him at their door with sadness. "We are humiliated," she said. "Cielito is reneging. She agreed only to gain our relief from the conscription; now that we are free, she is reneging. Father will talk with you."

Mr. Lindo did. "This is terrible," the sister translated. "We had no idea. We are in debt to you, and can't pay it off. We owe you a bride."

Zak realized two things. First, that if Cielito really did not want to marry him, it would be folly to make her do so. Second, that she had deceived him and her own family to achieve her end. That was not the sort of woman he should marry either; in time she would deceive him worse.

"We must make the effort," Mr. Lindo continued. "Will you consider our youngest in lieu? She is not yet of age, but has potential and will try very hard."

This offer surprised Zak. Take another girl? He did not want to throw the offer in the family's face, as it was clear they were trying to make it right. So he temporized. "Maybe I should meet her."

(Voila came to the fore, looking very young and skittish.)

They brought her immediately. She was thirteen and barely breasted. Zak touched her hand, and she dissolved into frightened giggles. (Voila did.) This was no good.

"Or the older sister," the plain one translated reluctantly. "She is smart, reliable, and eighteen." (Now the sunlight fully illuminated Flame, garbed in old working clothes, quite lean and plain, with her hair bound tightly back.)

She looked as if she wanted to be a thousand miles away, but she had to do her job of communication, even when speaking of herself in the third person. Zak had the impression she was used to that role, clarifying things for others, not for herself.

This was obviously little better. But he did not wish to hurt the family's feelings, or the girl's. "What is your name?" he asked her directly.

"Atalanta. Because I can run swiftly." She was not evincing pride. Indeed she was tall and lean: a runner's body, not a lover's.

"The virgin huntress?" he asked, remembering the classic myth.

"Half right," she agreed wryly. "I never hunted anything. Zachary, this is not my idea." She was feminine enough to blush.

"I know." About to turn her down, he became aware of the tension in the parents. They were desperate to settle accounts honorably, and had few resources. They were honorable in a way Cielito was not. She had severely embarrassed them. He did not want to make it worse for them.

Then he thought of something he had read about once. "Compromise," he said. "Give me three days with her, to decide. If after that—" He shrugged.

"This is outrageous," Atalanta said under her breath. But she translated.

The parents smiled. "Si!" Señor Lindo said. "Three days. You will like her." His faint hope was painful to see.

Atalanta winced as she translated. "You have bought yourself three days of misery."

She was surely right, but what else was there? So they made the deal, and Atalanta went home with Zak that day.

He regretted it immediately. He could see that she felt extremely awkward in his room. "We both know this is merely postponing the inevitable," he said. "I don't want to be with you and you don't want to be with me. We can ease the discomfort somewhat. Do you have somewhere else to stay for three days?"

"No."

"Then I will rent you a separate room at this hotel. There will be no need to tell your family about that."

"You misunderstand," she said reluctantly. "I did not say I do not want to be with you."

He was taken aback. "I understood this was no more voluntary on your part than on mine."

"That is correct. But it is my duty to—to make you want me in lieu of my sister. I know it is hopeless, but I must at least do my part."

"But that means—"

"To share your room. Your bed. You may do what you choose with me. I will not resist or protest."

"Atalanta, I am not trying to make you do anything of the kind! I would never force myself on an unwilling woman."

"I know. You did not touch my sister."

"Not because I didn't want to! But we were a dancing couple. I would not presume beyond that."

"Yes. You are an honorable man."

"So it is best that you have the nights, at least, to yourself. By day we must keep company; that's the deal."

She gritted her teeth visibly. "I hate this. I want not to be humiliated. But I have to tell the truth."

"There is no need."

"My sister was always highly appealing to men, even as a child. They always wanted her, and she obliged many of them."

"Even as a child?" he asked, surprised.

"Yes. And I—I would get crushes on her boyfriends, who never looked at me. My family didn't know; I kept it secret. But you—I would be a liar if I did not tell."

"Me, also?" he asked, amazed. "A crush?"

"Yes. So you could not force yourself on me. Of course you would not want to. But for other reasons than protecting my virtue. Please do not tell."

Zak assessed this case. "Don't tell—that I left you alone?"

"Yes. Leave me that bit of dignity. Let others wonder."

"I will, of course. It was never my purpose to embarrass you. Stay here; you can have the bed. I'll sleep on the floor."

She did not reply. He realized that this was another miscue. "You don't want that."

"I have no right to ask."

"Look, Atalanta, you are a women. In bed, in the dark—I am a man."

"Yes."

"Here is the problem. I might clasp you in darkness, but still not want to marry you. You would be risking everything for nothing."

"No. I would pretend you truly desired me. I would remember that illusion."

She wanted the illusion. He appreciated that. He was sorry that that was all it could ever be.

"Let's leave that in abeyance for now," he decided. "I will take you out for dinner. When we return here, if you still want to share my bed, with its attendant risks, you may do so."

She ventured a smile. "The risk of being ravished—or ignored." Then she focused on something else. "I can't be seen with you in my work clothes. I must return home to fetch a dress."

"I will buy you one," he said expansively.

"It is better not to waste your money."

"What do you care how I spend my money?" he asked somewhat peevishly.

"Waste is not good. We would starve if we wasted anything. You should not waste either."

Ouch. Cielito had had a contrary philosophy, eager to accept anything he offered. "I apologize. I should not have snapped at you. But I do not regard this as a waste. It is what I would do for a—" He broke off, realizing that he was about to insult her.

"For a woman you cared for," she finished for him.

"I apologize also for that unkind thought."

She flashed a smile. "I appreciate honesty, whatever its nature."

"So do I." He considered a moment. "Atalanta, we are here together to see whether I might like to accept you in lieu of your lovely sister. We must at least make a pretense. I must treat you as a girl—as a woman I value. You must allow it. For her I would buy a dress. In fact, I did."

She nodded. "Your reasoning prevails. May I select it?"

He did not fully trust this. "Let's find one we agree on. You surely know where to shop for it."

"I surely do," she agreed, smiling again.

"More honesty: you look nice when you smile."

She shrugged. "I am becoming comfortable with you, on whatever basis. We seem to understand each other."

They went to a shop she knew. She selected the cheapest, plainest dress that fit her. She was saving him money.

"Bear with me," he murmured. "Translate this: What dress would most enhance this woman?"

She hesitated, but translated. The shop proprietress smiled. She brought out a much fancier dress, replete with jewelry.

"This is no good," Atalanta said. "She wants to make a big sale."

"Compromise," he said. "Try it on. Then we'll decide."

Reluctantly she took the dress to the changing booth. She emerged a moment later wearing it. The woman clapped her hands in delight: it was the perfect outfit.

Zak nodded. She was correct. Atalanta looked much better. Not beautiful—she could never be that—but almost elegant. The dress did enhance her lean frame, feminizing it.

Unasked, the woman took hold of the girl's hair, unbound it, and fetched a tiara to frame it. Suddenly the hair was glorious, a red cascade. She got dainty slipper-like shoes to replace the boots, and the feet became delicate. Then she got makeup and touched up the face.

"This is ludicrous," Atalanta muttered. "I feel like a clown."

"Look in the mirror."

She turned and gazed at herself. A handsome, almost pretty lady stared back at her. She was silent.

"We'll take it," Zak said.

The outfit was expensive; the woman had indeed promoted a big sale. But she had accomplished what Zak had asked for: making the most of its wearer.

They ate at a good restaurant. Atalanta tried to order the cheapest dish, but Zak made her ask the waiter for their recommended dinner, and they had that. Atalanta made no further protest, and ate well.

They talked, and he found her to be intelligent and intellectually well rounded. She was pleasant company.

They returned to the hotel late. "Now about the bed," Zak said.

"We are here to ascertain whether I am a girl you might wish to keep," she reminded him. "You can dress me and feed me, but unless I can be a woman to you, it won't work. You should at least make the effort."

He laughed. "You are almost too smart for me! You throw my own words back at me."

"Compromise," she said. "Get bare with me this night. Do what you choose. If you find it bad, we will both know there can be no further relationship. Then we won't have to struggle through two more days of discomfort."

It was indeed a fair test. Had she had more flesh on her bones he would have been eager to clasp her. As it was—he was not reluctant. There was that in him that wanted her to succeed, because he already knew that she was twice the woman her sister was.

(By this time the youngest children had grown bored and most had fallen asleep. That allowed the story to become more intimately adult.)

They undressed and washed up separately. She was in the bed before him. He liked her efficiency in this, too. Cielito had taken forever to get changed. He joined her in the darkness, lying beside her warm body.

"You must try," she reminded him. "I have no experience. Tell me what you want, and I will do it. Tell me in detail, lest I do it wrong."

Was she serious? Probably so, as she was a virgin. Suddenly he was concerned about hurting her, as could happen in a girl's first sexual experience. So it needed to be slow, and she needed the chance to change her mind.

"Lie on me," he said.

She did not question this. She rolled over and got carefully on him—then paused, aware of his erect member.

"Just our upper bodies," he said.

Evidently relieved, she adjusted. He felt her small breasts pressing against his chest; this position gave them more authority.

"Kiss me."

She slid up enough for her face to reach his face. She put her mouth to his.

It was as if a firework exploded. Suddenly his passion overwhelmed him. "Atta, forgive me," he said.

"Anything," she agreed, knowing what was coming.

(The narrator spread a sheet over their bodies, discreetly obscuring the immediate action. Let the villagers imagine it in whatever detail they preferred. To some it might seem that the actors were actually doing what was described. As if they were really in love.)

He rolled her over, got into position over her, and pushed his member into her cleft. She was lean, but definitely female there. He thrust, crashing through any barrier there might have been. Deep into her, he climaxed, pulsing repeatedly as he kissed her face.

Then, ashamed, he withdrew. "I'm sorry!" he gasped. "I couldn't help myself. I am a man."

"And I am a woman, now," she said.

"Did I hurt you?"

"Some." Then she reconsidered. "I think I am not supposed to say that."

"When you kissed me—"

"I know. It is all right, Zachary."

"I meant to be careful. But your kiss—"

"It's all right. May I kiss you again?"

"No!" Then he had to laugh, and she laughed with him. "I mean, not if it causes me to rape you."

"Then I had better kiss you before you are able to do it again."

She did, and he liked it as well as before, but she was right: he couldn't stiffen so soon after the first. So he merely kissed her back, in the darkness.

Still kissing avidly, they fell asleep.

In the morning he woke to find her up and about. She was cleaning up the room, having evidently cleaned herself and him up first, while he slept. "Virtual pigsty," she was muttering. "Men can't keep house."

"I apologize," he said.

"Oh! I thought you were asleep."

"I was. But I did not enlist you as a chore maid. I will have the hotel staff tackle my neglect."

"Do you always leave your rooms like this?"

"Yes. I am ashamed."

"You are a man." She finished the job. The room was much neater and cleaner now.

He got up and dressed. Atalanta was already dressed in her old work clothes.

"About last night—"

"Oh, please don't take that back!" she said, alarmed.

"I lost control. But you were wonderful."

She sat down quickly, looking faint.

"I'm sorry," he said quickly. "I took advantage. There was something about your kiss, in the dark."

"You kissed me, and desired me, and couldn't wait," she said. "My life is complete."

He pondered that. "I am unclear whether you are speaking figuratively or sarcastically."

"Figuratively, of course. It felt so good to be wanted. I was afraid you wouldn't."

"So was I," he admitted. "But in the dark—I mean—"

"When you couldn't see me. I know. At least now I know I can do it. That if we were otherwise compatible, that would not interfere."

Unfortunately now it was day, and she was as plain as ever. He felt no desire for her.

"We must eat," he said.

"Oh, I can fix it," she said. "I can do woman's work."

"I was thinking of the restaurant."

"As you wish. But I should do my exercises first. They aren't good on a full belly."

"As you wish," he echoed. She had an exercise routine? She kept surprising him.

He sat and watched as she went through a series of calisthenics and stretches. Her movements were precise. She had excellent coordination, as did her lovely sister. Perhaps it ran in the family.

Then he got an idea that struck him as hard and suddenly as his sexual urgency of the night before. "Atalanta, can you dance?"

"Nobody asks me to dance. I know the steps, but—" She shrugged.

"The tango."

"Oh, yes, of course. We all do the tango."

"Dance with me."

"It would look odd. I'm not lush like my sister."

"Do it anyway." He approached her and took her in his arms.

They danced the tango, silently. She did know it, and did it well. Then he tried her on a competition variant, and she stumbled. "Oh, I'm sorry."

"Don't apologize," he said. "Do it this way." He did the step himself, demonstrating.

She nodded. Then she did it with him, perfectly. She was as apt as Cielito, just not as sightly.

"There's a dance I know of in a neighboring town," he said. "Put on your new dress. I'm taking you there."

"But I would be a joke," she protested.

"It is a masquerade."

She paused, considering, then nodded. "Of course. But that dress is not suitable for dancing. It would fall apart."

"Wear it to the shop. We'll get you a dancing dress."

"But the expense!" she protested.

Before he knew it, he kissed her, closing his eyes. And the passion roiled up. "Damn!"

"Did I do something wrong?"

"Hardly. Get bare. Now. If you will."

Her mouth fell open. "By daylight?"

"By any light."

(The narrator held another sheet, and shrouded them as necessary.)

In moments they were both bare, and in the throes of it. He tried to hold back, but the urgency overwhelmed him, as before. He couldn't stop until he had jetted into her core.

"I suppose it would be hypocritical to apologize," he said as he dismounted.

"You desired me by day," she said in wonder.

"I'm sorry it was not a shared experience. There's just something about your kiss. It incites me beyond control."

"It *is* a shared experience," she said. "Just not the same way. I don't need the—the orgasm. I'm thrilled to have your passion. Twice now."

"You have it," he agreed, kissing her again. As before, his spent member was far less urgent, and he was able to clasp her and kiss her without requiring the culmination.

"Oh, Zak," she sighed. "I could endure this forever."

"I have made no promises," he reminded her.

"I know. But even three days of this is heaven for me."

Heaven for him too. Now he had to ask himself: was she right for him after all? He had been smitten by her sister's beauty, but Atalanta was actually far more woman in every other respect.

He needed time to think about it. "We must go to the shop," he said. Then he remembered: "We forgot breakfast!"

"I am not hungry now."

"Neither am I!" For they had found something better.

"Why did you kiss me?" she asked as they drove.

He thought back, remembering. "I said I would buy you a dancing dress. You protested the expense. You are so keen to save me money. You would make a good—" He caught himself. "It just, pleased me. I acted without thinking."

"Maybe you had better not kiss me in public," she said, smiling as she restored her conservative lipstick.

"It would be dangerous," he agreed.

They bought the new dress. It did for her what the prior dress had, only more so. She no longer looked lean; she looked slender, her modest curves amplified by the outfit. It was another significant transformation.

They stopped at the restaurant for lunch. Then he took her to the masquerade. Her mask was an angel face, his a devil's face.

Everyone was masked, identified only by large numbers on plaques they wore. There were many dances, and in some they were required to change partners, as random numbers were matched up. Zak danced perfectly, of course. But so did Atalanta. In fact she was much in demand by other males. They loved the coordinated angel. It was easy to see why; she made any partner look good, because she was always perfectly in step, yet lacked the body to distract attention from her partner.

Even so, that body, enhanced by the motions of the dance, was compelling. Watching her dance with others, as well as with him, he appreciated the animation of it. She was beautiful.

At the end of the evening they were awarded in informal plaque as the best dancing couple. Atalanta seemed almost ready to faint behind her mask.

Back in the car, he hesitated, then spoke. "I want to kiss you."

"Fold down the seats."

They did, laughing, and he kissed her, and they went at it in their clothing. This time no explanations or apologies were needed. Both were flush with the joy of the dance.

"You were phenomenal," he told her belatedly.

"Dance or sex?" she asked archly.

"Both."

"Atalanta, will you marry me?"

She stiffened. "Please do not tease me."

"Never that! We're only half through the trial period, but already I know you are the woman for me. Please marry me so we can be together forever."

"Yes."

They kissed again. Then they reassembled themselves and he drove the car back to the hotel.

"It's not just sex," he said. "But that did make the difference. I hope you don't mind."

"I will never mind."

Back in the hotel room, Atalanta was nervous. "Are you afraid I'll want to kiss you again?" he asked. "If so, it is well-founded."

"I am afraid you won't," she said. "There is one more thing I must tell you."

"As long as it's not that you have changed your mind, now that I have discovered you."

"It is this," she said seriously. "I am not really Cielito's sister."

He was astonished. "But the family—the deal—everything. You said you had a crush on me."

"I do," she said. "I love you, Zachary. But I can't let our association be based on a lie. I must confess. Then you may banish me from your life, if that is the way you feel."

"Atalanta, you are making me nervous. What is it?"

"I have known you for years," she said. "Loved you for years. I have watched all your recent dances. But with my plain face and lean body, how could I ever hope to win you? So when the Lindo family needed help, I went to them and made them a deal. Thus I became their elder daughter."

"You took her place?" he asked, still amazed.

"Yes. If you like me and keep me, their debt to you is paid, and I have my love realized. It's a fair deal for both parties. They gave me an avenue, I gave them possible settlement. If you reject me, then we are no worse off than before. But it has to be on the basis of truth; I will not take you because of a lie."

"This elder daughter—what of her?"

"She is lame. She can't dance. She's a nice person, and if you prefer to try her, it is your prerogative."

She couldn't dance. That doomed that. "I'll stick with you. At least you can dance. Superlatively."

"About that—"

"Yes. Why didn't you tell me at the outset how well you could dance? I probably would have chosen you for my partner."

"Because I didn't want a purely platonic and professional relationship of the sort you had with your regular partner. I wanted your love. I had to win that before I could risk dancing."

That set him back. Her reasoning was dead on. He would have treated her as a sterile business partner, as was his policy. Only with Cielito Lindo had he realized that he wanted both together. "Well figured," he agreed. "You did it correctly."

"I wanted you because you are the finest dancer I have seen. But for me dancing and emotion are not separated."

"Nor for me, any more."

"I am not done."

"There is more?" he asked warily.

"Two more bits. It is true that Ceilito is not eager to marry you. But she will if her father directs her to, and he will do that if it is the only way to settle the debt. You can still have Ceilito."

"Still have her!"

"She will dance with you, and bear your children."

"But never really love me, and always resent the need."

"She might come to love you. You are a worthy person. Marriages are often arranged, and they work out as well as the love matches do. It is feasible."

"You are arguing her case!"

She nodded. "I would rather argue my own case. But you know it already."

He fixed on something else. "But the kisses—I got carried away, and virtually ravished you when I never expected it. You couldn't have arranged that."

"But I did, Zachary. That is the other bit. I wear a special hormone cream in my lips that has a potent effect on a male. As you discovered."

"That too!" he exclaimed.

"I felt that if you liked me sexually, you would be disposed in my favor, even if my face is not pretty."

His head was spinning. "No effect on you?"

"Some effect. It makes me desire sex. But I am already in love with you, and want you close to me, so it doesn't matter."

He considered. This young woman had known what she wanted, waited her opportunity, and made her play. He discovered he liked that; she could be a very useful ally professionally. She had done what she had to to get his attention, and he was satisfied to have hers.

But that hormone. Would he like her without it? That was critical. "Atalanta, clean that stuff off your mouth."

"Of course," she said sadly. She brought out cold cream, applied it, and wiped it away. "I am clean."

"Now kiss me."

"But there will be no effect."

"Precisely. Do it."

She approached him and tentatively kissed him on the mouth. There was no sudden passion. Then he kissed her back, held her close, and bore her on to the bed. In moments her legs were spread and he was thrusting into the crevice between them. He climaxed explosively, still kissing her. This time she joined him; he felt her channel flexing, and saw the flush of her skin.

"But how could this be?" she asked as he lay panting beside her. "There is only—me."

"I am a man. I like sex. I don't need a hormone, if I like the girl."

"Are you teasing me?"

"I wasn't sure myself, especially after learning how you deceived me. Now I know: you're fine, sexually. I'm sure you'll be fine emotionally, as I come to know you better. Meanwhile, the dancing is great."

"Well, yes, I can dance. But as I explained—"

"Marry me."

"But—"

"If you turn me on without the hormone, it's real. After this, you are welcome to use it. I just needed to know."

"Yes," she breathed.

"Yes you know, yes you'll use the hormone, or yes you'll marry me?"

"All three," she said blissfully.

"And of course we'll be dancing, competing in tournaments, not just the tango. You have a problem with that?"

She burst out laughing, and he joined her. They were, indeed, well-matched.

Now the story was done, Fifth and Flame were kissing for themselves, the hour was finished, and the Male Spirit's power was fading. They had outlasted him, and balked the takeover. Gale was relieved, pleased, and proud. Her children had come through in marvelous fashion, artistically as well as magically.

The audience stood and applauded. They had forgotten about the threat they were avoiding, during the story. That was another special victory.

Then a small vision appeared before Gale. It was the personification of the male spirit. "Are you satisfied?"

He was devious, as she well knew. What was he up to now? "Affirmation. For the moment."

"I want to fuck you again."

"Regret."

"Have you seen your husband recently?"

She looked beside her. Havoc was gone. "Question?"

"I have him."

"Negation. You can't hold a Glamor."

"I fetched his ikon."

Gale froze. The male spirit had learned about ikons? This was mischief. *Havoc!* she called mentally.

Apology, came his faint response. *I had an emergency call from Monochrome, so went immediately. It was fake, and a trap. I am captive in a Yellow Chroma zone, my ikon also.*

I will help you!

Negation. He is after your ikon too. All the ikons. Warn the kids.

"I see you understand," the Male Spirit's illusion said. "Come to me, and your husband will not suffer as long as you keep me satisfied."

Gale was appalled. The enemy had once again distracted them and outwitted them. What could she do, but oblige him while she tried to figure out a way to rescue Havoc?

"Voila," she murmured. "Havoc's captive. I must go to him. Read my mind."

Her daughter gazed at her. Then she vanished.

Gale grimly set herself. Then she oriented on Havoc, and teleported herself there. She would be nearly helpless, but Voila would know what to do. She hoped.

Chapter 20
Ifrit

Need. It was Voila's thought, sent to him only.

Iolo was ranging alone, in his natural vapor state, seeding selected regions with infant ifrits. That task was just about finished, so he had time, though he would have heeded Voila regardless. They had been close friends all their lives. He had taught her cloud formation, and she had taught him solid teleportation. They would have been lovers, had they not been so close so long; as it was they had merely practiced sex together to get the details straight, not for personal feeling. That was the way of all of their interactions.

Ask. He knew already that it was serious.

Father's captive. Mother's foolish. Help her.

Ah. Voila was the most powerful human Glamor ever grown on Charm, and sometimes she was impatient with her slow parents. Iolo was a bit more objective, and knew that they had mature, sensible qualities, and used their powers generally wisely. They were not to blame if they could not see as far along the paths as their children could.

Deal. He oriented on Elder Idyll for information as Voila's thought faded.

Grandmother Idyll, he called. Telepathy was another useful talent learned from the humans. Normally ifrits communicated via touches, their vapors conveying everything needful. But that did not work when they were not on the same planet. Idyll was with a human, on Mino, in space. So telepathy was necessary.

Welcome, Iolo. It was Idyll, her thought familiar, encompassing, and reassuring.

Voila requires me to help Gale, who seeks to rescue Havoc, who is captive of the Male Spirit.

There was no hesitation; the Ifrit Glamor had seen this coming in the near future paths. *Correct. Join her and Monochrome. Go with them to the Spirit's redoubt.*

That was enough. Iolo could not see the future paths farther than a few seconds, but his contact with Idyll more than made up for it. He contracted his cloud to solid form, then used telportation to conjure himself to the Human Glamor Gale's presence in Continent Australia.

She was no longer there. She had just teleported herself to the North American continent, a redoubt in the Rocky Mountains. A castle constructed in the ancient Earthy style, replete with very solid walls, conical turrets, deep dungeons, and an oubliette. It was part of a wealthy estate now overrun by the wild magic of the local Yellow Chroma volcano.

He landed beside her. She was in a stony cell near the one that held Havoc. She was theoretically hiding from the Male Spirit until she could decide on a way to rescue Havoc. "Iolo!" she exclaimed.

"Wait," he said. "I must fetch Monochrome."

"But she's busy defending Earth!"

"Idyll directs."

Gale nodded. "Apology. I lost my perspective when I learned of Havoc's capture. I will wait."

Iolo teleported to Antarctica, joining Monochrome in her apartment. "Greeting," he said.

"You are Voila's companion," the woman said. "The six-legged ifrit dog."

"Ifrit," he agreed. "Read my mind." Actually no human being could read the mind of an ifrit being without being in cloud form, but Iolo had learned to set up a plate of thoughts and impressions for human consumption.

"Havoc!" she exclaimed. "I thought he was in Australia. It was a trap? The Male Spirit got his ikon! And Gale wants to help? And she needs help? I can do that. But if Havoc is caught in a Chroma zone, my power will be limited."

"It is the right path," Iolo said. "Voila sent me."

She smiled. "And Voila can read the future in a manner none of the rest of us can. Well, show me where, Iolo. I'll follow."

"All we say there the Spirit knows."

"Of course."

Iolo traveled back to join Gale, making his route clear for the Mistress to follow. They arrived almost together.

I will watch, Iolo sent, and dissolved into his natural state. He had learned to do this rapidly. He remained attuned to the dialogue of the women. *Do not reveal my nature.* Because he was, as Havoc would have put it, the wild card. The Male Spirit did not yet know his full capacities. So far he seemed merely to be a talking dog.

The two women hugged. "Appreciation for coming," Gale said. "I don't know how to proceed. Havoc is chained to a stone wall and guarded by brutish men seeking a pretext to torture him. His ikon is here, and he has no magic stone left. The Male Spirit wants me to oblige him sexually in return for not torturing Havoc. I can't think straight."

"I am in a similar position," Monochrome said sympathetically. "He will do the same with me, if he catches me here outside my sphere of power. But we both know the Spirit will never let Havoc or us go voluntarily. I fear it was a mistake for either of us to come here."

Both of them were covering for Iolo, giving him time to fade out. All of them knew that the Male Spirit had to be aware of everything that was occurring in this castle.

"Negation," Gale said. "The paths decree it."

"You have great confidence in your daughter's perception."

"Clarification: there are three who read the future well. Voila sees the near future, Idyll the intermediate future, and Mino the far future. They are working together to fathom the paths that most benefit us. That is why they allowed Havoc to be captured."

"They saw it coming—and let it happen?" Monochrome asked, appalled.

"Affirmation. It is the only way to save your planet. The Male Spirit also saw this coming, and is playing to benefit himself. It is a complex game with the outcome as yet undecided."

That was technically true, but if there were any way for the Male Spirit to be defeated, they would be on the path for it. The Spirit thought that the advantage was his, because all of the paths he fathomed favored him. It was best that he continue to think that.

Meanwhile Iolo diffused through the castle. Men were busy throughout, tending to the operation of the castle, bringing in food, cleaning chambers, repairing cracks, and doing the myriad other things required. He identified the Male Spirit in the form of a large muscular human man, his host for the occasion. The Spirit was sitting in a private chamber with his eyes closed, but was not sleeping; evidently he was thinking. Then Iolo moved on and found Havoc standing against a wall, naked, chained to the wall by his wrists. The ifrit settled in and touched him. *Iolo. I will free you for a while.*

Havoc nodded almost imperceptibly. *The women?*

Both here, covering for us.

Iolo coalesced portions of his substance around the manacles on Havoc's wrists. He infiltrated the mechanism and pushed the tumblers aside. The manacles opened, releasing the man.

Havoc was without Glamor magic, but he remained a strong and smart man. He knew he was being observed, but played the game. He was absolutely quiet as he moved through the dark dungeon passages, seeking an exit. He was at no particular disadvantage in darkness; his ears, nose, and fingers guided him.

He found the oubliette. This was a deep well set in the middle of the dungeon floor, so constructed that anyone who fell in would find it almost impossible to climb out, because it was larger at the base than at the top and the stones were slick. He avoided it and moved on.

He found a stone stairway, but it was booby-trapped. The third step was on a hinge that would release a mechanism to drop a block on the head of whoever was there. *Beware* Iolo cautioned.

Havoc smiled. His fingers had already found the hinge and withdrew. He passed the stairs by.

Meanwhile Gale and Monochrome continued to converse. "You love him, of course," Gale said.

"I do, as do you," the Mistress agreed. "Do you object?"

"Negation. He needs a mistress, and you are the best on Earth. But what about when Havoc leaves Earth?"

"I will retire from my position here and go with him."

"Question: won't that leave Earth ungoverned?"

"No. There will be a new Mistress of Mistresses. It is a position, not a person."

"But won't you then be mortal?"

"I will be mortal. But the magic of your planet may help me retain my appearance for a time. Regardless, I will do it for love."

"Conjecture: you won't have to retire. You will learn to travel between planets."

"Is that possible?"

"Affirmation. For a Glamor."

"Wonderful!"

"Welcome to the life." They embraced again.

The male spirit ran out of patience. "You girls are playing me along," he said, appearing before them.

So the Male Spirit had been watching them all along. He must have been telepathically or clairvoyantly tuning in on the women. That meant he had seen Iolo dissolve. But did he know the ifrit's full nature?

"You saw us!" Gale said, looking horrified.

"Can the act, honey. You knew I was onto you. It's that nice clairvoyance you have. That's why this syrupy little dialogue with your arch rival."

"We are not rivals," Monochrome protested.

"The hell you aren't, sweetcakes. You pretend to want merely to be Havoc's mistress, but that's only until you displace his wife. Then he'll be all yours."

"Doubt," Gale said.

"Fuck that, sister; naturally you are in denial, or pretending to be. But it's academic; neither of you will have him. Instead you will both have me, as concubines, while he watches and learns."

"Negation!" Gale said for them both.

The spirit smiled. "We shall see, sweetheart. Come join me in my parlor."

The scene shifted to the castle's main hall. On one side was Havoc, now manacled naked to a large cross. On the other was a throne on which the Male Spirit sat, similarly naked. Between them stood the two lovely women garbed like queens. Iolo wasn't sure whether the Male Spirit had conjured them all there, or forced them to move themselves there. It hardly mattered; this was merely the setting for the Spirit's further mischief.

"I am curious how you freed yourself, Havoc," the male spirit said. "Your manacles just seemed to open of their own accord. Yet you have no remaining magic I know of. Therefore there must be something I don't know of. What is it?"

Havoc was silent. He was protecting Iolo's secret.

"I could torture you to my heart's content, and you would never answer my question," the Spirit said, not seeming disappointed. "You are a man's man, the kind I prefer. So it is useless to question you directly. But there are indirect ways. That is why I asked you several folk to meet me here."

The man paused, but no one responded. They were waiting for his next move.

"Now here is the deal," the spirit said. "I am being hosted by the body of a stout minion who gets to feel what I feel. I want to give him some nice action before I settle down to serious business. Gale, sweetie, come kiss my right buttock."

Gale merely stood there, unspeaking.

"The penalty for future balks will be pain to Havoc's right side." A man garbed as a torturer lifted a red-hot rod from a brazier and walked toward Havoc. He poked the tip of the rod toward Havoc's right buttock, halting just shy of the skin. "He can handle it, of course, but can you, dear? It will be your responsibility."

Gale merely stood, her face impassive. But Iolo knew she was nervous and angry.

"Monochrome, you albino dear, come kiss my left ear."

"Unlikely."

"The penalty for future balks on your part will be pain to Havoc's left side." A second torturer lifted a large metal pincers toward Havoc's left ear.

Gale and Monochrome exchanged a glance, both appalled.

"Now I know I can't hold either of you here," the Spirit said. "One of you is a Glamor whose ikon I have not yet acquired, and the other is the Mistress of Mistresses whose power on Earth is supreme everywhere except here, at least until I resume my rightful role as Master of Masters." He paused, gazing at each of them, openly fingering his penis. "You can both take off, and I can't stop you. But if you do, the man you love will be slowly tortured to death. You know this is no bluff. So neither of you will be going anywhere at the moment. I believe we are all clear on that."

Iolo could see that they all were clear. The male spirit was merciless. He made threats not so much to intimidate as to establish the rules of his game.

"We'll start with the entertainment," the Spirit continued after a moment. "When that palls, we'll get serious. Ladies, perform as directed."

The two women hesitated. The two torturers started to move toward Havoc. The women immediately walked to the spirit. Gale kneeled and kissed his right buttock. Monochrome kissed his left ear.

"I see you have made your decision," the Spirit said. "There is one other thing: I am not completely obtuse about the dynamics of the situation. If I kill Havoc now, I will have no further hold over you, and will lose you as playmates. That would annoy me. So I will kill him only if it is clear I have lost your favors. But that leaves considerable play for pain. He will wish to die, but will not be allowed that release. So I suggest you make no attempt to deceive or harm me, as I anger easily and will strike at him in retaliation." He glanced at each woman. "Have you any questions?"

"Affirmation," Gale said. "Are we permitted honest expression?"

"Such as calling me a despicable turd? Yes, I welcome it. In time I will have your love, but in the interim I prefer your hate. There's a special pleasure in possessing an openly unwilling woman." He glanced significantly at Monochrome, whose lip curled in contempt. Iolo knew that the spirit had forced her to suffer orgasm at his instigation in a prior interaction; it was in their minds.

"Are we permitted dishonest expression?" Monochrome asked.

"That comes under the heading 'Deception.' Not permitted."

"But we are at war. Deception is part of the game."

The spirit nodded. "So it is. And of course I can read your minds whenever I choose. So a reversal: deception is permitted, if you can get away with it."

Iolo knew that the Spirit was mistaken about reading their minds. Glamors knew how to mask their real thoughts while leaving superficial ones to be read. That was his liability.

"We're set," the Spirit said. "Havoc, are you watching? If you close your eyes, my minions will pin them open with bamboo splinters."

"I am watching," Havoc replied grimly.

Iolo was perplexed. Why had Havoc allowed himself to be captured like this? Surely he had known the fake Monochrome from the real one, and his vision of the near future would have warned him about the trap. By stepping into it he had precipitated an ugly sequence that gave the Spirit considerable advantage. Iolo had come to know Havoc well, in the course of his close association with Viola; the man maintained a reputation for barbarian ignorance and lack of caution, but he was a supremely smart and savvy person. This was quite unlike him.

Then it came to him: Havoc had done it deliberately. He had seen the trap and walked into it. Why?

And there was another answer: because Voila had told him to. She, together with Mino and Idyll, had seen the future paths, and this was one that led more surely to eventual victory. The paths governed everything, in this complicated siege.

Yet how could becoming captive, and thus causing both his wife and his mistress to become effective captives also, be a winning strategy? Iolo couldn't see it.

And a third answer: if Iolo couldn't see it, neither could the Male Spirit, even if he had some future seeing. So the Spirit was playing into the strategy, thinking it meant his victory.

"Gale, honeypot, kiss my ass."

"I just did, simpleton."

"Not so. You kissed my buttock. Now kiss my dirty brown rectum." The man bent over, exposing it to her.

Gale grimaced and put her face into his crack.

"Lick it while you're there," the spirit said, keeping his gaze on Havoc. "Run your tongue in. Ream it out."

Havoc, watching, did not react. Now Iolo understood why: this was the devious path to victory. The Glamors were doing what they had to do, immune to personal aversion.

"You're disgusting," Monochrome said.

"And you, luscious bimbo, put your sweet boobs up against my face so I can suck them."

The Mistress obeyed, bracing her breasts with her hands and presenting them to the man's lowered face. He fastened his mouth on the left nipple and sucked. Then he paused. "Secrete some milk in there; I'm thirsty."

Monochrome did not argue that this was contrary to nature. As a Glamor she could produce milk at will. Iolo read her mind and knew she had done it on occasion for particular lovers. So she was not freaked out by this act; it was within her milieu. But she strongly disliked doing it for this man—which was the point of the demand.

The Spirit rocked back and forth a little, savoring the breast at one orifice and the tongue at the other. Iolo read Havoc's mind and discovered that he was turned on by this sight, but was suppressing his masculine reaction. His wife and mistress, two outstandingly beautiful women, were indulging in sexual interplay with another man, and it was a turn-on despite its involuntary and ugly nature. Which, again, was part of the Spirit's purpose. It was hard to evoke disgust without at least some concurrent desire.

"Now get your mouth down there and suck my cock, bovine beauty," the Spirit said.

Monochrome did so, sitting on the floor beneath him and raising her head to take his member in. The two women were working his penis and rectum simultaneously. Still Havoc watched without visible reaction.

"Oh, that's great, floozies! Do it harder." Then, as they obliged, his orgasm came. "Hoooo!" His member jetted into Monochrome's mouth while his anus clenched on Gale's probing tongue. Iolo picked this up from the minds of all three of them.

"Quit, succubi." They did, and the Spirit stepped away from them. "We'll do it that way every day, when I'm in charge."

The women stood beside each other, neither looking pleased. One had a smear of brown on her mouth, the other a driblet of white. The point, of course, was to degrade them. The Spirit had not succeeded in making them balk, but had rubbed their faces literally in his nether region.

"Now kiss each other," the spirit said.

"Outrage!" Gale snapped.

The spirit glanced at the torturers. They moved as if to burn and pinch Havoc.

The two women kissed. The spirit had established that he could use Havoc to control the two women. They would do anything rather than see Havoc tortured. All ultimately in the interest of following the correct path to the favorable future.

"Let's see what other entertainment you can provide, girls. You both love Havoc, right? The one wants to keep him, the other wants to take him. You are either natural enemies, or natural friends. Your choice: fight or make love."

They two did not hesitate. They set about making love, stripping away their dresses and underclothing, becoming nude, then kissing and stroking each others' breasts. Iolo was not remotely human, but he could assume human form when he chose, and knew that this would be a strong turn-on for any ordinary human male.

"That is some sight," the spirit said, evidently disgruntled. "Two bitches in heat." It was clear that he had lost whatever points he had wanted to score, as he had not managed to make them balk. In fact they were doing it right. His spent member was coming back to life.

"Why don't you come have sex with *me*, penis-puss?" Havoc asked.

For an instant the Spirit was transported by rage. Then he controlled it. Havoc had scored on him, and anything he did to Havoc now would merely affirm that. Iolo couldn't smile when in cloud form, but he felt the urge. Two women having sex together—the implication was that the Male Spirit liked same-sex sex.

"Enough!" the man snapped. "We've moving on to the next scene." The women stopped.

A literal scene appeared, an illusion holo showing an open field. On one side was a haphazard army of men bearing pitchforks, kitchen knives, clubs fashioned from broken furniture, torches, and rocks. On the other was a peaceful town going about its normal business.

Neither woman spoke. They simply sat and watched.

"Question," Havoc said.

Thus prompted, the Spirit felt free to answer. "This is middle North America. The revolution has begun. My troops lack proper weapons because of the milquetoast policies of the past millennium, but that will be rectified once I return to proper power. Maybe before then; the weapons exist, but have been mothballed in out of the way vaults. We will start liberating them soon, and that will facilitate progress."

"Those guns led to phenomenal useless slaughter," Monochrome said. "As did war, which we also largely abolished, legends to the contrary."

"You run a dull planet," the Spirit agreed. "It is past time for a change."

"How did you get rebels in the middle of an area controlled by the Female Spirit?" Gale asked. "You can't have any direct power there."

"Direct power," the Spirit agreed. "That is the key. I wield *indirect* power. I have minions who are promised the spoils of war. Top lieutenants report to me here, then go out to recruit and command lower forces. Greed, anger, lust are powerful motivators. As we shall see."

The rag-tag army swept across the field to the town. They surrounded and torched the outlying houses. In moments people came running out, not knowing what was happening.

The invaders with clubs clubbed the men. "We don't need them," the Spirit said. Those with rocks bashed in the skulls of the older women. "Or them." Those with pitchforks rounded up the children. "They will make useful slaves." Those with knives grabbed the young women, threatening them with death as they tore off their clothing and raped them. "There's always a market for unspoiled maidens."

Other men were entering the burning houses, not to extinguish the flames, but to haul out what loot they could find. "The spoils of war," the Spirit said. "A real motivator."

Iolo was neither human nor fleshly, but such brutal destruction bothered him. All this mischief, just to sate the greed and lust of a few disreputable men?

"The news will spread," Monochrome said. "My police will converge on the perpetrators and bring them to justice."

"They'll have a big job, whitelips," the Spirit said. "Similar risings are occurring all across the planet. This has been building for some time."

"The Glamors will help," Gale said.

The Spirit nodded. "Indeed they will, asskiss. That should be interesting."

Iolo was perplexed. The Spirit *wanted* the Glamors to intervene?

Then the scene showed the Red Glamor's arrival. She appeared, shiningly lovely, like a living red garnet. She spread her hands—and the weapons flew from the hands of the rebels to land in a pile.

Seeing this, the townsmen took heart. They started fighting back effectively. Their weapons had not flown, and they greatly outnumbered the enemy. They beat back the rebels as the girls tore themselves free.

The townsmen were not great fighters, having had much of a millennium of peace. But they were outraged by the wanton mayhem, the rapes, and killing. They closed in on the rebels, who were showing much less courage now that the disadvantage was theirs.

"Simply confine them," the Red Glamor said. "We need to find out who sent them, and why."

"The rebellion does not seem to be going well," Gale remarked, satisfied.

"You straightforward folk are perpetually naïve about feints," the male spirit remarked. "Observe what your red babe is doing."

She was doing magic—but now there was a faint red line connecting her to a distant region. To a Red Chroma zone, where her ikon gathered and broadcast its power. The Spirit had made that connection visible.

"You Glamors draw power from your ikons," the Spirit said. "Which in turn draw it from their environments. So Red is tied to a Red Chroma volcano. It is volcano magic that powers her."

"You seem to understand the principle," Gale said. "It is true for all of us. But you can't touch an ikon."

"But my minions can." Now the scene oriented on a brute man wearing goggles as he tramped across the landscape. This was another locale of the planet, near one of the converted volcanoes. Indeed, the red of the zone was coming into view ahead.

Iolo realized that this was leading up to. The minion was going after the Red Glamor's ikon!

They watched as the man forged into the Red Chroma zone, following the made-visible line. The line obligingly changed color as it entered the zone, so that it was not lost in the background color. It proceeded straight to the volcano, which was murkily quiescent at the moment.

"It seems that the Glamor's attention is taken by the rebellion," the Spirit said. "She doesn't realize that I have perfected a Science-Magic method of coloring the power fluxes, so as to be able to trace them to their origins. They are invisible until they are used; then they show up, at least to those wearing the right lenses."

"Oh, no," Gale breathed.

"Oh, yes, honey tongue. You may not be truly captive yet, but it will soon happen, because you can not protect your ikon. Once I have all your ikons, the game will be mine."

"Why didn't we see this?" Gale asked, almost rhetorically.

"Because you didn't think to look, candy lips. There are too many paths."

"You know about the paths," Gale said, realizing.

"I know about the paths," the Spirit agreed. "This about that: something like ninety nine percent of them favor me. The odds are greatly in my favor. You had to have known that. So why are you still fighting me? I thought about it, and realized that you are zeroing in on the few paths that favor you. Ninety nine percent is useless, if you steer reality to the one percent."

Gale, Monochrome, and Havoc were all looking it him now. The Spirit was speaking truth—a truth they had thought he was ignorant about. He was on to them.

"And you may be interested to know that I am systematically closing off those paths," the Spirit continued. "Catching the Glamors is most of it. You won't be able to oppose me without your Glamor powers. So I am forging the path that closes off the wrong paths. Odd that it didn't seem to occur to you that I would do this."

He was taunting them. Iolo wondered, though. Couldn't Voila, Mino, and Idyll have seen this bad path and avoided it? Something was missing from this picture.

We did foresee it, Idyll thought. *And steered toward it. It is part of our strategy.*

Meanwhile the minion was closing in on the Red Glamor's ikon. He made his way fearlessly to the shaking edge of the volcano and found the crevice where the ikon rested. He picked it up.

"Three down," the Spirit said. "Now I have Havoc's, the Yellow Glamor's, and the Red Glamor's. The others will be taken soon enough. When they are complete, my victory should be close."

But this will lose the planet, Iolo protested to Idyll.

Affirmation.

Iolo was shocked, a mood he had learned from the humans. *You are letting the malign Male Spirit win?*

Confirmation.

He did not question her further. There was obviously something he did not understand.

"It seems we focused too much on the specific sites," Gale said. "We did not know you were aware of the paths."

"You did not know I was telepathic, either." The spirit smiled again, enjoying their renewed shock. "Which was my main clue to the nature of your ifrit companion. He is the one who opened Havoc's manacles."

"We did not discuss that telepathically," Havoc said.

"But you thought of that when I asked you. Then I got the story of the cloud-creature who is even now watching us."

Oh, no! Had the spirit also picked up on Iolo's dialogue with Idyll?

"Yes I did, vapor spook. Idyll at least shows the sense to know when she is beaten. She sees the intermediate future and knows there is no way to stop me. I find that reassuring. But that does not mean I will relax until it is accomplished."

Ifrit emotions were by no means the same as those of living folk, let alone the human species. But Iolo had learned a number of human ones from Voila. The relevant ones at this point were dismay and recrimination. How could they have been so blithe about such fundamental magic powers as clairvoyance, future paths, and telepathy? Why hadn't anyone checked the male spirit for such powers? It should have been easy to do. Now they were in deep trouble.

"Overconfidence goes before a fall," the Spirit said with smug satisfaction.

Iolo had no mental response to that. He withdrew from active participation in the dialogue.

And retreated to his nether mind, the one that could not be road by any outsider. In fact there was no evidence of its existence. This was a device Havoc had taught his four children, and Iolo too, and they had all learned it well. It was like a private chamber, hidden from the world, where the most secret and precious things were kept.

Such as the larger truth of this campaign. Havoc, Gale, and the other Glamors all knew that the Male Spirit either possessed or could develop such powers, because the Female Spirit, Monochrome, had done so. But Monochrome did not know of the secret inner mind, not because Havoc would not have trusted her with it, but because of her inherent affinity to the Male Spirit. They were two aspects of the greater Earth Spirit, and what one possessed, the other surely did also. So to best help the Female Spirit to survive in power, they had had to keep some secrets from her.

Havoc had walked deliberately into this trap, for several reasons. He needed to make the Male Spirit think he was prevailing, and he needed to learn as much about the Male Spirit as possible. Gale had come for similar reasons. Some forms of mind probing were best done at very close range. When Gale got touchingly close to the Spirit at the same time as the Spirit was enjoying his orgasm, Gale had been able to ascertain the limits of his powers. Thus she had surely confirmed that the Spirit lacked either the hidden mind, or any knowledge of it. She had also marked him, so that hereafter she would always know where on Earth he was. The Glamors had a secret weapon.

There were others, such as the succubus Gale had tamed long ago, Swale. She could have sucked out the male spirit's soul during his orgasm, but had not done so, as it would only have been the soul of the human host. The Spirit himself was beyond any such entrapment. It would have nullified the host, but the Spirit would simply have sought another. It was better to deal with the one they knew.

Because the larger issue remained cloudy. None of them could be quite certain which side would win.

"Ifrit!" The Male Spirit's tone was peremptory.

Iolo come out of his private shell. *What is your concern, Malign demon?*

"I want all the Glamors to assemble here and cease opposing me. You, with your teleportation and cloudy nature, can get anywhere. Go notify them of my directive."

Iolo was annoyed, another learned human emotion. *I do not serve you, Spirit.*

"On pain of Havoc's torture. Show them a picture of what we have here, so they understand. If all are not here by sundown, the torture will proceed."

Iolo hesitated. He was supposed to facilitate the malign purpose of this thing? He oriented on Havoc, but the man was impassive and not communicating.

"Please," Gale said.

She wanted to spare Havoc torture, and had already demeaned herself for that. Yet this was unlike her. Why wasn't she furiously fighting?

"Because she knows she's on the losing side," the Spirit said. "She has learned that cooperation will spare her husband torture. It makes sense. I don't do torture for the fun of it; it's a business decision."

Iolo spread out, starting his mission. He was sure the Glamors had something in mind, but he could not fathom what it was. All he could do was cooperate and hope for the best.

He spread his awareness. The closest Glamor was Black, suppressing a pocket of rebellion in the north west portion of the continent termed Alaska.

He moved to join the Glamor in his own way: by diffusing a trace amount of his substance rapidly in that direction, forming a very thin string, until it reached the spot. Then he funneled his main mass along that string, until his cloud form was there.

It took a moment to orient at the new location. This was a hilly region with few trees or permanent human houses. There was what appeared to be a mining camp there, where men and women worked to extract precious stones from the ground.

However, they were not working now. Rough-hewn raiders were performing their usual mayhem, killing the men, raping the prettier women, and rounding up children for slavery. This was another spot rebellion, which was of course why the Glamor had come to it.

Even as Iolo formed his impression of the scene, the Black Glamor acted. He stirred the air, and a whirling cloud formed. In fact it was a vortex around a spot vacuum, like a miniature Black Chroma volcano inruption. The cloud became a funnel cloud, a tornado, traveling toward the raiders.

Iolo immediately took evasive action, because strongly moving air was dangerous. It pulled apart the cells and rendered an ifrit null. The best defense was to condense to solid state, which was far less vulnerable. That was of course one reason the solid state had evolved; it was needed when an ifrit got caught by a sudden storm or eruption. He pressed himself down closely to the ground and drew in his substance, coalescing as the winds stirred around him.

Fortunately he was not too close to the funnel.

But the others were. Suddenly the raiders were swept up in the rushing air, their weapons flying out to land on the ground beyond. The remarkable thing was that the abused women were not touched. Somehow the terrible blast passed them by with no more than a stirring of their hair and what clothing remained on them. This was no ordinary storm.

But of course Glamor magic was hardly ordinary. The Glamors had decades or even centuries of experience with special magic, and could do it well.

Glamor, Iolo thought.

"A greeting, ifrit," Black said, recognizing him. "Apology for forcing your coalescence; I was not before aware of your presence. What is your mission?"

Now he spoke in the sonic human manner, as his form was solid. "I bring a warning and a demand."

The Glamor's main attention had been on the action. Now it focused on Iolo. "Question?"

"The Male Spirit of Earth is behind these uprisings, and he has captured Havoc's icon, and thus Havoc himself. He is searching out the other ikons. Yours is threatened. Meanwhile he demands your attendance at his castle, lest he commence torturing Havoc."

If the Glamor realized that there was something missing from this picture, he did not express it. "Anger."

"Concurrence."

"How is he able to fetch the ikons?"

"It seems he has spies who watched their placement. He also can make their lines of power visible. Now men are going to take the ikons."

"And the spot rebellions are mere distractions," the Glamor concluded.

"Agreement."

"This is extremely annoying." This was not the Black Glamor's normal manner of expression, so Iolo knew he was speaking for the ears of the Male Spirit. "But perhaps only a bluff. Can you verify whether my ikon is threatened?"

"Affirmation. But I do not care to diffuse in the presence of these strong winds." For the tornado remained in place, keeping the rebels occupied while the defenders collected the scattered weapons and formed a cadre to deal with the rebels. Some of the women looked extremely angry; they were ready to kill, the moment the opportunity presented.

"Diffuse to the southeast; it will not touch you."

"Appreciation." Iolo did so, and the winds remained clear of that region.

When he was completely back to his natural state, he extended his awareness, orienting on the Black Glamor's ikon, which was a small black Mobius strip: a band of flexible material twisted back on itself so that one side traced to the other, endlessly. This was deep in a Black Chroma zone, in a niche near the volcano. It should have been almost impossible to find, short of a massive search. But a man was proceeding toward it, equipped with grappling hooks to catch hold of the swept black ground, in case of an inruption. He was following the identifying signal, and would soon have the ikon.

Iolo returned his attention to the Alaska site. *Your ikon is immediately threatened,* he reported from his cloud state.

"Expletive!" the Glamor swore.

Pain Iolo agreed.

"There is no help for it. I must repair to the malign Spirit's lair. Disgust."
Resignation, Iolo thought.

The defendants had taken over the region. The winds subsided, letting the rebels drop to the ground. Some were unconscious, others woozy. The angry women ran at them, swinging captured clubs. There could hardly be any doubt: they were not pleased about getting raped. The loyal men did not try to restrain them; it was their right.

"Guide me," the Glamor said. Iolo did, showing the way to the Male Spirit's redoubt.

Now he oriented on the next closest Glamor. This was Red, in the east Asian extremity, putting down another insurrection. As he siphoned across to join her, he saw that she was doing it in her special fashion. The Black Glamor had generated a vacuum-based whirlwind, as befitted the nature of the Black Chroma inrupting volcanoes. The Red Glamor's clientele was the human species, and she specialized in sex. This was leading to an interesting scene.

The ragtag rebels were advancing on an isolated village, brandishing their weapons, intent on rapine and destruction. But the natives had seen them coming and were ranging out to meet them. The defenders were all young and pretty women, wearing robes that were fastened open in front to display their bare breasts and crotches. They carried no weapons, only open hands. Their banner said **MAKE LOVE NOT WAR**.

This made the rebels pause. They had been promised sex, but this promised better sex. They halted, uncertain. Then their leader signaled two men: "Go fuck them. See what happens." He was speaking in the local language—Earth was a grab-bag of diverse languages—but Iolo could get the meaning from his thoughts.

The two men were glad to obey. They set aside their weapons so that these could not be grabbed and used against them during their distraction, and advanced on the line of women. Two especially shapely women went out to intercept them, arms open. The men entered those welcoming embraces, kissed the girls, and quickly got them down on the ground for sex. They opened their trousers, brought out their stiffened members, and shoved them into the ready apertures of the women.

In moments, the men got up again, closed up their pants, and walked away. "Hey!" the leader called. "Where you going?"

"Home," a man replied.

"You can't go home! We got a war to fight!"

"We don't feel like fighting any more." The men walked away, and soon were gone.

The leader was not a fool. "No more fucking!" he commanded. "Kill them instead!" But the women beckoned, smiling, and the men, aroused by the sight of the sex just consummated, crowded forward, ignoring the commands of the leader. They lacked good discipline, being *ad hoc* recruits, and the women were simply too tempting. Soon the ground was strewn with copulating couples, and the remaining men were eagerly waiting their turns.

And as each man had sex, the Red Glamor touched his distracted mind, instilling an aversion to any further violence. It was the trick the succubi used: catch a man in his most vulnerable state, the moment of orgasm. Only in this case no souls were being sucked out; a new and better directive was implanted. It seemed as if it was the sex that softened the men, but that was just the cover.

It set them up, and none of them were likely to protest.

I am rather proud of my ploy, the Red Glamor remarked telepathically. *For one thing, it will make rebels everywhere afraid to have sex, lest they cease being rebels. And it is a far more positive way to handle the situation.*

It was indeed. There would be no overt violence here, no damage done, not even to the rebels.

The leader was made of sterner stuff. He drew the long knife he carried and ran at the nearest woman.

This one is mine the Red Glamor thought for Iolo's benefit. She intercepted the man invisibly, one hand catching the knife wrist, the other opening his trousers and drawing out his stiffening member. She guided it to her cleft and pressed down on it so that it penetrated her fully. Before he knew it, he was in the throes of sex with an invisible woman.

The waiting men stared at the leader, who seemed to be having sex with himself. He thrust and jetted into seeming air, while Red touched his mind as she had the others. Then she drew herself off him, leaving him with a detumescing member and a pacifistic attitude. Confused and embarrassed, he hastily put his instrument away and departed.

Iolo was not human, but he had learned human ways, including an appreciation for sex. He found himself wishing he could be participating in this mass orgy of willing sex. But of course that was not feasible.

Negation. It was the Red Glamor. *I will oblige you, friend.*

But I am in cloud form and you are busy. There is no time.

Coalesce only your member; that will suffice.

Now there was a concept! *But it would simply fall to the ground, unsupported by any other solid body.*

Negation. Try it.

He shrugged, mentally, and began forming his member. And the Glamor took hold of it with her invisible hand and guided it into her cleft, so that as it became firm it was supported by her body. Anyone watching would have seen a human style penis form in the air and move slightly. He lacked any support for thrusting, but she handled that too, using her hand to thrust it in and back. Soon he climaxed, and the feeling was strong despite the lack of a body to generate ejaculate.

Appreciation! he thought in the throes of it.

We value your assistance, Iolo. Take good care of Voila. She gave him a last rippling squeeze, then relaxed with the member still embedded, giving him time to dissolve it back into vapor. It was good to have a truly understanding and competent partner.

Appreciation for not dropping it on the ground, he thought wryly.

Acknowledged. She waited just long enough, then moved on to her next charge, for there were many men yet to touch.

It was evident that this spot rebellion was under control. Iolo was about to depart, when he remembered his mission. *Red.*

I read it in your mind during your joy of manhood, she responded. *I must report to the malign Spirit by dusk, lest Havoc be tortured. And they are after my ikon.*

Confirmation. Disgust.

She was not concerned. *There is more than meets the present mind.*

He hoped so. *Parting.*

Parting, she echoed.

Iolo oriented on the next nearest Glamor. This was Voila, in the region of China in southern Asia. The rebels there consisted of a mutinous unit of the local military force, well trained and disciplined. This would not be easy to stop.

"Welcome, Iolo!" Voila said, aware the moment he transferred in. She kissed his vapor. "I know your message, infuriating as it is."

What form is this? he asked, because it was not at all human.

"I am assuming the form of a local dragon," she explained. "Earthly dragons are not like real dragons. They are basically sinuous serpents with legs and wings and horrendous heads. But they carry considerable social clout, considering they are magical while this is a science planet. I believe the local troops will heed the word of their dragon." She continued to shape the weird creature, invisibly. She would make it visible when the appropriate time came, and of course she was reading that time in the future paths.

Are you really going to go to the Male Spirit? Iolo inquired, for he was unable to read Voila's future paths.

"Why, are you jealous?" she asked merrily.

Affirmation, he responded dutifully. Jealously was another human emotion he had studied and tried to emulate. *I don't want him possessing you in any sense. After all, we may marry when we are eighteen.*

"We may indeed," she agreed. "If circumstances warrant. We will know when the time comes. We will always be friends, regardless."

Red had sex with me.

"The bitch!" she said, laughing. "How can I preserve your virginity if she messes in?"

He had to laugh too, mentally. He and Voila considered sex many times, playing in childhood at being man and woman, and it had become a quite pleasant pastime. They had also discussed marriage, because they understood each other completely and it would be a challenging thing for a human and ifrit to do. But Idyll indicated that there was only a 50-50 intermediate future chance of it.

"It depends largely on the outcome of this Second Crisis," she said, answering his thought. "And on its relation to the Third Crisis. The welfare of the planets comes first."

Which was the problem with loving this particular woman: she was too important to the fate of several worlds. She could not marry for love or convenience; it had to contribute to the proper paths. It was ironic—another human concept—that it was their mutual understanding of this that generated much of their love for each other. They got along perfectly, because of their awareness of the near futures and the interaction of their cultures. But that same understanding meant that neither could quarrel with the necessary choices. *Affirmation.*

"But between crises we can get together and pretend," she said. "I'll be the innocent but nubile and lovely human girl, and you'll be the alien man with a dark secret who sacrifices all to get into my luscious little cleft. We'll be the ultimate fools."

Fools he agreed fondly. Something they could never afford to be in reality.

"Iolo, there'll be part of a scene when I arrive at the malign Spirit's redoubt," she said. "You won't like it, but you must bear with it. Do not throttle him."

Agreement he thought reluctantly. She could see farther into the future than he could, especially when buttressed by Idyll and Mino. That was why she was the effective leader of this earth mission, and prime architect of their handling of the Second Crisis. But if she said he wouldn't like it, that was surely the case. He had a trial coming.

"Regret," she said softly, and kissed his space. "Now get on with your mission. Watch out for winds."

Parting. He extended toward the next closest Glamor, which was Gray.

Unfortunately, there was a violent storm in progress in that area. It forced Iolo to coalesce immediately, lest his substance be too far disturbed by the gusty winds and descending sheets of rain. Then he realized that the Gray Glamor was using this storm to help the defenders against the rebels, just as the Black Glamor had with the tornado. Gray Chroma magic was noted mainly for its ability to nullify magic outside its zone, but no magic was limited to its specialty. The Gray Glamor could conjure a storm, or more economically, divert an existing one. But how should that stop the rebels?

It's a cover, ifrit, the Gray Glamor's thought came. *I am nulling science magic in this area, but prefer they not know, as my range is limited.*

Oh, of course. Iolo completed his condensation to his human form. He could assume any solid form, but the one he had practiced so long with Voila was the fastest and easiest because of its familiarity. He had become the dog for the journey to this planet, but there was no longer any point in pretending he was an animal of limited intellect.

Now he saw how this was operating. This was an urban setting, and the rebel troops had been assembled from a local military barracks. The men had chafed because of inaction, which was no coincidence; the female authorities had placed the roughest men in this unit and kept it well away from temptation, distrusting its nature. Unfortunately that had made it a prime conversion target for the Male Spirit, who had surely promised violence, rapine, and wealth as the spoils of war. There was enough disturbance here to show that such action had gotten fairly started before the arrival of the Glamor.

The storm was soaking everything, including especially the Science Chroma guns and grenades of the rebels. That should not ordinarily have rendered them inoperative, but served as a pretext. Gray had suppressed science magic in this area, so that no guns, grenades, cars, or electric devices operated. That rendered the rebels relatively helpless against the resurging defendants, who were confined to crude clubs, knives, and ropes. Those simple non-magic implements worked. By the time the rebels realized that their "hi-tech" weapons no longer worked, they were being overrun and taken prisoner. They were cursing the weather, thinking that if it wasn't the water getting in the works, it must be the electrical effects of the lightning.

Seeing the situation coming under control, the Gray Glamor turned his majority attention on Iolo. *You come bearing uncomfortable news, ifrit.* He used telepathy, because he was a bird without the ability to speak human sonics, though he was by no means otherwise silent. In fact, he was an impressive bird, apart from his Glamor status: he stood about as tall as a man, on a single three-toes leg, with three bright eyes placed around his head. He seemed to be in a cloak, but that was deceptive; it was formed by his two wings. Actually he was what was defined on Charm as a three-legged species, with those extremities forming feet or wings as required. When he flew, it was with three wings and no feet. He was not flying here, as this would have amazed the natives to an inconvenient extent. Here on Earth, birds had only two wings, along with several other extremities.

"Agreement, Glamor. The Male Spirit demands that you and all Glamors report to his lair by nightfall at that region, or he will torture Havoc, whom he holds captive."

Incredulity!

"He has sent out minions to fetch the ikons, whose positions he knows or can trace. Yours is also being targeted. He believes that since he has Havoc's ikon, Havoc can not oppose him. He is using Havoc as a lever against the other Glamors, believing that Havoc is the most important, being the king."

Havoc can not be tortured.

"We know that, but it seems the Male Spirit does not. Thus he is showing his hand, and it is a cruel hand. He made Havoc's wife and mistress have sex with him, then with each other, in Havoc's presence. They acceded, lest Havoc be tortured."

I am not human, but I find this amusing, as humans surely do. How can the Spirit believe that fear of torture makes these women respond?

"I wonder myself. I conjecture that the Spirit knows less of us than he supposes, or that he is playing a deeper game, trying to force us to show our further abilities. Or it may simply be diversion for his effort to close off all future paths that do not favor him."

That becomes dangerous.

"Yet Voila and Idyll know it, and tolerate it."

We must trust their judgment. They can see farther into the future than we can.

"Agreement."

I will be there.

"Appreciation. Parting."

Acknowledged. The Glamor returned his attention to the messy battle.

Iolo diffused and moved on to the next Glamor. He was getting the job done, distasteful as it was.

He turned to the Spirit's lair by dusk, his message delivered. All the Chroma Glamors were there, but none of Havoc's children.

The Spirit was openly impressed by the animal Glamors. "A white six-legged billy goat," he remarked. "A brown wormy thing you call a dragon. A giant silver spider. A gray bird-like thing. And an orange sphinx. You certainly have variety on your frontier world!"

None of the creatures or people responded. They were not here by choice, and made no pretense to liking it.

"Black, green, and translucent men, together with one invisible one. And a luscious red woman," the Spirit continued. "A handsome blue woman. And a really nice yellow one. But of course I already know about you, honey, since yours was the first ikon I captured, so I was able to nullify you and take over your Chroma zone. I look forward to a sexual threesome with you coloreds. You surely know some nice tricks."

The three human female Glamors did not reply.

The Spirit's visage hardened. "But we are missing four. The king's children. So it must be time to make a demonstration, so that all you become aware that I did not bluff and will not be gainsaid." He glanced at the two torturers, who stepped forward. "Gentlemen, proceed."

Then the four siblings appeared: Warp, Weft, Flame, and Voila. "Touch him and you die," Flame said grimly.

The Male Spirit smiled. "Oh, really, firehead? Let's call that bluff. You know my nature: this is merely the body I am occupying at the moment, one that can readily be replaced. But if I have to go to that trouble, I will be annoyed, and I will naturally take it out on Havoc. So come here, redhead, and give me a kiss."

Flame hesitated, scowling. "Better do it, Sis," Warp murmured. "He isn't bluffing."

With evident extreme reluctance, Flame stepped toward the Spirit. She was in her Amazon garb, with a knife at her side. He smiled, relishing the encounter. "Here are the ground rules, doxie. You strike me or offer anything other than token resistance, the torture starts. Let's see what it takes to make you balk."

"Leave her alone," Gale snapped. "She's not grown."

He glanced at her. "Ah, the mother speaks. I can make the mother ream out my rectum with her tongue, but she won't tolerate a little garden variety smooching with her daughter? Go ahead, mother: tell her to balk."

Gale was grimly silent. Monochrome took her hand supportively. Iolo found this an interesting example of human interaction: the mistress comforting the wife.

Flame reached the spirit. He took hold of her and hauled her in for a kiss. She yielded, barely, her arms down by her sides. Then he reached down and pinched her tight bottom. She remained still.

"It's not quite enough," the Spirit said. "Take off your clothes."

Gale made a strangled sound but did not move or speak. Flame slowly began working on her shirt.

"Too slow, girl." The man put his hand at her throat and ripped her shirt down the front.

Flame's hand went for her knife. Iolo knew that this was for show, because it was far too slow; she could have had the knife out and slashing his throat in the time she took to touch the blade.

Weft jumped forward. "Don't do it, Sis! He'll torture Dad!" She interposed herself, her perky bosom coming between Flame and the man.

"Well now," the Spirit said. "Isn't this a nice piece! Let's get a close look." He ripped her blouse similarly open. Her beautiful breasts emerged, and Iolo knew that this too was artifice: she was making them prominent, as an effective distraction.

"I'll take it," the Spirit said, putting his hands on those full orbs and squeezing. Weft faced him, proffering no resistance.

He caught his fingers in her skirt band and yanked. The skirt came down, along with her underwear, exposing her bottom and legs. He grabbed that bottom and fondled it fiercely. "Prime meat here," he said approvingly. "You do know how to fuck, don't you honey? Let's do it now. Show your daddy what you're made of."

"No!" It was Voila. "She's not for you."

He turned to her. "Oh? Then it must be that you are the one for me. Come here, you young tidbit. Got boobs yet?"

"Stay back, Sis," Weft warned. "This guy's mean."

"On the contrary," the Spirit said. "Come here, little girl. I understand you are the strongest of the Glamors. What are you going to do to me, to make me destroy your father?"

Voila approached him, looking very young. "I am going to nullify you," she said evenly. "But not yet."

"I am so glad to hear that, cherub. Meanwhile let's fuck. That should be real fun, considering the audience."

"You are trying to make one of us balk, so you have a pretext to torture Father," Voila said. "This will not work."

"No? And why not, my pretty?"

"Because you can't control him, or any of us."

"You forget I have your ikons, sweetie."

"They do not suffice. Now we are tired of this game, and will depart."

"Not until I'm satisfied, nymphet." He grabbed for her. But his hand passed through her substance without resistance.

"Parting," Voila said, fading from the scene.

"That's a balk! Torture him!"

The hooded men stepped forward—and stared. For Havoc was no longer there. Instead there was only a vaguely man shaped cloud of vapor. Havoc was diffusing, as he could have at any point.

Gale smiled. "You never had any of us, cretin. Glamors can't be controlled. All your posturing was done by our sufferance. Now we are through playing such games. We are leaving you, having demonstrated our power."

Then all the Glamors vanished, one by one. In moments only the other three king's children remained. They smiled and vanished.

The Male Spirit was left staring. Iolo knew, because he was really the last to leave, invisibly. The point had been made. The Glamors had not lost their powers, regardless of their ikons. Indeed, they had powers beyond those shown before. The Male Spirit had been had. They had distracted him until the proper future path was ready, gaining an advantage.

The sight of the Spirit's scowl of fury was wonderful. Of course Iolo knew that this was by no means the end of the matter. The Spirit's program of conquest was still being waged, and was still gaining. But it was a nice episode.

Iolo just hoped that they had played it correctly. Hereafter the Spirit would be far more careful, and that would be dangerous.

Chapter 21
Assignment

Monochrome was distraught. They had trumped the foul Male Spirit, but that was merely another pyrrhic victory. The Glamors had used up most of the rest of their Chroma stones and now were largely powerless. The Spirit's collection of their icons had effectively cut off their local sources of magic power. Only when they were in their home chroma zones could they function effectively. That meant that the main regions of the planet were no longer magically defended.

They were losing the war. More rebellions were springing up all across the planet, too many for the Glamors to handle even had they had full powers. The tide was inevitably turning toward destruction. Only here on Antarctica did the existing order seem secure. Even here, she realized, there had been episodes, such as the initial attempt to kill the entire party from Charm. Voila had thwarted that, giving Caveat the credit, and thwarted a later attempt on her life, giving Mistress Modesty credit. They had been early salvos in the Male Spirit's rebellion.

"Oh Havoc, I hate this," she wailed in his arms. "Earth is going to be lost on my watch."

"Not necessarily," he reassured her. "The future paths don't read clearly when Glamor opposes Glamor, but Voila has been guiding us to our best probabilities. Statistics are not my domain, but I understand they can be deceptive. Our chances are better than they appear."

"But the malign Spirit is systematically closing off every path that doesn't favor him—and Voila is letting him. Where is the sense in that?"

"Let's ask her." He lifted one hand and snapped his fingers.

Voila appeared. "You summoned me, father?" They hugged, though they had been together only hours before, at the Male Spirit's lair.

Monochrome had to laugh. They were playing stern father, dutiful daughter, though in reality the daughter was governing the operation.

"I am trying to explain to Chrome how statistics can be deceiving, especially when it comes to losing a planet or two. But my ailing elder mind is not smart enough to handle it. Can you clarify it?"

Voila nodded. "It is time for that." Monochrome realized that Havoc had read the near future and timed his summons for when his daughter was about to appear anyway. They were both too busy to waste time on incidental dialogues.

"You have something else on your mind," Monochrome told the girl. "Don't waste time catering to my ignorance."

"Necessary," Voila said seriously. "In your immunization programs you need to know which diseases are most threatening, so as not to waste resources fighting the wrong ones. Sometimes you merely test for suspected diseases."

"True." Monochrome was surprised the girl had picked up on this aspect of Earth culture, as it did not exist on Charm.

"If you have a test that is one hundred percent accurate, you are sure of catching all the cases."

"True." It was a statistical certainty.

"So if five percent of the population has the disease, you have identified them all, and need treat only those ones. The positives."

"True." Where was this leading?

"But if you are one of those tested, and the verdict is positive, there may only a fifty percent chance that you actually have the disease."

"That's what gets me," Havoc said. "How a hundred percent becomes fifty percent."

"Well, you have to allow for the false positives," Monochrome said. "The test may indicate that ten percent of the population has it, when only five percent really does. That makes that chances of an individual testee who tests positive even."

"It is one hundred percent likely that the Male Spirit will win the planet," Voila said. "But only fifty percent that he will prevail in this struggle for power."

"That's not the same!" Monochrome protested. Then she reconsidered. "But I appreciate the principle. He needs not only to win the planet, but to keep it. You are reading the further future."

"Agreement. We regret the difficulty this puts you into, but it is the way of it. This rebellion has been brewing for some time; the volcano conversion was merely the trigger, not the cause. Your chances of thwarting it were one in three; with our help they are one in two."

"Yet if we had not set out to reclaim Colony Charm, that trigger would not have occurred."

"Affirmation. But the rebellion would have come at a later date, perhaps when some other Mistress was in power, and been more certain of success. It is better to tackle it now."

Monochrome nodded. "I do appreciate that insight. Was this what you came to clarify for me?"

"In part. Do you trust me?"

Monochrome was taken aback. "Have I expressed distrust? I did not mean to."

"Negation. But further trust is necessary. Are you satisfied that your oath of friendship with my father was warranted?"

"Oh, yes! It led me to love him. That is a rather rare and wonderful thing for me."

"I did it reluctantly," Havoc said. "But it was right."

"Now you must go to Planet Charm and learn diffusion."

"But Earth is in peril! I can't desert my planet in its hour of greatest need. I am the representative of the Female Spirit."

Voila did not argue the case. She merely waited.

"Idea," Havoc said after a moment. "The Male Spirit wants to gain control of your body. He will be able to, when he wins power. Only if you are off-planet will he be balked."

"I would not flee for personal safety!"

"My ability to diffuse saved me from torture," Havoc continued. "The Male Spirit did not know that we Glamors mastered that mechanism, learning it from the ifrits. It is in that sense alien magic. In fact it is independent of Chroma zones, and can't be stifled by the environment. If you learn it also, he will not be able to hold you, because this is also independent of ikons. That would guarantee your safety."

The notion had considerable if alarming appeal. She distrusted it. "Are you sure you don't simply want me out of the way while you yield the planet?" Monochrome demanded, not facetiously.

"We do want that," Voila agreed. "But you are also needed on Charm at this time."

Monochrome was shocked. "Your planet needs *me*, the leader of your erstwhile enemy planet? Your awareness of the future paths make this the proper course?"

"Affirmation," Voila said.

Did she trust the girl that far? Monochrome had to take a moment to ponder.

"But what will I do for sex if she's gone?" Havoc asked, also not entirely facetiously.

Now Voila smiled. "Father, there is always mother. She does know how. I understand she is even good at it, when she tries. Flame's lover Fifth swears by her, and he doesn't even like full-fleshed women. Perhaps you could persuade her to substitute for the Mistress."

Havoc laughed. "I am answered. Not to mention that I love her, and begot you by her."

"Appreciation, father." She kissed him on the cheek. "I hope some day to win your confidence."

He patted her shoulder reassuringly. "Some day you surely will, daughter."

Their banter had an insidious effect. They plainly loved and respected each other, Monochrome decided. "I defer to your judgment. I will go to Charm."

"I will take you to Mino," Voila said, instantly serious. "There you will meet Havoc's oath friend Ennui. Take Idyll from her and go to Charm."

"But I have no idea how to—" Monochrome broke off, realizing that the path had been cleared. She turned to Havoc. "Kiss me, beloved, and return to your wife."

Havoc did, with gusto. Then Monochrome took Voila's hand—and found herself in what appeared to be a small spaceship, facing a severe elder woman. Voila was gone. "Ennui, I presume?"

"Monochrome," the woman responded, her Colony accent almost unintelligible. "Question: Is it true?"

Her mind made the context clear. "Yes, I am Havoc's oath friend, as are you. But it was involuntary, with me. Now we are lovers, and in love." The two were not at all synonymous.

"Alignment. It was involuntary with me too," Ennui said. "We were in an ugly situation and he wanted my cooperation, but I was afraid of him and demanded the barbarian oath. That made all the difference. He became king and I became his personal secretary, effectively governing the planet for him. The details, I mean; he was more for the big picture."

"I, too, understand about governing. Both the show aspects and the duller but more important details. But now I am supposed to leave Earth and go to Colony Charm with you to learn diffusion."

"It is worth learning." Ennui paused, then shrugged. "So it seems we are oath sisters. We must trust each other. It is surely for the best."

"Surely," Monochrome agreed. "I see you are no more comfortable with this than I am."

The woman nodded. "Jealousy would be too unkind a word. But it is difficult to share oath friendship. It is such a special thing. Gale was not pleased when she learned of me, though she later reconciled."

"I do believe I understand," Monochrome said. "Oh—and he said I was to take Idyll from you. I don't understand what that means."

Ennui winced. "Symbol had to give up her ikon. Now I must give up Idyll. That pains me, but Idyll confirms it."

"I don't mean to cause discomfort, or to take anything that isn't mine."

"Clarification: this is not that. It means that you need her guidance. Hold my hand."

Monochrome reached out to take her hand. Something vast, spiritual, and kind crossed from Ennui's body to Monochrome's body.

Greeting. I am Idyll Ifrit, or an imprint of her. The full entity resides on planet Counter Charm.

"The one who sees the intermediate future," Monochrome said. "Voila's mentor."

Agreement. She and I work with Mino, who sees the far future. The linkages are not perfect, but together we have a fair appreciation of the future paths.

"Something I don't understand. How can losing Earth be better than keeping it?"

What is best for the immediate future is not necessarily best for the intermediate or far future. It is necessary for the male spirit to establish his dominion, using his most trusted and capable minions. Then when he is overthrown, those minions will be nullified, and there will be no further unrest for some time. This is merely one thread of a much larger pattern.

Monochrome saw that this could make a significant difference. Had she known who the rebels were going to be, she could have dealt with them preemptively and perhaps saved herself a revolution.

"Why did I have to take you from Ennui, who is surely sorry to lose you?"

I must teach you diffusion, which you will need for the Third Crisis, and guide you as you govern Charm. Ennui will be too busy to be with you throughout.

"Govern Charm! I am the Mistress of Earth, whom Charm is opposing." Yet Voila had said that Charm needed her, and governance was her area of expertise.

No longer. The situation is more complicated than we could fathom before interacting directly with Earth, and we learned you were never our enemy. All the Glamors are gone, from Charm, and the situation there is also complicating. A Glamor is required to handle the more difficult challenges, especially in the absence of the king, and the people will accept you. You must do what Havoc did, making appearances, solving problems directly, while the real government of the planet continues without significant change.

"Havoc is a figurehead?"

Not at all. Merely the most visible executive. The one the people look to. As long as they love Havoc, they accept the laws he enforces with little question.

While the real work was quietly done by the bureaucracy. This was ever the way of government. She understood it well enough. She just had never expected to do it for the colony planet Earth was theoretically at war with.

"Amazement," Monochrome said, lapsing into the colony summary convention.

Ennui smiled, seemingly not confused by the one-sided dialogue. "I know it's confusing. But Idyll will guide you well."

Now we must go to Planet Counter Charm, my home. Take Ennui's hand, as she can't transport herself.

Monochrome looked at Ennui. "I am supposed to—"

"Understanding." Ennui took her hand.

Then they were in a pleasant glade. Monochrome knew immediately that this was not Earth; the gravity differed slightly, and the trees were unlike any she had seen before. The air was fresh and fragrant, with a bracing, almost intoxicating tinge.

This is my home, Idyll thought. *Would you prefer that I made a human emulation for sonic communication?*

"Actually, I would. So much is so suddenly new that I think I would relate better."

Mist swirled before them. It coalesced into a human-sized shape, which then became defined as a pretty young woman. She was nymphly in her lovely nudity. "Greeting," she said. "I am the emulation. But I am also inside you."

Confirmation, the thought came.

"She had to be within you to transport you, the first time," Ennui explained. "The Glamors can travel between planets, but have to have ikons or aspects to orient on. Idyll means you no harm; she is a significant part of our effort."

"The Second Crisis requires the most of each of us," the nymphly Idyll said.

"I am not sure I quite understand these crises," Monochrome said. "Havoc spoke of them also."

"The First Crisis was Mino," Idyll said. "He is the advance scout sent to prepare our worlds for eventual mining by the machine culture. This would destroy them, so we had to nullify him. He is now our ally. The Second Crisis is the effort by Earth to reclaim Charm as a colony; this would also have deleterious effect on us. The Third Crisis is the arrival of the Machine culture in force, in response to the signal Mino sent at light-speed before he was converted. As it happens, the same group of people are handling all three. We are fortunate that Havoc came on the scene to organize these efforts; otherwise we would have lost by default."

"Havoc," Monochrome repeated. "I love him."

"So do I, in my fashion. We have made love many times here in my demesnes. This emotion helps unify our species, which are not otherwise at all similar."

Monochrome took stock. "You are a completely alien life form, yet you can relate sexually?"

The woman smiled. "Not even a life form as we understand it. We are of demonic origin. But we learned sex from the humans, and they enjoy it so much that we have learned to like it also. Any interaction with Havoc is a pleasure, and he is especially keen on this."

"So I discovered!" Monochrome agreed, laughing, and Idyll laughed with her. The ifrits had learned humor, too.

"Now sometimes we even condense to human form and do it between ourselves," Idyll said. "But we prefer it with real humans, because of their extreme appreciation." She shrugged prettily. "Both our species have gained much from our association."

After seeing Havoc diffuse into vapor, thwarting the Male Spirit, Monochrome appreciated this. But she had a separate issue. "You spoke of my governing Charm. I do have training and competence in governance, but are you sure the natives will accept me?"

"Affirmation. You will introduce yourself to them tomorrow. Now we must instruct you in diffusing."

"By that you mean vaporizing, becoming a cloud?" She wanted to be quite sure, for this was an astonishing thing.

"Affirmation. It is not difficult once you have the pattern. Its advantage is that it is not dependent on an ikon or particular Chroma zone. You will be able to do it anywhere, and escape any prison."

"Havoc did that, and told me that," Monochrome agreed. "I was amazed."

"Some abilities are best concealed until the need comes."

"I can appreciate that. But I have no idea how to do it."

"Follow me." The nymph lifted one hand. Vapor rose from it as her fingers dissolved.

Monochrome lifted her hand. The entity within her focused. She felt her substance changing, loosening its physical bonds without sacrificing their interconnections. She saw the vapor rising from her fingers. She was awed.

"Comment: It is impressive," Ennui said. "But safe, when you know how."

"Thank you for that reassurance."

The nymph's head dissolved, forming an expanding cloud. Monochrome felt her own head going, becoming tenuous. She felt no fear, only wonder.

The nymph's upper body fuzzed and evaporated. So did Monochrome's. They were forming two clouds.

Keep our substances separate, the ifrit's thought came. *We can interact, but until you are fully conversant with your cloud form, you should be discrete.*

Discrete, Monochrome agreed, liking the concept.

The process continued, until they had become two adjacent clouds within the glade, extending beyond it through the trees. Now she was aware of Ennui in a new way, not seeing her so much as feeling her with her diffuse substance, knowing her shape, temperature, water content, and animation. *Ennui,* she thought.

"I am here," the woman replied sonically.

I am around you, and in you where you breathe.

"Affirmation. I feel your soft cohesion on my skin."

Idyll extended a pseudopod of mist. "Touch her," Ennui said.

Monochrome found she could shape her vapor, slowly. She extended a somewhat ragged projection to meet the other.

The two clouds made contact. *Congratulations*, Idyll thought with much greater clarity. *You have achieved cloud form.*

She had indeed. Not only was she conscious, she was phenomenally alert. Her mind seemed to be working better than it ever had. There was no seeming solid resistance between the neurons; they connected at light-speed without having to grow links. She was exhilarated. This was better than being solid!

Suddenly Monochrome was nervous. Was she becoming intoxicated or delusional? That was dangerous. *I want to return to my own form.*

I will guide you.

The ifrit did. Monochrome coalesced, her cloud condensing, solidifying at the base. She felt her human feet taking form beside the pile of clothing she had vacated. Clothing was not animate, and not subject to direct control of the will. Her ankles formed, and built up to her knees, as though a mannequin was being developed from clay. There was no spurting blood; she wasn't sure how that worked. She could feel her toes, though her upper body remained vapor.

Her thighs coalesced, and joined to form her torso. Her belly built up to her waist, and on to her chest. Her headless body stood there, its breasts prominent. The arms developed at the sides. Then at last the head formed, throat, chin, face, and cranium, with hair appearing full length. That was interesting, because hair was essentially dead material; how could it be part of this animate process?

Magic, or our equivalent, Idyll's thought came. *You are thinking scientifically.*

So she was. This was a magic planet; the rules differed.

Her body complete, she walked around, flexing her arms and legs. She seemed to be exactly as she had been. She picked up her clothing and got into it. It fit perfectly.

Still, this experience had shaken her. She had seen Havoc do it, and knew that he had returned to normal, but it was different when she did it herself. She had long since accepted the reality of magic, but aspects of it required more assimilation than others. And this was not exactly magic, as she had been informed.

"Now you need to come with me to Charm," Ennui said. "And to Triumph City. Tomorrow you will introduce yourself to the people, so that they will accept you as their temporary queen."

"I'm not anyone's queen!" Monochrome protested. "There is no monarchy on Earth."

"But there is on Charm. You will govern by Havoc's authority, as queen regent. The need is urgent."

Monochrome did not question why Havoc and Gale had not returned to do this job. She knew Voila had decreed that they must stay on Earth. Monochrome had become expendable in the defense of Earth; thus the job was hers, ironically.

Affirmation, Idyll's thought came. The nymph had not re-formed; it was not the ifrit's normal form. *I will help as needed. I am familiar with most of the folk you will encounter, and Ennui will backstop you.*

"I suspect I should get some rest and sleep," Monochrome said. "I don't change worlds often, and I am not accustomed to it."

Ennui laughed. "I know the feeling. It was like that when Havoc became king and I had to steer him straight."

"Will it be all right simply to sleep here?"

"Negation. You must sleep at the king's palace."

She had briefly lost track of that in her adjustment to the idea of diffusion and coalescing. "Havoc said nothing about my taking his place."

"I suspect Havoc did not know. There are things even Glamors do not know, lest they inadvertently betray secrets by thinking of them. But Voila informed me."

Confirmation, Idyll thought.

"And Voila governs," Monochrome said, bemused. "A sixteen year old girl."

"And the strongest Glamor we know of. I love Havoc, and will never betray him, but in this respect he is a figurehead. He is smart, dedicated, and more man than any other, but he depends on others for the details. In fact I have effectively run the planet for some time, as I mentioned, and must get back to work now."

So was Monochrome to be a temporary figurehead, in the manner of Havoc, while Ennui did the real work?

Negation, Idyll thought. *Ennui does not govern the planet, she runs it. Havoc gives directives she implements; you will do the same.*

Ah. That clarified it. She could do that. "Then I think we are ready for the palace," Monochrome said. "I trust you will introduce me to a suitable guide, so that you can work."

"Agreement."

Then they were standing in a wooden chamber, before a large wood desk. "My office," Ennui said. She lifted her voice. "Lady."

Another older woman appeared. She was elegant, and carried herself with a certain royal grace. The two embraced, then Ennui turned to Monochrome. "Lady Aspect, this is Monochrome, Mistress of Mistresses of Earth, the effective ruler, here by Voila's directive and Havoc's acquiescence. Monochrome, this is the Lady Aspect, wife of the former King Deal, now Havoc's social authority. You may trust her in all things."

"Greeting," the Lady Aspect said graciously. If she was amazed by this sudden development, she took it in stride.

Again, Monochrome was aware of the strong Colony accent. *This won't do,* she thought. *I will not be able to communicate effectively with these people. In a thousand years the language has diverged too far.* But something bothered her about that: the four King's children had spoken without accents from the start. How was that possible?

They read the minds of the Earthers on the ship, Idyll explained. *They knew from the minds what the words meant, and quickly learned them. You will do the same.*

But I barely know telepathy!

For this, you know enough. You have been doing it with Ennui.

Not that I am aware of.

Correction, Ennui's thought came. *I read her meaning, and projected mine to her.*

Accepted, the ifrit thought. *Now she will do it herself.*

Meanwhile the Lady Aspect stood without reaction, letting the telepathic dialogue proceed. Monochrome realized with another start that she too was telepathic, so understood exactly.

"Hello," Monochrome said. "It seems I am to govern the planet temporarily, in Havoc's stead. We are oath friends."

The Lady nodded. "That explains it. Come with me; we shall leave Ennui to her business."

"Gratitude," Ennui murmured, taking a seat at her desk, where papers had accumulated. But she sent a thought: *Best not to mind read beyond that purpose at present, lest it betray your ability.*

This belatedly startled Monochrome, as she had not realized before this dialogue that Ennui was telepathic, or that Ennui knew that she herself was telepathic; the woman had given no sign. She nodded, appreciating the warning.

Aspect brought her to an elaborate suite. "This is Havoc's apartment. You will occupy it for now." She projected her meaning with her words, so that it seemed almost as if she were speaking Earther dialect.

"Oh, no, I'd prefer not!" Monochrome protested, trying to do the same.

That's it, the woman thought encouragingly. "But if you are to govern—"

"I did not seek this, but will perform as required. But I prefer some place to sleep I can call my own, and not be displaced when Havoc and Gale return." It was already becoming easier.

"There is only the royal mistress' suite now vacant. I'm not sure—"

"That will do. I am Havoc's mistress."

The Lady paused momentarily, assimilating this. "I see. Some might consider this to be a lesser post."

"I love him. I must be with him. The title hardly matters."

Aspect considered. "You are beautiful, yet I think older."

"I am fifty. Age is immaterial. They call me a Glamor."

"A Glamor! Do you know what that signifies?"

"I do."

"Then I will perform for you as I do for Havoc, guiding you in the protocols of this kingdom. But I think for convenience you need some servants."

"I am unclear why."

"It is the royal way. To suitably impress the populace you need the accouterments. I will prepare a gown for you, but they will attend you constantly."

Monochrome sighed inwardly. "As you wish."

Aspect frowned. "Observation: it is my impression that the functionaries down the line who implement the directives from above are aware of your origin and are negative toward you. They are not providing you with the best. They are sending a girl who harbors a secret sexual appetite that makes others nervous, a boy who is in treatment as a thief, and a Chroma representative whose wife is currently away seeking her fourth: that is, sex with another man for the purpose of getting pregnant. This is both legitimate and necessary, by our convention, but leaves her husband on edge both because of the denial of her favors and the knowledge that she is granting them to another man. He may be distracted and irritable. Recommendation: reject these people and require more suitable assistants."

Monochrome considered. She could handle appetites and thievery, and could surely console the man in marital distress in her fashion. "I am sure they are worthy people in their separate fashions, and deserving of their chances. I will accept them as they are."

"Acquiescence. The girl is available immediately. She is sixteen and sexually appealing, as bath girls are. I will see to the others in due course." *Practice your communication with them.*

I will. Appreciation.

The Lady snapped her fingers. A lovely teen-aged girl appeared. "This is Scent, who will be your bath girl. She will make you clean and comfortable for the night. Scent, this is the Lady Monochrome, temporary Queen of Charm. She is unfamiliar with local protocols, so you will guide her appropriately. Feed her tonight, see that she rests well, and have her ready for her introductory speech at the assigned hour tomorrow morning."

"Understood, Lady."

Aspect departed. Monochrome realized she had been passed along to another guide. She concentrated on projection. "I am not sure—"

"Does my lady prefer a shower or a bath?" Without the telepathy that question would have been prohibitively obscure.

"A hot bath!" Monochrome agreed gladly.

Soon she was pleasantly soaking in a marvelous bubble bath in a giant tub. The girl was indeed competent; everything was right. Monochrome hardly needed to think of anything she might want before the girl had it ready. Colony Charm evidently had well-trained bath attendants. But she also fathomed the secret appetite: a rape fantasy common to many young girls, but more intense in this one. Scent wanted to be ravished, but in her own fashion.

"Is it permissible to talk for a while?" Monochrome asked. She had the additional motive of needing to practice her telepathic attuning.

"Anything my Lady desires is permissible."

"Do you know my identity?"

"No, Lady. Just that you are the Lady Monochrome of Earth, occupying the suite of the king's mistress."

"Delicately put! I am King Havoc's new mistress. But I am also the ruler of Planet Earth, being mistress in two senses. Are you curious to know more?"

The girl smiled. "Desperately, Mistress! But I am not permitted to pry."

"I gather you are to be my body servant for the duration of my stay on this planet. Does that mean that your prime loyalty is to me?"

"Yes, Lady, by definition. Until the Lady Aspect says otherwise."

"Then let us get to know more about each other." Because Monochrome did not want any miscues or embarrassments. There was one huge one she needed to identify at the outset. "You are assigned to serve me. What is your private personal opinion of me?"

"Lady, I am allowed no such opinion!" the girl protested.

"But you are obliged to give it when asked," Monochrome said shrewdly. The telepathy certainly helped, but she was heeding Ennui's advice not to use it for that purpose. The dialogue interpretation was challenge enough.

"I must not give offense," Scent said nervously.

"Risk it. I must know the truth."

The girl winced, but obliged. "I do not know you, Lady, but I did know the Lady Symbol, Havoc's former mistress, whom you are displacing. A remarkably sexy older woman I much admire. My private loyalty is to her. You are—" she was unable to finish.

"An impostor?"

Pained, the girl nodded.

"And will this be the private opinion of others I encounter here?"

"Yes, probably, Lady," Scent agreed faintly.

"Appreciation," Monochrome said, using the local shorthand. "At such time as that changes, let me know. We will speak no more of it at this time."

"Appreciation," the girl echoed.

It was as she had suspected: Monochrome had been given an assignment, and her regal authority would be supported. But she would have to win the personal support of the people on her own. This was usually that way of it when a new officer came to an existing situation.

Nicely handled, Idyll thought. *Both language and dialogue. The girl does not realize how different your natural speech is.*

Monochrome had forgotten the ifrit's presence. *I have had experience. A new person always has to prove herself, if she is to function efficiently.*

She had a nice private meal, and an excellent night's sleep in a comfortable bed. Scent was there in the morning to bring her breakfast and dress her for the coming occasion. Dialogue was considerably more comfortable; she was learning the words and accent, so as to be less dependent on telepathy.

She would have to give an introductory speech. It would help if she knew what specific challenges she faced, apart from accent. "Scent, is there someone I should check with, before I meet the people?"

"Yes, Lady. The Green Chroma representative. He has been assigned to travel with you to the Chroma zones. The Lady Aspect summoned him and he is near."

"How soon can I meet him?"

"Very soon, if you wish, Lady."

"Now, then."

The girl tapped on a panel in the wall. "On my way," a male voice said. And in a few minutes a Green Chroma man appeared, the color extending to his hair and uniform. "The Lady summoned?"

She paused, realizing as she touched his mind that he was telepathic— and that he was similarly touching her mind. She had no choice but to trust his discretion.

"You know my identity and mission. Please tell me what is expected of me in the next few days."

"Gladly, Lady," he said curtly.

There was a pause. "Beginning now," she said.

"You will meet your third immediate associate, the handyman, who will see to routine chores and comforts. Then you will present yourself before the city assemblage for a speech. The manner of it will largely determine your reception at Planet Charm. Thereafter Secretary Ennui will acquaint you with the most pressing matters for your consideration. These will range from easy to formidable. I will be on hand to facilitate diplomatic negotiations."

"What may I call you, representative?"

"Green will do; it is my office. I normally represent the interests of my Chroma, but in this case that is extended to the interests of the planet."

So he was the one who would be keeping tabs on her, and reporting back to the Chroma authorities. He was avoiding the use of a personal name, maintaining his distance. "Appreciation, Green."

"This is not a social liaison, Lady. I am not your friend. No appreciation need be spoken."

Just so. "Call me Mistress. This is my office." *And keep my secrets.*

"As you wish, Mistress." He remained stiffly formal. "In what sense?"

"In all senses, as perhaps you will see. Is the handyman present?"

Green rapped on the wall. A curly-headed young-teen boy appeared. "Lady, I am Wrench."

"Call me Mistress." Now she was aware of Green mentally monitoring her continuing effort to speak so that the natives had no trouble understanding her. "What can you do for me?"

"I can carry baggage, summon transport, run errands—anything Mistress wishes."

"How did you come by this position?"

"Question?"

"Answer with candor," Green snapped. Monochrome appreciated the support, and knew he read that appreciation in her mind. He might not like her, but he was being true to his assignment.

The boy quailed but obeyed. "I am in treatment for thievery. We received news of an inclement assignment. We drew lots. I lost."

Monochrome smiled. "Appreciation, Wrench. Do you wish to be rid of your inclination to steal?"

"Yes, Mistress. It is mischief, gaining me nothing."

"Wrench, I asked for candor. I can cure you of the urge, but will not do so unless you truly desire to be free of it. Do you so desire?"

He hesitated, seeming on the verge of tears. "Mistress, I want to get along and be accepted, but I also want to retain my ability in case I ever need it, and to remain me. I have seen some who have been magically cured, and they look normal but their souls are gone. That frightens me."

She nodded. "Well spoken, Wrench. Come here."

"Acquiescence, Mistress." He approached her, plainly ill at ease.

She took his hand. "This is the cure. Let go of me when you feel your soul slipping away." She exerted her gentle force of persuasion.

His eyes widened. "This is different!" he exclaimed. "This feels good!"

"You are coming to be a little in love with me. You want only what I want. I want you to be yourself, without compulsion, master of your urges."

"I am, Mistress!" His expression and mind were filled with the wonder of it, and his new admiration of her.

Green, too, took note. *This is impressive magic, Mistress.*

It is my kind, that helps me govern people. I use it only beneficially.

Understanding.

She let go of the boy's hand. The cure had been effected. "Now fetch Scent."

The girl appeared. "I am here, Mistress." News of her preferred title had evidently spread rapidly.

"Prepare me for the presentation. Wrench, carry word that I am on my way. Green, guide me there: proper place, proper time."

The girl got busy adjusting her dress and hair, prettifying her. She was competent. Monochrome could have done it herself, having had decades experience at being beautiful, but wanted to ascertain Scent's ability. She also was not completely conversant with the local standards of appearance. And she was working on the speech she was about to give.

"I saw what you did with Wrench, Mistress," the girl murmured. "Could you do that with me?"

Monochrome smiled. "There is no need, Scent. You are like me: you like sex almost too well. This will not be a liability at such time as you marry."

"But my dreams—sometimes they frighten me."

"When you have your chance, implement them. As long as a thing is desired by all parties participating, there is no offense. Merely be discreet."

"Amazement. Relief."

"I have had considerable experience in this regard. Be at ease."

The girl nodded, almost glowing.

"Time, Mistress," Green murmured.

Monochrome stood. "Is there a formality of entrance?"

"The Lady Aspect will introduce you. You may, if you wish, take my arm."

She took his arm and walked with him through the wooden passages. As yet she had not seen the city, only the royal chambers. She would surely have time for sight-seeing later.

The Lady Aspect was awaiting her at the theater entrance. "Pause," she murmured. Then she walked to the central dais.

Monochrome waited with Green. She could not see the audience yet, but could tell by the hushed sounds of it that it was large, surely capacity for the theater. Many people wanted to see the new temporary ruler. Had she learned the local dialect well enough? She had been doing well enough in individual dialogues, but could not project to an entire audience.

You have it well enough, Green thought. *They will expect some accent.*

She hoped he was correct.

Aspect spoke without any fancy preamble. "Greeting, folk."

"Greeting, Lady," hundreds of voices responded.

"As you know, King Havoc, Queen Gale, and others in authority have gone to Planet Earth to stifle the invasion it contemplated. The need for governance remains. Havoc has appointed Mistress Monochrome of Earth to govern in his stead during the interim. She will now make herself known." She turned toward Monochrome and nodded, then vacated the dais.

Monochrome walked to the dais. It overlooked a three-quarter audience chamber that was impressive. It was several stories deep, with decks of chairs at each level. The acoustics were excellent; the Lady Aspect had been audible throughout, and Monochrome knew she would be too. Every seat was filled.

"Greeting, folk," she said, emulating Aspect.

"Greeting, Lady," they replied almost in unison.

Monochrome smiled. "Correction," she said. "My title is Mistress. Mistress Monochrome, for my lack of color. I am the Mistress of Mistresses of Planet Earth, the effective monarch. I am also the sexual mistress of King Havoc. I assure you I am competent in each employment. Shall we try it again?" She paused, then said "Greeting, folk." Had she handled the accent well enough?

"Greeting, Mistress," they replied.

"Appreciation. I do not expect you to trust me at the outset, as I govern the planet you regard as an enemy. But for the time you come to believe it, the news is this: Earth is no longer your enemy, if it ever was. Earth is under siege by a force that can make it an enemy, but Havoc and the Glamors are working with me to oppose that force. At this point we do not know which side will prevail. I am therefore here at Havoc's behest to do the job he is unable to do at the moment. My interest is your interest: to enable the planet to function for the benefit of all. I will appreciate your cooperation in this."

But as she spoke, she saw that she was not persuading them. This was not a problem with her accent, as she did seem to have conquered that problem. It was that they did not trust her, and did not want her here. They would not directly oppose her, because they did trust the Lady Aspect. But they would not help her any more than they had to.

Monochrome tried another tack. "You might wonder why I agreed to come here, as I am largely unfamiliar with your world, and have a world of my own to occupy my attention. I can tell you it was not entirely voluntary. But I love Havoc, and want to be with him forever, as his mistress. I will not be able to do that unless Planet Charm is stable. So it is in my interest to ensure its stability."

She still wasn't getting through. They heard her words, but did not really believe in her conviction. Why should they? They had, really, only her word about her good will. They did not know her nature.

Then she noted something. A woman in the third row of the lowest floor was crying. She was not making any fuss, and her face was straight, but tears were leaking from her closed eyes and crossing her cheeks. Beside her sat a stolid man, unaware.

She could work with this. Her modest ability to read the clairvoyant near future showed her a potent path.

"You," she said, fixing her gaze on the woman. "Come here."

The woman's eyes popped open. "Mistress!" she protested. "I was not asleep, merely reflecting on something personal. I meant no affront."

"I know, dear, and I have taken none. I want to know your problem. Perhaps I can address it, in the interest of interplanetary harmony."

"There is no help for me," the woman said.

"We shall see. Come."

Reluctantly the woman stood and walked to the stage. She came to stand before Monochrome. The remaining audience, surprised by this diversion, was paying close attention.

"What are you called?" She fathomed the name from the woman's mind, but was schooling herself not to depend on that.

"Chunky, Mistress."

That did describe her, cruelly. She must have been heavyset throughout life.

"What is making you weep, Chunky?" Monochrome asked.

"My husband wishes to leave me for the woman whose fourth he sired," the woman said. "She is younger and sexier, and I have borne and raised our four so have no further hold on him. But I still love him."

Just so. Monochrome look at the man who had been seated beside her. "Are you her husband?"

"Affirmation, Mistress," he agreed nervously.

"Join us here. What is your name?"

"Carrot, Mistress."

He did have reddish hair, but she suspected the name was more for another portion of his anatomy, considering his strong sex drive. He was heavyset, like his wife, but handsome in a crude way.

"Is it true?"

"Affirmation," he agreed, looking slightly ashamed.

Monochrome turned to Chunky. "I am going to solve your problem."

"Mistress, you can't order me to stay with a woman I no longer love," Carrot protested.

Monochrome turned back to face him. "Nor would I try. Instead I am going to enchant you. If you object, I will release you. Does this seem fair?"

"Question." He was understandably confused.

"How old is your wife"

"Fifty, Mistress."

"I am fifty." Monochrome glanced around. "Is there a telepath in the house?"

Green stepped forward. "I am, Mistress." Now it was in the open.

"Verify my statement."

"You are fifty, Mistress," Green said, plainly amazed. It was nice acting; he had already fathomed her age. The audience's amazement was real, however.

"Look at me, Carrot." He looked. "Hereafter, when your wife smiles at you, she will look like this." She took his head in her hands, put her face close to his, and smiled. She had a smile that could illuminate a mine shaft, as friends had put it long ago. This smile was buttressed by her special magic of persuasion, a quality of her Mistresshood.

The man's face went slack. He was dazed by the smile, and half in love with her already.

"Hereafter, when your wide removes her clothing," Monochrome continued, "her body will look like this." She opened her elaborate gown and stepped out of it, gloriously naked. She heard the gasp of the audience, perhaps somewhat because of her temerity in exposing herself, but mainly because of her stunning beauty of form.

Carrot just stared. He was indeed ensorceled.

"When you touch her, she will feel like this," Monochrome continued. She took his right hand and set it on her left breast.

The man might as well have been a statue, except for his visibly racing pulses. The audience was much the same, hardly breathing.

"Now look at Chunky," Monochrome said, not letting his hand drop.

He turned his head to look.

"Smile," she said to the woman.

Tentatively, Chunky smiled.

"Telepath: what does he see?"

"Your image, Mistress. To him, she looks like you. He desires her, as he does you. The other woman can't compare."

She addressed the man again. "And when she kisses you, you will have thirty seconds until eruption—within her or without her. Every time." The man's trousers were bulging, he was already near eruption.

She moved her face close to his, then halted. "I am not going to kiss you." Then she let him go.

The audience burst out laughing. They laughed loud and long, and by the time they subsided, Monochrome knew she did not need to say any more. She had won them over.

"Find this couple a private room," she told Wrench. "Protect their privacy. It will require only a minute or so."

Man and wife hurried after the boy. Monochrome returned to the audience. "I do things my own way," she said. "But I do get them done. I hope we will be able to work together for the benefit of the planet."

A number of the men were staring. Belatedly she realized she had not returned to her clothing. Scent brought it to her and she dressed before the audience without shame. Only then did the applause begin.

"Oh Mistress, that was so romantic!" Scent said. "You saved their marriage." She, too, had been won over.

"A remarkable show," Green said. "The public nudity was a nice touch; the people always appreciate that sort of thing. But of course a striking body is no necessary indication of administrative competence." He had been swayed, but not won.

"That reminded me of Havoc," the Lady Aspect said approvingly. "The barbaric flair, mainly."

"Introductions are best accomplished with flair," Monochrome agreed. "Now it is time to tackle the serious work." She knew the main challenge remained ahead. Planetary problems were not necessarily resolved by flair alone.

Chapter 22
Chaos

Havoc shook his head. They had fought the good fight, but the malign Male Spirit had been too cunning for them, going after their ikons and removing them from their Chroma zones so that they no longer broadcast magic power. That left all but the White Science Chroma Glamor shackled by lack of magic, and the White ikon he had placed in a different Chroma zone, nullifying it too. They had no remaining super powers.

However, they did retain some depleted Chroma stones, and these enabled them to do minimal low-energy magic. Nearby clairvoyance, a minute or so's future path reading, close illusion, and of course telepathy. Such abilities were better than nothing. It was frustrating to be unable to teleport, conjure, or transform, other than diffusion, which worked in any magic environment including this Science one. But they were far from helpless.

While the Glamors had been taming the rogue new Chroma zones and putting down spot insurrections, the Male Spirit had been closing off the remaining future paths that threatened his dominance. Now he had stifled the last path, and the balance was shifting, transferring the background power from Female to Male. After a thousand years, he was returning.

"Imperative: Voila says we have to rescue the mistresses before the fall," Gale reminded him. "They are like ikons, funneling power to the Mistress of Mistresses. The Male will try to destroy them all so that Monochrome will have no slightest chance of return."

"At least he can't get her," Havoc said. "Voila saw that coming, and sent her off-planet. Mino says Idyll says she is doing well."

"Governing Charm better than you did," Gale said teasingly. "And you wanted to keep her here for sex."

"Well, she's good at it."

"And I am not?" she asked archly.

"You're familiar. You have become dull."

"Oh, really?" She took his hands and pressed them against her breasts. He loved it when she did that. She was, for his taste, still the most beautiful woman of Planet Charm.

"I caught that thought," she murmured. "Appreciation." Then she changed her mind. "But we have a rescue to perform. Sex will have to wait." He hated it when she did that, though of course they were both teasing each other. They had been having plenty of sex between spot crises, and it was always new and exciting.

"What rescue is ours?" he asked with resignation.

"The Mistress Modesty, the one Voila worked with. Voila can't do it herself, so we must."

"Putting her chore on us," he grumbled. "Somebody should have taught that girl responsibility."

"Somebody's father," she agreed.

"Somebody's mother."

"Enough." She kissed him, shutting him up. This was of course more teasing, and dialogue for any possible eavesdropper. They both knew that Voila had been exquisitely trained, and had thorough responsibility. She was the de facto leader of this entire expedition to planet Earth. She had passed this task along to her parents because she had critical work elsewhere.

"Where?" he inquired as he squeezed her bottom.

"Paris, Europe, Asia, where she stepped into the play. Mistress Modesty remains there, but must be expeditiously removed. The Male Spirit means to rape, torture, and kill all the mistresses he catches, so as to destroy the network and make it impossible for Monochrome ever to resume power. He is thorough."

"So you said before. He's an anal sphincter. After what he made you and Chrome do—"

"We could have escaped any time. It was only sex."

"He made it filthy."

"Deliberately. He was trying to break us, and especially you."

"And Voila decreed that we had to let him do it. So it's her fault."

Gale nodded. "I will be most annoyed if it turns out there was not critical reason."

Havoc nodded. They were still talking for the Male Spirit's spies. Gale had had solid reason: to identify and mark the Male Spirit's identity so they could unerringly track him, regardless of the body he used. "I have known you some time, Gale, and I trust you. But I was afraid you would chomp that sneering creature's ass."

"Temptation," she agreed. "But we had to follow the script. You weren't tempted to burst out of those manacles and flatten him?"

"Temptation," he agreed. "Speaking of which: Are you sure we can't—?"

"Let's check." She joined him in checking the near future paths.

There was an opportunity. "Take the second capsule," he said. They were in the station, about to board a capsule leading to the rocket port. They stepped back, and in a moment the capsule door closed, and it proceeded without them.

They kissed while waiting for the next. Then it arrived, and sure enough: it was empty. They boarded, waited for it to start moving, then jammed against the wall for a frenzy of kissing, feeling, and clothed penetration. "Love!" she exclaimed.

"Sex," he said, pushing deeper into her.

She made as if to swat him. "You think I'm good for only one thing."

"Oh? What is that?"

She struggled to break his embrace, but he held her close. "Beast!"

But their actions and dialogue were mere covering for their real dialogue, which was conducted in very short-range telepathy that required close physical contact for transmission. No one would snoop on this, or even know it was occurring.

You know we are walking into a trap, he thought as he continued pumping inside her. *The paths show it.*

Agreement. She continued kissing him avidly. *The Male Spirit knows we mean to rescue Modesty, and will seek to capture us when we approach her.*

I wish we could see the paths more clearly. "Joy!" For he was in his first climax.

When Glamor wars with Glamor, the paths fuzz beyond the immediate time; you know that. It is only the juxtaposition of many paths that betrays the coming trap. But they fuzz for him too, so we are as much protected as endangered. "Is that the best you can do, sex fiend? That little bit of drool? Is your member even stiff?"

"Outrage! I will show you stiff." *So no one knows the outcome. But it is going to be violent.*

Violent, she agreed, shuddering with more than her own first orgasm. "That's more like it, Havoc. Now put more oomph into it."

It involves the man. Objection.

Caveat, she corrected him. *The homosexual man they put guiding Voila so she couldn't seduce him.*

He smiled. "Here I came again." He bucked harder into her. *She could if she wanted to.*

"Oh, I feel it spouting," she said. And of course she did. *She did, one time, just to prove she could. She has a crush on him. He's a good man.*

He'd better be, if he had my daughter. "That's just the beginning, wench. Keep your channel hot."

"It's burning. Give me some balm to cool it. I think you've been holding back." *Voila wants him saved too. She fears the Male Spirit will punish him to get at her.*

"Have a gusher." He jetted again. *It's the way that turd works.*

"Is that what you give Chrome? Three feeble squirts? I want more." *Voila says we can win this one, but not the campaign.*

"More, you female hound? I'll wash you into tomorrow!" *We depend on Voila—but isn't her future seeing clouded also? Could she be leading us into doom?*

"I'm ready!" *Negation. Remember, we aren't depending on her alone. Idyll and Mino see the intermediate and far future, and they indicate that this course is correct. We can win the battle, lose the campaign, but win the war.*

For a fifty percent chance.

For a fifty percent chance.

They concluded their phenomenal sex as the capsule slowed, coming to the next station. They cleaned up hastily, and were ready when it stopped. Their private dialogue had been less sanguine than their sexual one.

The rockets were still running, as there was far less public evidence of the underlying strife. Most people supposed that the revolutionary outbreaks were isolated events; they did not know their unifying theme. This was not because of suppression of the planetary news; it was because only the Glamors truly knew what was going on.

They slept on the rocket, and woke as it landed near Paris. This was to be a straight routine pickup. Theoretically.

Of course they knew that it was nothing of the kind. They had made no long-range plan because that would be fathomed by the Male Spirit, and his minions would be there to stop it. They would have to depend on their spot paths awareness, being otherwise essentially random.

Havoc kissed her just before they left the rocket. *Where?* he inquired.

Napoleon's Tomb.

Question?

Voila left word for them to hide there.

Ah. *What tourist sites are near?*

I haven't reviewed the guide in detail. All I remember is the Eiffel Tower about a mile west of the tomb.

Satisfaction.

They broke the long kiss, as others were beginning to take notice. "Well, I love her," Havoc explained to the crowd.

Smiles broke out. This was the correct local explanation, as he had fathomed. The folk of this section of Earth took pride in their ability to love and be loved. They also spoke a different language, but were bi- or tri-lingual, and understood the language spoken on Charm. Havoc and Gale had refined their dialect since coming to Earth, and now spoke it well enough.

They were theoretically tourists. "I want to see the Eyefull Tower," Havoc announced as they left the rocket.

"But we have a pass to see Napoleon's Tomb. They rebuilt it after World War Three, the same was it was. The least we can do is admire it."

"Grumble. I did not know Napoleon, so don't care where he was buried. Tower next."

She kissed him. "Eiffel Tower next, love."

There was a moving walk with seats to carry them north to the Tomb. It seemed it was a popular tourist destination. Havoc looked around as they rode, having no need to pretend fascination. The houses and costumes of this planet were intriguing, along with its universal nonChroma coloration. It seemed that this came with the default Chroma, whatever it was, in this case Science. He was impressed with the artifacts of Science, which seemed as thorough as those of any of the Chroma zones of Charm.

Meanwhile Gale, acting like a tourist wife, following his cues, was actually focusing on the paths. They might be opaque beyond a minute or so, but even that minute could make an enormous difference.

"Big river," he said, poring over the little guidebook. "I want to see it."

"The Seine," she said. "In due course."

They reached the Tomb, an impressive edifice. "This is as big as Triumph City!" he exclaimed.

"Larger," she agreed tolerantly.

They followed the guidance of the paths admixed with token clairvoyance, and seemingly coincidentally came across a handsome man and a woman standing in an alcove. The woman was older but beautiful. Mistress Modesty, Voila's friend. She reminded him of Monochrome, by no particular coincidence. They were similar only in being lovely, shapely, poised older women with that certain flair that was the sign of the magic of the Glamor. Modesty was of course equivalent to an ikon; that nevertheless gave her a special presence. If he had sex with her, he would think of Monochrome amidst it.

"I am Voila's mother," Gale murmured to Modesty as they paused. "Follow quietly."

They two followed, as if other interested tourists in a party. "There will be a trap sprung," Havoc murmured to the man without looking at him. "Soon. Stay close." For the paths were converging on an unavoidable scene of violence.

"So we understand," the man, Caveat, said. "We tried to dissuade Voila from putting you at such risk, but she is headstrong."

Both Havoc and Gale laughed. "So are we," Havoc said.

"Trust us," Gale said.

"We do."

Men appeared, surrounding them. "Come with us, you four. Don't make a scene."

Havoc let them get close, unobtrusively wrapping his hands in metallic sheathing, then exploded into action. No magic was required for this, and he used none. He struck one in the head with a mailed fist, and another in the solar plexus. Both went down as Gale caught Modesty and Caveat by the hands and led them to a deep recess. Two more men tried to follow them, but Havoc was on them, cutting them down with simultaneous blows to their necks. It seemed the Male Spirit hadn't counted on Havoc's martial arts training, and had sent unprepared thugs to apprehend them.

The melee, of course, attracted attention. "No quarreling here," a guard cried, advancing. The remaining two men hung back, frustrated; they were not supposed to attract undue attention, because of course their attempted abduction was illicit.

Havoc made sure the pursuit had been stifled, then followed Gale's party. She was leading them into a labyrinth of columns and passages, following a devious random course. Soon they had lost themselves in the tomb.

But this was merely the beginning. The Male Spirit had other agents, and some of the police now answered to him, bribed by promises. "We have to get back to the rocket port," Gale said. "We have passes."

"But they'll ambush us there," Caveat protested.

"Affirmation," Havoc said, and led them west, away from the Tomb environs. Reading the necessary signal clairvoyantly, he flagged down a local taxi. "Rocketport," he said, giving the drive a fistful of local currency.

"Sure. Get in."

"No ride. Just go there. Fast. Avoid pursuit."

Amazed, the driver guided his vehicle south. The amount of currency was more than enough to make such a chase worth his while.

"You have no passes," Caveat said, realizing. "It was a ruse."

"Agreement," Gale said.

They walked rapidly west, skulking around buildings, avoiding the main streets of the city as much as possible. Because their route was completely unexpected, they were not immediately spotted by the Spirit's minions. That was an advantage of deliberate randomness; it was hard to read in the near-future paths. But the minions were out there, and soon enough would locate them. The paths had more violence ahead—much more. It could not be avoided.

In due course they came to the Eiffel Tower rising beside the river. Havoc paused to admire it, gawking like the veriest tourist. "What a sight!"

"It is one of the nation's most famous artifacts," Caveat said. "Do you wish to explore it?"

"Affirmation!" Who would expect them to pause for sightseeing during such pursuit?

They approached the base of the Tower. The four corners of it curved outward as they neared the ground, lending a dynamic atmosphere. "This, too, was destroyed in the holocaust of World War Three," Modesty said. "It was reconstructed almost exactly as the original, only with stronger metal and springing. There is a restaurant up at the convergence."

"Food!" Havoc said with proper barbaric appetite.

The mistress smiled. "And you are hungry, of course, after beating up those thugs. That was an amazing feat."

Havoc shrugged. "And you are an amazing actress, according to Voila."

She laughed. "*She* says that of *me*?"

"It is surely true," Gale said.

There was an admission station barring access to the Tower. "You have passes?" the guard inquired sternly.

They did not, as that would have signaled their destination. But Mistress Modesty stepped forward. "We beg your indulgence," she said, placing her small hand on the guard's arm.

"Mistress, of course!" he said, recognizing her. Nothing was denied the mistresses.

They took the elevator to the high restaurant, where Modestly got them seated immediately. But as the food was served, Gale took Havoc's hand. It was time to check the paths, combining their minds for extra power.

It was a shock. The violence was frighteningly close. "Emergency. No time to eat," Havoc said with deep regret. They had misjudged its incipience, checking the paths separately.

They rose and fled the restaurant. "Shouldn't the other patrons be warned?" Caveat inquired, concerned.

"Negation," Havoc said tightly. "They would panic and do more damage than the threat. The best thing for them is for us to get away from here and lead the pursuit away."

They went to the elevator, but Havoc knew it would be too slow. "I must stop them."

Gale nodded. "Do what you must, love. We'll be here." She kissed him. *I will hide them if I can.*

He ran to the outer framework, wrapping his hands. There was a way in which the hugely curving struts resembled giant tree trunks. He got on the outside and let himself slide rapidly down, holding on loosely with his shielded hands. The increasing curvature near the ground helped slow him. It was a feat he was pretty sure few if any Earthers could have done, which was a reason why the Male Spirit's minions had not anticipated it.

As he reached the ground, he saw them converging: brute men, this time with guns. They would shoot anyone who tried to leave the Tower. But Havoc spread a magic impression of being one of them, and was able to pass their formation unchallenged.

However, this was only the enclosure. How would the thugs get in to find the fugitives before the regular police came to stop them? They had only minutes to accomplish their purpose.

Then he saw the big machines. These were earth movers, used to clear regions of dirt and debris for new construction. They were rolling toward the

Eiffel Tower.

In a moment he fathomed it. They were going to knock it down! If they couldn't capture their prey, they would kill it—and hundreds of innocent by-standers. The Male Spirit didn't care; in fact such an act would further disrupt the orderly society and foment revolution.

How could he stop it? Havoc had neither the time nor the mental power to fathom the perfect counter. He had to find something *now*, imperfect as it might be.

He followed his best path, and it brought him to a historical museum. "Question?" he asked himself aloud.

Then he fathomed it. This particular wing celebrated some of the ancient war machines. Here, in perfect working order, fueled and ready for the morrow's demonstration, was a pre-holocaust tank: a heavily armored wheel-tracked vehicle used in warfare to crush troops and buildings alike. This would do.

Havoc clambered onto it, and into it, his spot clairvoyance showing him how. He lowered the turret lid, strapped himself into the driving compartment, turned on the power, oriented the external sensors, and put it into motion. The giant machine lumbered forward, its tracks crunching over the decorative railing. It crashed through the large glassy window and rumbled outside the building. This was fun!

He drove with increasing competence toward the Tower. The first earth mover was tackling the nearest supportive strut, starting to bash it out of the way. The Tower was big and strong and stable, but too much determined dozing would inevitably undermine it and topple it.

Havoc extended his clairvoyance to fathom the mechanism of the tank's cannon. He oriented it on the lead earth mover, rapidly learning the aiming mechanism. He locked it onto its target. He fired it.

The earth mover burst into flame from the explosive shell. It was out of action. Havoc oriented on the second, and soon it too was flaming.

Now the Male Spirit evidently caught on. The other earth movers swung about and trundled slowly toward Havoc's tank. But they were outgunned. Havoc took out a third, and a fourth, before they got the message and desisted.

Now the local police were arriving in force. Havoc deserted his tank and slunk out of sight and awareness. His job was done, for the moment. He had saved his friends—and the Eiffel Tower.

Later he reunited with Gale, Modesty, and Caveat. "Now I think I more properly understand your name," Caveat said, clearly shaken.

"Havoc," Gale said fondly. "His trademark: wreaking havoc. I have tried to smooth it out of him, but he's a barbarian."

"And you're a barbarian wench," Havoc retorted, as fondly.

"At the risk of interrupting a romantic moment," Caveat said, "I suspect that the Spirit's men have not yet yielded the issue. I doubt it will be safe to try to use those rocket tickets."

"What tickets?" Gale inquired innocently. All four burst out laughing.

But the matter was serious. "We need a new plan," Havoc said. "They'll be coming after us with weapons."

"And we lack long-range magic," Gale said.

"I presume you can diffuse, the way Havoc can," Caveat said to Gale. "They can't stop that."

"But you and Modesty can't," she replied. "We are here to conduct both of you to safety."

"That hardly seems worth the risk," Modesty said. "We are but bit players."

"Players Voila values."

"A coincidence of association."

"Only to a degree."

Havoc stayed out of it. The fact was that both Earthers were vital, because they were close to Voila, and Voila was the major target of the Male Spirit. They had to be protected, and not merely because Voila liked them; they were, unwittingly, key players. But it was not feasible to tell them that, for the very telling would affect the paths to a risky extent. So they clothed it in sentiment, but it was far more serious than that.

Meanwhile they had to get their party to a safe Chroma zone. Havoc knew which one it was, but could not afford to say it, for the Male Spirit had minions everywhere.

Including here. Men appeared ahead of them. These were armed with pistols: squat little machines with forward-pointing snouts, that ejected hard little spheres. Those spheres were dangerous.

"Stay between us," Havoc said tersely, facing forward. Gale turned to face backward, to watch the men who would be coming from that direction.

"Perhaps I can help," Caveat said. "I am familiar with the armament of Earth. Those are ball pistols, with an effective range of up to fifty feet, normally used to pacify unruly crowds without injuring people."

"We do not believe in injuring people if there is any alternative," Mistress Modesty said.

This was useful information: non-lethal weapons. "Question," Havoc said. "Type. Countering."

"They will be one of three main types," Caveat said. "All fire balls, but the balls differ. The silver-colored ones deliver a disorienting shock to any person they strike. They are best countered by avoidance, or intercepting them with highly insulated material. The brown ones explode into clinging strings that quickly harden in place, effectively trussing up the fugitive. They are countered again by avoidance, or wrapping them in tough material that prevents the strings from spreading. The green-colored ones are fluid balls that fragment and splatter evaporating sleep gas. Avoidance is generally ineffective; they must be prevented from striking anything nearby, and may be caught carefully and thrown away."

Havoc nodded. "So I can catch a green or brown ball, but not a silver ball. I can let a silver or brown ball go by, but not a green one."

"All of them are mischief," Modesty said. "We need to escape these ruffians entirely, if possible, at least until the gendarmes arrive."

"There seems to be an opening to the north," Caveat said. "But I distrust this."

"They are herding us," Havoc agreed. "We'll take them on directly, surprising them."

The two Earthers clearly believed this was unwise, even foolish, but did not protest.

"In my footsteps," Havoc said, and walked rapidly toward the rebels in front. The others fell in behind him: Modesty, Caveat, and Gale, glancing back.

The rebels were surprised, but quickly rallied. They fired a few silver balls. Havoc, anticipating them magically, dived for a gutter and swept up a child's bat that had evidently been lost. He swung it at the first ball, batting it back toward the rebels. It dropped to the ground and flashed, discharging.

The next ball was brown. "Don't hit it!" Caveat called.

Havoc didn't. He caught it gently in one hand, then hurled it back. This one did not hit the ground; it hurtled toward the rebels, who flung themselves to either side, avoiding it.

The third was green. Havoc caught it, carefully, held it a moment, then flipped it directly at the closest rebel. The man tried to avoid it, but it struck him on the back and puffed into fluid and vapor. The man dropped, unconscious.

They were through the line, and now the gendarmes were converging, as Modesty had predicted. The spot crisis had passed.

"I doubt this is over," Caveat said. "I repeat, we two are unlikely to be worth the risk when you two have a planet to save. Better to abandon us and get on with your serious business."

"I concur," Modesty said. "I doubt Voila would want to put her parents at serious risk on our behalf."

"Negation," Gale said as Havoc led them through devious streets. "You both are important."

"I regret bringing this up," Caveat said. "But there is something you should know that might change your mind. I—seduced your daughter."

Both Havoc and Gale burst out laughing. "This is gallant of you, trying to protect her reputation," Gale said. "But we know better. She seduced you, in a way that made you helpless."

"I forgot your telepathy," Caveat said, disconcerted. "Still, it means you need have no particular regard for my safety, as I can only be an embarrassment to you. I am—not normal."

"Question?" Havoc asked, though he knew what the man was trying to say.

It was Modesty who answered. "Caveat was put in charge of Voila because the Mistress of Mistresses feared she might seduce him and turn him away from his assignment. He is homosexual, not attracted to women. But it seems she found a way anyway, and now he loves her, as do I."

"Confirmation?" Gale asked. She was taking up the dialogue while Havoc explored the nearest future paths, steering their group to what scant safety was available.

"I do love her," Caveat agreed. "But I cannot be her lover. The relationship was doomed before it started."

"She has decreed that you be saved, regardless," Gale said.

"She has a crush on me. For that reason, also, it may be better that I be removed from her life."

"This about Voila," Gale said seriously. "She is young, and she has emotions, and much yet to learn. But she does not let emotions sway her judgment. None of our children do. Flame had to kill her Earther lover, and it broke her heart, but she did what she had to do. Voila would too. Any of them would. She wants you preserved because there is valid reason for it, regardless of her crush. We mean to rescue you with or without your cooperation, but it will make it easier if you help."

"I am answered," Caveat said.

"As, surely, am I," Modesty agreed.

"Another crisis is coming," Havoc said. "I have steered us clear as long as is feasible, but the rebels are determined, and have set another ambush for us. This time their directive is to kill us if they can't capture us. We can survive, but you must obey us implicitly."

"Agreed," Modesty said with a weak smile.

"Follow Gale!" Havoc snapped. Gale ran to the right while Havoc dived left. He caught hold of a low awning as a flight of balls landed in the place they had vacated, bursting with string, flashes, and spreading vapor. He ripped the awning free of its moorings and tossed it over the vapor before it could spread farther.

Then he turned and charged the hidden men who had fired the barrage. He was among them before they could react. He swept a pistol from the hand of one, aimed it down, and fired it. A green ball shot out and shattered on the pavement. By the time the men tried to escape, they were caught by its puffing vapor, and dropped to the ground unconscious.

Gale quickly skirted the region and rejoined Havoc, followed by Caveat and Modesty. "May I say: nicely handled," Caveat said.

"We must go to the rocket port," Havoc said. "They don't expect us there."

"Because we have no passes," Gale said. "They will have verified that, after being fooled before."

"If that is your only problem, I can abate it," Modesty said. "Mistresses can travel where they choose. With whom they choose, without tickets. We try not to abuse the privilege, and the populace knows that."

And that was one reason she was along, Havoc realized. To facilitate their surprise travels. "Appreciation."

They intercepted the moving walk and boarded it. Several gendarmes were already on it, routinely coming off duty and riding home. They looked askance at the party, evidently uncertain whether to challenge it. Armed rebels were already coming into sight. "Fix it," Havoc murmured to Modesty.

Mistress Modesty approached the ranking gendarme, a stout grizzled man. "I am Mistress Modesty. Perhaps you know of me."

"Yes, Mistress," he agreed, abruptly positive. "It is a pleasure to meet you, however informally. Your plays are great."

"Thank you." She smiled winningly. "We are traveling to the rocket port, but certain ruffians have been harassing us along the way. I would appreciate it if you could prevent them from bothering us." She kissed him.

"Of course, Mistress," he agreed immediately. He signaled, and the other gendarmes stood, hands lightly touching weapons, gazing out to either side to be sure no ruffians were approaching. That very action was enough to cause them to stay clear; Havoc could see that rebels had been approaching the belt, and now had stopped. It would not be good form to directly oppose gendarmes. In a moment they faded out of sight.

"If you have time, sir," Modesty said, and led the leader into a curtained off section. She was rewarding him with sex, as was her nature. Even as old as she was, it was surely a marvelous experience for him.

In due course they emerged, and the Mistress took another gendarme in. By the time they reached the rocket port, all of them had been rewarded, and no rebels had approached the traveling belt. The other passengers smiled knowingly, appreciating the way of the mistresses. They would be telling the story to their friends and families, in due course.

Gale squeezed Havoc's hand. "It's a pleasure to see a mistress in action," she murmured.

"Agreement." He wished he could take her similarly out of view, but the next crisis was too close.

They reached the rocket port, and the gendarmes formed an informal honor guard escorting the party to the ship. There was no chance for rebels to intercept them.

"What ship?" Caveat inquired.

"Whatever is taking off soonest," Havoc said. It wasn't like him to be that sloppy, but something prompted him.

"That would be the one to what we call Moscow," Caveat said. "But I have to say, I doubt this is wise. The rebels will simply close in on that landing port there, and we will be unable to leave the rocket without being attacked."

"I must concur," Modesty said. "We are surely safer here, where I have friends." Her gaze flicked to indicate the gendarmes.

They were making sense. Havoc glanced at Gale. "Look deep," she murmured, then looked surprised.

Look deep? Where? For a moment Havoc was baffled. Then he turned his attention inward—and discovered a new lower level in his hidden mind. It was marked by the letter V. Voila had put it there, telepathically—without his knowing. That amazed him, first that she had been able to access his private mind like that, and second, that she had done so without his knowledge of it. That was why Gale was surprised; she had discovered something added to her own mind.

It was like a sub-cellar, a chamber excavated below his secret chamber. He mentally tugged at the V, and the chamber opened to reveal the message: "Take the ship—now."

Havoc looked around. They were walking past another rocket access. He turned and entered it. "This one."

"But that's the rocket to Turkey," Caveat protested. "It doesn't leave for another hour."

Havoc refused to argue. "We're taking it."

"Then allow me," Modesty said as they approached the dock's ticket window. "I am Mistress Modesty, with a party of four. It is urgent that we board this ship."

"Mistress, it is already full," the man protested.

She held his gaze. "Please."

"I will see what I can do," he said, disgruntled.

"I appreciate it." She walked to the entrance to his office, entered, and in a moment took his hand and led him away. She was rewarding him for his cooperation.

And well within the hour four passengers had yielded their seats to the new party. They strapped in as the countdown for takeoff proceeded. The rocket was roughly saucer shaped, with a large passenger compartment in the center and concentric rings of seats. The pretty stewardesses set their apparatus in the open center and used the radiating aisles to serve token nuts and beverages to the two hundred passengers. It was pleasant enough. Their party was in the smallest center circle.

"Hijack it to Rome, Italy, father," Voila's voice said in his mind, without telepathy. It was another implanted message.

Havoc touched Caveat's hand. "Request: how do I hijack this ship to Rome, Italy?"

The man's mouth fell open for an instant. Then he rallied. "Follow me." He unstrapped himself and rose from his seat.

The two of them walked along an aisle to the rim, and thence up a ramp to the pilot's cockpit above the main compartment. Gale and Modesty remained seated, as if nothing unusual were happening; Gale would have had a cautionary message from her daughter.

"The compartment is locked," Caveat said. "We need the key."

Havoc invoked his clairvoyance and spoke a small series of numbers and letters. The door opened to admit them. They entered and were with the seated pilot. "You must reprogram the destination," Caveat told the pilot. "To Rome."

"This is impossible!" the pilot said. "What are you doing in this restricted area?"

Havoc put his hand on the pilot's neck, using a precious bit of magic to change the man's mind. The impossible became possible, as the pilot reprogrammed the ship's destination.

"You will not cancel that new destination when I leave you," Havoc said. "And you will not notify the port authority of the change until you are approaching Rome."

"I find it impossible to object," the pilot said. "Though I know I will be in serious trouble for this irregularity."

"Negation: this is a hijacking. You are not at fault."

The man had to believe it, and it was true.

They returned to their seats. "It is an education to know you," Caveat said.

"It is Voila's doing. Check your mind; she may have left you a message."

The man paused, then looked surprised. "She did! It's a kiss."

"Humor."

"Surely so. She knew from the outset that I was not for her. But she pretends we have a future together."

"Affirmation. But she knows the future paths, and is realistic. She will surely let you go when her maidenly crush fades."

"That would be best," Caveat agreed.

Gale leaned across and took his hand. "Observation: These are strained times."

"And you, Madame, her mother: do you not object to our association?"

"Negation. We raised our children to make sensible judgments," Gale said seriously. "We know that in due course Voila will choose a man who is right for her. He will have to be extremely understanding and tolerant, because there is no other woman like her. It may be that she chooses you for now because it can't be permanent. That will make the breakup less difficult."

"It is already difficult. I do love her. Any way she chooses to be loved, regardless of my nature."

"So do we. It is not easy for us to accept our immature child as our governess, but this is the way of it. We are all creatures of passing necessity, during this war of worlds."

"Amen!" he agreed.

Then the muted roar and pressure of the takeoff stifled conversation for a time.

In due course the pilot announced their destination for the passengers. "This rocket has been hijacked, and is bound for Rome. The authorities will try to obtain passage on another rocket for your original destination."

There was immediate pandemonium. "Hijacked!" "Are they going to kill us all?" "Are there parachutes?"

Modesty stood and faced the other passengers. "Please," she said, and the hush spread across as they recognized a Mistress. "I am Mistress Modesty, hitherto of the Paris region, but I have traveled with my plays, some of which you may have seen."

"The Option!" a girl exclaimed. "So romantic! He married her after all!"

"The Option," Modesty agreed, having established her credential. "We are not in the old uncivilized days of popular fiction, when hijackings were likely to mean murders or crashing into buildings. In this case it merely means that the rocket has been involuntarily rerouted, and will land in Rome rather than Ankara. This will be an inconvenience, but none of you will be hurt or seriously threatened. We will try to get you expeditiously on your way. We appreciate your cooperation."

"But who hijacked it, Mistress?" a man asked.

Modesty smiled. "I did." She paused just long enough for the shock to sink in, then continued. "I am in the company of Caveat, a noted official working with the Mistress of Mistresses." She nodded to Caveat, who stood and made a turning bow. "And the rulers of Colony Charm, who are here to help us manage our crisis of colored volcanoes: King Havoc and Queen Gale." Havoc and Gale stood and bowed. The people stared, then applauded.

"Some rebel ruffians wished us ill," Modesty continued. "In fact they were firing balls at us. We managed to escape, but they pursued. We believe they will be lurking at the port where this ship is scheduled to land, so we have somewhat arbitrarily changed the destination. In this manner we hope to escape their malice and continue our efforts to safeguard this world for the authority of Mistress Monochrome. We apologize for disrupting your journey, but we have been under some pressure." She smiled with practiced weariness.

"Forgiven!" a man called, and in a moment the others echoed it. This had become an adventure.

Distract them. It was Voila's thought, coming from somewhere. There was surely reason; it might be that panic was threatening despite the reassurance of the Mistress.

Havoc sent a thought to Gale. *The Watching.* She nodded. Then he stood, stepped into the center, and addressed the passengers. "It is our custom on Planet Charm to exchange favors. You are doing us the favor of helping us escape an assassination attempt. We will do you the favor of entertaining you while we are with you. My wife and I are minstrels as well as rulers, and will put on a small play for two. We hope you enjoy it." He paused. "It is a bit risqué; does anyone object?"

There was laughter. These were adults and teens.

"I must explain how we do plays on Charm," Havoc said. "There is a narrator and actors, and the narrator may also act, but his primary purpose is to make the story clear to the audience. We normally perform in the round, so that people in a full circle around us can see; there is no front or back of the stage. Props are minimal; we make do with what we have at hand." He turned slowly around as he spoke, so that at some time he faced each member of the audience.

He struck a pose, commencing the play. "Way back in the bad old days before the good days, when anarchy was never far from erupting, there was a concern that Earth might be invaded by bug-eyed aliens. There was some reason for this apprehension, because an alien artifact had been discovered in a crater of the moon. It seemed ancient, but that did not necessarily mean that it was dead; in fact it seemed to have some hidden source of power that could make it function if activated." He looked around. "Suppose it was a weapon waiting for the return of its masters? Should it be destroyed? No, because that would alert the aliens that it had been found, and might cause them to invade immediately. So they did not touch it; instead they put a watch on it, a signal device that would flash briefly in black light if the device ever did come to life. They set up stations on Earth with telescopes trained on the crater, watching for that signal. If it flashed, they would know the aliens were coming, and could take precautions. If it did not flash, they had nothing to worry about. They did not alert the Earth population, lest there be panic; they merely set up the hidden telescopes and waited and watched, ceaselessly. The telescopes were buried underground in complete darkness so as not to give away their presence. The watchers were anonymous, unknown even to each other, so that the secret would be less likely to leak out. It was all very quiet, but well paid."

Havoc paused, assessing his audience. He had its attention, perhaps as much for the novelty of his being a king, or the hijacking, as for the story itself. That was fine; this was merely the preliminary.

"Because the work was dull, and in the dark, there was the risk of inattention, or even falling asleep. That might be dangerous. So they set up pairs of people for one hour sessions, instructed to change off every five minutes, one watching, the other making sure the watcher was fully alert. Even a five second lapse might be too long. Even so, it was necessary to change the roster of watches often, so that none became too familiar and thus indifferent to the process. No special training was needed, merely the quality of being unattached, and the ability and willingness to concentrate. Watchers were sworn to secrecy before, during, and after their service. This was effective; there was no leak, and the news never got out."

Havoc paused again. "Have any of you heard of it?" When no one in the audience spoke, he gestured expressively. "See, the secret was well kept. It remains unknown to this day." That brought a murmur of laughter; it was a nice way to mask a pure invention.

Havoc continued the narration, living it himself as Gale stepped up to join him. The fact of his speaking faded from his awareness, and perhaps that of the audience.

One day it was the turn of Bates. That was not his real name, merely the name he was assigned for this duty, keeping him anonymous. He entered the chamber, found the prior watcher in the darkness, and touched his shoulder. "Shift change," he said. The other drew back, and Bates moved forward to put his eye to the eyepiece and his hands on the stabilizing bar. This was the position he was bound to hold for five minutes. Now he could see the crater dimly outlined, with its black hole of a center. The transfer had taken only two seconds, and the flash would have had a duration of at least three seconds, so nothing was missed. If he should see the flash, he would squeeze the bar, alerting headquarters.

Meanwhile the other watcher for this hour entered, replacing the companion. When the door closed, and they were in complete darkness, Bates spoke. "Hello. I am Bates."

"Hello. I am Zenda."

He was startled. "A woman!"

"They are short of personnel," she said, her tone a mixture of humor and annoyance.

"Normally it's man and man, woman and woman."

"There are exceptions. You may lodge a complaint after your shift."

Bates laughed. "No complaint! I like it. Relieves the monotony."

"Oh? What did you have in mind?"

"Nothing. It's just more interesting with a woman."

"Really?" There was something in her tone.

Then there was a soft ding. His first five minutes were up. "Change," he said tersely, stepping back and to the side

"Done," Zenda agreed, stepping up and in to take his place. "No flash."

"Very good."

"What did you mean about it being more interesting with a woman?"

"Well, of course it depends on the woman."

"Oh? You mean if she's young and pretty?"

Her attitude annoyed him. "Yes, really."

"What about the man?"

"Better if he is young and handsome. Though in the dark it might not matter much."

"This puts me in mind of a game," she said. "Are you familiar with 'begging'?"

"A child's game," he said.

"Not necessarily."

"One child has to stand still, no matter what. The other tries to tickle him. They take turns, and the one who first begs the other to stop is the loser."

"Adults can play it too. I challenge you."

"To tickle you?" he asked, amazed.

"To make me beg. Before I make you beg. It will keep us awake."

"But I'd have to—to touch you. Where you're ticklish. Under your clothing."

"Well, if you lack the nerve, then don't."

"You are—are giving me permission to—to touch you like that? Anywhere?"

"Anywhere I can touch you. I bet I can make you beg first."

"But what about the watching? That's what we're here for."

"The one watching must continue watching, while the other touches. Under no circumstances must the watcher interrupt the watching. Five minute turns."

"You're on!" he said. The prospect excited him.

"And it should keep us awake and alert."

He realized it was true. Suddenly they would not be bored or sleepy. But that made him think of another aspect. "You know, this could get embarrassing. I don't know what you look like, but—"

"Oh, if I'm ugly you don't want to play?"

She made it sound so unkind! Yet it was true. "I apologize. I'm an ordinary guy, and I assume you're—well—similar."

She mellowed. "Let's try one round, and quit after that if either one wants to."

"Done. We'll start when my turn watching comes. You set the pace."

There was a ding. Five minutes were up. It had hardly seemed that long. "Watcher change," she said.

They made the change, and he viewed the moon crater. "No flash," he murmured routinely.

"First base," she said. Her hands touched his head, smoothing his hair, brushing his ears, rubbing his neck. Her fingers were slender, cool, and agile.

"You have nice hands, Zenda," he said.

"Thank you. I was a manicurist before I decided to try moon-watching."

"But this isn't going to make me beg."

"I'm just scouting the terrain. How's this?" She tickled the back of his neck.

Bates caught his breath. The tickle was far more effective than he expected. "You're good! But I'm not begging." Neither was he removing his eyes from the eyepiece or his hands from the bar; those had to remain in place no matter what.

She tried under his chin, and again he had to steel himself, but survived. Then she touched his mouth. He sucked in his breath as the tickle was much worse, but did not beg her to stop.

"I see this will be a challenge," she said. "Let's try another kind."

"What do you—" he started. Then he was cut off by her next touch on his mouth. She was kissing him.

The effect was electric. His mouth seemed to be on soft fire, and his head was floating.

After a brief eternity she drew back. "You were saying?"

"I think you used something other than your hands," he said, feeling dizzy.

"Are you crying foul?"

"No! It just surprised me."

"Hands aren't the only things that can tickle." Now her lips moved to his neck, and he felt her tongue licking his skin. That was evocative in another way.

There was the ding. "Change," he said, almost regretfully. They swapped places.

Now it was his turn, as she was bound to the eyepiece and bar and had to submit to his tickling. First he felt her head, exploring it as she had his. She had fair-length hair bound back into a ponytail, and her features seemed regular: surely attractive, could they just be seen. Then he tickled her ears and neck, but couldn't make her beg for mercy. So he kissed her mouth, and that was a mistake, because he suspected the contact had more impact on him than on her. He followed that with kisses on her ears, which had delicate earrings.

Then the dinger dinged, and they changed places again. This time she unbuttoned his shirt and slid her hands across his chest and around to his sides. Her light touch thrilled him; it was extremely suggestive. When she tickled his ribs he made an exclamation more to encourage her than as any ticklishness, because the pleasure of her touch overruled any negative aspect. When she put her face down and kissed his belly he suffered the masculine reaction. She surely knew it, but gave no indication.

Ding, and they changed again. Now it was his turn to do her upper half. He opened her blouse and stroked her belly and bra. She was finely formed with no surplus fat on her, just pleasingly rounded. Then he removed the bra and tickled her breasts. That got to her; she giggled and quivered.

"Are you begging?" he inquired.

"No!" she cried breathlessly.

So he put his face down and licked her breasts, then kissed her nipples. She writhed and a moan escaped her, but she did not yield. It occurred to him that she had set this up so she could be treated to exactly this kind of attention by an anonymous stranger, with no danger of commitment. Well, he was game.

They changed places again. This time she took down his trousers and undershorts and stroked his legs. His member stood proudly erect in the darkness. She addressed it, circling the shaft with her fingers and working it. The thing surged in her hands, making ready to erupt.

"Now I can cause this to jettison into space," she murmured. "Or to find a more comfortable lodging. Which do you prefer?"

"The lodging!" he said eagerly.

"For that you will have to beg."

She had him. Her fingers squeezed the rod, bringing it almost to the point; obviously she was experienced in this respect. He was about to climax.

"I'm begging!" he cried. "Please!"

She turned in the darkness, put her bottom to his groin, and guided his member into her cleft just as the finale came. He spurted deep within her, again and again, the sheer delight of it transporting him. But he never removed his eyes or hands from their assignments.

"You lose," she said with satisfaction as his passion blissfully faded.

"You won," he agreed. Then the dinger sounded, and they exchanged places.

"We will never meet again," she said.

"Oh, Zenda, I wish—" But what could he say? It was her decision, part of the deal.

"But it has been fun," she continued.

"Fun," he agreed weakly.

By the time their shift was done, they were both fully clothed again and in order. They had not seen the flash. Zenda gave him a final kiss, then exited through her door. She was gone.

That was all there was to it, but Bates could not let it go. The feel of Zenda was with him, and he wanted to be with her. But he had no knowledge of her real identity. For all he knew, she could even be married; that would explain both her desire to be private, and her sexual competence. It hardly mattered; he wanted her.

But how could he find her? He had many subsequent watching shifts, some with women, but none were her. She probably had quit the program.

He pondered, then tried the direct way. He ran an ad in the seeking-partners network. BATES SEEKING ZENDA.

He received several answers from women named Zenda, but follow-up dialogue showed that none were the one he sought. His first question was HOW DID WE MEET, and their answers were wrong. Then came a live prospect. IN DARKNESS.

WHERE?

YOU TELL ME.

That set him back at first. Then he realized that she needed to verify his identity too, lest he simply be on the make for any woman of that name. WATCHING THE MOON. WHAT DID WE DO?

WE PLAYED BEG. WHO WON?

It really was her! YOU DID.

But she remained cautious. "HOW?

YOU TOOK ME IN. I THINK I LOVE YOU.

She was reassured. YOU DON'T KNOW ME. YOU'VE NEVER EVEN SEEN ME.

TRUE. IT'S A PASSION THING.

She became more candid. I HAD JUST BEEN JILTED. I TOOK IT OUT ON YOU. I MEANT NEVER TO MEET YOU AGAIN.

I KNOW. BUT I'M BEGGING.

I FOUND I DID HAVE A HANKERING FOR YOU, THOUGH I DON'T KNOW

YOU. YOU PLAYED THE GAME MANFULLY AND ACCEPTED YOUR LOSS.
SOME LOSS! he replied. YOU GAVE ME GREAT SEX.
BUT FACE IT: RELATIONSHIPS ARE BASED ON MORE THAN SEX.
FIFTY FIFTY WHETHER IT WORKS. I'M GAME. Would she respond fa-
vorably?
ME TOO. And there it was. They would give it a try. Maybe it wouldn't
work out in the long term, but at least it would abate their temporary passion
for each other.
The story ended there. Havoc stood with Gale, both naked. They had put
on quite a show, in the supposed darkness.
After a moment, the applause began. The story, dramatized as it had been,
had gone over well.
The pilot's voice came: "We are now descending on Naples, Italy. Please
fasten your seat belts."
"Naples!" Someone exclaimed. "You said Rome!"
"It changed," the pilot said. "The Rome port was too crowded to accom-
modate us. The same support will be available at Naples."
And that was what the distraction of the story had covered: their additional change of course. Another surprise for the pursuing rebels, and it put
them quite close to their destination: the Green Chroma zone around Mount
Vesuvius.
"It was worth it," another man said. "What a story!" He meant what a
show; Gale nude was a treat for any observer, and Gale teasing a man was that
much more.
The rocket landed. *Hide*, Voila's thought came.
Havoc stood and addressed the other passengers. "We beg a favor. We four
would prefer to depart surrounded by others, so as not to be obvious targets.
You will run the risk of being attacked."
"What will you pay?" a woman called.
"A kiss and a feel. We kiss and you feel."
They laughed. Then they formed clusters around each member of the party:
women around Havoc and Caveat, men around Gale and Modesty. They pressed
in so closely that it would be difficult for any outside to distinguish the targeted
individuals.
They left the rocket. Women and girls surrounded Havoc, taking their
feels as they moved along; hands were constantly touching him in public and
private places. When they reached the moving walk area, Havoc selected one
clearly smitten teen girl, put his arms around her, and kissed her lingeringly.
He added one feel of her pert bottom and let her go.
Fortunately others caught her as she swooned.
Gale and Modesty were doing similar with their men, both of them dishev-
eled from the touchings. Even Caveat had played along; this was business for
him, and he was a handsome man.
But they still had to get to the Green Chroma zone. The rebels were locat-
ing them and closing in. "Coordination," Havoc murmured to Gale, and sent a
detailed thought.
"Acquiescence," she said.
Havoc took Mistress Modesty by the elbow. "Come with me. There is dan-
ger."
Modesty nodded, and accompanied him without protest. They stepped

onto a conveyer belt, rode it to the nearest rest stop, and stepped off. Meanwhile Gale was taking Caveat in another direction. The pursuing rebels would have to split their attention to track both parties.

Havoc and Modesty entered a toilet booth. "Change your appearance," Havoc whispered tersely. He was already changing his own, reversing his shirt and putting on a skullcap he had brought. "Heed me as we move."

"Oh, yes," she agreed, rapidly becoming another kind of woman.

They left the booth together. "Down!" Havoc snapped, dropping himself low. She dropped with him, as a green ball flew just over their bodies and shattered against a wall. They ran away before the spreading mist could catch them.

"Your clairvoyance is useful," Modesty remarked as they ducked behind another building.

"Agreement," he said, smiling. "Along with the nearest future paths."

"I gather you merely select one that avoids the worst mischief, a path being perhaps no more than a momentary position as a ball misses."

"Concurrence. You grasp magic readily."

"I came to admire it in your daughter, a fine girl and consummate actress."

"Appreciation. Problem: five rebels are encircling our location. We can avoid them, but that leads to their discovery of Gale and Caveat before they are ready. We need to hold their attention a little longer."

"How may I help?"

"If you are willing to flash them, to give me time to act—"

She smiled. "Say when."

"Walk forth now, alone."

She stepped away from the wall. Immediately several thuggish men appeared. "Hey, look what we flushed!" one called.

Now, Havoc thought.

Mistress Modesty opened her gown as she faced the men.

"Hoo!" one man exclaimed, his pupils dilating. "I thought you said she was old!"

"A mistress is never old," the other replied, his own eyes fixed on her form.

"Can I have her?"

"Not yet. We haven't flushed the man."

Havoc moved. He was on the nearest man without warning, knocking him down and out with a precisely placed blow. He turned on the second, catching him around the neck and putting him down with a key nerve block. He took that man's pistol, aimed it at the third man, and fired a silver ball. It struck the man's lifting arm, and he went down in literal shock.

The remaining two rebels faded out, avoiding further conflict. "Follow," Havoc said, running after them.

Wordlessly, Modesty followed. Havoc ducked around a building, then into a tool shed. He closed the door behind Modesty as she entered, breathing hard. "My apology for delaying you," she gasped. "I am not accustomed to such exertion."

"Needless. We must wait here fifteen minutes, then proceed. You have time to recover." She was of senior age, but the rebels were right: she had a figure to conjure with, as most mistresses did. Suddenly he missed Monochrome.

She pulled her open robe together, covering her heaving breasts. Then she paused, noting his gaze. "You are so competent, I forget you are a man. I believe you call it no fault?"

Havoc did not hesitate. He took her in his arms and kissed her passionately, then penetrated her with her ready assistance. He was competent in martial arts; she was as competent in sex. "No fault," he agreed belatedly.

"There is after all no sense in wasting opportunity," she said, stroking his buttocks with a touch that was marvelously evocative even immediately after his climax.

"Appreciation. You understand men."

She laughed pleasantly. "I do. All of us do. But I was thinking also of myself."

"You desired this?" he asked, surprised. "I assumed you were merely catering to my need."

"Read my mind, Havoc."

He read it, and discovered raging passion. She did desire him, and she had not yet had her will of him. "Surprise." He had not withdrawn from her; now his member surged back into rigidity.

"You are already something of a legend, Havoc. We mistresses are trained to service men, and we do it gladly, but you are a man among men. I had hoped this chance would come."

"Caution. You want more than sex. But I can make no larger commitment."

"No fault, as agreed. I want more than routine sex. I want a rare experience. Let me lead, if you will."

He let her lead, and she caressed and kissed his head and body while massaging his member internally. He withheld his second climax, waiting on her pleasure. Only when she slowly worked into her orgasm did he allow himself to join her. They held each other in mutual ecstasy, letting it take them where it would. The experience was, for him, better than the first. The mutuality was what did it.

Now the spare time was done. They put themselves together and moved out. The rebels had lost track of them and were far afield, and they made it to the Green Chroma zone without further event.

Gale and Caveat were already there. "Appreciation for your diversion," Gale said. "We slipped by unmolested."

They proceeded through the zone, going toward Mount Vesuvius, now erupting green fire and ash. White Dynamo and green Naive intercepted them and guided them to the villa they had set up. Other mistresses were still arriving, rescued by the other Glamors. This was to be their sanctuary while the battle for Earth continued beyond.

Voila appeared. "You made it!" she exclaimed, girlishly, as if there had been doubt. She hugged Modesty, then Caveat. "I'm so glad you'll be safe during the final battle for Earth. The Male Spirit won't be able to take any more hostages."

"Except one," Caveat said grimly.

They looked at him. Then Voila recoiled in horror. "Oh no!"

"Oh, yes," he said, smiling wolfishly. "I am the Male Spirit, and I have taken a body that you will not want to hurt. Now we shall wait here while my forces slowly overwhelm the planet and make it mine. Then, my little dear, I will make *you* mine. I look forward to that a good deal more than you do, I'm sure."

They stood there, having no reply. It seemed the Spirit had outmaneuvered them. Again.

Chapter 23
Charm

They repaired to Ennui's office to see about Monochrome's place in governing the planet. "I can handle most of it," Ennui said. "But one is major, and requires high-profile authority."

"That is the one," Monochrome agreed.

"A new Blue Chroma volcano is erupting in an established Red Chroma zone. This is causing considerable disruption. The Red Chroma folk in that area must be efficiently evacuated, and some kind of settlement made for their loss of territory. They are on the verge of panic, and I think will truly heed only the king or an equivalent representative." She paused, eying Monochrome. "The Lady Aspect might handle it, as she is held in high regard, but she lacks organizational skills."

"I possess them," Monochrome said. "Are there any of Dynamo's trainees remaining on this planet?"

"Only a few dropouts," Ennui said, surprised. "They would not be competent."

"Bring them here. I will make them competent. Now I need detailed background on the region, the people, and especially the existing local government. Can you provide authorities?"

"The Red and Blue Chroma representatives. But they do not get along well with each other, and I doubt either respects you, Mistress."

"Bring them to me, regardless. I will talk with them while we travel to the site."

Ennui glanced at Green. "Bring them," he agreed.

"I will expect the trainees and Chroma representatives here in an hour."

"Mistress, that can't be—" Ennui broke off, reconsidering. "As you wish."

"It seems we have a vacant hour," Monochrome said to her assistants. "Come with me."

Scent, Wrench, Green, and the Lady Aspect accompanied her to her suite. "Outfit me with clothing suitable for traveling, but nevertheless capable of sex appeal," she said to Scent. "A slightly tight blouse, slightly short skirt, hair bound back in a youthful ponytail."

The girl got busy, undressing and changing her as she talked with the others. The Green Chroma man and nonChroma boy looked on without comment; they had already learned that the Mistress had her own ways of doing things.

"Lady Aspect, do you have criminals on Charm?"

It was Aspect's turn to be surprised. "They are normally executed or banished to Limbo. There are some few who simply don't fit in our society. We call them brigands. They tend to prey on travelers between Chroma zones, where the magic is lacking. Roughnecks without consciences."

"Bring me one scheduled for execution."

"Mistress, this is not wise," Green protested.

"Desperate situations require desperate measures. I am going to need a bodyguard."

"You can't trust a brigand!"

"I believe I can." She glanced at Aspect, who shrugged and departed.

Soon Aspect returned with a crude, muscular man chained at ankles and wrists, but wearing knives and a club. "This is Grudge, an incorrigible brigand. He is a formidable martial artist and leader of men, cunning enough to have evaded capture for five years despite striking frequently, and is considered too dangerous to live. He remains armed because he has sworn to die before giving up his weapons. He knows that the moment he uses them here, he will die; there is a magical geis on him." She paused. "Beware, Mistress."

Monochrome faced the man. "Greeting, Grudge."

"Obscenity, Mistress. Looking for a real fuck you don't have to live with after? I'm your man."

"Perhaps you are, Grudge. Here is the deal I proffer: I will give you one supreme sexual experience, and in the process enchant you so that you will love me without reservation thereafter. My whim will become your command, and you will serve me utterly. You will be my love slave, knowing that your love may never be indulged again. In return for this service, you will not be executed and the geis will be lifted; you will remain as my servant and bodyguard until I am through with you. Then you will be released to pursue your own designs, still guided by my imprint. You will not return to brigandry. Do you agree?"

He stared at her. "Joke?"

"Literal."

"Agreement."

"His word is worthless," Green said. "He means to betray you as soon as he has had you."

"Of course," Monochrome agreed. "But you are witness that he has agreed to my offer. Remove his manacles."

"Mistress, he will kill you!"

Monochrome quirked a smile. "Then you will be rid of me, Green, victim of my own foolishness. The Lady Aspect will testify to that."

"I agree with Green," Aspect said. "You are placing yourself in completely unnecessary peril."

"Wrench," Monochrome said.

Wrench stepped forward, and in a moment had the manacles off the brigand. In that moment Monochrome drew down her skirt and stood with her nether section bare. "Do not interfere," she murmured to the others.

Grudge didn't hesitate. He leaped forward, swept her into his hungry embrace, kissed her, and pressed her back against the wall, his rigid penis emerging to ram into her cleft. He thrust and climaxed in one motion, panting. She made no effort to hinder him. Instead she focused her personal power on his body and mind, exerting a much stronger force than she had on Carrot. It was like a trap snapping on a rat. Such acquisition required very close contact, which she had in this moment. It was a succubus-like technique she and Gale had exerted when the Male Spirit of Earth had thought he was using them sexually. The brigand was caught in his moment of ecstasy.

Green, Wrench, and Scent were staring, mesmerized by the scene. But there was a certain fascination in Scent's expression; this was a rape fantasy being enacted.

Grudge withdrew, spent, looking surprised. "Question: What's wrong with me?"

"Brigand, you are mine," she informed him. "I own your soul. You will obey me without question. Acknowledge."

For an instant he seemed to try to fight. Then he yielded. "Acknowledged, Mistress."

"You will be my bodyguard in the field and my submissive companion elsewhere. Any person who proffers me physical harm will have to get through you. You will not kill him unless it is quite necessary, but you may knock him to the ground, indulging your appetite for violence. You will not otherwise try to harm anyone, especially not these four here with me now: the Lady Aspect, Scent, Wrench, and Green."

"Agreement," Grudge said, in wonder.

"Get him better clothing," Monochrome told Scent. "And wash him so he no longer smells."

"But Mistress, he will rape me!" There was a tinge of desire in that fear.

Monochrome turned to Grudge. "Will you rape her?"

"No, Mistress."

"Why not?"

"Because she is not you, and you do not want it."

"But he could just be saying that," Scent protested fearfully. It seemed that despite her fantasies, she was not eager for real rape. "Until he gets hold of me."

"Green?" Monochrome inquired.

"Negation," Green said. "His mind is completely captive. You can trust him, now."

Still dubious, the girl fetched clothing and approached the brigand. "Remember, you can't touch me." Yet it was almost like an invitation. Fear and desire overlapping. He was a captive rapist, therefore fascinating.

"Endorsement. No touching. Not that I wouldn't want to," Grudge told her. "You're a pretty little piece, and there's something about you. And I would if she told me to. But she told me no, and that's it."

"True," Green said.

The girl got to work changing the brigand's clothing. When she had him naked, she washed him with sponges and a basin of water. He let her, doing nothing, though his member rose when she washed that portion. That did not bother her; as a bath girl she was used to this reaction in men. In fact she seemed rather intrigued by the size and firmness of it, washing it almost caressingly. Her confidence increased as the truth of Monochrome's statement was borne out. The brigand was no longer dangerous to the members of this party.

"Question," Wrench said.

Monochrome turned to him. "Speak."

"First you did it with Carrot. Now with Grudge. You have amazing power. You know I don't want to be here. Why didn't you do it to me? I mean, you could simply have compelled me, without taking the trouble to help me. You didn't. You changed no more of me than you needed to."

Monochrome smiled. "It isn't necessary. You will do what you are supposed to do regardless, and in time you will be satisfied to work with me."

"I'm satisfied now, Mistress." And it was true: he had been converted, in significant part by the wonders he had seen her perform.

"And you know it is of your own volition, and not because I enchanted you," she said. "I merely deleted your urge to steal."

"Revelation!" he agreed, not really surprised.

"One or two remaining," Green said wryly. Neither he nor the Lady Aspect had been converted. But it would happen in due course.

"Feed him," Monochrome said. "He is hungry. In fact, feed us all, quickly. We can have the same meal he has."

Aspect summoned a servant and gave a directive. Sandwiches and beer rapidly appeared.

"You know, Mistress," Grudge remarked as he gulped down his rations, "I could get to like you even if I didn't already love you."

"I am a likable person," she agreed without vanity.

As the hour finished, Grudge was halfway handsome in a military uniform, and the others no longer shied away from him. All were satisfied with the quick meal, and Scent was a bit tipsy, evidently unused to beer. Grudge steadied her elbow unobtrusively, and she did not flinch. "Next time take it slower, girl," he advised. "Men use that stuff to make girls willing, or at least unable to resist."

"Willing," she echoed dizzily.

Ennui appeared. "The people you requested are in the assembly room."

"Very good," Monochrome said briskly. "We will join them immediately."

They did so. There was a fair assortment of Chroma folk, as well as the Red and Blue Chroma representatives. Not all of them were pleased to be there, and it showed.

Monochrome addressed them directly. "There is a Chroma crisis we must handle expeditiously. I am depending on you to assist me in this. We will save lives and abate confusion. As we travel I will talk with each of you, and you will be competent to perform your roles. But at this moment all I will do is touch you. Hold forth your hands."

Bemused, they did so. She walked to each and touched his or her hand with a single finger. Their eyes widened as she did so; suddenly they were persuaded that she was competent to do the job—and that they were competent also. It was semi-hypnotic, but also true. It was her special personal magic, motivating people, giving them confidence.

Then they went out for their transportation to the crisis zone, for this was to be a hands-on operation. She got fleeting glimpses of the wooden city, which she understood was a giant floating pyramid, and the lake on which it floated, and the surrounding development. Then they were at the loading zone and boarding carriages. She traveled with Scent, Wrench, Grudge, Green, and the two other Chroma representatives.

The coach was made for six, but Scent sat on Grudge's lap, having entirely lost her fear of him. He held her in place but took no liberties whatever. "If she hadn't bound me, you little tease, I'd be in you right now," he murmured. "You got the nicest hot little ass."

"Concurrence," she agreed, wiggling her bottom.

The Chroma representatives maintained straight faces. Wrench looked uncomfortable.

"Now while we travel, I need to learn all about your two Chroma," Monochrome told the Red and Blue Chroma representatives. "So I can best serve them. I expect to work through the existing governmental apparatus, displacing no one, but I will need their names and descriptions."

"Mistress, this can hardly be assimilated in an hour," the Blue Chroma man protested.

"I am constrained to agree," the Red Chroma man said. The two Chroma representatives sat spaced as far apart as possible in the crowded coach, not concealing their aversion for each other.

"It can and will be," Monochrome said firmly. "As it is a Red Chroma zone, the Red Chroma officials are the ones I must know best. You surely know them all, Red. Speak them rapidly to me."

The man shrugged. "This particular zone is governed by a woman, the Lady Fussy. This is not humor; it describes her, and she is proud of it. She is excellent on details, and requires them to be exactly correct." He continued naming and describing lesser officials. In about half an hour he was through.

Monochrome turned to the Blue Chroma man. "What will be the earliest need relating to the new zone forming?"

"For Blue Chroma inhabitants to tame its wildness, Mistress," he replied. "This will be risky, because new volcanoes are unpredictable. Special volunteers will be required. This normally involves an extended process of recruitment."

"I don't have time for that. I need those volunteers this day."

"Unfeasibility."

"We have some Blue Chroma executive trainees in the other coaches. These will be competent to recruit immediately. But we will require your intercession to legitimize the recruitment in the closest Blue Chroma zones. What are the officials in the three closest zones?"

The blue man's mouth tightened, but he answered. He listed the leaders and their primary subordinates, with their individual natures and quirks. It was a lot of information.

She privately noted the Green Chroma representative's smug expression. He thought she was assimilating little if any of this.

By the time the man finished his spiel, the coach was descending. Only now did Monochrome gaze out the small window. "We are airborne!" she remarked. She had been too preoccupied to pick up on this, until she felt the drop.

None of the Chroma representatives spoke. Wrench and Scent did not because they felt it was not their place. That left Grudge. "Yes, Mistress. This is my first flight, too. We nonChroma ground criminals don't get to see much magic."

She smiled at him, and he went still, affected by the expression. He loved her, and any such token gesture had special impact. "Nor we visitors from other planets," she agreed.

"Mistress—when we land—I've never been a bodyguard before, but this may be out in the wilds where my kind roams. If you please, I should go out first to scout the scene."

"Agreement. All of those present here are to be protected, as most will lack magic outside their Chroma."

The coach landed. "Gotta move you off, cutie," Grudge told Scent. "But it's been fun."

"Not half what it would have been alone, muscles," she replied. She was actually flirting with him.

Grudge heaved out of his place, setting Scent there instead, and wedged out of the coach. In a moment he called back. "Scene's clear, Mistress."

"Appreciation." She climbed out.

They were at the edge of the Red Chroma zone, and it was chaotic. The emerging vent of the Blue Chroma volcano was straight ahead, sending out puffs of blue ash. The air was swirling, forming scattered funnel clouds where the contesting Chroma interacted.

Red people were everywhere, walking away from the advancing blueness. They looked harried, and tired, and desperate.

Monochrome turned to the Red Chroma representative. "Surely these folk have magic. Why have they not simply conjured themselves to safety?"

"Conjuring living people is advanced magic that not many peasants master," he replied. "They normally settle for simple magic to help feed and clothe themselves. In addition, all magic becomes chancy when Chroma zones collide. It is safest for them to stay on their feet."

"And they may have no place to go," Monochrome added. "Because the other territories are already occupied."

"Agreement."

"Assemble as many refugees as feasible here, so I can address them," she said. "But first I must speak with the Lady Fussy."

A red woman appeared before them. "I am here, Mistress. What is your interest?" She spoke with formal respect, but her aspect hinted at moderate contempt for the outsider.

"I wish to get these refugees settled compatibly. I gather there is little room for them elsewhere in your zone."

"True, Mistress. It will take months to find them new situations."

Monochrome turned to the Blue Chroma representative. "Take the carriage to the zone of Appetite. Ask him to come here immediately." That was the leader of the nearest Blue Chroma zone.

Wordlessly, the Blue man turned and went back to the coach. In a moment it floated up, lifted by the local magic, and moved away.

"What can that fraud do here?" Fussy demanded.

"He can make resources available to facilitate the travel of the Red Chroma refugees through his zone and on to their destination. Food, clothing, temporary shelter, and so on; they can be treated like tourists."

"Question: why would that tightwad do that?"

"It will make economic and social sense."

"This I must see happen," Fussy said dubiously.

The Lady Aspect approached from another coach. "News, Mistress: Ennui has located a prospect. But it is on the far side of the planet."

That was excellent timing, not entirely coincidental. The Lady Aspect was in telepathic contact with the Lady Ennui. Monochrome had asked them to locate a newly erupting Red Chroma volcano.

"Mistress, the refugees are assembled," the Red Chroma representative said.

She smiled at him, impressing him against his will. "Appreciation, Red. Guide me there."

He did so. The ragged group was waiting passively, fearing there was no real hope. Red people in a red scene; she still wasn't quite used to that color effect. Red Chroma rescue workers were providing them with food and temporary sanitary facilities, but it was a token effort.

"Amplify my voice," Monochrome murmured. Red nodded.

Then she spoke. "Greeting." Her voice carried magically.

"Greeting," they echoed weakly.

"I am Mistress Monochrome, here to assist you in finding compatible new residence. Unfortunately it is far across the planet, so you will have to leave this zone. I regret this, but you know you can't remain here."

They nodded disconsolately; they knew.

"Nor in this Chroma zone; it is filled and there is no room for refugees."

They knew.

"But there is a place for you to go. We have located a new Red Chroma volcano even now expanding its terrain. This will be wild magic, of course, a special challenge. But all yours to tame and settle. You will be pioneers, in just the way the Blue Chroma folk coming here will be. You will set up your own government, answer to your own leaders, and fashion your own community. There are ways in which this may be regarded an an improvement."

They perked up. There were indeed some positive aspects, especially considering the alternative of perpetual refugee status.

"But there is also a negative aspect. It is far away. The far side of the planet. You will lose many of your former neighbors. I trust you will be able to handle this."

They were considering, and concluding that they could.

"Soon you will have to make a trek to the nearby Blue Chroma zone, where we expect them to treat you like tourists and guests, and to provide magic transport around the planet. So that aspect should not be difficult. The real challenge will be when you arrive at the new Red Chroma zone. Can you handle it?"

They nodded. They could handle this too.

"You gave them hope," Red murmured appreciatively. "And it seems you are implementing your promise. This will not be forgotten in our circle."

"Appreciation," she replied.

The coach returned. The Blue representative conducted a stout blue man to the site. "Expletive!" the visitor exclaimed. "What nonsense is this, Earth Mistress?"

"And it is good to meet you, too, Appetite," she said, and quickly kissed him lightly on the lips.

He stood a moment, while several in their party smiled knowingly. "Apology," he said. "I listen."

"Accepted. Here is the plan: you will locate a number of Blue Chroma zone folk who for whatever reason are eager to settle new territory, led by competent officials." She named several people: lesser officials who did not get along well with the existing authority. "You will grant them a very special opportunity to colonize a new Blue Chroma zone." She gestured, indicating the burgeoning blue on the horizon. "They will merely have to give up their present homes and goods, which they will have no further use for anyway. This will revert to the common good, to be handled as you see fit. Thus you will be doing significant favors while gaining significant properties and goods. In return you will of course facilitate the progress of these unfortunate refugees who are involuntarily giving up their residences to your colonists. You will arrange for them to be magically transported around the planet to the new Blue Chroma volcano just now erupting. You will treat them like the honored guests they are, so that they have no complaints about your uncommon courtesy, and they will be gone as soon as you arrange it. Thereafter this challenging new zone is yours to populate. Does this make sense to you?"

The crafty thoughts were almost visibly coursing through his greedy head. He could gain significant power and influence, while simultaneously ridding himself of some troublesome misfits. And he would be on record with the King's court as having done it a favor.

It did not take him long to decide. "Enthusiasm!"

She kissed him again, lightly. "Pleasure."

He wavered a moment, recovering, then turned about to return to the coach. He was already snapping directives to his aides as he entered. This would be expeditiously accomplished.

"I think our job here is largely done," Monochrome said. "But I suspect it best to remain here until we see the refugees being moved out. Is there a house for my party?

"Affirmation! There is a mansion for your party!" Lady Fussy said with no irony. "You have solved my problem."

"This was my intention. It is why the king's authority exists: to deal with interChroma problems."

Later, after a sumptuous dinner that Monochrome insisted be shared with the refugees, Green approached her. "I am persuaded, Mistress. You remembered the names, and played beautifully on internal rivalries. I have not seen such ad hoc competence and flair since Havoc."

"Well, I love Havoc," she said, as if that explained everything. Then she considered. "No fault?"

His jaw dropped momentarily. "Agreement," he said, awed.

After the first eager bout of sex, she explained. "I wanted to persuade you without duress or temptation. I wanted you to be satisfied that I am competent to handle this position. Now that you are satisfied, perhaps we can be friends. I like being with men. But I love only Havoc."

"Understanding," he breathed, more than satisfied. "You have overwhelmed my doubt, Mistress."

There was more sex, of course; men always wanted a lot at the outset of a sexual relationship. But she enjoyed it too, especially after his edge was off and he was amenable to subtle guidance. In the darkness, in her shielded private mind, she pretended he was Havoc, knowing that neither Green nor Havoc would mind, if they knew.

They slept, woke for another bout, slept, bouted, and slept until early morning. Then, after one more bout, Green rose to garb himself. "Statement: My understanding is that this night delimits it," he said. "You surely already know that it was the best night of my life."

"I am competent, in whatever manner," she repeated with a smile. "But there may be other nights, as circumstances facilitate." For his wife remained out seeking her fourth, and this was a fair distraction for him.

"Gratitude, Mistress. Now I shall see about further organization of the refugee emigration."

"Appreciation for your assistance." Because there was still a fair amount of detail work to be accomplished. He departed the chamber, not concerned that others should know where he had nighted. No fault was no fault, a convention Monochrome found she liked. And of course other men would envy him his night; that enhanced his status.

She got up, washed efficiently, dressed, and went out. Grudge was there, awaiting her pleasure. "You know I have some magic," she murmured.

"Confirmation, Mistress," he said, smiling. "You are a Glamor."

"My clairvoyance is not yet perfect, but it indicates that there is something I need to handle. I will take a private morning walk; trail me inconspicuously and act when you see fit."

"Affirmation."

She departed the red village, where men were doing early chores and women were preparing breakfast. Monochrome would eat later, with the Lady Fussy, as a matter of protocol. Right now she needed to discover what was nagging her.

The village was surrounded by fields where all manner of red plants grew. Some resembled Earth vegetables; some did not. Six-legged cows grazed, and six-legged dogs ranged out, keeping the cows contained. The area was open, but there was no sign of Grudge. The man was good at hiding.

She came to a red forest that bordered a red river. She smiled: the Red River Valley? She followed a path along the river bank. The nagging was stronger.

The red faded, giving way to normal coloration, by her Earthly definition. The river continued to flow red, carrying its magic into other realms.

Ahead she spied a ford: a shallow section with a series of large stones set up across the river so that people could step from one to another to reach the other side. A young Red Chroma girl was setting foot on the first stone.

Suddenly a brutish nonChroma man appeared at the far side. "Come here, girlie; I've got a treat for you." He opened his front to let his erect member spring out.

Horrified, she turned to flee—but two more men appeared behind her. She tried to run between them, but one caught her and heaved her off her feet. He wrestled her around to face him, then pushed her head down so that he was holding her bent over before him, her legs kicking the air with futility. She screamed, but the sound was muffled in part by her own body.

"Gotcha," the first man said with satisfaction as he stepped from stone to stone, his ready penis leading the way.

These were brigands, and he was contemplating the rape of a child. "No!" Monochrome cried.

The third man wheeled to face her, drawing his knife, while the second continued to hold the inverted girl and the first closed on her dangling legs. Monochrome realized she was in trouble. She could nullify one man with a touch, but there were three, and their weapons could reach her before she could touch them all. Yet she could not allow the rape to proceed; this was what had nagged her. She hesitated.

A knife seemed to sprout from the first brigand's chest. He toppled into the river. Then Grudge appeared, catching the third man by the throat and levering him to the ground.

"Don't kill him!" Monochrome cried. "Just nullify him."

Grudge kneed the man in the jaw and left him lying unconscious. He turned on the second man. That man released the girl, who dropped as a heap on the ground. Monochrome went to her, touching her with calming, fetching her in to weep on her shoulder. "You are safe now," she murmured comfortingly.

Meanwhile Grudge dispatched the brigand and left him lying unconscious beside his comrade. Then he went to the river to recover his knife from the dead brigand. By the time he had it out, cleaned, and back in its sheath, Monochrome had the girl in order.

"How did you come here?" she asked the girl.

"I got separated from my family. I thought they had crossed the river."

"No, the rendezvous with the evacuation coaches is the other direction. I will take you there now."

"Appreciation," the girl said, wiping away the last tear. "I was foolish, I know."

"We all do foolish things, when there are frightening disruptions."

They walked back to the village, where Scent and Wrench were out looking for them. "Take this girl to the rendezvous and find her family," Monochrome told Scent. "Inform the Red Chroma authorities that there are three brigands somewhat the worse for wear at the river ford," she told Wrench. "We must talk," she said to Grudge.

"Apology if I have done wrong, Mistress," he said humbly.

"Needless. I want to know why you took out the farthest man first, as he was no immediate threat to me."

"He would have had time to draw his weapon. Then he would have been a threat. He would have knifed me while I handled the other two. Brigands tend to operate in threes for that reason: two may be caught with hands encumbered or in bad position, but the third can act when he is somewhat apart."

She nodded. "Now I understand. You did right, and I am glad I trusted your judgment. Why was the second brigand holding the girl upside down?"

"For efficient rape. Brigands usually don't have much time to operate before the screams of the victims bring help in force. They have to do it fast and get away."

"But she was in no position for—" She broke off, seeing his grim expression. "I fear I am being naïve."

"Negation, Mistress," he said insincerely.

Scent, Wrench, and Green returned. "The four of you join me in my chamber," Monochrome said.

In her chamber, with better privacy, she tackled it again. "Perhaps a demonstration will alleviate my ignorance. How was this rape to have been accomplished?"

Grudge glanced at Scent. "You know I won't hurt you."

"Affirmation."

"Say you're the victim, like that Red Chroma girl. A man grabs you like this." He took hold of her, turned her around to face him, and pushed her head down so that her back was against his belly, her feet dangling outward. It was the position the Red girl had been in. "Now Wrench, say you're the second brigand. Come up and pull down her pants."

Wrench glanced at Monochrome, who nodded. He approached the girl's legs. "Resist," Grudge murmured to her.

Scent kicked her feet, but it was ineffective. Wrench got close from the side and put his hands on her panties. So she spread her legs wide, preventing them from coming off. Wrench ducked under and came up between them. "Now he's got them apart," Grudge said. "He can push the pants aside and jam into her. She can kick, but it'll just make it more fun for him. If she didn't spread her legs, I could choke her a little, until she relaxed. Either way, she'll be raped in seconds. Then he'll hold her for me. Three men can do a girl that way in hardly a minute. Then, if they have time, they can do her again at leisure, other positions. It's very efficient."

"So I now appreciate," Monochrome said. "Yet in this position, the female channel slants downward. That seems less than comfortable for a man, whose member when he is standing will angle upward."

"True, Mistress. But we brigands are used to it. In fact we like it that way. We call it dipping the stick. It's easy enough when you know how."

Wrench remained standing between the girl's legs, staring into her crotch, bemused. It was obvious that he had never had this particular view before. He had gotten far more of a peek than he had anticipated, and though he was young yet, he evidently appreciated it enough to get an erection.

"Pull them aside," Scent told him mischievously. "Like a real rapist. I dare you!"

Thus challenged, aware that she was teasing him, thinking he wouldn't, Wrench reached forward and drew the panties to the side. He froze, stunned by the close view of her wet open cleft.

Then she lifted her legs and clamped her thighs on his head. "Gotcha, dope!" she exclaimed. "How you going to rape me now?"

"Confusion," the boy confessed. "Wonder." For his eyes were still locked on that open channel.

"Wedge your face forward," Grudge said. "Lick her slot. If that doesn't do it, bite her clit."

Scent immediately released the boy's head, laughing. "Obscenity! Slurped by a brigand boy."

Wrench backed away, blushing furiously. She had certainly gotten the better of him despite her position.

Grudge set Scent back on her feet. "Sorry about raping you," he said. "You have a really nice little bottom, as I said before."

"Forgiven," Scent said, with part of a smile. "You must have done it for real, many times."

"Agreement. I'm a brigand. Never go unprotected into isolated nonChroma zones; brigands like to wait in ambush, as those three did. Chroma folk can't protect themselves with magic, there."

"And had I not had you to guard me, I would have been treated the same," Monochrome said.

"Negation, Mistress. You'd have nulled one as you did me."

"That requires special energy. I am glad I did not have to expend it." She shrugged. "Lesson learned."

"Question," Green said. "What of brigand women? Are they treated like that?"

"Negation. As long as they give sex on demand, they get to choose the position. But some brigand molls, well, they like it brigand style. Provides them the illusion of being forced, as if they are succulent young captives."

"Which they aren't," Scent said, clearly turned on by this dialogue. "What do they do when there are male captives? Castrate them?"

"Sometimes," Grudge agreed. "But mostly the molls prefer to play with them. Tie them to stakes, upright, naked, and tease them to erection, especially if the captive men don't want it. Tonguing and fingering always work. If they get two or more men at once, have a contest to see who can make them spurt into space first and farthest. Ugly women love to get a man like that and make him perform several times. Maybe then bring a brigand girl who never had sex and put her in the position and shove her on. So she learns rough sex early. One moll folded a spent man over a rail and plumbed his ass with a huge dildo."

"Gruesome," Scent breathed raptly. Wrench and Green seemed quite interested despite their aversion. Sex was that way, evoking both sublime and degraded impulses.

"Intriguing sub-culture," Monochrome said. "We try to discourage forced sex on Earth, but all these variants are tolerated when practiced voluntarily. Now we must go eat and facilitate the emigration."

They got to work, and in due course the emigration was complete. They traveled to the other end, where the former trainees and some Chroma officials were efficiently directing the immigrants to suitable sites within the expanding Blue Chroma zone. Monochrome assisted, knowing the names of both the trainees and the officials; like Havoc, she had eidetic memory, and she had done her homework.

The job finished, they returned to the capital city of Triumph. This time she enjoyed the variegated scenery throughout, as the coach floated over some zones and was carried by hugely tentacular plants or giant animals or the robots they called golems across others. This was a weird and wonderful world, and she was falling in love with it, not just because it was Havoc's home planet.

When they camped for the night, as it took more than a day to traverse the planet, Monochrome thought to practice her diffusion. To do this properly she had to be outside, which meant she could be discovered. So she took precautions. "Scent, Wrench, Grudge, and Green—we are working closely together and I have no complaint about your service. Now I must trust your discretion. There is a thing I must practice that I wish to keep private."

"We shall of course respect your privacy," Green said, speaking for the four of them. He had become her lover and friend, and a useful source of information and contacts. "As we respect your person and your authority. We have come to know you and to love you, in our several fashions." He glanced around, and received affirmative nods.

"Appreciation. I am about to diffuse."

"Ifrit style?" he asked, startled.

"Affirmation. An ifrit is teaching me."

"Question," Grudge said.

Green answered. "The ifrits are cloud beings from Planet Counter Charm who can condense to solid form when they choose. They taught certain others, mainly Glamors, this art. King Havoc and Queen Gale know it, though they did not demonstrate it publicly. It seems that Mistress Monochrome is being honored with this ability also. We are about to be privileged to witness her practice session, which will surely be impressive. We will not speak elsewhere of what we see, as that would endanger her by revealing her special ability to potential enemies. We should all make minor oaths of discretion, for her protection. I hereby make mine."

There was a pause. Then Grudge spoke. "Made."

"Made," Scent said, looking pale.

"Made," Wrench said.

"We are so bound," Green said.

"Appreciation. As I diffuse, I will be around you and even inside you as you breathe. Do not be concerned; I mean you no harm."

They laughed, a bit uneasily.

"Then join me outside, and keep watch. Cover for me if necessary."

They joined her outside. This was a nonChroma park, large enough so that no Chroma zones showed. The other coaches were parked nearby. They stood in a glade in the forest, with her four companions in an approximate circle, alert for intrusion.

Monochrome proceeded to diffuse. At first she couldn't get it started, but then Idyll interceded, showing her how. Her head started to fuzz into vapor.

"Mistress!" Scent exclaimed, horrified.

"Reassurance," Green said. "This is how it is accomplished. Do not distract her during the process."

As she diffused into an increasingly large cloud, Monochrome expanded to surround the four. *I am here* she thought.

"Awe," Wrench murmured.

Finally she was all cloud. This was only her second time, but it felt surprisingly good. Her mind seemed somehow more powerful, her sensations sharper.

Then someone came. It was only a young man and woman, two of the trainees who had served so well. The four friends faded into the forest, as it would be difficult for them to explain their presence here in the early evening, leaving the glade seeming vacant.

It was a Yellow Chroma man and a Silver Chroma woman. He juggled a ball of fire, typical of his Chroma, while she snapped electric sparks from her fingers, typical of hers. They found a comfortable spot in the center of the glade and lay down. They were lovers! Monochrome surrounded them, feeling their aroused bodies. This was an experience she had not sought but was delighted to have.

"Tickle & Peek?" the man inquired.

"Acquiescence."

He touched her on her side. "Eeeek!" she screamed, wildly waving her hands and legs, managing to display a considerable amount of intimate flesh. It was obviously deliberate.

Then she addressed him. "Did you Peek here?" She touched his chest.

"Affirmation."

"Then I get to Peek there too." She tugged at his shirt, and he cooperated, until his upper body was bare. "Did you Peek here?" She touched his crotch.

"Affirmation."

She pulled off his trousers. Now he was completely bare, with a standing erection. "Oh, I can't stand it," she said. "I want a different game." In a moment she was out of her own clothing and sitting astride him, settling her cleft on his member. "If you can climax after me, you win," she said, bouncing vigorously.

"I lose," he gasped, thrusting into her.

"Spoilsport!" She lay on him, keeping him inside her. Soon she too climaxed, her bottom flexing as she milked him.

In due course they separated, dressed, and departed, their tryst complete. As such things went, it was purely routine; folk met all the time for no fault liaisons.

Monochrome was thoroughly experienced in sex, but the novelty of this nevertheless excited her. She had surrounded the two as they connected, and felt their passion physically and telepathically. She knew it affected the others too, as the two men had erections and so did the boy. The girl was clenching her legs together. There was something about voyeuristic spying that enhanced sexual appreciation.

She thought to coalesce, but knew she could not do it nearly fast enough to satisfy her, and she didn't want to have sex with Green in public. So she hovered invisible, surrounding them, absorbing their words and minds. Something interesting was about to happen; the near future paths practically glowed with it. Sex was on all their minds, its urgency battering them. It had to find its expression.

The girl was the first to break. "Grudge, please—no fault," Scent said, going to him as she lifted her skirt. "I've wanted your member ever since I washed it."

"I shouldn't," the brigand said. "Though sorely tempted. I have a conscience now. I am not to molest you."

"Beseeching," she said. "Absolutely no fault. The Mistress told me to indulge my fantasy."

"Do it," Green said tersely. "I will answer to the Mistress." He was correct in that; Monochrome's concern was that any sex be voluntary, and the girl truly was desperate for it. Her surging hormones were mixing with the cloud substance as Monochrome felt her cleft and infiltrated some vapor inside it. Scent had been truly named: she had hormonal scent. No man could resist that odor long.

Granted that release, Grudge went at it with a will, embracing Scent and kissing her as he ran his hands under her skirt and squeezed her plush bottom. "Damned nice ass," he murmured. "I've wanted it ever since I saw it that time. The way you clamped Wrench's head! You give a man ideas. You're some girl."

"Agreement. Brigand style," she said.

"But that's rape!"

"Beseeching. It turns me on something awful. My rape fantasy."

Grudge looked helplessly at Green. Green shrugged. "She has a right to the way she wants it. I will hold her."

"Appreciation," she said.

Green carefully picked her up the way Grudge had demonstrated before, getting her with her back to his front, her head down, and her legs extending before him. She spread them wide as Grudge moved in. She had no panties, having doffed them before. "Now!" she gasped. "Dip your stick, brigand!"

Grudge set his rigid member at her widely exposed cleft and pushed cautiously in and down. Monochrome felt every nuance of that entry. The man was afraid she would change her mind and did not dare rape her in reality.

"Harder!" she cried. "Drive it in there! I want it to feel like rape!"

"She does want that," Green said, reading her mind. "She's afire with lust."

Grudge pumped his swollen member vigorously, distending her tight avenue, and in a moment groaned as he spurted inside her. Then she climaxed too, gasping with the force of her orgasm. Monochrome felt all of it, her vaporous substance enclosing them both. They were turned on? So was she!

They held the tableau a moment, then Grudge withdrew. "Unharmed, friend?" he asked, concerned.

"Great!" she said. "Now him!"

"Question?" Green asked, startled as he set her down.

"Three men can rape a girl rapidly, this way. This is my chance. Do me. You know you want to, Green. You too, Wrench, after Green. No fault, no fault! Make me come again. I want to be triply violated!"

Grudge spread his hands. "She does want it." He picked her up, turned her around, and put her into the position.

"I hope I can justify this to the Mistress," Green said. Then he proceeded to penetrate her, soon climaxing. Scent did so too, responding to the novelty of a second man so soon. Monochrome felt all of this as well, including the jetting, as her vapor was everywhere. It was a rare experience, unlike any she had had before.

When Green was done, the girl called to the hesitant Wrench. "Come on, boy! Become a man! You know you want to." Grudge held her in place, her bared bottom inviting.

She was right: at this point he was desperate to do it. But he was extremely nervous. He stood there, his member pushing at his trousers, but did not approach her.

"Do it, or I'll fold you over a rail and ream your ass with a dildo!" she cried. The two men had to laugh, remembering the description of the way brigand molls treated captive men.

That did it. Wrench approached, bared his stiff member, and oriented it. Green mischievously set his hands at the lad's back and shoved him forward, so that he had sudden full entry. That was enough; he spurted immediately. Again Scent joined him, and so did Monochrome.

Now at last they were done. Grudge set her back on her feet. All three men seemed somewhat ashamed as they restored their clothing, fearing they had done wrong, but the girl was radiant. "What an experience!" she cried as she cleaned out the accumulated ejaculate. "It was just as good as I dreamed."

"But perhaps there will be no need to talk about this elsewhere," Green said. Grudge and Wrench nodded agreement.

Scent considered, then also agreed. She had managed to indulge her wild sexual fantasy, but that would not do her reputation as a discreet bath girl a lot of credit. "Yet if we are ever private again, the same four of us—"

"You vixen!" Grudge exclaimed. "You'd make us do it again!"

"And you would, wouldn't you," she said smugly.

The men exchanged glances, unable to deny it. The simulated rapes had turned them on too. That was why they were ashamed.

"And if we all had time off, or maybe at night, and I suggested a place and time, you would come," she continued. Then she laughed. "All three of you. In me."

No one denied it. There were rueful smiles. The four of them had a tacit understanding.

Now Monochrome coalesced. She formed back into her physical self. The four had resumed their prior stations.

She looked around. "I trust nothing happened while I was diffused?" she inquired.

"A couple came by," Green said.

"A tryst," Scent said.

"We watched them," Wrench said.

"So you got some vicarious sex. That's fine. Thank you for maintaining guard during my practice."

"Welcome," Green said a bit awkwardly. She couldn't blame them for not wishing to detail what they had done, and didn't push it. It was all voluntary, as she knew intimately. They seemed to have forgotten that she had been there too, diffused around them, and that she had communicated with them telepathically. They had to know she knew, on some suppressed level.

And at such time as they did it again, she would make sure to be watching, one way or another. The fact that they chose not to know she had observed their lusty game enhanced her own joy of the occasion. Secrets could be a lot of fun.

Next day they completed their journey to the capital city. Triumph, viewed at leisure, was amazing. It was a huge hollow four-sided pyramid, technically a tetrahedron, constructed of wood with metal sheathing, two thousand feet on a side, big enough to accommodate a hundred thousand people. It was the primary and really the only city on the planet, as the rest was mostly forest and farmland. The people lived on ten large floors, the poorest at the bottom, the better established toward the top. There was no monetary system to indicate wealth, but a system of barter that served a similar purpose.

They reported to Ennui's office. "How did it go?" Ennui asked, as if she didn't know.

"We managed," Monochrome said.

"We have another problem: Air Chroma and Brown Chroma are overlapping in one area, causing friction, as each wants to dominate. Can you handle it?"

"The invisible folk, and the golem folk," Monochrome said. "We'll muddle through somehow. We're a team."

Her companions did not comment, but she felt their pleasure at being so credited. They also wanted to continue as a group, for their own very private reason.

They handled that crisis, and the following ones. Each was its own challenge, but each had its own keys to solution. With dedication, expertise, innovation, and genuine caring, they made the best of each.

Every so often the four others did manage another tryst, addicted to the secret naughtiness of it. The fact was that Scent was blossoming into an extremely attractive young woman, and her eagerness for pseudo-violent sex was a potent turn-on. At other times they all worked hard and got along well, despite the considerable difference in their various stations. Green was a married man, and Scent was supposed to be pristine for service to the king at such time as he might desire her, while Grudge was of course a brigand. Only Wrench was truly free, but he was so young that no normal girl would take him seriously. It was no fault, and thus all right, but they would all keep the secret. As would Monochrome. And Idyll ifrit, who found the situation amusing.

Monochrome made frequent contact with Chroma individuals in the various crises, doing her best to ease small problems as well as large ones. The news evidently spread, because the people became distinctly friendly, even in completely new regions. It was a pleasure all around.

She practiced diffusion when she could, and had become proficient at it, no longer requiring the ifrit's direct guidance. She had not used it in handling a crisis, but was very glad to have the ability. She had not forgotten how Havoc had vaporized, escaping supposed captivity. She might do the same, some day.

A month passed. Then, abruptly, as they were about to go out to handle another crisis, Monochrome lost her magic. She felt it fade. She had become a normal woman, no longer a Glamor.

It is true, Idyll thought. *I have been focusing on maintaining your ikonical connection to your home planet, so that your magic remained available to you. But the Male Spirit has now prevailed, and absorbed the power.*

"Oh, I should have been there! I deserted my post!"

Negation, Mistress. The fall was inevitable. We needed to get you to safety so that the Male Spirit could not ravage and destroy your body once he prevailed.

"You saved me at the expense of my planet. I must return to do whatever I can to salvage the situation, whatever the cost."

Negation. It is now in the hands of Voila.

"And the other Glamors, of course. Still—"

The others will depart Earth soon. This final battle is for Voila alone.

"But she is a child! Extremely talented, but still too young and inexperienced to hope to deal with a monster like the Male Spirit. How can you leave her to be sacrificed? I love her, in my fashion, and can't abide such neglect."

I love her too, and am with her to the degree necessary. She is young, agreed, and lacks the experience we would have preferred for this engagement. But she is the most powerful human Glamor ever invoked, and has trained all her life for this encounter.

"You saw it coming, of course. But having strong magic is hardly enough. How strong is she?"

Extremely strong. She has contested in practice with her siblings, and established that she can defeat the three of them together—and they are the strongest Glamors after her. She could if she chose defeat all the adult Glamors together. We have kept her true magnitude masked, but now it will come into play.

"I had no idea! But I suppose that was part of the plan. Still, experience is if anything even more important than raw power. The Male Spirit has the experience of a billion years, and lacks all conscience. It is no fair match."

We are addressing the matter of experience in two ways. First, I am with her, and though I am alien I have planetary experience beyond that of any human being. Second, she has Swale with her.

"Swale? As in a dip in a landscape? I do not follow."

Swale is the name of a succubus. She travels to men, entices them into sex, and takes their souls at the moment of ejaculation. Queen Gale tamed her two decades ago, and now she serves our purposes. Her powers have been enhanced, and she no longer has to occupy a living woman to address a man. She can generate a tactile illusion of a woman. That enables her to take out any man she chooses. Her services will enable Voila to nullify any male Earther she needs to. The succubus also has considerable experience with men that Voila will be able to draw on at need.

"That is reassuring," Monochrome said somewhat dryly. "But is it enough?"

We don't know. Her chances are even. That is the best we can do, in a war between planets.

"And I am on the side of Charm!"

And of Earth. We hope to return that planet to you, Mistress.

"I hope you succeed, Idyll. But still I fear for Voila."

Everything rests with her, the ifrit agreed.

She called the four companions together immediately. "I have lost my power," she said. "We shall have to stop."

"Why, Mistress?" Scent asked.

"Without my special magic, I will not be able to influence folk to facilitate solutions. That could be disaster."

"It makes no difference to us," the girl said. "We love you anyway."

"Appreciation," Monochrome said wryly. "However, it requires more than your affection to solve the problems of this world."

"Clarification," Green said. "What I believe she means is that if we accept you, so do the people. We were by no means eager to join you, but you won us over by magic, competence, and caring. The citizens of this planet, too, love you, Mistress. I know this telepathically; it is unfeigned. You have been solving problems mainly by your intelligence and organizational proficiency, but also by your sincere appreciation of individual people of any station. You retain those qualities. We will continue to support you in your work, and so will the people. We all honor the King's Mistress. Acting in lieu of King Havoc, you have done him proud."

"That is exactly what I meant," Scent said, smiling.

"Ditto," Wrench agreed.

"Confirmation, for what a brigand's word is worth," Grudge said. "You took me by magical force, but you have made me more of a man than I ever was before, and you are doing the same for the planet."

Green nodded. "But if you remain in doubt, Mistress, check with the Ladies Ennui and Aspect."

Monochrome did so. "It is true," Aspect said. "You have won the hearts of the people of this planet, Mistress. You have utterly charmed them. They do love you, and want you to remain. They will do their utmost to please you. Your mere presence goes far to solve the typical crisis."

She had charmed the folk of Charm. There was a certain pleasant alignment in that. "But now I will become my true age, and look it. My beauty will fade. The people will notice."

Aspect smiled. "Mistress, I am older than you, and I retain such beauty as I choose, without the benefit of magic. I will gladly share my secrets with you. Please: remain on duty as before, until Havoc returns. We all need you."

Monochrome did something she had not done in decades: she wept. It was not a negative thing.

Chapter 24
Voila

Voila stared at the man she had known as Caveat. Now he was the Male Spirit, her revolting nemesis. She projected all the attributes of surprise, horror, and fear.

"And rest assured, baby," the body said, "I do not share my host's sexual orientation. I mean to plumb your petite crevice to its tight little depth, your screams of protest music to my mind."

She retreated fearfully. "Never, you beast." But her denial was faint.

"Starting now," he said. He advanced on her.

Havoc strode forward to intercept him. "Negation."

The Spirit paused. "Ah yes, the protective father playing his role. How are you going to negate me, yokel, without your magic? A little bit of clairvoyance won't suffice, you know."

Havoc reached for him, but his hands stopped just shy of the man's neck. The Spirit had gained power and was protected from physical assault.

"Let him be, father," Voila said. "He can't touch me any more than you can touch him."

"Not yet, Liebchin," the Spirit agreed. "But every day, every hour I am gaining power, and once the balance shifts in my favor, I will be able to overwhelm your fading resistance. You will be privileged to watch it happen, while my minions lay siege to this fortress zone. Soon enough they will capture it, and put all of you into my power."

The dialogue continued, and Voila maintained her timorous side of it. But she was acting, maintaining the pretense of her innocence and vulnerability. She needed to have the Spirit believe that her capture was incipient. Because she needed to keep him close enough so that she could constantly monitor the twisted paths of their shifting interactive future. She could not afford to miss the key one. The key to liberty, for herself, her people, and her planet. For both planets: Charm and Earth.

For the Green Chroma zone was indeed under siege. The Spirit's minions were gathering from all across the planet, encircling it, making ready to invade. Their Science magic weapons would not work within the green, but their knives, clubs, and brute strength would. They would batter, rape and kill the local population, which as yet lacked magic to oppose them. That was why the Glamors and Charm trainees were here: to protect the natives from the worst of the assault. But they would be thinly spaced, unable to hold out indefinitely. The rebels would inevitably prevail, in due course.

And that was necessary for success in the farther future. The Spirit had to win Earth, so that he could lose it. He had closed off all the paths that balked him, except for one: Voila's. He had to engage that one for the final decision. So did she.

"In fact my minions are coming in now," the Spirit said. "I suggest that you Glamors see to the security of your zone, lest you lose it at the outset."

"It's true," the Green Glamor said tersely. "They are coming in a thick mass."

"It's called a human sea," the Spirit said. "A way to overwhelm an enemy despite facing superior firepower. As it happens, I have a fair number of supporters in this area." He smiled, not at all nicely. "Your surprise destination was not a complete surprise to me, it seems."

Havoc looked disgusted. "All that ducking around, and you knew where we were going?"

"It was hardly secret, barbarian. The Glamors were all leaving their posts and coming here. It was almost as if they were running out of magic and needed to withdraw to a supposedly safe place."

"Father, you should help them hold the zone," Voila said.

"And what of you, honey?" he asked. "This pig wants your ass."

"You bet I do," the Spirit agreed. "I haven't plumbed a chaste little teen ass in centuries."

"I can take care of myself, father," Voila insisted with a show of false bravado.

"We need your help," the Green Glamor said. "They are pressing us hard."

"Go, father."

Havoc hesitated a moment more, then with evident reluctance went with the Green Glamor.

"You too, mother," Voila said bravely.

Gale was even more reluctant. "Dear, I'm not sure you understand quite what this monster has in mind."

"He can't touch me," Voila said. "I can vaporize if I have to."

Gale nodded. "True. But keep Iolo with you, just in case." She too departed with evident reluctance.

The other Glamors had gone to help defend the perimeter. Only Iolo remained, in six legged dog form.

"So now it is just you and me," the Spirit said, stepping toward her.

"And Iolo," she said, stepping back.

"Ah yes, your alien dog. The ifrit, I believe you call him. Well, honeybuns, I have learned something about those creatures in the interim. I can handle him." He walked to a closed chest, opened it, and rummaged. Then he took another step toward her.

Iolo growled and moved to intercept the Spirit. The man produced a rod-like device. "Do you know what this is, dogface? It's a Science magic gimmick called a cattle prod. Want to know what it does? I will gladly show you." He lunged at the ifrit with the rod.

"Get away!" Voila cried with alarm.

Iolo was already retreating, avoiding the touch of the thing.

"Too bad," the Spirit said, returning to the chest. "I really wanted to make a demonstration. This may be a Green Chroma zone, but I carry my brand of magic with me and can make my gimmicks work here. Your cur would have gotten one hell of a shock. Maybe there will be another chance."

"Maybe you'd better dissolve, Iolo," Voila said. "He can't shock you then."

"That depends, cutie," the man said, stepping forward again as she retreated. He was clearly enjoying himself. "It seems I have another device, thanks to my minions who left my supply chest here for me to find. A field generator that will charge the molecules in its vicinity and cause them to line up incorrectly. Your ifrit can vaporize, but he won't be able to function at all well, assuming he survives. So come on, ifrit. Make my day."

"You beast!" Voila said.

"You have it wrong, precious. It's the alien beast that will feel this effect. The solid forms will be left alone; it's designed for that. But don't take my word; let me demonstrate."

"You're just such a monster," she said, obviously intimidated.

"With a hankering at the moment for fresh young flesh," he agreed, grabbing for her.

She turned and fled far enough to establish a reasonably safe distance between them. Iolo paced her, at least keeping her company. *Is he really that stupid?* he asked telepathically.

Hardly. He's playing a game of cat and mouse.

"Right on, lovey," the Spirit agreed as he returned to the chest. He brought out several items of clothing and efficiently donned them, not caring that in the process of changing he exposed his genital section. Boots, long-sleeved plaid shirt, heavy denim trousers, leather gloves, and an extremely wide-brimmed hat. "Where's the fun in ravishing a helpless maiden? I want her to struggle first, and to try to fight the rape as long as she can."

"You can't rape me," Voila said, running toward the volcano. Now she realized that the Spirit had clothed himself for this, while she was in a light print dress, bare-headed, bare-armed, and with shoes hardly more than slippers. Definitely unsuitable for a nervous volcano. He had, it seemed, foreseen this encounter better than she had.

"Now that's debatable," the Spirit said, pursuing her without straining himself. It was her misfortune that Caveat's body was a good one; the man was in excellent physical condition. "I surely can't kill you, any more than you can kill me. But I can hold you down, because we have about the same amount of magic in this setting, by whatever name. You have only a fraction of your normal quota. Short range telepathy, close clairvoyance, spot glimpses of the nearest future paths. None of these will do you any good when trying to fend off another Glamor; our abilities cancel each other out. So it comes down to the purely physical. I have greater muscular strength than you do, so can overcome you. I'm betting that a small blunt penetration of your body in a place that is made to be penetrable won't count as damage. So yes, I think I can rape you, and I am eager to verify the case. If you prove to be impenetrable, I'll regretfully admit my misjudgment."

"You don't know anything," Voila gasped as she ascended the steepening slope. The volcano wasn't erupting at the moment, but the green rock and debris hinted at the recency of the last one, and incipience of the next.

"Well, if you're so sure, why don't you stop running, lie down conveniently, and spread your sweet little legs? We'll soon know whether it is feasible."

"That would be cooperation," she said, evincing desperation. "I can cooperate when I choose; I did with Caveat. But I won't cooperate with you."

"Nor would I expect you to, sweetie-pie. Welcome to let me catch you, and
you try to keep your nicely fleshed thighs together. You can readily prove your
case, if it exists. I think you know it doesn't. Your only chance is avoidance—
and you can't avoid me long."

"Yes I can. I'm from the volcano world, and this is a Chroma volcano. I
know its tricks."

"This is Vesuvius," he retorted. "Perhaps the most famous of Earth's volcanoes. I know much about it, and have come prepared, as you can see."

Now the slope was getting hot. She stepped carefully, avoiding the occasional greenly steaming vents. "What do you know about it?"

He was, it seemed, happy to show off his knowledge. Villains loved to brag,
according to Earther legend. "Its most historically notable eruption was in the
time of the Romans. That was back when I governed the planet, as it happens.
We need Romans again; I may see to it, when I resume power, soon."

"Romans," she said, now using her clairvoyance to avoid hot patches. "They
were a local clan?"

He laughed. "So you might say! They started here in central Italy, and
thanks to a superior ability at warfare, managed to spread their empire until it
encompassed virtually the whole of Europe. My kind of men. In time they grew
soft and careless and barbarians finally overran them."

"Barbarians?" She wanted to keep him talking.

"That's right: you are a barbarian daughter. You'd side with them. But to
others it seemed like the end of civilization for a thousand years. At any rate,
amidst the Roman hegemony, Mt. Vesuvius erupted and attracted some attention, especially when it buried two Roman towns in ash and lava. That did not
much please the townsmen, but it did do one thing: it preserved the towns of
Pompeii and Herculaneum as virtually pristine examples of Roman culture,
including some lovely erotic murals. So why, you may will inquire, did those
towns develop so close to such a dangerous mountain?"

"Because of the Chroma magic," she said before she thought. "The strongest magic is at the volcano."

He laughed again. "Beautiful! Of course you would see it that way, darling.
And perhaps it is true, for Science magic requires fertile soil for growing plants,
and the most fertile is what forms from the issue of a volcano. The vineyards of
Pompeii ran far up the slopes of Vesuvius and were renowned. But then came
the eruption, with a series of waves of debris formed from shattered rocks, hot
mud, and swirling gases flowing rapidly downhill burying everything. Ash and
hot lava pellets rained down, poisoning the air, smothering those buried. Pum-
ice splashed into the water of the sea, sizzling as it floated. Bolts of lightning
arched everywhere. Expanding gases issued from vents and fried whoever they
caught. Hardly anyone remaining in the cities survived, though of course the
smarter ones had fled the moment the volcano gave first warning."

Voila realized that folk of the Science Chroma could not protect themselves telekinetically; if they did not have shelters, they were pelted with the
burning stones. Neither could they teleport themselves out of the danger zone.
They were oddly helpless before the fury of the eruption.

Now, of course, Vesuvius was erupting green magic. Established Green
Chroma folk had little need to fear it, because that same magic enhanced their

powers. But that was not her Chroma, and she had to depend on avoidance. She was dodging constantly to avoid the burning green balls descending from the sky. This was not a major eruption, but it was awkward enough. She would have to retreat, getting a bit more distance from the worst of it.

And of course the Spirit was below her on the slope, preventing her from making that retreat. His protective clothing shielded him from the worst of it. "There have been a number of eruptions in the past thousand years," he continued as if nothing were amiss. "But better warning systems and alertness have minimized the lethality. Only fools approach during an actual eruption, however small."

"I must be a fool," she agreed. Then she headed for the bunker she had sensed, made long ago as an observation station, recording the tremors of the mountain. It was unoccupied, housing only its instruments, but stout enough to protect occupants from all but the worst volcanic sieges.

"A cute one," he said. "With spirit. Vulcan would surely like you."

"Question?"

"Vulcan, the Greek God of Fire, and thus of volcanoes: Vulcan-o. You hail from the volcano planet, you brown-haired honey, and did not know that?"

"We are not current with Earthly gods. We honor only our own planetary spirit."

"Sensible. Do you pray to it?"

"Question?"

"Pray: to beg some favor, such as good luck or beauty or the desire of a favored man."

"We have our own ways to evoke male desire, and need ask no fictional entity."

"Well retorted, frail flower! You are evoking mine. I love the way your small but well-formed breasts bounce as you run. I'm sure the effect is even better when you run nude."

The eruption was intensifying, making her safety difficult. She had thought to make the Spirit fall back, but he clung like a leach. He surely had his own clairvoyant avoidance ability. There was no help for it: she had to go to the bunker, and he would follow her there. This would not be fun.

She turned and proceeded directly to it, scrambling in the low entry way as the falling ash became a green blanket. Iolo dived in after her, followed by the Spirit.

"I though you'd never come in here," he said. "It is getting uncomfortable out there."

"I noticed," she said tersely. The bunker was small but high enough to stand in, and well-equipped. There was bottled water and a fireproof safe with hard loaves of bread and hanging bags of cheese. This would do for some time.

"Ah, wine," he said. "Naturally a fine vintage. We shall have to get drunk together, dissolving inhibitions."

"The wine is all yours," she said.

"You should drink at least some of it. That will dull your revulsion when I rape you."

"You aren't going to rape anyone."

He removed his clothing and stood with his genital bare. "We shall have most of a day and a night to make the proof of that, doxy. Unless you prefer to spoil the effect by simply volunteering your body for the duration."

"Negation." His sexual references were constant; that was part of his campaign.

"I doubt you'll be going out into the storm." He glanced out the open hole, where the air flared erratically with the landing of green volcanic bombs. "You'd scorch your sweet tender pinkies."

"Affirmation." She rummaged in a storage bin for bedding. "This side is mine and Iolo's; that side is yours. Stay where you belong."

"And if I don't?" he inquired. "What will you do, scream faintly?"

"I will vaporize."

That made him pause momentarily. "You think I'm bluffing about zapping ifrits?"

"Negation. But just as I don't want to hurt your current host body, who I know as a decent man I have a crush on, you don't want to hurt me physically, because then you would never get a chance to seduce, rape, or humiliate me. If you attack me and I dissolve, you will have to choose between destroying me or letting me escape. You might win Earth, but lose your personal desire for mastery of significant young flesh."

He nodded. "You have figured it out. I *can't* rape you. Yet. Once I take over Earth I should be able to capture you regardless. So I am forced to wait a tedious bit longer."

"Affirmation."

"Still, there are gradients. Suppose I gave Caveat some say in the matter? He does have a guilty passion for you, which colors my possession of this body. Would you let him possess you, knowing that I share it?"

"Negation. You will have to free him entirely—and if you do, you will not be able to recover him."

"How so? This interests me."

"Give me your hand."

Bemused, he reached toward her with one hand. She took it and focused a portion of her power, including a glimpse of certain future paths.

He nodded again. "So you aren't bluffing. You made his body single-access before I took it. There are things I can learn from you. And will, when you are mine."

"Unlikely."

"Things will change when I recover my planet. You are seeing only a portion of my power."

She shrugged, letting go of his hand. "*If* you recover it. The odds remain even."

"Which is an oddity. I have closed off all the adverse paths, with the exception of the one you bestride. When I close off yours, there will be none. How can you regard this as even?"

"Because one path is all I need. It is the hole in your bucket."

"A hole in the bucket," he repeated. "That's a nice primitive analogy. But once I plug that hole, and I mean that in the most literally sexual way, there will be no paths and Earth will be mine."

"Negation." But her denial lacked force. "Now I want to clean up and rest. Turn your back."

He laughed uproariously. "How precociously innocent! You actually expect me to avoid gazing on your dawning nubility when I have the chance?"

She frowned. "I suppose I expected some show of chivalry. I was of course naïve."

"You were indeed! But since you make an issue of this, I will make you a deal: I will turn my back if you give me a kiss."

"Outrage! I don't want to kiss you."

"Then I will watch. There is something special about a girl whose body is just getting there."

She hesitated. "One kiss. No tongue. Promise?"

"Promise," he agreed, amused.

She walked slowly to him, evincing nervousness. He stood still, letting her come to him. She put her hands on his elbows, lifted up on tiptoes, and gave him a delicate kiss on the lips.

He enfolded her, his hands taking hold of her buttocks.

"Foul!" she exclaimed, jerking her head back.

"I didn't say I wouldn't feel you. Just no tongue."

She turned, wrenching herself away. "I should have known I couldn't trust you."

"You just didn't nail the contract down tight. Consider it a lesson. You have a nice bottom."

"Conceded," she said through gritted teeth. "Now turn your back, and don't peek."

"You concede the contract or the bottom?"

"The contract," she said with girlish fury. "Now will you turn, or will you openly renege?"

He turned his back. She fetched a basin of green water from the bunker supply, got a washcloth and towel, and stripped. The refuse of the volcano was all over her, the green grit chafing under her clothing. She washed it all off, then turned to find new clothing from the bunker closet.

The Male Spirit was leering at her. "A really nice bottom."

"You promised!" she exclaimed, dismayed.

"I did not promise to stay turned. You left another loophole."

"Oh, you're impossible!" She scrambled into the first thing her hand fell on, a bath robe.

"I am the essence of maleness. Men exist to appreciate the tender flesh of young women."

"Well, we don't give it to any man who wants it. Only to ones worthy of it."

"You give it to any man who succeeds in taking it. As I expect to, soon enough."

"Never!" But there remained that devastating uncertainty. She lay on the bunk she had chosen, trying with imperfect success to keep the robe closed. "Keep your distance."

"Of course," he agreed, slowly approaching.

"I mean it! I'll vaporize."

"You prefer destruction to the company of a man? I think not."

"Oh, you don't know anything!"

"Would you prefer that I give Caveat some play?"

That made her pause, considering. Part of what she hated about this was that Caveat was hostage to the Spirit's meanness. Could she help him to this slight extent, or would it make it even worse for him? She would have to gamble. "Affirmation."

The man's posture shifted subtly. A different personality was governing.

"Beware, Voila. He means you ill."

"Caveat!"

"You have given him too much leeway already. He will destroy you. Don't let my body be the agency of that."

"Caveat, are you all right, apart from being suppressed?"

"I am. But I am immaterial. Don't let him touch you. All he wants is to possess you before he destroys you."

"Confirmation. But will he let you survive, after his use of your body is done?"

"Doubtful, Voila. I love you, in my fashion, and you like me in yours. That is reason for him to destroy me."

"But I want you to be free!"

He shook his head in the exact way Caveat had. "I am doomed regardless, Voila. Don't let him use me to get at you. Get away while you can. You have no idea of the cynicism the Malign Spirit has."

"I think I do. Caveat, you don't deserve this. I want to save you if I can."

"Don't, Voila. I am no more than a lever against you."

"How can I help you?"

"Voila, no!"

"Answer."

"The foul Spirit requires me to answer. He offers to spare my life and sanity when he is through with me, if you let him seduce you sexually. You are the one he wants, not me. But I urge you not to—"

The man froze, then the subtle signals changed back. "I believe that suffices," the Spirit said. "Do we have a deal?"

"Negation! I can't trust your deals."

"You can when I have nothing to gain by reneging. I will have no further use for this host when this is over. It will be easiest just to let him go. But if you annoy me, I will treat him unkindly, to spite you."

"You're good at spite." But she was fighting a rearguard action, knowing that what he said made sense. She did want to save Caveat.

He came to the bed. "Move over, honey; give me room."

"Negation!"

He sat on the edge of the bunk, forcing her to move over. He ran his hand into her robe, stroking her bare breast beneath, while she sat frozen. "You know you want it," he murmured.

"Negation! I just don't want you to hurt Caveat." But her nipple was rising under his touch.

"Tell me to desist," he said.

"Desist!"

"As if you mean it."

"I do mean it. Don't touch me." But her force was weak.

"It's late for that." Now his other hand stroked across her belly and found her delicate pubic region. One finger tickled the closed cleft. Her legs parted involuntarily.

"No," she said faintly. "I won't tolerate rape."

"You are not facing rape at the moment. Merely decent treatment for your gay paramour."

"It is nevertheless rape, because I don't want to do it."

"It is a deal, for which you pay in sex. Women do that all the time. Sex is their prime currency."

"I am not that kind of woman." She was no longer resisting, physically.

He put his mouth down to kiss a quivering breast. "Delicious."

"Go back to your side of the bunker." But she made no effort to push him away.

"In a moment." He stretched out beside her. His clothing had departed somewhere along the way.

"Please," she whimpered.

"I thought you'd never ask." He rolled over onto her, holding her down.

She struggled, but was unable to escape. "I'll vaporize."

"You're cute when you make empty threats." His member was wedging its way through to the unwilling channel. The broad tip found the secret aperture and pressed urgently onward.

"No!" she cried despairingly.

"Yes," he said, and thrust, pushing deeply into her.

"Stop! Don't do it! I beg you!" But she was already too late.

"I love it when you beg." He thrust again, harder, distending her avenue mercilessly. He was now at full depth, her vagina pulled painfully thin around his turgid member.

She struggled again, sobbing. "No, no."

He held her in place as his climax came, pumping hot fluid into her, inflating her further. "Phenomenal!"

She lay without moving, until at last he subsided and withdrew the penetration. He lay beside her, breathing hard.

"Are you done?" she inquired with an edge.

"For now, precious."

"Did you enjoy it?"

"It was glorious."

"That's good." Her tone had changed. She was no longer crying.

He propped his head on his arm and gazed at her. "What's your angle?"

"You had more of an orgasm than you perhaps knew."

"I had the most intense, durable orgasm ever. There's just something about conquering tight young flesh."

"There may be something you don't know."

He smiled. "But you are going to tell me, eh, child?"

"We have on Charm a magic entity called a succubus."

"A demon of the night who seduces sleeping men. We have this myth on Earth too."

"But on Charm it is more than that. She takes over the body of a living woman and uses it to seduce an unwary man. At the moment of orgasm, the succubus takes his soul, leaving a mere mortal husk. Pubescent boys are taught to be wary."

"How fortunate I am not pubescent, nor can my soul be taken. I am the Earth Male Spirit."

"My mother was invaded by a succubus when young. She fought the thing and won. She tamed it, and then allowed it to remain with her. It became her friend, doing her bidding. Sometimes she lends it to other women, to make them especially seductive. It is unmatched at sex."

"Fascinating! Are you about to tell me that the succubus is with you?"

"Affirmation. Her name is Swale. She made me sexually irresistible. She gave you your most potent orgasm."

"That she did," he agreed heartily.

"And she locked you into your present body. She could not take your soul in the moment of your rapture, but she could reverse her normal ploy and confine it. Only two releases are possible: the death of your host will free you, and you will not enjoy that demise. Or I may allow you to go, after you acknowledge defeat."

"You have an imagination, child. I can not be confined. I travel from host to host as pleases me."

"Then travel now, spook." There was nothing frail or fainting in her present tone.

"In due course. I am not yet done with you."

"Yes you are. But if you prefer, make a partial effort, just to see whether it is possible."

He shrugged. "As you wish." Then his expression changed. "You little bitch! It's true. You have locked me in."

"I have locked you in," she agreed. "Rather, Swale has. I had merely to get you close enough for her to do her job." She smiled, not nicely. "It was hardly difficult. You were so intent on brute seduction you were not wary of the trap. An all-too-typical male failing."

He stared at her. "You're an actress! You suckered me!"

"I am good at the role of ingenue."

"You traitorous brat! I'll beat you into a pulp!"

"Beat me," she agreed, smiling with more teeth than necessary.

He struck at her with his fist. She lifted her hand and caught it, readily blocking it. He swung with the other fist. She caught that hand too. Then she squeezed. His knuckles cracked. "Damnation!" he cried as he wrenched his hands away.

"A fair description of your situation, you fool."

He focused on her. Energy crackled. Lightning speared out at her—and deflected harmlessly.

"This is not possible," he said. "You have no such power. I have your ikon hostage."

"Really? Then I must be imagining this." A lightning strike speared from her to him. He stiffened momentarily, electrocuted, before casting it out.

He roared and sprang at her. She spread her arms and clasped him to her. She kissed him, and blue fire coursed from her lips to his, stunning his mouth. "Rape me again, hotshot. I'll burn your member off."

He jerked away. "You have more magic stones hidden on you. They can't last long at this rate."

She stood, throwing off her robe to be naked. It was obvious she was concealing nothing. "Where? Do you think I ate them? They would be toxic to my flesh."

"I don't understand."

"Explanation: I have another ikon, one beyond your reach. I possess my full Glamor power, which matches yours. You can not impose your will on me."

"Another ikon! When? Where?"

"For some time, cretin. I could have stopped you at any time, but I needed your orgasm. It is on Jupiter's Moon Io."

"That's far from Earth! It can't work that far away."

"How unfortunate for me. While you were collecting ikons, I was getting mine properly placed. It is beyond your reach, but functions perfectly for me. Io is a wellspring of nonChroma magic; it is bursting constantly out of its volcanoes. All of it is mine to draw on: a full planetful. I am as strong as you, even on your home planet."

"Ludicrous, you bratty child. You need to be spanked."

She presented her bare bottom. "Spank me, idiot."

He bristled with power, advancing again on her. She let him come close, then shoved him back with a telekinetic kick to his groin. Sparks flew as force met force.

It took him some time to concede that she matched him in power, because it was not news he desired. He did try to rape her, and she allowed him to penetrate part way, then toasted his member with projected heat until he was forced to desist. Her vagina was like a kiln. She slept, and when he tried to sneak up on her she sprouted thorns and gave him a stabbing welcome he did not favor. He had forgotten that Iolo was with them; the ifrit watched him constantly, and warned her telepathically.

Next day his temper was hardly improved. "You little bitch, you have locked me into this body when I have business elsewhere."

"Really?" she inquired with mock innocence. "Whatever would that business be?"

"The completion of the conquest of Earth. My minions have labored constantly to disrupt the prior system, and the tide is about to turn. I must establish the new order."

"You can't do that as long as I remain on Earth. I have no immediate plan to depart."

"No? Watch this." He gestured, forming a holo, which was the Science equivalent of an illusion picture. It showed mayhem in one city after another. Buildings were burning, and streets were swarming with armed men.

"The mistresses governed a world in peace and prosperity," Voila said. "You have brought war and destruction. This is your pride?"

"Conquest is necessarily violent. Things will settle down when the new order gets established."

"*If* the new order gets established."

"You can look on this and think your weak-water mistresses have a chance?"

"They have to have a chance. Your way is doom, as it was before."

He stood, lifting his arms. New power imbued him. "Ah—it comes, it comes! The balance has shifted. The world is mine!"

"The wreckage is yours."

He turned on her. "I lacked full power before. Now I have it. I will destroy you."

"You seem to be a slow learner. You can't touch me. There is not sufficient power in all Earth to harm me."

"Die, bitch!" Phenomenal electrical intensity engulfed her.

And had no effect. "One Glamor can't prevail against another when both have their strength. One world can't overcome another. All of Io stands against you."

"A mere distant moon!"

"Animated by the strongest Glamor extant. I have prepared all my young life to handle you."

He paused, thinking. "Your parents, your siblings—they don't have similar ikons. I'll destroy them to get at you."

"All of them are gone to where you can't reach them. So are Monochrome and the lesser mistresses. You can't touch any of them."

"But they were going out to fight the siege of this zone."

"That was a ruse. They were departing. Their job here is done. Mine is beginning."

"Well, I can touch others you may value. I can torture ordinary women until their blood swamps you."

"And I can torture your men until they die."

"You lack the guts, cutie. You're just a child."

She smiled grimly. "Try me, man-turd."

The holo showed a picture of two men hauling a struggling young woman to a stage. They held her while a third man bared his member and raped her. Then he drew a knife and stabbed her in the belly. She collapsed in her pooling blood. "So?" the Spirit inquired.

Then the rapist stiffened in another manner. His eyes stared at something unseen. His hands grasped at empty air. His body bucked as if suffering an epileptic seizure. Then he collapsed and lay on the floor unconscious amidst the slain woman's blood. He was followed by the two who had held the woman. First one, then the other writhed similarly on the stage, also coated by the woman's spreading blood. "So," Voila said evenly.

He gazed at her with new assessment. "So you *can* spill blood."

"I do not get pleasure from it, but I can do it when it is warranted. Any of your men who kill women will die. And you will remain here with me, unable to go to them."

"Really?" He went to the bunker entrance.

"Really." A sudden wash of green fire engulfed the opening. "You are captive in this Chroma zone."

"But my men have taken it!"

"Your men are dead." She did not explain how.

He looked telepathically, and blanched. She was not bluffing. "I have to hand it to you, sweetie. You are much tougher than I suspected."

"You would have suspected, had you had the wit to look."

"Belatedly I am coming to appreciate why your siblings and parents deferred to you. I thought they were merely being polite, to encourage you."

"They acknowledge reality. I am the one Glamor you should never have clasped."

"Caveat is horrified."

She nodded. "I am sorry, Caveat. We could never have been a couple, for reasons other than your sexual orientation. I regret having to deceive you on that and other things. It was necessary to lure and trap the Male Spirit."

"Caveat is oddly pleased."

"He is pleased to have a part in your confinement."

"He will suffer."

"You will suffer similarly. You are bound to him in feeling as well as body."

"I doubt it."

She smiled. "Experiment."

After a moment he winced. "That is some spell."

"You will be free of it only when you depart that host, if I let you, and you will not be able to return to it."

"He will suffer after I leave. I will have him tortured."

"You misunderstand the nature of the enchantment. It has two parts: physical and psychic. You may leave physically when I allow it, but the psychic will remain. You will feel his pain, of whatever nature, as long as you occupy any human host. If you annoy him, he may even hurt himself, just to be sure you hurt. You will be better advised to see that he lives a pain-free life, physically and emotionally."

"But he's a fag!"

"Which may complicate your own sexual enjoyment hereafter."

"You utter bitch!"

"Appreciation."

He considered. "All the patterns of rescue, saving the Mistresses—to get me with Caveat and you with me?"

She nodded. "Idyll the Ifrit Glamor specializes in the intermediate future paths. She guided me, as the strongest Glamor ever to exist. This was my mission from my birth on. I confess to being surprised how it happened, but not *that* it happened. You have to be nullified; the welfare of Earth depends on it."

"And I have to vanquish you, or I am stuck in stasis."

"Confirmation. The paths are obscure; even now we judge the chances even, for either of us."

He paced the floor. "How long have you been the strongest of your ilk, considering you are the youngest?"

"Since my first year. My elder siblings trained me, knowing that I was destined to govern them. My parents did the same, knowing the same. We all knew that the crisis would come within twenty years, and that I would have to be ready for it. Had it come later, I would have been able to win outright; as it is, I can't be sure of it."

"Such a comfort," he muttered ironically.

"And of course we triggered it by seeding Earth's volcanoes. Idyll saw a huge opacity therefrom, but it was our best seeming ploy to stop Earth from conquering our planet. Now we find ourselves aligned with that same government to sustain it, ironically."

"Had the triggering come later, I would have taken over more readily. I have had to make my move too early."

"Affirmation. Mino saw that."

"Mino."

"Our machine ally who sees the far future paths. Idyll would have had us avoid the volcano seeding, but Mino said it was best, so we did it. Now we are experiencing the consequence, but it also provides us the chance for victory. The future is complicated."

"So I am up against three types: those who see the near future, as I do, and those who see the intermediate future as Idyll does, and one who sees the far future, as your robot does. I would seem to be overmatched, even on my own planet."

"Normally a planetary Spirit can hold his planet against any outer force. But you are only half the spirit; you war against the Female Spirit, thus dividing your force. Otherwise our chances would be significantly diminished."

"So interesting to know. Too bad I encountered the wrong opposition."

"Unfortunate," she agreed.

The Male Spirit exploded, coming at her with body and magic simultaneously. Voila had seen it coming and was ready. She caught his two hands with hers, but was borne back by the force of his rush. She beat back the magic, but it pressed her sorely. She landed on her back on the floor, his body on top of her, his stiff member probing her groin.

She held the other two aspects off, but let his member penetrate slightly. Then she heated her cleft, intensely.

He hurled himself back, crying out in pain. She had come close to cooking the tip of his member. It was a trick Swale had taught her. She was literally unrapable by any human flesh. In his ire he had forgotten.

The other attacks abated. She got up and went to the Spirit where he lay on his back, groaning. "I will heal you, this time," she said. "I suspect you have learned your lesson."

She took his member in her hands, surrounding it, applying her healing magic. He stopped groaning immediately; the first effect was the relief of pain. He lay still, allowing her to proceed. The reddened flesh paled, and in due course the shrunken tissue expanded, becoming not only healthy but fully erect.

"Why?" he asked.

"Because I value your host, Caveat, and do not want him hurt. I want him to have his normal life, once this is done." She kneaded the penis, giving Swale leave, and in a moment it spouted a jet of fluid.

"A damned hand job," the Spirit said, disgusted.

"We can entertain each other, while we are at impasse," she said. "I will even let you have normal sex with me, now that you know you can't force me. We may have a long wait."

"A long wait for what?"

"For you to yield the issue and return Earth to the Female Spirit."

"I will not yield the issue."

"Then I will not let you go. You have taken over Earth, but I hold you hostage here in the Green Chroma zone. For the lifetime of your present host. It may get dull."

"Why would you enliven it by giving me sex?"

"Because I do have a crush on Caveat. With your presence he can have normal sex with me. That won't be possible once you depart this host."

"This is outrageous."

"Really?" she asked, and sent a pulse into his now-flaccid member. It stiffened immediately. She sent another pulse, and the host body's desire for her intensified. This was the work of the succubus, again, evoking the male desire.

"Damn you, you are making him want you, and that makes *me* want you."

"Here are my terms for the interim," she said calmly as the member throbbed incipiently in her hand. "Give Caveat control, and I will give him sex every hour for the duration. In that manner he can love me fully, until we part, and I can be thrilled in his embrace. You will share his pleasure, which will be considerable."

"Suppose I take over as I penetrate your sweet little pussy?"

"I will fry you," she said simply. It was no bluff; she would know the moment the host's status changed.

He considered. She sent another mini-pulse into him, causing the member to swell eagerly. "Damn, I've got to have you, bitch-girl! I agree to your terms of association. That does not mean I'm yielding the planet."

"Naturally not." She got up, went to her bunk, and lay down on it.

"You are weird," Caveat said, following her. "You have made me hetero-sexual."

"Only with me, only while the Spirit is in you. Your underlying nature has not changed. This is a compromise."

"Thank you." He got on her, kissed her breasts, then entered her and climaxed. "I love you, Voila," he gasped.

"And I love you, Caveat," she responded as he withdrew. "For the nonce. After this we will go our separate ways, our own lifestyles, remembering only our joy of this occasion."

"The Spirit wants more."

"He wants the planet."

"More sex. His own."

She considered momentarily. "Very well, Spirit. Compromise. One for you each time there is one for him. The more he enjoys it, the more you will. Take it now." She gave Swale rein to handle him.

"Thanks, bitch." The man was on her and in her in an instant, thrusting and spurting.

He lay on her a while longer, not withdrawing. "Your turn is over," she murmured, and started heating.

He quickly withdrew. Caveat laughed. "He got the message. You are in control."

"Agreement. I am the mistress."

This was the onset of the contest of wills. The Spirit would not yield the planet, and Voila would not let him go until he did. He continued to have his minions take over the various offices of the planet, but they continued to have seizures and expire the moment they abused any women.

"How do you do it?" he finally asked, frustrated.

Now she explained. "Swale is doing it. The succubus. She can travel rapidly anywhere she wants. She orients on the abusive man, generates the illusion of a lovely and phenomenally sexy naked woman, tempts him into sex, and steals his soul as he climaxes. It's what succubi do."

"But there is nothing there to see! And anyway, they can't touch an illusion."

"The illusion is three-fold: sight, sound, and touch. It appears only to the man addressed. He embraces her, kisses her, penetrates her, and expires in orgasmic bliss." She made a moue. "A better fate than he deserves. Of course it may appear otherwise to those who don't see the illusion."

"As he thrusts into her," the spirit agreed. "Not a seizure, but a sexual climax. What a fiendish plot."

"Appreciation."

"And my men invading this green zone—that's what happened to them too?"

"Agreement. Swale has been extremely busy, but rose to the occasion."

"Their souls—what does she do with them?"

"She feeds on them, gaining energy for further exploits. Touch illusions require considerably more energy than mere sight illusions."

His energy crackled. "I could deal with her."

"If you were free to range the planet," she agreed. "As it is, she is near you only when with me, and thus under my protection."

"I am seeing my best men killed."

"Not if they treat women well."

"Then the Female Spirit might as well be in control."

She smiled. "Are you yielding the planet?"

"No, fuck it, bitch."

"Then you will inherit anarchy. I suggest you come to terms with me before even victory will leave you with ruin."

"A damned pyrrhic victory."

"Question?"

"Earth ancient history, again. Pyrrhus was a Greek king and general who fought the Romans. He was a brilliant strategist, but the Romans were so tenacious that when he won the battle he lost so many men that he said he could not afford another such victory. Thus the concept of pyrrhic victory: a win that is hardly worth it."

She clapped her hands in girlish glee. "Concurrence! I shall name you Pyrrhus."

"Bitch," he muttered.

"Appreciation."

Meanwhile she was having a wonderful affair with Caveat. Sometimes she shifted her form to resemble a boy, so as to let him enjoy sex his way. This disgusted the Male Spirit, but he was unable to protest, because he now shared the host's imperatives. She was pressuring him to come to larger terms with her on the personal basis as well as the planetary one.

"If I had it to do over, I'd put a warship into orbit around Moon Io," he said. "And occupy a different host."

"Mino would blast it out of existence." She assumed boy form. "As for the host: are you sure you don't want sex now, Pyrrhus?

"Go moon the moon, bitch."

She pouted artfully. "There was a time when you were desperate to seduce me."

"I thought you were a girl, not a praying mantis."

She laughed. "A nice analogy. The females eat the males, after mating, don't they?"

"Exactly."

It was two weeks before the Spirit was ready to compromise. Even constant sex palled when a man had global ambitions put on hold, and what she provided him was not exactly constant. She had known he would wear down in time. "How can we settle the issue?" he asked.

"We can play a game, Pyrrhus," she said.

"A game! This is no game. The planet is at stake."

"A game we devised to show the way of the future paths. The game will not determine the victor, but will show the likely winner. Thereafter it will be pointless to continue, as it will only delay the inevitable."

"You know this from your near-future paths?"

"From Idyll's intermediate-future paths."

"Show me."

She extended her hand. He took it and received the complex skein of paths. It was persuasive, because the paths could not be denied.

"Give me one last fuck, bitch. Then we'll see."

"It is not necessarily the last, Pyrrhus," she said, spreading her legs.

"Whatever." He was on her and in her one more time, pulsing immediately. "That succubus sure can make it go."

"Swale lives for sex," she agreed. "I can take it or leave it."

"You've been taking it for a fortnight."

"From Caveat. Swale has attended to you." Indeed, the succubus had had a lot of fun with the Spirit when not destroying his far flung minions.

"Sure." But he was disgruntled. "Now what's the game?"

"Icons."

"Ikons? You want those back?"

"Icons, Pyrrhus. These are game pieces. We each start with twenty assorted figurines that become creatures when invoked. We each occupy our creature and interact. The one who leads in points when the last icon has been played is the victor. That will indicate prospects."

"And if I win, you will leave Earth to me?"

"Affirmation. I will have no choice."

"You could stay on Earth and fuck me some more."

"I would expire of boredom."

He shook his head. "You Glamors really like sex, whatever you say. You'd miss it."

"We like sex with the right partners. You aren't right. Fortunately Swale never gets tired of it."

"Let's see the icons."

Voila snapped her fingers, and two boxes of icons appeared. "The black ones are yours, the white ones mine. They are identical, apart from color."

"Then you won't mind exchanging them."

She shrugged. "As you wish." She took the black ones and poured them out on the bed. Each was different: dog, cat, hawk, shark, rhino, and so on, each rendered in exquisite detail. Artisans on Charm had crafted them carefully. "Each has both Earthly and Charmly aspects, so you can invoke it as either. I suspect you will prefer to invoke your familiar Earthly forms, instead of, for example, a six-legged dog. But it is entirely your choice."

"One of these is a human man," he said as he sorted them.

"Merely a variety of animal. With this, as as with each, you may invoke it either male or female."

"Why would I want to be a woman?"

"To seduce my male human invocation."

"Ah. Seduction results in a point?"

"Negation. Points are scored only with a killing, and there may be only one killing in a contest, or several. The one with the most points when the final icons are expended wins."

"Then what is the point of sex?"

"When male and female of the same species meet, either can invoke the pheromones that promote sex. A woman might do it just before the man clubs her to death; then he will have sex with her instead, and they must finish and separate before resuming competition. If a woman is about to knife a man from behind, and he sees her but can't avoid the stroke, he can invoke sex and she will stop immediately. It is a spot nullification ploy, useful only when male and female of the same species interact."

"But if we choose icons independently, chances of matching animals are small."

"Negation. If one is a mouse and the other a cat, the mouse may become a cat as the easiest way to nullify without thinking. If the genders match, there is a catfight; if not, there may be sex."

"But aren't the icons chosen and invoked simultaneously?"

"Negation. They are chosen and invoked by turns. If the first invokes a mouse, the second may invoke a cat—and can't change again until after the mouse does."

"And if the mouse hides in a hole and avoids the cat?"

"After half an hour in one form with no decision, the position is null, and that one must invoke a new icon."

"Why delay that long, if the end is the same?"

"The cat might find a way to get the mouse. Also, to make the cat use more time, so it has to change in half an hour even if the mouse becomes an ant."

"Why would anyone become an ant?"

"All the icons must be invoked before the game is done. The ant must be invoked at some point."

He gazed at the icons. "Now I grasp it. There is strategy in the order of invoking. If you are a horse I can be an ant and escape you, then become a spider when your ant is your last icon and must be invoked."

"Concurrence. The strategy of invocations is vital. But there is no guaranteed victory; a spider may kill an ant, but not if it can't catch it, and the ant may lead the spider into a trap. There is advantage only, not certainty."

"And terrain would make a difference. What is it?"

"Highly varied: trees, ponds, hills, caves, sand, villages, rivers. The setting is the first thing invoked." She tapped her box. "When both boxes are invoked, they expand and interact, forming a unique landscape. We can't know ahead exactly what it will be."

"Except by near-future clairvoyance?"

"Not when Glamor opposes Glamor. The paths are obscure."

He concentrated. "So I see, as it were. I think I like this game. It has intriguing elements."

"It can be as devious as the future itself. That is why it is a fair indication of our situation. Whoever can handle the game best can likely handle reality best."

He counted off the icons. "Dog, cat, bear, duck, hawk, rhino, shark, human, monkey, mouse, crocodile, horse, ant, spider, bat, frog, turtle, dragonfly, snake, goat. Twenty animals."

"We tried to make a fair selection. Since the sets are the same, it doesn't matter very much which animals."

"If you invoke Charm variants, it may. I understand you call them by the same turns, but they are not at all the same creatures."

She nodded. "We can limit it to the Earth variants if you prefer."

"I do prefer. But why would you agree to that?"

"I made it a point to learn the Earth variants. I can play them readily enough."

"What penalty if you invoke a Charm variant?"

"Loss of that life."

"That will do. I shall retire for a day to consider strategies. Tomorrow we shall settle the issue via the game."

"As you wish. I shall sleep."

"You have confidence!"

"I know the game. It will be as it will be."

He glanced at her slantwise. "You've got an angle. Are you going to invoke male animals, hoping I'll be female and you can screw me?"

"I prefer my own gender, as I suspect do you."

"So you'll commit to our own sexes for the game, for all the animals?"

"If you prefer. Female is considered to be a slight liability when the species match, but the pheromones are a compensating aspect."

"Ah. Invoking sex. But the male can do it too."

"Agreement. But the male is always interested in sex anyway, so it makes less difference. The female has a choice. She won't try to mate with him unless there is reason."

He laughed. "Reason! Naturally you would see it that way. But about having a choice: It makes a difference who chooses first. I prefer last, so as to respond to your choices."

She shrugged. "Agreement."

"You are ready to play with Earth animals on Earth turf, and limit your choices to female, and give me the advantage of second choice, and prepare by sleeping? Where's the catch?"

"The essence of the game is beyond such details. It will show the nature of the future regardless."

"Suppose I play and lose, and renege?"

"You would be inviting grief. The game is only an indication."

"So you said." He shook his head. "I don't quite understand you. That bugs me."

"Appreciation." She lay on her bunk and closed her eyes.

"How about one last fuck?"

Could he really have sex that much on his mind? "You may expend all your remaining energy copulating, if you wish, though it does suggest that you fear there will be no further chance after the game."

"How about an ass fuck?"

He was still trying to annoy her. "If that is your preference." She had rehearsed all varieties of sexual contact, preparing for this siege; he could not make her balk.

"You're too damned obliging? What's your angle?"

"Swale is bored. She wants some fun before the distraction of the game. She is familiar with all variants."

He paused. "The succubus. Let her do for me what she did for my men, except that she won't be able to take my soul. Make a fucking illusion."

"Welcome." Privately she warned Swale: *He means to get you separate from me, and destroy you, thereby perhaps lifting the curse of confinement you laid on him. Beware.*

Protect me. For the succubus alone would be no match for the Male Spirit; he could indeed destroy her if allowed.

Agreed.

Then the succubus exited her womb and hovered before the Male Spirit. She assumed the form of an almost impossibly buxom young woman, naked and radiating sex appeal. "Fuck me, animal," she said. "I love it." It was what was termed an imaginary illusion, apparent only to the person it was oriented on, but Voila could perceive those too.

"You got it, demoness," he said heartily. He clasped her and kissed her, squeezing her breasts and buttocks. "Damn, you feel real!"

"I *am* real, Pyrrhus. Merely not physical. You are clasping, kissing, and feeling air."

"I know it. But it's great air. After I win the game and the bitch girl goes home, suppose you stay here for more fucking? I'll even give you men to suck dry, to keep your energy up. How about it?"

Voila remained lying with her eyes closed, but she was paying full attention. She had not before been close when Swale tackled a man this way, and was curious. She was also completely alert for the Spirit's coming effort of destruction, which would immediately follow his climax. He was trying to lull her by his words.

"Maybe, man-thing. Depends how well you fuck."

"This well," he said, dispensing with further foreplay and ramming into her vulva. He was literally penetrating air, his penis thrusting into nothing.

"Harder," Swale murmured appreciatively as her soul-substance invisibly enclosed the rod.

He thrust again, and this time jetted into space. And without pause blasted her with all his magic power.

Voila, ready at the precise moment, encased the succubus in protective magic, shielding her. The illusion figure glowed with the phenomenal clash of energies. It was like a volcanic eruption contained within an invulnerable bottle. "Ooo, that's what I call one hot fuck!" Swale said. "Do it again, Pyrrhus."

"Damn!" He had been balked, and knew it. "Bitch."

"Appreciation," Swale said, and faded, returning to Voila. The man was left standing with dripping penis, his treacherous ploy balked. Around him the floor of the bunker had melted from the heat of the stifled magic, becoming concave. The stink of it suffused the air.

It had been another test of power, and again Voila had matched him. No one else could have. Now that the alignment of the planet was his, he had hideous force. Had she not seen his attempt in the near future paths, and been thoroughly braced for it with a specific protocol to counter it, he would have succeeded. As it was, he had come closer than was comfortable.

The succubus was suffering despite her brave response; some of the power had singed her tenuous substance. She coalesced in Voila's uterus, slowly recovering. She would not be able to function for a while. But the paths suggested that she would not need to.

Voila remained as she was, seemingly asleep. The Male Spirit glanced at her and turned away, disgruntled again.

Next day they set up for it. "The landscape is largely imaginary," she explained as she set the two boxes on the floor between them. "Our bodies will remain here, while our minds animate the icons. It will seem real, but is no more so than the succubus' illusory body. It is a game of the imagination, which is what makes it relevant to the mutable future. It is possible to cheat, but pointless, as it will merely skew the apparent results of the contest, not the real ones. By game's end we should both better know our future."

"Perhaps," he agreed grimly.

They reviewed the incidental protocols, and were ready. Voila invoked her box, and Pyrrhus invoked his. Both expanded, interacting, forming the setting.

It was beautiful: a warm Earthly landscape replete with forests, fields, lakes, mountains, and caves, all visible as the scene expanded and became more detailed. Soon much of it passed beyond immediate view, too large as it approached life size. It came to rest with them in the center: a grassy glade in a forest where rabbits grazed. Part of the challenge was to grasp the layout in sufficient detail to take advantage of it; that initial glimpse of the whole was the only one.

Voila invoked her first icon: the duck. It was a fine-looking female mallard, except that it was black. She could have chosen any variety of duck, but it had to be her color, for clear identification.

She had the scene to herself. The white animal could not be invoked until she interacted with one of the background creatures, such as a rabbit. If she took half an hour by herself, she would have to invoke her next—and her opponent would get to choose for her. That would likely put her into difficulty, and give him a chance to take half an hour without penalty.

She did not waste time. She waddled up to the nearest rabbit. It saw her and spooked, bounding to the cover of the nearest bush.

A white mouse appeared, with a loud ping! announcing its presence. Hiding was not an option; they would always know where both of them were.

A mouse? He was trying to expend one of his weaker icons where her animal represented no danger to it.

She became the cat, a female leopard, capable of catching the mouse in an instant, and of fighting off most other animals.

He became the dog, in this case a giant male timber wolf, a likely match for the leopard but no certain victor. Did he want a fight? If the wolf injured her, that injury would carry through to the next form. It would also take her thirty seconds to make the change, while they were in contact, giving him time to kill her if he could. That might be his strategy.

Voila did not choose to fight. She fled as she assessed the situation. She came to a lake where she might become the crocodile. She could change instantly as long as there was no physical contact. That was preferable. She turned and leaped to a tree overhanging the water, landing on a low branch. The wolf pursued, but was unable to reach her. He paced below, looking up.

She became a black spider, a poisonous breed. She sprang down toward the white wolf.

He became a white bat, flying up to meet her, jaws gaping.

She had thought to surprise him, but he had surprised her by being ready for her ploy. She had to react immediately, because the moment the bat touched the spider, it would take her thirty seconds to change again, and he would chomp her to death in two seconds. It was already too late to avoid contact.

She invoked her hawk, ready to chomp the bat. But he became another hawk. Then they collided. There would be a fight. She was female, he male, with greater size and power; she would be at a disadvantage.

She invoked the pheromones. That was possible during contact. Now he was desperate to mate with her. But they affected her too; she couldn't simply flee teasingly, or attack him while he sought sex. They wrestled around to get in position, mating vigorously in flight. She had thought this would be a burden, because of the effort of doing it while not crashing to the ground, but flight became automatic, and the sex was actually quite rewarding. In real life she doubted that Earth hawks mated except in their seasons, but in the game it was not only feasible but fun.

They finished and separated. They had to get a certain distance apart before they could resume hostilities. This time the pheromones would not work; they had been expended for this creature. She had won her reprieve, but now she had to flee, fight, or change.

She fled. He pursued. She came to a lake and dived toward its surface. He could not change until she did; with luck she could make him land in the water. That would set him up for a lethal strike, or force him to change without proper thought.

He pursued, gaining. He was almost on her tail. So she struck the water, changing to shark form. She turned in place, ready to chomp him—only to find a horse. He had changed almost the same time as she, anticipating her choice. The horse was too big for the shark to handle.

So she became the rhinoceros, which was thought of as a dry land creature, but it could handle water too. She whipped her horn about, trying to spear the horse.

It almost worked. But he sheered away and became another rhino. Again she was female, he male, larger, stronger. So again she invoked the pheromones, and they made love not war. This time the mating was not at all airborne; it was ponderous and violent as he rose up on his hind legs and jammed hard into her from behind. But as a rhino she liked it that way, and was quite satisfied with his massive effort. She braced her stout legs to hold her place, ensuring that he rammed to full depth with each thrust, savoring each internal collision.

However, she was not comfortable with the larger situation. The male spirit was playing too aptly. Neither of them could see future paths for this, yet he seemed to anticipate her moves. How could that be?

She pondered as they continued the sex. Evidently rhinos took their time, and that was fine for thinking. He must have analyzed the game carefully, and formulated prepared choices to match her choices. So he could react rapidly, catching her off-guard. How could she mess that up, converting it to her advantage?

By making random or seemingly foolish changes that he could not anticipate. That might interfere with his prepared responses, perhaps even tricking him into bad ones.

They finished the engagement with a shuddering joint climax as his copious ejaculate pressured into her willing chamber, and finally separated. Then she charged back at him. He seemed surprised but was ready; he braced, ready to meet her head-on.

She became the monkey, just before the collision. She clambered onto his head and clasped it. Now they were in contact and he could not change forms within thirty seconds.

He flung his head about, trying to dislodge her, but she clung to his horn, refusing to be dislodged. She had, indeed, surprised him. Good.

It took him a while to realize that he had to change, and then thirty seconds to make the change. She counted off seconds, then flung herself away just before he changed so that she would suffer no similar delay.

He became the shark. A great white shark, of course. But she became a horse: a solid black mare. The lake here was shallow enough so her four legs reached the bottom muck. She turned and delivered a one rear-footed kick. It scored on the shark's side, surely denting some cartilage. She had injured him. That put her ahead; if there were no killing by game's end, that would win for her.

He became the turtle, swimming away so as not to be in contact while at a physical disadvantage. She pursued him, splashing vigorously, but could not match the reptile's speed.

So she became a black crocodile, forging forward to catch the white turtle in her powerful jaws. She caught it—and he did not have time to change before she chomped him to death.

She did so, crunching him repeatedly. First she got his hind legs, then his forelegs, and finally his head as he struggled desperately to escape. The first kill was hers.

The scene faded. They were back in the bunker. Sitting across from each other.

"So you took one, bitch," he said. "The game's not over."

"Concurrence. You must assume your next form."

"Ready."

The scene formed again. Pyrrhus became a white male crocodile, a form that would have saved him a point before.

Voila invoked her ant icon. Her black ant raced up the trunk of a tree overhanging the shore of the lake. The crocodile could see her, but could not reach her. It was surely frustrating for him. Avoidance was as good as a fight or sex.

The crocodile circled below the branch, eying the ant. Then he gathered speed and launched himself upward. It was futile; he could not hurl himself clear of the water, and even if he could, he would not be able to catch the ant with those teeth. It was wasted effort.

Then he became the frog, leaping from the water, flying through the air. The tongue speared out and caught the ant. Voila was suddenly dead.

The scene faded again. "Even," the Spirit said with satisfaction.

He was right. She had been careless, and paid the price.

They started again. This time she invoked the black dragonfly. That was a strong flyer, able to maneuver in any direction, and with eyes to observe everything. She would change the moment he took a dangerous form.

He became a white monkey. He pursued her, but she rose higher, out of his reach. He swept up a stick and threw at at her, but she had no trouble avoiding it. She remained almost within range, however, leading him to a rocky slope. He could not change until she did; he had no choice but to keep after her. He followed, throwing stones he found.

She came to rest on a larger stone. He paused, knowing she could fly before he could reach her. She rested, teasing him. He moved slowly toward her, trying to reduce the range. She waited.

When he got close enough, he pounced, swinging a stick at her. And she invoked her snake icon. A black rattlesnake, quickly coiling and striking. Her teeth were closing on the back of the monkey's leg.

And he was the white ant, too small to be caught that way. She had used her spider form, so could not drop on him with that.

She became the mouse, which tried to step on or catch the ant in her mouth.

And he became the cat.

As he pounced, grasping his opportunity, she became the goat. The cat landed almost on her horns. She shook him violently off, and charged him where he fell, butting him mercilessly; if she could maintain contact, she could kill him before he could change.

But he got an instant's leeway between butts, and became the bear. He wrapped her in his crushing bear-hug.

She had no choice: she had to fight. She angled her head, orienting a horn, and bucked her head up, spearing his eye. That made him relax in pain, and she got a moment's separation. She used it to become another bear.

She stood on her hind legs and spread her forelegs, ready to give him a bear hug while he was distracted by the lost eye. But he was too canny to be caught that way. He became the dragonfly and dodged away.

Still, she had him on the run. One of the insect's eyes was crushed, interfering with its maneuvering. She became the bat and flew after it; a half-blinded dragonfly could not maneuver better than a bat.

However, her ribs here hurting, from the squeezing his bear had given her. This slowed her flight, giving him time to change again.

He did, to the duck. A one-eyed drake. The bat could not do much to that; it was a standoff.

But she had something else in mind. She looped around, heading for the cave she had seen before. She swooped into it, using her echo location, rapidly exploring its interior.

It was empty. There was only a small fallen stalactite stuck in the ground. There was no other exit. Anyone entering this cave would be trapped in it.

She had learned what she needed to. She returned to the duck and became the dog, lunging for the bird.

Who became the snake, a cobra, orienting on the dog.

She turned turtle, proof against the poisonous fangs.

He become the goat, a fierce buck, charging with his horns, trying to butt her into a tree trunk.

She became the frog, hopping out of the way. He tried to pursue, but she was smaller and thus more agile than he.

He had only two animals left. He took the one he didn't want to finish with: the spider.

Bad choice. She hopped toward him, to come in range to snap him up with her tongue. But he scuttled into a tangle of grass, protecting himself from that tongue. She couldn't get him.

So she took her final form: human. She became herself, naked, because all animals were natural. She leaped forward, stomping on the grass with her bare feet, trying to squish the spider. But he changed too, becoming a large muscular naked man.

She turned and fled immediately. He pursued her. She ran for the cave she had explored in bat form. Because she knew her body, and the route, she was fleet, and managed to stay ahead of him. But he was gaining.

She plunged into the cave just ahead of him. But its darkness did not enable her to escape. He blocked the entrance, then entered carefully, ready to catch her the moment she tried to escape. He did not need two eyes for this.

This would be the time to invoke the pheromones. She knew he expected that. It would postpone the end, but not change it: he had the clear advantage. She was weak because of her bruised ribs; she couldn't fight well regardless.

His hand brushed her shoulder as she stooped in the darkness. Immediately he grasped it and hauled her roughly toward him.

She stabbed him with the stout, sharp stalactite she had just picked up. The stone sank into his gut. He grunted, surprised and pained.

She yanked her spike out, but did not step back. She stabbed him again, using both hands: this time in the chest. She knew exactly where the heart of a man was.

He fell, mortally wounded.

The scene faded. They were back in the bunker, her ribs unbruised, his eye whole, and no stab wounds.

"Victory," she said.

"It's only a game. You got a break."

"I made my break. I located that stalactite, and went for it when I needed it. I out-thought you, Pyrrhus."

He shook his head. "I don't think so. I think you're trying to convince me I'm a loser, so you won't have to fight me."

"You are a loser, Pyrrhus. If we fight, you will lose. The game shows it. The paths are clarifying."

"Show me the paths."

She extended her hand, and he took it. The paths were there in their twisting skein, showing that Earth was returning soon to the Female Spirit. Voila's acquisition of full magic power via her Io ikon had given her the advantage, and she would win a direct confrontation.

"Damn!" he said, retaining contact. "I don't believe it. I think you're faking the paths."

"Negation."

"I'm taking Earth, though hell should bar the way."

"Hell does bar the way, Pyrrhus. You can make this difficult, but you will lose if you challenge it. It would be better for you to yield quietly."

"The hell I will!" He hauled her in to him. "I'm going to fuck you till your eyeballs pop, you little bitch, then choke you till your tongue falls out of your face. Our magic powers cancel out, but physically I can destroy you. See where your paths go once you are safely dead, you presumptuous foreign tart."

She had of course expected this. "Clasp me, and I will take you to hell. You do not know what you face, Pyrrhus."

"I'll damn well find out, gamine." He squeezed her cruelly tight, his hard penis probing.

"Clarification," she said, her cleft heating warningly. "I mean to stay close to you throughout, as long as you remain in power on Earth, and you can not banish me. Do you have any idea how bitchy I can be? You will have sex only with me, on my terms. No other woman will get close to you, and you will have scar tissue on your member."

"You're bluffing, baby." But the heat was preventing him from penetrating her; she did have control.

"And I won't necessarily be pretty." She became hideous, a wrinkled warty witch. Now her cleft cooled, and surrounded his member, wetly slurping it, drawing it in.

"Bitch!" He put his hands to her neck and tried to throttle her.

"So you have decided," she said, returning to her natural form. But her neck was like an iron column, impervious to his choking. She put her own arms about him and held him so tightly that the air hissed out of his mouth. Then she took him to hell.

They sank through the floor of the bunker, down through the rock. Old magma filled in over their heads.

"Hey!" he exclaimed.

"I warned you, Pyrrhus. Now I must unleash my minions."

"Your minions!" he exclaimed as their motion continued. "You have no minions! All your people have gone home to their backward planet."

"Negation. They retired from the field for a time. Now they will return to deal with you."

"You're bluffing, tike."

She did not answer. She merely held him as they continued inexorably downward. Now the cold old rock warmed, and they dropped into a glowing green magma chamber. They were completely surrounded by molten rock.

As a Glamor she could handle it. Her concern was the Male Spirit: this was the heart of his domain. The paths were clarifying, but could she really beat him in his own realm as the game suggested? Now she was nervous.

She remembered her early dialogue with her father. "You are the one who can see the future paths most clearly, Voila," he said. "You are the one who is most likely to discover new things. We named you aptly, perhaps anticipating your ability. But this also puts you on the spot."

"Question?" she asked. She was only three years old, and was discovering new things at a ferocious rate.

"Because when the Second Crisis comes, you will be the one to see it first, and you will have to handle it, as you did the First. You have the key power. All we can do is prepare you to use it when you have to."

"But won't you be there to keep me safe, father?"

"Honey, I will always be there when you need me. But it still will not be easy."

"What of mother? Won't she be there too?"

"Yes, she too, and your siblings. We will all support you. But you will have to prepare the ground yourself."

"Why, father?"

"Because you are the most powerful Glamor ever, Voila. No one else can do what you can do. But you will face challenges that may destroy you. You must prepare diligently."

"I will, father," she promised.

And she had, knowing that her life depended on it.

That time had come.

Voila finally let the Spirit go. "Now we set the scene," she said.

The magma wavered and faded. A new scene formed: a copy of the icons game background they had recently contested in.

"What the hell is this?" he demanded.

"This is hell, as you agree. And here are your demons."

"What are you talking about? This is an illusion scene."

"A setting for our reality. Prepare yourself for your fate, Pyrrhus."

He laughed. "Your quaint hell scene can't hurt me. I'm still going to fuck you to death. I can make myself invulnerable to your heat." He advanced on her again.

Voila opened her mouth wide. She made an ululating sound. Something emerged from her mouth: a swirling coil of smoke. It expanded rapidly and become the form of a man. In fact it was Havoc.

"We have unfinished business, cretin," Havoc said.

"So that's where you hid, barbarian! In your brat's mouth!"

Havoc strode forward, swinging. He connected to Pyrrhus' chin, knocking him off his feet. "You've got to get through me if you want to rape her."

"You have no power here! I have your ikon."

"Not any more, dunce. I recovered it during your distraction. I'm at full strength now."

"Impossible! My minions guard those ikons with their lives."

"But not with their penises, idiot. The female minions under the direction of the mistresses seduced them and took the ikons while you played games with my daughter. You should have been more alert."

"The bitch!"

"From him, that is a compliment, father," Voila said.

"I still fucked your wife, mistress, and daughter," the spirit said. "Fucked them all and made them like it."

"Something about that, turd," Havoc said. "Did you ever wonder why Gale let you make her ream your wretched ass when you thought we were hostages, or why I allowed it?"

"Seeing your wife playing dirty with another man must have turned you on, barbarian."

"She needed to reach the core of your soul, your essence, buried in the center of your physical host, well-protected by being encased in flesh. Swale could not evoke it in the manner of a normal man; your essence can't be stolen. You gave Gale access, and she touched it with her tongue."

"Best ass reaming I ever had," the Spirit agreed. "So what if she verified my nature? It's hardly secret."

"She marked you. Thereafter she always knew exactly where you were, regardless which body you used. You could never again hide from us. That was a key factor in countering your activities—and of course in verifying that you remained occupied with Voila while we recovered our ikons."

"But I took over this host body without her knowing."

"The hell you did, idiot. You took it just before we came to you in Paris, and laid low, giving Caveat his head. Gale made sure to stay with you throughout, guiding you to Voila. To this trap, imbecile."

Now the Male Spirit paused, realizing that he had indeed been had. "Damn, what a cunning bitch!"

"Thank you," Gale said. She had emerged from Voila after Havoc, followed by the three siblings. "A man is always a fool about sex, thinking it's all about him."

"Hey!" Havoc protested.

She smiled. "Some are nicer fools than others."

"Appreciation," Havoc said wryly. He returned his attention to Pyrrhus. "But now it is time for the games to end, and to send you back into your hole, creep. We don't need your kind governing Earth."

"As if you have any choice, barbarian. I am tired of your posturing; I'm going to return to the surface and organize my minions to run my empire."

"You are going nowhere, Pyrrhus. Except out of power."

"Welcome to try to stop me." Pyrrhus turned and walked away from Havoc.

That brought him to face Voila. "You can't pass me until you have dealt with my minions," she said. "I am the Glamor of Amoeba. They are everywhere, and I am where they are."

"The hell I can't, sweetie pie." He barged on toward her.

And halted, encountering a wall of energy. She was blocking his passage, and he would have to destroy her before getting through. He knew that would be no easy task. "Bitch," he muttered, and turned to the side.

Only to encounter Weft. She was stunningly beautiful in an evening gown. "My clientele is the bacteria," she said. "Here is a sample." A ragged glob appeared. "You may be immune, but your human host isn't. Do you know what deadly disease bacteria can do to him? They will eat him alive, literally. Do you care to verify this, scumball?"

Pyrrhus sent a blast of energy at her, but it bounced off harmlessly. He turned and went the opposite way.

There was Warp, floating. "And I am the Glamor of Fungus. I have made contact with the Earthly varieties, and they accept me as their representative." Fungus sprouted on his hands. "Not all are friendly. Would you like to discover what they can do to living flesh when they try?"

This, too, promised to be messy. Pyrrhus dropped through the floor, seeking an avenue below.

There was Flame. "I am the Glamor of Viruses. You made me kill my Earther lover," she said. "I will roast you for that." A ball of fire appeared before her. "You will feel what your mortal host feels as he burns to death. He does not deserve it, but you do."

The fireball hurtled toward the Male Spirit. He shot upward, escaping it.

There was Gale standing above him. "Say, lover, I love your gams," he said, peering up under her skirt.

"And I am the Glamor of Mosses and Lichen," she said evenly, hurling a mass down at him. It struck before he could dodge. Greenish plant-like things sprouted all over his body, and all around him. "You sought to molest my daughter? My creatures will consume your corpse."

Green glaze covered the man's eyes and mouth. He erupted in fire, burning the moss away. But he also retreated; this, too, was too complicated to handle at the moment.

He was back before Havoc. "This is all a vision," he said. "A game setting. Even with your ikon, you can't prevail against me in my home territory."

"Well, we'll give it a try," Havoc said with gusto. "I let you touch my wife, but I didn't like it. Then you touched my daughter, and I liked it less. Now it's time to make you pay."

"In fact, you're all just images conjured by the bitch girl. You have no more power than she has, by definition."

Havoc nodded. "Know, O miscreant, that we are animated to be as she saw us when she formed her first permanent memories of us. Her elder siblings are far more dangerous than they seem, and her mother is quietly deadly."

"And what of you, barbarian? What do you have?"

"This." Havoc focused—and a blast of power came that blew away the entire top of the mountain, forming a giant roiling cloud in the sky. The Spirit was sent spinning into the maelstrom. "Impossibly potent," Havoc said conversationally. "Larger than life. No one dare oppose me, lest there be havoc, of course."

"Well, spooks don't faze me," the Spirit said. But he had surely been taken aback. The volcano itself could hardly have blown away the mountain that way.

"They should," Havoc said. "Our power is greater than yours. The game demonstrated that. We can't destroy you, but we can drive you out of that body and out of power. It will take you another thousand years to recover. Earth will return to the Female Spirit and prosper, with our help."

"Ha ha," Pyrrhus said. "Over my dead—"

Then, suddenly, he was caught by six beams of power, from above, below, and the four sides. One beam from each of the Glamors. He fought to repel them, and for a moment succeeded. But then they drilled in harder, and turned him incandescent. Slowly he burned away, becoming smaller, flaring as he fought, but overcome.

At last there was nothing left but an ash. The malign Male Spirit had been destroyed or rendered null.

The scene faded. Voila was left in the bunker with Caveat and Iolo. The Glamors had been mere imprints in her consciousness; the real people were with Mino, awaiting the decision of the battle for Earth. All their demonstrated powers had actually been hers. Pyrrhus, at the end, had known it. She truly was stronger than he.

"He's gone," Caveat said, amazed.

"He's gone," Voila said. "We banished him. Now you can resume your normal life, and I will return to Charm."

"My normal life," he said, awed. "I thought I had been burned to a cinder."

"It was merely a vision, a framework for animating the settlement. The Spirit had to go. We merely wanted to do it with minimal destruction of the landscape."

"In a dream sequence?" He shrugged.

"I could have done it purely physically, but there were constraints."

"You didn't want to hurt me," he agreed. "The Male Spirit counted on that. Would you have done it, if you had to?"

"Affirmation. I had a hold on him too: he did not want to be confined to your body, especially if it was crippled or in constant pain. Once I satisfied him that I was ready to do that, and that he had no way out of such imprisonment except to yield the field, he did."

"Hell for me, hell for him. And you really would have done it."

"Regret," she agreed. "The planet is more important than a single man."

"I agree. I would not have it otherwise. But I'm glad it wasn't necessary." He was plainly being brave; he had been severely shaken by the possession and the manner of its exorcism. "But you know, you couldn't have banished him unless he really wanted to go. Your threat about staying always with him, driving off other women, making him hurt for sex—he knew you meant it, and that daunted him."

"Agreement. We could not oust him by our will alone; only a massive shift in global sentiment could do that. The force was merely for show, on both sides. He could have hung on for a century or two, to Earth's enormous detriment. We had to make him see the futility of staying. He would have none of the benefits, because I was stronger and would balk him."

"Yet the prospect of your continued association doesn't bother me."

"You're not insatiably heterosexual."

Caveat laughed. "How right you are! So he is locked in to me, and can't return until I die, freeing him to occupy another host."

"Clarification: he can't return until *I* die—and I'm immortal. A thousand years is merely a concept."

"Voila, you're absolutely beautiful! You saved me from hell."

"Kiss me, Caveat. Then we will commence our separate lives. I am sorry we could not be together; you are a good man. I would have liked to make a life with you, but that can not be."

"Because of my orientation?"

"That, too," she agreed. She kissed him. "Because of what I am."

He did not debate the point. He had seen too much. "Thanks for not changing me."

"Question?"

"Don't play innocent with me, Voila. I know you could have done it, had you chosen to."

"Temptation," she confessed. "But I love you as you are."

He nodded appreciatively. "And I love you as you are, your hideous power and nerve notwithstanding. But you are right; we are not for each other." He sighed. "I hope we can remain friends."

"Agreement." She was relieved; he was accepting it. "With us the sexual element is restrained, so friendship is possible."

"No offense intended, but you seemed to be quite free with sex despite opposing the Spirit."

"Explanation: with normal folk, men crave sex while women can take it or leave it. That gives women a tactical advantage. Culturally and practically, it is a tool that we employ as convenient. It is part of our colonial culture, reflected mainly in no fault relationships: temporary liaisons where the women give the men willing sex in return for protection, food, transportation or other things of value. Most women learn the art of it early; there is little reticence because of ignorance or fear. With Glamors this is exaggerated; men crave it passionately and are indefatigable, while women can enjoy it, particularly if they telepathically receive the mental pleasure of the male orgasm. But they don't *have* to have it. They can satisfy the men with full, partial, or no pleasure themselves, as they prefer, and the men know it. My seeming naïveté was a ruse he foolishly chose to believe; I have not been innocent in that respect since early childhood." She smiled fondly. "You were my first true human loving man-woman sex, Caveat, but that was a technicality. So then I demonstrated to Pyrrhus that I could make his mortal host's existence endlessly delightful, or satisfactory, or awful, as I chose, and he would have no alternative satisfaction with any other woman. That put him into extreme disadvantage. I was teasing him cruelly, and promised him no relief."

He shook his head, ruefully appreciative. "You are correct. He cursed himself for falling for it, yet he desired you more than ever. It seems there is something about sex with another Glamor that is phenomenally appealing."

"Agreement. We are highly sexed, as he knew. But he more than I, as he also knew."

"And you were merciless in exploiting it."

"True. It was my lever. I am a much harder woman than I pretend."

"And I, perhaps as foolishly, still love you despite knowing that, though without sexual inclination."

She nodded. "I confess to being touched by that."

"I have a question you may prefer not to answer: did you really have a crush on me?"

"I did, Caveat, in my fashion, and still do. It may be compounded mainly of my desire to experience some of the human emotions of my parents and siblings, or to play my ingénue role more effectively—"

"Please, Voila. The initial statement will do. I have my own caveats, as my name suggests. I understand the qualifications and prefer to ignore them."

She laughed. "So do I! Kiss me and enhance the illusion."

He did, and for a moment she was the sweet girl again. She savored the nuance of first love, however qualified.

He held her and gazed at her. "I am curious, Voila. I know something of your nature, but not enough. Are you a girl with Glamor powers, or a Glamor emulating a girl?"

"The latter, now. But my time on Earth was my chance to play at being a girl; they did not know me here. I tried very hard to be naïve and sweet, in action and thought, for the time allowed. You helped."

"Because I was 'safe'!" he said. "You knew I would never expect a continuing romantic relationship. So you wouldn't have to hurt me emotionally when you left me. Because your girlhood is a mere speck on the vortex of raw magic power that is your real nature, barely clothed by your human form."

"Exaggeration," she said. But it was not much of one. In this respect she was jealous of her siblings: they were governed to an extent by their human qualities. She could never be. Even Swale the succubus was more human than Voila. It was her necessary curse. She had to be that way, to handle the three crises. The third one was coming in about five years, according to the clarifying paths. She would then be twenty one and at her full strength. Even so, it might not be enough.

He changed the subject. "Will Mistress Monochrome return?"

"She should, but there is a problem."

"A problem? I understood she was safe on your planet."

"She is. But the people don't want to let her go. They like her too well, and she likes them. Father will have to try to persuade her to spend at least some time on Earth."

Caveat laughed. "She's his mistress. She'll go where he goes."

"Agreement. In the interim, mother will have to serve on Earth, with my siblings. It should work out."

"It should," he agreed. "Gale is some woman. Reminiscent of you, in some ways."

"Appreciation." There was no humor in either statement.

"I don't envy your Glamors' chore of helping to restore Earth to a peaceful, prosperous existence. The Male Spirit's minions have done a great deal of damage in a short time."

"Agreement. With Mistress Monochrome spending half her time on Charm, she must have help. We will need a really competent administrator to implement the necessary policies."

"There is Dynamo."

"He married a Chroma woman, so his attention will be divided. He will handle the Chroma zones. We need a single man for the main portion of the planet."

"There are surely many prospects." He paused, for she was looking at him. "Oh, no!"

"Oh, yes, Caveat. The Mistress of Mistresses already knows and trusts you, as do I. So will the people. You will be the Prime Minister of Earth."

He gazed at her a moment longer, then nodded, accepting it. He really didn't have a choice.

They left the bunker with the ifrit. Caveat stared. The ground was covered with lichen. "How much of that vision was real?" he asked.

"Enough. We regret the collateral damage, but the Male Spirit refused to go entirely gently. A token demonstration of physical power was necessary. The mistresses supervised a mass evacuation in time."

"In time?"

She gestured toward the volcano. He looked—and stared.

The entire top of the mountain was gone. All around it was desolation. Nothing alive remained besides themselves. The volcano seemed to have suffered a phenomenal eruption. Would anyone else ever know what had actually happened?

"A token demonstration," he echoed, awed.

"Agreement. To accomplish the necessary."

"Ozymandias," he murmured.

"Question?"

"A local reference. A commentary on the vanity and futility of a tyrant's power. He thought his works would last forever, but they were completely forgotten."

"Apt," she agreed. "I trust that Pyrrhus will be similarly disappointed." Then she took his hand and transported them both to Naples. They had a planet to organize.

Author's Note

I had been writing these ChroMagic novels every two years on even years: 1998, 2000, 2002. Then I got sidetracked into other projects in 2004, so wrote *Key to Liberty* mostly in 2005. And something else came up.

I had intended to take December 2004 off to watch videos and otherwise relax, as I'm a workaholic and need consciously to plan for relaxation or I don't do it. I eat right, exercise mind and body, make sure to get enough sleep, and try to keep my home life placid: all ingredients of a healthy life style. But play time is also part of the formula, so I do try to do some things just for fun. It's an effort. So what happened? Well, we'd had two hurricanes pass our way in September, with attendant complications such as a week-long power outage, and I'd had to scramble to get Xanth #30 *Stork Naked* completed on schedule in November. Then I pondered *Liberty*, because I really wanted to know what those four Glamor kids were going to be up to, and I kept getting drawn back to make more notes on the novel. What about Warp, Weft, Flame, and Voila? They would go to Earth; then what? What about the old folk back home, Havoc, Gale, Ennui? I had to *know*. And in December I lost control and ditched the relaxation, instead plunging into writing it. It turned out to be my second best writing month ever, at about 77,500 words. (My best was on Xanth #29, *Pet Peeve*: 81,000.)

As it turned out, it was well I did so, because my family life is complicating, and I would not have been able to complete the novel in 2005 had I not had that phenomenal start. I wrote 50,000 words in January, still decent, then 18,000 in February, 17,000 in March, 24,000 in April, 30,000 in May, 26,000 in June, and edited the 256,000 word novel in July. I had to have it clear by then, because I had Xanth #31 *Air Apparent* to do on a deadline. So it was a close call; those reduced figures represent not laziness but desperate scrambling for writing time.

So what happened? Well, I was diagnosed with a crushed disk, which gives me fairly constant low back discomfort, or pain if I'm careless moving around. I also had a prostate biopsy, but fortunately that showed it was inflammation, not cancer. So those things did not slow me much. It was my wife. She had been slowly weakening the prior year, and I was riding into town with her to help with grocery shopping and the like. She couldn't walk far, so I pushed her around the grocery store in their riding cart that had a place for her to sit behind the basket. It felt like driving a semi-trailer truck backwards, but it was ideal, getting her through the shopping without wearing her out. Even so, she had a number of falls, the last of which sprained her left ankle badly enough to take her entirely off her feet for six weeks. But when that healed, she could no longer walk; her general weakness and loss of muscle tissue prevented her. I took over the driving, and did the grocery shopping on my own, as it was a chore for her even to make it to the car. The wheelchair we got for her was invaluable; she practically lived in it for several months. I had to heave her from bed to wheelchair, and from wheelchair to wherever else, as she could no longer stand. This became a precise maneuver, as she weighed as much as I did, and her arms were too weak for her to help me by hanging on. I would brace my feet, put my arms around her, and give a mighty heave. Thank fate I was in good physical condition!

Then at last the mystified doctors got the diagnosis: Chronic Inflammatory Demyelinating Polyneuropathy. Inflammation was eating away the myelin, which was the protective sheathing around her nerves, so that in effect they shorted out, and the signals could not get through. Then her muscles atrophied from lack of use. The cause was idiopathic: no, not idiotic, it just means they don't know what causes it. But it's devastating. Fortunately there's a treatment: a series of IV infusions of fabulously expensive immunoglobulin G had a nearly miraculous effect, and she gradually recovered the use of her body. And I correspondingly recovered some of my writing time. By the time the novel was finished, she was making solid progress, though still using the wheelchair. We had our 49th anniversary as she got better. Thus the course of this novel covered the worst of her illness. I hope the challenge and sometimes near despair of the situation did not translate to the novel.

It was fun researching Earth volcanoes, but of course I could use only a fraction of what I found. That's the problem with research; you have to do far more than shows. I also enjoyed making an original culture for post-holocaust Earth. Do I really believe that men are warlike and women are peaceful? To a degree, but that's not the point. This is really the Male Spirit vs. the Female Spirit, with men and women on both sides. I see the violent horrors of this world, leading toward destruction of our resources, environment, and inevitably ourselves, and I wish there were a better governing principle. The world is obviously run mostly by males. Maybe a takeover by the Female Spirit would help.

What of the missing element I realized as I finished the last novel: when did the funguses, bacteria, viruses and amoeba colonize Planet Charm? It never occurred to me when writing *Liberty*, so it seems it will have to wait for the next. Writing can be like that: you overlook a key element until too late.

So what of that next novel, *Key to Survival*, when the machine culture comes to take over and exploit these planets on its way to becoming a galactic power? At this writing I don't know. It may be several more years before I figure it out. But at least you know the cast of characters.

—Piers Anthony, July 2005

About the Author

Piers Anthony is one of the world's most prolific and popular authors. His fantasy Xanth novels have been read and loved by millions of readers around the world, and have appeared on the *New York Times* Best Seller list 21 times.

Although Piers is mostly known for fantasy and science fiction, he has written novels in other genres as well, including historical fiction, martial arts, and horror.

Piers Anthony's official website is HI PIERS at www.hipiers.com, where he publishes his bi-monthly online newsletter. Piers lives with his wife in Central Florida.

Printed in the United States
99985LV00004B/8/A

9 781594 263828